COMPLETE STORIES

Dorothy Parker was born to J. Henry and Elizabeth Rothschild on August 22, 1893. Parker's childhood was not a happy one. Her mother died young, and Dorothy did not enjoy a good relationship with her father and stepmother. She began her education at a Catholic convent school in Manhattan before being sent away to Miss Dana's School in Morristown, New Jersey. In 1916, Frank Crowninshield gave Parker an editorial position at *Vogue*, following its publication of a number of her poems. The following year she moved on to write for *Vanity Fair*, where she would later become the theater critic. That same year she met and married Edwin Pond Parker II, whom she divorced a few years later. It was at *Vanity Fair* that Parker met her associates with whom she would form the Algonquin Round Table, the famed New York literary circle. In 1925, Parker also began writing short stories for a new magazine called *The New Yorker*. Her relationship with that publication would last, off and on, until 1957. Parker went abroad in the 1930s, continuing to write poetry and stories. In Europe she met Alan Campbell, whom she married in 1933. The couple divorced in 1947 but remarried in 1950, remaining together until Campbell's death in 1963. Throughout this period in her life, Parker continued to publish collections of her work, including *Enough Rope* (1926), *Sunset Gun* (1928), *Laments for the Living* (1930), and *Death and Taxes* (1931). Her last great work was a play, *The Ladies of the Corridor*, which she wrote with Arnaud d'Usseau, published in 1954. Parker died on June 7, 1967.

Colleen Breese teaches in the English Department at the University of Toledo and is the author of *Excuse My Dust: The Art of Dorothy Parker's Serious Fiction*. She resides with her family in Sylvania, Ohio.

Regina Barreca, a professor of English and feminist theory at the University of Connecticut, is the author of *Sweet Revenge: The Wicked Delights of Getting Even*, *Untamed and Unabashed: Essays on Women and Humor in Literature*, *Perfect Husbands (and other Fairy Tales)*, and *They Used to Call Me Snow White, but I Drifted*. She lives with her husband in Storrs, Connecticut.

DOROTHY PARKER

COMPLETE STORIES

EDITED BY
COLLEEN BREESE

WITH AN INTRODUCTION BY
REGINA BARRECA

PENGUIN BOOKS

PENGUIN BOOKS
Published by the Penguin Group
Penguin Books USA Inc., 375 Hudson Street, New York, New York 10014, U.S.A.
Penguin Books Ltd, 27 Wrights Lane, London W8 5TZ, England
Penguin Books Australia Ltd, Ringwood, Victoria, Australia
Penguin Books Canada Ltd, 10 Alcorn Avenue,
Toronto, Ontario, Canada M4V 3B2
Penguin Books (N.Z.) Ltd, 182–190 Wairau Road,
Auckland 10, New Zealand

Penguin Books Ltd, Registered Offices:
Harmondsworth, Middlesex, England

First published in Penguin Books 1995

9   10

"The Custard Heart" was originally published in Dorothy Parker's *Here Lies*, The Viking Press,
1939. The other selections first appeared in the following periodicals: *American Mercury, The
Bookman, Cosmopolitan, Esquire, Harper's Bazaar, Ladies' Home Journal, The New Republic,
The New Yorker, Pictorial Review, Scribner's, Smart Set, Vanity Fair,* and *Woman's Home
Companion.*

"The Banquet of Crow" is reprinted by permission of *The New Yorker.* "As the Spirit Moves,"
"An Apartment House Anthology," "Men I'm Not Married To," "Welcome Home," "Our Own
Crowd," and "Professional Youth" are reprinted by permission of *Saturday Evening Post.*

LIBRARY OF CONGRESS CATALOGING IN PUBLICATION DATA
Parker, Dorothy, 1893–1967.
[Short stories]
Complete stories / Dorothy Parker ; edited by Colleen Breese ; with
an introduction by Regina Barreca.
p. cm.
ISBN 0 14 01.8939 4 (pbk.)
1. United States—Social life and customs—20th century—Fiction.
I. Breese, Colleen. II. Title.
.PS3531.A5855A6   1995
813'.52—dc20   95-15524

Printed in the United States of America
Set in Sabon

CONTENTS

INTRODUCTION

Why is it that many critics seem so intent on defusing the power of Dorothy Parker's writing that she appears more like a terrorist bomb than what she really is: one, solitary, unarmed American writer of great significance? Is it because so many of her critics—one might hesitate to underscore the obvious: so many of her *male* critics—seem to resent, half-consciously, her unwillingness to appease their literary appetites? Is it because Parker did not list among her many talents The Ability to Play Well with Others?

Dorothy Parker wrote strong prose for most of her life, and she wrote a lot of it, remaining relentlessly compassionate regarding, and interested in, the sufferings primarily of those who could not extricate themselves from the emotional tortures of unsuccessful personal relationships. Her stories were personal, yes, but also political and have as their shaping principles the larger issues of her day—which remain for the most part the larger issues of our own day (with Prohibition mercifully excepted).

Parker depicted the effects of poverty, economic and spiritual, upon women who remained chronically vulnerable because they received little or no education about the real world—the "real world" being the one outside the fable of love and marriage. But Parker also addressed the ravages of racial discrimination, the effects of war on marriage, the tensions of urban life, and the hollow space between fame and love. Of her domestic portraits one is tempted to say that, for Parker, the words "dysfunctional family" were redundant. She wrote about abortion when you couldn't write the word and wrote about chemical and emotional addiction when the concepts were just a gleam in the analysts' collective eye.

Parker approached these subjects with the courage and intelligence of a woman whose wit refused to permit the absurdities of life to continue along without comment. Irreverent toward anything held sacred —from romance or motherhood to literary teas and ethnic stereotypes —Parker's stories are at once playful, painful, and poignant. Her own characteristic refusal to sit down, shut up, and smile at whoever was footing the bill continues to impress readers who come to her for the first time and delight those who are already familiar with the routine.

Her humor intimidates some readers, but those it scares off are the ones she wouldn't have wanted anyway.

She didn't court or need the ineffectual. She would not, for example, have wept too long for having frightened good old Freddie from the sketch titled "Men I'm Not Married To." Freddie, she tells us, "is practically a whole vaudeville show in himself. He is never without a new story of what Pat said to Mike as they were walking down the street, or how Abie tried to cheat Ikie, or what old Aunt Jemima answered when she was asked why she had married for the fifth time. Freddie does them in dialect, and I have often thought it is a wonder that we don't all split our sides." There, in brief, lies the difference between Parker's gift and much of what passed for humor in her own (and in our own) time: Parker's wit caricatures the self-deluded, the powerful, the autocratic, the vain, the silly, and the self-important; it does not rely on mean and small formulas, and it never ridicules the marginalized, the sidelined, or the outcast. When Parker goes for the jugular, it's usually a vein with blue blood in it.

Certainly the portraits of deleriously pretentious intelligentsia Parker poured onto her pages tweaked at certain readers, and it's probable that Parker herself was aware of the wince-inducing effect of some of her sharper prose as she left it out of the earlier collections of her work. What is certain is that a number of the stories printed here for the first time since their initial publication in various periodicals contain moments of satire so spectacular that those certain readers mentioned earlier might shrivel up in the manner of a vampire shown a silver cross.

Her silver crosses are fashioned along the lines of this miniature, presented in Parker's previously uncollected early sketch "An Apartment House Anthology":

> The minute you step into her apartment you realize that Mrs. Prowse is a woman of fine sensibilities. They stick out, as you might say, all over the place. You can see traces of them in the handmade candles dripping artistically over the polychrome candlesticks; in the single perfect blossom standing upright in a roomy bowl; in the polychrome bust of Dante on the mantel—taken, by many visitors, to be a likeness of William Gibbs McAdoo; most of all in the books left all about, so that Mrs. Prowse, no matter where she is sitting, always can have one at hand, to lose herself in. They are, mainly, collections of verse, both free and under control, for Mrs. Prowse is a regular glutton for poetry.

In passage after passage, Parker not only grasps the petit points made by self-proclaimed cognoscenti in order to mock them, but she grasps them hard 'round the throat, and hard enough to put them out of their misery.

Parker went about the business of writing in a very practical way: she did it and got paid for it. But it seems as if there is a fraternity of disgruntled critics who would like to make her pay for her achievement with her reputation. They speak of her "exile" to Hollywood, where she had the audacity to be successful as a screenwriter and the nerve to be nominated for an Academy Award for writing the cinematic masterpiece *A Star Is Born*. They argue that she "sold out" and "wasted" herself by writing about narrow topics.

Let's clear up this business about narrow topics: Parker concerns herself primarily with the emotional and intellectual landscape of women, the places where a thin overlay of social soil covers the minefields of very personal disaffection, rejection, betrayal, and loss. She manages throughout it all to make her work funny (and that she is funny is one of the most important things about her) while tilling away at this dangerous garden; and for that generations of women and men have thanked her by reading her, memorizing her, making movies about her, performing plays based on her, and writing books analyzing her—but also castigating her most ruthlessly, passing on untruths behind her back and since 1967 speaking most ill of the dead.

Narrow topics? It is true that Parker often viewed her large subjects through small lenses, and that sometimes—sometimes—her fanatic attention to detail can be mistaken for a passion for minutiae instead of a passion for sharply focused observation. But those disparaging Parker's accomplishments usually make only passing (if not parenthetical) reference to the fact that she has remained a popular writer for more than sixty years, a woman who constructed a literary reputation for herself by writing satirical and witty prose and poetry when women were not supposed to have a sense of humor, and writing about the battle between the classes with as much appetite and bite as she brought to the struggle between the sexes.

You might say that Dorothy Parker should be placed at the head of her generation's class, given her ability to willfully and wickedly push, prod, and pinch her readers into thought, emotion, laughter, and the wish to change the world as we've always known it. You might say that she has surely earned recognition by articulating that which is ubiquitous but unspoken, or you might say that she deserves kudos because she managed to say with wit and courage what most of us are too cowardly or silly to admit. Usually when authors manage to do this—

write powerfully and passionately about an important and universal topic—they are rewarded.

Not so with Parker. Parker has been slammed for at least thirty years. One recent critic complains that Parker had "no disinterestedness, no imagination," and another bows low to introduce Parker with the gallant phrase "The span of her work is narrow and what it embraces is often slight." It's clear, however, that such critics write not out of their own convictions but out of their own prejudices. How else could they have read Parker with such blinkered vision?

Parker's work is anything—anything—but slight, concerning as it does life, death, marriage, divorce, love, loss, dogs, and whisky. Given the comprehensive nature of her catalog, it is clear that the only important matters untouched by Parker boil down to the impact of microchip technology, sports, and cars. And if you look carefully at her prose, Parker does deal with cars—if only in passing, and only those passing in the fast lane.

Not that Parker had a great wish to be counted among Those Who Appeal to the Well-Read. Her portrait of literary types, in both her fiction and her nonfiction, is about as flattering as a broken tooth. In another previously uncollected sketch, "Professional Youth," we are introduced to "one of the leading boy authors, hailed alike by friends and relatives as the thirty-one-year-old child wonder"—uncannily resembling his modern counterparts, who continue to make up the vast population of large parties in large cities celebrating small achievements. Parker informs us about the way in which the junior author declares his greatness and originality:

> Perhaps you have read his collected works, that celebrated five-inch shelf. As is no more than fair, his books—*Annabelle Takes to Heroin*, *Gloria's Neckings*, and *Suzanne Sobers Up*—deal with the glamorous adventures of our young folks. Even if you haven't read them, though, there is no need for you to go all hot and red with nervous embarrassment when you are presented to their author. . . . He has the nicest, most reassuring way of taking it all cozily for granted that not a man or a woman and but few children in these loosely United States could have missed a word that he has written. . . .

And what exactly is the original contribution to thought made by this radical young band of renegade writers?

They come clean with the news that war is a horrible thing, that injustice still exists in many parts of the globe even to this day, that the very rich are apt to sit appreciably prettier than the very poor. Even the tenderer matters are not smeared over with romance for them. They have taken a calm look at this marriage thing and they are there to report that it is not always a lifelong trip to Niagara Falls. You will be barely able to stagger when the evening is over. In fact, once you have heard the boys settling things it will be no surprise to you if any day now one of them works it all out that there is nothing to this Santa Claus idea.

Not that reading fares all that much better than writing. Parker implies that language should be considered a controlled substance, parceled out according to need and only in small amounts. Listen to what, in her classic late-night-alone monologue "The Little Hours," she has to say about what she might call the "gorgeous" effects of books taken at a high dosage:

> Reading—there's an institution for you. Why, I'd turn on the light and read, right this minute, if reading weren't what contributed toward driving me here. I'll show it. God, the bitter misery that reading works in this world! Everybody knows that—everybody who *is* everybody. All the best minds have been off reading for years. Look at the swing La Rochefoucauld took at it. He said that if nobody had ever learned to read, very few people would be in love. There was a man for you, and that's what *he* thought of it. Good for you, La Rochefoucauld; nice going, boy. I wish I'd never learned to read. I wish I'd never learned to take off my clothes. Then I wouldn't have been caught in this jam at half-past four in the morning. If nobody had ever learned to undress, very few people would be in love. No, his is better. Oh, well, it's a man's world.

"If nobody had ever learned to undress, very few people would be in love" is one of Parker's witty lines. It is not her autobiography. When an author's words are confused with her deeds, they too often act as substitutions for a truly conscientious consideration of her work and life. Yes, Parker married a few times, divorced a few times, drank, and wrote her heart out. Except for the astonishing ability with which she completed this last task, she lived a life much like those of the other writers of her day. It seems odd, then, for an article written on the centenary of her birth (in *The New Yorker*, ironically enough) despairingly to announce the shocking discovery that for Parker "success did not bring happiness."

Why this prevailing wish to preserve Parker as a twentieth-century version of Dickens's Miss Havisham, a phantom swaying over the ghostly remains of the Algonquin Round Table, murmuring rhyming verse to herself, alone and abandoned? Why the wish to see her long life as a failure of the will to die rather than the triumph of a will to survive? Perhaps because the idea of a successful woman writer, one who deflated daily the pretensions of the world around her with a stiletto irreverence aimed at the hypocrisies of the cultural avant-garde, is unnerving even in this day and age. Why else preserve not the image of a wickedly laughing woman who enjoyed her heart's rush into the territories where angels feared to tread, but the vision of a sad, unfunny used up little old lady? (Who *was* that little old lady, anyway? Certainly not Parker. At seventy Parker wanted to start writing a column for *Esquire* and to publish a new collection of stories.)

On a bad day it's not hard to dream up a conspiracy plot which demands that all women writers who speak successfully with a satirical tongue get lacerated critically or, worse, that such women are presented as sad, shriveled shells of frivolous femininity, or—worse still, worst ever—that women who don't act nicely *get left alone*. But then such bad days are usually provoked by the realization that the woman writer is still regarded by certain critics as an intellectual and moral idiot because she doesn't write about fly fishing or pontificate on the bounty of the world so lovingly created (by men, need we add?) as her playground.

But Dorothy Parker was not meant to be Betty Crocker; the joys of womanhood were not on her agenda.

The complications, delights, humor, and frustrations of womanhood were, however, unflinchingly examined by Parker. Her business was to make fun of the ideal, whatever it was, and trace the split between the vision of a woman's life as put forth by the social script and the way real women lived real lives. The ordinary is the very heart of her material. It is the essence of much of her humor. In "Dusk Before Fireworks," for example, we are privy to the following timeless exchange between a "very good-looking young man indeed, shaped to be annoyed," and a "temperately pretty" woman who "half a year before . . . had been sweeter to see," which takes place after the beleaguered girlfriend has just protested a little too much: "You know I haven't got a stitch of jealousy in me. Jealous! Good heavens, if I were going to be jealous, I'd be it about someone worth while, and not about any silly, stupid, idle, worthless, selfish, hysterical, vulgar, promiscuous, sex-ridden—"

Delicately annoyed, the young man stops her tirade with the word

"Darling!" Using the term as a means of punctuation rather than a declaration of affection, he interrupts her only to ask the age-old question:

> "Why do you want to work up all this? I watched you just sit there and deliberately talk yourself into it, starting right out of nothing. Now what's the idea of that? Oh, good Lord, what's the matter with women, anyway?"
>
> "Please don't call me 'women,' " she said.
>
> "I'm sorry, darling," he said. "I didn't mean to use bad words." He smiled at her. She felt her heart go liquid, but she did her best to be harder won.

The gap between how life is dressed up to appear and what it looks like underneath its fancy trimmings is the gap where interesting writing begins, especially when that writing is satiric. The female satirist makes some people nervous. They don't feel all that easy around a woman who puts her "femininity" aside in order to make a point or a joke—and heaven help her if she wants to take a humorous perspective on a serious point.

But heaven help Parker, then, because she was nothing if not irreverent; nothing to her was sacred save human dignity. For the woman in "The Little Hours" who finds herself awake as a kind of penance for having retired early, in bed with only La Rochefoucauld for company, Parker can offer a virtual litany of irreverence. Listen to how well she mimics the authoritative voice, only to slash it to pieces with the edge of reality; listen to the way she demonstrates her perfect knowledge of the lines (making reference to, among others, Shakespeare, Browning, Milton, Marvell, Keats, Shelley, and Walter Savage Landor). Only after establishing proficiency in that most acceptable of lofty literary languages does Parker go on to savage its meaning by tossing it all into the blender:

> This above all, to thine own self be true and it must follow, as the night the day, thou canst not then be false to any man. Now they're off. And once they get started, they ought to come like hot cakes. Let's see. Ah, what avail the sceptered race and what the form divine, when every virtue, every grace, Rose Aylmer, all were thine. Let's see. They also serve who only stand and wait. If Winter comes, can Spring be far behind? Lilies that fester smell far worse than weeds. Silent upon a peak in Darien. Mrs. Porter and her daughter wash their feet in soda-water. And Agatha's Arth is a hug-the-hearth, but my true love is false. Why did you die when lambs

were cropping, you should have died when apples were dropping. Shall be together, breathe and ride, so one day more am I deified, who knows but the world will end tonight. And he shall hear the stroke of eight and not the stroke of nine. They are not long, the weeping and the laughter; love and desire and hate I think will have no portion in us after we pass the gate. But none, I think, do there embrace. I think that I shall never see a poem lovely as a tree. I think I will not hang myself today. Ay tank Ay go home now.

Smart as a kick in the shins and as on target as a stealth flyer, maybe Parker is more concerned with being considered witty than with being considered nice, especially if "nice" is synonymous with "agreeable" and "orthodox." It's tough to be funny when you have to be nice, and Parker made it her business to be funny. Readers clearly adore her humor; critics have often disparaged it as shrill and self-indulgent. This can be put into perspective, however, when we realize that women who argue against their own subjugation are called shrill and those who point out the absurdities in life without offering an accompanying twelve-step program to fix it all up are deemed ethically irresponsible. A recent critic charmingly claimed that Parker remained "morally a child" all of her life. Parker was many things, but naive wasn't among them, and the idea of her suffering from a case of moral arrested development because she occupied her time in confronting emotional and social issues can hardly be regarded as a rational argument.

If Parker's work can be dismissed as narrow and easy, then so can the work of Austen, Eliot, and Woolf. Now that it's mentioned, their writing was also dismissed as small prose-potatoes for quite some time. Maybe Parker is in good company there in the crowded margins, along with all the other literary paragons of her sex. Aphra Behn didn't get cut much critical slack, either, when she was writing social satire in the 1670s; and like many women writers after her, she was said to have been unencumbered by the necessity of being ladylike.

(Wasn't it Behn who wrote in an introduction to one of her plays that she appeared as a woman, not as a playwright, to her critics, and that often her work was attacked for one reason alone: it "had no other misfortune but that of coming out for a woman's: had it been owned by a man, though the most dull, unthinkably rascally scribbler in town, it had been a most admirable" piece of writing? Surely the same can be claimed for Parker. This leads me to think that perhaps Parker should be pictured as seated at a table with these, her literary predecessors, rather than chained by the ankle and fixed in one amber moment at the restaurant of a middling Manhattan hotel surrounded by the boys. Perhaps we should place Parker among her peers, not merely her contemporaries. Surely Behn, Austen, Eliot, and Woolf have more in common with Parker than Benchley ever did, even if we imagine that Parker would have rather played with Robert than with Aphra.)

Parker can be summed up as a writer of depth and substance; to hiss merely that she was a rapid burn-out case is to sneer, when what is called for is prolonged and sincere applause. It's like saying that Virginia Woolf was melancholic, George Eliot couldn't handle her relationships, and Jane Austen wasn't much fun at a dance: you'd imagine that throwing rocks at the glass houses of major writers would get tiring after a while and certain critics would pack up their pebbles, heading home, where at least in their sleep they could do little harm. The trajectory of Parker's critical acceptance has often been charted far below that of her popular acclaim, a curious reversal of the situation of many other midtwentieth-century writers, who are so often pushed to the front of the group by their very own personal critics, the authors looking a great deal like reluctant children, aware of their limitations, who are shoved onto the stage by aggressively solicitous parents eager for them to perform so that their own talents can be validated.

With Parker, the job is simplified. There is no need to resurrect her, because she has remained an author whose work has continued to sell strongly year after year, her readership gleefully resistant to the condescension of literary types who damn her with faint praise. But there is now, as there is every so often, a need to re-establish her footing in the "canon." The stories collected here are evidence of that. The fact that these works have captured the flag of the reading world's attention and held it since 1944, when the first *Portable Dorothy Parker* was published, is additional evidence, should it be needed, of her strength and originality.

That Parker is brutally funny is no joke: the unforgiving nature of the humor she directed not only towards herself but towards any figures who took themselves too seriously is her trademark. Her wit is not a surprise to those who have read more than two or three of her works, whether stories, poems, plays, or reviews; the patterns of her humor become quickly familiar even to her new readers, since the effects of her style depend not so much on the ambush of the unexpected as on the anticipation of the inevitable.

You know that the woman—cleverly named Dorothy Parker by the author—in the 1928 *New Yorker* story "The Garter," newly collected here, is best friends with the women in Parker's better-known monologues "A Telephone Call," "The Little Hours," and "The Waltz." When her garter breaks as she sits alone in the middle of a party, "a poor, heartsick orphan . . . in the midst of a crowd," she muses "To think of a promising young life blocked, halted, shattered by a garter! In happier times, I might have been able to use the word 'garter' in a sentence. Nearer, my garter thee, nearer to thee." At this point, of course, she's off and running once again, with the applause and hollers of the audience a mere blur:

> It doesn't matter; my life's over, anyway. I wonder how they'll be able to tell when I'm dead. It will be a very thin line of distinction between me sitting here holding my stocking, and just a regulation dead body. . . . If I could have just one more chance, I'd wear corsets. Or else I'd go without stockings, and play I was the eternal Summer girl. Once they wouldn't let me in the Casino at Monte Carlo because I didn't have any stockings on. So I went and found my stockings, and then came back and lost my shirt. Dottie's Travel Diary: or Highways and Byways in Picturesque Monaco, by One of Them. I wish I were in Monte Carlo right this minute. I wish I were in Carcassonne. Hell, it would look like a million dollars to me to be on St. Helena. . . . Suppose somebody asks me to dance. I'll just have to rock my head and say, "No spik Inglese," that's all. Can this be me, praying that nobody will come near me?

If Parker isn't sure that it's her, we can reassure her on the matter: the voice is virtuoso Parker, and "The Garter" is one of her best monologues.

You know, too, that the supercilious mother in "Lolita" will be undone by her predatory envy towards the daughter who happily marries the man coveted by the mother herself; when the wry narrator informs the reader at the story's conclusion that Lolita's mother was "not a woman who easily abandoned hope," you know that the mother's hope is a poisonous one, aimed to strike at her daughter's success. You know that the wise older woman in "Advice to the Little Peyton Girl" will herself duplicate the unwise habits of the younger woman seeking her advice, that she cannot live out the counsel she passes along. Perhaps, Parker implies, it is impossible for a flesh-and-blood human being to be as coolly manipulative, controlling, and controlled as thirty-nine-ish Miss Marion appears to be when she suggests to her nineteen-year-old friend Sylvie Peyton that she not permit herself to "become insecure," and that she conquer her fears that her boyfriend will leave her by being "always calm." Miss Marion coos, "You must wait, Sylvie, and it's a bad task. You must not telephone him again, no matter what happens. Men cannot admire a girl who—well, it's a hard word, but I must say it—pursues them. . . . Talk to him gaily and graciously when you see him, and never hint of the sorrow he has caused you. Men hate reminders of sadness."

Who would like to bet there and then that, after the little Peyton girl has left Miss Marion alone with her own needy demons, the coolly collected older woman will not catastrophically pick up her telephone—more than once in the space of a few minutes—to call a certain Mr. Lawrence? Are we shocked to hear her inner voice send up the familiar lament "Oh, he said he'd call, he said he'd call. He said there was nothing the trouble, he said of course he'd call. Oh, he said so." All the good advice is invalidated in a shadowy, lonely late afternoon for a single woman approaching forty.

In presenting the pattern for examination, Parker exploits the apparently trivial—telephone calls, social invitations—in order first to extract, and then to reveal, a theory concerning the larger implications of the difference between the sexes. The theory goes something like this, as she put it in a 1957 story titled "The Banquet of Crow": "Two people can't go on and on and on, doing the same things year after year, when only one of them likes doing them . . . and still be happy." It's a simple statement, but not an easy one to live through, especially for the likes of Miss Marion or, Parker implies, for the rest of us who cannot mummify our emotions.

You need not have read much Parker to know how these stories will turn out, but then her skill does not depend on the breathless rush towards the unknown but instead on the breathless rush towards the known—even, or especially, when that which is known is what should be known and avoided. The voraciously vulnerable woman will be hurt; the casually unfaithful man will call another more-than-willing victim to his side; the shopgirl who longs for jewels in a window will learn just how far from her reach these pearls lie; the son of a selfish mother will turn up on her doorstep hoping for unselfishness; the woman who dances with a lout will have her instep stepped on and will keep on waltzing.

The waltzing woman will inevitably keep her subtext to herself, and let her partner in on only those phrases he will be able to endure, telling him, "I was watching you do it when you were dancing before. It's awfully effective when you look at it." She then goes on to tell us what she really thinks, and it isn't as winsome as what he hears:

It's awfully effective when you look at it. I bet I'm awfully effective when you look at me. My hair is hanging along my cheeks, my skirt is swaddling about me, I can feel the cold damp of my brow. I must look like something out of "The Fall of the House of Usher." This sort of thing takes a fearful toll of a woman my age. And he worked up his little step himself, he with his degenerate cunning.

Not that the reader is certain, by the story's end, whose voice is in ascendancy. The man is a figure to be satirized internally, perhaps; but that doesn't mean you shouldn't keep your arms around him just the same. The twinned-voice belongs to a woman who laughs at her partner but doesn't quite want to let him go. It's sad, Parker knows it's sad, and you know it's sad when Parker writes it. And yet we laugh.

Parker's characters are in most danger—and are most dangerous—when they threaten to break the silence. When the young woman in "New York to Detroit" calls to demand some verbal reassurance, she gets only the literalization of the bad connection that has no doubt existed between the lovers for months before his departure from Manhattan. We flinch to hear her say, no doubt against all her better instincts, "Darling, it hurts so terribly when they ask me about you, and I have to say I don't—" only to have him reply, "This is the damndest, lousiest connection I ever saw in my life. . . . What hurts? What's the matter?" The repetition of her sentiment more than undermines its effectiveness; it renders her speech so useless that she attempts surrender: "I said, it hurts so terribly when people ask me about you . . . and I have to say—Oh, never mind. Never mind." But she can't quite give up, and asks him for some sweetness to get her through the night—only to have him ring off to join a bunch of his friends who have just dropped by for a party. If you have to ask for love, according to Parker, you won't get it; but who, according to Parker, can manage to go through life without asking for love?

When she writes about a woman waiting for a telephone call, anyone who has ever waited by the phone can understand what Parker's character is putting herself through, sensing the ferocity of the struggle against speech when words can only lead to further ruin:

I must think about something else. This is what I'll do. I'll put the clock in the other room. Then I can't look at it. If I do have to look at it, then I'll have to walk into the bedroom, and that will be something to do. Maybe, before I look at it again, he will call me. I'll be so sweet to him, if he calls me. If he says he can't see me tonight, I'll say, "Why, that's all right, dear. Why, of course it's all right." I'll be the way I was when I first met him. Then maybe he'll like me again. I was always sweet, at first. Oh, it's so easy to be sweet to people before you love them. . . . They don't like you to tell them they've made you cry. They don't like you to tell them you're unhappy because of them. If you do, they think you're possessive and exacting. And then they hate you. They hate you whenever you say anything you really think. You always have to keep playing little games. Oh, I thought we didn't have to; I thought this was so big I could say whatever I meant. I guess you can't, ever. I guess there isn't ever anything big enough for that.

Writing with the full force of true passion—writing the way this character speaks—Parker has indeed been chastised for believing that the literary world was big enough to let her say, in all honesty, whatever she meant. Even as her character misgauges her beloved, so did Parker misgauge a gang of critics who sought to punish her for the authenticity and lack of pretense in her writing. And yet even as her character makes us look at ourselves, and makes us the laugh in the mirror image presented, so does Parker hold a glass up to life, lightly. She wins, finally, because her success affords her the last laugh.

—Regina Barreca

SUGGESTIONS FOR FURTHER READING

CRITICISM

Bunkers, Suzanne L. " 'I am Outraged Womanhood': Dorothy Parker as Feminist and Social Critic." *Regionalism and the Female Imagination* 4 (1978): 25–35.

Douglas, George. *Women of the Twenties*. New York: Saybrook, 1989.

Gray, James. "Dream of Unfair Women: Nancy Hale, Clare Booth Luce, and Dorothy Parker." In James Gray, *On Second Thought*. Minneapolis: University of Minnesota Press, 1946.

Hagopian, John. "You Were Perfectly Fine." *Insight I: Analyses of American Literature*. Frankfurt: A. M. Hirschgraben, 1962.

Labrie, Ross. "Dorothy Parker Revisited." *Canadian Review of American Studies* 7 (1976): 48–56.

Kinney, Arthur F. *Dorothy Parker*. Boston: Twayne, 1978.

Miller, Nina. "Making Love Modern: Dorothy Parker and Her Public." *American Literature* 64, no. 4 (1992): 763–784.

Shanahan, William. "Robert Benchley and Dorothy Parker: Punch and Judy in Formal Dress." *Rendevous* 3, no. 1 (1968): 23–34.

Toth, Emily. "Dorothy Parker, Erica Jong, and New Feminist Humor." *Regionalism and the Female Imagination* 2, no. 2 (1977): 70–85.

Trichler, Paula A. "Verbal Subversions in Dorothy Parker: 'Trapped Like a Trap in a Trap.' " *Language and Style: An International Journal* 13, no. 4 (1980): 46–61.

Walker, Nancy. "Fragile and Dumb: The 'Little Woman' in Woman's Humor, 1900–1940." *Thalia: Studies in Literary Humor* 5 (1982), no. 2: 24–49.

Yates, Norris. "Dorothy Parker's Idle Men and Women." In Norris Wilson Yates, *The American Humorist: Conscience of the Twentieth Century*. Ames: Iowa State University Press, 1964.

BACKGROUND

Capron, Marion. "Dorothy Parker." *Writers at Work: The Paris Review Interviews*. Edited by Malcolm Cowley. New York: Viking, 1957. Reprinted in *Women Writers at Work*. Edited by George Plimpton. New York: Penguin, 1989.

Case, Frank. *Tales of a Wayward Inn*. New York: Frederick A. Stokes, 1938.

Douglas, Ann. *Terrible Honesty: Mongrel Manhattan in the 1920s*. New York: Farrar, Straus & Giroux, 1995.

Drennan, Robert, ed. *The Algonquin Wits*. New York: Citadel Press, 1968.

Gaines, James R. *Wit's End: Days and Nights of the Algonquin Round Table*. New York: Harcourt, 1977.

Grant, Jane. *Ross, The New Yorker, and Me*. New York: Raynel & Morrow, 1968.

Harriman, Margaret Case. *The Vicious Circle: The Story of the Algonquin Round Table*. New York: Harcourt, 1977.

Kramer, Dale. *Ross and The New Yorker*. New York: Doubleday, 1951.

Kunkel, Thomas. *Genius at Work: Harold Ross of The New Yorker*. New York: Random House, 1995.

DOROTHY PARKER BIOGRAPHIES

Frewin, Leslie. *The Late Mrs. Dorothy Parker*. New York: Macmillan, 1986.

Keats, John. *You Might As Well Live: The Life and Times of Dorothy Parker*. New York: Simon & Schuster, 1970.

Meade, Marion. *Dorothy Parker: What Fresh Hell Is This?* New York: Villard Books, 1988.

ANTHOLOGY

The Viking Portable Library: Dorothy Parker. New York: Viking, 1944. Republished as *The Indispensable Dorothy Parker*. New York: Book Society, 1944. Published again as *Selected Short Stories*. New York: Editions for the Armed Services, 1944. Revised and enlarged as *The Portable Dorothy Parker*. New York: Viking, 1973; revised, 1976. Republished as *The Collected Dorothy Parker*. London: Duckworth, 1973.

CHRONOLOGY

1893   August 22: Born in West End, New Jersey, to J. Henry Rothschild and Eliza A. (Marston) Rothschild.

1897   July 20: Mother dies.

1900–   Student at Blessed Sacrament Convent, New York City, and
1908   Miss Dana's School, Morristown, New Jersey. Formal education ends abruptly at age fourteen.

1913   December 28: Father dies.

1914   September: First published poem for money ($12), "Any Porch," *Vanity Fair*.

1915   First job, on *Vogue*; light verse published by Franklin P. Adams (F.P.A.).

1917–   Staff writer for *Vanity Fair*; April 1918–March 1920: replaces
1920   P. G. Wodehouse as drama reviewer.

1917   June 30: Marries Edwin ("Eddie") Pond Parker II, of Hartford, Connecticut, descendant of prominent Congregational clergy family.

1919   June: Algonquin Round Table meets for the first time.

1920   January: *High Society* with Frank Crowninshield and George S. Chappell. Fired from *Vanity Fair* for outspoken criticism; named drama reviewer for *Ainslee's* (May 1920–July 1923). Contributes free-lance verse and prose to *Life*.

1920–   Contributes essays and verse to *Saturday Evening Post*, *Ladies'*
1923   *Home Journal*, *Everybody's*, and *Life*.

1922   April 30: Writes song for *No Siree!* and acts in production; writes "Nero" with Robert Benchley for *The 49ers*. Publishes first book, *Women I'm Not Married To; Men I'm Not Married To* (with F.P.A.). Fall: Has abortion.

1924   December 1: Play, *Close Harmony* (with Elmer Rice), opens.

1925   Collaborates on novel, *Bobbed Hair* (*Collier's*, January 17). First film script, *Business Is Business* (with George S. Kaufman).

1926   *Enough Rope* (poems) becomes a best-seller; first European trip.

1927   October 1–March 1931: Book reviewer for *The New Yorker* as "Constant Reader"; also contributes fiction and poems. August 11: Marches against execution of Sacco and Vanzetti in Boston.

1928   March 31: Divorces Eddie Parker. *Sunset Gun* (collected poems) another best-seller; column for *McCall's*.

1929   "Big Blonde" wins O. Henry Award as year's best short story.

1930   *Laments for the Living* (collected fiction).

1931   *Death and Taxes* (collected poems); contributes drama reviews to *The New Yorker* and lyrics to *Shoot the Works* by Heywood Broun. On three-month contract for MGM in Hollywood.

1933   *After Such Pleasures* (collected stories) published.

1934   June 18: Marries Alan Campbell; contributes to dialogue of *Here Is My Heart* and *One Hour Late* (both Paramount). Helps organize Screen Writers Guild.

1935   Contributes to dialogue, *The Case Against Mrs. Ames, Mary Burns, Fugitive*; to screenplay construction, *Hands Across the Table*; and to treatment, *Paris in Spring* (all Paramount). Lyrics, *Big Broadcast of 1936* (Paramount).

1936   *Not So Deep as a Well* (collected poems); joint screenplays, *Three Married Men* and *Lady, Be Careful* (both Paramount) and *Suzy* (MGM); additional dialogue, *The Moon's Our Home* (Paramount). June: Helps found the Anti-Nazi League.

1937   Joint screenplay, *A Star Is Born*, for David Selznick; nominated for Academy Award for the screenplay; joint screenplay, *Woman Chases Man* (United Artists). Reports on Loyalist cause from Spain for *New Masses*.

1938   Joint screenplay, *Sweethearts* (MGM); *Trade Winds* (United Artists).

1939   *Here Lies* (collected stories) published.

1941   Joint screenplay, *Weekend for Three*; additional dialogue, *The Little Foxes* (both RKO).

1942   *Collected Stories*; joint original screenplay, *Saboteur* (Universal).

1944   *The Viking Portable Library: Dorothy Parker*, poems and stories chosen by Parker.

1947   Joint original story, *Smash-Up: The Story of a Woman* (Universal-International). Nominated for a second Academy Award, for best original story. May 27: Divorces Campbell.

1949   Joint screenplay, *The Fan* (20th Century–Fox). Play *The Coast of Illyria* (with Ross Evans) has three-week run in Dallas. Blacklisted in Hollywood.

1950   Remarries Alan Campbell; "Horsie" a basis for *Queen for a Day* (United Artists).

1952–   Testimony against her before HUAC.
1953

1953   Play *The Ladies of the Corridor* (with Arnaud d'Usseau).

1955   Called before New York State joint legislative committee; pleads Fifth Amendment.
1956   Additional lyrics for *Candide* (musical).
1957–   Book reviewer for *Esquire*; a total of 46 columns, 208 books
1963   reviewed.
1958   Marjorie Peabody Waite Award, American Academy of Arts and Letters. Publishes last short story, "Bolt Behind the Blue," in December *Esquire*.
1959   Inducted into American Academy of Arts and Letters.
1963   June 14: Alan Campbell dies, apparent suicide, age fifty-nine.
1963–   Distinguished Visiting Professor of English, California State
1964   College at Los Angeles.
1964   Records stories and poems for Spoken Arts, Verve; publishes final magazine piece in December *Esquire*.
1965   *Short Story* anthology, co-edited with Frederick B. Shroyer.
1967   June 7: Discovered dead of a heart attack in her room at Hotel Volney, New York City, at age seventy-three.

A NOTE ON THE TEXT

The stories are republished here from the texts of their original sources except in those instances where Dorothy Parker herself emended them in subsequent collections. The original sources are noted at the end of each story; variants and emendations are noted below. Minor orthographic emendations have been silently incorporated throughout the collection.

"The Wonderful Old Gentleman" (1926) was originally subtitled "A Story Proving that No One Can Hate Like a Close Relative." The subtitle was dropped when the story was first collected in *Laments for the Living* (1930) and subsequently in *The Viking Portable Library: Dorothy Parker* (1944).

"Lucky Little Curtis" (1927) was retitled simply "Little Curtis" in *Laments for the Living* and thereafter in the *Portable*.

"Long Distance" (1928), subtitled "Wasting Words, or an Attempt at a Telephone Conversation Between New York and Detroit," was retitled "New York to Detroit" in *Laments for Living* and in the *Portable*.

"The Waltz" (1933): The $50 figure at the end of the story was retained in Parker's collection *After Such Pleasures* (1933) but changed to $20 in Parker's *Here Lies* (1939) and the *Portable*.

"The Custard Heart" first appeared in *Here Lies* (1939). Unlike her other stories, there was no original magazine publication.

"The Game" (1948) was co-authored by Ross Evans, Parker's collaborator on the play *The Coast of Illyria* (1949).

STORIES

Such a Pretty Little Picture

Mr. Wheelock was clipping the hedge. He did not dislike doing it. If it had not been for the faintly sickish odor of the privet bloom, he would definitely have enjoyed it. The new shears were so sharp and bright, there was such a gratifying sense of something done as the young green stems snapped off and the expanse of tidy, square hedge-top lengthened. There was a lot of work to be done on it. It should have been attended to a week ago, but this was the first day that Mr. Wheelock had been able to get back from the city before dinnertime.

Clipping the hedge was one of the few domestic duties that Mr. Wheelock could be trusted with. He was notoriously poor at doing anything around the house. All the suburb knew about it. It was the source of all Mrs. Wheelock's jokes. Her most popular anecdote was of how, the past winter, he had gone out and hired a man to take care of the furnace, after a seven-years' losing struggle with it. She had an admirable memory, and often as she had related the story, she never dropped a word of it. Even now, in the late summer, she could hardly tell it for laughing.

When they were first married, Mr. Wheelock had lent himself to the fun. He had even posed as being more inefficient than he really was, to make the joke better. But he had tired of his helplessness, as a topic of conversation. All the men of Mrs. Wheelock's acquaintance, her cousins, her brother-in-law, the boys she went to high school with, the neighbors' husbands, were adepts at putting up a shelf, at repairing a lock, or making a shirtwaist box. Mr. Wheelock had begun to feel that there was something rather effeminate about his lack of interest in such things.

He had wanted to answer his wife, lately, when she enlivened some neighbor's dinner table with tales of his inadequacy with hammer and wrench. He had wanted to cry, "All right, suppose I'm not any good at things like that. What of it?"

He had played with the idea, had tried to imagine how his voice would sound, uttering the words. But he could think of no further argument for his case than that "What of it?" And he was a little relieved, somehow, at being able to find nothing stronger. It made it reassuringly impossible to go through with the plan of answering his wife's public railleries.

Mrs. Wheelock sat, now, on the spotless porch of the neat stucco house. Beside her was a pile of her husband's shirts and drawers, the price-tags still on them. She was going over all the buttons before he wore the garments, sewing them on more firmly. Mrs. Wheelock never waited for a button to come off, before sewing it on. She worked with quick, decided movements, compressing her lips each time the thread made a slight resistance to her deft jerks.

She was not a tall woman, and since the birth of her child she had gone over from a delicate plumpness to a settled stockiness. Her brown hair, though abundant, grew in an uncertain line about her forehead. It was her habit to put it up in curlers at night, but the crimps never came out in the right place. It was arranged with perfect neatness, yet it suggested that it had been done up and got over with as quickly as possible. Passionately clean, she was always redolent of the germicidal soap she used so vigorously. She was wont to tell people, somewhat redundantly, that she never employed any sort of cosmetics. She had unlimited contempt for women who sought to reduce their weight by dieting, cutting from their menus such nourishing items as cream and puddings and cereals.

Adelaide Wheelock's friends—and she had many of them—said of her that there was no nonsense about her. They and she regarded it as a compliment.

Sister, the Wheelocks' five-year-old daughter, played quietly in the gravel path that divided the tiny lawn. She had been known as Sister since her birth, and her mother still laid plans for a brother for her. Sister's baby carriage stood waiting in the cellar, her baby clothes were stacked expectantly away in bureau drawers. But raises were infrequent at the advertising agency where Mr. Wheelock was employed, and his present salary had barely caught up to the cost of their living. They could not conscientiously regard themselves as being able to afford a son. Both Mr. and Mrs. Wheelock keenly felt his guilt in keeping the bassinet empty.

Sister was not a pretty child, though her features were straight, and her eyes would one day be handsome. The left one turned slightly in toward the nose, now, when she looked in a certain direction; they would operate as soon as she was seven. Her hair was pale and limp, and her color bad. She was a delicate little girl. Not fragile in a picturesque way, but the kind of child that must be always undergoing treatment for its teeth and its throat and obscure things in its nose. She had lately had her adenoids removed, and she was still using squares of surgical gauze instead of handkerchiefs. Both she and her mother somehow felt that these gave her a sort of prestige.

She was additionally handicapped by her frocks, which her mother bought a size or so too large, with a view to Sister's growing into them—an expectation which seemed never to be realized, for her skirts were always too long, and the shoulders of her little dresses came halfway down to her thin elbows. Yet, even discounting the unfortunate way she was dressed, you could tell, in some way, that she was never going to wear any kind of clothes well.

Mr. Wheelock glanced at her now and then as he clipped. He had never felt any fierce thrills of father-love for the child. He had been disappointed in her when she was a pale, large-headed baby, smelling of stale milk and warm rubber. Sister made him feel ill at ease, vaguely irritated him. He had had no share in her training; Mrs. Wheelock was so competent a parent that she took the places of both of them. When Sister came to him to ask his permission to do something, he always told her to wait and ask her mother about it.

He regarded himself as having the usual paternal affection for his daughter. There were times, indeed, when she had tugged sharply at his heart—when he had waited in the corridor outside the operating room; when she was still under the anesthetic, and lay little and white and helpless on her high hospital bed; once when he had accidentally closed a door upon her thumb. But from the first he had nearly acknowledged to himself that he did not like Sister as a person.

Sister was not a whining child, despite her poor health. She had always been sensible and well-mannered, amenable about talking to visitors, rigorously unselfish. She never got into trouble, like other children. She did not care much for other children. She had heard herself described as being "old-fashioned," and she knew she was delicate, and she felt that these attributes rather set her above them. Besides, they were rough and careless of their bodily well-being.

Sister was exquisitely cautious of her safety. Grass, she knew, was often apt to be damp in the late afternoon, so she was careful now to stay right in the middle of the gravel path, sitting on a folded newspaper and playing one of her mysterious games with three petunias that she had been allowed to pick. Mrs. Wheelock never had to speak to her twice about keeping off wet grass, or wearing her rubbers, or putting on her jacket if a breeze sprang up. Sister was an immediately obedient child, always.

II

Mrs. Wheelock looked up from her sewing and spoke to her husband. Her voice was high and clear, resolutely good-humored. From her habit of calling instructions from her upstairs window to Sister playing on the porch below, she spoke always a little louder than was necessary.

"Daddy," she said.

She had called him Daddy since some eight months before Sister was born. She and the child had the same trick of calling his name and then waiting until he signified that he was attending before they went on with what they wanted to say.

Mr. Wheelock stopped clipping, straightened himself and turned toward her.

"Daddy," she went on, thus reassured, "I saw Mr. Ince down at the post office today when Sister and I went down to get the ten o'clock mail—there wasn't much, just a card for me from Grace Williams from that place they go to up on Cape Cod, and an advertisement from some department store or other about their summer fur sale (as if I cared!), and a circular for you from the bank. I opened it; I knew you wouldn't mind.

"Anyway, I just thought I'd tackle Mr. Ince first as last about getting in our cordwood. He didn't see me at first—though I'll bet he really saw me and pretended not to—but I ran right after him. 'Oh, Mr. Ince!' I said. 'Why, hello, Mrs. Wheelock,' he said, and then he asked for you, and I told him you were finely, and everything. Then I said, 'Now, Mr. Ince,' I said, 'how about getting in that cordwood of ours?' And he said, 'Well, Mrs. Wheelock,' he said, 'I'll get it in soon's I can, but I'm short of help right now,' he said.

"Short of help! Of course I couldn't say anything, but I guess he could tell from the way I looked at him how much I believed it. I just said, 'All right, Mr. Ince, but don't you forget us. There may be a cold snap coming on,' I said, 'and we'll be wanting a fire in the living-room. Don't you forget us,' I said, and he said, no, he wouldn't.

"If that wood isn't here by Monday, I think you ought to do something about it, Daddy. There's no sense in all this putting it off, and putting it off. First thing you know there'll be a cold snap coming on, and we'll be wanting a fire in the living-room, and there we'll be! You'll be sure and 'tend to it, won't you, Daddy? I'll remind you again Monday, if I can think of it, but there are so many things!"

Mr. Wheelock nodded and turned back to his clipping—and his thoughts. They were thoughts that had occupied much of his leisure lately. After dinner, when Adelaide was sewing or arguing with the maid, he found himself letting his magazine fall face downward on his knee, while he rolled the same idea round and round in his mind. He had got so that he looked forward, through the day, to losing himself in it. He had rather welcomed the hedge-clipping; you can clip and think at the same time.

It had started with a story that he had picked up somewhere. He couldn't recall whether he had heard it or had read it—that was probably it, he thought, he had run across it in the back pages of some comic paper that someone had left on the train.

It was about a man who lived in a suburb. Every morning he had gone to the city on the 8:12, sitting in the same seat in the same car, and every evening he had gone home to his wife on the 5:17, sitting in the same seat in the same car. He had done this for twenty years of his life. And then one night he didn't come home. He never went back to his office any more. He just never turned up again.

The last man to see him was the conductor on the 5:17.

"He come down the platform at the Grand Central," the man reported, "just like he done every night since I been working on this road. He put one foot on the step, and then he stopped sudden, and he said 'Oh, hell,' and he took his foot off of the step and walked away. And that's the last anybody see of him."

Curious how that story took hold of Mr. Wheelock's fancy. He had started thinking of it as a mildly humorous anecdote; he had come to accept it as fact. He did not think the man's sitting in the same seat in the same car need have been stressed so much. That seemed unimportant. He thought long about the man's wife, wondered what suburb he had lived in. He loved to play with the thing, to try to feel what the man felt before he took his foot off the car's step. He never concerned himself with speculations as to where the man had disappeared, how he had spent the rest of his life. Mr. Wheelock was absorbed in that moment when he had said "Oh, hell," and walked off. "Oh, hell" seemed to Mr. Wheelock a fine thing for him to have said, a perfect summary of the situation.

He tried thinking of himself in the man's place. But no, he would have done it from the other end. That was the real way to do it.

Some summer evening like this, say, when Adelaide was sewing on buttons, up on the porch, and Sister was playing somewhere about. A pleasant, quiet evening it must be, with the shadows lying long on the street that led from their house to the station. He would put down the garden shears, or the hose, or whatever he happened to be puttering with—not throw the thing down, you know, just put it quietly aside—and walk out of the gate and down the street, and that would be the last they'd see of him. He would time it so that he'd just make the 6:03 for the city comfortably.

He did not go ahead with it from there, much. He was not especially anxious to leave the advertising agency forever. He did not particularly dislike his work. He had been an advertising solicitor since he had gone to work at all, and he worked hard at his job and, aside from that, didn't think about it much one way or the other.

It seemed to Mr. Wheelock that before he had got hold of the "Oh, hell" story he had never thought about anything much, one way or the other. But he would have to disappear from the office, too, that was certain. It would spoil everything to turn up there again. He thought dimly of taking a train going West, after the 6:03 got him to the Grand Central Terminal—he might go to Buffalo, say, or perhaps Chicago. Better just let that part take care of itself and go back to dwell on the moment when it would sweep over him that he was going to do it, when he would put down the shears and walk out the gate—

The "Oh, hell" rather troubled him. Mr. Wheelock felt that he would like to retain that; it completed the gesture so beautifully. But he didn't quite know to whom he should say it.

He might stop in at the post office on his way to the station and say it to the postmaster; but the postmaster would probably think he was only annoyed at there being no mail for him. Nor would the conductor of the 6:03, a train Mr. Wheelock never used, take the right interest in it. Of course the real thing to do would be to say it to Adelaide just before he laid down the shears. But somehow Mr. Wheelock could not make that scene come very clear in his imagination.

III

"Daddy," Mrs. Wheelock said briskly.

He stopped clipping, and faced her.

"Daddy," she related, "I saw Doctor Mann's automobile going by the house this morning—he was going to have a look at Mr. Warren, his rheumatism's getting along nicely—and I called him in a minute, to look us over."

She screwed up her face, winked, and nodded vehemently several times in the direction of the absorbed Sister, to indicate that she was the subject of the discourse.

"He said we were going ahead finely," she resumed, when she was sure that he had caught the idea. "Said there was no need for those t-o-n-s-i-l-s to c-o-m-e o-u-t. But I thought, soon's it gets a little cooler, some time next month, we'd just run in to the city and let Doctor Sturges have a look at us. I'd rather be on the safe side."

"But Doctor Lytton said it wasn't necessary, and those doctors at the hospital, and now Doctor Mann, that's known her since she was a baby," suggested Mr. Wheelock.

"I know, I know," replied his wife. "But I'd rather be on the safe side."

Mr. Wheelock went back to his hedge.

Oh, of course he couldn't do it; he never seriously thought he could, for a minute. Of course he couldn't. He wouldn't have the shadow of an excuse for doing it. Adelaide was a sterling woman, an utterly faithful wife, an almost slavish mother. She ran his house economically and efficiently. She harried the suburban trades people into giving them dependable service, drilled the succession of poorly paid, poorly trained maids, cheerfully did the thousand fussy little things that go with the running of a house. She looked after his clothes, gave him medicine when she thought he needed it, oversaw the preparation of every meal that was set before him; they were not especially inspirational meals, but the food was always nourishing and, as a general thing, fairly well cooked. She never lost her temper, she was never depressed, never ill.

Not the shadow of an excuse. People would know that, and so they would invent an excuse for him. They would say there must be another woman.

Mr. Wheelock frowned, and snipped at an obstinate young twig. Good Lord, the last thing he wanted was another woman. What he

wanted was that moment when he realized he could do it, when he
would lay down the shears—

Oh, of course he couldn't; he knew that as well as anybody. What
would they do, Adelaide and Sister? The house wasn't even paid for
yet, and there would be that operation on Sister's eye in a couple of
years. But the house would be all paid up by next March. And there
was always that well-to-do brother-in-law of Adelaide's, the one who,
for all his means, put up every shelf in that great big house with his
own hands.

Decent people didn't just go away and leave their wives and
families that way. All right, suppose you weren't decent; what of
it? Here was Adelaide planning what she was going to do when
it got a little cooler, next month. She was always planning
ahead, always confident that things would go on just the same.
Naturally, Mr. Wheelock realized that he couldn't do it, as well as
the next one. But there was no harm in fooling around with the
idea. Would you say the "Oh, hell" now, before you laid down
the shears, or right after? How would it be to turn at the gate and
say it?

Mr. and Mrs. Fred Coles came down the street arm-in-arm, from
their neat stucco house on the corner.

"See they've got you working hard, eh?" cried Mr. Coles genially, as
they paused abreast of the hedge.

Mr. Wheelock laughed politely, marking time for an answer.

"That's right," he evolved.

Mrs. Wheelock looked up from her work, shading her eyes with her
thimbled hand against the long rays of the low sun.

"Yes, we finally got Daddy to do a little work," she called brightly.
"But Sister and I are staying right here to watch over him, for fear he
might cut his little self with the shears."

There was general laughter, in which Sister joined. She had risen
punctiliously at the approach of the older people, and she was looking
politely at their eyes, as she had been taught.

"And how is my great big girl?" asked Mrs. Coles, gazing fondly at
the child.

"Oh, much better," Mrs. Wheelock answered for her. "Doctor
Mann says we are going ahead finely. I saw his automobile passing
the house this morning—he was going to see Mr. Warren,
his rheumatism's coming along nicely—and I called him in a minute to
look us over."

She did the wink and the nods, at Sister's back. Mr. and Mrs. Coles nodded shrewdly back at her.

"He said there's no need for those t-o-n-s-i-l-s to c-o-m-e o-u-t," Mrs. Wheelock called. "But I thought, soon's it gets a little cooler, some time next month, we'd just run in to the city and let Doctor Sturges have a look at us. I was telling Daddy, 'I'd rather be on the safe side,' I said."

"Yes, it's better to be on the safe side," agreed Mrs. Coles, and her husband nodded again, sagely this time. She took his arm, and they moved slowly off.

"Been a lovely day, hasn't it?" she said over her shoulder, fearful of having left too abruptly. "Fred and I are taking a little constitutional before supper."

"Oh, taking a little constitutional?" cried Mrs. Wheelock, laughing.

Mrs. Coles laughed also, three or four bars.

"Yes, just taking a little constitutional before supper," she called back.

Sister, weary of her game, mounted the porch, whimpering a little. Mrs. Wheelock put aside her sewing, and took the tired child in her lap. The sun's last rays touched her brown hair, making it a shimmering gold. Her small, sharp face, the thick lines of her figure were in shadow as she bent over the little girl. Sister's head was hidden on her mother's shoulder, the folds of her rumpled white frock followed her limp, relaxed little body.

The lovely light was kind to the cheap, hurriedly built stucco house, to the clean gravel path, and the bits of closely cut lawn. It was gracious, too, to Mr. Wheelock's tall, lean figure as he bent to work on the last few inches of unclipped hedge.

Twenty years, he thought. The man in the story went through with it for twenty years. He must have been a man along around forty-five, most likely. Mr. Wheelock was thirty-seven. Eight years. It's a long time, eight years is. You could easily get so you could say that final "Oh, hell," even to Adelaide, in eight years. It probably wouldn't take more than four for you to know that you could do it. No, not more than two. . . .

Mrs. Coles paused at the corner of the street and looked back at the Wheelocks' house. The last of the light lingered on the mother and child group on the porch, gently touched the tall, white-clad figure of the husband and father as he went up to them, his work done.

Mrs. Coles was a large, soft woman, barren, and addicted to sentiment.

"Look, Fred; just turn around and look at that," she said to her husband. She looked again, sighing luxuriously. "Such a pretty little picture!"

Smart Set, December 1922

Too Bad

"My dear," Mrs. Marshall said to Mrs. Ames, "I never was so surprised in my life. Never in my life. Why, Grace and I were like that—just like *that*."

She held up her right hand, the upstanding first and second fingers rigidly close together, in illustration.

Mrs. Ames shook her head sadly, and offered the cinnamon toast.

"Imagine!" said Mrs. Marshall, refusing it though with a longing eye. "We were going to have dinner with them last Tuesday night, and then I got this letter from Grace from this little place up in Connecticut, saying she was going to be up there she didn't know how long, and she thought, when she came back, she'd probably take just one big room with a kitchenette. Ernest was living down at the club, she said."

"But what did they do about their apartment?" Mrs. Ames's voice was high with anxiety.

"Why, it seems his sister took it, furnished and all—by the way, remind me, I must go and see her," said Mrs. Marshall. "They wanted to move into town, anyway, and they were looking for a place."

"Doesn't she feel terribly about it—his sister?" asked Mrs. Ames.

"Oh—terribly." Mrs. Marshall dismissed the word as inadequate. "My dear, think how everybody that knew them feels. Think how I feel. I don't know when I've had a thing depress me more. If it had been anybody but the Weldons!"

Mrs. Ames nodded.

"That's what I said," she reported.

"That's what everybody says." Mrs. Marshall quickly took away any undeserved credit. "To think of the Weldons separating! Why, I always used to say to Jim. 'Well, there's one happily married couple, anyway,' I used to say, 'so congenial, and with that nice apartment, and all.' And then, right out of a clear sky, they go and separate. I simply can't understand what on earth made them do it. It just seems too awful!"

Again Mrs. Ames nodded, slowly and sadly.

"Yes, it always seems too bad, a thing like that does," she said. "It's too bad."

II

Mrs. Ernest Weldon wandered about the orderly living-room, giving it some of those little feminine touches. She was not especially good as a touch-giver. The idea was pretty, and appealing to her. Before she was married, she had dreamed of herself as moving softly about her new dwelling, deftly moving a vase here or straightening a flower there, and thus transforming it from a house to a home. Even now, after seven years of marriage, she liked to picture herself in the gracious act.

But, though she conscientiously made a try at it every night as soon as the rose-shaded lamps were lit, she was always a bit bewildered as to how one went about performing those tiny miracles that make all the difference in the world to a room. The living-room, it seemed to her, looked good enough as it was—as good as it would ever look, with that mantelpiece and the same old furniture. Delia, one of the most thoroughly feminine of creatures, had subjected it to a long series of emphatic touches earlier in the day, and none of her handiwork had since been disturbed. But the feat of making all the difference in the world, so Mrs. Weldon had always heard, was not a thing to be left to servants. Touch-giving was a wife's job. And Mrs. Weldon was not one to shirk the business she had entered.

With an almost pitiable air of uncertainty, she strayed over to the mantel, lifted a small Japanese vase, and stood with it in her hand, gazing helplessly around the room. The white-enameled bookcase caught her eye, and gratefully she crossed to it and set the vase upon it, carefully rearranging various ornaments to make room. To relieve the congestion, she took up a framed photograph of Mr. Weldon's sister in evening gown and eye-glasses, again looked all about, and then set it timidly on the piano. She smoothed the piano-cover ingratiatingly, straightened the copies of "A Day in Venice," "To a Wild Rose," and Kreisler's "Caprice Viennois," which stood ever upon the rack, walked over to the tea-table and effected a change of places between the cream-jug and the sugar-bowl.

Then she stepped back, and surveyed her innovations. It was amazing how little difference they made to the room.

Sighing, Mrs. Weldon turned her attention to a bowl of daffodils, slightly past their first freshness. There was nothing to be done there; the omniscient Delia had refreshed them with clear water, had clipped their stems, and removed their more passé sisters. Still Mrs. Weldon bent over them pulling them gently about.

She liked to think of herself as one for whom flowers would thrive, who must always have blossoms about her, if she would be truly happy. When her living-room flowers died, she almost never forgot to stop in at the florist's, the next day, and get a fresh bunch. She told people, in little bursts of confidence, that she loved flowers. There was something almost apologetic in her way of uttering her tender avowal, as if she would beg her listeners not to consider her too bizarre in her taste. It seemed rather as though she expected the hearer to fall back, startled, at her words, crying, "Not really! Well, what *are* we coming to?"

She had other little confessions of affection, too, that she made from time to time; always with a little hesitation, as if understandably delicate about baring her heart, she told her love for color, the country, a good time, a really interesting play, nice materials, well-made clothes, and sunshine. But it was her fondness for flowers that she acknowledged oftenest. She seemed to feel that this, even more than her other predilections, set her apart from the general.

Mrs. Weldon gave the elderly daffodils a final pat, now, and once more surveyed the room, to see if any other repairs suggested themselves. Her lips tightened as the little Japanese vase met her gaze; distinctly, it had been better off in the first place. She set it back, the irritation that the sight of the mantel always gave her welling within her.

She had hated the mantelpiece from the moment they had first come to look at the apartment. There were other things that she had always hated about the place, too—the long, narrow hall, the dark dining-room, the inadequate closets. But Ernest had seemed to like the apartment well enough, so she had said nothing, then or since. After all, what was the use of fussing? Probably there would always be drawbacks, wherever they lived. There were enough in the last place they had had.

So they had taken the apartment on a five-year lease—there were four years and three months to go. Mrs. Weldon felt suddenly weary. She lay down on the davenport, and pressed her thin hand against her dull brown hair.

Mr. Weldon came down the street, bent almost double in his battle with the wind from the river. His mind went over its nightly dark thoughts on living near Riverside Drive, five blocks from a subway station—two of those blocks loud with savage gales. He did not much like their apartment, even when he reached it. As soon as he had seen that dining-room, he had realized that they must always breakfast by artificial light—a thing he hated. But Grace had never appeared to notice it, so he had held his peace. It didn't matter much, anyway, he explained to himself. There was pretty sure to be something wrong, everywhere. The dining-room wasn't much worse than that bedroom on the court, in the last place. Grace had never seemed to mind that, either.

Mrs. Weldon opened the door at his ring.

"Well!" she said, cheerily.

They smiled brightly at each other.

"Hel-lo," he said. "Well! You home?"

They kissed, slightly. She watched with polite interest while he hung up his hat and coat, removed the evening papers from his pocket, and handed one to her.

"Bring the papers?" she said, taking it.

She preceded him along the narrow hall to the living-room, where he let himself slowly down into his big chair, with a sound between a sigh and a groan. She sat opposite him, on the davenport. Again they smiled brightly at each other.

"Well, what have you been doing with yourself today?" he inquired.

She had been expecting the question. She had planned before he came in, how she would tell him all the little events of her day—how the woman in the grocer's shop had had an argument with the cashier, and how Delia had tried out a new salad for lunch with but moderate success, and how Alice Marshall had come to tea and it was quite true that Norma Matthews was going to have another baby. She had woven them into a lively little narrative, carefully choosing amusing phrases of description; had felt that she was going to tell it well and with spirit, and that he might laugh at the account of the occurrence in the grocer's. But now, as she considered it, it seemed to her a long, dull story. She had not the energy to begin it. And he was already smoothing out his paper.

"Oh, nothing," she said, with a gay little laugh. "Did you have a nice day?"

"Why—" he began. He had had some idea of telling her how he had finally put through that Detroit thing, and how tickled J. G. had seemed to be about it. But his interest waned, even as he started to speak. Besides, she was engrossed in breaking off a loose thread from the wool fringe on one of the pillows beside her.

"Oh, pretty fair," he said.

"Tired?" she asked.

"Not so much," he answered. "Why—want to do anything tonight?"

"Why, not unless you do," she said, brightly. "Whatever you say."

"Whatever *you* say," he corrected her.

The subject closed. There was a third exchange of smiles, and then he hid most of himself behind his paper.

Mrs. Weldon, too, turned to the newspaper. But it was an off night for news—a long speech of somebody's, a plan for a garbage dump, a proposed dirigible, a four-day-old murder mystery. No one she knew had died or become engaged or married, or had attended any social functions. The fashions depicted on the woman's page were for Miss Fourteen-to-Sixteen. The advertisements ran mostly to bread, and sauces, and men's clothes and sales of kitchen utensils. She put the paper down.

She wondered how Ernest could get so much enjoyment out of a newspaper. He could occupy himself with one for almost an hour, and then pick up another and go all through the same news with unabated interest. She wished that she could. She wished, even more than that, that she could think of something to say. She glanced around the room for inspiration.

"See my pretty daffy-down-dillies?" she said, finding it. To anyone else, she would have referred to them as daffodils.

Mr. Weldon looked in the direction of the flowers.

"M-m-mm," he said in admission, and returned to the news.

She looked at him, and shook her head despondently. He did not see, behind the paper; nor did she see that he was not reading. He was waiting, his hands gripping the printed sheet till their knuckles were blue-white, for her next remark.

It came.

"I love flowers," she said, in one of her little rushes of confidence.

Her husband did not answer. He sighed, his grip relaxed, and he went on reading.

Mrs. Weldon searched the room for another suggestion.

"Ernie," she said, "I'm so comfortable. Wouldn't you like to get up and get my handkerchief off the piano for me?"

He rose instantly. "Why, certainly," he said.

The way to ask people to fetch handkerchiefs, he thought as he went back to his chair, was to ask them to do it, and not try to make them think that you were giving them a treat. Either come right out and ask them, would they or wouldn't they, or else get up and get your handkerchief yourself.

"Thank you ever so much," his wife said with enthusiasm.

Delia appeared in the doorway. "Dinner," she murmured bashfully, as if it were not quite a nice word for a young woman to use, and vanished.

"Dinner, Ern," cried Mrs. Weldon gaily, getting up.

"Just minute," issued indistinctly from behind the newspaper.

Mrs. Weldon waited. Then her lips compressed, and she went over and playfully took the paper from her husband's hands. She smiled carefully at him, and he smiled back at her.

"You go ahead in," he said, rising. "I'll be right with you. I've just got to wash up."

She looked after him, and something like a volcanic eruption took place within her. You'd think that just one night—just one little night—he might go and wash before dinner was announced. Just one night—it didn't seem much to ask. But she said nothing. God knew it was aggravating, but after all, it wasn't worth the trouble of fussing about.

She was waiting, cheerful and bright, courteously refraining from beginning her soup, when he took his place at the table.

"Oh, tomato soup, eh?" he said.

"Yes," she answered. "You like it, don't you?"

"Who—me?" he said. "Oh, yes. Yes, indeed."

She smiled at him.

"Yes, I thought you liked it," she said.

"You like it, too, don't you?" he inquired.

"Oh, yes," she assured him. "Yes, I like it ever so much. I'm awfully fond of tomato soup."

"Yes," he said, "there's nothing much better than tomato soup on a cold night."

She nodded.

"I think it's nice, too," she confided.

They had had tomato soup for dinner probably three times a month during their married life.

The soup was finished, and Delia brought in the meat.

"Well, that looks pretty good," said Mr. Weldon, carving it. "We haven't had steak for a long time."

"Why, yes, we have, too, Ern," his wife said eagerly. "We had it—let me see, what night were the Baileys here?—we had it Wednesday night—no, Thursday night. Don't you remember?"

"Did we?" he said. "Yes, I guess you're right. It seemed longer, somehow."

Mrs. Weldon smiled politely. She could not think of any way to prolong the discussion.

What did married people talk about, anyway, when they were alone together? She had seen married couples—not dubious ones but people she really knew were husbands and wives—at the theater or in trains, talking together as animatedly as if they were just acquaintances. She always watched them, marvelingly, wondering what on earth they found to say.

She could talk well enough to other people. There never seemed to be enough time for her to finish saying all she wanted to to her friends; she recalled how she had run on to Alice Marshall, only that afternoon. Both men and women found her attractive to listen to; not brilliant, not particularly funny, but still amusing and agreeable. She was never at a loss for something to say, never conscious of groping around for a topic. She had a good memory for bits of fresh gossip, or little stories of some celebrity that she had read or heard somewhere, and a knack of telling them entertainingly. Things people said to her stimulated her to quick replies, and more amusing narratives. They weren't especially scintillating people, either; it was just that they talked to her.

That was the trick of it. If nobody said anything to you, how were you to carry on a conversation from there? Inside, she was always bitter and angry at Ernest for not helping her out.

Ernest, too, seemed to be talkative enough when he was with others. People were always coming up and telling her how much they had enjoyed meeting her husband, and what fun he was. They weren't just being polite. There was no reason why they should go out of their way to say it.

Even when she and Ernest had another couple in to dinner or bridge, they both talked and laughed easily, all evening long. But as soon as the guests said good-night and what an awfully nice evening it had been, and the door had closed behind them, there the Weldons were again, without a word to say to each other. It would have been intimate and amusing to have talked over their guests' clothes and skill at bridge and probable domestic and financial affairs, and she would do it the next day, with great interest, too, to Alice Marshall, or some other one of her friends. But she couldn't do it with Ernest. Just as she started to, she found she simply couldn't make the effort.

So they would put away the card-table and empty the ash-receivers, with many "Oh, I beg your pardon's" and "No, no—I was in your way's," and then Ernest would say, "Well, I guess I'll go along to bed," and she would answer, "All right—I'll be in in a minute," and they would smile cheerfully at each other, and another evening would be over.

She tried to remember what they used to talk about before they were married, when they were engaged. It seemed to her that they never had had much to say to each other. But she hadn't worried about it then;

indeed, she had felt the satisfaction of the correct, in their courtship, for she had always heard that true love was inarticulate. Then, besides, there had been always kissing and things, to take up your mind. But it had turned out that true marriage was apparently equally dumb. And you can't depend on kisses and all the rest of it to while away the evenings, after seven years.

You'd think that you would get used to it, in seven years, would realize that that was the way it was, and let it go at that. You don't, though. A thing like that gets on your nerves. It isn't one of those cozy, companionable silences that people occasionally fall into together. It makes you feel as if you must do something about it, as if you weren't performing your duty. You have the feeling a hostess has when her party is going badly, when her guests sit in corners and refuse to mingle. It makes you nervous and self-conscious, and you talk desperately about tomato soup, and say things like "daffy-down-dilly."

Mrs. Weldon cast about in her mind for a subject to offer her husband. There was Alice Marshall's new system of reducing—no, that was pretty dull. There was the case she had read in the morning's paper about the man of eighty-seven who had taken, as his fourth wife, a girl of twenty—he had probably seen that, and as long as he hadn't thought it worth repeating, he wouldn't think it worth hearing. There was the thing the Baileys' little boy had said about Jesus—no, she had told him that the night before.

She looked over at him, desultorily eating his rhubarb pie. She wished he wouldn't put that greasy stuff on his head. Perhaps it was necessary, if his hair really was falling out, but it did seem that he might find some more attractive remedy, if he only had the consideration to look around for one. Anyway, why must his hair fall out? There was something a little disgusting about people with falling hair.

"Like your pie, Ernie?" she asked vivaciously.

"Why, I don't know," he said, thinking it over. "I'm not so crazy about rhubarb, I don't think. Are you?"

"No, I'm not so awfully crazy about it," she answered. "But then, I'm not really crazy about any kind of pie."

"Aren't you really?" he said, politely surprised. "I like pie pretty well—some kinds of pie."

"Do you?" The polite surprise was hers now.

"Why, yes," he said. "I like a nice huckleberry pie, or a nice lemon meringue pie, or a—" He lost interest in the thing himself, and his voice died away.

He avoided looking at her left hand, which lay on the edge of the table, palm upward. The long, grey-white ends of her nails protruded beyond the tips of her fingers, and the sight made him uncomfortable. Why in God's name must she wear her finger nails that preposterous length, and file them to those horrible points? If there was anything that he hated, it was a woman with pointed finger nails.

They returned to the living-room, and Mr. Weldon again eased himself down into his chair, reaching for the second paper.

"Quite sure there isn't anything you'd like to do tonight?" he asked solicitously. "Like to go to the movies or anything?"

"Oh, no," she said. "Unless there's something you want to do."

"No, no," he answered. "I just thought maybe you wanted to."

"Not unless you do," she said.

He began on his paper, and she wandered aimlessly about the room. She had forgotten to get a new book from the library, and it had never in her life occurred to her to reread a book that she had once completed. She thought vaguely of playing solitaire, but she did not care enough about it to go to the trouble of getting out the cards, and setting up the table. There was some sewing that she could do, and she thought that she might presently go into the bedroom and fetch the nightgown that she was making for herself. Yes, she would probably do that, in a little while.

Ernest would read industriously, and, along toward the middle of the paper, he would start yawning aloud. Something happened inside Mrs. Weldon when he did this. She would murmur that she had to speak to Delia, and hurry to the kitchen. She would stay there rather a long time, looking vaguely into jars and inquiring half-heartedly about laundry lists, and, when she returned, he would have gone in to get ready for bed.

In a year, three hundred of their evenings were like this. Seven times three hundred is more than two thousand.

Mrs. Weldon went into the bedroom, and brought back her sewing. She sat down, pinned the pink satin to her knee, and began whipping narrow lace along the top of the half-made garment. It was fussy work. The fine thread knotted and drew, and she could not get the light adjusted so that the shadow of her head did not fall on her work. She grew a little sick, from the strain on her eyes.

Mr. Weldon turned a page, and yawned aloud. "Wah-huh-huh-huh-huh," he went, on a descending scale. He yawned again, and this time climbed the scale.

III

"My dear," Mrs. Ames said to Mrs. Marshall, "don't you really think that there must have been some other woman?"

"Oh, I simply couldn't think it was anything like that," said Mrs. Marshall. "Not Ernest Weldon. So devoted—home every night at half-past six, and such good company, and so jolly, and all. I don't see how there *could* have been."

"Sometimes," observed Mrs. Ames, "those awfully jolly men at home are just the kind."

"Yes, I know," Mrs. Marshall said. "But not Ernest Weldon. Why, I used to say to Jim, 'I never saw such a devoted husband in my life,' I said. Oh, not Ernest Weldon."

"I don't suppose," began Mrs. Ames, and hesitated. "I don't suppose," she went on, intently pressing the bit of sodden lemon in her cup with her teaspoon, "that Grace—that there was ever anyone—or anything like that?"

"Oh, Heavens, no," cried Mrs. Marshall. "Grace Weldon just gave her whole life to that man. It was Ernest this and Ernest that every minute. I simply can't understand it. If there was one earthly reason— if they ever fought, or if Ernest drank, or anything like that. But they got along so beautifully together—why, it just seems as if they must have been crazy to go and do a thing like this. Well, I can't begin to tell you how blue it's made me. It seems so awful!"

"Yes," said Mrs. Ames, "it certainly is too bad."

Mr. Durant

Not for some ten days had Mr. Durant known any such ease of mind. He gave himself up to it, wrapped himself, warm and soft, as in a new and an expensive cloak. God, for Whom Mr. Durant entertained a good-humored affection, was in His heaven, and all was again well with Mr. Durant's world.

Curious how this renewed peace sharpened his enjoyment of the accustomed things about him. He looked back at the rubber works, which he had just left for the day, and nodded approvingly at the solid red pile, at the six neat stories rising impressively into the darkness. You would go far, he thought, before you would find a more up-and-coming outfit, and there welled in him a pleasing, proprietary sense of being a part of it.

He gazed amiably down Center Street, noting how restfully the lights glowed. Even the wet, dented pavement, spotted with thick puddles, fed his pleasure by reflecting the discreet radiance above it. And to complete his comfort, the car for which he was waiting, admirably on time, swung into view far down the track. He thought, with a sort of jovial tenderness, of what it would bear him to; of his dinner—it was fish-chowder night—of his children, of his wife, in the order named. Then he turned his kindly attention to the girl who stood near him, obviously awaiting the Center Street car, too. He was delighted to feel a sharp interest in her. He regarded it as being distinctly creditable to himself that he could take a healthy notice of such matters once more. Twenty years younger—that's what he felt.

Rather shabby, she was, in her rough coat with its shagginess rubbed off here and there. But there was a something in the way her cheaply smart turban was jammed over her eyes, in the way her thin young figure moved under the loose coat. Mr. Durant pointed his tongue, and moved it delicately along his cool, smooth upper lip.

The car approached, clanged to a stop before them. Mr. Durant stepped gallantly aside to let the girl get in first. He did not help her to enter, but the solicitous way in which he superintended the process gave all the effect of his having actually assisted her.

Her tight little skirt slipped up over her thin, pretty legs as she took the high step. There was a run in one of her flimsy silk stockings. She was doubtless unconscious of it; it was well back toward the seam, extending, probably from her garter, half-way down the calf. Mr. Durant had an odd desire to catch his thumbnail in the present end of the run, and to draw it on down until the slim line of the dropped stitches reached to the top of her low shoe. An indulgent smile at his whimsy played about his mouth, broadening to a grin of affable evening greeting for the conductor, as he entered the car and paid his fare.

The girl sat down somewhere far up at the front. Mr. Durant found a desirable seat toward the rear, and craned his neck to see her. He could catch a glimpse of a fold of her turban and a bit of her brightly rouged cheek, but only at a cost of holding his head in a strained, and presently painful, position. So, warmed by the assurance that there would always be others, he let her go, and settled himself restfully. He had a ride of twenty minutes or so before him. He allowed his head to fall gently back, to let his eyelids droop, and gave himself to his thoughts. Now that the thing was comfortably over and done with, he could think of it easily, almost laughingly. Last week, now, and even part of the week before, he had had to try with all his strength to force it back every time it wrenched itself into his mind. It had positively affected his sleep. Even though he was shielded by his newly acquired amused attitude, Mr. Durant felt indignation flood within him when he recalled those restless nights.

He had met Rose for the first time about three months before. She had been sent up to his office to take some letters for him. Mr. Durant was assistant manager of the rubber company's credit department; his wife was wont to refer to him as one of the officers of the company, and, though she often spoke thus of him to people in his presence, he never troubled to go more fully into detail about his position. He rated a room, a desk, and a telephone to himself; but not a stenographer. When he wanted to give dictation or to have some letters typewritten, he telephoned around to the various other offices until he found a girl who was not busy with her own work. That was how Rose had come to him.

She was not a pretty girl. Distinctly, no. But there was a rather sweet fragility about her, and an almost desperate timidity that Mr. Durant had once found engaging, but that he now thought of with a prickling irritation. She was twenty, and the glamour of youth was around her. When she bent over her work, her back showing white through her sleazy blouse, her clean hair coiled smoothly on her thin neck, her straight, childish legs crossed at the knee to support her pad, she had an undeniable appeal.

But not pretty—no. Her hair wasn't the kind that went up well, her eyelashes and lips were too pale, she hadn't much knack about choosing and wearing her cheap clothes. Mr. Durant, in reviewing the thing, felt a surprise that she should ever have attracted him. But it was a tolerant surprise, not an impatient one. Already he looked back on himself as being just a big boy in the whole affair.

It did not occur to him to feel even a flicker of astonishment that Rose should have responded so eagerly to him, an immovably married man of forty-nine. He never thought of himself in that way. He used to tell Rose, laughingly, that he was old enough to be her father, but neither of them ever really believed it. He regarded her affection for him as the most natural thing in the world—there she was, coming from a much smaller town, never the sort of girl to have had admirers; naturally, she was dazzled at the attentions of a man who, as Mr. Durant put it, was approaching the prime. He had been charmed with the idea of there having been no other men in her life; but lately, far from feeling flattered at being the first and only one, he had come to regard it as her having taken a sly advantage of him, to put him in that position.

It had all been surprisingly easy. Mr. Durant knew it would be almost from the first time he saw her. That did not lessen its interest in his eyes. Obstacles discouraged him, rather than led him on. Elimination of bother was the main thing.

Rose was not a coquettish girl. She had that curious directness that some very timid people possess. There were her scruples, of course, but Mr. Durant readily reasoned them away. Not that he was a master of technique, either. He had had some experiences, probably a third as many as he habitually thought of himself as having been through, but none that taught him much of the delicate shadings of wooing. But then, Rose's simplicity asked exceedingly little.

She was never one to demand much of him, anyway. She never thought of stirring up any trouble between him and his wife, never besought him to leave his family and go away with her, even for a day. Mr. Durant valued her for that. It did away with a lot of probable fussing.

It was amazing how free they were, how little lying there was to do. They stayed in the office after hours—Mr. Durant found many letters that must be dictated. No one thought anything of that. Rose was busy most of the day, and it was only considerate that Mr. Durant should not break in on her employer's time, only natural that he should want as good a stenographer as she was to attend to his correspondence.

Rose's only relative, a married sister, lived in another town. The girl roomed with an acquaintance named Ruby, also employed at the rubber works, and Ruby, who was much taken up with her own affairs of the emotions, never appeared to think it strange if Rose was late to dinner, or missed the meal entirely. Mr. Durant readily explained to his wife that he was detained by a rush of business. It only increased his importance, to her, and spurred her on to devising especially pleasing dishes, and solicitously keeping them hot for his return. Sometimes, important in their guilt, Rose and he put out the light in the little office and locked the door, to trick the other employees into thinking that they had long ago gone home. But no one ever so much as rattled the doorknob, seeking admission.

It was all so simple that Mr. Durant never thought of it as anything outside the usual order of things. His interest in Rose did not blunt his appreciation of chance attractive legs or provocative glances. It was an entanglement of the most restful, comfortable nature. It even held a sort of homelike quality, for him.

And then everything had to go and get spoiled. "Wouldn't you know?" Mr. Durant asked himself, with deep bitterness.

Ten days before, Rose had come weeping to his office. She had the sense to wait till after hours, for a wonder, but anybody might have walked in and seen her blubbering there; Mr. Durant felt it to be due only to the efficient management of his personal God that no one had. She wept, as he sweepingly put it, all over the place. The color left her cheeks and collected damply in her nose, and rims of vivid pink grew around her pale eyelashes. Even her hair became affected; it came away from the pins, and stray ends of it wandered limply over her neck. Mr. Durant hated to look at her, could not bring himself to touch her.

All his energies were expended in urging her for God's sake to keep quiet; he did not ask her what was the matter. But it came out, between bursts of unpleasant-sounding sobs. She was "in trouble." Neither then nor in the succeeding days did she and Mr. Durant ever use any less delicate phrase to describe her condition. Even in their thoughts, they referred to it that way.

She had suspected it, she said, for some time, but she hadn't wanted to bother him about it until she was absolutely sure. "Didn't want to bother me!" thought Mr. Durant.

Naturally, he was furious. Innocence is a desirable thing, a dainty thing, an appealing thing, in its place; but carried too far, it is merely ridiculous. Mr. Durant wished to God that he had never seen Rose. He explained this desire to her.

But that was no way to get things done. As he had often jovially remarked to his friends, he knew "a thing or two." Cases like this could be what people of the world called "fixed up"—New York society women, he understood, thought virtually nothing of it. This case could be fixed up, too. He got Rose to go home, telling her not to worry, he would see that everything was all right. The main thing was to get her out of sight, with that nose and those eyes.

But knowing a thing or two and putting the knowledge into practice turned out to be vastly different things. Mr. Durant did not know whom to seek for information. He pictured himself inquiring of his intimates if they could tell him of "someone that this girl he had heard about could go to." He could hear his voice uttering the words, could hear the nervous laugh that would accompany them, the terrible flatness of them as they left his lips. To confide in one person would be confiding in at least one too many. It was a progressing town, but still small enough for gossip to travel like a typhoon. Not that he thought for a moment that his wife would believe any such thing, if it reached her; but where would be the sense in troubling her?

Mr. Durant grew pale and jumpy over the thing as the days went by. His wife worried herself into one of her sick spells over his petulant refusals of second helpings. There daily arose in him an increasing anger that he should be drawn into conniving to find a way to break the law of his country—probably the law of every country in the world. Certainly of every decent, Christian place.

It was Ruby, finally, who got them out of it. When Rose confessed to him that she had broken down and told Ruby, his rage leaped higher than any words. Ruby was secretary to the vice-president of the rubber company. It would be pretty, wouldn't it, if she let it out? He had lain wide-eyed beside his wife all that night through. He shuddered at the thought of chance meetings with Ruby in the hall.

But Ruby had made it delightfully simple, when they did meet. There were no reproachful looks, no cold turnings away of the head. She had given him her usual smiling "good-morning," and added a little upward glance, mischievous, understanding, with just the least hint of admiration in it. There was a sense of intimacy, of a shared secret binding them cozily together. A fine girl, that Ruby!

Ruby had managed it all without any fuss. Mr. Durant was not directly concerned in the planning. He heard of it only through Rose, on the infrequent occasions when he had had to see her. Ruby knew, through some indistinct friends of hers, of "a woman." It would be twenty-five dollars. Mr. Durant had gallantly insisted upon giving Rose the money. She had started to sniffle about taking it, but he had finally prevailed. Not that he couldn't have used the twenty-five very nicely himself, just then, with Junior's teeth, and all!

Well, it was all over now. The invaluable Ruby had gone with Rose to "the woman"; had that very afternoon taken her to the station and put her on a train for her sister's. She had even thought of wiring the sister beforehand that Rose had had influenza and must have a rest.

Mr. Durant had urged Rose to look on it as just a little vacation. He promised, moreover, to put in a good word for her whenever she wanted her job back. But Rose had gone pink about the nose again at the thought. She had sobbed her rasping sobs, then had raised her face from her stringy handkerchief and said, with an entirely foreign firmness, that she never wanted to see the rubber works or Ruby or Mr. Durant again. He had laughed indulgently, had made himself pat her thin back. In his relief at the outcome of things, he could be generous to the pettish.

He chuckled inaudibly, as he reviewed that last scene. "I suppose she thought she'd make me sore, saying she was never coming back," he told himself. "I suppose I was supposed to get down on my knees and coax her."

It was fine to dwell on the surety that it was all done with. Mr. Durant had somewhere picked up a phrase that seemed ideally suited to the occasion. It was to him an admirably dashing expression. There was something stylish about it; it was the sort of thing you would expect to hear used by men who wore spats and swung canes without self-consciousness. He employed it now, with satisfaction.

"Well, that's that," he said to himself. He was not sure that he didn't say it aloud.

The car slowed, and the girl in the rough coat came down toward the door. She was jolted against Mr. Durant—he would have sworn she did it purposely—uttered a word of laughing apology, gave him what he interpreted as an inviting glance. He half rose to follow her, then sank back again. After all, it was a wet night, and his corner was five blocks farther on. Again there came over him the cozy assurance that there would always be others.

In high humor, he left the car at his street, and walked in the direction of his house. It was a mean night, but the insinuating cold and the black rain only made more graphic his picture of the warm, bright house, the great dish of steaming fish chowder, the well-behaved children and wife that awaited him. He walked rather slowly to make them seem all the better for the wait, humming a little on his way down the neat sidewalk, past the solid, reputably shabby houses.

Two girls ran past him, holding their hands over their heads to pro-

tect their hats from the wet. He enjoyed the click of their heels on the
pavement, their little bursts of breathless laughter, their arms upraised
in a position that brought out all the neat lines of their bodies. He knew
who they were—they lived three doors down from him, in the house
with the lamp-post in front of it. He had often lingeringly noticed their
fresh prettiness. He hurried, so that he might see them run up the steps,
their narrow skirts sliding up over their legs. His mind went back to the
girl with the run in her stocking, and amusing thoughts filled him as he
entered his own house.

His children rushed, clamoring, to meet him, as he unlocked the
door. There was something exciting going on, for Junior and Charlotte
were usually too careful-mannered to cause people discomfort by rushing and babbling. They were nice, sensible children, good at their les-
sons, and punctilious about brushing their teeth, speaking the truth, and
avoiding playmates who used bad words. Junior would be the very picture of his father, when they got the bands off his teeth, and little Charlotte strongly resembled her mother. Friends often commented on what
a nice arrangement it was.

Mr. Durant smiled good-naturedly through their racket, carefully
hanging up his coat and hat. There was even pleasure for him in the
arrangement of his apparel on the cool, shiny knob of the hatrack.
Everything was pleasant, tonight. Even the children's noise couldn't ir-
ritate him.

Eventually he discovered the cause of the commotion. It was a little
stray dog that had come to the back door. They were out in the kitchen
helping Freda, and Charlotte thought she heard something scratching,
and Freda said nonsense, but Charlotte went to the door, anyway, and
there was this little dog, trying to get in out of the wet. Mother helped
them give it a bath, and Freda fed it, and now it was in the living-room.
Oh, Father, couldn't they keep it, please, couldn't they, couldn't they,
please, Father, couldn't they? It didn't have any collar on it—so you
see it didn't belong to anybody. Mother said all right, if he said so, and
Freda liked it fine.

Mr. Durant still smiled his gentle smile. "We'll see," he said.

The children looked disappointed, but not despondent. They would
have liked more enthusiasm, but "we'll see," they knew by experience,
meant a leaning in the right direction.

Mr. Durant proceeded to the living-room, to inspect the visitor. It
was not a beauty. All too obviously, it was the living souvenir of a
mother who had never been able to say no. It was a rather stocky little
beast with shaggy white hair and occasional, rakishly placed patches of

black. There was a suggestion of Sealyham terrier about it, but that was almost blotted out by hosts of reminiscences of other breeds. It looked, on the whole, like a composite photograph of Popular Dogs. But you could tell at a glance that it had a way with it. Scepters have been tossed aside for that.

It lay, now, by the fire, waving its tragically long tail wistfully, its eyes pleading with Mr. Durant to give it a fair trial. The children had told it to lie down there, and so it did not move. That was something it could do toward repaying them.

Mr. Durant warmed to it. He did not dislike dogs, and he somewhat fancied the picture of himself as a soft-hearted fellow who extended shelter to friendless animals. He bent, and held out a hand to it.

"Well, sir," he said, genially. "Come here, good fellow."

The dog ran to him, wriggling ecstatically. It covered his cold hand with joyous, though respectful kisses, then laid its warm, heavy head on his palm. "You are beyond a doubt the greatest man in America," it told him with its eyes.

Mr. Durant enjoyed appreciation and gratitude. He patted the dog graciously.

"Well, sir, how'd you like to board with us?" he said. "I guess you can plan to settle down." Charlotte squeezed Junior's arm wildly. Neither of them, though, thought it best to crowd their good fortune by making any immediate comment on it.

Mrs. Durant entered from the kitchen, flushed with her final attentions to the chowder. There was a worried line between her eyes. Part of the worry was due to the dinner, and part to the disturbing entrance of the little dog into the family life. Anything not previously included in her day's schedule threw Mrs. Durant into a state resembling that of one convalescing from shellshock. Her hands jerked nervously, beginning gestures that they never finished.

Relief smoothed her face when she saw her husband patting the dog. The children, always at ease with her, broke their silence and jumped about her, shrieking that Father said it might stay.

"There, now—didn't I tell you what a dear, good father you had?" she said in the tone parents employ when they have happened to guess right. "That's fine, Father. With that big yard and all, I think we'll make out all right. She really seems to be an awfully good little——"

Mr. Durant's hand stopped sharply in its patting motions, as if the dog's neck had become red-hot to his touch. He rose, and looked at his wife as at a stranger who had suddenly begun to behave wildly.

"She?" he said. He maintained the look and repeated the word. "She?"

Mrs. Durant's hands jerked.

"Well—" she began, as if about to plunge into a recital of extenuating circumstances. "Well—yes," she concluded.

The children and the dog looked nervously at Mr. Durant, feeling something was gone wrong. Charlotte whimpered wordlessly.

"Quiet!" said her father, turning suddenly upon her. "I said it could stay, didn't I? Did you ever know Father to break a promise?"

Charlotte politely murmured, "No, Father," but conviction was not hers. She was a philosophical child, though, and she decided to leave the whole issue to God, occasionally jogging Him up a bit with prayer.

Mr. Durant frowned at his wife, and jerked his head backward. This indicated that he wished to have a few words with her, for adults only, in the privacy of the little room across the hall, known as "Father's den."

He had directed the decoration of his den, had seen that it had been made a truly masculine room. Red paper covered its walls, up to the wooden rack on which were displayed ornamental steins, of domestic manufacture. Empty pipe-racks—Mr. Durant smoked cigars—were nailed against the red paper at frequent intervals. On one wall was an indifferent reproduction of a drawing of a young woman with wings like a vampire bat, and on another, a watercolored photograph of "September Morn," the tints running a bit beyond the edges of the figure as if the artist's emotions had rendered his hand unsteady. Over the table was carefully flung a tanned and fringed hide with the profile of an unknown Indian maiden painted on it, and the rocking-chair held a leather pillow bearing the picture, done by pyrography, of a girl in a fencing costume which set off her distressingly dated figure.

Mr. Durant's books were lined up behind the glass of the bookcase. They were all tall, thick books, brightly bound, and they justified his pride in their showing. They were mostly accounts of favorites of the French court, with a few volumes on odd personal habits of various monarchs, and the adventures of former Russian monks. Mrs. Durant, who never had time to get around to reading, regarded them with awe, and thought of her husband as one of the country's leading bibliophiles. There were books, too, in the living-room, but those she had inherited or been given. She had arranged a few on the living-room table; they looked as if they had been placed there by the Gideons.

Mr. Durant thought of himself as an indefatigable collector and an insatiable reader. But he was always disappointed in his books, after he had sent for them. They were never so good as the advertisements had led him to believe.

Into his den Mr. Durant preceded his wife, and faced her, still frowning. His calm was not shattered, but it was punctured. Something annoying always had to go and come up. Wouldn't you know?

"Now you know perfectly well, Fan, we can't have that dog around," he told her. He used the low voice reserved for underwear and bathroom articles and kindred shady topics. There was all the kindness in his tones that one has for a backward child, but a Gibraltar-like firmness was behind it. "You must be crazy to even think we could for a minute. Why, I wouldn't give a she-dog houseroom, not for any amount of money. It's disgusting, that's what it is."

"Well, but, Father——" began Mrs. Durant, her hands again going off into their convulsions.

"Disgusting," he repeated. "You have a female around, and you know what happens. All the males in the neighborhood will be running after her. First thing you know, she'd be having puppies—and the way they look after they've had them, and all! That would be nice for the children to see, wouldn't it? I should think you'd think of the children, Fan. No, sir, there'll be nothing like that around here, not while I know it. Disgusting!"

"But the children," she said. "They'll be just simply——"

"Now you just leave all that to me," he reassured her. "I told them the dog could stay, and I've never broken a promise yet, have I? Here's what I'll do—I'll wait till they're asleep, and then I'll just take this little dog and put it out. Then, in the morning, you can tell them it ran away during the night, see?"

She nodded. Her husband patted her shoulder, in its crapy-smelling black silk. His peace with the world was once more intact, restored by this simple solution of the little difficulty. Again his mind wrapped itself in the knowledge that everything was all fixed, all ready for a nice, fresh start. His arm was still about his wife's shoulder as they went on in to dinner.

American Mercury, September 1924

A Certain Lady

My friend, Mrs. Legion, is one of those few, as tradition numbers them, who are New Yorkers by birth. This gives her an appreciable edge on the parvenus who are Manhattanites only by migration. The Legions occupy an apartment on upper Riverside Drive, in a building called "The Emdor"—an apt and amicable blending of the name of the owner's wife, Emma, with that of his daughter, Doris. Thus, at one crack, are any possible hard feelings averted, and a happy literary effect achieved. "Isn't it a cute idea?" Mrs. Legion asks you, when she has explained the origin of the title. "Isn't it," you answer, without an interrogation point. And there you both are, ready to start all over again.

Shortly—oh, anywhere from seven to ten minutes—after she has met you, Mrs. Legion is supplying you with all the ground floor information as to why she lives on Riverside Drive, instead of Park Avenue. There is all the sun they get, and that big kitchen, and the superintendent is so obliging, and just look how convenient the busses are. Not for worlds, she promises you, would she dwell in any other section of the city. Yet, oddly enough—just about enough—she may be found frequently inspecting and pricing Park Avenue apartments, and hopefully calling up real estate agents to inquire if the rents in that part of town have taken a change for the better since her last inquiry.

Although she lives as far from Park Avenue as it is possible to do and still keep out of Jersey, Mrs. Legion is cozily conversant of all the comings and goings, or what have you, of the Avenue dwellers. Breathlessly she pursues the society notes in the daily papers; promptly on their days of publication she buys the magazines dealing with the activities of the socially elect. Only drop a hat, and she can give you anything you want to know in the way of dates, and maiden names, and who married whom, and how they are getting along, if any. She employs nicknames, in referring to members of the favored few hundred, with an easy casualness that gives her remarks a truly homey flavor.

Naturally, it eats into her time to keep so admirably posted on these matters. And Mrs. Legion is pretty hard pressed for time. You might think, with her husband earning a cheery income, with Junior and Barbara safely in school, and a pleasant sufficiency of maids—two will do it nicely—around the apartment, that Mrs. Legion's life would follow the course made celebrated by the proverbial Riley; but the days are all too short for her to complete her business. She is always late for her appointments, rushing in a bit breathless, almost embarrassingly apologetic for those things that lack of time has forced her to leave undone. You simply must excuse the way she looks, but she didn't have a minute to get her hair waved, or, goodness, she must try to crowd in a manicure somehow, or for heaven's sake, remind her to stop at the baker's on her way home—she didn't have a second all morning. Her life is passed in an oddly imperceptible process known as "getting around" to things,—getting around to answer a letter, getting around to having her fur coat done over, getting around to having a talk with Junior's teacher.

And then, of course, there is all her shopping to do. Mrs. Legion's shopping has never yet reached a stage even approaching completion. Rarely a day passes that she must not visit the stores, if not to purchase, then to look around and get an idea or so. To look at her, you realize instantly that it must indeed take time and thought and research for her to assemble her costumes, to get them so faithfully like those worn by all other women of her circumstances. Mrs. Legion and her friends dress with the uniformity of the Tiller girls. Their hats are of the same shape and worn at the same angle, their coiffures meticulously alike, their dresses follow one another closely in material and design, their shoes are of the same last. Not until she has sedulously effaced all traces of individuality does Mrs. Legion feel that she is smart enough to appear in public.

Duties aside, Mrs. Legion must have her fun, being only human. Her good times consist in meeting her women friends almost daily, either at her house or at one of theirs, and having a real old-fashioned talk. Sometimes this is staged over the bridge table, sometimes over the Mah Jong tiles, sometimes a bit of silky and lacy sewing. The Legion school of conversationalists deals entirely with personalities, nor does it fear to probe deep into the intimate affairs of absent acquaintances. Detailed stories of miserable matrimony and racking separation, of lingering illness and agonizing childbirth and ancestral insanity, of heartbreak and poverty and desertion burble melodiously from the ladies' cool, smooth, expensively rouged lips.

The talk is interrupted by the serving of a lavish and imaginative tea, of which Mrs. Legion partakes generously. She is always going to begin dieting next Monday morning.

For her further diversion, there are literature and the drama. Mrs. Legion is by her own admission a great reader. She has long been a member of the circulating library contained in the stationer's nearest her. She is saved the wear and tear of selecting appropriate reading matter—there is the nicest girl there, who knows just the sort of thing she likes. Mrs. Legion can seldom tell you the title of a book she reads, and never the author's name, but she can always give you a pretty comprehensive résumé of the plot. She likes a book because there is the cutest girl in it, or the most attractive man, or because the author says the rawest things,—well, my dear, simply nothing is left to your imagination. And the lifting of any strain on the imagination is regarded, in the Legion circle, as the king of assets.

In the theatre, she likes best to patronize, even though she must wait weeks to obtain desirable seats, those exhibits which she euphemistically describes as "my dear, they say it's the most off-color thing you ever saw. I do hope the police don't stop it before we can get tickets." She does not care for drama of the drab, the every-day, or the underworld. As she says, she does love to see pretty clothes.

Sporadically, Mrs. Legion goes in for culture in a really big way, and signs up for a course of lectures on Flemish paintings or current events or interior decoration. The first lecture of the series is largely attended and faithfully quoted: along about the sixth or seventh, only the first row of gilt chairs is occupied. Mrs. Legion has looked on this world for some thirty-seven years, and she has not failed to draw conclusions. So clear are her views that she can dismiss any subject with a single sentence. Of politics, she says that Mrs. Coolidge is awfully sweet looking, and they say she is very popular in Washington. Of the unemployment situation, that these beggars you see in the streets all have big bank accounts and probably most of them own tenement buildings. Of married life, that she honestly believes that Fred Legion would eat steak every night if you'd give it to him. Of the race question, that these Swedes and Irish girls are so independent that she has half a mind to get a couple of darkie servants. Of art and belles lettres, that she wouldn't live in Greenwich Village if you gave her the place. Of motherhood, that it certainly is hard to know how to dress children when they're at that awkward age. Of the relation of the sexes, that it's terrible what women have to go through in this world.

My friend, Mrs. Legion. Heiress of the ages.

The New Yorker, February 28, 1925

The Wonderful Old Gentleman

If the Bains had striven for years, they could have been no more successful in making their living-room into a small but admirably complete museum of objects suggesting strain, discomfort, or the tomb. Yet they had never even tried for the effect. Some of the articles that the room contained were wedding-presents; some had been put in from time to time as substitutes as their predecessors succumbed to age and wear; a few had been brought along by the Old Gentleman when he had come to make his home with the Bains some five years before.

It was curious how perfectly they all fitted into the general scheme. It was as if they had all been selected by a single enthusiast to whom time was but little object, so long as he could achieve the eventual result of transforming the Bain living-room into a home chamber of horrors, modified a bit for family use.

It was a high-ceilinged room, with heavy, dark old woodwork, that brought long and unavoidable thoughts of silver handles and weaving worms. The paper was the color of stale mustard. Its design, once a dashing affair of a darker tone splashed with twinkling gold, had faded into lines and smears that resolved themselves, before the eyes of the sensitive, into hordes of battered heads and tortured profiles, some eyeless, some with clotted gashes for mouths.

The furniture was dark and cumbersome and subject to painful creakings—sudden, sharp creaks that seemed to be wrung from its brave silence only when it could bear no more. A close, earthy smell came from its dulled tapestry cushions, and try as Mrs. Bain might, furry gray dust accumulated in the crevices.

The center-table was upheld by the perpetually strained arms of three carved figures, insistently female to the waist, then trailing discreetly off into a confusion of scrolls and scales. Upon it rested a row of blameless books, kept in place at the ends by the straining shoulder-muscles of two bronze-colored plaster elephants, forever pushing at their tedious toil.

On the heavily carved mantel was a gayly colored figure of a curly-headed peasant boy, ingeniously made so that he sat on the shelf and dangled one leg over. He was in the eternal act of removing a thorn from his chubby foot, his round face realistically wrinkled with the cruel pain. Just above him hung a steel-engraving of a chariot-race, the dust flying, the chariots careening wildly, the drivers ferociously lashing their maddened horses, the horses themselves caught by the artist the moment before their hearts burst, and they dropped in their traces.

The opposite wall was devoted to the religious in art; a steel-engraving of the Crucifixion, lavish of ghastly detail; a sepia-print of the martyrdom of Saint Sebastian, the cords cutting deep into the arms writhing from the stake, arrows bristling in the thick, soft-looking body; a water-color copy of a "Mother of Sorrows," the agonized eyes raised to a cold heaven, great, bitter tears forever on the wan cheeks, paler for the grave-like draperies that wrapped the head.

Beneath the windows hung a painting in oil of two lost sheep, huddled hopelessly together in the midst of a wild blizzard. This was one of the Old Gentleman's contributions to the room. Mrs. Bain was wont to observe of it that the frame was worth she didn't know how much.

The wall-space beside the door was reserved for a bit of modern art that had once caught Mr. Bain's eye in a stationer's window—a colored print, showing a railroad-crossing, with a train flying relentlessly toward it, and a low, red automobile trying to dash across the track before the iron terror shattered it into eternity. Nervous visitors who were given chairs facing this scene usually made opportunity to change their seats before they could give their whole minds to the conversation.

The ornaments, placed with careful casualness on the table and the upright piano, included a small gilt lion of Lucerne, a little, chipped, plaster Laocoön, and a savage china kitten eternally about to pounce upon a plump and helpless china mouse. This last had been one of the Old Gentleman's own wedding-gifts. Mrs. Bain explained, in tones low with awe, that it was very old.

The ash-receivers, of Oriental manufacture, were in the form of grotesque heads, tufted with bits of gray human hair, and given bulging, dead, glassy eyes and mouths stretched into great gapes, into which those who had the heart for it might flick their ashes. Thus the smallest details of the room kept loyally to the spirit of the thing, and carried on the effect.

But the three people now sitting in the Bains' living-room were not in the least oppressed by the decorative scheme. Two of them, Mr. and Mrs. Bain, not only had had twenty-eight years of the room to accustom themselves to it, but had been stanch admirers of it from the first. And no surroundings, however morbid, could close in on the aristocratic calm of Mrs. Bain's sister, Mrs. Whittaker.

She graciously patronized the very chair she now sat in, smiled kindly on the glass of cider she held in her hand. The Bains were poor, and Mrs. Whittaker had, as it is ingenuously called, married well, and none of them ever lost sight of these facts.

But Mrs. Whittaker's attitude of kindly tolerance was not confined to her less fortunate relatives. It extended to friends of her youth, working people, the arts, politics, the United States in general, and God, Who had always supplied her with the best of service. She could have given Him an excellent reference at any time.

The three people sat with a comfortable look of spending the evening. There was an air of expectancy about them, a not unpleasant little nervousness, as of those who wait for a curtain to rise. Mrs. Bain had brought in cider in the best tumblers, and had served some of her nut cookies in the plate painted by hand with clusters of cherries—the plate she had used for sandwiches when, several years ago, her card club had met at her house.

She had thought it over a little tonight, before she lifted out the cherry plate, then quickly decided and resolutely heaped it with cookies. After all, it was an occasion—informal, perhaps, but still an occasion. The Old Gentleman was dying upstairs. At five o'clock that afternoon the doctor had said that it would be a surprise to him if the Old Gentleman lasted till the middle of the night—a big surprise, he had augmented.

There was no need for them to gather at the Old Gentleman's bedside. He would not have known any of them. In fact, he had not known them for almost a year, addressing them by wrong names and asking them grave, courteous questions about the health of husbands or wives or children who belonged to other branches of the family. And he was quite unconscious now.

Miss Chester, the nurse who had been with him since "this last stroke," as Mrs. Bain importantly called it, was entirely competent to attend and watch him. She had promised to call them if, in her tactful words, she saw any signs.

So the Old Gentleman's daughters and son-in-law waited in the warm living-room, and sipped their cider, and conversed in low, polite tones.

Mrs. Bain cried a little in pauses in the conversation. She had always cried easily and often. Yet, in spite of her years of practice, she did not do it well. Her eyelids grew pink and sticky, and her nose gave her no little trouble, necessitating almost constant sniffling. She sniffled loudly and conscientiously, and frequently removed her pince-nez to wipe her eyes with a crumpled handkerchief, gray with damp.

Mrs. Whittaker, too, bore a handkerchief, but she appeared to be holding it in waiting. She was dressed, in compliment to the occasion, in her black crepe de Chine, and she had left her lapis-lazuli pin, her olivine bracelet, and her topaz and amethyst rings at home in her bureau drawer, retaining only her lorgnette on its gold chain, in case there should be any reading to be done.

Mrs. Whittaker's dress was always studiously suited to its occasion; thus, her bearing had always that calm that only the correctly attired may enjoy. She was an authority on where to place monograms on linen, how to instruct working folk, and what to say in letters of condolence. The word "lady" figured largely in her conversation. Blood, she often predicted, would tell.

Mrs. Bain wore a rumpled white shirt-waist and the old blue skirt she saved for "around the kitchen." There had been time to change, after she had telephoned the doctor's verdict to her sister, but she had not been quite sure whether it was the thing to do. She had thought that Mrs. Whittaker might expect her to display a little distraught untidiness at a time like this; might even go in for it in a mild way herself.

Now Mrs. Bain looked at her sister's elaborately curled, painstakingly brown coiffure, and nervously patted her own straggling hair, gray at the front, with strands of almost lime-color in the little twist at the back. Her eyelids grew wet and sticky again, and she hung her glasses over one forefinger while she applied the damp handkerchief. After all, she reminded herself and the others, it was her poor father.

Oh, but it was really the best thing, Mrs. Whittaker explained in her gentle, patient voice.

"You wouldn't want to see Father go on like this," she pointed out. Mr. Bain echoed her, as if struck with the idea. Mrs. Bain had nothing to reply to them. No, she wouldn't want to see the Old Gentleman go on like this.

Five years before, Mrs. Whittaker had decided that the Old Gentleman was getting too old to live alone with only old Annie to cook for him and look after him. It was only a question of a little time before it "wouldn't have looked right," his living alone, when he had his children to take care of him. Mrs. Whittaker always stopped things before they got to the stage where they didn't look right. So he had come to live with the Bains.

Some of his furniture had been sold; a few things, such as his silver, his tall clock, and the Persian rug he had bought at the Exposition, Mrs. Whittaker had found room for in her own house; and some he brought with him to the Bains'.

Mrs. Whittaker's house was much larger than her sister's, and she had three servants and no children. But, as she told her friends, she had held back and let Allie and Lewis have the Old Gentleman.

"You see," she explained, dropping her voice to the tones reserved for not very pretty subjects, "Allie and Lewis are—well, they haven't a great deal."

So it was gathered that the Old Gentleman would do big things for the Bains when he came to live with them. Not exactly by paying board—it is a little too much to ask your father to pay for his food and lodging, as if he were a stranger. But, as Mrs. Whittaker suggested, he could do a great deal in the way of buying needed things for the house and keeping everything going.

And the Old Gentleman did contribute to the Bain household. He bought an electric heater and an electric fan, new curtains, storm-windows, and light-fixtures, all for his bedroom; and had a nice little bathroom for his personal use made out of the small guest-room adjoining it.

He shopped for days until he found a coffee-cup large enough for his taste; he bought several large ash-trays, and a dozen extra-size bath-towels, that Mrs. Bain marked with his initials. And every Christmas and birthday he gave Mrs. Bain a round, new, shining ten-dollar gold piece. Of course, he presented gold pieces to Mrs. Whittaker, too, on like appropriate occasions. The Old Gentleman prided himself always on his fair-mindedness. He often said that he was not one to show any favoritism.

Mrs. Whittaker was Cordelia-like to her father during his declining years. She came to see him several times a month, bringing him jelly or potted hyacinths. Sometimes she sent her car and chauffeur for him, so that he might take an easy drive through the town, and Mrs. Bain might be afforded a chance to drop her cooking and accompany him. When Mrs. Whittaker was away on trips with her husband, she almost never neglected to send her father picture post-cards of various points of interest.

The Old Gentleman appreciated her affection, and took pride in her. He enjoyed being told that she was like him.

"That Hattie," he used to tell Mrs. Bain, "she's a fine woman—a fine woman."

As soon as she had heard that the Old Gentleman was dying Mrs. Whittaker had come right over, stopping only to change her dress and have her dinner. Her husband was away in the woods with some men, fishing. She explained to the Bains that there was no use in disturbing him—it would have been impossible for him to get back that night. As soon as—well, if anything happened she would telegraph him, and he could return in time for the funeral.

Mrs. Bain was sorry that he was away. She liked her ruddy, jovial, loud-voiced brother-in-law.

"It's too bad that Clint couldn't be here," she said, as she had said several times before. "He's so fond of cider," she added.

"Father," said Mrs. Whittaker, "was always very fond of Clint." Already the Old Gentleman had slipped into the past tense.

"Everybody likes Clint," Mr. Bain stated.

He was included in the "everybody." The last time he had failed in business, Clint had given him the clerical position he had since held over at the brush works. It was pretty generally understood that this had been brought about through Mrs. Whittaker's intervention, but still they were Clint's brush works, and it was Clint who paid him his salary. And forty dollars a week is indubitably forty dollars a week.

"I hope he'll be sure and be here in time for the funeral," said Mrs. Bain. "It will be Wednesday morning, I suppose, Hat?"

Mrs. Whittaker nodded.

"Or perhaps around two o'clock Wednesday afternoon," she amended. "I always think that's a nice time. Father has his frock coat, Allie?"

"Oh, yes," Mrs. Bain said eagerly. "And it's all clean and lovely. He has everything. Hattie, I noticed the other day at Mr. Newton's funeral they had more of a blue necktie on him, so I suppose they're wearing them—Mollie Newton always has everything just so. But I don't know——"

"I think," said Mrs. Whittaker firmly, "that there is nothing lovelier than black for an old gentleman."

"Poor Old Gentleman," said Mr. Bain, shaking his head. "He would have been eighty-five if he just could have lived till next September. Well, I suppose it's all for the best."

He took a small draft of cider and another cooky.

"A wonderful, wonderful life," summarized Mrs. Whittaker. "And a wonderful, wonderful old gentleman."

"Well, I should say so," said Mrs. Bain. "Why, up to the last year he was as interested in everything! It was, 'Allie, how much do you have to give for your eggs now?' and 'Allie, why don't you change your butcher?—this one's robbing you,' and 'Allie, who was that you were talking to on the telephone?' all day long! Everybody used to speak of it."

"And he used to come to the table right up to this stroke," Mr. Bain related, chuckling reminiscently. "My, he used to raise Cain when Allie didn't cut up his meat fast enough to suit him. Always had a temper, *I'll* tell you, the Old Gentleman did. Wouldn't stand for us having anybody in to meals—he didn't like that worth a cent. Eighty-four years old, and sitting right up there at the table with us!"

They vied in telling instances of the Old Gentleman's intelligence and liveliness, as parents cap one another's anecdotes of precocious children.

"It's only the past year that he had to be helped up- and downstairs," said Mrs. Bain. "Walked up-stairs all by himself, and more than eighty years old!"

Mrs. Whittaker was amused.

"I remember you said that once when Clint was here," she remarked, "and Clint said, 'Well, if you can't walk up-stairs by the time you're eighty, when are you going to learn?' "

Mrs. Bain smiled politely, because her brother-in-law had said it. Otherwise she would have been shocked and wounded.

"Yes, sir," said Mr. Bain. "Wonderful."

"The only thing I could have wished," Mrs. Bain said, after a pause—"I could have wished he'd been a little different about Paul. Somehow I've never felt quite right since Paul went into the navy."

Mrs. Whittaker's voice fell into the key used for the subject that has been gone over and over and over again.

"Now, Allie," she said, "you know yourself that was the best thing that could have happened. Father told you that himself, often and often. Paul was young, and he wanted to have all his young friends running in and out of the house, banging doors and making all sorts of racket, and it would have been a terrible nuisance for father. You must realize that father was more than eighty years old, Allie."

"Yes, I know," Mrs. Bain said. Her eyes went to the photograph of her son in his seaman's uniform, and she sighed.

"And besides," Mrs. Whittaker pointed out triumphantly, "now that Miss Chester's here in Paul's room, there wouldn't have been any room for him. So you see!"

There was rather a long pause. Then Mrs. Bain edged toward the other thing that had been weighing upon her.

"Hattie," she said, "I suppose—I suppose we'd ought to let Matt know?"

"I shouldn't," said Mrs. Whittaker composedly. She always took great pains with her "shall's" and "will's." "I only hope that he doesn't see it in the papers in time to come on for the funeral. If you want to have your brother turn up drunk at the services, Allie, *I* don't."

"But I thought he'd straightened up," said Mr. Bain. "Thought he was all right since he got married."

"Yes, I know, I know, Lewis," Mrs. Whittaker said wearily. "I've heard all about that. All I say is, *I* know what Matt is."

"John Loomis was telling me," reported Mr. Bain, "he was going through Akron, and he stopped off to see Matt. Said they had a nice little place, and he seemed to be getting along fine. Said she seemed like a cracker-jack housekeeper."

Mrs. Whittaker smiled.

"Yes," she said, "John Loomis and Matt were always two of a kind—you couldn't believe a word either of them said. Probably she did seem to be a good housekeeper. I've no doubt she acted the part very well. Matt never made any bones of the fact that she was on the stage once, for almost a year. Excuse me from having that woman come to Father's funeral. If you want to know what *I* think, *I* think that Matt marrying a woman like that had a good deal to do with hastening Father's death."

The Bains sat in awe.

"And after all Father did for Matt, too," added Mrs. Whittaker, her voice shaken.

"Well, I should think so," Mr. Bain was glad to agree. "I remember how the Old Gentleman used to try and help Matt get along. He'd go down, like it was to Mr. Fuller, that time Matt was working at the bank, and he'd explain to him, 'Now, Mr. Fuller,' he'd say, 'I don't know whether you know it, but this son of mine has always been what you might call the black sheep of the family. He's been kind of a drinker,' he'd say, 'and he's got himself into trouble a couple of times, and if you'd just keep an eye on him, so's to see he keeps straight, it'd be a favor to me.'

"Mr. Fuller told me about it himself. Said it was wonderful the way the Old Gentleman came right out and talked just as frankly to him. Said *he'd* never had any idea Matt was that way—wanted to hear all about it."

Mrs. Whittaker nodded sadly.

"Oh, I know," she said. "Time and again Father would do that. And then, as like as not, Matt would get one of his sulky fits, and not turn up at his work."

"And when Matt would be out of work," Mrs. Bain said, "the way

Father'd hand him out his car-fare, and I don't know what all! When Matt was a grown man, going on thirty years old, Father would take him down to Newins & Malley's and buy him a whole new outfit— pick out everything himself. He always used to say Matt was the kind that would get cheated out of his eye-teeth if he went into a store alone."

"My, Father hated to see anybody make a fool of themselves about money," Mrs. Whittaker commented. "Remember how he always used to say, 'Anybody can make money, but it takes a wise man to keep it'?"

"I suppose he must be a pretty rich man," Mr. Bain said, abruptly restoring the Old Gentleman to the present.

"Oh—rich!" Mrs. Whittaker's smile was at its kindliest. "But he managed his affairs very well, Father did, right up to the last. Everything is in splendid shape, Clint says."

"He showed you the will, didn't he, Hat?" asked Mrs. Bain, forming bits of her sleeve into little plaits between her thin, hard fingers.

"Yes," said her sister. "Yes, he did. He showed me the will. A little over a year ago, I think it was, wasn't it? You know, just before he started to fail, that time."

She took a small bite of cooky.

"*Awfully* good," she said. She broke into a little bubbly laugh, the laugh she used at teas and wedding receptions and fairly formal dinners. "You know," she went on, as one sharing a good story, "he's gone and left all that old money to me. 'Why, Father!' I said, as soon as I'd read that part. But it seems he'd gotten some sort of idea in his head that Clint and I would be able to take care of it better than anybody else, and you know what Father was, once he made up that mind of his. You can just imagine how *I* felt. I couldn't say a thing."

She laughed again, shaking her head in amused bewilderment.

"Oh, and Allie," she said, "he's left you all the furniture he brought here with him, and all the things he bought since he came. And Lewis is to have his set of Thackeray. And that money he lent Lewis, to try and tide him over in the hardware business that time—that's to be regarded as a gift."

She sat back and looked at them, smiling.

"Lewis paid back most all of that money Father lent him that time," Mrs. Bain said. "There was only about two hundred dollars more, and then he would have had it all paid up."

"That's to be regarded as a gift," insisted Mrs. Whittaker. She leaned over and patted her brother-in-law's arm. "Father always liked you, Lewis," she said softly.

"Poor Old Gentleman," murmured Mr. Bain.

"Did it—did it say anything about Matt?" asked Mrs. Bain.

"Oh, Allie!" Mrs. Whittaker gently reproved her. "When you think of all the money Father spent and spent on Matt, it seems to me he did more than enough—more than enough. And then when Matt went way off there to live, and married that woman, and never a word about it—Father hearing it all through strangers—well, I don't think any of us realize how it hurt Father. He never said much about it, but I don't think he ever got over it. I'm always so thankful that poor dear mother didn't live to see how Matt turned out."

"Poor Mother," said Mrs. Bain shakily, and brought the grayish handkerchief into action once more. "I can hear her now, just as plain. 'Now, children,' she used to say, 'do for goodness' sake let's all try and keep your father in a good humor.' If I've heard her say it once, I've heard her say it a hundred times. Remember, Hat?"

"Do I remember!" said Mrs. Whittaker. "And do you remember how they used to play whist, and how furious Father used to get when he lost?"

"Yes," Mrs. Bain cried excitedly, "and how Mother used to have to cheat, so as to be sure and not win from him? She got so she used to be able to do it just as well!"

They laughed softly, filled with memories of the gone days. A pleasant, thoughtful silence fell around them.

Mrs. Bain patted a yawn to extinction, and looked at the clock.

"Ten minutes to eleven," she said. "Goodness, I had no idea it was anywhere near so late. I wish—" She stopped just in time, crimson at what her wish would have been.

"You see, Lew and I have got in the way of going to bed early," she explained. "Father slept so light, we couldn't have people in like we used to before he came here, to play a little bridge or anything, on account of disturbing him. And if we wanted to go to the movies or anywhere, he'd go on so about being left alone that we just kind of gave up going."

"Oh, the Old Gentleman always let you know what he wanted," said Mr. Bain, smiling. "He was a wonder, *I'll* tell you. Nearly eighty-five years old!"

"Think of it," said Mrs. Whittaker.

A door clicked open above them, and feet ran quickly and not lightly down the stairs. Miss Chester burst into the room.

"Oh, Mrs. Bain!" she cried. "Oh, the Old Gentleman! Oh, he's gone! I noticed him kind of stirring and whimpering a little, and he seemed to be trying to make motions at his warm milk, like as if he wanted some. So I put the cup up to his mouth, and he sort of fell over, and just like that he was gone, and the milk all over him."

Mrs. Bain instantly collapsed into passionate weeping. Her husband put his arm tenderly about her, and murmured a series of "Now-now's."

Mrs. Whittaker rose, set her cider-glass carefully on the table, shook out her handkerchief, and moved toward the door.

"A lovely death," she pronounced. "A wonderful, wonderful life, and now a beautiful, peaceful death. Oh, it's the best thing, Allie; it's the best thing."

"Oh, it is, Mrs. Bain; it's the best thing," Miss Chester said earnestly. "It's really a blessing. That's what it is."

Among them they got Mrs. Bain up the stairs.

Pictorial Review, January 1926

Dialogue at Three in the Morning

"Plain water in mine," said the woman in the petunia-colored hat. "Or never mind about the water. Hell with it. Just straight Scotch. What I care? Just straight. That's me. Never gave anybody any trouble in my life. All right, they can say what they like about me, but I know—I know—I never gave anybody any trouble in my life. You can tell them that from me, see? What I care?"

"Listen," said the man with the ice-blue hair. And he leaned across the table toward her, and frowned heavily at the designs he drew with the plated knife. "Listen. I just want you to get this thing clear——"

"Yeah," she said. "Get things clear. That's good. That gives me a big laugh. That's laughable, a thing like that is. Say, if there's anybody around here that's going to get things clear, I'm going to be the one around here that's going to get things clear. What you do, you go back to Jeannette, see, and you tell her I know what she's saying about me. I don't want to get you into this, but you tell her that from me. You can keep out of it. You don't have to tell her you told me. You don't even have to tell her you saw me. Say, if you're ashamed to tell people you know me, that's all right with me, see? I'm not going to give anybody any trouble. If you're ashamed to tell your friends you're a friend of mine, what I care? I guess I'll be able to stand that, all right. I've stood a lot of things."

"Ah, listen," he said. "Listen. Will you please listen just a minute?"

"Yeah, listen," she said. "That's fine. Listen. Well, I'm through with this listening stuff. You can tell them all from me, see, I'm going to be the one that's going to do the talking from now on. You can tell Jeannette that. What I care? You can run right to her and blab that. Says I look fat in my red dress, does she? That's a nice thing to have anybody say about you. Makes you feel great, that does. You can tell Miss Jeannette she's got a lot to do to make cracks about a person's red dress. That's pretty laughable, that is. Say, when I ask her to pay for anything I wear, then it will be time for her to crack. Her or anybody else. I make my own living, thank God, and I don't have to ask anybody for anything. You can tell them all that. You or anybody else."

"Will you do me a favor?" he said. "Will you do me one little favor? Will you? Will you listen just——"

"Yeah, favors," she said. "Nobody's got to do me any favors. I make my own living, and I don't have to ask any favors off of anybody. I never gave anybody any trouble in my life. And if they don't like it, they know what they can do. Tiffany's window, see? The whole lot of them. Oh, did I break that glass? Oh, isn't that terrible. All right—if it's broken it's broken. Isn't it? Hell with it. Hell with them all."

"If you'd listen," he said. "There isn't anything for you to get sore about. Just listen——"

"Who's sore?" she said. "I'm not sore. I'm all right. You don't have to worry about me. You or Jeannette or anybody else. Sore. Say, if a person's not going to get sore about a thing like that, what kind of a thing is a person expected to get sore about? After all I've done for her. Trouble with me is, I'm too kind-hearted. That's what everybody always told me. 'Trouble with you is, you're too kind-hearted,' they said. And now look what she goes around and says about me. And you let her say a thing like that to you, and you're ashamed to say you're a friend of mine. All right, you don't have to. You can go back to Jeannette and stay there. The whole lot of you."

"Now listen, sweetheart," he said. "Haven't I always been your friend? Haven't I? Well now, wouldn't you listen to your friend just for a——"

"Friends," she said. "Friends. Fine lot of friends I got. Go around cutting your throat. That's what you get for being kind-hearted. Just a big kind-hearted slob. That's me. Oh, hell with the water. I'll drink it straight. I make my own living, and go around not giving anybody any trouble, and then the whole lot of them turn on me. After the way I was brought up, and the home we used to have, and all, and they go around making cracks about me. Work all day long, and don't ask anything off of anybody. And here I am with a weak heart, besides. I'd just as soon I was dead. What've I got to live for, anyway? Kindly answer me that one question. What've I got to live for?"

Tears striped her cheeks.

The man with the ice-blue hair reached across the Scotch-soaked tablecloth and took her hand.

"Ah, listen," he said. "Listen."

From the unknown, a waiter appeared. He chirped and fluttered about them. Presently, you felt, he would cover them with leaves. . . .

The New Yorker, February 13, 1926

The Last Tea

The young man in the chocolate-brown suit sat down at the table, where the girl with the artificial camellia had been sitting for forty minutes.

"Guess I must be late," he said. "Sorry you been waiting."

"Oh, goodness!" she said. "I just got here myself, just about a second ago. I simply went ahead and ordered because I was dying for a cup of tea. I was late, myself. I haven't been here more than a minute."

"That's good," he said. "Hey, hey, easy on the sugar—one lump is fair enough. And take away those cakes. Terrible! Do I feel terrible!"

"Ah," she said, "you do? Ah. Whadda matter?"

"Oh, I'm ruined," he said. "I'm in terrible shape."

"Ah, the poor boy," she said. "Was it feelin' mizzable? Ah, and it came way up here to meet me! You shouldn't have done that—I'd have understood. Ah, just think of it coming all the way up here when it's so sick!"

"Oh, that's all right," he said. "I might as well be here as any place else. Any place is like any other place, the way I feel today. Oh, I'm all shot."

"Why, that's just awful," she said. "Why, you poor sick thing. Goodness, I hope it isn't influenza. They say there's a lot of it around."

"Influenza!" he said. "I wish that was all I had. Oh, I'm poisoned. I'm through. I'm off the stuff for life. Know what time I got to bed? Twenty minutes past five, A.M., this morning. What a night! What an evening!"

"I thought," she said, "that you were going to stay at the office and work late. You said you'd be working every night this week."

"Yeah, I know," he said. "But it gave me the jumps, thinking about going down there and sitting at that desk. I went up to May's—she was throwing a party. Say, there was somebody there said they knew you."

"Honestly?" she said. "Man or woman?"

"Dame," he said. "Name's Carol McCall. Say, why haven't I been told about her before? That's what I call a girl. What a looker she is!"

"Oh, really?" she said. "That's funny—I never heard of anyone that thought that. I've heard people say she was sort of nice-looking, if she

49

wouldn't make up so much. But I never heard of anyone that thought she was pretty."

"Pretty is right," he said. "What a couple of eyes she's got on her!"

"Really?" she said. "I never noticed them particularly. But I haven't seen her for a long time—sometimes people change, or something."

"She says she used to go to school with you," he said.

"Well, we went to the same school," she said. "I simply happened to go to public school because it happened to be right near us, and Mother hated to have me crossing streets. But she was three or four classes ahead of me. She's ages older than I am."

"She's three or four classes ahead of them all," he said. "Dance! Can she step! 'Burn your clothes, baby,' I kept telling her. I must have been fried pretty."

"I was out dancing myself, last night," she said. "Wally Dillon and I. He's just been pestering me to go out with him. He's the most wonderful dancer. Goodness! I didn't get home till I don't know what time. I must look just simply a wreck. Don't I?"

"You look all right," he said.

"Wally's crazy," she said. "The things he says! For some crazy reason or other, he's got it into his head that I've got beautiful eyes, and, well, he just kept talking about them till I didn't know where to look, I was so embarrassed. I got so red, I thought everybody in the place would be looking at me. I got just as red as a brick. Beautiful eyes! Isn't he crazy?"

"He's all right," he said. "Say, this little McCall girl, she's had all kinds of offers to go into moving pictures. 'Why don't you go ahead and go?' I told her. But she says she doesn't feel like it."

"There was a man up at the lake, two summers ago," she said. "He was a director or something with one of the big moving-picture people—oh, he had all kinds of influence!—and he used to keep insisting and insisting that I ought to be in the movies. Said I ought to be doing sort of Garbo parts. I used to just laugh at him. Imagine!"

"She's had about a million offers," he said. "I told her to go ahead and go. She keeps getting these offers all the time."

"Oh, really?" she said. "Oh, listen, I knew I had something to ask you. Did you call me up last night, by any chance?"

"Me?" he said. "No, I didn't call you."

"While I was out, Mother said this man's voice kept calling up," she said. "I thought maybe it might be you, by some chance. I wonder who it could have been. Oh—I guess I know who it was. Yes, that's who it was!"

"No, I didn't call you," he said. "I couldn't have seen a telephone, last night. What a head I had on me, this morning! I called Carol up, around ten, and she said she was feeling great. Can that girl hold her liquor!"

"It's a funny thing about me," she said. "It just makes me feel sort of sick to see a girl drink. It's just something in me, I guess. I don't mind a man so much, but it makes me feel perfectly terrible to see a girl get intoxicated. It's just the way I am, I suppose."

"Does she carry it!" he said. "And then feels great the next day. There's a girl! Hey, what are you doing there? I don't want any more tea, thanks. I'm not one of these tea boys. And these tea rooms give me the jumps. Look at all those old dames, will you? Enough to give you the jumps."

"Of course, if you'd rather be some place, drinking, with I don't know what kinds of people," she said, "I'm sure I don't see how I can help that. Goodness, there are enough people that are glad enough to take me to tea. I don't know how many people keep calling me up and pestering me to take me to tea. Plenty of people!"

"All right, all right, I'm here, aren't I?" he said. "Keep your hair on."

"I could name them all day," she said.

"All right," he said. "What's there to crab about?"

"Goodness, it isn't any of my business what you do," she said. "But I hate to see you wasting your time with people that aren't nearly good enough for you. That's all."

"No need worrying over me," he said. "I'll be all right. Listen. You don't have to worry."

"It's just I don't like to see you wasting your time," she said, "staying up all night and then feeling terribly the next day. Ah, I was forgetting he was so sick. Ah, I was mean, wasn't I, scolding him when he was so mizzable. Poor boy. How's he feel now?"

"Oh, I'm all right," he said. "I feel fine. You want anything else? How about getting a check? I got to make a telephone call before six."

"Oh, really?" she said. "Calling up Carol?"

"She said she might be in around now," he said.

"Seeing her tonight?" she said.

"She's going to let me know when I call up," he said. "She's probably got about a million dates. Why?"

"I was just wondering," she said. "Goodness, I've got to fly! I'm having dinner with Wally, and he's so crazy, he's probably there now. He's called me up about a hundred times today."

"Wait till I pay the check," he said, "and I'll put you on a bus."

"Oh, don't bother," she said. "It's right at the corner. I've got to fly. I suppose you want to stay and call up your friend from here?"

"It's an idea," he said. "Sure you'll be all right?"

The New Yorker, September 11, 1926

Oh! He's Charming!

"Mr. Pawling," said the hostess, "this is a great admirer of your books. Miss Waldron, Mr. Pawling. Miss Waldron, oh, she's a great admirer of yours."

She laughed heartily and highly, and melted away through the crowd, toward the depleted tea-table. Her lips were scrolled in sunshine, but in her eyes was the look of the caged thing, the look of the tortured soul who is wondering what in hell has become of that fresh supply of toast.

"Want to sit down?" said the author. "Here's a couple of chairs. Might as well grab them."

"Ooh, let's!" said the great admirer. "Let's do!"

So they did.

"God, I'm tired," said the author. "Dead, I am. Terrible party, this is. Terrible people. Everybody here's terrible. Lot of lice."

"Oh, you must get so sick of parties!" said the great admirer. "You must be simply bored to death. I suppose people are after you every second with invitations."

"I never answer them," he said. "I won't even go to the telephone any more. But they get you, anyhow. Look at me now. Stuck."

"Oh, it must be simply terrible," she said. "I was thinking, when I was watching you, before. Everybody crowding around you every minute."

"What's a person going to do?" he said.

"No, but really," she said, "you can't blame them, you know. Naturally everybody wants to meet you. My heavens, I've been just simply dying to, ever since I read *Some Ladies in Agony*. I just love every word of that book. I've read it over and over. But my heavens, I suppose so many people tell you how they love your books, it would simply bore you to death to hear me rave about them."

"Not at all," he said. "That's quite all right."

"Oh, I do," she said. "I love them. I've often thought 'I'd just love to sit down and write Freeman Pawling a little letter.' But I couldn't get up the nerve to. I was simply scared to death of you. Do you mind if I say something awfully personal? I had no idea you'd be so young!"

"That so?" he said.

"Why, I thought you'd have gray hair, at least," she said. "I thought anybody would have to be old, to know as much as you do."

"That so?" he said.

"My heavens," she said, "the things you know! Why, I thought nobody but me knew them. Do you mind if I ask you an awfully personal question? How on earth did you ever find out so much about women?"

"Oh, my God," he said, "I've known a million of them. All over the world."

"You don't have to tell me," she said. "I bet you have. I bet you've left broken hearts wherever you've gone. Haven't you?"

"Well," he said.

"It must be just simply awful for any woman you know," she said. "The way you see right through and through them. I'd better be terribly careful what I say. First thing I know, you'll be putting me in a book. Look, I'm going to ask you something awfully personal. Do you mind? Look, was Cicely Celtic in *Various Knights and a Lady* drawn from real life?"

"She was," he said, "and she wasn't. Partly she was, and partly she wasn't."

"That's what I thought," she said. "She was rather an amusing little thing," he said, "the real Cicely. Girl named Nancy James—very good family. A lady. Possessive as the devil, though. She's dead, now. Shot herself."

"Ooh," she said. "Just like in the book!"

"Yes," he said. "I thought I might as well use it. After all the trouble she was. God, what a jealous little ape."

"Are you writing anything now?" she said.

"Oh, it's coming slowly," he said. "Coming slowly. It doesn't do to hurry it."

"I was in at the library yesterday," she said. "Isn't it funny, I was just asking them if you had anything new out, and they said no. They said no, you didn't. I always ask them what's good, and they sort of save out books for me. I got a lot. There's one of them by Sherwood Anderson. The *Dark* something, or something."

"Don't read it," he said. "It's a louse. Poor Anderson's all through."

"Oh, I'm awfully glad you told me," she said. "Now I won't have to waste my time over it. Then I got this Dreiser thing, only it's in two books, and it looks terribly long."

"Dreiser trying to write," he said. "That's one of the funniest things in the world. He can't write."

"Well, I'm glad to know that," she said. "I won't have to bother with it. Let's see—oh, I got this new Ring Lardner book. Short stories or something."

"Who?" he said.

"You know," she said. "He used to write funny things. You know, all those funny things. Everything spelled wrong, and everything."

"What's his name?" he said.

"Lardner," she said. "Ring Lardner. It's a funny name, isn't it?"

"It's a new one on me," he said.

"Well, I really just got it mostly for Daddy," she said. "He's crazy about baseball and things. I thought he'd probably be crazy about it. I just can't seem to find any books I like, any more. My heavens, I wish you'd hurry up and finish your new one. I wish I had the nerve to ask you something awfully personal. I wonder if you'd mind. What's your new book like?"

"It's different," he said. "Entirely different. I have evolved a different form. The trouble with novelists is their form. It's their form, if you see what I mean. In this book, I have taken an entirely different form: It's evolved from the *Satyricon* of Petronius."

"Ooh," she said. "Ooh. Exciting!"

"A good deal of the scene," he said, "is laid in Egypt. I think they're about ready for it."

"How gorgeous!" she said. "I simply love anything about Egypt. I'm just crazy to go there. Have you ever been?"

"No," he said. "I'm sick of traveling. It's the same thing everywhere. People giving parties. Terrible."

"Oh, I know," she said. "It must be awful. Look, I don't want you to think I'm being awfully personal, but I was just thinking I'd simply love to have you come up to the house for tea some time. I wonder if you would."

"God, I'm through for the year," he said. "This is the last time they get me out."

"But just quietly," she said. "Just a few people that are crazy about your things, too. Or just nobody, if you like."

"For God's sake, when would I have any time?" he said.

"Well, just in case you ever do," she said, "it's in the telephone book. D. G. Waldron. Do you think you can remember that or shall I write it down?"

"Don't write it," he said. "I never carry women's addresses around with me. It's hot as hell in here. I'm going to duck. Well, good-bye."

"Oh, are you going?" she said. "Well, good-bye, then. I can't tell you how exciting it's been, meeting you and all. I hope to goodness I

haven't bored you to death, raving about your books. But if you knew
how I read them and read them! I simply can't wait to tell everybody
I've really met Freeman Pawling!"

"Not at all," he said.

"And any time you're not just terribly busy," she said, "it's in the
telephone book. You know!"

"Well, good-bye," he said.

He was out the door in eight seconds flat, with no time out for
farewells to his hostess.

The great admirer crossed the room to the tea-table, and clutched
the hostess by her weary and flaccid hand.

"Oh, my dear," she said, "it was just simply too thrilling for anything. Oh, he's charming!"

"Isn't he?" said the hostess. "I knew you'd think so, too."

The New Yorker, October 9, 1926

Travelogue

The woman in the spangled black dress left the rest of the party, and made room on the sofa for the sunburned young man with the quiet eyes.

"You just sit yourself right down here this minute," she said. "And give an account of yourself. The idea! Running away for nearly two years, and not even a post-card out of you! Aren't you ashamed? Answer Muvver. Izzun you tebble shame you'self?"

"I'm rotten about writing letters," he said. "I'm sorry. I guess I'm hopeless. I always mean to write, and I never seem to get around to it. It isn't because I don't think of people. It's just I'm terrible about writing letters."

"Where have you been, anyway?" she said. "Nearly two years! Where dat bad boy been teepin' himself?"

"Well, I was in Arabia, mostly," he said.

"You're crazy," she said. "Just simply crazy. What on earth did you want to go to a place like that for?"

"I don't know," he said. "I just sort of thought I'd like to see it."

"Oh, I know," she said. "You don't have to tell me. I'm just like you. I love traveling. Freddy always says, just give me a couple of trunks and a letter of credit, and I'm all right. Well, you ask Freddy. It's the funniest thing, but I was saying to him only last night at dinner—we were all alone, the Allens were coming, but their baby was sick at the last minute, the poor little thing, it's so delicate it would scare you to death to see it, oh, my God, I must call up Kate Allen and find out how it is, I told Freddy to remind me—I was telling him, 'One of these fine days,' I said, 'you won't see me sitting here,' I said. 'I'm going to just pack up a toothbrush and an extra pair of stockings,' I said, 'and the next you'll hear of me, I'll be in Egypt or India or somewhere,' I said. Oh, I'm a born traveler!"

"Really?" he said.

"Arabia!" she said. "Well, just imagine that. Tell me all about it. How did you like it, anyway?"

"Why, I had a good time," he said.

"Imagine," she said. "Way off there. Well, I've often wondered about

Arabia. Tell me some more about it. Isn't there an awful lot of sand and everything?"

"Well, there is," he said. "But, you see—"

"Sand!" she said. "Don't sand me! After this summer down at Dune Harbor, I've had enough of sand, thank you. I could write a book about sand. Always in your shoes, no matter what you did, and the children tracking it into the house till I thought I'd go crazy. I did. I thought I'd simply go crazy. Ever been to Dune Harbor?"

"No," he said. "No, I haven't."

"Well, don't," she said. "Nothing but sand, sand, sand. You can get all the sand you want right there, without going off to any Arabia."

"Well, you see," he said, "the way it is in Arabia—"

"And Freddy on that beach!" she said. "You'd have died. The first day he got down there he just lay out there, and lay out there, and the first thing you knew, his shoulders! I thought about you, right away. I said if you could have seen those shoulders of his, you just simply would have died."

"It must have been awfully funny," he said. "You see, what I was going to say, in Arabia—"

"That's right," she said. "That's just exactly what I want you to do. Tell me all about your trip. I want to hear every single thing. What was it like? What are the people like? Are they all Arabs and everything?"

"Well, of course," he said, "there's a lot of—"

"Imagine!" she said. "Arabs! Isn't it exactly like something in a book? Oh, it must be just the way I pictured it. Tell me about all these Arabs. What are they like, anyway?"

"Why, they're pretty much like everybody else," he said. "Some of them are great, and some of them aren't so good. Most of them are pretty—"

"You know," she said, "I've always been sure I could get along with people like that. Arabs and everything. I'm so interested in people, they just seem to know, and they let me see their inside selves. Oh, I'm always making friends with the darndest people! You just ask Freddy. 'Well,' he said to me, 'nobody could ever call you a snob,' he said. And you know, I took it for a compliment. Arabs! Oh, I'd love anything like that. Well, go on, tell me about it. Where did you stay?"

"Why, a lot of the time," he said, "I lived right with the natives. You see, I wanted to—"

"Imagine! Right with them!" she said. "But wasn't it terribly uncomfortable and everything?"

"They were darn decent to me," he said. "And as soon as you got used to it, you—"

"Oh, I could do it," she said. "I could do it in a minute. I don't care what I have to put up with, just as long as I'm traveling and seeing new things. When we were in Milan, three years ago, we went to this little hotel—the place was so crowded, there was nothing but Americans, wherever you went. I used to say to Freddy, 'You'd think some of them would have sense enough to stay home.' So we stayed at this little hotel, and do you know what we got? Well, I'll tell you, because you're an old friend, but if you ever—! We got fleas. Absolutely. Fleas. Freddy was nearly crazy, you know how he is, but I just said to him, 'Well, that's the kind of thing you've got to expect when you're traveling.' Oh, that's the way I am. Nothing fazes me. But look, these Arabs. Don't they all have a lot of wives or something?"

"Why, lots of them have more than one wife," he said. "You see, the way they look at it, it's a question of—"

"Aren't they terrible?" she said. "Imagine, more than one wife! Isn't that the Oriental of it, for you? They're terrible. And don't they all pretend to be terribly religious or something?"

"Their religion seems to mean a lot to them," he said. "No matter how poor a man is, or no matter where he goes, he always has his little mat, to—"

"Yes, I know," she said. "Prayer rugs. That's what they call them. Prayer rugs. I'll never forget, before I was married, we had this perfectly beautiful prayer rug in the living-room, right in front of the piano. We girls used to have a regular joke about it. We used to keep teasing Father, which one of us he was going to give it to—oh, he thought the world and all of that prayer rug! So then Father got married again, and of course, he kept the prayer rug right there. Oh, we often have a good laugh about that prayer rug!"

"Is that so?" he said.

"Oh, yes," she said. "My, that prayer rug! Oh, it was a beautiful thing, to anybody that appreciated it. Blue and yellow and I don't know what all colors. And everything in the design meant something. Oh, they're awfully clever that way, those Arabs. They make some really lovely things. I suppose you've seen a lot of them."

"Yes," he said. "Yes, I have."

"I'm crazy about their work," she said. "I'd love to see them doing it. I've often thought, what I'd like to do, I'd like to— Oh, there's Freddy, over in the door. He wants to go home. Isn't he just the old stick-in-the-mud? Always wants to go home at half-past eleven. I say to him, 'You're as good as a clock,' I tell him. 'Whenever we're out at a party I can always tell when it's half-past eleven.' Honestly. I just tease the life out of him. But he never minds what I say. He just laughs. Well, I'm pretty dead, myself. Been shopping all day—it just kills me. I just put it off till the last minute, I hate it so. Now, listen, you've got to come and see us. We're pretty hurt, the way you've acted. Will you come soon? Please? Please?"

"Thank you very much," he said.

"And it was simply too wonderful," she said, "to hear all about Arabia. My, you've made me feel as if I was in an awful rut, just living here. But I'm going to do it some day. I warn you. One of these fine days you'll wake up and I'll be way off the other side of the world. That's the way I am—I've just got to do it, sooner or later. Will you look at Freddy scowling! He probably thinks you and I are fixing up a plan to elope, sitting here so long. Oh, he knows what you travelers are! Now you *are* coming soon, aren't you? There's heaps more things I want to ask you about. You needn't think you're done with Arabia yet, by any manner of means. You come soon! Now you mind Muvver! Don't you be bad, naughty, wicked, tebble boy ever adain. You hear me?"

"Thank you very much," he said.

"Nighty-ni'," she said. "S'eet d'eams."

"Good-night," he said.

She went on away to Freddy.

The New Yorker, October 30, 1926

Little Curtis

Mrs. Matson paused in the vestibule of G. Fosdick's Sons' Department Store. She transferred a small parcel from her right hand to the crook of her left arm, gripped her shopping-bag firmly by its German-silver frame, opened it with a capable click, and drew from its orderly interior a little black-bound book and a neatly sharpened pencil.

Shoppers passing in and out jostled her as she stood there, but they neither shared in Mrs. Matson's attention nor hurried her movements. She made no answer to the "Oh, I *beg* your pardons" that bubbled from the lips of the more tender-hearted among them. Calm, sure, gloriously aloof, Mrs. Matson stood, opened her book, poised her pencil, and wrote in delicate, prettily slanting characters: "4 crepe-paper candy-baskets, $.28."

The dollar-sign was gratifyingly decorative, the decimal point clear and deep, the 2 daintily curled, the 8 admirably balanced. Mrs. Matson looked approvingly at her handiwork. Still unhurried, she closed the book, replaced it and the pencil in the bag, tested the snap to see that it was indisputably shut, and took the parcel once more in her right hand. Then, with a comfortable air of duty well done, she passed impressively, and with a strong push, from G. Fosdick's Sons' Department Store by means of a portal which bore a placard with the request, "Please Use Other Door."

Slowly Mrs. Matson made her way down Maple Street. The morning sunshine that flooded the town's main thoroughfare caused her neither to squint nor to lower her face. She held her head high, looking about her as one who says, "Our good people, we are pleased with you."

She stopped occasionally by a shop-window, to inspect thoroughly the premature autumn costumes there displayed. But her heart was unfluttered by the envy which attacked the lesser women around her. Though her long black coat, of that vintage when coats were puffed of sleeve and cut sharply in at the waist, was stained and shiny, and her hat had the general air of indecision and lack of spirit that comes with age, and her elderly black gloves were worn in patches of rough gray, Mrs. Matson had no yearnings for the fresh, trim costumes set temptingly before her. Snug in her was the thought of the rows of recent garments, each one in its flowered cretonne casing, occupying the varnished hangers along the poles of her bedroom closet.

She had her unalterable ideas about such people as gave or threw away garments that might still be worn, for warmth and modesty, if not for style. She found it distinctly lower-class to wear one's new clothes "for every day"; there was an unpleasant suggestion of extravagance and riotous living in the practice. The working classes, who, as Mrs. Matson often explained to her friends, went and bought themselves electric ice-boxes and radios the minute they got a little money, did such things.

No morbid thought of her possible sudden demise before the clothes in her closet could be worn or enjoyed irked her. Life's uncertainty was not for those of her position. Mrs. Matsons pass away between seventy and eighty; sometimes later, never before.

A blind colored woman, a tray of pencils hung about her neck, with a cane tapping the pavement before her, came down the street. Mrs. Matson swerved sharply to the curb to avoid her, wasting a withering glance upon her. It was Mrs. Matson's immediate opinion that the woman could see as well as *she* could. She never bought of the poor on the streets, and was angry if she saw others do so. She frequently remarked that these beggars all had big bank-accounts.

She crossed to the car-tracks to await the trolley that would bear her home, her calm upset by her sight of the woman. "Probably owns an apartment-house," she told herself, and shot an angry glance after the blind woman.

However, her poise was restored by the act of tendering her fare to the courteous conductor. Mrs. Matson rather enjoyed small and legitimate disbursements to those who were appropriately grateful. She gave him her nickel with the manner of one presenting a park to a city, and swept into the car to a desirable seat.

Settled, with the parcel securely wedged between her hip and the window, against loss or robbery, Mrs. Matson again produced the book and pencil. "Car-fare, $.05," she wrote. Again the exquisite handwriting, the neat figures, gave her a flow of satisfaction.

Mrs. Matson, regally without acknowledgment, accepted the conductor's aid in alighting from the car at her corner. She trod the sunsplashed pavement, bowing now and again to neighbors knitting on their porches or bending solicitously over their iris-beds. Slow, stately bows she gave, unaccompanied by smile or word of greeting. After all, she was Mrs. Albert Matson; she had been Miss Laura Whitmore, of

the Drop Forge and Tool Works Whitmores. One does not lose sight
of such things.

She always enjoyed the first view of her house as she walked toward
it. It amplified in her her sense of security and permanence. There it
stood, in its tidy, treeless lawns, square and solid and serviceable. You
thought of steel-engravings and rows of Scott's novels behind glass, and
Sunday dinner in the middle of the day, when you looked at it. You
knew immediately that within it no one ever banged a door, no one
clattered up- and down-stairs, no one spilled crumbs or dropped ashes
or left the light burning in the bathroom.

Expectancy pervaded Mrs. Matson as she approached her home. She
spoke of it always as her home. "You must come to see me in my home
some time," she graciously commanded new acquaintances. There was
a large, institutional sound to it that you didn't get in the word "house."

She liked to think of its cool, high-ceilinged rooms, of its busy maids,
of little Curtis waiting to deliver her his respectful kiss. She had adopted
him almost a year ago, when he was four. She had, she told her friends,
never once regretted it.

In her absence her friends had been wont to comment sadly upon
what a shame it was that the Albert Matsons had no child—and with
all the Matson and Whitmore money, too. Neither of them, the friends
pointed out, could live forever; it would all have to go to the Henry
Matsons' children. And they were but quoting Mrs. Albert Matson's
own words when they observed that those children would be just the
kind that would run right through it.

Mr. and Mrs. Matson held a joint view of the devastation that would
result if their nephews and nieces were ever turned loose among the
Matson and Whitmore money. As is frequent in such instances, their
worry led them to pay the other Matson family the compliment of the
credit for schemes and desires that had never edged into their thoughts.

The Albert Matsons saw their relatives as waiting, with a sort of
stalking patience, for the prayed-for moment of their death. For years
they conjured up ever more lurid pictures of the Matson children going
through their money like Sherman to the sea; for years they carried
about with them the notion that their demise was being eagerly awaited,
was being made, indeed, the starting-point of bacchanalian plans.

The Albert Matsons were as one in everything, as in this. Their
thoughts, their manners, their opinions, their very locutions were phenomena of similarity. People even pointed out that Mr. and Mrs. Matson looked alike. It was regarded as the world's misfortune that so

obviously Heaven-made a match was without offspring. And of course—you always had to come back to it, it bulked so before you—there was all that Matson and Whitmore money.

No one, though, ever directly condoled with Mrs. Matson upon her childlessness. In her presence one didn't speak of things like having children. She accepted the fact of babies when they were shown to her; she fastidiously disregarded their mode of arrival.

She had told none of her friends of her decision to adopt a little boy. No one knew about it until the papers were signed and he was established in the Matson house. Mrs. Matson had got him, she explained, "at the best place in New York." No one was surprised at that. Mrs. Matson always went to the best places when she shopped in New York. You thought of her selecting a child as she selected all her other belongings: a good one, one that would last.

She stopped abruptly now, as she came to her gate, a sudden frown creasing her brow. Two little boys, too absorbed to hear her steps, were playing in the hot sun by the hedge—two little boys much alike in age, size, and attire, compact, pink-and-white, good little boys, their cheeks flushed with interest, the backs of their necks warm and damp. They played an interminable, mysterious game with pebbles and twigs and a small tin trolley-car.

Mrs. Matson entered the yard.

"Curtis!" she said.

Both little boys looked up, startled. One of them rose and hung his head before her frown.

"And who," said Mrs. Matson deeply, "who told Georgie he could come here?"

No answer. Georgie, still squatting on his heels, looked inquiringly from her to Curtis. He was interested and unalarmed.

"Was it you, Curtis?" asked Mrs. Matson.

Curtis nodded. You could scarcely tell that he did, his head hung so low.

"Yes, mother dear!" said Mrs. Matson.

"Yes, mother dear," whispered Curtis.

"And how many times," Mrs. Matson inquired, "have I told you that you were not to play with Georgie? How many times, Curtis?"

Curtis murmured vaguely. He wished that Georgie would please go.

"You don't know?" said Mrs. Matson incredulously. "You don't know? After all mother does for you, you don't know how many times she has told you not to play with Georgie? Don't you remember what mother told you she'd have to do if you ever played with Georgie again?"

A pause. Then the nod.

"Yes, mother dear!" said Mrs. Matson.

"Yes, mother dear," said Curtis.

"Well!" Mrs. Matson said. She turned to the enthralled Georgie. "You'll have to go home now, Georgie—go right straight home. And you're not to come here any more, do you understand me? Curtis is not allowed to play with you—not ever."

Georgie rose.

" 'By," he said philosophically, and walked away, his farewell unanswered.

Mrs. Matson gazed upon Curtis. Grief disarranged her features.

"Playing!" she said, her voice broken with emotion. "Playing with a furnaceman's child! After all mother does for you!"

She took him by a limp arm and led him, unresisting, along the walk to the house; led him past the maid that opened the door, up the stairs to his little blue bedroom. She put him in it and closed the door.

Then she went to her own room, placed her package carefully on the table, removed her gloves, and laid them, with her bag, in an orderly drawer. She entered her closet, hung up her coat, then stooped for one of the felt slippers that were set scrupulously, in the first dancing position, on the floor beneath her nightgown. It was a lavender slipper, with scallops and a staid rosette; it had a light, flexible leather sole, across which was stamped its name, "Kumfy-Toes."

Mrs. Matson grasped it firmly by the heel and flicked it back and forth. Carrying it, she went to the little boy's room. She began to speak as she turned the door-knob.

"And before mother had time to take her hat off, too," she said. The door closed behind her.

She came out again presently. A scale of shrieks followed her.

"That will do!" she announced, looking back from the door. The shrieks faded obediently to sobs. "That's quite enough of that, thank you. Mother's had just about plenty for one morning. And today, too, with the ladies coming this afternoon, and all mother has to attend to! Oh, I'd be ashamed, Curtis, if I were you—that's what I'd be."

She closed the door, and retired, to remove her hat.

The ladies came in mid-afternoon. There were three of them. Mrs. Kerley, gray and brittle and painstaking, always thoughtful about sending birthday-cards and carrying glass jars of soup to the sick. Mrs.

Swan, her visiting sister-in-law, younger, and given to daisied hats and crocheted lace collars, with her transient's air of bright, determined interest in her hostess's acquaintances and activities. And Mrs. Cook. Only she did not count very much. She was extremely deaf, and so pretty well out of things.

She had visited innumerable specialists, spent uncounted money, endured agonizing treatments, in her endeavors to be able to hear what went on about her and to have a part in it. They had finally fitted her out with a long, coiling, corrugated speaking-tube, rather like a larger intestine. One end of this she placed in her better ear, and the other she extended to those who would hold speech with her. But the shining black mouthpiece seemed to embarrass people and intimidate them; they could think of nothing better to call into it than "Getting colder out," or "You keeping pretty well?" To hear such remarks as these she had gone through years of suffering.

Mrs. Matson, in her last spring's blue taffeta, assigned her guests to seats about the living-room. It was an afternoon set apart for fancy-work and conversation. Later there would be tea, and two triangular sandwiches apiece made from the chopped remnants of last night's chicken, and a cake which was a high favorite with Mrs. Matson, for its formula required but one egg. She had gone, in person, to the kitchen to supervise its making. She was not entirely convinced that her cook was wasteful of materials, but she felt that the woman would bear watching.

The crepe-paper baskets, fairly well filled with disks of peppermint creams, were to enliven the corners of the tea-table. Mrs. Matson trusted her guests not to regard them as favors and take them home.

The conversation dealt, and favorably, with the weather. Mrs. Kerley and Mrs. Swan vied with each other in paying compliments to the day.

"So clear," said Mrs. Kerley.

"Not a cloud in the sky," augmented Mrs. Swan. "Not a one."

"The air was just lovely this morning," reported Mrs. Kerley. "I said to myself, 'Well, this is a beautiful day if there ever *was* one.' "

"There's something so balmy about it," said Mrs. Swan.

Mrs. Cook spoke suddenly and overloudly, in the untrustworthy voice of the deaf.

"Phew, this is a scorcher!" she said. "Something terrible out."

The conversation went immediately to literature. It developed that Mrs. Kerley had been reading a lovely book. Its name and that of its author escaped her at the moment, but her enjoyment of it was so keen that she had lingered over it till 'way past ten o'clock the night before.

Particularly did she commend its descriptions of some of those Italian places; they were, she affirmed, just like a picture. The book had been drawn to her attention by the young woman at the Little Booke Nooke. It was, on her authority, one of the new ones.

Mrs. Matson frowned at her embroidery. Words flowed readily from her lips. She seemed to have spoken on the subject before.

"I haven't any use for all these new books," she said. "I wouldn't give them house-room. I don't see why a person wants to sit down and write any such stuff. I often think, I don't believe they know what they're writing about themselves half the time. I don't know who they think wants to read those kind of things. I'm sure I don't."

She paused to let her statements sink deep.

"Mr. Matson," she continued—she always spoke of her husband thus; it conveyed an aristocratic sense of aloofness, did away with any suggestion of carnal intimacy between them—"Mr. Matson isn't any hand for these new books, either. He always says, if he could find another book like *David Harum*, he'd read it in a minute. I wish," she added longingly, "I had a dollar for every time I've heard him say that."

Mrs. Kerley smiled. Mrs. Swan threw a rippling little laugh into the pause.

"Well, it's true, you know, it really is true," Mrs. Kerley told Mrs. Swan.

"Oh, it is," Mrs. Swan hastened to reassure her.

"I don't know what we're coming to, *I'm* sure," announced Mrs. Matson.

She sewed, her thread twanging through the tight-stretched circle of linen in her embroidery-hoop.

The stoppage of conversation weighed upon Mrs. Swan. She lifted her head and looked out the window.

"My, what a lovely lawn you have!" she said. "I couldn't help noticing it, first thing. We've been living in New York, you know."

"I often say I don't see what people want to shut themselves up in a place like that for," Mrs. Matson said. "You know, you exist, in New York—we live, out here."

Mrs. Swan laughed a bit nervously. Mrs. Kerley nodded. "That's right," she said. "That's pretty good."

Mrs. Matson herself thought it worthy of repetition. She picked up Mrs. Cook's speaking-tube.

"I was just saying to Mrs. Swan," she cried, and called her epigram into the mouthpiece.

"Live where?" asked Mrs. Cook.

Mrs. Matson smiled at her patiently. "New York. You know, that's where I got my little adopted boy."

"Oh, yes," said Mrs. Swan. "Carrie told me. Now, wasn't that lovely of you!"

Mrs. Matson shrugged. "Yes," she said, "I went right to the best place for him. Miss Codman's nursery—it's absolutely reliable. You can get awfully nice children there. There's quite a long waiting-list, they tell me."

"Goodness, just think how it must seem to him to be up here," said Mrs. Swan, "with this big house, and that lovely, smooth lawn, and everything."

Mrs. Matson laughed slightly. "Oh—well," she said.

"I hope he appreciates it," remarked Mrs. Swan.

"I think he will," Mrs. Matson said capably. "Of course," she conceded, "he's pretty young right now."

"So lovely," murmured Mrs. Swan. "So sweet to get them young like this and have them grow up."

"Yes, I think that's the nicest way," agreed Mrs. Matson. "And, you know, I really enjoy training him. Naturally, now that we have him here with us, we want him to act like a little gentleman."

"Just think of it," cried Mrs. Swan, "a child like that having all this! And will you have him go to school later on?"

"Oh, yes," Mrs. Matson replied. "Yes, we want him to be educated. You take a child going to some nice little school near here, say, where he'll meet only the best children, and he'll make friends that it will be a pretty good thing for him to know some day."

Mrs. Swan waxed arch. "I suppose you've got it all settled what he's going to be when he grows up," she said.

"Why, certainly," said Mrs. Matson. "He's to go right straight into Mr. Matson's business. My husband," she informed Mrs. Swan, "is the Matson Adding Machines."

"Oh-h-h," said Mrs. Swan on a descending scale.

"I think Curtis will do very well in school," prophesied Mrs. Matson. "He's not at all stupid—picks up everything. Mr. Matson is anxious to have him brought up to be a good, sensible business man—he says that's what this country needs, you know. So I've been trying to teach him the value of money. I've bought him a little bank. I don't think you can begin too early. Because probably some day Curtis is going to have— well——"

Mrs. Matson drifted into light, anecdotal mood.

"Oh, it's funny the way children are," she remarked. "The other day

Mrs. Newman brought her little Amy down to play with Curtis, and when I went up to look at them, there he was, trying to give her his brand-new flannel rabbit. So I just took him into my room, and I sat him down, and I said to him, 'Now, Curtis,' I said, 'you must realize that mother had to pay almost two dollars for that rabbit—nearly two hundred pennies,' I said. 'It's very nice to be generous, but you must learn that it isn't a good idea to give things away to people. Now you go in to Amy,' I said, 'and you tell her you're sorry, but she'll have to give that rabbit right back to you.' "

"And did he do it?" asked Mrs. Swan.

"Why, I told him to," Mrs. Matson said.

"Isn't it splendid?" Mrs. Swan asked of the company at large. "Really, when you think of it. A child like that, just suddenly having everything all at once. And probably coming of poor people, too. Are his parents—living?"

"Oh, no, no," Mrs. Matson said briskly. "I couldn't be bothered with anything like that. Of course, I found out all about them. They were really quite nice, clean people—the father was a college man. Curtis really comes of a very nice family, for an orphan."

"Do you think you'll ever tell him that you aren't—that he isn't— tell him about it?" inquired Mrs. Kerley.

"Dear me, yes, just as soon as he's a little older," Mrs. Matson answered. "I think it's so much nicer for him to know. He'll appreciate everything so much more."

"Does the little thing remember his father and mother at all?" Mrs. Swan asked.

"*I* really don't know if he does or not," said Mrs. Matson.

"Tea," announced the maid, appearing abruptly at the door.

"Tea is served, Mrs. Matson," said Mrs. Matson, her voice lifted.

"Tea is served, Mrs. Matson," echoed the maid.

"I don't know what I'm going to do with her," Mrs. Matson told her guests when the girl had disappeared. "Here last night she had company in the kitchen till nearly eleven o'clock at night. The trouble with me is I'm too good to servants. The only way to do is to treat them like cattle."

"They don't appreciate anything else," said Mrs. Kerley.

Mrs. Matson placed her embroidery in her sweet-grass workbasket, and rose.

"Well, shall we go have a cup of tea?" she said.

"Why, how lovely!" cried Mrs. Swan.

Mrs. Cook, who had been knitting doggedly, was informed, via the speaking-tube, of the readiness of tea. She dropped her work instantly, and led the way to the dining-room.

The talk, at the tea-table, was of stitches and patterns. Praise, benignly accepted by Mrs. Matson, was spread by Mrs. Swan and Mrs. Kerley upon the sandwiches, the cake, the baskets, the table-linen, the china, and the design of the silver.

A watch was glanced at, and there arose cries of surprise at the afternoon's flight. There was an assembling of workbags, a fluttering exodus to the hall to put on hats. Mrs. Matson watched her guests.

"Well, it's been just too lovely," Mrs. Swan declared, clasping her hand. "I can't *tell* you how much I've enjoyed it, hearing about the dear little boy, and all. I *hope* you're going to let me see him some time."

"Why, you can see him now, if you'd like," said Mrs. Matson. She went to the foot of the stairs and sang, "*Cur*-tis, *Cur*-tis."

Curtis appeared in the hall above, clean in the gray percale sailor-suit that had been selected in the thrifty expectation of his "growing into it." He looked down at them, caught sight of Mrs. Cook's speaking-tube, and watched it intently, his eyes wide open.

"Come down and see the ladies, Curtis," commanded Mrs. Matson.

Curtis came down, his warm hand squeaking along the banister. He placed his right foot upon a step, brought his left foot carefully down to it, then started his right one off again. Eventually he reached them.

"Can't you say how-do-you-do to the ladies?" asked Mrs. Matson.

He gave each guest, in turn, a small, flaccid hand.

Mrs. Swan squatted suddenly before him, so that her face was level with his.

"My, what a nice boy!" she cried. "I just love little boys like you, do you know it? Ooh, I could just eat you up! I could!"

She squeezed his arms. Curtis, in alarm, drew his head back from her face.

"And what's *your* name?" she asked him. "Let's see if you can tell me what your name is. I just *bet* you can't!"

He looked at her.

"Can't you tell the lady your name, Curtis?" demanded Mrs. Matson.

"Curtis," he told the lady.

"Why, what a *pretty* name!" she cried. She looked up at Mrs. Matson. "Was that his real name?" she asked.

"No," Mrs. Matson said, "they had him called something else. But I named him as soon as I got him. My mother was a Curtis."

Thus might one say, "My name was Guelph before I married."

Mrs. Cook spoke sharply. "Lucky!" she said. "Pretty lucky, that young one!"

"Well, I should say so," echoed Mrs. Swan. "Aren't you a pretty lucky little boy? Aren't you, aren't you, aren't you?" She rubbed her nose against his.

"Yes, Mrs. Swan." Mrs. Matson pronounced and frowned at Curtis. He murmured something.

"Ooh—*you*!" said Mrs. Swan. She rose from her squatting posture. "I'd like to *steal* you, in your little sailor-suit, and all!"

"Mother bought that suit for you, didn't she?" asked Mrs. Matson of Curtis. "Mother bought him all his nice things."

"Oh, he calls you mother? Now, isn't that sweet!" cried Mrs. Swan.

"Yes, I think it's nice," said Mrs. Matson.

There was a brisk, sure step on the porch; a key turned in the lock. Mr. Matson was among them.

"Well," said Mrs. Matson upon seeing her mate. It was her invariable evening greeting to him.

"Ah," said Mr. Matson. It was his to her.

Mrs. Kerley cooed. Mrs. Swan blinked vivaciously. Mrs. Cook applied her speaking-tube to her ear in the anticipation of hearing something good.

"I don't think you've met Mrs. Swan, Albert," remarked Mrs. Matson. He bowed.

"Oh, I've heard so much about Mr. Matson," cried Mrs. Swan.

Again he bowed.

"We've been making friends with your dear little boy," Mrs. Swan said. She pinched Curtis's cheek. "You sweetie, you!"

"Well, Curtis," said Mr. Matson, "haven't you got a good-evening for me?"

Curtis gave his hand to his present father with a weak smile of politeness. He looked modestly down.

"That's more like it," summarized Mr. Matson. His parental duties accomplished, he turned to fulfill his social obligations. Boldly he caught up Mrs. Cook's speaking-tube. Curtis watched.

"Getting cooler out," roared Mr. Matson. "I thought it would."

Mrs. Cook nodded. "That's good!" she shouted.

Mr. Matson pressed forward to open the door for her. He was of generous proportions, and the hall was narrow. One of the buttons-of-leisure on his coat-sleeve caught in Mrs. Cook's speaking-tube. It fell, with a startling crash, to the floor, and writhed about.

Curtis's control went. Peal upon peal of high, helpless laughter came

from him. He laughed on, against Mrs. Matson's cry of "Curtis!,"
against Mr. Matson's frown. He doubled over with his hands on his
little brown knees, and laughed mad laughter.

"Curtis!" bellowed Mr. Matson. The laughter died. Curtis straightened himself, and one last little moan of enjoyment escaped him.

Mr. Matson pointed with a magnificent gesture. "Upstairs!" he
boomed.

Curtis turned and climbed the stairs. He looked small beside the
banister.

"Well, of all the—" said Mrs. Matson. "I never knew him to do a
thing like that since he's been here. I never heard him do such a thing!"

"That young man," pronounced Mr. Matson, "needs a good talking to."

"He needs more than that," his spouse said.

Mr. Matson stooped with a faint creaking, retrieved the speaking-
tube, and presented it to Mrs. Cook. "Not at all," he said in anticipation
of the thanks which she left unspoken. He bowed.

"Pardon me," he ordered, and mounted the stairs.

Mrs. Matson moved to the door in the wake of her guests. She was
bewildered and, it seemed, grieved.

"I never," she affirmed, "never knew that child to go on that way."

"Oh, children," Mrs. Kerley assured her, "they're funny sometimes
—especially a little boy like that. You can't expect so much. My goodness, you'll fix all that! I always say I don't know any child that's getting any better bringing up than that young one—just as if he was
your own."

Peace returned to the breast of Mrs. Matson. "Oh—goodness!" she
said. There was almost a coyness in her smile as she closed the door on
the departing.

Pictorial Review, February 1927

The Sexes

The young man with the scenic cravat glanced nervously down the sofa at the girl in the fringed dress. She was examining her handkerchief; it might have been the first one of its kind she had seen, so deep was her interest in its material, form, and possibilities. The young man cleared his throat, without necessity or success, producing a small, syncopated noise.

"Want a cigarette?" he said.

"No, thank you," she said. "Thank you ever so much just the same."

"Sorry I've only got these kind," he said. "You got any of your own?"

"I really don't know," she said. "I probably have, thank you."

"Because if you haven't," he said, "it wouldn't take me a minute to go up to the corner and get you some."

"Oh, thank you, but I wouldn't have you go to all that trouble for anything," she said. "It's awfully sweet of you to think of it. Thank you ever so much."

"Will you for God's sakes stop thanking me?" he said.

"Really," she said, "I didn't know I was saying anything out of the way. I'm awfully sorry if I hurt your feelings. I know what it feels like to get your feelings hurt. I'm sure I didn't realize it was an insult to say 'thank you' to a person. I'm not exactly in the habit of having people swear at me because I say 'thank you' to them."

"I did not swear at you!" he said.

"Oh, you didn't?" she said. "I see."

"My God," he said, "all I said, I simply asked you if I couldn't go out and get you some cigarettes. Is there anything in that to get up in the air about?"

"Who's up in the air?" she said. "I'm sure I didn't know it was a criminal offense to say I wouldn't dream of giving you all that trouble. I'm afraid I must be awfully stupid, or something."

"Do you want me to go out and get you some cigarettes; or don't you?" he said.

"Goodness," she said, "if you want to go so much, please don't feel you have to stay here. I wouldn't have you feel you had to stay for anything."

"Ah, don't be that way, will you?" he said.

"Be what way?" she said. "I'm not being any way."

"What's the matter?" he said.

"Why, nothing," she said. "Why?"

"You've been funny all evening," he said. "Hardly said a word to me, ever since I came in."

"I'm terribly sorry you haven't been having a good time," she said. "For goodness' sakes, don't feel you have to stay here and be bored. I'm sure there are millions of places you could be having a lot more fun. The only thing, I'm a little bit sorry I didn't know before, that's all. When you said you were coming over tonight, I broke a lot of dates to go to the theater and everything. But it doesn't make a bit of difference. I'd much rather have you go and have a good time. It isn't very pleasant to sit here and feel you're boring a person to death."

"I'm not bored!" he said. "I don't want to go any place! Ah, honey, won't you tell me what's the matter? Ah, please."

"I haven't the faintest idea what you're talking about," she said. "There isn't a thing on earth the matter. I don't know what you mean."

"Yes, you do," he said. "There's something the trouble. Is it anything I've done, or anything?"

"Goodness," she said, "I'm sure it isn't any of my business, anything you do. I certainly wouldn't feel I had any right to criticize."

"Will you stop talking like that?" he said. "Will you, please?"

"Talking like what?" she said.

"You know," he said. "That's the way you were talking over the telephone today, too. You were so snotty when I called you up, I was afraid to talk to you."

"I beg your pardon," she said. "What did you say I was?"

"Well, I'm sorry," he said. "I didn't mean to say that. You get me so balled up."

"You see," she said, "I'm really not in the habit of hearing language like that. I've never had a thing like that said to me in my life."

"I told you I was sorry, didn't I?" he said. "Honest, honey, I didn't mean it. I don't know how I came to say a thing like that. Will you excuse me? Please?"

"Oh, certainly," she said. "Goodness, don't feel you have to apologize to me. It doesn't make any difference at all. It just seems a little bit funny to have somebody you were in the habit of thinking was a gentleman come to your home and use language like that to you, that's all. But it doesn't make the slightest bit of difference."

"I guess nothing I say makes any difference to you," he said. "You seem to be sore at me."

"I'm sore at you?" she said. "I can't understand what put that idea in your head. Why should I be sore at you?"

"That's what I'm asking you," he said. "Won't you tell me what I've done? Have I done something to hurt your feelings, honey? The way you were, over the phone, you had me worried all day. I couldn't do a lick of work."

"I certainly wouldn't like to feel," she said, "that I was interfering with your work. I know there are lots of girls that don't think anything of doing things like that, but I think it's terrible. It certainly isn't very nice to sit here and have someone tell you you interfere with his business."

"I didn't say that!" he said. "I didn't say it!"

"Oh, didn't you?" she said. "Well, that was the impression I got. It must be my stupidity."

"I guess maybe I better go," he said. "I can't get right. Everything I say seems to make you sorer and sorer. Would you rather I'd go?"

"Please do just exactly whatever you like," she said. "I'm sure the last thing I want to do is have you stay here when you'd rather be some place else. Why don't you go some place where you won't be bored? Why don't you go up to Florence Leaming's? I know she'd love to have you."

"I don't want to go up to Florence Leaming's!" he said. "What would I want to go up to Florence Leaming's for? She gives me a pain."

"Oh, really?" she said. "She didn't seem to be giving you so much of a pain at Elsie's party last night, I notice. I notice you couldn't even talk to anybody else, that's how much of a pain she gave you."

"Yeah, and you know why I was talking to her?" he said.

"Why, I suppose you think she's attractive," she said. "I suppose some people do. It's perfectly natural. Some people think she's quite pretty."

"I don't know whether she's pretty or not," he said. "I wouldn't know her if I saw her again. Why I was talking to her was you wouldn't even give me a tumble, last night. I came up and tried to talk to you, and you just said, 'Oh, how do you do'—just like that, 'Oh, how do you do'—and you turned right away and wouldn't look at me."

"I wouldn't look at you?" she said. "Oh, that's awfully funny. Oh, that's marvelous. You don't mind if I laugh, do you?"

"Go ahead and laugh your head off," he said. "But you wouldn't."

"Well, the minute you came in the room," she said, "you started making such a fuss over Florence Leaming, I thought you never wanted to see anybody else. You two seemed to be having such a wonderful time together, goodness knows I wouldn't have butted in for anything."

"My God," he said, "this what's-her-name girl came up and began talking to me before I even saw anybody else, and what could I do? I couldn't sock her in the nose, could I?"

"I certainly didn't see you try," she said.

"You saw me try to talk to you, didn't you?" he said. "And what did you do? 'Oh, how do you do.' Then this what's-her-name came up again, and there I was, stuck. Florence Leaming! I think she's terrible. Know what I think of her? I think she's a damn little fool. That's what I think of her."

"Well, of course," she said, "that's the impression she always gave me, but I don't know. I've heard people say she's pretty. Honestly I have."

"Why, she can't be pretty in the same room with you," he said.

"She has got an awfully funny nose," she said. "I really feel sorry for a girl with a nose like that."

"She's got a terrible nose," he said. "You've got a beautiful nose. Gee, you've got a pretty nose."

"Oh, I have not," she said. "You're crazy."

"And beautiful eyes," he said, "and beautiful hair and a beautiful mouth. And beautiful hands. Let me have one of the little hands. Ah, look atta little hand! Who's got the prettiest hands in the world? Who's the sweetest girl in the world?"

"I don't know," she said. "Who?"

"You don't know!" he said. "You do so, too, know."

"I do not," she said. "Who? Florence Leaming?"

"Oh, Florence Leaming, my eye!" he said. "Getting sore about Florence Leaming! And me not sleeping all last night and not doing a stroke of work all day because you wouldn't speak to me! A girl like you getting sore about a girl like Florence Leaming!"

"I think you're just perfectly crazy," she said. "I was not sore! What on earth ever made you think I was? You're simply crazy. Ow, my new pearl beads! Wait a second till I take them off. There!"

The New Republic, July 13, 1927

Arrangement in Black and White

The woman with the pink velvet poppies twined round the assisted gold of her hair traversed the crowded room at an interesting gait combining a skip with a sidle, and clutched the lean arm of her host.

"Now I got you!" she said. "Now you can't get away!"

"Why, hello," said her host. "Well. How are you?"

"Oh, I'm finely," she said. "Just simply finely. Listen, I want you to do me the most terrible favor. Will you? Will you please? Pretty please?"

"What is it?" said her host.

"Listen," she said. "I want to meet Walter Williams. Honestly, I'm just simply crazy about that man. Oh, when he sings! When he sings those spirituals! Well, I said to Burton, 'It's a good thing for you Walter Williams is colored,' I said, 'or you'd have lots of reason to be jealous.' I'd really love to meet him. I'd like to tell him I've heard him sing. Will you be an angel and introduce me to him?"

"Why, certainly," said her host. "I thought you'd met him. The party's for him. Where is he, anyway?"

"He's over there by the bookcase," she said. "Let's wait till those people get through talking to him. Well, I think you're simply marvelous, giving this perfectly marvelous party for him, and having him meet all these white people, and all. Isn't he terribly grateful?"

"I hope not," said her host.

"I think it's really terribly nice," she said. "I do. I don't see why on earth it isn't perfectly all right to meet colored people. I haven't any feeling at all about it—not one single bit. Burton—oh, he's just the other way. Well, you know, he comes from Virginia, and you know how they are."

"Did he come tonight?" said her host.

"No, he couldn't," she said. "I'm a regular grass widow tonight. I told him when I left, 'There's no telling what I'll do,' I said. He was just so tired out, he couldn't move. Isn't it a shame?"

"Ah," said her host.

"Wait till I tell him I met Walter Williams!" she said. "He'll just about die. Oh, we have more arguments about colored people. I talk to him like I don't know what, I get so excited. 'Oh, don't be so silly,' I say. But I must say for Burton, he's heaps broader-minded than lots of these Southerners. He's really awfully fond of colored people. Well, he says himself, he wouldn't have white servants. And you know, he had this old colored nurse, this regular old nigger mammy, and he just simply loves her. Why, every time he goes home, he goes out in the kitchen to see her. He does, really, to this day. All he says is, he says he hasn't got a word to say against colored people as long as they keep their place. He's always doing things for them—giving them clothes and I don't know what all. The only thing he says, he says he wouldn't sit down at the table with one for a million dollars. 'Oh,' I say to him, 'you make me sick, talking like that.' I'm just terrible to him. Aren't I terrible?"

"Oh, no, no, no," said her host. "No, no."

"I am," she said. "I know I am. Poor Burton! Now, me, I don't feel that way at all. I haven't the slightest feeling about colored people. Why, I'm just crazy about some of them. They're just like children—just as easy-going, and always singing and laughing and everything. Aren't they the happiest things you ever saw in your life? Honestly, it makes me laugh just to hear them. Oh, I like them. I really do. Well, now, listen, I have this colored laundress, I've had her for years, and I'm devoted to her. She's a real character. And I want to tell you, I think of her as my friend. That's the way I think of her. As I say to Burton, 'Well, for Heaven's sakes, we're all human beings!' Aren't we?"

"Yes," said her host. "Yes, indeed."

"Now this Walter Williams," she said. "I think a man like that's a real artist. I do. I think he deserves an awful lot of credit. Goodness, I'm so crazy about music or anything, I don't care *what* color he is. I honestly think if a person's an artist, nobody ought to have any feeling at all about meeting them. That's absolutely what I say to Burton. Don't you think I'm right?"

"Yes," said her host. "Oh, yes."

"That's the way I feel," she said. "I just can't understand people being narrow-minded. Why, I absolutely think it's a privilege to meet a man like Walter Williams. Yes, I do. I haven't any feeling at all. Well, my goodness, the good Lord made him, just the same as He did any of us. Didn't He?"

"Surely," said her host. "Yes, indeed."

"That's what I say," she said. "Oh, I get so furious when people are narrow-minded about colored people. It's just all I can do not to say something. Of course, I do admit when you get a bad colored man, they're simply terrible. But as I say to Burton, there are some bad white people, too, in this world. Aren't there?"

"I guess there are," said her host.

"Why, I'd really be glad to have a man like Walter Williams come to my house and sing for us, some time," she said. "Of course, I couldn't ask him on account of Burton, but I wouldn't have any feeling about it at all. Oh, can't he sing! Isn't it marvelous, the way they all have music in them? It just seems to be right *in* them. Come on, let's us go on over and talk to him. Listen, what shall I do when I'm introduced? Ought I to shake hands? Or what?"

"Why, do whatever you want," said her host.

"I guess maybe I'd better," she said. "I wouldn't for the world have him think I had any feeling. I think I'd better shake hands, just the way I would with anybody else. That's just exactly what I'll do."

They reached the tall young Negro, standing by the bookcase. The host performed introductions; the Negro bowed.

"How do you do?" he said.

The woman with the pink velvet poppies extended her hand at the length of her arm and held it so for all the world to see, until the Negro took it, shook it, and gave it back to her.

"Oh, how do you do, Mr. Williams," she said. "Well, how do you do. I've just been saying, I've enjoyed your singing so awfully much. I've been to your concerts, and we have you on the phonograph and everything. Oh, I just enjoy it!"

She spoke with great distinctness, moving her lips meticulously, as if in parlance with the deaf.

"I'm so glad," he said.

"I'm just simply crazy about that 'Water Boy' thing you sing," she said. "Honestly, I can't get it out of my head. I have my husband nearly crazy, the way I go around humming it all the time. Oh, he looks just as black as the ace of— Well. Tell me, where on earth do you ever get all those songs of yours? How do you ever get hold of them?"

"Why," he said, "there are so many different——"

"I should think you'd love singing them," she said. "It must be more fun. All those darling old spirituals—oh, I just love them! Well, what are you doing, now? Are you still keeping up your singing? Why don't you have another concert, some time?"

"I'm having one the sixteenth of this month," he said.

"Well, I'll be there," she said. "I'll be there, if I possibly can. You can count on me. Goodness, here comes a whole raft of people to talk to you. You're just a regular guest of honor! Oh, who's that girl in white? I've seen her some place."

"That's Katherine Burke," said her host.

"Good Heavens," she said, "is that Katherine Burke? Why, she looks entirely different off the stage. I thought she was much better-looking. I had no idea she was so terribly dark. Why, she looks almost like— Oh, I think she's a wonderful actress! Don't you think she's a wonderful actress, Mr. Williams? Oh, I think she's marvelous. Don't you?"

"Yes, I do," he said.

"Oh, I do, too," she said. "Just wonderful. Well, goodness, we must give someone else a chance to talk to the guest of honor. Now, don't forget, Mr. Williams, I'm going to be at that concert if I possibly can. I'll be there applauding like everything. And if I can't come, I'm going to tell everybody I know to go, anyway. Don't you forget!"

"I won't," he said. "Thank you so much."

The host took her arm and piloted her into the next room.

"Oh, my dear," she said. "I nearly died! Honestly, I give you my word, I nearly passed away. Did you hear that terrible break I made? I was just going to say Katherine Burke looked almost like a nigger. I just caught myself in time. Oh, do you think he noticed?"

"I don't believe so," said her host.

"Well, thank goodness," she said, "because I wouldn't have embarrassed him for anything. Why, he's awfully nice. Just as nice as he can be. Nice manners, and everything. You know, so many colored people, you give them an inch, and they walk all over you. But he doesn't try any of that. Well, he's got more sense, I suppose. He's really nice. Don't you think so?"

"Yes," said her host.

"I liked him," she said. "I haven't any feeling at all because he's a colored man. I felt just as natural as I would with anybody. Talked to him just as naturally, and everything. But honestly, I could hardly keep a straight face. I kept thinking of Burton. Oh, wait till I tell Burton I called him 'Mister'!"

The New Yorker, October 8, 1927

A Telephone Call

Please, God, let him telephone me now. Dear God, let him call me now. I won't ask anything else of You, truly I won't. It isn't very much to ask. It would be so little to You, God, such a little, little thing. Only let him telephone now. Please, God. Please, please, please.

If I didn't think about it, maybe the telephone might ring. Sometimes it does that. If I could think of something else. If I could think of something else. Maybe if I counted five hundred by fives, it might ring by that time. I'll count slowly. I won't cheat. And if it rings when I get to three hundred, I won't stop; I won't answer it until I get to five hundred. Five, ten, fifteen, twenty, twenty-five, thirty, thirty-five, forty, forty-five, fifty. . . . Oh, please ring. Please.

This is the last time I'll look at the clock. I will not look at it again. It's ten minutes past seven. He said he would telephone at five o'clock. "I'll call you at five, darling." I think that's where he said "darling." I'm almost sure he said it there. I know he called me "darling" twice, and the other time was when he said good-by. "Good-by, darling." He was busy, and he can't say much in the office, but he called me "darling" twice. He couldn't have minded my calling him up. I know you shouldn't keep telephoning them—I know they don't like that. When you do that, they know you are thinking about them and wanting them, and that makes them hate you. But I hadn't talked to him in three days—not in three days. And all I did was ask him how he was; it was just the way anybody might have called him up. He couldn't have minded that. He couldn't have thought I was bothering him. "No, of course you're not," he said. And he said he'd telephone me. He didn't have to say that. I didn't ask him to, truly I didn't. I'm sure I didn't. I don't think he would say he'd telephone me, and then just never do it. Please don't let him do that, God. Please don't.

"I'll call you at five, darling." "Good-by, darling." He was busy, and he was in a hurry, and there were people around him, but he called me "darling" twice. That's mine, that's mine. I have that, even if I never see him again. Oh, but that's so little. That isn't enough. Nothing's enough, if I never see him again. Please let me see him again, God. Please, I want him so much. I want him so much. I'll be good, God. I will try to be better, I will, if You will let me see him again. If You will let him telephone me. Oh, let him telephone me now.

Ah, don't let my prayer seem too little to You, God. You sit up there, so white and old, with all the angels about You and the stars slipping by. And I come to You with a prayer about a telephone call. Ah, don't laugh, God. You see, You don't know how it feels. You're so safe, there on Your throne, with the blue swirling under You. Nothing can touch You; no one can twist Your heart in his hands. This is suffering, God, this is bad, bad suffering. Won't You help me? For Your Son's sake, help me. You said You would do whatever was asked of You in His name. Oh, God, in the name of Thine only beloved Son, Jesus Christ, our Lord, let him telephone me now.

I must stop this. I mustn't be this way. Look. Suppose a young man says he'll call a girl up, and then something happens, and he doesn't. That isn't so terrible, is it? Why, it's going on all over the world, right this minute. Oh, what do I care what's going on all over the world? Why can't that telephone ring? Why can't it, why can't it? Couldn't you ring? Ah, please, couldn't you? You damned, ugly, shiny thing. It would hurt you to ring, wouldn't it? Oh, that would hurt you. Damn you, I'll pull your filthy roots out of the wall, I'll smash your smug black face in little bits. Damn you to hell.

No, no, no. I must stop. I must think about something else. This is what I'll do. I'll put the clock in the other room. Then I can't look at it. If I do have to look at it, then I'll have to walk into the bedroom, and that will be something to do. Maybe, before I look at it again, he will call me. I'll be so sweet to him, if he calls me. If he says he can't see me tonight, I'll say, "Why, that's all right, dear. Why, of course it's all right." I'll be the way I was when I first met him. Then maybe he'll like me again. I was always sweet, at first. Oh, it's so easy to be sweet to people before you love them.

I think he must still like me a little. He couldn't have called me "darling" twice today, if he didn't still like me a little. It isn't all gone, if he still likes me a little; even if it's only a little, little bit. You see, God, if You would just let him telephone me, I wouldn't have to ask You anything more. I would be sweet to him, I would be gay, I would be just the way I used to be, and then he would love me again. And then I would never have to ask You for anything more. Don't You see, God? So won't You please let him telephone me? Won't You please, please, please?

Are You punishing me, God, because I've been bad? Are You angry with me because I did that? Oh, but, God, there are so many bad people—You could not be hard only to me. And it wasn't very bad; it couldn't have been bad. We didn't hurt anybody, God. Things are only bad when they hurt people. We didn't hurt one single soul; You know that. You know it wasn't bad, don't You, God? So won't You let him telephone me now?

If he doesn't telephone me, I'll know God is angry with me. I'll count five hundred by fives, and if he hasn't called me then, I will know God isn't going to help me, ever again. That will be the sign. Five, ten, fifteen, twenty, twenty-five, thirty, thirty-five, forty, forty-five, fifty, fifty-five . . . It was bad. I knew it was bad. All right, God, send me to hell. You think You're frightening me with Your hell, don't You? You think Your hell is worse than mine.

I mustn't. I mustn't do this. Suppose he's a little late calling up—that's nothing to get hysterical about. Maybe he isn't going to call—maybe he's coming straight up here without telephoning. He'll be cross if he sees I have been crying. They don't like you to cry. He doesn't cry. I wish to God I could make him cry. I wish I could make him cry and tread the floor and feel his heart heavy and big and festering in him. I wish I could hurt him like hell.

He doesn't wish that about me. I don't think he even knows how he makes me feel. I wish he could know, without my telling him. They don't like you to tell them they've made you cry. They don't like you to tell them you're unhappy because of them. If you do, they think you're possessive and exacting. And then they hate you. They hate you whenever you say anything you really think. You always have to keep playing little games. Oh, I thought we didn't have to; I thought this was so big I could say whatever I meant. I guess you can't, ever. I guess there isn't ever anything big enough for that. Oh, if he would just telephone, I wouldn't tell him I had been sad about him. They hate sad people. I would be so sweet and so gay, he couldn't help but like me. If he would only telephone. If he would only telephone.

Maybe that's what he is doing. Maybe he is coming on here without calling me up. Maybe he's on his way now. Something might have happened to him. No, nothing could ever happen to him. I can't picture anything happening to him. I never picture him run over. I never see him lying still and long and dead. I wish he were dead. That's a terrible wish. That's a lovely wish. If he were dead, he would be mine. If he were dead, I would never think of now and the last few weeks. I would remember only the lovely times. It would be all beautiful. I wish he were dead. I wish he were dead, dead, dead.

This is silly. It's silly to go wishing people were dead just because they don't call you up the very minute they said they would. Maybe the clock's fast; I don't know whether it's right. Maybe he's hardly late at all. Anything could have made him a little late. Maybe he had to stay at his office. Maybe he went home, to call me up from there, and somebody came in. He doesn't like to telephone me in front of people. Maybe he's worried, just a little, little bit, about keeping me waiting. He might even hope that I would call him up. I could do that. I could telephone him.

I mustn't. I mustn't, I mustn't. Oh, God, please don't let me telephone him. Please keep me from doing that. I know, God, just as well as You do, that if he were worried about me, he'd telephone no matter where he was or how many people there were around him. Please make me know that, God. I don't ask You to make it easy for me—You can't do that, for all that You could make a world. Only let me know it, God. Don't let me go on hoping. Don't let me say comforting things to myself. Please don't let me hope, dear God. Please don't.

I won't telephone him. I'll never telephone him again as long as I live. He'll rot in hell, before I'll call him up. You don't have to give me strength, God; I have it myself. If he wanted me, he could get me. He knows where I am. He knows I'm waiting here. He's so sure of me, so sure. I wonder why they hate you, as soon as they are sure of you. I should think it would be so sweet to be sure.

It would be so easy to telephone him. Then I'd know. Maybe it wouldn't be a foolish thing to do. Maybe he wouldn't mind. Maybe he'd like it. Maybe he has been trying to get me. Sometimes people try and try to get you on the telephone, and they say the number doesn't answer. I'm not just saying that to help myself; that really happens. You know that really happens, God. Oh, God, keep me away from that telephone. Keep me away. Let me still have just a little bit of pride. I think I'm going to need it, God. I think it will be all I'll have.

Oh, what does pride matter, when I can't stand it if I don't talk to him? Pride like that is such a silly, shabby little thing. The real pride, the big pride, is in having no pride. I'm not saying that just because I want to call him. I am not. That's true, I know that's true. I will be big. I will be beyond little prides.

Please, God, keep me from telephoning him. Please, God.

I don't see what pride has to do with it. This is such a little thing, for me to be bringing in pride, for me to be making such a fuss about. I may have misunderstood him. Maybe he said for me to call him up, at five. "Call me at five, darling." He could have said that, perfectly well. It's so possible that I didn't hear him right. "Call me at five, darling." I'm almost sure that's what he said. God, don't let me talk this way to myself. Make me know, please make me know.

I'll think about something else. I'll just sit quietly. If I could sit still. If I could sit still. Maybe I could read. Oh, all the books are about people who love each other, truly and sweetly. What do they want to write about that for? Don't they know it isn't true? Don't they know it's a lie, it's a God damned lie? What do they have to tell about that for, when they know how it hurts? Damn them, damn them, damn them.

I won't. I'll be quiet. This is nothing to get excited about. Look. Suppose he were someone I didn't know very well. Suppose he were another girl. Then I'd just telephone and say, "Well, for goodness' sake, what happened to you?" That's what I'd do, and I'd never even think about it. Why can't I be casual and natural, just because I love him? I can be. Honestly, I can be. I'll call him up, and be so easy and pleasant. You see if I won't, God. Oh, don't let me call him. Don't, don't, don't.

God, aren't You really going to let him call me? Are You sure, God? Couldn't You please relent? Couldn't You? I don't even ask You to let him telephone me this minute, God; only let him do it in a little while. I'll count five hundred by fives. I'll do it so slowly and so fairly. If he hasn't telephoned then, I'll call him. I will. Oh, please, dear God, dear kind God, my blessed Father in Heaven, let him call before then. Please, God. Please.

Five, ten, fifteen, twenty, twenty-five, thirty, thirty-five . . .

The Bookman, January 1928

A Terrible Day Tomorrow

The woman in the leopard-skin coat and the man with the gentian-blue muffler wormed along the dim, table-bordered lanes of the speakeasy.

"Sit down any place you see," he said. "It's only just for a minute. Here's a table—this'll do, won't it?"

"Oh, yes," she said. "This is perfectly all right."

They sat down. A stocky lad in his shirt sleeves, and those rolled up, appeared beside the table, and made a friendly grin.

"Hello, there, Gus," said the man with the gentian-blue muffler. "We're only going to be here just a minute. You might bring us a couple of specials—that what you want, dear? All right, Gus, a couple of specials, and hurry them along, will you? I've got to get home early—I've got a terrible day tomorrow."

Gus vanished.

"Want to take your coat off?" said the man with the gentian-blue muffler.

"Oh, I don't think so," said the woman in the leopard-skin coat. "It isn't worth while."

"No, it isn't, really," he said. "I've simply got to get to bed early. I've got to be in the office at crack o' dawn. I mean it. What a day I've got ahead of me! Boy, what a day!"

"Ah," she said. "You poor lamb."

"That guy from Detroit is going to be there at nine," he said, "and I've got a meeting at half-past ten, and we've got to fix up those contracts at twelve, and then I have to have lunch with J. G. and give him that report, and I've got God knows how many appointments all afternoon. Oh, I haven't got much to do tomorrow. Not very much!"

"Ah," she said.

"I've got to get downtown at crack o' dawn," he said. "I can't rock into the office around eleven o'clock, the way I've been—All right, Gus put them right here. Well, here we go. Yours all right?"

"Oh, it's lovely," she said. "Oo, it's strong, though."

"They are pretty powerful," he said. "It'll do you good. Can't hurt anybody, if you just have one or two, and get to bed early. It's this staying up till crack o' dawn that knocks the hell out of you. I'm not going to do it any more. Starting tonight, I'm just going to have a couple of drinks, and go to bed before twelve. Then I'll feel more like getting down to work at crack o' dawn."

"I think that's terribly sensible," she said.

"It's the only thing to do," he said. "I'm through with this stuff. I've been drinking too damn much. Everybody's been telling me I look terrible. Don't I look terrible?"

"Why, I don't think you do at all," she said. "You look a little bit tired sometimes, the way everybody does. But I think you look fine. You look lovely."

"That's what you say!" he said. "I look terrible. I know it. Go on and finish yours, and we'll have one more. Oh, Gus! Couple of specials, will you? I should have told him to hurry. We've got to get out of here right away. What a day I've got tomorrow!"

"Oh, I know," she said. "Poor boy."

"Loosen your coat, why don't you?" he said. "You'll be cold when you go out."

"All right, I will," she said. "Hadn't you better take your muffler off?"

"Well, I might as well," he said. "It's hot in here. Rotten air, in these places. Bad for you. I'm not going to sit around speakeasies any more. Worst thing you can do. Thanks, Gus. That's what I call service. Well, here we go."

"Oo, they taste strong," she said. "Lord knows what they'll do to us."

"Can't hurt you, if you do like this," he said, "—just have a couple and then go home. It's all right to stay up and drink if you can sleep all the next day, but it's a different proposition when you've got to be downtown at crack o' dawn. I'm not going to get plastered and stay out all night any more. Except maybe Saturday nights."

"I think that's a terribly good idea," she said.

"You know what I may do?" he said. "I may go on the wagon altogether. It wouldn't hurt me a bit to go on for a while. It wouldn't hurt you, either."

"I don't drink so terribly much," she said.

"Oh, you do pretty well, there, baby," he said. "Everybody drinks too much. It's enough to poison you. I don't see how we're alive, the stuff we drink. I'm going on the wagon. Come ahead and finish your drink. Want another?"

"No, thanks," she said.

"Sure?" he said.

"No, really," she said.

"Tell you what I thought we might do," he said. "As long as I'm going on the wagon—and it would do you a lot of good to go on, too, dear, honestly it would—I thought we might have another little drink, tonight. What about it?"

"Why—if you want to," she said. "As a matter of fact, these haven't done anything at all to me."

"Me, either," he said. "They're cheating us. Hey, Gus! Two more specials, and put something in them this time, will you? And don't forget we're in a hurry. God, I've got to get down to that office on time tomorrow! I've got the worst day I ever had in my life."

"Ah, I know," she said.

"That's right, take your coat off," he said. "It's hot as hell in here. Wait a minute till I get mine off, and I'll help you. There. You all right, sweet?"

"Oh, I'm fine," she said. "Isn't it funny, the way those drinks didn't touch me?"

"That's because we've all been drinking too much," he said. "That's the beauty about going on the wagon. When you fall off and have a couple of drinks, it gives you such a nice glow you don't need any more. But if you've been drinking, see what I mean, you've got to keep it up before you can get anything. See? Oh, thanks, Gus. That's fine. Well, here we go."

"That's a nice one," she said.

"Sure," he said. "It's got something in it, for a change. They'll gyp the life out of you in these places if you don't watch them every minute. I'm through with them. I'm damn glad I'm going on the wagon. That's the best idea I've had in a long while. Hey, don't nurse it along like that, dear. Drink it quick. See, like this."

"Like this?" she said.

"That's more like it," he said. "Now maybe you'll hear from it. You'll never get anywhere, sipping a drink. Come on, now, one more swallow. Good girl. Oh, Gus! Couple more, while you're up."

"Are you crazy?" she said. "We haven't finished these ones yet."

"We'll be through by the time he brings the others," he said. "Then we won't have to sit around and wait. See? We've got to get along. Honestly, I've got to be in the office at crack o' dawn, tomorrow. What a day!"

"Yes," she said. "I know."

"Do I know!" he said. "Hurry up, dear. Drink your drink. Finished? Oh, come on and finish it—stop stalling. That's the way. Here's Gus; pretty work, Gus. Gus is my friend, aren't you Gus? Sure you are. Gus and I are old friends. Well, here we go, dear. Have a little nightcap. Make you sleep."

"I usually always sleep pretty well," she said.

"No use talking, I've got to get more sleep," he said. "I look terrible. My mother worries her head off about me. Every time she writes me a letter, she says, 'Take care of yourself.' Yeah. I take fine care of myself. She's got a right to worry. I'm a nice guy, I am. You know what? I haven't written to my mother for three weeks. That's nice, isn't it?"

"You ought to write to her," she said.

"Where the hell do I get time to write?" he said. "I haven't got any time to write letters. God, I ought to write to my mother. I'll write to her tomorrow. Oh, Judas, I can't write tomorrow. I've got a terrible day tomorrow. Terrible!"

"Really?" she said.

"I've got so much to do tomorrow, I won't even have time to write to my poor, sweet mother," he said. "That's only how busy I'm going to be. It's no wonder my poor, sweet mother worries. She worries the head off herself about me. You don't love me."

"I do so!" she said.

"Yes, you do!" he said.

"I certainly do!" she said. "What do you want to say a thing like that for?"

"I know," he said. "I know."

"You know a lot, don't you?" she said. "It must be great to know as much as you do. You make me sick."

"I know I do," he said. "I know I make you sick."

"You do not!" she said.

"Oh, I know," he said.

"What you know is, you know perfectly well I love you," she said. "You don't love me, that's what's the trouble."

"Yes, I don't!" he said.

"I suppose you don't think I can tell," she said. "Well, I can. I know you don't love me. You never even think about me. All you think about's yourself. You don't think about anything but your old office. 'Oh, I've got to get down to the office, oh, I've got to get down to the office. Oh, I've got to be at the dear, sweet, darling, precious office at crack o' dawn.' That's all you ever say."

"Well, I do," he said. "I told you I've got to get down early tomorrow. I've got an awful day."

"Oh, shut up!" she said.

"Thank you," he said. "Thank you very much. That's awfully sweet of you. I'm much obliged. Gus! Where the hell've you been? What's the matter, can't I get a drink here? Am I a nigger, or something? Bring a couple of specials, and try and hurry up a little bit about it, will you? God's sweet sake!"

"I thought you weren't going to drink any more," she said.

"What difference does it make to you?" he said. "What do you care whether I drink or not? I could drink myself stiff, for all you care. You don't care about me."

"You mustn't talk like that," she said. "You know I care, don't you? Don't you? Don't you know I care?"

"Do you honestly care a little bit?" he said.

"Ah, darling," she said.

"Maybe you do," he said. "Maybe you care a little bit. If you cared anything at all about me, you'd finish your drink, so we could have a little nightcap. That's the way! Aren't you ashamed of yourself, talking to me the way you did? Weren't you a bad girl? You know you went for me like a regular bulldog? Do you know that? Bulldog, bulldog, bow, wow, wow, Eli Yale; for it's a bulldog, bulldog, bow, wow, wow, our team will never fail; when the sons of Eli—Why, here's Gus! Well, well, well, if it isn't my old friend, Gus. And look what he's got. Look what Gus brought us, dear. Well, here we go. That's a nice little night-cap. Nightcap, nightcap, bow, wow, wow, Eli—"

"I love to hear you sing," she said. "It sounds—oo, that is a nice drink. That's the nicest one we've had."

"Drink it!" he said. "Really, dear, you've got to get over that habit of sipping your drinks. That's what keeps you up so late. If you'd learn to drink quickly, you could get home before crack o' dawn. Cracko-dawn, crackodawn, bow, wow, wow, Eli Yale; for it's a crackodawn, crackodawn, bow, wow, wow, our team will never—No, but seriously, sweet, I want to talk to you seriously about that. You know, you ought, seriously—what the hell was I going to say? Can you imagine that? I had something very important I wanted to talk to you about, and I can't remember what it was. What did I start saying to you, anyway?"

"When?" she said.

"Nope, it's gone," he said. "Well, I guess it couldn't have been anything very important. Let it ride. How're you coming with your drink? Know what we're going to do when you finish it? We're going to have a little nightcap. Hurry up, won't you, dear? Honestly, we haven't got all night. I've got to get some sleep. I've got a terrible day, tomorrow. Terrible, terrible, bow, wow, wow, Eli Yale; for it's a terrible, terrible, bow,—Oh Gus! Hey, Gus! Listen, Gus, you're a friend of mine, aren't you? Then how about getting us a couple more specials? Will you, Gus? Just for me and the girl friend—you know the girl friend, don't you? Sure he does. All right, Gus, two more little specials."

And so on.

The New Yorker, February 11, 1928

Just a Little One

I like this place, Fred. This is a nice place. How did you ever find it? I think you're perfectly marvelous, discovering a speakeasy in the year 1928. And they let you right in, without asking you a single question. I bet you could get into the subway without using anybody's name. Couldn't you, Fred?

Oh, I like this place better and better, now that my eyes are getting accustomed to it. You mustn't let them tell you this lighting system is original with them, Fred; they got the idea from the Mammoth Cave. This is you sitting next to me, isn't it? Oh, you can't fool me. I'd know that knee anywhere.

You know what I like about this place? It's got atmosphere. That's what it's got. If you would ask the waiter to bring a fairly sharp knife, I could cut off a nice little block of the atmosphere, to take home with me. It would be interesting to have for my memory book. I'm going to start keeping a memory book tomorrow. Don't let me forget.

Why, I don't know, Fred—what are you going to have? Then I guess I'll have a highball, too; please, just a little one. Is it really real Scotch? Well, that will be a new experience for me. You ought to see the Scotch I've got home in my cupboard; at least it was in the cupboard this morning—it's probably eaten its way out by now. I got it for my birthday. Well, it was something. The birthday before, all I got was a year older.

This is a nice highball, isn't it? Well, well, well, to think of me having real Scotch; I'm out of the bush leagues at last. Are you going to have another one? Well, I shouldn't like to see you drinking all by yourself, Fred. Solitary drinking is what causes half the crime in the country. That's what's responsible for the failure of prohibition. But please, Fred, tell him to make mine just a little one. Make it awfully weak; just cambric Scotch.

It will be nice to see the effect of veritable whisky upon one who has been accustomed only to the simpler forms of entertainment. You'll like that, Fred. You'll stay by me if anything happens, won't you? I don't think there will be anything spectacular, but I want to ask you one thing, just in case. Don't let me take any horses home with me. It doesn't matter so much about stray dogs and kittens, but elevator boys get awfully stuffy when you try to bring in a horse. You might just as well know that about me now, Fred. You can always tell that the crash is coming when I start getting tender about Our Dumb Friends. Three highballs, and I think I'm St. Francis of Assisi.

But I don't believe anything is going to happen to me on these. That's because they're made of real stuff. That's what the difference is. This just makes you feel fine. Oh, I feel swell, Fred. You do too, don't you? I knew you did, because you look better. I love that tie you have on. Oh, did Edith give it to you? Ah, wasn't that nice of her? You know, Fred, most people are really awfully nice. There are darn few that aren't pretty fine at heart. You've got a beautiful heart, Fred. You'd be the first person I'd go to if I were in trouble. I guess you are just about the best friend I've got in the world. But I worry about you, Fred. I do so, too. I don't think you take enough care of yourself. You ought to take care of yourself for your friends' sake. You oughtn't to drink all this terrible stuff that's around; you owe it to your friends to be careful. You don't mind my talking to you like this, do you? You see, dear, it's because I'm your friend that I hate to see you not taking care of yourself. It hurts me to see you batting around the way you've been doing. You ought to stick to this place, where they have real Scotch that can't do you any harm. Oh, darling, do you really think I ought to? Well, you tell him just a little bit of a one. Tell him, sweet.

Do you come here often, Fred? I shouldn't worry about you so much if I knew you were in a safe place like this. Oh, is this where you were Thursday night? I see. Why, no, it didn't make a bit of difference, only you told me to call you up, and like a fool I broke a date I had, just because I thought I was going to see you. I just sort of naturally thought so, when you said to call you up. Oh, good Lord, don't make all that fuss about it. It really didn't make the slightest difference. It just didn't seem a very friendly way to behave, that's all. I don't know—I'd been believing we were such good friends. I'm an awful idiot about people, Fred. There aren't many who are really your friend at heart. Practically anybody would play you dirt for a nickel. Oh, yes, they would.

Was Edith here with you, Thursday night? This place must be very becoming to her. Next to being in a coal mine, I can't think of anywhere she could go that the light would be more flattering to that pan of hers. Do you really know a lot of people that say she's good-looking? You must have a wide acquaintance among the astigmatic, haven't you, Freddie, dear? Why, I'm not being any way at all—it's simply one of those things, either you can see it or you can't. Now to me, Edith looks like something that would eat her young. Dresses well? *Edith* dresses

well? Are you trying to kid me, Fred, at my age? You mean you mean
it? Oh, my God. You mean those clothes of hers are *intentional*? My
heavens, I always thought she was on her way out of a burning building.

Well, we live and learn. Edith dresses well! Edith's got good taste!
Yes, she's got sweet taste in neckties. I don't suppose I ought to say it
about such a dear friend of yours, Fred, but she is the lousiest necktie-
picker-out I ever saw. I never saw anything could touch that thing you
have around your neck. All right, suppose I did say I liked it. I just said
that because I felt sorry for you. I'd feel sorry for anybody with a thing
like that on. I just wanted to try to make you feel good, because I
thought you were my friend. My friend! I haven't got a friend in the
world. Do you know that, Fred? Not one single friend in this world.

All right, what do you care if I'm crying, I can cry if I want to, can't
I? I guess you'd cry, too, if you didn't have a friend in the world. Is my
face very bad? I suppose that damned mascara has run all over it. I've
got to give up using mascara, Fred; life's too sad. Isn't life terrible? Oh,
my God, isn't life awful? Ah, don't cry, Fred. Please don't. Don't you
care, baby. Life's terrible, but don't you care. You've got friends. I'm
the one that hasn't got any friends. I am so. No, it's me. I'm the one.

I don't think another drink would make me feel any better. I don't
know whether I want to feel any better. What's the sense of feeling
good, when life's so terrible? Oh, all right, then. But please tell him just
a little one, if it isn't too much trouble. I don't want to stay here much
longer. I don't like this place. It's all dark and stuffy. It's the kind of
place Edith would be crazy about—that's all I can say about this place.
I know I oughtn't to talk about your best friend, Fred, but that's a
terrible woman. That woman is the louse of this world. It makes me
feel just awful that you trust that woman, Fred. I hate to see anybody
play you dirt. I'd hate to see you get hurt. That's what makes me feel
so terrible. That's why I'm getting mascara all over my face. No, please
don't, Fred. You mustn't hold my hand. It wouldn't be fair to Edith.
We've got to play fair with the big louse. After all, she's your best friend,
isn't she?

Honestly? Do you honestly mean it, Fred? Yes, but how could I help
thinking so, when you're with her all the time—when you bring her
here every night in the week? Really, only Thursday? Oh, I know—I
know how those things are. You simply can't help it, when you get
stuck with a person that way. Lord, I'm glad you realize what an awful
thing that woman is. I was worried about it, Fred. It's because I'm your
friend. Why, of course I am, darling. You know I am. Oh, that's just
silly, Freddie. You've got heaps of friends. Only you'll never find a better

friend than I am. No, I know that. I know I'll never find a better friend than you are to me. Just give me back my hand a second, till I get this damned mascara out of my eye.

Yes, I think we ought to, honey. I think we ought to have a little drink, on account of our being friends. Just a little one, because it's real Scotch, and we're real friends. After all, friends are the greatest things in the world, aren't they, Fred? Gee, it makes you feel good to know you have a friend. I feel great, don't you, dear? And you look great, too. I'm proud to have you for a friend. Do you realize, Fred, what a rare thing a friend is, when you think of all the terrible people there are in this world? Animals are much better than people. God, I love animals. That's what I like about you, Fred. You're so fond of animals.

Look, I'll tell you what let's do, after we've had just a little highball. Let's go out and pick up a lot of stray dogs. I never had enough dogs in my life, did you? We ought to have more dogs. And maybe there'd be some cats around, if we looked. And a horse, I've never had one single horse, Fred. Isn't that rotten? Not one single horse. Ah, I'd like a nice old cab-horse, Fred. Wouldn't you? I'd like to take care of it and comb its hair and everything. Ah, don't be stuffy about it, Fred, please don't. I need a horse, honestly I do. Wouldn't you like one? It would be so sweet and kind. Let's have a drink and then let's you and I go out and get a horsie, Freddie—just a little one, darling, just a little one.

The New Yorker, May 12, 1928

The Mantle of Whistler

The hostess, all smiles and sparkles and small, abortive dance-steps, led the young man with the side-burns across the room to where sat the girl who had twice been told she looked like Clara Bow.

"There she is!" she cried. "Here's the girl we've been looking for! Miss French, let me make you acquainted with Mr. Bartlett."

"Pleased to meet up with you social," said Mr. Bartlett.

"Pardon my wet glove," said Miss French.

"Oh, you two!" said the hostess. "I've just been dying to get you two together. I knew you'd get on just like nothing at all. Didn't I tell you he had a marvelous line, Alice? What'd I tell you, Jack—didn't I say over and over again she was a scream? And she's always like this. You wait till you know her as well as I do! Goodness, I just wish I could stay here and listen to you."

However, frustrated in her desire, she smiled heartily, waved her hand like a dear little baby shaking bye-bye, and schottisched across the floor to resume the burdens of hospitality.

"Hey, where have you been all my life?" said the young man who had a marvelous line.

"Don't be an Airedale," said the girl who was always like this.

"Any objection if I sit down?" he said.

"Go right ahead," she said. "Sit down and take a load off your feet."

"I'll do that little thing for you," he said. "Sit down before I fall down, what? Some party, isn't it? What a party this turned out to be!"

"And how!" she said.

" 'And how' is right," he said. " 'S wonderful."

" 'S marvelous," she said.

" 'S awful nice," he said.

" 'S Paradise," she said.

"Right there with the comeback, aren't you?" he said. "What a girl you turned out to be! Some girl, aren't you?"

"Oh, don't be an Airedale," she said.

"Just a real good girl," he said. "Some little looker, too. Where did you get those big, blue eyes from, anyway? Don't you know I'm the guy that always falls for big, blue eyes?"

"You would," she said. "You're just the tripe."

"Hey, listen, listen," he said. "Lay off for a minute, will you? Come on, now, get regular. Aren't you going to tell me where you got those big, blue eyes?"

"Oh, don't be ridic," she said. "They are not big! Are they?"

"Are they big!" he said. "You don't know they're big, do you? Oh, no, nobody ever told you that before. And you don't know what you do to me, when you look up like that, do you? Yes, you don't!"

"I wouldn't know about that," she said.

"Ah, stop that, will you?" he said. "Go ahead, now, come clean. Tell me where you got those big, blue eyes."

"What's your idea in bringing that up?" she said.

"And your hair's pretty cute, too," he said. "I suppose you don't know you've got pretty cute hair. You wouldn't know about that, would you?"

"Even if that was good, I wouldn't like it," she said.

"Come on, now," he said. "Don't you know that hair of yours is pretty cute?"

" 'S wonderful," she said. " 'S marvelous."

"That you should care for me?" he said.

"Oh, don't be an Airedale," she said.

"I could care for you in a big way," he said. "What those big, blue eyes of yours do to me is nobody's business. Know that?"

"Oh, I wouldn't know about that," she said.

"Hey, listen," he said, "what are you trying to do—run me ragged? Don't you ever stop kidding? When are you going to tell me where you got your big, blue eyes?"

"Oh, pull yourself together," she said.

"I'd have to have a care with a girl like you," he said. "Watch my step, that's what I'd have to do."

"Don't be sil," she said.

"You know what?" he said. "I could get a girl like you on the brain."

"The what?" she said.

"Ah, come on, come on," he said. "Lay off that stuff, will you? Tell me where you've been keeping yourself, anyhow. Got any more like you around the house?"

" 'S all there is," she said. " 'R' isn't any more."

"That's Oke with me," he said. "One like you's enough. What those eyes of yours do to me is plenty! Know it?"

"I wouldn't know about that," she said.

"That dress of yours slays me," he said. "Where'd you get the catsy dress? Hm?"

"Don't be an Airedale," she said.

"Hey, where'd you get that expression, anyway?" he said.

"It's a gift," she said.

" 'Gift' is right," he said. "It's a honey."

"You ain't heard nothin' yet," she said.

"You slay me," he said. "I'm telling you. Where do you get all your stuff from?"

"What's your idea in bringing that up?" she said.

The hostess, with enhanced sparkles, romped over to them.

"Well, for heaven's sakes!" she cried. "Aren't you two even going to look at anybody else? What do you think of her, Jack? Isn't she cute?"

"Is she cute!" he said.

"Isn't he marvelous, Alice?" asked the hostess.

"You'd be surprised," she said.

The hostess cocked her head, like a darling, mischievous terrier puppy, and sparkled whimsically at them.

"Oh, you two!" she said. "Didn't I tell you you'd get on just like nothing at all?"

"And how!" said the girl.

" 'And how' is right!" said the young man.

"You two!" cooed the hostess. "I could listen to you all night."

The New Yorker, August 18, 1928

The Garter

There it goes! That would be. That would happen to me. I haven't got enough trouble. Here I am, a poor, lone orphan, stuck for the evening at this foul party where I don't know a soul. And now my garter has to go and break. That's the kind of thing they think up to do to me. Let's see, what shall we have happen to her now? Well, suppose we make her garter break; of course, it's an old gag, but it's always pretty sure-fire. A lot they've got to do, raking up grammar-school jokes to play on a poor, heartsick orphan, alone in the midst of a crowd. That's the bitterest kind of loneliness there is, too. Anybody'll tell you that. Anybody that wouldn't tell you that is a rotten egg.

This couldn't have happened to me in the perfumed sanctity of my boudoir. Or even in the comparative privacy of the taxi. Oh, no. That would have been too good. It must wait until I'm cornered, like a frightened rat, in a room full of strangers. And the dressing-room forty yards away—it might as well be Sheridan. I would get that kind of break. Break, break, break, on thy cold gray stones, O sea, and I would that my tongue could utter the thoughts that arise in me. Boy, do I would that it could! I'd have this room emptied in thirty seconds, flat.

Thank God I was sitting down when the crash came. There's a commentary on existence for you. There's a glimpse of the depths to which a human being can sink. All I have to be thankful for in this world is that I was sitting down when my garter busted. Count your blessings over, name them one by one, and it will surprise you what the Lord hath done. Yeah. I see.

What is a person supposed to do in a case like this? What would Napoleon have done? I've got to keep a cool head on my shoulders. I've got to be practical. I've got to make plans. The thing to do is to avert a panic at all costs. Tell the orchestra for God's sake to keep on playing. Dance, you jazz-mad puppets of fate, and pay no attention to me. I'm all right. Wounded? Nay, sire, I'm healthy. Oh, I'm great.

The only course I see open is to sit here and hold on to it, so my stocking won't come slithering down around my ankle. Just sit here and sit here and sit here. There's a rosy future. Summer will come, and bright, bitter Autumn, and jolly old King Winter. And here I'll be, hanging on to this damned thing. Love and fame will pass me by, and I shall never know the sacred, awful joy of holding a tiny, warm body in my grateful arms. I may not set down imperishable words for posterity to marvel over; there will be for me nor travel nor riches nor wise, new friends, nor glittering adventure, nor the sweet fruition of my gracious womanhood. Ah, hell.

Won't it be nice for my lucky hosts, when everybody else goes home, and I'm still sitting here? I wonder if I'll ever get to know them well enough to hang my blushing head and whisper my little secret to them. I suppose we'll have to get pretty much used to one another. I'll probably live a long time; there won't be much wear on my system, sitting here, year in, year out, holding my stocking up. Maybe they could find a use for me, after a while. They could hang hats on me, or use my lap for an ash-tray. I wonder if their lease is up, the first of October. No, no, no, now I won't hear a word of it; you all go right ahead and move, and leave me here for the new tenants. Maybe the landlord will do me over for them. I expect my clothes will turn yellow, like Miss Havisham's, in *Great Expectations*, by Charles Dickens, an English novelist, 1812–1870. Miss Havisham had a broken heart, and I've got a broken garter. The Frustration Girls. The Frustration Girls on an Island, The Frustration Girls at the World's Fair, The Frustration Girls and Their Ice-Boat, The Frustration Girls at the House of All Nations. That's enough of that. I don't want to play that any more.

To think of a promising young life blocked, halted, shattered by a garter! In happier times, I might have been able to use the word "garter" in a sentence. Nearer, my garter thee, nearer to thee. It doesn't matter; my life's over, anyway. I wonder how they'll be able to tell when I'm dead. It will be a very thin line of distinction between me sitting here holding my stocking, and just a regulation dead body. A demd, damp, moist, unpleasant body. That's from *Nicholas Nickleby*. What am I having, anyway— An Evening with Dickens? Well, it's the best I'll get, from now on.

If I had my life to live over again, I'd wear corsets; corsets with lots of firm, true, tough, loyal-hearted garters attached to them all the way around. You'd be safe with them; they wouldn't let you down. I wouldn't trust a round garter again as far as I could see it. I or anybody else. Never trust a round garter or a Wall Street man. That's what life has taught me. That's what I've got out of all this living. If I could have just one more chance, I'd wear corsets. Or else I'd go without stockings, and play I was the eternal Summer girl. Once they wouldn't let me in the Casino at Monte Carlo because I didn't have any stockings on. So I went and found my stockings, and then came back and lost my shirt. Dottie's Travel Diary: or Highways and Byways in Picturesque Monaco, by One of Them. I wish I were in Monte Carlo right this minute. I wish I were in Carcassonne. Hell, it would look like a million dollars to me to be on St. Helena.

I certainly must be cutting a wide swath through this party. I'm making my personality felt. Creeping into every heart, that's what I'm doing. Oh, have you met Dorothy Parker? What's she like? Oh, she's terrible. God, she's poisonous. Sits in a corner and sulks all evening—never opens her yap. Dumbest woman you ever saw in your life. You know, they say she doesn't write a word of her stuff. They say she pays this poor little guy, that lives in some tenement on the lower East Side, ten dollars a week to write it and she just signs her name to it. He has to do it, the poor devil, to help support a crippled mother and five brothers and sisters; he makes buttonholes in the daytime. Oh, she's terrible.

Little do they know, the blind fools, that I'm all full of tenderness and affection, and just aching to give and give and give. All they can see is this unfortunate exterior. There's a man looking at it now. All right, baby, go on and look your head off. Funny, isn't it? Look pretty silly, don't I, sitting here holding my knee? Yes, and I'm the only one that's going to hold it, too. What do you think of that, sweetheart?

Heaven send that no one comes over here and tries to make friends with me. That's the first time I ever wished that, in all my life. What shall I do if anyone comes over? Suppose they try to shake hands with me. Suppose somebody asks me to dance. I'll just have to rock my head and say, "No spik Inglese," that's all. Can this be me, praying that nobody will come near me? And when I was getting dressed, I thought, "Maybe this will be the night that romance will come into my life." Oh, if I only had the use of both my hands, I'd just cover my face and cry my heart out.

That man, that man who was looking! He's coming over! Oh, now what? I can't say, "Sir, I have not the dubious pleasure of your acquaintance." I'm rotten at that sort of thing. I can't answer him in perfect French. Lord knows I can't get up and walk haughtily away. I wonder how he'd take it if I told him all. He looks a little too Brooks Brothers to be really understanding. The better they look, the more they think you are trying to get new with them, if you talk of Real Things, Things That Matter. Maybe he'd think I was just eccentric. Maybe he's got a humane streak, somewhere underneath. Maybe he's got a sister or a mother or something. Maybe he'll turn out to be one of Nature's noblemen.

How do you do? Listen, what would you do if you were I, and . . . ?

The New Yorker, September 8, 1928

New York to Detroit

"All ready with Detroit," said the telephone operator.

"Hello," said the girl in New York.

"Hello?" said the young man in Detroit.

"Oh, Jack!" she said. "Oh, darling, it's so wonderful to hear you. You don't know how much I—"

"Hello?" he said.

"Ah, can't you hear me?" she said. "Why, I can hear you just as if you were right beside me. Is this any better, dear? Can you hear me now?"

"Who did you want to speak to?" he said.

"You, Jack!" she said. "You, you. This is Jean, darling. Oh, please try to hear me. This is Jean."

"Who?" he said.

"Jean," she said. "Ah, don't you know my voice? It's Jean, dear. Jean."

"Oh, hello there," he said. "Well. Well, for heaven's sake. How are you?"

"I'm all right," she said. "Oh, I'm not, either, darling. I—oh, it's just terrible. I can't stand it any more. Aren't you coming back? Please, when are you coming back? You don't know how awful it is, without you. It's been such a long time, dear—you said it would be just four or five days, and it's nearly three weeks. It's like years and years. Oh, it's been so awful, sweetheart—it's just——"

"Hey, I'm terribly sorry," he said, "but I can't hear one damn thing you're saying. Can't you talk louder, or something?"

"I'll try, I'll try," she said. "Is this better? Now can you hear?"

"Yeah, now I can, a little," he said. "Don't talk so fast, will you? What did you say, before?"

"I said it's just awful without you," she said. "It's such a long time, dear. And I haven't had a word from you. I—oh, I've just been nearly crazy, Jack. Never even a post-card, dearest, or a——"

"Honestly, I haven't had a second," he said. "I've been working like a fool. God, I've been rushed."

"Ah, have you?" she said. "I'm sorry, dear. I've been silly. But it was just—oh, it was just hell, never hearing a word. I thought maybe you'd telephone to say good-night, sometimes,—you know, the way you used to, when you were away."

"Why, I was going to, a lot of times," he said, "but I thought you'd probably be out, or something."

"I haven't been out," she said. "I've been staying here, all by myself. It's—it's sort of better, that way. I don't want to see people. Everybody says, 'When's Jack coming back?' and 'What do you hear from Jack?' and I'm afraid I'll cry in front of them. Darling, it hurts so terribly when they ask me about you, and I have to say I don't——"

"This is the damndest, lousiest connection I ever saw in my life," he said. "What hurts? What's the matter?"

"I said, it hurts so terribly when people ask me about you," she said, "and I have to say—Oh, never mind. Never mind. How are you, dear? Tell me how you are."

"Oh, pretty good," he said. "Tired as the devil. You all right?"

"Jack, I—that's what I wanted to tell you," she said. "I'm terribly worried. I'm nearly out of my mind. Oh, what will I do, dear, what are we going to do? Oh, Jack, Jack, darling!"

"Hey, how can I hear you when you mumble like that?" he said. "Can't you talk louder? Talk right into the what-you-call-it."

"I can't scream it over the telephone!" she said. "Haven't you any sense? Don't you know what I'm telling you? Don't you know? Don't you know?"

"I give up," he said. "First you mumble, and then you yell. Look, this doesn't make sense. I can't hear anything, with this rotten connection. Why don't you write me a letter, in the morning? Do that, why don't you? And I'll write you one. See?"

"Jack, listen, listen!" she said. "You listen to me! I've got to talk to you. I tell you I'm nearly crazy. Please, dearest, hear what I'm saying. Jack, I——"

"Just a minute," he said. "Someone's knocking at the door. *Come in. Well, for cryin' out loud! Come on in, bums. Hang your coats up on the floor, and sit down. The Scotch is in the closet, and there's ice in that pitcher. Make yourselves at home—act like you were in a regular bar. Be with you right away.* Hey, listen, there's a lot of crazy Indians just come in here, and I can't hear myself think. You go ahead and write me a letter tomorrow. Will you?"

"Write you a letter!" she said. "Oh, God, don't you think I'd have written you before, if I'd known where to reach you? I didn't even know that, till they told me at your office today. I got so——"

"Oh, yeah, did they?" he said. "I thought I—*Ah, pipe down, will you? Give a guy a chance. This is an expensive talk going on here.* Say, look, this must be costing you a million dollars. You oughtn't to do this."

"What do you think I care about that?" she said. "I'll die if I don't talk to you. I tell you I'll die, Jack. Sweetheart, what is it? Don't you want to talk to me? Tell me what makes you this way. Is it—don't you really like me any more? Is that it? Don't you, Jack?"

"Hell, I can't hear," he said. "Don't what?"

"Please," she said. "Please, please. Please, Jack, listen. When are you coming back, darling? I need you so. I need you so terribly. When are you coming back?"

"Why, that's the thing," he said. "That's what I was going to write you about tomorrow. *Come on, now, how about shutting up just for a minute? A joke's a joke.* Hello. Hear me all right? Why, you see, the way things came out today, it looks a little bit like I'd have to go on to Chicago for a while. Looks like a pretty big thing, and it won't mean a very long time, I don't believe. Looks as if I'd be going out there next week, I guess."

"Jack, no!" she said. "Oh, don't do that! You can't do that. You can't leave me alone like this. I've got to see you, dearest. I've got to. You've got to come back, or I've got to come there to you. I can't go through this. Jack, I can't, I——"

"Look, we better say good-night now," he said. "No use trying to make out what you say, when you talk all over yourself like that. And there's so much racket here—*Hey, can the harmony, will you? God, it's terrible. Want me to be thrown out of here?* You go get a good night's sleep, and I'll write you all about it tomorrow."

"Listen!" she said. "Jack, don't go 'way! Help me, darling. Say something to help me through tonight. Say you love me, for God's sake say you still love me. Say it. Say it."

"Ah, I can't talk," he said. "This is fierce. I'll write you first thing in the morning. 'By. Thanks for calling up."

"Jack!" she said. "Jack, don't go. Jack, wait a minute. I've got to talk to you. I'll talk quietly. I won't cry. I'll talk so you can hear me. Please, dear, please——"

"All through with Detroit?" said the operator.

"No!" she said. "No, no, no! Get him, get him back again right away! Get him back. No, never mind. Never mind it now. Never——"

Big Blonde

Hazel Morse was a large, fair woman of the type that incites some men when they use the word "blonde" to click their tongues and wag their heads roguishly. She prided herself upon her small feet and suffered for her vanity, boxing them in snub-toed, high-heeled slippers of the shortest bearable size. The curious things about her were her hands, strange terminations to the flabby white arms splattered with pale tan spots—long, quivering hands with deep and convex nails. She should not have disfigured them with little jewels.

She was not a woman given to recollections. At her middle thirties, her old days were a blurred and flickering sequence, an imperfect film, dealing with the actions of strangers.

In her twenties, after the deferred death of a hazy widowed mother, she had been employed as a model in a wholesale dress establishment—it was still the day of the big woman, and she was then prettily colored and erect and high-breasted. Her job was not onerous, and she met numbers of men and spent numbers of evenings with them, laughing at their jokes and telling them she loved their neckties. Men liked her, and she took it for granted that the liking of many men was a desirable thing. Popularity seemed to her to be worth all the work that had to be put into its achievement. Men liked you because you were fun, and when they liked you they took you out, and there you were. So, and successfully, she was fun. She was a good sport. Men like a good sport.

No other form of diversion, simpler or more complicated, drew her attention. She never pondered if she might not be better occupied doing something else. Her ideas, or, better, her acceptances, ran right along with those of the other substantially built blondes in whom she found her friends.

When she had been working in the dress establishment some years she met Herbie Morse. He was thin, quick, attractive, with shifting lines about his shiny, brown eyes and a habit of fiercely biting at the skin around his finger nails. He drank largely; she found that entertaining. Her habitual greeting to him was an allusion to his state of the previous night.

"Oh, what a peach you had," she used to say, through her easy laugh. "I thought I'd die, the way you kept asking the waiter to dance with you."

She liked him immediately upon their meeting. She was enormously amused at his fast, slurred sentences, his interpolations of apt phrases from vaudeville acts and comic strips; she thrilled at the feel of his lean arm tucked firm beneath the sleeve of her coat; she wanted to touch the wet, flat surface of his hair. He was as promptly drawn to her. They were married six weeks after they had met.

She was delighted at the idea of being a bride; coquetted with it, played upon it. Other offers of marriage she had had, and not a few of them, but it happened that they were all from stout, serious men who had visited the dress establishment as buyers; men from Des Moines and Houston and Chicago and, in her phrase, even funnier places. There was always something immensely comic to her in the thought of living elsewhere than New York. She could not regard as serious proposals that she share a western residence.

She wanted to be married. She was nearing thirty now, and she did not take the years well. She spread and softened, and her darkening hair turned her to inexpert dabblings with peroxide. There were times when she had little flashes of fear about her job. And she had had a couple of thousand evenings of being a good sport among her male acquaintances. She had come to be more conscientious than spontaneous about it.

Herbie earned enough, and they took a little apartment far uptown. There was a Mission-furnished dining-room with a hanging central light globed in liver-colored glass; in the living-room were an "over-stuffed suite," a Boston fern, and a reproduction of the Henner "Magdalene" with the red hair and the blue draperies; the bedroom was in gray enamel and old rose, with Herbie's photograph on Hazel's dressing-table and Hazel's likeness on Herbie's chest of drawers.

She cooked—and she was a good cook—and marketed and chatted with the delivery boys and the colored laundress. She loved the flat, she loved her life, she loved Herbie. In the first months of their marriage, she gave him all the passion she was ever to know.

She had not realized how tired she was. It was a delight, a new game, a holiday, to give up being a good sport. If her head ached or her arches throbbed, she complained piteously, babyishly. If her mood was quiet, she did not talk. If tears came to her eyes, she let them fall.

She fell readily into the habit of tears during the first year of her marriage. Even in her good sport days, she had been known to weep lavishly and disinterestedly on occasion. Her behavior at the theater was a standing joke. She could weep at anything in a play—tiny garments, love both unrequited and mutual, seduction, purity, faithful servitors, wedlock, the triangle.

"There goes Haze," her friends would say, watching her. "She's off again."

Wedded and relaxed, she poured her tears freely. To her who had laughed so much, crying was delicious. All sorrows became her sorrows; she was Tenderness. She would cry long and softly over newspaper accounts of kidnaped babies, deserted wives, unemployed men, strayed cats, heroic dogs. Even when the paper was no longer before her, her mind revolved upon these things and the drops slipped rhythmically over her plump cheeks.

"Honestly," she would say to Herbie, "all the sadness there is in the world when you stop to think about it!"

"Yeah," Herbie would say.

She missed nobody. The old crowd, the people who had brought her and Herbie together, dropped from their lives, lingeringly at first. When she thought of this at all, it was only to consider it fitting. This was marriage. This was peace.

But the thing was that Herbie was not amused.

For a time, he had enjoyed being alone with her. He found the voluntary isolation novel and sweet. Then it palled with a ferocious suddenness. It was as if one night, sitting with her in the steam-heated living-room, he would ask no more; and the next night he was through and done with the whole thing.

He became annoyed by her misty melancholies. At first, when he came home to find her softly tired and moody, he kissed her neck and patted her shoulder and begged her to tell her Herbie what was wrong. She loved that. But time slid by, and he found that there was never anything really, personally, the matter.

"Ah, for God's sake," he would say. "Crabbing again. All right, sit here and crab your head off. I'm going out."

And he would slam out of the flat and come back late and drunk.

She was completely bewildered by what happened to their marriage. First they were lovers; and then, it seemed without transition, they were enemies. She never understood it.

There were longer and longer intervals between his leaving his office and his arrival at the apartment. She went through agonies of picturing him run over and bleeding, dead and covered with a sheet. Then she lost her fears for his safety and grew sullen and wounded. When a

person wanted to be with a person, he came as soon as possible. She
desperately wanted him to want to be with her; her own hours only
marked the time till he would come. It was often nearly nine o'clock
before he came home to dinner. Always he had had many drinks, and
their effect would die in him, leaving him loud and querulous and bristling for affronts.

He was too nervous, he said, to sit and do nothing for an evening.
He boasted, probably not in all truth, that he had never read a book in
his life.

"What am I expected to do—sit around this dump on my tail all
night?" he would ask, rhetorically. And again he would slam out.

She did not know what to do. She could not manage him. She could
not meet him.

She fought him furiously. A terrific domesticity had come upon her,
and she would bite and scratch to guard it. She wanted what she called
"a nice home." She wanted a sober, tender husband, prompt at dinner,
punctual at work. She wanted sweet, comforting evenings. The idea of
intimacy with other men was terrible to her; the thought that Herbie
might be seeking entertainment in other women set her frantic.

It seemed to her that almost everything she read—novels from the
drug-store lending library, magazine stories, women's pages in the
papers—dealt with wives who lost their husbands' love. She could bear
those, at that, better than accounts of neat, companionable marriage
and living happily ever after.

She was frightened. Several times when Herbie came home in the
evening, he found her determinedly dressed—she had had to alter those
of her clothes that were not new, to make them fasten—and rouged.

"Let's go wild tonight, what do you say?" she would hail him. "A
person's got lots of time to hang around and do nothing when they're
dead."

So they would go out, to chop houses and the less expensive cabarets.
But it turned out badly. She could no longer find amusement in watching
Herbie drink. She could not laugh at his whimsicalities, she was so
tensely counting his indulgences. And she was unable to keep back her
remonstrances—"Ah, come on, Herb, you've had enough, haven't you?
You'll feel something terrible in the morning."

He would be immediately enraged. All right, crab; crab, crab, crab,
crab, that was all she ever did. What a lousy sport *she* was! There would
be scenes, and one or the other of them would rise and stalk out in
fury.

She could not recall the definite day that she started drinking, herself.

There was nothing separate about her days. Like drops upon a window-pane, they ran together and trickled away. She had been married six months; then a year; then three years.

She had never needed to drink, formerly. She could sit for most of a night at a table where the others were imbibing earnestly and never droop in looks or spirits, nor be bored by the doings of those about her. If she took a cocktail, it was so unusual as to cause twenty minutes or so of jocular comment. But now anguish was in her. Frequently, after a quarrel, Herbie would stay out for the night, and she could not learn from him where the time had been spent. Her heart felt tight and sore in her breast, and her mind turned like an electric fan.

She hated the taste of liquor. Gin, plain or in mixtures, made her promptly sick. After experiment, she found that Scotch whisky was best for her. She took it without water, because that was the quickest way to its effect.

Herbie pressed it on her. He was glad to see her drink. They both felt it might restore her high spirits, and their good times together might again be possible.

" 'Atta girl," he would approve her. "Let's see you get boiled, baby."

But it brought them no nearer. When she drank with him, there would be a little while of gaiety and then, strangely without beginning, they would be in a wild quarrel. They would wake in the morning not sure what it had all been about, foggy as to what had been said and done, but each deeply injured and bitterly resentful. There would be days of vengeful silence.

There had been a time when they had made up their quarrels, usually in bed. There would be kisses and little names and assurances of fresh starts. . . . "Oh, it's going to be great now, Herb. We'll have swell times. I was a crab. I guess I must have been tired. But everything's going to be swell. You'll see."

Now there were no gentle reconciliations. They resumed friendly relations only in the brief magnanimity caused by liquor, before more liquor drew them into new battles. The scenes became more violent. There were shouted invectives and pushes, and sometimes sharp slaps. Once she had a black eye. Herbie was horrified next day at sight of it. He did not go to work; he followed her about, suggesting remedies and heaping dark blame on himself. But after they had had a few drinks—"to pull themselves together"—she made so many wistful references to her bruise that he shouted at her and rushed out and was gone for two days.

Each time he left the place in a rage, he threatened never to come back. She did not believe him, nor did she consider separation. Somewhere in her head or her heart was the lazy, nebulous hope that things would change and she and Herbie settle suddenly into soothing married life. Here were her home, her furniture, her husband, her station. She summoned no alternatives.

She could no longer bustle and potter. She had no more vicarious tears; the hot drops she shed were for herself. She walked ceaselessly about the rooms, her thoughts running mechanically round and round Herbie. In those days began the hatred of being alone that she was never to overcome. You could be by yourself when things were all right, but when you were blue you got the howling horrors.

She commenced drinking alone, little, short drinks all through the day. It was only with Herbie that alcohol made her nervous and quick in offense. Alone, it blurred sharp things for her. She lived in a haze of it. Her life took on a dream-like quality. Nothing was astonishing.

A Mrs. Martin moved into the flat across the hall. She was a great blonde woman of forty, a promise in looks of what Mrs. Morse was to be. They made acquaintance, quickly became inseparable. Mrs. Morse spent her days in the opposite apartment. They drank together, to brace themselves after the drinks of the nights before.

She never confided her troubles about Herbie to Mrs. Martin. The subject was too bewildering to her to find comfort in talk. She let it be assumed that her husband's business kept him much away. It was not regarded as important; husbands, as such, played but shadowy parts in Mrs. Martin's circle.

Mrs. Martin had no visible spouse; you were left to decide for yourself whether he was or was not dead. She had an admirer, Joe, who came to see her almost nightly. Often he brought several friends with him—"The Boys," they were called. The Boys were big, red, good-humored men, perhaps forty-five, perhaps fifty. Mrs. Morse was glad of invitations to join the parties—Herbie was scarcely ever at home at night now. If he did come home, she did not visit Mrs. Martin. An evening alone with Herbie meant inevitably a quarrel, yet she would stay with him. There was always her thin and wordless idea that, maybe, this night, things would begin to be all right.

The Boys brought plenty of liquor along with them whenever they came to Mrs. Martin's. Drinking with them, Mrs. Morse became lively and good-natured and audacious. She was quickly popular. When she had drunk enough to cloud her most recent battle with Herbie, she was excited by their approbation. Crab, was she? Rotten sport, was she? Well, there were some that thought different.

Ed was one of The Boys. He lived in Utica—had "his own business" there, was the awed report—but he came to New York almost every week. He was married. He showed Mrs. Morse the then current photographs of Junior and Sister, and she praised them abundantly and sincerely. Soon it was accepted by the others that Ed was her particular friend.

He staked her when they all played poker; sat next her and occasionally rubbed his knee against hers during the game. She was rather lucky. Frequently she went home with a twenty-dollar bill or a ten-dollar bill or a handful of crumpled dollars. She was glad of them. Herbie was getting, in her words, something awful about money. To ask him for it brought an instant row.

"What the hell do you do with it?" he would say. "Shoot it all on Scotch?"

"I try to run this house half-way decent," she would retort. "Never thought of that, did you? Oh, no, his lordship couldn't be bothered with that."

Again, she could not find a definite day, to fix the beginning of Ed's proprietorship. It became his custom to kiss her on the mouth when he came in, as well as for farewell, and he gave her little quick kisses of approval all through the evening. She liked this rather more than she disliked it. She never thought of his kisses when she was not with him.

He would run his hand lingeringly over her back and shoulders.

"Some dizzy blonde, eh?" he would say. "Some doll."

One afternoon she came home from Mrs. Martin's to find Herbie in the bedroom. He had been away for several nights, evidently on a prolonged drinking bout. His face was gray, his hands jerked as if they were on wires. On the bed were two old suitcases, packed high. Only her photograph remained on his bureau, and the wide doors of his closet disclosed nothing but coat-hangers.

"I'm blowing," he said. "I'm through with the whole works. I got a job in Detroit."

She sat down on the edge of the bed. She had drunk much the night before, and the four Scotches she had had with Mrs. Martin had only increased her fogginess.

"Good job?" she said.

"Oh, yeah," he said. "Looks all right."

He closed a suitcase with difficulty, swearing at it in whispers.

"There's some dough in the bank," he said. "The bank book's in your top drawer. You can have the furniture and stuff."

He looked at her, and his forehead twitched.

"God damn it, I'm through, I'm telling you," he cried. "I'm through."

"All right, all right," she said. "I heard you, didn't I?"

She saw him as if he were at one end of a cannon and she at the other. Her head was beginning to ache bumpingly, and her voice had a dreary, tiresome tone. She could not have raised it.

"Like a drink before you go?" she asked.

Again he looked at her, and a corner of his mouth jerked up.

"Cockeyed again for a change, aren't you?" he said. "That's nice. Sure, get a couple of shots, will you?"

She went to the pantry, mixed him a stiff highball, poured herself a couple of inches of whisky and drank it. Then she gave herself another portion and brought the glasses into the bedroom. He had strapped both suitcases and had put on his hat and overcoat.

He took his highball.

"Well," he said, and he gave a sudden, uncertain laugh. "Here's mud in your eye."

"Mud in your eye," she said.

They drank. He put down his glass and took up the heavy suitcases.

"Got to get a train around six," he said.

She followed him down the hall. There was a song, a song that Mrs. Martin played doggedly on the phonograph, running loudly through her mind. She had never liked the thing.

> "Night and daytime,
> Always playtime.
> Ain't we got fun?"

At the door he put down the bags and faced her.

"Well," he said. "Well, take care of yourself. You'll be all right, will you?"

"Oh, sure," she said.

He opened the door, then came back to her, holding out his hand.

" 'By, Haze," he said. "Good luck to you."

She took his hand and shook it.

"Pardon my wet glove," she said.

When the door had closed behind him, she went back to the pantry.

She was flushed and lively when she went in to Mrs. Martin's that evening. The Boys were there, Ed among them. He was glad to be in town, frisky and loud and full of jokes. But she spoke quietly to him for a minute.

"Herbie blew today," she said. "Going to live out west."

"That so?" he said. He looked at her and played with the fountain pen clipped to his waistcoat pocket.

"Think he's gone for good, do you?" he asked.

"Yeah," she said. "I know he is. I know. Yeah."

"You going to live on across the hall just the same?" he said. "Know what you're going to do?"

"Gee, I don't know," she said. "I don't give much of a damn."

"Oh, come on, that's no way to talk," he told her. "What you need—you need a little snifter. How about it?"

"Yeah," she said. "Just straight."

She won forty-three dollars at poker. When the game broke up, Ed took her back to her apartment.

"Got a little kiss for me?" he asked.

He wrapped her in his big arms and kissed her violently. She was entirely passive. He held her away and looked at her.

"Little tight, honey?" he asked, anxiously. "Not going to be sick, are you?"

"Me?" she said. "I'm swell."

II

When Ed left in the morning, he took her photograph with him. He said he wanted her picture to look at, up in Utica. "You can have that one on the bureau," she said.

She put Herbie's picture in a drawer, out of her sight. When she could look at it, she meant to tear it up. She was fairly successful in keeping her mind from racing around him. Whisky slowed it for her. She was almost peaceful, in her mist.

She accepted her relationship with Ed without question or enthusiasm. When he was away, she seldom thought definitely of him. He was good to her; he gave her frequent presents and a regular allowance. She was even able to save. She did not plan ahead of any day, but her wants were few, and you might as well put money in the bank as have it lying around.

When the lease of her apartment neared its end, it was Ed who suggested moving. His friendship with Mrs. Martin and Joe had become strained over a dispute at poker; a feud was impending.

"Let's get the hell out of here," Ed said. "What I want you to have is a place near the Grand Central. Make it easier for me."

So she took a little flat in the Forties. A colored maid came in every day to clean and to make coffee for her—she was "through with that housekeeping stuff," she said, and Ed, twenty years married to a passionately domestic woman, admired this romantic uselessness and felt doubly a man of the world in abetting it.

The coffee was all she had until she went out to dinner, but alcohol kept her fat. Prohibition she regarded only as a basis for jokes. You could always get all you wanted. She was never noticeably drunk and seldom nearly sober. It required a larger daily allowance to keep her misty-minded. Too little, and she was achingly melancholy.

Ed brought her to Jimmy's. He was proud, with the pride of the transient who would be mistaken for a native, in his knowledge of small, recent restaurants occupying the lower floors of shabby brownstone houses; places where, upon mentioning the name of an habitué friend, might be obtained strange whisky and fresh gin in many of their ramifications. Jimmy's place was the favorite of his acquaintances.

There, through Ed, Mrs. Morse met many men and women, formed quick friendships. The men often took her out when Ed was in Utica. He was proud of her popularity.

She fell into the habit of going to Jimmy's alone when she had no engagement. She was certain to meet some people she knew, and join them. It was a club for her friends, both men and women.

The women at Jimmy's looked remarkably alike, and this was curious, for, through feuds, removals, and opportunities of more profitable contacts, the personnel of the group changed constantly. Yet always the newcomers resembled those whom they replaced. They were all big women and stout, broad of shoulder and abundantly breasted, with faces thickly clothed in soft, high-colored flesh. They laughed loud and often, showing opaque and lusterless teeth like squares of crockery. There was about them the health of the big, yet a slight, unwholesome suggestion of stubborn preservation. They might have been thirty-six or forty-five or anywhere between.

They composed their titles of their own first names with their husbands' surnames—Mrs. Florence Miller, Mrs. Vera Riley, Mrs. Lilian Block. This gave at the same time the solidity of marriage and the glamour of freedom. Yet only one or two were actually divorced. Most of them never referred to their dimmed spouses; some, a shorter time separated, described them in terms of great biological interest. Several were mothers, each of an only child—a boy at school somewhere, or a girl being cared for by a grandmother. Often, well on towards morning, there would be displays of kodak portraits and of tears.

They were comfortable women, cordial and friendly and irrepressibly matronly. Theirs was the quality of ease. Become fatalistic, especially about money matters, they were unworried. Whenever their funds dropped alarmingly, a new donor appeared; this had always happened. The aim of each was to have one man, permanently, to pay all her bills, in return for which she would have immediately given up other admirers and probably would have become exceedingly fond of him; for the affections of all of them were, by now, unexacting, tranquil, and easily arranged. This end, however, grew increasingly difficult yearly. Mrs. Morse was regarded as fortunate.

Ed had a good year, increased her allowance and gave her a sealskin coat. But she had to be careful of her moods with him. He insisted upon gaiety. He would not listen to admissions of aches or weariness.

"Hey, listen," he would say, "I got worries of my own, and plenty. Nobody wants to hear other people's troubles, sweetie. What you got to do, you got to be a sport and forget it. See? Well, slip us a little smile, then. That's my girl."

She never had enough interest to quarrel with him as she had with Herbie, but she wanted the privilege of occasional admitted sadness. It was strange. The other women she saw did not have to fight their moods. There was Mrs. Florence Miller who got regular crying jags, and the men sought only to cheer and comfort her. The others spent whole evenings in grieved recitals of worries and ills; their escorts paid them deep sympathy. But she was instantly undesirable when she was low in spirits. Once, at Jimmy's, when she could not make herself lively, Ed had walked out and left her.

"Why the hell don't you stay home and not go spoiling everybody's evening?" he had roared.

Even her slightest acquaintances seemed irritated if she were not conspicuously light-hearted.

"What's the matter with you, anyway?" they would say. "Be your age, why don't you? Have a little drink and snap out of it."

When her relationship with Ed had continued nearly three years, he moved to Florida to live. He hated leaving her; he gave her a large check and some shares of a sound stock, and his pale eyes were wet when he said good-by. She did not miss him. He came to New York infrequently, perhaps two or three times a year, and hurried directly from the train to see her. She was always pleased to have him come and never sorry to see him go.

Charley, an acquaintance of Ed's that she had met at Jimmy's, had long admired her. He had always made opportunities of touching her and leaning close to talk to her. He asked repeatedly of all their friends if they had ever heard such a fine laugh as she had. After Ed left, Charley became the main figure in her life. She classified him and spoke of him as "not so bad." There was nearly a year of Charley; then she divided her time between him and Sydney, another frequenter of Jimmy's; then Charley slipped away altogether.

Sydney was a little, brightly dressed, clever Jew. She was perhaps nearest contentment with him. He amused her always; her laughter was not forced.

He admired her completely. Her softness and size delighted him. And he thought she was great, he often told her, because she kept gay and lively when she was drunk.

"Once I had a gal," he said, "used to try and throw herself out of the window every time she got a can on. Jee-*zuss*," he added, feelingly.

Then Sydney married a rich and watchful bride, and then there was Billy. No—after Sydney came Ferd, then Billy. In her haze, she never recalled how men entered her life and left it. There were no surprises. She had no thrill at their advent, nor woe at their departure. She seemed to be always able to attract men. There was never another as rich as Ed, but they were all generous to her, in their means.

Once she had news of Herbie. She met Mrs. Martin dining at Jimmy's, and the old friendship was vigorously renewed. The still admiring Joe, while on a business trip, had seen Herbie. He had settled in Chicago, he looked fine, he was living with some woman—seemed to be crazy about her. Mrs. Morse had been drinking vastly that day. She took the news with mild interest, as one hearing of the sex peccadilloes of somebody whose name is, after a moment's groping, familiar.

"Must be damn near seven years since I saw him," she commented. "Gee. Seven years."

More and more, her days lost their individuality. She never knew dates, nor was sure of the day of the week.

"My God, was that a year ago!" she would exclaim, when an event was recalled in conversation.

She was tired so much of the time. Tired and blue. Almost everything could give her the blues. Those old horses she saw on Sixth Avenue— struggling and slipping along the car-tracks, or standing at the curb, their heads dropped level with their worn knees. The tightly stored tears would squeeze from her eyes as she teetered past on her aching feet in the stubby, champagne-colored slippers.

The thought of death came and stayed with her and lent her a sort of drowsy cheer. It would be nice, nice and restful, to be dead.

There was no settled, shocked moment when she first thought of killing herself; it seemed to her as if the idea had always been with her. She pounced upon all the accounts of suicides in the newspapers. There was an epidemic of self-killings—or maybe it was just that she searched for the stories of them so eagerly that she found many. To read of them roused reassurance in her; she felt a cozy solidarity with the big company of the voluntary dead.

She slept, aided by whisky, till deep into the afternoons, then lay abed, a bottle and glass at her hand, until it was time to dress to go out for dinner. She was beginning to feel towards alcohol a little puzzled distrust, as toward an old friend who has refused a simple favor. Whisky could still soothe her for most of the time, but there were sudden, inexplicable moments when the cloud fell treacherously away from her, and she was sawed by the sorrow and bewilderment and nuisance of all living. She played voluptuously with the thought of cool, sleepy retreat. She had never been troubled by religious belief and no vision of an after-life intimidated her. She dreamed by day of never again putting on tight shoes, of never having to laugh and listen and admire, of never more being a good sport. Never.

But how would you do it? It made her sick to think of jumping from heights. She could not stand a gun. At the theater, if one of the actors drew a revolver, she crammed her fingers into her ears and could not even look at the stage until after the shot had been fired. There was no gas in her flat. She looked long at the bright blue veins in her slim wrists—a cut with a razor blade, and there you'd be. But it would hurt, hurt like hell, and there would be blood to see. Poison—something tasteless and quick and painless—was the thing. But they wouldn't sell it to you in drugstores, because of the law.

She had few other thoughts.

There was a new man now—Art. He was short and fat and exacting and hard on her patience when he was drunk. But there had been only occasionals for some time before him, and she was glad of a little stability. Too, Art must be away for weeks at a stretch, selling silks, and that was restful. She was convincingly gay with him, though the effort shook her.

"The best sport in the world," he would murmur, deep in her neck. "The best sport in the world."

One night, when he had taken her to Jimmy's, she went into the dressing-room with Mrs. Florence Miller. There, while designing curly mouths on their faces with lip-rouge, they compared experiences of insomnia.

"Honestly," Mrs. Morse said, "I wouldn't close an eye if I didn't go to bed full of Scotch. I lie there and toss and turn and toss and turn. Blue! Does a person get blue lying awake that way!"

"Say, listen Hazel," Mrs. Miller said, impressively, "I'm telling you I'd be awake for a year if I didn't take veronal. That stuff makes you sleep like a fool."

"Isn't it poison, or something?" Mrs. Morse asked.

"Oh, you take too much and you're out for the count," said Mrs. Miller. "I just take five grains—they come in tablets. I'd be scared to fool around with it. But five grains, and you cork off pretty."

"Can you get it anywhere?" Mrs. Morse felt superbly Machiavellian.

"Get all you want in Jersey," said Mrs. Miller. "They won't give it to you here without you have a doctor's prescription. Finished? We'd better go back and see what the boys are doing."

That night, Art left Mrs. Morse at the door of her apartment; his mother was in town. Mrs. Morse was still sober, and it happened that there was no whisky left in her cupboard. She lay in bed, looking up at the black ceiling.

She rose early, for her, and went to New Jersey. She had never taken the tube, and did not understand it. So she went to the Pennsylvania Station and bought a railroad ticket to Newark. She thought of nothing in particular on the trip out. She looked at the uninspired hats of the women about her and gazed through the smeared window at the flat, gritty scene.

In Newark, in the first drug-store she came to, she asked for a tin of talcum powder, a nailbrush, and a box of veronal tablets. The powder and the brush were to make the hypnotic seem also a casual need. The clerk was entirely unconcerned. "We only keep them in bottles," he said, and wrapped up for her a little glass vial containing ten white tablets, stacked one on another.

She went to another drug-store and bought a face-cloth, an orange-wood stick, and a bottle of veronal tablets. The clerk was also uninterested.

"Well, I guess I got enough to kill an ox," she thought, and went back to the station.

At home, she put the little vials in the drawer of her dressing-table and stood looking at them with a dreamy tenderness.

"There they are, God bless them," she said, and she kissed her finger-tip and touched each bottle.

The colored maid was busy in the living-room.

"Hey, Nettie," Mrs. Morse called. "Be an angel, will you? Run around to Jimmy's and get me a quart of Scotch."

She hummed while she awaited the girl's return.

During the next few days, whisky ministered to her as tenderly as it had done when she first turned to its aid. Alone, she was soothed and vague, at Jimmy's she was the gayest of the groups. Art was delighted with her.

Then, one night, she had an appointment to meet Art at Jimmy's for an early dinner. He was to leave afterward on a business excursion, to be away for a week. Mrs. Morse had been drinking all the afternoon; while she dressed to go out, she felt herself rising pleasurably from drowsiness to high spirits. But as she came out into the street the effects of the whisky deserted her completely, and she was filled with a slow, grinding wretchedness so horrible that she stood swaying on the pavement, unable for a moment to move forward. It was a gray night with spurts of mean, thin snow, and the streets shone with dark ice. As she slowly crossed Sixth Avenue, consciously dragging one foot past the other, a big, scarred horse pulling a rickety express-wagon crashed to his knees before her. The driver swore and screamed and lashed the beast insanely, bringing the whip back over his shoulder for every blow, while the horse struggled to get a footing on the slippery asphalt. A group gathered and watched with interest.

Art was waiting, when Mrs. Morse reached Jimmy's.

"What's the matter with you, for God's sake?" was his greeting to her.

"I saw a horse," she said. "Gee, I—a person feels sorry for horses. I—it isn't just horses. Everything's kind of terrible, isn't it? I can't help getting sunk."

"Ah, sunk, me eye," he said. "What's the idea of all the bellyaching? What have you got to be sunk about?"

"I can't help it," she said.

"Ah, help it, me eye," he said. "Pull yourself together, will you? Come on and sit down, and take that face off you."

She drank industriously and she tried hard, but she could not overcome her melancholy. Others joined them and commented on her gloom, and she could do no more for them than smile weakly. She made little dabs at her eyes with her handkerchief, trying to time her movements so they would be unnoticed, but several times Art caught her and scowled and shifted impatiently in his chair.

When it was time for him to go to his train, she said she would leave, too, and go home.

"And not a bad idea, either," he said. "See if you can't sleep yourself out of it. I'll see you Thursday. For God's sake, try and cheer up by then, will you?"

"Yeah," she said. "I will."

In her bedroom, she undressed with a tense speed wholly unlike her usual slow uncertainty. She put on her nightgown, took off her hair-net and passed the comb quickly through her dry, vari-colored hair. Then she took the two little vials from the drawer and carried them into the bathroom. The splintering misery had gone from her, and she felt the quick excitement of one who is about to receive an anticipated gift.

She uncorked the vials, filled a glass with water and stood before the mirror, a tablet between her fingers. Suddenly she bowed graciously to her reflection, and raised the glass to it.

"Well, here's mud in your eye," she said.

The tablets were unpleasant to take, dry and powdery and sticking obstinately half-way down her throat. It took her a long time to swallow all twenty of them. She stood watching her reflection with deep, impersonal interest, studying the movements of the gulping throat. Once more she spoke aloud.

"For God's sake, try and cheer up by Thursday, will you?" she said. "Well, you know what he can do. He and the whole lot of them."

She had no idea how quickly to expect effect from the veronal. When she had taken the last tablet, she stood uncertainly, wondering, still with a courteous, vicarious interest, if death would strike her down then and there. She felt in no way strange, save for a slight stirring of sickness from the effort of swallowing the tablets, nor did her reflected face look at all different. It would not be immediate, then; it might even take an hour or so.

She stretched her arms high and gave a vast yawn.

"Guess I'll go to bed," she said. "Gee, I'm nearly dead."

That struck her as comic, and she turned out the bathroom light and went in and laid herself down in her bed, chuckling softly all the time.

"Gee, I'm nearly dead," she quoted. "That's a hot one!"

III

Nettie, the colored maid, came in late the next afternoon to clean the apartment, and found Mrs. Morse in her bed. But then, that was not unusual. Usually, though, the sounds of cleaning waked her, and she did not like to wake up. Nettie, an agreeable girl, had learned to move softly about her work.

But when she had done the living-room and stolen in to tidy the little square bedroom, she could not avoid a tiny clatter as she arranged the objects on the dressing-table. Instinctively, she glanced over her shoulder at the sleeper, and without warning a sickly uneasiness crept over her. She came to the bed and stared down at the woman lying there.

Mrs. Morse lay on her back, one flabby, white arm flung up, the wrist against her forehead. Her stiff hair hung untenderly along her face. The bed covers were pushed down, exposing a deep square of soft neck and a pink nightgown, its fabric worn uneven by many launderings; her great breasts, freed from their tight confiner, sagged beneath her armpits. Now and then she made knotted, snoring sounds, and from the corner of her opened mouth to the blurred turn of her jaw ran a lane of crusted spittle.

"Mis' Morse," Nettie called. "Oh, Mis' Morse! It's terrible late."

Mrs. Morse made no move.

"Mis' Morse," said Nettie. "Look, Mis' Morse. How'm I goin' get this bed made?"

Panic sprang upon the girl. She shook the woman's hot shoulder.

"Ah, wake up, will yuh?" she whined. "Ah, please wake up."

Suddenly the girl turned and ran out in the hall to the elevator door, keeping her thumb firm on the black, shiny button until the elderly car and its Negro attendant stood before her. She poured a jumble of words over the boy, and led him back to the apartment. He tiptoed creakingly in to the bedside; first gingerly, then so lustily that he left marks in the soft flesh, he prodded the unconscious woman.

"Hey, there!" he cried, and listened intently, as for an echo.

"Jeez. Out like a light," he commented.

At his interest in the spectacle, Nettie's panic left her. Importance was big in both of them. They talked in quick, unfinished whispers, and it was the boy's suggestion that he fetch the young doctor who lived on the ground floor. Nettie hurried along with him. They looked forward to the limelit moment of breaking their news of something untoward, something pleasurably unpleasant. Mrs. Morse had become the medium of drama. With no ill wish to her, they hoped that her state was serious, that she would not let them down by being awake and normal on their return. A little fear of this determined them to make the most, to the doctor, of her present condition. "Matter of life and death," returned to Nettie from her thin store of reading. She considered startling the doctor with the phrase.

The doctor was in and none too pleased at interruption. He wore a yellow and blue striped dressing-gown, and he was lying on his sofa, laughing with a dark girl, her face scaly with inexpensive powder, who perched on the arm. Half-emptied highball glasses stood beside them, and her coat and hat were neatly hung up with the comfortable implication of a long stay.

Always something, the doctor grumbled. Couldn't let anybody alone after a hard day. But he put some bottles and instruments into a case, changed his dressing-gown for his coat and started out with the Negroes.

"Snap it up there, big boy," the girl called after him. "Don't be all night."

The doctor strode loudly into Mrs. Morse's flat and on to the bedroom, Nettie and the boy right behind him. Mrs. Morse had not moved; her sleep was as deep, but soundless, now. The doctor looked sharply at her, then plunged his thumbs into the lidded pits above her eyeballs and threw his weight upon them. A high, sickened cry broke from Nettie.

"Look like he tryin' to push her right on th'ough the bed," said the boy. He chuckled.

Mrs. Morse gave no sign under the pressure. Abruptly the doctor abandoned it, and with one quick movement swept the covers down to the foot of the bed. With another he flung her nightgown back and lifted the thick, white legs, cross-hatched with blocks of tiny, iris-colored veins. He pinched them repeatedly, with long, cruel nips, back of the knees. She did not awaken.

"What's she been drinking?" he asked Nettie, over his shoulder.

With the certain celerity of one who knows just where to lay hands on a thing, Nettie went into the bathroom, bound for the cupboard where Mrs. Morse kept her whisky. But she stopped at the sight of the two vials, with their red and white labels, lying before the mirror. She brought them to the doctor.

"Oh, for the Lord Almighty's sweet sake!" he said. He dropped Mrs. Morse's legs, and pushed them impatiently across the bed. "What did she want to go taking that tripe for? Rotten yellow trick, that's what a thing like that is. Now we'll have to pump her out, and all that stuff. Nuisance, a thing like that is; that's what it amounts to. Here, George, take me down in the elevator. You wait here, maid. She won't do anything."

"She won't die on me, will she?" cried Nettie.

"No," said the doctor. "God, no. You couldn't kill her with an ax."

IV

After two days, Mrs. Morse came back to consciousness, dazed at first, then with a comprehension that brought with it the slow, saturating wretchedness.

"Oh, Lord, oh, Lord," she moaned, and tears for herself and for life striped her cheeks.

Nettie came in at the sound. For two days she had done the ugly, incessant tasks in the nursing of the unconscious, for two nights she had caught broken bits of sleep on the living-room couch. She looked coldly at the big, blown woman in the bed.

"What you been tryin' to do, Mis' Morse?" she said. "What kine o' work is that, takin' all that stuff?"

"Oh, Lord," moaned Mrs. Morse, again, and she tried to cover her eyes with her arms. But the joints felt stiff and brittle, and she cried out at their ache.

"Tha's no way to ack, takin' them pills," said Nettie. "You can thank you' stars you heah at all. How you feel now?"

"Oh, I feel great," said Mrs. Morse. "Swell, I feel."

Her hot, painful tears fell as if they would never stop.

"Tha's no way to take on, cryin' like that," Nettie said. "After what you done. The doctor, he says he could have you arrested, doin' a thing like that. He was fit to be tied, here."

"Why couldn't he let me alone?" wailed Mrs. Morse. "Why the hell couldn't he have?"

"Tha's terr'ble, Mis' Morse, swearin' an' talkin' like that," said Nettie, "after what people done for you. Here I ain' had no sleep at all for two nights, an' had to give up goin' out to my other ladies!"

"Oh, I'm sorry, Nettie," she said. "You're a peach. I'm sorry I've given you so much trouble. I couldn't help it. I just got sunk. Didn't you ever feel like doing it? When everything looks just lousy to you?"

"I wouldn' think o' no such thing," declared Nettie. "You got to cheer up. Tha's what you got to do. Everybody's got their troubles."

"Yeah," said Mrs. Morse. "I know."

"Come a pretty picture card for you," Nettie said. "Maybe that will cheer you up."

She handed Mrs. Morse a post-card. Mrs. Morse had to cover one eye with her hand, in order to read the message; her eyes were not yet focusing correctly.

It was from Art. On the back of a view of the Detroit Athletic Club he had written: "Greeting and salutations. Hope you have lost that gloom. Cheer up and don't take any rubber nickles. See you on Thursday."

She dropped the card to the floor. Misery crushed her as if she were between great smooth stones. There passed before her a slow, slow pageant of days spent lying in her flat, of evenings at Jimmy's being a good sport, making herself laugh and coo at Art and other Arts; she saw a long parade of weary horses and shivering beggars and all beaten, driven, stumbling things. Her feet throbbed as if she had crammed them into the stubby champagne-colored slippers. Her heart seemed to swell and harden.

"Nettie," she cried, "for heaven's sake pour me a drink, will you?"

The maid looked doubtful.

"Now you know, Mis' Morse," she said, "you been near daid. I don' know if the doctor he let you drink nothin' yet."

"Oh, never mind him," she said. "You get me one, and bring in the bottle. Take one yourself."

"Well," said Nettie.

She poured them each a drink, deferentially leaving hers in the bathroom to be taken in solitude, and brought Mrs. Morse's glass in to her.

Mrs. Morse looked into the liquor and shuddered back from its odor. Maybe it would help. Maybe, when you had been knocked cold for a few days, your very first drink would give you a lift. Maybe whisky would be her friend again. She prayed without addressing a God, without knowing a God. Oh, please, please, let her be able to get drunk, please keep her always drunk.

She lifted the glass.

"Thanks, Nettie," she said. "Here's mud in your eye."

The maid giggled. "Tha's the way, Mis' Morse," she said. "You cheer up, now."

"Yeah," said Mrs. Morse. "Sure."

The Bookman, February 1929

You Were Perfectly Fine

The pale young man eased himself carefully into the low chair, and rolled his head to the side, so that the cool chintz comforted his cheek and temple.

"Oh, dear," he said. "Oh, dear, oh, dear, oh, dear. Oh."

The clear-eyed girl, sitting light and erect on the couch, smiled brightly at him.

"Not feeling so well today?" she said.

"Oh, I'm great," he said. "Corking, I am. Know what time I got up? Four o'clock this afternoon, sharp. I kept trying to make it, and every time I took my head off the pillow, it would roll under the bed. This isn't my head I've got on now. I think this is something that used to belong to Walt Whitman. Oh, dear, oh, dear, oh, dear."

"Do you think maybe a drink would make you feel better?" she said.

"The hair of the mastiff that bit me?" he said. "Oh, no, thank you. Please never speak of anything like that again. I'm through. I'm all, all through. Look at that hand; steady as a humming-bird. Tell me, was I very terrible last night?"

"Oh, goodness," she said, "everybody was feeling pretty high. You were all right."

"Yeah," he said. "I must have been dandy. Is everybody sore at me?"

"Good heavens, no," she said. "Everyone thought you were terribly funny. Of course, Jim Pierson was a little stuffy, there for a minute at dinner. But people sort of held him back in his chair, and got him calmed down. I don't think anybody at the other tables noticed it at all. Hardly anybody."

"He was going to sock me?" he said. "Oh, Lord. What did I do to him?"

"Why, you didn't do a thing," she said. "You were perfectly fine. But you know how silly Jim gets, when he thinks anybody is making too much fuss over Elinor."

"Was I making a pass at Elinor?" he said. "Did I do that?"

"Of course you didn't," she said. "You were only fooling, that's all. She thought you were awfully amusing. She was having a marvelous time. She only got a little tiny bit annoyed just once, when you poured the clam-juice down her back."

"My God," he said. "Clam-juice down that back. And every vertebra a little Cabot. Dear God. What'll I ever do?"

"Oh, she'll be all right," she said. "Just send her some flowers, or something. Don't worry about it. It isn't anything."

"No, I won't worry," he said. "I haven't got a care in the world. I'm sitting pretty. Oh, dear, oh, dear. Did I do any other fascinating tricks at dinner?"

"You were fine," she said. "Don't be so foolish about it. Everybody was crazy about you. The maître d'hôtel was a little worried because you wouldn't stop singing, but he really didn't mind. All he said was, he was afraid they'd close the place again, if there was so much noise. But he didn't care a bit, himself. I think he loved seeing you have such a good time. Oh, you were just singing away, there, for about an hour. It wasn't so terribly loud, at all."

"So I sang," he said. "That must have been a treat. I sang."

"Don't you remember?" she said. "You just sang one song after another. Everybody in the place was listening. They loved it. Only you kept insisting that you wanted to sing some song about some kind of fusiliers or other, and everybody kept shushing you, and you'd keep trying to start it again. You were wonderful. We were all trying to make you stop singing for a minute, and eat something, but you wouldn't hear of it. My, you were funny."

"Didn't I eat any dinner?" he said.

"Oh, not a thing," she said. "Every time the waiter would offer you something, you'd give it right back to him, because you said that he was your long-lost brother, changed in the cradle by a gypsy band, and that anything you had was his. You had him simply roaring at you."

"I bet I did," he said. "I bet I was comical. Society's Pet, I must have been. And what happened then, after my overwhelming success with the waiter?"

"Why, nothing much," she said. "You took a sort of dislike to some old man with white hair, sitting across the room, because you didn't like his necktie and you wanted to tell him about it. But we got you out, before he got really mad."

"Oh, we got out," he said. "Did I walk?"

"Walk! Of course you did," she said. "You were absolutely all right. There was that nasty stretch of ice on the sidewalk, and you did sit down awfully hard, you poor dear. But good heavens, that might have happened to anybody."

"Oh, sure," he said. "Louisa Alcott or anybody. So I fell down on the sidewalk. That would explain what's the matter with my—Yes. I see. And then what, if you don't mind?"

"Ah, now, Peter!" she said. "You can't sit there and say you don't remember what happened after that! I did think that maybe you were just a little tight at dinner—oh, you were perfectly all right, and all that, but I did know you were feeling pretty gay. But you were so serious, from the time you fell down—I never knew you to be that way. Don't you know, how you told me I had never seen your real self before? Oh, Peter, I just couldn't bear it, if you didn't remember that lovely long ride we took together in the taxi! Please, you do remember that, don't you? I think it would simply kill me, if you didn't."

"Oh, yes," he said. "Riding in the taxi. Oh, yes, sure. Pretty long ride, hmm?"

"Round and round and round the park," she said. "Oh, and the trees were shining so in the moonlight. And you said you never knew before that you really had a soul."

"Yes," he said. "I said that. That was me."

"You said such lovely, lovely things," she said. "And I'd never known, all this time, how you had been feeling about me, and I'd never dared to let you see how I felt about you. And then last night—oh, Peter dear, I think that taxi ride was the most important thing that ever happened to us in our lives."

"Yes," he said. "I guess it must have been."

"And we're going to be so happy," she said. "Oh, I just want to tell everybody! But I don't know—I think maybe it would be sweeter to keep it all to ourselves."

"I think it would be," he said.

"Isn't it lovely?" she said.

"Yes," he said. "Great."

"Lovely!" she said.

"Look here," he said, "do you mind if I have a drink? I mean, just medicinally, you know. I'm off the stuff for life, so help me. But I think I feel a collapse coming on."

"Oh, I think it would do you good," she said. "You poor boy, it's a shame you feel so awful. I'll go make you a whisky and soda."

"Honestly," he said, "I don't see how you could ever want to speak to me again, after I made such a fool of myself, last night. I think I'd better go join a monastery in Tibet."

"You crazy idiot!" she said. "As if I could ever let you go away now! Stop talking like that. You were perfectly fine."

She jumped up from the couch, kissed him quickly on the forehead, and ran out of the room.

The pale young man looked after her and shook his head long and slowly, then dropped it in his damp and trembling hands.

"Oh, dear," he said. "Oh, dear, oh, dear, oh, dear."

The New Yorker, February 23, 1929

The Cradle of Civilization

The two young New Yorkers sat on the cool terrace that rose sharp from the Mediterranean, and looked into deep gin fizzes, embellished, in the Riviera manner, with mint. They were dressed, the girl and the young man, in identical garments; but anyone could easily have distinguished between him and her. Their costumes seemed to have been assembled in compliment to the general region of their Summer visit, lest any one district feel slighted; they wore berets, striped fishing-shirts, wide-legged cotton trousers, and rope-soled *espadrilles*. Thus, a Frenchman, summering at an American resort, might have attired himself in a felt sombrero, planter's overalls, and rubber hip-boots.

A bay of smooth, silent water stretched between their backs and the green and white island where the Man in the Iron Mask had been prisoned, his face shrouded in black velvet and hope in his sick heart. To their right, back of the long rocks, lay the town the Phoenicians founded, and beyond it the four-pointed fort that the wise had proclaimed, when Vauban planned it, would end all war for all time. The mild harbor to which Napoleon had come back from Elba dented the shore to their left. Far in the hills above their lowered eyes hung the little vertical city from the walls of which the last of the relayed signal fires had risen, to flame back to Italy the news of Caesar's fresh conquests in Gaul. . . .

"Come on, sea-pig," the young man said. "Get rid of that, and we'll fasten onto another. Oh, garçon. Encore deux jeen feezes, tou de suite."

"Yes, sir," his waiter said.

"And mettez un peu more de jeen in them cette fois, baby," the young man said. "Atta boy. Wonderful little yellow race, these French."

"They're crazy," the girl said. "You should have seen that poor nut Bill and I crashed into, driving back from the Casino at four o'clock this morning. My God, all we did was bust his bumper a little, and you'd have thought we'd killed him. He kept screaming all this stuff about why did these Americans come over here, anyway. And there was Bill, so tight he couldn't see, yelling right back at him, 'Yes, and if we hadn't come over, this would be Germany now.' I never laughed so hard in my life."

"Casino any good last night?" he said.

"Oh, it was all right," she said. "Bill lost eighty-five thousand francs."

"How much is that in money?" he said.

"Lord knows," she said. "I can't be bothered figuring. We didn't stay long. I was in bed by half-past four."

"I got in at seven," he said. "And woke up at eleven o'clock, still stewed."

"What did you do all evening?" she said.

"I don't remember much about it," he said. "I must have barged all around. There was one place where I got up and led the orchestra—I guess that must have been at the Splendide. Oh, yes, I remember now. And Bob Weed got this idea in his head he wanted to play a violin, and this Frog violinist they have in the orchestra wouldn't let him have his, and the thing got broken in the struggle, and the Frog cried. Honestly. Cried his head off. Bob gave him five hundred francs."

"He's crazy," she said. "A hundred would have been more than enough."

"Well, Bob was drunk," he said.

"I'm crazy about the Splendide," she said. "It's just like the Desert Club, back in New York."

"There was a good crowd there last night," he said. "Lady Sylvia Goring was giving a big party."

"Was she tight?" she said.

"Oh, sure," he said. "To the eyes. Gosh, she's an attractive jane. I think I'll have to go to work on that."

"You haven't a chance," she said. "She only likes chauffeurs and sailors. Who else was there?"

"Oh, tout le monde," he said. "The whole bunch."

"I wish we'd gone," she said. "But Bill couldn't have made it. He couldn't have kept on his feet for the President of France—whoever that may be."

"It's Poincare or however you say it, isn't it?" he said. "Or somebody."

"Well, it's my idea of nothing to worry about," she said. "I've got other things to think of. Oh, look. See that girl over there?"

She pointed to a neighboring table where sat four other heirs of the ages, two young women and two young men, all with New York in their voices, all dressed in fishing-shirts and berets and wide trousers.

"The one that forgot her brassiere?" he said.

"No," she said, "the one with her feet in the man's lap. Well, she's the one that gave that marvelous party last week, where a lot of people got tight and went in swimming off the rocks with nothing on, and she had big searchlights played on them. Isn't that the most divine idea?"

"That was before I came down from Paris," he said. "I was still trying to get out of the Ritz bar, last week. Who's the pansy she's got her feet on?"

"I think he writes or something," she said. "There's an awful mob of those kind of people around here. Somebody said What's-his-name was here last year—you know, writes all those plays. Oh, *you* know. Shaw."

"He must have looked great," he said, "in swimming with a beard on."

"Oh, they're all nuts," she said. "I wasn't here last year. They say there's a much better crowd this Summer. Did you know Peggy Joyce has taken a villa?"

"This Riviera gets them all," he said. "It's a darned good little dump. I think I'll stay another week, if the life doesn't get me."

"I'm getting sort of fed," she said. "These French people get on my nerves."

"Where did you see any French people?" he said.

"Oh, you can't help knowing they're all around," she said. "It gets on your nerves. They're so damn dumb, they make me sick. Why, they don't even speak English in the post-office."

"They're a hot lot," he said. "Hey, garçon, you big stiff. Oh, garçon. Encore deux jeen feezes, and vitez it up a little, s' i' vous plaît."

He tilted his chair, stretched himself vastly, and yawned in loud arpeggio, his head sliding from side to side to the slow rhythm. The sheet of Mediterranean caught his eye.

"Hey, look at that damn mill-pond, will you?" he said. "Blue as a fool. Know what they used to call that puddle? The cradle of civilization, they called it. How's that—am I educated, or aren't I?"

"Oh, you're a knockout in every line," she said. She glanced over her shoulder at the sea. "I don't think I'll go in swimming again."

"What?" he said. "Not in the cradle of civilization?"

"Oh, shut up," she said. "I suppose you'll be pulling that for the next year. No, I'm not going in. The water's rotten today."

"You're right, at that," he said. "It's lousy."

The New Yorker, September 21, 1929

But the One on the Right

I knew it. I knew if I came to this dinner, I'd draw something like this baby on my left. They've been saving him up for me for weeks. Now, we've simply got to have him—his sister was so sweet to us in London; we can stick him next to Mrs. Parker—she talks enough for two. Oh, I should never have come, never. I'm here against my better judgment. Friday, at eight-thirty, Mrs. Parker vs. her better judgment, to a decision. That would be a good thing for them to cut on my tombstone: Wherever she went, including here, it was against her better judgment. This is a fine time of the evening to be thinking about tombstones. That's the effect he's had on me, already, and the soup hardly cold yet. I should have stayed at home for dinner. I could have had something on a tray. The head of John the Baptist, or something. Oh, I should not have come.

Well, the soup's over, anyway. I'm that much nearer to my Eternal Home. Now the soup belongs to the ages, and I have said precisely four words to the gentleman on my left. I said, "Isn't this soup delicious?"; that's four words. And he said, "Yes, isn't it?"; that's three. He's one up on me.

At any rate, we're in perfect accord. We agree like lambs. We've been all through the soup together, and never a cross word between us. It seems rather a pity to let the subject drop, now we've found something on which we harmonize so admirably. I believe I'll bring it up again; I'll ask him if that wasn't delicious soup. He says, "Yes, wasn't it?" Look at that, will you; perfect command of his tenses.

Here comes the fish. Goody, goody, goody, we got fish. I wonder if he likes fish. Yes, he does; he says he likes fish. Ah, that's nice. I love that in a man. Look, he's talking! He's chattering away like a veritable magpie! He's asking me if I like fish. Now does he really want to know, or is it only a line? I'd better play it cagey. I'll tell him, "Oh, pretty well." Oh, I like fish pretty well; there's a fascinating bit of autobiography for him to study over. Maybe he would rather wrestle with it alone. I'd better steal softly away, and leave him to his thoughts.

I might try my luck with what's on my right. No, not a chance there. The woman on his other side has him cold. All I can see is his shoulder. It's a nice shoulder, too; oh, it's a nice, *nice* shoulder. All my life, I've been a fool for a nice shoulder. Very well, lady; you saw him first. Keep your Greek god, and I'll go back to my Trojan horse.

Let's see, where were we? Oh, we'd got to where he had confessed his liking for fish. I wonder what else he likes. Does he like cucumbers? Yes, he does; he likes cucumbers. And potatoes? Yes, he likes potatoes, too. Why, he's a regular old Nature-lover, that's what he is. I would have to come out to dinner, and sit next to the Boy Thoreau. Wait, he's saying something! Words are simply pouring out of him. He's asking me if I'm fond of potatoes. No, I don't like potatoes. There, I've done it! I've differed from him. It's our first quarrel. He's fallen into a moody silence. Silly boy, have I pricked your bubble? Do you think I am nothing but a painted doll with sawdust for a heart? Ah, don't take it like that. Look, I have something to tell you that will bring back your faith. I do like cucumbers. Why, he's better already. He speaks again. He says, yes, he likes them, too. Now we've got that all straightened out, thank heaven. We both like cucumbers. Only he likes them twice.

I'd better let him alone now, so he can get some food. He ought to try to get his strength back. He's talked himself groggy.

I wish I had something to do. I hate to be a mere drone. People ought to let you know when they're going to sit you next to a thing like this, so you could bring along some means of occupation. Dear Mrs. Parker, do come to us for dinner on Friday next, and don't forget your drawn-work. I could have brought my top bureau drawer and tidied it up, here on my lap. I could have made great strides towards getting those photographs of the groups on the beach pasted up in the album. I wonder if my hostess would think it strange if I asked for a pack of cards. I wonder if there are any old copies of *St. Nicholas* lying about. I wonder if they wouldn't like a little help out in the kitchen. I wonder if anybody would want me to run up to the corner and get a late paper.

I could do a little drinking, of course, all by myself. There's always that. Oh, dear, oh, dear, oh, dear, there's always that. But I don't want to drink. I'll get *vin triste*. I'm melancholy before I even start. I wonder what this stiff on my left would say, if I told him I was in a fair way to get *vin triste*. Oh, look at him, hoeing into his fish! What does he care whether I get *vin triste* or not? His soul can't rise above food. Purely physical, that's all he is. Digging his grave with his teeth, that's what he's doing. Yah, yah, ya-ah! Digging your grave with your tee-eeth! Making a god of your stommick! Yah, yah, ya-ah!

He doesn't care if I get *vin triste*. Nobody cares. Nobody gives a damn. And me so nice. All right, you baskets, I'll drink myself to death, right in front of your eyes, and see how you'll feel. Here I go. . . . Oh, my God, it's Chablis. And of a year when the grapes failed, and they used Summer squash, instead. Fifteen dollars for all you can carry home on your shoulder. Oh, now, listen, where I come from, we feed this to the pigs. I think I'll ask old Chatterbox on my left if this isn't rotten wine. That ought to open up a new school of dialectics for us. Oh, he says he really wouldn't know—he never touches wine. Well, that fairly well ends that. I wonder how he'd like to step to hell, anyway. Yah, yah, ya-ah! Never touches wi-yine! Don't know what you're miss-sing! Yah, yah, ya-ah!

I'm not going to talk to him any more. I'm not going to spend the best years of my life thinking up pearls to scatter before him. I'm going to stick to my Chablis, rotten though it be. From now on, he can go his way, and I'll go mine. I'm better than anybody at this table. Ah, but am I really? Have I, after all, half of what they have? Here I am lonely, unwanted, silent, and me with all my new clothes on. Oh, what would Louiseboulanger say if she saw her gold lamé going unnoticed like this? It's life, I suppose. Poor little things, we dress, and we plan, and we hope—and for what? What is life, anyway? A death sentence. The longest distance between two points. The bunch of hay that's tied to the nose of the tired mule. The——

Well, well, well, here we are at the *entrecôte*. Button up your *entrecôte*, when the wind is free—no, I guess not. Now I'll be damned if I ask old Loquacity if he likes meat. In the first place, his likes and dislikes are nothing to me, and in the second—well, look at him go after it! He must have been playing hard all afternoon; he's Mother's Hungry Boy, tonight. All right, let him worry it all he wants. As for me, I'm on a higher plane. I do not stoop to him. He's less than the dust beneath my chariot wheel. Yah, yah, ya-ah! Less than the du-ust! Before I'd be that way. Yah, yah, ya-ah!

I'm glad there's red wine now. Even if it isn't good, I'm glad. Red wine gives me courage. The Red Badge of Courage. I need courage. I'm in a thin way, here. Nobody knows what a filthy time I'm having. My precious evening, that can never come again, ruined, ruined, ruined, and all because of this Somewhat Different Monologist on my left. But he can't lick me. The night is not yet dead, no, nor dying. You know, this really isn't bad wine.

Now what do you suppose is going on with the Greek God on my right? Ah, no use. There's still only the shoulder—the nice, *nice* shoulder. I wonder what the woman's like, that's got him. I can't see her at all. I wonder if she's beautiful. I wonder if she's Greek, too. When Greek meets immovable body—you might be able to do something with that, if you only had the time. I'm not going to be spineless any longer. Don't think for a minute, lady, that I've given up. He's still using his knife and fork. While there's hands above the table, there's hope.

Really, I suppose out of obligation to my hostess, I ought to do something about saying a few words to this macaw on my left. What shall I try? Have you been reading anything good lately, do you go much to the play, have you ever been to the Riviera? I wonder if he would like to hear about my Summer on the Riviera; hell, no, that's no good without lantern slides. I bet, though, if I started telling him about That One Night, he'd listen. I won't tell him—it's too good for him. Anybody that never touches wine can't hear that. But the one on the right—he'd like that. He touches wine. Touches it, indeed! He just threw it for a formidable loss.

Oh, look, old Silver Tongue is off again! Why, he's mad with his own perfume! He's rattling away like lightning. He's asking me if I like salad. Yes, I do; what does he want to make of that? He's telling me about salad through the ages. He says it's so good for people. So help me God, if he gives me a talk on roughage, I'll slap his face. Isn't that my life, to sit here, all dressed up in my best, and listen to this thing talk about romaine? And all the time, right on my right——

Well, I thought you were never going to turn around. . . . You haven't? . . . You have? Oh, Lord, I've been having an awful time, too. . . . Was she? . . . Well, you should have seen what I drew. . . . Oh, I don't see how we could. . . . Yes, I know it's terrible, but how can we get out of it? . . . Well. . . . Well, yes, that's true. . . . Look, right after dinner, I'll say I have this horrible headache, and you say you're going to take me home in your car, and——

The New Yorker, October 19, 1929

Here We Are

The young man in the new blue suit finished arranging the glistening luggage in tight corners of the Pullman compartment. The train had leaped at curves and bounced along straightaways, rendering balance a praiseworthy achievement and a sporadic one; and the young man had pushed and hoisted and tucked and shifted the bags with concentrated care.

Nevertheless, eight minutes for the settling of two suitcases and a hat-box is a long time.

He sat down, leaning back against bristled green plush, in the seat opposite the girl in beige. She looked as new as a peeled egg. Her hat, her fur, her frock, her gloves were glossy and stiff with novelty. On the arc of the thin, slippery sole of one beige shoe was gummed a tiny oblong of white paper, printed with the price set and paid for that slipper and its fellow, and the name of the shop that had dispensed them.

She had been staring raptly out of the window, drinking in the big weathered signboards that extolled the phenomena of codfish without bones and screens no rust could corrupt. As the young man sat down, she turned politely from the pane, met his eyes, started a smile and got it about half done, and rested her gaze just above his right shoulder.

"Well!" the young man said.

"Well!" she said.

"Well, here we are," he said.

"Here we are," she said. "Aren't we?"

"I should say we were," he said. "Eeyop. Here we are."

"Well!" she said.

"Well!" he said. "Well. How does it feel to be an old married lady?"

"Oh, it's too soon to ask me that," she said. "At least—I mean. Well, I mean, goodness, we've only been married about three hours, haven't we?"

The young man studied his wrist-watch as if he were just acquiring the knack of reading time.

"We have been married," he said, "exactly two hours and twenty-six minutes."

"My," she said. "It seems like longer."

"No," he said. "It isn't hardly half-past six yet."

"It seems like later," she said. "I guess it's because it starts getting dark so early."

"It does, at that," he said. "The nights are going to be pretty long from now on. I mean. I mean—well, it starts getting dark early."

"I didn't have any idea what time it was," she said. "Everything was so mixed up, I sort of don't know where I am, or what it's all about. Getting back from the church, and then all those people, and then changing all my clothes, and then everybody throwing things, and all. Goodness, I don't see how people do it every day."

"Do what?" he said.

"Get married," she said. "When you think of all the people, all over the world, getting married just as if it was nothing. Chinese people and everybody. Just as if it wasn't anything."

"Well, let's not worry about people all over the world," he said. "Let's don't think about a lot of Chinese. We've got something better to think about. I mean. I mean—well, what do we care about them?"

"I know," she said. "But I just sort of got to thinking of them, all of them, all over everywhere, doing it all the time. At least, I mean— getting married, you know. And it's—well, it's sort of such a big thing to do, it makes you feel queer. You think of them, all of them, all doing it just like it wasn't anything. And how does anybody know what's going to happen next?"

"Let them worry," he said. "We don't have to. We know darn well what's going to happen next. I mean. I mean—well, we know it's going to be great. Well, we know we're going to be happy. Don't we?"

"Oh, of course," she said. "Only you think of all the people, and you have to sort of keep thinking. It makes you feel funny. An awful lot of people that get married, it doesn't turn out so well. And I guess they all must have thought it was going to be great."

"Come on, now," he said. "This is no way to start a honeymoon, with all this thinking going on. Look at us—all married and everything done. I mean. The wedding all done and all."

"Ah, it was nice, wasn't it?" she said. "Did you really like my veil?"

"You looked great," he said. "Just great."

"Oh, I'm terribly glad," she said. "Ellie and Louise looked lovely, didn't they? I'm terribly glad they did finally decide on pink. They looked perfectly lovely."

"Listen," he said. "I want to tell you something. When I was standing up there in that old church waiting for you to come up, and I saw those two bridesmaids, I thought to myself, I thought, 'Well, I never

knew Louise could look like that!' Why, she'd have knocked anybody's
eye out."

"Oh, really?" she said. "Funny. Of course, everybody thought her
dress and hat were lovely, but a lot of people seemed to think she looked
sort of tired. People have been saying that a lot, lately. I tell them I
think it's awfully mean of them to go around saying that about her. I
tell them they've got to remember that Louise isn't so terribly young
any more, and they've got to expect her to look like that. Louise can
say she's twenty-three all she wants to, but she's a good deal nearer
twenty-seven."

"Well, she was certainly a knock-out at the wedding," he said.
"Boy!"

"I'm terribly glad you thought so," she said. "I'm glad some one did.
How did you think Ellie looked?"

"Why, I honestly didn't get a look at her," he said.

"Oh, really?" she said. "Well, I certainly think that's too bad. I don't
suppose I ought to say it about my own sister, but I never saw anybody
look as beautiful as Ellie looked today. And always so sweet and unselfish, too. And you didn't even notice her. But you never pay attention
to Ellie, anyway. Don't think I haven't noticed it. It makes me feel just
terrible. It makes me feel just awful, that you don't like my own sister."

"I do so like her!" he said. "I'm crazy for Ellie. I think she's a
great kid."

"Don't think it makes any difference to Ellie!" she said. "Ellie's got
enough people crazy about her. It isn't anything to her whether you like
her or not. Don't flatter yourself she cares! Only, the only thing is, it
makes it awfully hard for me you don't like her, that's the only thing.
I keep thinking, when we come back and get in the apartment and
everything, it's going to be awfully hard for me that you won't want
my own sister to come and see me. It's going to make it awfully hard
for me that you won't ever want my family around. I know how you
feel about my family. Don't think I haven't seen it. Only, if you don't
ever want to see them, that's your loss. Not theirs. Don't flatter
yourself!"

"Oh, now, come on!" he said. "What's all this talk about not wanting your family around? Why, you know how I feel about your family.
I think your old lady—I think your mother's swell. And Ellie. And your
father. What's all this talk?"

"Well, I've seen it," she said. "Don't think I haven't. Lots of people
they get married, and they think it's going to be great and everything,

and then it all goes to pieces because people don't like people's families, or something like that. Don't tell me! I've seen it happen."

"Honey," he said, "what is all this? What are you getting all angry about? Hey, look, this is our honeymoon. What are you trying to start a fight for? Ah, I guess you're just feeling sort of nervous."

"Me?" she said. "What have I got to be nervous about? I mean. I mean, goodness, I'm not nervous."

"You know, lots of times," he said, "they say that girls get kind of nervous and yippy on account of thinking about—I mean. I mean— well, it's like you said, things are all so sort of mixed up and everything, right now. But afterwards, it'll be all right. I mean. I mean—well, look, honey, you don't look any too comfortable. Don't you want to take your hat off? And let's don't ever fight, ever. Will we?"

"Ah, I'm sorry I was cross," she said. "I guess I did feel a little bit funny. All mixed up, and then thinking of all those people all over everywhere, and then being sort of 'way off here, all alone with you. It's so sort of different. It's sort of such a big thing. You can't blame a person for thinking, can you? Yes, don't let's ever, ever fight. We won't be like a whole lot of them. We won't fight or be nasty or anything. Will we?"

"You bet your life we won't," he said.

"I guess I will take this darned old hat off," she said. "It kind of presses. Just put it up on the rack, will you, dear? Do you like it, sweetheart?"

"Looks good on you," he said.

"No, but I mean," she said, "do you really like it?"

"Well, I'll tell you," he said. "I know this is the new style and every-thing like that, and it's probably great. I don't know anything about things like that. Only I like the kind of a hat like that blue hat you had. Gee, I liked that hat."

"Oh, really?" she said. "Well, that's nice. That's lovely. The first thing you say to me, as soon as you get me off on a train away from my family and everything, is that you don't like my hat. The first thing you say to your wife is you think she has terrible taste in hats. That's nice, isn't it?"

"Now, honey," he said, "I never said anything like that. I only said——"

"What you don't seem to realize," she said, "is this hat cost twenty-two dollars. Twenty-two dollars. And that horrible old blue thing you think you're so crazy about, that cost three ninety-five."

"I don't give a darn what they cost," he said. "I only said—I said I liked that blue hat. I don't know anything about hats. I'll be crazy about this one as soon as I get used to it. Only it's kind of not like your other hats. I don't know about the new styles. What do I know about women's hats?"

"It's too bad," she said, "you didn't marry somebody that would get the kind of hats you'd like. Hats that cost three ninety-five. Why didn't you marry Louise? You always think she looks so beautiful. You'd love her taste in hats. Why didn't you marry her?"

"Ah, now, honey," he said. "For heaven's sakes!"

"Why didn't you marry her?" she said. "All you've done, ever since we got on this train, is talk about her. Here I've sat and sat, and just listened to you saying how wonderful Louise is. I suppose that's nice, getting me all off here alone with you, and then raving about Louise right in front of my face. Why didn't you ask her to marry you? I'm sure she would have jumped at the chance. There aren't so many people asking her to marry them. It's too bad you didn't marry her. I'm sure you'd have been much happier."

"Listen, baby," he said, "while you're talking about things like that, why didn't you marry Joe Brooks? I suppose he could have given you all the twenty-two-dollar hats you wanted, I suppose!"

"Well, I'm not so sure I'm not sorry I didn't," she said. "There! Joe Brooks wouldn't have waited until he got me all off alone and then sneered at my taste in clothes. Joe Brooks wouldn't ever hurt my feelings. Joe Brooks has always been fond of me. There!"

"Yeah," he said. "He's fond of you. He was so fond of you he didn't even send a wedding present. That's how fond of you he was."

"I happen to know for a fact," she said, "that he was away on business, and as soon as he comes back he's going to give me anything I want, for the apartment."

"Listen," he said. "I don't want anything he gives you in our apartment. Anything he gives you, I'll throw right out the window. That's what I think of your friend Joe Brooks. And how do you know where he is and what he's going to do, anyway? Has he been writing to you?"

"I suppose my friends can correspond with me," she said. "I didn't hear there was any law against that."

"Well, I suppose they can't!" he said. "And what do you think of that? I'm not going to have my wife getting a lot of letters from cheap traveling salesmen!"

"Joe Brooks is not a cheap traveling salesman!" she said. "He is not! He gets a wonderful salary."

"Oh yeah?" he said. "Where did you hear that?"

"He told me so himself," she said.

"Oh, he told you so himself," he said. "I see. He told you so himself."

"You've got a lot of right to talk about Joe Brooks," she said. "You and your friend Louise. All you ever talk about is Louise."

"Oh, for heaven's sakes!" he said. "What do I care about Louise? I just thought she was a friend of yours, that's all. That's why I ever even noticed her."

"Well, you certainly took an awful lot of notice of her today," she said. "On our wedding day! You said yourself when you were standing there in the church you just kept thinking of her. Right up at the altar. Oh, right in the presence of God! And all you thought about was Louise."

"Listen, honey," he said, "I never should have said that. How does anybody know what kind of crazy things come into their heads when they're standing there waiting to get married? I was just telling you that because it was so kind of crazy. I thought it would make you laugh."

"I know," she said. "I've been all sort of mixed up today, too. I told you that. Everything so strange and everything. And me all the time thinking about all those people all over the world, and now us here all alone, and everything. I know you get all mixed up. Only I did think, when you kept talking about how beautiful Louise looked, you did it with malice and forethought."

"I never did anything with malice and forethought!" he said. "I just told you that about Louise because I thought it would make you laugh."

"Well, it didn't," she said.

"No, I know it didn't," he said. "It certainly did not. Ah, baby, and we ought to be laughing, too. Hell, honey lamb, this is our honeymoon. What's the matter?"

"I don't know," she said. "We used to squabble a lot when we were going together and then engaged and everything, but I thought everything would be so different as soon as you were married. And now I feel so sort of strange and everything. I feel so sort of alone."

"Well, you see, sweetheart," he said, "we're not really married yet. I mean. I mean—well, things will be different afterwards. Oh, hell. I mean, we haven't been married very long."

"No," she said.

"Well, we haven't got much longer to wait now," he said. "I mean—well, we'll be in New York in about twenty minutes. Then we can have dinner, and sort of see what we feel like doing. Or I mean. Is there anything special you want to do tonight?"

"What?" she said.

"What I mean to say," he said, "would you like to go to a show or something?"

"Why, whatever you like," she said. "I sort of didn't think people went to theaters and things on their—I mean, I've got a couple of letters I simply must write. Don't let me forget."

"Oh," he said. "You're going to write letters tonight?"

"Well, you see," she said. "I've been perfectly terrible. What with all the excitement and everything. I never did thank poor old Mrs. Sprague for her berry spoon, and I never did a thing about those book ends the McMasters sent. It's just too awful of me. I've got to write them this very night."

"And when you've finished writing your letters," he said, "maybe I could get you a magazine or a bag of peanuts."

"What?" she said.

"I mean," he said, "I wouldn't want you to be bored."

"As if I could be bored with you!" she said. "Silly! Aren't we married? Bored!"

"What I thought," he said, "I thought when we got in, we could go right up to the Biltmore and anyway leave our bags, and maybe have a little dinner in the room, kind of quiet, and then do whatever we wanted. I mean. I mean—well, let's go right up there from the station."

"Oh, yes, let's," she said. "I'm so glad we're going to the Biltmore. I just love it. The twice I've stayed in New York we've always stayed there, Papa and Mamma and Ellie and I, and I was crazy about it. I always sleep so well there. I go right off to sleep the minute I put my head on the pillow."

"Oh, you do?" he said.

"At least, I mean," she said. " 'Way up high it's so quiet."

"We might go to some show or other tomorrow night instead of tonight," he said. "Don't you think that would be better?"

"Yes, I think it might," she said.

He rose, balanced a moment, crossed over and sat down beside her. "Do you really have to write those letters tonight?" he said.

"Well," she said, "I don't suppose they'd get there any quicker than if I wrote them tomorrow."

There was a silence with things going on in it.

"And we won't ever fight any more, will we?" he said.

"Oh, no," she said. "Not ever! I don't know what made me do like that. It all got so sort of funny, sort of like a nightmare, the way I got thinking of all those people getting married all the time; and so many of them, everything spoils on account of fighting and everything. I got all mixed up thinking about them. Oh, I don't want to be like them. But we won't be, will we?"

"Sure we won't," he said.

"We won't go all to pieces," she said. "We won't fight. It'll all be different, now we're married. It'll all be lovely. Reach me down my hat, will you, sweetheart? It's time I was putting it on. Thanks. Ah, I'm sorry you don't like it."

"I do so like it!" he said.

"You said you didn't," she said. "You said you thought it was perfectly terrible."

"I never said any such thing," he said. "You're crazy."

"All right, I may be crazy," she said. "Thank you very much. But that's what you said. Not that it matters—it's just a little thing. But it makes you feel pretty funny to think you've gone and married somebody that says you have perfectly terrible taste in hats. And then goes and says you're crazy, beside."

"Now, listen here," he said. "Nobody said any such thing. Why, I love that hat. The more I look at it the better I like it. I think it's great."

"That isn't what you said before," she said.

"Honey," he said. "Stop it, will you? What do you want to start all this for? I love the damned hat. I mean, I love your hat. I love anything you wear. What more do you want me to say?"

"Well, I don't want you to say it like that," she said.

"I said I think it's great," he said. "That's all I said."

"Do you really?" she said. "Do you honestly? Ah, I'm so glad. I'd hate you not to like my hat. It would be—I don't know, it would be sort of such a bad start."

"Well, I'm crazy for it," he said. "Now we've got that settled, for heaven's sakes. Ah, baby. Baby lamb. We're not going to have any bad starts. Look at us—we're on our honeymoon. Pretty soon we'll be regular old married people. I mean. I mean, in a few minutes we'll be getting in to New York, and then we'll be going to the hotel, and then everything will be all right. I mean—well, look at us! Here we are married! Here we are!"

"Yes, here we are," she said. "Aren't we?"

Cosmopolitan, March 31, 1931

Lady with a Lamp

Well, Mona! Well, you poor sick thing, you! Ah, you look so little and white and *little,* you do, lying there in that great big bed. That's what you do—go and look so childlike and pitiful nobody'd have the heart to scold you. And I ought to scold you, Mona. Oh, yes, I should so, too. Never letting me know you were ill. Never a word to your oldest friend. Darling, you might have known I'd understand, no matter what you did. What do I mean? Well, what do you *mean* what do I mean, Mona? Of course, if you'd rather not talk about—Not even to your oldest friend. All I wanted to say was you might have known that I'm always for you, no matter what happens. I do admit, sometimes it's a little hard for me to understand how on earth you ever got into such—well. Goodness knows I don't want to nag you now, when you're so sick.

All right, Mona, then you're *not* sick. If that's what you want to say, even to me, why, all right, my dear. People who aren't sick have to stay in bed for nearly two weeks, I suppose; I suppose people who aren't sick look the way you do. Just your nerves? You were simply all tired out? I see. It's just your nerves. You were simply tired. Yes. Oh, Mona, Mona, why don't you feel you can trust me?

Well—if that's the way you want to be to me, that's the way you want to be. I won't say anything more about it. Only I do think you might have let me know that you had—well, that you were so *tired,* if that's what you want me to say. Why, I'd never have known a word about it if I hadn't run bang into Alice Patterson and she told me she'd called you up and that maid of yours said you had been sick in bed for ten days. Of course, I'd thought it rather funny I hadn't heard from you, but you know how you are—you simply let people go, and weeks can go by like, well, like *weeks,* and never a sign from you. Why, I could have been dead over and over again, for all you'd know. Twenty times over. Now, I'm not going to scold you when you're sick, but frankly and honestly, Mona, I said to myself this time, "Well, she'll have a good wait before I call her up. I've given in often enough, goodness knows. Now she can just call me first." Frankly and honestly, that's what I said!

And then I saw Alice, and I did feel mean, I really did. And now to see you lying there—well, I feel like a complete *dog*. That's what you do to people even when you're in the wrong the way you always are, you wicked little thing, you! Ah, the poor dear! Feels just so awful, doesn't it?

Oh, don't keep trying to be brave, child. Not with me. Just give in—it helps so much. Just tell me all about it. You know I'll never say a word. Or at least you ought to know. When Alice told me that maid of yours said you were all tired out and your nerves had gone bad, I naturally never said anything, but I thought to myself, "Well, maybe that's the only thing Mona could say was the matter. That's probably about the best excuse she could think of." And of course *I'll* never deny it—but perhaps it might have been better to have said you had influenza or ptomaine poisoning. After all, people don't stay in bed for ten whole days just because they're nervous. All right, Mona, then they *do*. Then they do. Yes, dear.

Ah, to think of you going through all this and crawling off here all alone like a little wounded animal or something. And with only that colored Edie to take care of you. Darling, oughtn't you have a trained nurse, I mean really oughtn't you? There must be so many things that have to be done for you. Why, Mona! Mona, please! Dear, you don't have to get so excited. Very well, my dear, it's just as you say—there isn't a single thing to be done. I was mistaken, that's all. I simply thought that after— Oh, now, you don't have to do that. You never have to say you're sorry, to *me*. I understand. As a matter of fact, I was glad to hear you lose your temper. It's a good sign when sick people are cross. It means they're on the way to getting better. Oh, I know! You go right ahead and be cross all you want to.

Look, where shall I sit? I want to sit some place where you won't have to turn around, so you can talk to me. You stay right the way you're lying, and I'll— Because you shouldn't move around, I'm sure. It must be terribly bad for you. All right, dear, you can move around all you want to. All right, I must be crazy. I'm crazy, then. We'll leave it like that. Only please, please don't excite yourself that way.

I'll just get this chair and put it over—oops, I'm sorry I joggled the bed—put it over here, where you can see me. There. But first I want to fix your pillows before I get settled. Well, they certainly are *not* all right, Mona. After the way you've been twisting them and pulling them, these last few minutes. Now look, honey, I'll help you raise yourself ve-ry, ve-ry slo-o-ow-ly. Oh. Of course you can sit up by yourself, dear. Of course you can. Nobody ever said you couldn't. Nobody ever thought of such a thing. There now, your pillows are all smooth and lovely, and you lie right down again, before you hurt yourself. Now, isn't that better? Well, I should think it was!

Just a minute, till I get my sewing. Oh, yes, I brought it along, so we'd be all cozy. Do you honestly, frankly and honestly, think it's pretty? I'm so glad. It's nothing but a tray-cloth, you know. But you simply can't have too many. They're a lot of fun to make, too, doing this edge—it goes so quickly. Oh, Mona dear, so often I think if you just had a home of your own, and could be all busy, making pretty little things like this for it, it would do so *much* for you. I worry so about you, living in a little furnished apartment, with nothing that belongs to you, no roots, no nothing. It's not right for a woman. It's all wrong for a woman like you. Oh, I wish you'd get over that Garry McVicker! If you could just meet some nice, sweet, considerate man, and get married to him, and have your own lovely place—and with your *taste*, Mona!—and maybe have a couple of children. You're so simply adorable with children. Why, Mona Morrison, are you crying? Oh, you've got a cold? You've got a cold, *too*? I thought you were crying, there for a second. Don't you want my handkerchief, lamb? Oh, you have yours. Wouldn't you have a pink chiffon handkerchief, you nut! Why on earth don't you use cleansing tissues, just lying there in bed with no one to see you? You little idiot, you! Extravagant little fool!

No, but really, I'm serious. I've said to Fred so often, "Oh, if we could just get Mona married!" Honestly, you don't know the feeling it gives you, just to be all secure and safe with your own sweet home and your own blessed children, and your own nice husband coming back to you every night. That's a woman's *life*, Mona. What you've been doing is really horrible. Just drifting along, that's all. What's going to happen to you, dear, whatever is going to become of you? But no—you don't even think of it. You go, and go falling in love with that Garry. Well, my dear, you've got to give me credit—I said from the very first, "He'll never marry her." You know that. What? There was never any thought of marriage, with you and Garry? Oh, Mona, now listen! Every woman on earth thinks of marriage as soon as she's in love with a man. Every woman, I don't care who she is.

Oh, if you were only married! It would be all the difference in the world. I think a child would do everything for you, Mona. Goodness knows, I just can't speak *decently* to that Garry, after the way he's treated you—well, you know perfectly well, *none* of your friends can— but I can frankly and honestly say, if he married you, I'd absolutely let bygones be bygones, and I'd be just as happy as happy, for you. If he's what you want. And I will say, what with your lovely looks and what with good-looking as he is, you ought to have simply *gorgeous* children. Mona, baby, you really have got a rotten cold, haven't you? Don't you want me to get you another handkerchief? Really?

I'm simply sick that I didn't bring you any flowers. But I thought the place would be full of them. Well, I'll stop on the way home and send you some. It looks too dreary here, without a flower in the room. Didn't Garry send you any? Oh, he didn't know you were sick. Well, doesn't he send you flowers anyway? Listen, hasn't he called up, all this time, and found out whether you were sick or not? Not in ten days? Well, then, haven't you called him and told him? Ah, now, Mona, there *is* such a thing as being too much of a heroine. Let him worry a little, dear. It would be a very good thing for him. Maybe that's the trouble—you've always taken all the worry for both of you. Hasn't sent any flowers! Hasn't even telephoned! Well, I'd just like to talk to that young man for a few minutes. After all, this is all *his* responsibility.

He's away? He's *what*? Oh, he went to Chicago two weeks ago. Well, it seems to me I'd always heard that there were telephone wires running between here and Chicago, but of course— And you'd think since he's been back, the least he could do would be to do something. He's not back yet? He's not *back* yet? Mona, what are you trying to tell me? Why, just night before last— Said he'd let you know the minute he got home? Of all the rotten, low things I ever heard in my life, this is really the— Mona, dear, please lie down. Please. Why, I didn't mean anything. I don't know what I was going to say, honestly I don't, it couldn't have been anything. For goodness' sake, let's talk about something else.

Let's see. Oh, you really ought to see Julia Post's living-room, the way she's done it now. She has brown walls—not beige, you know, or tan or anything, but brown—and these cream-colored taffeta curtains and— Mona, I tell you I absolutely don't know what I was going to say, before. It's gone completely out of my head. So you see how unimportant it must have been. Dear, please just lie quiet and try to relax. Please forget about that man for a few minutes, anyway. No man's worth getting that worked up about. Catch me doing it! You know you can't expect to get well quickly, if you get yourself so excited. You know that.

What doctor did you have, darling? Or don't you want to say? Your own? Your own Doctor Britton? You don't mean it! Well, I certainly never thought he'd do a thing like— Yes, dear, of course he's a nerve specialist. Yes, dear. Yes, dear. Yes, dear, of course you have perfect confidence in him. I only wish you would in me, once in a while; after we went to school together and everything. You might know I absolutely sympathize with you. I don't see how you could possibly have done anything else. I know you've always talked about how you'd give anything to have a baby, but it would have been so terribly unfair to the child to bring it into the world without being married. You'd have had to go live abroad and never see anybody and— And even then, somebody would have been sure to have told it sometime. They always do. You did the only possible thing, *I* think. Mona, for heaven's sake! Don't scream like that. I'm not deaf, you know. All right, dear, all right, all right, all right. All right, of course I believe you. Naturally I take your word for anything. Anything you say. Only please do try to be quiet. Just lie back and rest, and have a nice talk.

Ah, now don't keep harping on that. I've told you a hundred times, if I've told you once, I wasn't going to say anything at all. I tell you I don't remember *what* I was going to say. "Night before last"? When did I mention "night before last"? I never said any such— Well. Maybe it's better this way, Mona. The more I think of it, the more I think it's much better for you to hear it from me. Because somebody's bound to tell you. These things always come out. And I know you'd rather hear it from your oldest friend, wouldn't you? And the good Lord knows, anything I could do to make you see what that man really is! Only do relax, darling. Just for me. Dear, Garry isn't in Chicago. Fred and I saw him night before last at the Comet Club, dancing. And Alice saw him Tuesday night at El Rhumba. And I don't know how many people have said they've seen him around at the theater and night clubs and things. Why, he couldn't have stayed in Chicago more than a day or so—if he went at all.

Well, he was with *her* when we saw him, honey. Apparently he's with her all the time; nobody ever sees him with anyone else. You really must make up your mind to it, dear; it's the only thing to do. I hear all over that he's just simply *pleading* with her to marry him, but I don't know how true that is. I'm sure I can't see why he'd want to, but then you never can tell what a man like that will do. It would be just good enough *for* him if he got her, that's what *I* say. Then he'd see. She'd never stand for any of his nonsense. She'd make him toe the mark. She's a smart woman.

But, oh, so *ordinary*. I thought, when we saw them the other night, "Well, she just looks cheap, that's all she looks." That must be what he likes, I suppose. I must admit he looked very well. I never saw him look better. Of course you know what I think of him, but I always had to say he's one of the handsomest men I ever saw in my life. I can understand how any woman would be attracted to him—at first. Until they found out what he's really like. Oh, if you could have seen him with that awful, common creature, never once taking his eyes off her, and hanging on every word she said, as if it was pearls! It made me just——

Mona, angel, are you *crying*? Now, darling, that's just plain silly. That man's not worth another thought. You've thought about him entirely too much, that's the trouble. Three years! Three of the best years of your life you've given him, and all the time he's been deceiving you with that woman. Just think back over what you've been through—all the times and times and times he promised you he'd give her up; and you, you poor little idiot, you'd believe him, and then he'd go right back to her again. And *everybody* knew about it. Think of that, and then try telling me that man's worth crying over! Really, Mona! I'd have more pride.

You know, I'm just glad this thing happened. I'm just glad you found out. This is a little too much, this time. In Chicago, indeed! Let you know the minute he came home! The kindest thing a person could possibly have done was to tell you, and bring you to your senses at last. I'm not sorry I did it, for a second. When I think of him out having the time of his life and you lying here deathly sick all on account of him, I could just— Yes, it is on account of him. Even if you didn't have an— well, even if I was mistaken about what I naturally thought was the matter with you when you made such a secret of your illness, he's driven you into a nervous breakdown, and that's plenty bad enough. All for that man! The skunk! You just put him right out of your head.

Why, of course you can, Mona. All you need to do is to pull yourself together, child. Simply say to yourself, "Well, I've wasted three years of my life, and that's that." Never worry about *him* any more. The Lord knows, darling, he's not worrying about you.

It's just because you're weak and sick that you're worked up like this, dear. I know. But you're going to be all right. You can make something of your life. You've got to, Mona, you know. Because after all—well, of course, you never looked sweeter, I don't mean that; but you're—well, you're not getting any younger. And here you've been throwing away your time, never seeing your friends, never going out, never meeting anybody new, just sitting here waiting for Garry to telephone, or Garry to come in—if he didn't have anything better to do. For three years, you've never had a thought in your head but that man. Now you just forget him.

Ah, baby, it isn't good for you to cry like that. Please don't. He's not even worth talking about. Look at the woman he's in love with, and you'll see what kind he is. You were much too good for him. You were much too sweet to him. You gave in too easily. The minute he had you, he didn't want you any more. That's what he's like. Why, he no more loved you than——

Mona, don't! Mona, stop it! Please, Mona! You mustn't talk like that, you mustn't say such things. You've got to stop crying, you'll be terribly sick. Stop, oh, stop it, oh, please stop! Oh, what am I going to do with her? Mona, dear—Mona! Oh, where in heaven's name is that fool maid?

Edie. Oh, Edie! Edie, I think you'd better get Dr. Britton on the telephone, and tell him to come down and give Miss Morrison something to quiet her. I'm afraid she's got herself a little bit upset.

Harper's Bazaar, April 1932

Dusk Before Fireworks

He was a very good-looking young man indeed, shaped to be annoyed. His voice was intimate as the rustle of sheets, and he kissed easily. There was no tallying the gifts of Charvet handkerchiefs, *art moderne* ash-trays, monogrammed dressing-gowns, gold keychains, and cigarette-cases of thin wood, inlaid with views of Parisian comfort stations, that were sent him by ladies too quickly confident, and were paid for with the money of unwitting husbands, which is acceptable any place in the world. Every woman who visited his small, square apartment promptly flamed with the desire to assume charge of its redecoration. During his tenancy, three separate ladies had achieved this ambition. Each had left behind her, for her brief monument, much too much glazed chintz.

The glare of the latest upholstery was dulled, now, in an April dusk. There was a soft blur of mauve and gray over chairs and curtains, in-stead of the daytime pattern of heroic-sized double poppies and small, sad elephants. (The most recent of the volunteer decorators was a lady who added interest to her ways by collecting all varieties of elephants save those alive or stuffed; her selection of the chintz had been made less for the cause of contemporary design than in the hope of keeping ever present the wistful souvenirs of her hobby and, hence, of herself. Unhappily, the poppies, those flowers for forgetfulness, turned out to be predominant in the pattern.)

The very good-looking young man was stretched in a chair that was legless and short in back. It was a strain to see in that chair any virtue save the speeding one of modernity. Certainly it was a peril to all who dealt with it; they were far from their best within its arms, and they could never have wished to be remembered as they appeared while eas-ing into its depths or struggling out again. All, that is, save the young man. He was a long young man, broad at the shoulders and chest and narrow everywhere else, and his muscles obeyed him at the exact instant of command. He rose and lay, he moved and was still, always in beauty. Several men disliked him, but only one woman really hated him. She was his sister. She was stump-shaped, and she had straight hair.

On the sofa opposite the difficult chair there sat a young woman, slight and softly dressed. There was no more to her frock than some dull, dark silk and a little chiffon, but the recurrent bill for it demanded, in bitter black and white, a sum well on toward the second hundred. Once the very good-looking young man had said that he liked women in quiet and conservative clothes, carefully made. The young woman was of those unfortunates who remember every word. This made living peculiarly trying for her when it was later demonstrated that the young man was also partial to ladies given to garments of slap-dash cut, and color like the sound of big brass instruments.

The young woman was temperately pretty in the eyes of most be-holders; but there were a few, mainly hand-to-mouth people, artists and such, who could not look enough at her. Half a year before, she had been sweeter to see. Now there was tension about her mouth and unease along her brow, and her eyes looked wearied and troubled. The gentle dusk became her. The young man who shared it with her could not see these things.

She stretched her arms and laced her fingers high above her head.

"Oh, this is nice," she said. "It's nice being here."

"It's nice and peaceful," he said. "Oh, Lord. Why can't people just be peaceful? That's little enough to ask, isn't it? Why does there have to be so much hell, all the time?"

She dropped her hands to her lap.

"There doesn't have to be at all," she said. She had a quiet voice, and she said her words with every courtesy to each of them, as if she respected language. "There's never any need for hell."

"There's an awful lot of it around, sweet," he said.

"There certainly is," she said. "There's just as much hell as there are hundreds of little shrill, unnecessary people. It's the second-raters that stir up hell; first-rate people wouldn't. You need never have another bit of it in your beautiful life if—if you'll pardon my pointing—you could just manage to steel yourself against that band of spitting hell-cats that is included in your somewhat overcrowded acquaintance, my lamb. Ah, but I mean it, Hobie, dear. I've been wanting to tell you for so long. But it's so rotten hard to say. If I say it, it makes me sound just like one of them—makes me seem inexpensive and jealous. Surely, you know, after all this time, I'm not like that. It's just that I worry so about you. You're so fine, you're so lovely, it nearly kills me to see you just eaten up by a lot of things like Margot Wadsworth and Mrs. Holt and Evie Maynard and those. You're so much better than that. You know that's why I'm saying it. You know I haven't got a stitch of jealousy in me. Jealous! Good heavens, if I were going to be jealous, I'd be it about someone worth while, and not about any silly, stupid, idle, worthless, selfish, hysterical, vulgar, promiscuous, sex-ridden——"

"Darling!" he said.

"Well, I'm sorry," she said. "I guess I'm sorry. I didn't really mean to go into the subject of certain of your friends. Maybe the way they behave isn't their fault, said she, lying in her teeth. After all, you can't expect them to know what it's about. Poor things, they'll never know how sweet it can be, how lovely it always is when we're alone together. It is, isn't it? Ah, Hobie, isn't it?"

The young man raised his slow lids and looked at her. He smiled with one end of his beautiful curly mouth.

"Uh-huh," he said.

He took his eyes from hers and became busy with an ash-tray and a spent cigarette. But he still smiled.

"Ah, don't," she said. "You promised you'd forget about—about last Wednesday. You said you'd never remember it again. Oh, whatever made me do it! Making scenes. Having tantrums. Rushing out into the night. And then coming crawling back. Me, that wanted to show you how different a woman could be! Oh, please, please don't let's think about it. Only tell me I wasn't as terrible as I know I was."

"Darling," he said, for he was often a young man of simple statements, "you were the worst I ever saw."

"And doesn't that come straight from Sir Hubert!" she said. "Oh, dear. Oh, dear, oh, dear. What can I say? 'Sorry' isn't nearly enough. I'm broken. I'm in little bits. Would you mind doing something about putting me together again?"

She held out her arms to him.

The young man rose, came over to the sofa, and kissed her. He had intended a quick, good-humored kiss, a moment's stop on a projected trip out to his little pantry to mix cocktails. But her arms clasped him so close and so gladly that he dismissed the plan. He lifted her to her feet, and did not leave her.

Presently she moved her head and hid her face above his heart.

"Listen," she said, against cloth. "I want to say it all now, and then never say it any more. I want to tell you that there'll never, never be anything like last Wednesday again. What we have is so much too lovely ever to cheapen. I promise, oh, I promise you, I won't ever be like—like anybody else."

"You couldn't be, Kit," he said.

"Ah, think that always," she said, "and say it sometimes. It's so sweet to hear. Will you, Hobie?"

"For your size," he said, "you talk an awful lot." His fingers slid to her chin and he held her face for his greater convenience.

After a while she moved again.

"Guess who I'd rather be, right this minute, than anybody in the whole world," she said.

"Who?" he said.

"Me," she said.

The telephone rang.

The telephone was in the young man's bedroom, standing in frequent silence on the little table by his bed. There was no door to the bed-chamber; a plan which had disadvantages, too. Only a curtained arch-way sequestered its intimacies from those of the living-room. Another archway, also streaming chintz, gave from the bedroom upon a tiny passage, along which were ranged the bathroom and the pantry. It was only by entering either of these, closing the door behind, and turning the faucets on to the full that any second person in the apartment could avoid hearing what was being said over the telephone. The young man sometimes thought of removing to a flat of more sympathetic design.

"There's that damn telephone," the young man said.

"Isn't it?" the young woman said. "And wouldn't it be?"

"Let's not answer it," he said. "Let's let it ring."

"No, you mustn't," she said. "I must be big and strong. Anyway, maybe it's only somebody that just died and left you twenty million dollars. Maybe it isn't some other woman at all. And if it is, what difference does it make? See how sweet and reasonable I am? Look at me being generous."

"You can afford to be, sweetheart," he said.

"I know I can," she said. "After all, whoever she is, she's way off on an end of a wire, and I'm right here."

She smiled up at him. So it was nearly half a minute before he went away to the telephone.

Still smiling, the young woman stretched her head back, closed her eyes and flung her arms wide. A long sigh raised her breast. Thus she stood, then she went and settled back on the sofa. She essayed whistling softly, but the issuing sounds would not resemble the intended tune and she felt, though interested, vaguely betrayed. Then she looked about the dusk-filled room. Then she pondered her finger nails, bringing each bent hand close to her eyes, and could find no fault. Then she smoothed her skirt along her legs and shook out the chiffon frills at her wrists. Then she spread her little handkerchief on her knee and with exquisite care traced the "Katherine" embroidered in script across one of its corners. Then she gave it all up and did nothing but listen.

"Yes?" the young man was saying. "Hello? Hello. I *told* you this is Mr. Ogden. Well, I *am* holding the wire. I've *been* holding the wire. *You're* the one that went away. Hello? Ah, now listen—Hello? Hey. Oh, what the hell *is* this? Come back, will you? Operator! Hello, *yes*, this is Mr. Ogden. Who? Oh, hello, Connie. How are you, dear? What? You're what? Oh, that's too bad. What's the matter? Why can't you? Where are you, in Greenwich? Oh, I see. When, now? Why, Connie, the only thing is I've got to go right out. So if you came in to town now, it really wouldn't do much—Well, I couldn't very well do that, dear. I'm keeping these people waiting as it is. I say I'm late now, I was just going out the door when you called. Why, I'd better not say that, Connie, because there's no telling when I'll be able to break away. Look, why don't you wait and come in to town tomorrow some time? What? Can't you tell me now? Oh— Well— Oh, Connie, there's no reason to talk like that. Why, of course I'd do anything in the world I could, but I tell you I can't tonight. No, no, no, no, no, it isn't that at all. No, it's nothing like that, I tell you. These people are friends of my sister's, and it's just one of those things you've got to do. Why don't you be a good girl and go to bed early, and then you'll feel better tomorrow? Hm? Will you do that? What? Of course I do, Connie. I'll try to later on if I can, dear. Well, all right, if you want to, but I don't know what time I'll be home. Of course I do. Of course I do. Yes, *do,* Connie. You be a good girl, won't you? 'By, dear."

The young man returned, through the chintz. He had a rather worn look. It was, of course, becoming to him.

"God," he said, simply.

The young woman on the sofa looked at him as if through clear ice.

"And how *is* dear Mrs. Holt?" she said.

"Great," he said. "Corking. Way up at the top of her form." He dropped wearily into the low chair. "She says she has something she wants to tell me."

"It can't be her age," she said.

He smiled without joy. "She says it's too hard to say over the wire," he said.

"Then it may be her age," she said. "She's afraid it might sound like her telephone number."

"About twice a week," he said, "Connie has something she must tell you right away, that she couldn't possibly say over the telephone. Usually it turns out she's caught the butler drinking again."

"I see," she said.

"Well," he said. "Poor little Connie."

"Poor little Connie," she said. "Oh, my God. That saber-toothed tigress. Poor little Connie."

"Darling, why do we have to waste time talking about Connie Holt?" he said. "Can't we just be peaceful?"

"Not while that she-beast prowls the streets," she said. "Is she coming in to town tonight?"

"Well, she was," he said, "but then she more or less said she wouldn't."

"Oh, she will," she said. "You get right down out of that fool's paradise you're in. She'll shoot out of Greenwich like a bat out of hell, if she thinks there's a chance of seeing you. Ah, Hobie, you don't really want to see that old thing, do you? Do you? Because if you do—Well, I suppose maybe you do. Naturally, if she has something she must tell you right away, you want to see her. Look, Hobie, you know you can see me any time. It isn't a bit important, seeing me tonight. Why don't you call up Mrs. Holt and tell her to take the next train in? She'd get here quicker by train than by motor, wouldn't she? Please go ahead and do it. It's quite all right about me. Really."

"You know," he said, "I knew that was coming. I could tell it by the way you were when I came back from the telephone. Oh, Kit, what makes you want to talk like that? You know damned well the last thing I want to do is see Connie Holt. You know how I want to be with you. Why do you want to work up all this? I watched you just sit there and deliberately talk yourself into it, starting right out of nothing. Now what's the idea of that? Oh, good Lord, what's the matter with women, anyway?"

"Please don't call me 'women,' " she said.

"I'm sorry, darling," he said. "I didn't mean to use bad words." He smiled at her. She felt her heart go liquid, but she did her best to be harder won.

"Doubtless," she said, and her words fell like snow when there is no wind, "I spoke ill-advisedly. If I said, as I must have, something to distress you, I can only beg you to believe that that was my misfortune, and not my intention. It seemed to me as if I were doing only a courteous thing in suggesting that you need feel no obligation about spending the evening with me, when you would naturally wish to be with Mrs. Holt. I simply felt that—Oh, the hell with it! I'm no good at this. Of course I didn't mean it, dearest. If you had said, 'All right,' and had gone and told her to come in, I should have died. I just said it because

I wanted to hear you say it was me you wanted to be with. Oh, I need to hear you say that, Hobie. It's—it's what I live on, darling."

"Kit," he said, "you ought to know, without my saying it. You know. It's this feeling you *have* to say things—that's what spoils everything."

"I suppose so," she said. "I suppose I know so. Only—the thing is, I get so mixed up, I just—I just can't go on. I've got to be reassured, dearest. I didn't need to be at first, when everything was gay and sure, but things aren't—well, they aren't the same now. There seem to be so many others that— So I need so terribly to have you tell me that it's me and not anybody else. Oh, I *had* to have you say that, a few minutes ago. Look, Hobie. How do you think it makes me feel to sit here and hear you lie to Connie Holt—to hear you say you have to go out with friends of your sister's? Now why couldn't you say you had a date with me? Are you ashamed of me, Hobie? Is that it?"

"Oh, Kit," he said, "for heaven's sake! I don't know why I did it. I did it before I even thought. I did it—well, sort of instinctively, I guess, because it seemed to be the easiest thing to do. I suppose I'm just weak."

"No!" she said. "You weak? Well! And is there any other news tonight?"

"I know I am," he said. "I know it's weak to do anything in the world to avoid a scene."

"Exactly what," she said, "is Mrs. Holt to you and you to her that she may make a scene if she learns that you have an engagement with another woman?"

"Oh, God!" he said. "I told you I don't give a damn about Connie Holt. She's nothing to me. Now will you for God's sake let it drop?"

"Oh, she's nothing to you," she said. "I see. Naturally, that would be why you called her 'dear' every other word."

"If I did," he said, "I never knew I was saying it. Good Lord, that doesn't mean anything. It's simply a—a form of nervousness, I suppose. I say it when I can't think what to call people. Why, I call telephone operators 'dear.' "

"I'm sure you do!" she said.

They glared. It was the young man who gave first. He went and sat close to her on the sofa, and for a while there were only murmurs. Then he said, "Will you stop? Will you stop it? Will you always be just like this—just sweet and the way you're meant to be and no fighting?"

"I will," she said. "Honest, I mean to. Let's not let anything come between us again ever. Mrs. Holt, indeed! Hell with her."

"Hell with her," he said. There was another silence, during which the young man did several things that he did extraordinarily well.

Suddenly the young woman stiffened her arms and pushed him away from her.

"And how do I know," she said, "that the way you talk to me about Connie Holt isn't just the way you talk to her about me when I'm not here? How do I know that?"

"Oh, my Lord," he said. "Oh, my dear, sweet Lord. Just when everything was all right. Ah, stop it, will you, baby? Let's just be quiet. Like this. See?"

A little later he said. "Look, sweet, how about a cocktail? Mightn't that be an idea? I'll go make them. And would you like the lights lighted?"

"Oh, no," she said. "I like it better in the dusk, like this. It's sweet. Dusk is so personal, somehow. And this way you can't see those lampshades. Hobie, if you knew how I hate your lampshades!"

"Honestly?" he said, with less injury than bewilderment in his voice. He looked at the shades as if he saw them for the first time. They were of vellum, or some substance near it, and upon each was painted a panorama of the right bank of the Seine, with the minute windows of the buildings cut out, under the direction of a superior mind, so that light might come through. "What's the matter with them, Kit?"

"Dearest, if you don't know, I can't ever explain it to you," she said. "Among other things, they're banal, inappropriate, and unbeautiful. They're exactly what Evie Maynard *would* have chosen. She thinks, just because they show views of Paris, that they're pretty darned sophisticated. She is that not uncommon type of woman that thinks any reference to la belle France is an invitation to the waltz. 'Not uncommon.' If that isn't the mildest word-picture that ever was painted of that——"

"Don't you like the way she decorated the apartment?" he said.

"Sweetheart," she said. "I think it's poisonous. You know that."

"Would you like to do it over?" he said.

"I should say not," she said. "Look, Hobie, don't you remember me? I'm the one that doesn't want to decorate your flat. Now do you place me? But if I ever *did,* the first thing I should do would be to paint these walls putty color—no, I guess first I'd tear off all this chintz and fling it to the winds, and then I'd——"

The telephone rang.

The young man threw one stricken glance at the young woman and then sat motionless. The jangles of the bell cut the dusk like little scissors.

"I think," said the young woman, exquisitely, "that your telephone is ringing. Don't let me keep you from answering it. As a matter of fact, I really must go powder my nose."

She sprang up, dashed through the bedroom, and into the bathroom. There was the sound of a closed door, the grind of a firmly turned key, and then immediately the noise of rushing waters.

When she returned, eventually, to the living-room, the young man was pouring a pale, cold liquid into small glasses. He gave one to her, and smiled at her over it. It was his wistful smile. It was of his best.

"Hobie," she said, "is there a livery stable anywhere around here where they rent wild horses?"

"What?" he said.

"Because if there is," she said, "I wish you'd call up and ask them to send over a couple of teams. I want to show you they couldn't drag me into asking who that was on the telephone."

"Oh," he said, and tried his cocktail. "Is this dry enough, sweet? Because you like them dry, don't you? Sure it's all right? Really? Ah, wait a second, darling. Let *me* light your cigarette. There. Sure you're all right?"

"I can't stand it," she said. "I just lost all my strength of purpose— maybe the maid will find it on the floor in the morning. Hobart Ogden, who was that on the telephone?"

"Oh, that?" he said. "Well, that was a certain lady who shall be nameless."

"I'm sure she should be," she said. "She doubtless has all the other qualities of a—Well. I didn't quite say it, I'm keeping my head. Ah, dearest, was that Connie Holt again?"

"No, that was the funniest thing," he said. "That was Evie Maynard. Just when we were talking about her."

"Well, well, well," she said. "Isn't it a small world? And what's on her mind, if I may so flatter her? Is *her* butler tight, too?"

"Evie hasn't got a butler," he said. He tried smiling again, but found it better to abandon the idea and concentrate on refilling the young woman's glass. "No, she's just dizzy, the same as usual. She's got a cocktail party at her apartment, and they all want to go out on the town, that's all."

"Luckily," she said, "you had to go out with these friends of your sister's. You were just going out the door when she called."

"I never told her any such thing!" he said. "I said I had a date I'd been looking forward to all week."

"Oh, you didn't mention any names?" she said.

"There's no reason why I should, to Evie Maynard," he said. "It's none of her affair, any more than what she's doing and who she's doing it with is any concern of mine. She's nothing in my life. You know that. I've hardly seen her since she did the apartment. I don't care if I never see her again. I'd *rather* I never saw her again."

"I should think that might be managed, if you've really set your heart on it," she said.

"Well, I do what I can," he said. "She wanted to come in now for a cocktail, she and some of those interior decorator boys she has with her, and I told her absolutely no."

"And you think that will keep her away?" she said. "Oh, no. She'll be here. She and her feathered friends. Let's see—they ought to arrive just about the time that Mrs. Holt has thought it over and come in to town. Well. It's shaping up into a lovely evening, isn't it?"

"Great," he said. "And if I may say so, you're doing everything you can to make it harder, you little sweet." He poured more cocktails. "Oh, Kit, why are you being so nasty? Don't do it, darling. It's not like you. It's so unbecoming to you."

"I know it's horrible," she said. "It's—well, I do it in defense, I suppose, Hobie. If I didn't say nasty things, I'd cry. I'm afraid to cry; it would take me so long to stop. I—oh, I'm so hurt, dear. I don't know what to think. All these women. All these awful women. If they were fine, if they were sweet and gentle and intelligent, I shouldn't mind. Or maybe I should. I don't know. I don't know much of anything, any more. My mind goes round and round. I thought what we had was so different. Well—it wasn't. Sometimes I think it would be better never to see you any more. But then I know I couldn't stand that. I'm too far gone now. I'd do anything to be with you! And so I'm just another of those women to you. And I used to come first, Hobie—oh, I did! I did!"

"You did!" he said. "And you do!"

"And I always will?" she said.

"And you always will," he said, "as long as you'll only be your own self. Please be sweet again, Kit. Like this, darling. Like this, child."

Again they were close, and again there was no sound.

The telephone rang.

They started as if the same arrow had pierced them. Then the young woman moved slowly back.

"You know," she said, musingly, "this is my fault. I did this. It was me. I was the one that said let's meet here, and not at my house. I said it would be quieter, and I had so much I wanted to talk to you about. I said we could be quiet and alone here. Yes, I said that."

"I give you my word," he said, "that damn thing hasn't rung in a week."

"It was lucky for me, wasn't it?" she said, "that I happened to be here the last time it did. I am known as Little Miss Horseshoes. Well. Oh, please do answer it, Hobie. It drives me even crazier to have it ring like this."

"I hope to God," the young man said, "that it's a wrong number." He held her to him, hard. "Darling," he said. Then he went to the telephone.

"Hello," he said into the receiver. "Yes? Oh, hello there. How are you, dear—how are you? Oh, did you? Ah, that's too bad. Why, you see I was out with these friends on my—I was out till quite late. Oh, you did? Oh, that's too bad, dear, you waited up all that time. No, I did *not* say that, Margot, I said I'd come if I possibly could. That's exactly what I said. I did so. Well, then you misunderstood me. Well, you must have. Now, there's no need to be unreasonable about it. Listen, what I said, I said I'd come if it was possible, but I didn't think there was a chance. If you think hard, you'll remember, dear. Well, I'm terribly sorry, but I don't see what you're making so much fuss about. It was just a misunderstanding, that's all. Why don't you calm down and be a good little girl? Won't you? Why, I can't tonight, dear. Because I *can't*. Well, I have a date I've had for a long time. Yes. Oh, no, it isn't anything like that! Oh, now, please, Margot! Margot, please don't! Now don't do that! I tell you I won't be here. All right, come ahead, but I won't be in. Listen, I can't talk to you when you're like this. I'll call you tomorrow, dear. I tell you I won't be *in*, dear! Please be good. Certainly I do. Look. I have to run now. I'll call you, dear. 'By."

The young man came back to the living-room, and sent his somewhat shaken voice ahead of him.

"How about another cocktail, sweet?" he said. "Don't you think we really ought—" Through the thickening dark, he saw the young woman. She stood straight and tense. Her fur scarf was knotted about her shoulders, and she was drawing on her second glove.

"What's this about?" the young man said.

"I'm so sorry," the young woman said, "but I truly must go home."

"Oh, really?" he said. "May I ask why?"

"It's sweet of you," she said, "to be interested enough to want to know. Thank you so much. Well, it just happens, I can't stand any more of this. There is somewhere, I think, some proverb about a worm's eventually turning. It is doubtless from the Arabic. They so often are. Well, good night, Hobie, and thank you so much for those delicious cocktails. They've cheered me up wonderfully."

She held out her hand. He caught it tight in both of his.

"Ah, now listen," he said. "Please don't do this, Kit. Please, don't, darling. Please. This is just the way you were last Wednesday."

"Yes," she said. "And for exactly the same reason. Please give me back my hand. Thank you. Well, good night, Hobie, and good luck, always."

"All right," he said. "If this is what you want to do."

"Want to do!" she said. "It's nothing *I* want. I simply felt it would be rather easier for you if you could be alone, to receive your telephone calls. Surely you cannot blame me for feeling a bit *de trop*."

"My Lord, do you think I want to talk to those fools?" he said. "What can I do? Take the telephone receiver off? Is that what you want me to do?"

"It's a good trick of yours," she said. "I gather that was what you did last Wednesday night, when I kept trying to call you after I'd gone home, when I was in holy agony there."

"I did not!" he said. "They must have been calling the wrong number. I tell you I was alone here all the time you were gone."

"So you said," she said.

"I don't lie to you, Kit," he said.

"That," she said, "is the most outrageous lie you have ever told me. Good night, Hobie."

Only from the young man's eyes and voice could his anger be judged. The beautiful scroll of his mouth never straightened. He took her hand and bowed over it.

"Good night, Kit," he said.

"Good night," she said. "Well, good night. I'm sorry it must end like this. But if you want other things—well, they're what you want. You can't have both them and me. Good night, Hobie."

"Good night, Kit," he said.

"I'm sorry," she said. "It does seem too bad. Doesn't it?"

"It's what you want," he said.

"I?" she said. "It's what *you* do."

"Oh, Kit, can't you understand?" he said. "You always used to. Don't you know how I am? I just say things and do things that don't mean anything, just for the sake of peace, just for the sake of not having a feud. That's what gets me in trouble. You don't have to do it, I know. You're luckier than I am."

"Luckier?" she said. "Curious word."

"Well, stronger, then," he said. "Finer. Honester. Decenter. All those. Ah, don't do this, Kit. Please. Please take those things off, and come sit down."

"Sit down?" she said. "And wait for the ladies to gather?"

"They're not coming," he said.

"How do you know?" she said. "They've come here before, haven't they? How do you know they won't come tonight?"

"I don't know!" he said. "I don't know what the hell they'll do. I don't know what the hell you'll do, any more. And I thought you were different!"

"I was different," she said, "just so long as you thought I was different."

"Ah, Kit," he said, "Kit. Darling. Come and be the way we were. Come and be sweet and peaceful. Look. Let's have a cocktail, just to each other, and then let's go out to some quiet place for dinner, where we can talk. Will you?"

"Well——" she said. "If you think——"

"I think," he said.

The telephone rang.

"Oh, my *God*!" shrieked the young woman. "Go answer it, you damned—you damned *stallion*!"

She rushed for the door, opened it, and was gone. She was, after all, different. She neither slammed the door nor left it stark open.

The young man stood, and he shook his remarkable head slowly. Slowly, too, he turned and went into the bedroom.

He spoke into the telephone receiver drearily at first, then he seemed to enjoy both hearing and speaking. He used a woman's name in address. It was not Connie; it was not Evie; it was not Margot. Glowingly he besought the unseen one to meet him; tepidly he agreed to await her coming where he was. He besought her, then, to ring his bell first three times and then twice, for admission. No, no, no, he said, this was not for any reason that might have occurred to her; it was simply that some business friend of his had said something about dropping in, and he wanted to make sure there would be no such intruders. He spoke of his hopes, indeed his assurances, of an evening of sweetness and peace. He said "good-by," and he said "dear."

The very good-looking young man hung up the receiver, and looked long at the dial of his wrist-watch, now delicately luminous. He seemed to be calculating. So long for a young woman to reach her home, and fling herself upon her couch, so long for tears, so long for exhaustion, so long for remorse, so long for rising tenderness. Thoughtfully he lifted the receiver from its hook and set it on end upon the little table.

Then he went into the living-room, and sped the dark before the tiny beams that sifted through the little open windows in the panoramas of Paris.

Harper's Bazaar, September 1932

A Young Woman in Green Lace

The young man in the sharply cut dinner jacket crossed the filled room and stopped in front of the young woman in green lace and possible pearls. He was, you must have said, a young man of imagination, strength of purpose, and a likable receptivity of the new, for such garments as his do not come about by accident; thought goes into their selection, and time, and both must be backed by a fine self-belief. From the young man's coat, more surely than from his palm, might be read the ingredients of his character. Whimsy peeped around the lapels of that coat; balance showed in the double march of its buttons; and the color of its material, the dreamy blue of a spring midnight, confessed a deep strain of sentiment. The face above the jacket was neat and spare, and wore, at the moment, a look of pleading.

"Good evening," the young man said. "At least, I beg your pardon. At least, I wonder if you'd mind if I sat down here beside of you. If you wouldn't mind, that is. If you'd let me, at least."

"But certainly," the young woman said, for she had recently returned from France. "But of course."

She lent him room on the little sofa where she sat, light and languid, and he rested none too easily beside her. He set his gaze upon her face, nor did he take it away.

"You know, this is terribly nice of you to let me do this," he said. "It's—well, what I mean is, I was afraid maybe you wouldn't."

"But no!" she said.

"You see," he said, "I've been looking at you all evening. At least, I couldn't get my eyes off of you. Honest. First thing I saw you, I tried to get Marge to introduce me, but she's been so busy fixing drinks and everything, I couldn't get near her. And then I saw you come and sit here, all by yourself, and I've been trying to get up my nerve to come over and talk to you. I thought you might be sore or something, at least. I'd get all set to start over, and then I'd think, 'Oh, she's so sweet and pretty, she'll just give me the bum's rush.' I thought you'd be sore or something, me coming over and talking to you without an introduction, I mean."

"Oh, *non*," she said. "Why, I'd never dream of being sore. Abroad, you know, they say the roof is an introduction."

"Beg pardon?" he said.

"That's what they say abroad," she said. "In Paris and places. You go to a party, and the person that's giving the party doesn't introduce anybody to anybody. They just take it for granted that everybody will talk to everybody else, because they take it for granted that their friends are their friends' friends. *Comprenez-vous?* Oh, I'm sorry. Slips. I *must* stop talking French. Only it's so hard, once you get into the habit of rattling it off. I mean, see what I mean? Why, I'd forgotten all about people having to be introduced to other people at a party."

"Well, I'm certainly glad you aren't sore," he said. "At least, it's wonderful for me. Only maybe you'd rather be alone, here. Would you?"

"Oh, *non, non, non, non, non,*" she said. "Goodness, no. I was just sitting here, watching everybody. I feel as if I don't know a soul since I've come back. But it's so interesting, just to sit and watch the way people behave and their clothes and everything. You feel as if you were in another world. Well, you know how you feel when you've come back from being abroad. Don't you?"

"I've never been abroad," he said.

"Oh, my," she said. "Oh, *là-là-là*. Haven't you really? Well, you must go, the very first minute you can. You'll adore it. I can tell just by looking at you you'll be crazy over it."

"Were you abroad long?" he said.

"I was in Paris over three weeks," she said.

"That's one place I'd like to go," he said. "I guess that must be tops."

"Oh, don't talk about it," she said. "It makes me so homesick I can't see straight. Oh, Paree, Paree, *ma chère* Paree. I just feel as though it's *my* city. Honestly, I don't know how I'm ever going to get along away from it. I'd like to go right straight back this minute."

"Hey, don't talk like that, will you?" he said. "We need you around here. At least, don't go back yet a while, will you please? I've only just met you."

"Oh, that's sweet of you," she said. "Goodness, so few American men know how to talk to a woman. I guess they're all too busy, or something. Everybody seems in such a hurry—no time for anything but money, money, money. Well, *c'est ça,* I suppose."

"We could find time for other things," he said. "There's a lot of fun we could have. There's a lot of fun around New York, at least."

"This old New York!" she said. "I don't believe I'll ever get used to it. There's nothing to *do* here. Now in Paris, it's so picturesque and everything, you're never blue a second. And there are all these cute little places where you can go and have a drink, when you want. Oh, it's wonderful."

"I know any amount of cute little places where you can go and have a drink," he said. "I can take you to any one of them in ten minutes."

"It wouldn't be like Paris," she said. "Oh, every time I think of it, I get *terriblement triste*. Darn it, there I go again. Will I *ever* remember?"

"Look," he said, "can't I get you a drink now? Why, you haven't been doing a thing. What would you like?"

"Oh, *mon dieu*, I don't know," she said. "I've got so in the habit of drinking champagne that really— What have they got? What do people drink here, anyway?"

"Well, there's Scotch and gin," he said, "and I think maybe there's some rye out in the dining-room. At least there may be."

"How funny!" she said. "You forget about the terrible things that people drink. Well, when in Rome— Gin, I guess."

"With ginger ale?" he said.

"Quel horreur!" she said. "No, just plain, I think, just—what do you call it?—straight."

"I'll be right back," he said, "and it'll be too long."

He left her and quickly returned, bearing little full glasses. Carefully he presented one to her.

"Merci mille fois," she said. "Oh, darn me. Thank you, I mean."

The young man sat down again beside her. He drank, but he did not look at the glass in his hand. He looked at the young woman.

"J'ai soif," she said. *"Mon dieu.* I hope you don't think I swear terribly. I've got so in the way of doing it, I really don't realize what I'm saying. And in French, you know, they don't think anything of it at all. Everybody says it. It isn't even like swearing. Ugh. My goodness, this is strong."

"It's all right, though," he said. "Marge has a good man."

"Marge?" she said. "A good man?"

"At least," he said, "the stuff isn't cut."

"Stuff?" she said. "Isn't cut?"

"She's got a good bootlegger, at least," he said. "I wouldn't be much surprised if he really did get it off the boat."

"Oh, please don't talk about boats!" she said. "It makes me so home-sick, I just nearly die. It makes me want to get right on a boat now."

"Ah, don't," he said. "Give me just a little chance. Lord, when I think I nearly passed up this party. Honestly, I wasn't going to come at first. And then the minute I saw you, I knew I'd never been so right in my life. At least, when I saw you sitting there and that dress and everything—well, I went for a loop, that's all."

"What, this old thing?" she said. "Why, it's old as the hills. I got it before I went abroad. I sort of didn't want to wear any of my French things tonight because—well, of course no one thinks anything of them over there, but I thought maybe these New York people might think they were pretty extreme. You know how Paris clothes are. They're so Frenchy."

"Would I like to see you in them," he said. "Boy! Why, I'd— Hey, there isn't anything in your glass. Here, let me fix that up for you. And don't move, will you?"

Again he went and came back, and again he bore glasses filled with colorless fluid. He resumed looking at the young woman.

"Well," she said. "*À votre santé*. Heavens, I wish I could stop that. I mean good luck."

"I've got it," he said, "ever since I met you. I wish—at least I wish we could get off somewhere away from here. Marge says they're going to roll back the rugs and dance, and everybody'll be wanting to dance with you, and I won't have a prayer."

"Oh, I don't want to dance," she said. "American men dance so badly, most of them. And I don't want to meet a lot of people, anyway. It's awfully hard for me to talk to them. I can't seem to understand what they're talking about, since I've been back. I suppose they think their slang is funny, but I don't see it."

"You know what we might do," he said, "if you would, at least? We might wait till they start dancing, and then just ease out. We might do the town for a while. What would you say, at least?"

"You know, that might be rather amusing," she said. "I'd really like to see some of your new little *bistros*—what do you call them?—oh, you know what I mean—speakeasies. I hear some of them are really quite interesting. I suppose this stuff is strong, but it doesn't seem to do anything at all to me. It must be because I haven't been used to anything but those wonderful French wines."

"Can I get you some more?" he said.

"Well," she said, "I might have a little. One has to do what everybody else does, don't you?"

"Same thing?" he said. "Straight gin?"

"*S'il vous plaît,*" she said. "But yes."

"Lady," he said, "can you take it! Are we going to have an evening!"

For the third time he went and came. For the third time he watched her though he drank.

"Ce n'est pas mal," she said. *"Pas du tout,* at all. There's a little place in one of the Boulevards—they're those big avenues they have— that has a sort of cordial that tastes almost exactly like this. My, I'd like to be there now."

"Ah, no, you wouldn't," he said. "Would you, really? You won't after a little while, anyway. There's a little place on Fifty-Second Street I want to take you first. Look, when they start dancing, what do you say you get your coat, or at least whatever you have, and meet me in the hall? There's no sense saying good-night. Marge will never know. I can show you a couple of places might make you forget Paris."

"Oh, don't say that," she said. "Please. As if I could ever forget my Paree! You just can't know how I feel about it. Every time anybody says 'Paris,' I just want to cry and cry."

"You can even do that," he said, "at least as long as you do it on my shoulder. It's waiting right here for you. What do you say we get started, baby? Mind if I call you baby? Let's go get ourselves a couple of pretty edges. How are you coming with that gin? Finished? Atta girl. How about it we go out now and get stinking?"

"But oke!" said the young woman in green lace.

They went out.

The New Yorker, September 24, 1932

Horsie

When young Mrs. Gerald Cruger came home from the hospital, Miss Wilmarth came along with her and the baby. Miss Wilmarth was an admirable trained nurse, sure and calm and tireless, with a real taste for the arranging of flowers in bowls and vases. She had never known a patient to receive so many flowers, or such uncommon ones; yellow violets and strange lilies and little white orchids poised like a bevy of delicate moths along green branches. Care and thought must have been put into their selection that they, like all the other fragile and costly things she kept about her, should be so right for young Mrs. Cruger. No one who knew her could have caught up the telephone and lightly bidden the florist to deliver her one of his five-dollar assortments of tulips, stock, and daffodils. Camilla Cruger was no complement to garden blooms.

Sometimes, when she opened the shiny boxes and carefully grouped the cards, there would come a curious expression upon Miss Wilmarth's face. Playing over shorter features, it might almost have been one of wistfulness. Upon Miss Wilmarth, it served to perfect the strange resemblance that she bore through her years; her face was truly complete with that look of friendly melancholy peculiar to the gentle horse. It was not, of course, Miss Wilmarth's fault that she looked like a horse. Indeed, there was nowhere to attach any blame. But the resemblance remained.

She was tall, pronounced of bone, and erect of carriage; it was somehow impossible to speculate upon her appearance undressed. Her long face was innocent, indeed ignorant, of cosmetics, and its color stayed steady. Confusion, heat, or haste caused her neck to flush crimson. Her mild hair was pinned with loops of nicked black wire into a narrow knot, practical to support her little high cap, like a charlotte russe from a bake-shop. She had big, trustworthy hands, scrubbed and dry, with nails cut short and so deeply cleaned with some small sharp instrument that the ends stood away from the spatulate finger-tips. Gerald Cruger, who nightly sat opposite her at his own dinner table, tried not to see her hands. It irritated him to be reminded by their sight that they must feel like straw matting and smell of white soap. For him, women who were not softly lovely were simply not women.

He tried, too, so far as it was possible to his beautiful manners, to keep his eyes from her face. Not that it was unpleasant—a kind face, certainly. But, as he told Camilla, once he looked he stayed fascinated, awaiting the toss and the whinny.

"I love horses, myself," he said to Camilla, who lay all white and languid on her apricot satin chaise-longue. "I'm a fool for a horse. Ah, what a noble animal, darling! All I say is, nobody has any business to go around looking like a horse and behaving as if it were all right. You don't catch horses going around looking like people, do you?"

He did not dislike Miss Wilmarth; he only resented her. He had no bad wish in the world for her, but he waited with longing the day she would leave. She was so skilled and rhythmic in her work that she disrupted the household but little. Nevertheless, her presence was an onus. There was that thing of dining with her every evening. It was a chore for him, certainly, and one that did not ease with repetition, but there was no choice. Everyone had always heard of trained nurses' bristling insistence that they be not treated as servants; Miss Wilmarth could not be asked to dine with the maids. He would not have dinner out; be away from *Camilla*? It was too much to expect the maids to institute a second dinner service or to carry trays, other than Camilla's, up and down the stairs. There were only three servants and they had work enough.

"Those children," Camilla's mother was wont to say, chuckling. "Those two kids. The independence of them! Struggling along on cheese and kisses. Why, they hardly let me pay for the trained nurse. And it was all we could do, last Christmas, to make Camilla take the Packard and the chauffeur."

So Gerald dined each night with Miss Wilmarth. The small dread of his hour with her struck suddenly at him in the afternoon. He would forget it for stretches of minutes, only to be smitten sharper as the time drew near. On his way home from his office, he found grim entertainment in rehearsing his table talk, and plotting desperate innovations to it.

Cruger's Compulsory Conversations: Lesson I, a Dinner with a Miss Wilmarth, a Trained Nurse. Good evening, Miss Wilmarth. Well! And how were the patients all day? That's good, that's fine. Well! The baby gained two ounces, did she? That's fine. Yes, that's right, she will be before we know it. That's right. Well! Mrs. Cruger seems to be getting stronger every day, doesn't she? That's good, that's fine. That's right, up and about before we know it. Yes, she certainly will. Well! Any visitors today? That's good. Didn't stay too long, did they? That's fine. Well! No, no, no, Miss Wilmarth—*you* go ahead. I wasn't going to say anything at all, really. No, really. Well! Well! I see where they found those two aviators after all. Yes, they certainly do run risks. That's right. Yes. Well! I see where they've been having a regular old-fashioned blizzard out west. Yes, we certainly have had a mild winter. That's right. Well! I see where they held up that jeweler's shop right in broad daylight on Fifth Avenue. Yes, I certainly don't know what we're coming to. That's right. Well! I see the cat. Do you see the cat? The cat is on the mat. It certainly is. Well! Pardon me, Miss Wilmarth, but must you look so much like a horse? Do you like to look like a horse, Miss Wilmarth? That's good, Miss Wilmarth, that's fine. You certainly do, Miss Wilmarth. That's right. Well! Will you for God's sake finish your oats, Miss Wilmarth, and let me get out of this?

Every evening he reached the dining-room before Miss Wilmarth and stared gloomily at silver and candle-flame until she was upon him. No sound of footfall heralded her coming, for her ample canvas oxfords were soled with rubber; there would be a protest of parquet, a trembling of ornaments, a creak, a rustle, and the authoritative smell of stiff linen; and there she would be, set for her ritual of evening cheer.

"Well, Mary," she would cry to the waitress, "you know what they say—better late than never!"

But no smile would mellow Mary's lips, no light her eyes. Mary, in converse with the cook, habitually referred to Miss Wilmarth as "that one." She wished no truck with Miss Wilmarth or any of the others of her guild; always in and out of a person's pantry.

Once or twice Gerald saw a strange expression upon Miss Wilmarth's face as she witnessed the failure of her adage with the maid. He could not quite classify it. Though he did not know, it was the look she sometimes had when she opened the shiny white boxes and lifted the exquisite, scentless blossoms that were sent to Camilla. Anyway, whatever it was, it increased her equine resemblance to such a point that he thought of proffering her an apple.

But she always had her big smile turned toward him when she sat down. Then she would look at the thick watch strapped to her wrist and give a little squeal that brought the edges of his teeth together.

"Mercy!" she would say. "My good mercy! Why, I had no more idea it was so late. Well, you mustn't blame me, Mr. Cruger. Don't you scold *me*. You'll just have to blame that daughter of yours. She's the one that keeps us all busy."

"She certainly is," he would say. "That's right."

He would think, and with small pleasure, of the infant Diane, pink and undistinguished and angry, among the ruffles and *choux* of her bassinet. It was her doing that Camilla had stayed so long away from him in the odorous limbo of the hospital, her doing that Camilla lay all day upon her apricot satin chaise-longue. "We must take our time," the doctor said, "just ta-a-ake our ti-yem." Yes; well, that would all be because of young Diane. It was because of her, indeed, that night upon night he must face Miss Wilmarth and comb up conversation. All right, young Diane, there you are and nothing to do about it. But you'll be an only child, young woman, that's what you'll be.

Always Miss Wilmarth followed her opening pleasantry about the baby with a companion piece. Gerald had come to know it so well he could have said it in duet with her.

"You wait," she would say. "Just you wait. You're the one that's going to be kept busy when the beaux start coming around. You'll see. That young lady's going to be a heart-breaker if ever I saw one."

"I guess that's right," Gerald would say, and he would essay a small laugh and fail at it. It made him uncomfortable, somehow embarrassed him to hear Miss Wilmarth banter of swains and conquest. It was unseemly, as rouge would have been unseemly on her long mouth and perfume on her flat bosom.

He would hurry her over to her own ground. "Well!" he would say. "Well! And how were the patients all day?"

But that, even with the baby's weight and the list of the day's visitors, seldom lasted past the soup.

"Doesn't that woman ever go out?" he asked Camilla. "Doesn't our Horsie ever rate a night off?"

"Where would she want to go?" Camilla said. Her low, lazy words had always the trick of seeming a little weary of their subject.

"Well," Gerald said, "she might take herself a moonlight canter around the park."

"Oh, she doubtless gets a thrill out of dining with you," Camilla said. "You're a man, they tell me, and she can't have seen many. Poor old horse. She's not a bad soul."

"Yes," he said. "And what a round of pleasure it is, having dinner every night with Not a Bad Soul."

"What makes you think," Camilla said, "that I am caught up in any whirl of gaiety, lying here?"

"Oh, darling," he said. "Oh, my poor darling. I didn't mean it, honestly I didn't. Oh, *lord,* I didn't mean it. How could I complain, after all you've been through, and I haven't done a thing? Please, sweet, please. Ah, Camilla, say you know I didn't mean it."

"After all," Camilla said, "you just have her at dinner. I have her around all day."

"Sweetheart, please," he said. "Oh, poor angel."

He dropped to his knees by the chaise-longue and crushed her limp, fragrant hand against his mouth. Then he remembered about being very, very gentle. He ran little apologetic kisses up and down her fingers and murmured of gardenias and lilies and thus exhausted his knowledge of white flowers.

Her visitors said that Camilla looked lovelier than ever, but they were mistaken. She was only as lovely as she had always been. They spoke in hushed voices of the new look in her eyes since her motherhood; but it was the same far brightness that had always lain there. They said how white she was and how lifted above other people; they forgot that she had always been pale as moonlight and had always worn a delicate disdain, as light as the lace that covered her breast. Her doctor cautioned tenderly against hurry, besought her to take recovery slowly— Camilla, who had never done anything quickly in her life. Her friends gathered, adoring, about the apricot satin chaise-longue where Camilla lay and moved her hands as if they hung heavy from her wrists; they had been wont before to gather and adore at the white satin sofa in the drawing-room where Camilla reclined, her hands like heavy lilies in a languid breeze. Every night, when Gerald crossed the threshold of her fragrant room, his heart leaped and his words caught in his throat; but those things had always befallen him at the sight of her. Motherhood had not brought perfection to Camilla's loveliness. She had had that before.

Gerald came home early enough, each evening, to have a while with her before dinner. He made his cocktails in her room, and watched her as she slowly drank one. Miss Wilmarth was in and out, touching flowers, patting pillows. Sometimes she brought Diane in on display, and those would be minutes of real discomfort for Gerald. He could not bear to watch her with the baby in her arms, so acute was his vicarious embarrassment at her behavior. She would bring her long head down close to Diane's tiny, stern face and toss it back again high on her rangy neck, all the while that strange words, in a strange high voice, came from her.

"Well, her wuzza boofull dirl. Ess, her wuzza. Her wuzza, wuzza, wuzza. Ess, her *wuzz*." She would bring the baby over to him. "See, Daddy. Isn't us a gate, bid dirl? Isn't us boofull? Say 'nigh-nigh,' Daddy. Us doe teepy-bye, now. Say 'nigh-nigh.' "

Oh, God.

Then she would bring the baby to Camilla. "Say 'nigh-nigh,' " she would cry. " 'Nigh-nigh,' Mummy."

"If that brat ever calls you 'Mummy,' " he told Camilla once, fiercely, "I'll turn her out in the snow."

Camilla would look at the baby, amusement in her slow glance. "Good night, useless," she would say. She would hold out a finger, for Diane's pink hand to curl around. And Gerald's heart would quicken, and his eyes sting and shine.

Once he tore his gaze from Camilla to look at Miss Wilmarth, surprised by the sudden cessation of her falsetto. She was no longer lowering her head and tossing it back. She was standing quite still, looking at him over the baby; she looked away quickly, but not before he had seen that curious expression on her face again. It puzzled him, made him vaguely uneasy. That night, she made no further exhortations to Diane's parents to utter the phrase "nigh-nigh." In silence she carried the baby out of the room and back to the nursery.

One evening, Gerald brought two men home with him; lean, easily dressed young men, good at golf and squash rackets, his companions through his college and in his clubs. They had cocktails in Camilla's room, grouped about the chaise-longue. Miss Wilmarth, standing in the nursery adjoining, testing the temperature of the baby's milk against her wrist, could hear them all talking lightly and swiftly, tossing their sentences into the air to hang there unfinished. Now and again she could distinguish Camilla's lazy voice; the others stopped immediately when she spoke, and when she was done there were long peals of laughter. Miss Wilmarth pictured her lying there, in golden chiffon and deep lace, her light figure turned always a little away from those about her, so that she must move her head and speak her slow words over her shoulder to them. The trained nurse's face was astoundingly equine as she looked at the wall that separated them.

They stayed in Camilla's room a long time, and there was always more laughter. The door from the nursery into the hall was open, and presently she heard the door of Camilla's room being opened, too. She had been able to hear only voices before, but now she could distinguish Gerald's words as he called back from the threshold; they had no meaning to her.

"Only wait, fellers," he said. "Wait till you see Seabiscuit."

He came to the nursery door. He held a cocktail shaker in one hand and a filled glass in the other.

"Oh, Miss Wilmarth," he said. "Oh, good evening, Miss Wilmarth. Why, I didn't know this door was open—I mean, I hope we haven't been disturbing you."

"Oh, not the least little bit," she said. "Goodness."

"Well!" he said. "I—we were wondering if you wouldn't have a little cocktail. Won't you please?" He held out the glass to her.

"Mercy," she said, taking it. "Why, thank you ever so much. Thank you, Mr. Cruger."

"And, oh, Miss Wilmarth," he said, "would you tell Mary there'll be two more to dinner? And ask her not to have it before half an hour or so, will you? Would you mind?"

"Not the least little bit," she said. "Of course I will."

"Thank you," he said. "Well! Thank you, Miss Wilmarth. Well! See you at dinner."

"Thank *you*," she said. "I'm the one that ought to thank *you*. For the lovely little cockytail."

"Oh," he said, and failed at an easy laugh. He went back into Camilla's room and closed the door behind him.

Miss Wilmarth set her cocktail upon a table, and went down to inform Mary of the impending guests. She felt light and quick, and she told Mary gaily, awaiting a flash of gaiety in response. But Mary received the news impassively, made a grunt but no words, and slammed out through the swinging doors into the kitchen. Miss Wilmarth stood looking after her. Somehow servants never seemed to— She should have become used to it.

Even though the dinner hour was delayed, Miss Wilmarth was a little late. The three young men were standing in the dining-room, talking all at once and laughing all together. They stopped their noise when Miss Wilmarth entered, and Gerald moved forward to perform introductions. He looked at her, and then looked away. Prickling embarrassment tormented him. He introduced the young men, with his eyes away from her.

Miss Wilmarth had dressed for dinner. She had discarded her linen uniform and put on a frock of dark blue taffeta, cut down to a point at the neck and given sleeves that left bare the angles of her elbows. Small, stiff ruffles occurred about the hips, and the skirt was short for its year. It revealed that Miss Wilmarth had clothed her ankles in roughened gray silk and her feet in black, casket-shaped slippers, upon which little bows quivered as if in lonely terror at the expanse before them. She had been busied with her hair; it was crimped and loosened, and ends that had escaped the tongs were already sliding from their pins.

All the length of her nose and chin was heavily powdered; not with a perfumed dust, tinted to praise her skin, but with coarse, bright white talcum.

Gerald presented his guests; Miss Wilmarth, Mr. Minot; Miss Wilmarth, Mr. Forster. One of the young men, it turned out, was Freddy, and one, Tommy. Miss Wilmarth said she was pleased to meet each of them. Each of them asked her how she did.

She sat down at the candle-lit table with the three beautiful young men. Her usual evening vivacity was gone from her. In silence she unfolded her napkin and took up her soup spoon. Her neck glowed crimson, and her face, even with its powder, looked more than ever as if it should have been resting over the top rail of a paddock fence.

"Well!" Gerald said.

"Well!" Mr. Minot said.

"Getting much warmer out, isn't it?" Mr. Forster said. "Notice it?"

"It is, at that," Gerald said. "Well. We're about due for warm weather."

"Yes, we ought to expect it now," Mr. Minot said. "Any day now."

"Oh, it'll be here," Mr. Forster said. "It'll come."

"I love spring," said Miss Wilmarth. "I just love it."

Gerald looked deep into his soup plate. The two young men looked at her.

"Darn good time of year," Mr. Minot said. "Certainly is."

"And how it is!" Mr. Forster said.

They ate their soup.

There was champagne all through dinner. Miss Wilmarth watched Mary fill her glass, none too full. The wine looked gay and pretty. She looked about the table before she took her first sip. She remembered Camilla's voice and the men's laughter.

"Well," she cried. "Here's a health, everybody!"

The guests looked at her. Gerald reached for his glass and gazed at it as intently as if he beheld a champagne goblet for the first time. They all murmured and drank.

"Well!" Mr. Minot said. "Your patients seem to be getting along pretty well, Miss Witmark. Don't they?"

"I should say they do," she said. "And they're pretty nice patients, too. Aren't they, Mr. Cruger?"

"They certainly are," Gerald said. "That's right."

"They certainly are," Mr. Minot said. "That's what they are. Well. You must meet all sorts of people in your work, I suppose. Must be pretty interesting."

"Oh, sometimes it is," Miss Wilmarth said. "It depends on the people." Her words fell from her lips clear and separate, sterile as if each had been freshly swabbed with boracic acid solution. In her ears rang Camilla's light, insolent drawl.

"That's right," Mr. Forster said. "Everything depends on the people, doesn't it? Always does, wherever you go. No matter what you do. Still, it must be wonderfully interesting work. Wonderfully."

"Wonderful the way this country's come right up in medicine," Mr. Minot said. "They tell me we have the greatest doctors in the world, right here. As good as any in Europe. Or Harley Street."

"I see," Gerald said, "where they think they've found a new cure for spinal meningitis."

"*Have* they really?" Mr. Minot said.

"Yes, I saw that, too," Mr. Forster said. "Wonderful thing. Wonderfully interesting."

"Oh, say, Gerald," Mr. Minot said, and he went from there into an account, hole by hole, of his most recent performance at golf. Gerald and Mr. Forster listened and questioned him.

The three young men left the topic of golf and came back to it again, and left it and came back. In the intervals, they related to Miss Wilmarth various brief items that had caught their eyes in the newspapers. Miss Wilmarth answered in exclamations, and turned her big smile readily to each of them. There was no laughter during dinner.

It was a short meal, as courses went. After it, Miss Wilmarth bade the guests good-night and received their bows and their "*Good* night, Miss Witmark." She said she was awfully glad to have met them. They murmured.

"Well, good night, then, Mr. Cruger," she said. "See you tomorrow!"

"Good night, Miss Wilmarth," Gerald said.

The three young men went and sat with Camilla. Miss Wilmarth could hear their voices and their laughter as she hung up her dark blue taffeta dress.

Miss Wilmarth stayed with the Crugers for five weeks. Camilla was pronounced well—so well that she could have dined downstairs on the last few nights of Miss Wilmarth's stay, had she been able to support the fardel of dinner at the table with the trained nurse.

"I really couldn't dine opposite that face," she told Gerald. "You go amuse Horsie at dinner, stupid. You must be good at it, by now."

"All right, I will, darling," he said. "But God keep me, when she asks for another lump of sugar, from holding it out to her on my palm."

"Only two more nights," Camilla said, "and then Thursday Nana'll be here, and she'll be gone forever."

" 'Forever,' sweet, is my favorite word in the language," Gerald said.

Nana was the round and competent Scottish woman who had nursed Camilla through her childhood and was scheduled to engineer the unknowing Diane through hers. She was a comfortable woman, easy to have in the house; a servant, and knew it.

Only two more nights. Gerald went down to dinner whistling a good old tune.

"The old gray mare, she ain't what she used to be,
    Ain't what she used to be, ain't what she used to be——"

The final dinners with Miss Wilmarth were like all the others. He arrived first, and stared at the candles until she came.

"Well, Mary," she cried on her entrance, "you know what they say—better late than never."

Mary, to the last, remained unamused.

Gerald was elated all the day of Miss Wilmarth's departure. He had a holiday feeling, a last-day-of-school jubilation with none of its faint regret. He left his office early, stopped at a florist's shop, and went home to Camilla.

Nana was installed in the nursery, but Miss Wilmarth had not yet left. She was in Camilla's room, and he saw her for the second time out of uniform. She wore a long brown coat and a brown rubbed velvet hat of no definite shape. Obviously, she was in the middle of the embarrassments of farewell. The melancholy of her face made it so like a horse's that the hat above it was preposterous.

"Why, there's Mr. Cruger!" she cried.

"Oh, good evening, Miss Wilmarth," he said. "Well! Ah, hello, darling. How are you, sweet? Like these?"

He laid a florist's box in Camilla's lap. In it were strange little yellow roses, with stems and leaves and tiny, soft thorns all of blood red. Miss Wilmarth gave a little squeal at the sight of them.

"Oh, the darlings!" she cried. "Oh, the boo-fuls!"

"And these are for you, Miss Wilmarth," he said. He made himself face her and hold out to her a square, smaller box.

"Why, Mr. Cruger," she said. "For me, really? Why, really, Mr. Cruger."

She opened the box and found four gardenias, with green foil and pale green ribbon holding them together.

"Oh, now, really, Mr. Cruger," she said. "Why, I never in all my life— Oh, now, you shouldn't have done it. Really, you shouldn't. My good mercy! Well, I never saw anything so lovely in all my life. Did you, Mrs. Cruger? They're *lovely*. Well, I just don't know how to *begin* to thank you. Why, I just—well, I just adore them."

Gerald made sounds designed to convey the intelligence that he was glad she liked them, that it was nothing, that she was welcome. Her squeaks of thanks made red rise in back of his ears.

"They're nice ones," Camilla said. "Put them on, Miss Wilmarth. And these are awfully cunning, Jerry. Sometimes you have your points."

"Oh, I didn't think I'd *wear* them," Miss Wilmarth said. "I thought I'd just take them in the box like this, so they'd keep better. And it's such a nice box—I'd like to have it. I—I'd like to keep it."

She looked down at the flowers. Gerald was in sudden horror that she might bring her head down close to them and toss it back high, crying "wuzza, wuzza, wuzza" at them the while.

"Honestly," she said, "I just can't take my eyes *off* them."

"The woman is mad," Camilla said. "It's the effect of living with us, I suppose. I hope we haven't ruined you for life, Miss Wilmarth."

"Why, Mrs. Cruger," Miss Wilmarth cried. "Now, really! I was just telling Mrs. Cruger, Mr. Cruger, that I've never been on a pleasanter case. I've just had the time of my life, all the time I was here. I don't know when I—honestly, I can't stop looking at my posies, they're so lovely. Well, I just can't thank you for all you've done."

"Well, we ought to thank you, Miss Wilmarth," Gerald said. "We certainly ought."

"I really hate to say 'good-by,'" Miss Wilmarth said. "I just hate it."

"Oh, don't say it," Camilla said. "I never dream of saying it. And remember, you must come in and see the baby, any time you can."

"Yes, you certainly must," Gerald said. "That's right."

"Oh, I will," Miss Wilmarth said. "Mercy, I just don't dare go take another look at her, or I wouldn't be able to leave, ever. Well, what am I thinking of! Why, the car's been waiting all this time. Mrs. Cruger simply insists on sending me home in the car, Mr. Cruger. Isn't she terrible?"

"Why, not at all," he said. "Why, of course."

"Well, it's only five blocks down and over to Lexington," she said, "or I really couldn't think of troubling you."

"Why, not at all," Gerald said. "Well! Is that where you live, Miss Wilmarth?"

She lived in some place of her own sometimes? She wasn't always disarranging somebody else's household?

"Yes," Miss Wilmarth said. "I have Mother there."

Oh. Now Gerald had never thought of her having a mother. Then there must have been a father, too, some time. And Miss Wilmarth existed because two people once had loved and known. It was not a thought to dwell upon.

"My aunt's with us, too," Miss Wilmarth said. "It makes it nice for Mother—you see, Mother doesn't get around very well any more. It's a little bit crowded for the three of us—I sleep on the davenport when I'm home, between cases. But it's so nice for Mother, having my aunt there."

Even in her leisure, then, Miss Wilmarth was a disruption and a crowd. Never dwelling in a room that had been planned only for her occupancy; no bed, no corner of her own; dressing before other people's mirrors, touching other people's silver, never looking out one window that was hers. Well. Doubtless she had known nothing else for so long that she did not mind or even ponder.

"Oh, yes," Gerald said. "Yes, it certainly must be fine for your mother. Well! Well! May I close your bags for you, Miss Wilmarth?"

"Oh, that's all done," she said. "The suitcase is downstairs. I'll just go get my hat-box. Well, good-by, then, Mrs. Cruger, and take care of yourself. And thank you a thousand times."

"Good luck, Miss Wilmarth," Camilla said. "Come see the baby."

Miss Wilmarth looked at Camilla and at Gerald standing beside her, touching one long white hand. She left the room to fetch her hat-box.

"I'll take it down for you, Miss Wilmarth," Gerald called after her.

He bent and kissed Camilla gently, very, very gently.

"Well, it's nearly over, darling," he said. "Sometimes I am practically convinced that there is a God."

"It was darn decent of you to bring her gardenias," Camilla said. "What made you think of it?"

"I was so crazed at the idea that she was really going," he said, "that I must have lost my head. No one was more surprised than I, buying gardenias for Horsie. Thank the Lord she didn't put them on. I couldn't have stood that sight."

"She's not really at her best in her street clothes," Camilla said. "She seems to lack a certain *chic*." She stretched her arms slowly above her head and let them sink slowly back. "That was a fascinating glimpse of her home life she gave us. Great fun."

"Oh, I don't suppose she minds," he said. "I'll go down now and back her into the car, and that'll finish it."

He bent again over Camilla.

"Oh, you look so lovely, sweet," he said. "So *lovely*."

Miss Wilmarth was coming down the hall, when Gerald left the room, managing a pasteboard hat-box, the florist's box, and a big leather purse that had known service. He took the boxes from her, against her protests, and followed her down the stairs and out to the motor at the curb. The chauffeur stood at the open door. Gerald was glad of that presence.

"Well, good luck, Miss Wilmarth," he said. "And thank you so much."

"Thank *you*, Mr. Cruger," she said. "I—I can't tell you how I've enjoyed it all the time I was here. I never had a pleasanter— And the flowers, and everything. I just don't know what to say. I'm the one that ought to thank *you*."

She held out her hand, in a brown cotton glove. Anyway, worn cotton was easier to the touch than dry, corded flesh. It was the last moment of her. He scarcely minded looking at the long face on the red, red neck.

"Well!" he said. "Well! Got everything? Well, good luck, again, Miss Wilmarth, and don't forget us."

"Oh, I won't," she said. "I—oh, I won't do that."

She turned from him and got quickly into the car, to sit upright against the pale gray cushions. The chauffeur placed her hat-box at her feet and the florist's box on the seat beside her, closed the door smartly, and returned to his wheel. Gerald waved cheerily as the car slid away. Miss Wilmarth did not wave to him.

When she looked back, through the little rear window, he had already disappeared in the house. He must have run across the sidewalk— run, to get back to the fragrant room and the little yellow roses and Camilla. Their little pink baby would lie sleeping in its bed. They would be alone together; they would dine alone together by candlelight; they would be alone together in the night. Every morning and every evening Gerald would drop to his knees beside her to kiss her perfumed hand and call her sweet. Always she would be perfect, in scented chiffon and deep lace. There would be lean, easy young men, to listen to her drawl and give her their laughter. Every day there would be shiny white boxes for her, filled with curious blooms. It was perhaps fortunate that no one looked in the limousine. A beholder must have been startled to learn that a human face could look as much like that of a weary mare as did Miss Wilmarth's.

Presently the car swerved, in a turn of the traffic. The florist's box slipped against Miss Wilmarth's knee. She looked down at it. Then she took it on her lap, raised the lid a little and peeped at the waxy white bouquet. It would have been all fair then for a chance spectator; Miss Wilmarth's strange resemblance was not apparent, as she looked at her flowers. They were her flowers. A man had given them to her. She had been given flowers. They might not fade maybe for days. And she could keep the box.

Harper's Bazaar, December 1932

Advice to the Little Peyton Girl

Miss Marion's eyes were sweet and steady beneath her folded honey-colored hair, and her mouth curved gently. She looked as white and smooth as the pond-lilies she had set floating in the blue glass bowl on the low table. Her drawing-room was all pale, clear colors and dark, satiny surfaces, and low light slanted through parchment—Miss Marion's room, from the whole world, hushed for her step, dim to enhance her luminous pallor and her soft and gracious garments. It was sanctuary to the little Peyton girl; and Miss Marion's voice was soothing as running water, and Miss Marion's words were like cool hands laid on her brow.

Before she had decided to do it, the little Peyton girl had told all her trouble. It was, as you looked at it, either a girl's fool worry or the worst of human anguish. For two weeks the little Peyton girl had not seen the Barclay boy. He had become preoccupied with other little girls.

"What shall I do, Miss Marion?" the little Peyton girl said.

Miss Marion's eyes, dark with compassion, dwelt on the small, worried face.

"You like him so much, Sylvie?" she said.

"I—yes, you see, I—" the girl said, and stopped to swallow. "It's so awful without him; it's so awful. You see, we saw each other every day—every single day, all summer. And he'd always telephone me, when he got home, even if he'd left me ten minutes before. And he'd always call me as soon as he woke up, to say good morning and tell me he was coming over. Every day. Oh, Miss Marion, you don't know how lovely it was."

"Yes, I do, dear," Miss Marion said. "I know, Sylvie."

"And then it just stopped," the girl said. "It just suddenly stopped."

"Really suddenly, Sylvie?" Miss Marion said.

"Well," Sylvie said. She tried a little smile. "Why, one night, you see, he'd been over at our house—we'd been sitting on the porch. And then he went home, and he didn't telephone me. And I waited and waited. I—I can't tell you how awful it was. You wouldn't think it would matter that much, that he didn't call up, would you? But it did."

"I know it did," Miss Marion said. "It does."

"I couldn't sleep, I couldn't do anything," Sylvie said. "It—oh, it got

184

to be half-past two. I couldn't imagine what had happened. I thought he'd smashed up in his car or something."

"I wonder if you really thought that, dear," Miss Marion said.

"Why, of course, I—" the girl said, and then she shook her head. "You know everything, Miss Marion, don't you? No, I—well, you see, there was a dance at the club and we'd sort of thought of going, only I—well, I didn't want to go to dances very much; it was much nicer just being alone with him. So I guess what I thought was he'd gone on to the dance when he left our house. And I just got so I couldn't stand it, and I called him up."

"Yes," Miss Marion said. "You called him up. How old are you, Sylvie? Nineteen, aren't you? And I've seen women of thirty-nine make just the same mistakes. It's strange. And was he home when you called him?"

"Yes," Sylvie said. "I—well, I woke him up, you see, and he wasn't very nice about it. And I asked him why he hadn't called me, and he—he said there wasn't any reason to call me, he'd been with me all evening, he didn't have anything to say. And he hadn't been to the dance, only—you see, I thought he had. I—I didn't believe him. And so I cried."

"He heard you cry?" Miss Marion said.

"Yes," Sylvie said. "He said—excuse me, Miss Marion—he said, 'Oh, for the love of God!' and he hung up. And I just couldn't bear that, not saying good night or anything, and so I—so I called him up again."

"Oh, my poor child," Miss Marion said.

"He said he was sorry he'd hung up," Sylvie said, "and everything was all right, only I asked him again wouldn't he please tell me honestly whether he'd been to the dance. And he—oh, he just talked *awfully*, Miss Marion. I can't tell you."

"Don't, dear," Miss Marion said.

"So after that," the girl said, "oh, I don't know—it went on, every day, for a while, and then lots of times he didn't telephone, and then there were days he didn't come over—he'd be playing tennis and things with other people. And then Kitty Grainger came back from Dark Harbor, and I—I guess he went over to her house a lot. They all do."

"Did you tell him you didn't like that?" Miss Marion said.

"Yes, I did, Miss Marion," Sylvie said. "I couldn't help it—it made me so mad. She's an awful girl; she's just awful. Why, she'd kiss *any-body*. She's the kind that always leaves dances and goes out on the golf course with some boy and doesn't come back for *hours*. It made me simply wild that he'd rather be with her than with me. Honestly, it wouldn't have been bad if it had been some terribly nice girl, some one miles more attractive than me. That wouldn't have been so bad, would it, Miss Marion?"

"I don't know, dear," Miss Marion said. "I'm afraid one never thinks a man leaves one for a finer woman. But Sylvie—one *never* points out the imperfections of his friends."

"Well, I couldn't help it," Sylvie said. "And so we had some terrible rows, you see. Kitty Grainger and those friends of hers—why, they're just the same kind she is! So, well, then I sort of saw him less and less, and, you see, every time he came over I was so scared it was the last time that I wasn't much fun, I guess. And I kept asking him what was the matter that he didn't come over every day the way he used to, and he said there wasn't a thing the matter. And I'd keep saying was it anything I'd done, and he said no, of course it wasn't. Honestly he did, Miss Marion. And now—well, I haven't seen him for two weeks. Two weeks. And I haven't heard a word from him. And—and I just don't think I can stand it, please, Miss Marion. Why, he *said* there was nothing the matter. I didn't know that you could see somebody every day, all the time, and then it would just stop. I didn't think it could stop."

"Weren't you ever afraid it would, Sylvie?" Miss Marion said.

"Oh, the last times I saw him, I was," the girl said. "And—well, I suppose I was, right from the start. It was so much fun, I thought it was too wonderful to last. He's so attractive and everything, I was always scared about other girls. I used to tell him, oh, I knew he'd throw me down. It was just fooling, of course; but it wasn't, too."

"You see, Sylvie," Miss Marion said, "men dislike dismal prophecies. I know Bunny Barclay is only twenty, but all men are the same age. And they all hate the same things."

"I wish I were like you, Miss Marion," Sylvie said. "I wish I always knew what to do. I guess I've done everything wrong. But still, he *said* there was nothing the matter. You don't know how awful it is not to be able to talk to him now. If we could just talk things over, if we could just get things straightened out, I think—"

"No, dear," Miss Marion said. "Men hate straightening out unpleasantness. They detest talking things over. Let the past die, my child, and go gaily on from its unmarked grave. Remember that when you see Bunny again, Sylvie. Behave as if you had been laughing together an hour before."

"But maybe I'll never see him again," the girl said. "I can't get near him. I've called him and I've called him and I've called him. Why, I telephoned him three times today! And he's never home. Well, he can't always be out, Miss Marion. Usually it's his mother that answers. And she'd say he was out, anyway. She hates me."

"Don't, child," Miss Marion said. "When one is unhappy, it is easy to think that the world is hostile; especially the part of the world that immediately surrounds the cause of one's unhappiness. Of course, Mrs. Barclay doesn't hate you, Sylvie. How could she?"

"Well, she always says he's out," Sylvie said; "and she never knows what time he'll be back. Maybe it's true. Oh, Miss Marion, do you think I'll ever see him again? Do you, truly?"

"Yes, I do," Miss Marion said, "and I believe you think so, too, dear. Of course, you will. Don't you go to the club to play tennis?"

"I haven't been for ages," the girl said. "I haven't gone anywhere. It makes Mother just frantic, but I don't want to go anywhere. I—I don't want to see him with Kitty and Elsie Taylor and all that crowd. I know he's with one or the other of them all the time—people tell me. And they say, 'What's the matter with you and Bunny, anyway? Did you have a fight?' And when I say there's nothing the matter, they look at me so queerly. But he *said* there wasn't anything the matter. Ah, why did he say that, Miss Marion? Didn't he mean it?"

"I'm afraid he didn't," Miss Marion said.

"Then what is it?" Sylvie said. "Oh, please tell me what to do. Tell me what you do, that every one loves you so. You must know everything, Miss Marion. I'll do anything on earth you say. It—oh, made my heart go all quick, when you said you thought I was going to see him again. Do you think—do you think maybe we could ever be the way we were?"

"Dear Sylvie," Miss Marion said, "listen. Yes, I think that you and Bunny may be close again, but it is you that must accomplish it. And it isn't going to be easy, child. It isn't going to be quick. There is no charm you can repeat to bring back love in a moment. You must have two things—patience and courage; and the first is much harder to summon than the second. You must wait, Sylvie, and it's a bad task. You must not telephone him again, no matter what happens. Men cannot admire a girl who—well, it's a hard word, but I must say it—pursues them. And you must go back to your friends, and go about with them. You are not to stay at home and pray for the telephone to ring—no, dear. Go out and make yourself gay, and gaiety will come to you. Don't be afraid that your friends will ask you questions or look at you queerly; you will give them no reason to. And people don't really say cruel things, dear; it is only in anticipation that pride is hurt.

"And when you meet Bunny again, it must all be different. For there was something the trouble, no matter what he says; something deeply the trouble. You showed him how much you cared for him, Sylvie, showed him he was all-important to you. Men do not like that. You would think they would find it sweet, but they do not. You must be light and you must be easy, for ease is the desire of all men. Talk to him gaily and graciously when you see him, and never hint of the sorrow he has caused you. Men hate reminders of sadness. And there must never be any reproaches, and there must never, never, never be any more 'terrible rows.' Nothing so embarrasses a man as to see a woman lose her dignity.

"And you must conquer your fears, dear child. A woman in fear for her love can never do right. Realize that there are times he will want to be away from you; never ask him why or where. No man will bear that. Don't predict unhappiness, nor foresee a parting; he will not slip away if you do not let him see that you are holding him. Love is like quicksilver in the hand, Sylvie. Leave the fingers open and it stays in the palm; clutch it, and it darts away. Be, above all things, always calm. Let it be peace to be with you.

"Never in this world make him feel guilty, no matter what he has done. If he does not call you when he has said he would, if he is late for an appointment with you, do not refer to it. Make him feel that all is well, always. Be sweet and gay and always, always calm.

"And trust him, Sylvie. He is not deliberately hurting you. He never will unless you suggest it. Trust yourself, too. Don't let yourself become insecure. It sounds an impudence to remind you that there are always others, when I know that it is only he you want; but it is a heartening thought. And he is not to know that he is the sun, that there is no life without him. He must never know that again.

"It is a long way, Sylvie, and a hard one, and you must watch every step you take along it. But it is the only way with a man."

"I see, Miss Marion," the girl said. She had not once taken her eyes from Miss Marion's. "I see what you must do. It—no, it isn't easy, is it? But if it will work—"

"It always has, dear," Miss Marion said.

The girl's face looked as if she beheld a rising sun. "I'm going to try, Miss Marion," she said. "I'm going to try never to do wrong things. I'm going to try—why, I'm going to try to be like you, and then he'd have to like me. It would be so wonderful to be like you: to be wise and lovely and gentle. Men must all adore you. You're—oh, you're just perfect. How do you know what is always the right thing to do?"

Miss Marion smiled. "Well, you see," she said, "I have had several more years than you in which to practice."

When the little Peyton girl had gone, Miss Marion moved slowly about the gracious room, touching a flower, moving a magazine. But her eyes did not follow her pale fingers, and her thoughts seemed absent from her small, unnecessary tasks. Once she looked at the watch on her wrist, and uttered an exclamation; and then she consulted it so frequently that the tiny minute-hand had little opportunity to move, between her glances. She lighted a cigarette, held it from her to consider the spiraling streamer of smoke, then crushed it cold. She rested in a low chair, rose from it and went to the sofa, then went back to the chair. She opened a large and glistening magazine, but turned no pages. Between the bands of honey-colored hair, her white brow was troubled.

Suddenly she rose again, put down the magazine, and with quick, firm steps that were not her habit swept across the room to the tall desk where the telephone rested. She dialed a number, with little sharp rips of sound.

"May I speak to Mr. Lawrence, please?" she said, after some seconds. "Oh, he isn't? Oh. Is this his secretary speaking? Could you tell me when he will be in, please? Oh, I see. Well, if he does come in, will you ask him please to call Miss Marion? No, Marion. No, that's all— that's the last name. Yes, he knows the number. Thank you so much."

Miss Marion replaced the receiver and sat looking at the telephone as if it offended her sight. She spoke aloud, and neither the tone nor the words seemed hers.

"Damn that woman," she said. "She knows damned well what my name is. Just because she hates me—"

For the next minutes, Miss Marion walked the room so rapidly that it was almost as if she ran. Her graceful gown was adapted to no such pace, and it dragged and twisted about her ankles. Her face was flushed with alien color when she went to the telephone again, and her hand shook as she turned the dial.

"May I speak to Mr. Lawrence, please?" she said. "Oh, hasn't he? Well, couldn't you please tell me where I could reach him? Oh, you don't know. I see. Have you any idea if he will be in later? I see. Thank you. Well, if he does come in, would you be good enough to ask him to telephone Miss Marion? Yes, Marion—Cynthia Marion. Thank you. Yes, I telephoned before. Please be sure to tell him to call me, will you? Thank you very much."

Slowly Miss Marion hung the receiver back in its place. Slowly her shoulders sagged, and her long, delicate body seemed to lose its bones. Then her arms were on the desk and her face buried in them, and the cool folds of her hair loosened and flew wild as she rolled her head from side to side. The room seemed to slip into shadow, as if to retreat from the sound of her sobs. Words jumbled among the moans in her throat.

"Oh, he said he'd call, he said he'd call. He said there was nothing the trouble, he said of course he'd call. Oh, he said so."

The knotted, choking noises died away presently, and she had been silent and still for some while before she raised her head and reached for the telephone. She was forced to stop twice during her turning of the dial, so that she might shake the tears from her eyes and see. When she spoke, her voice shook and soared.

"May I speak to Mr. Lawrence, please?" she said.

Harper's Bazaar, February 1933

From the Diary of a New York Lady
DURING DAYS OF HORROR, DESPAIR, AND WORLD CHANGE

MONDAY. Breakfast tray about eleven; didn't want it. The champagne at the Amorys' last night was *too* revolting, but what *can* you do? You can't stay until five o'clock on just *nothing*. They had those *divine* Hungarian musicians in the green coats, and Stewie Hunter took off one of his shoes and led them with it, and it *couldn't* have been funnier. He is *the* wittiest number in the *entire* world; he *couldn't* be more perfect. Ollie Martin brought me home and we both fell asleep in the car—*too* screaming. Miss Rose came about noon to do my nails, simply *covered* with *the* most divine gossip. The Morrises are going to separate *any minute*, and Freddie Warren *definitely* has ulcers, and Gertie Leonard simply *won't* let Bill Crawford out of her sight even with Jack Leonard *right there in the room,* and it's all *true* about Sheila Phillips and Babs Deering. It *couldn't* have been more thrilling. Miss Rose is *too* marvelous; I really think that a lot of times people like that are a lot more intelligent than a lot of people. Didn't notice until after she had gone that the damn fool had put that *revolting* tangerine-colored polish on my nails; *couldn't* have been more furious. Started to read a book, but too nervous. Called up and found I could get two tickets for the opening of "Run like a Rabbit" tonight for forty-eight dollars. Told them they had *the* nerve of the world, but what *can* you do? Think Joe said he was dining out, so telephoned some *divine* numbers to get someone to go to the theater with me, but they were all tied up. Finally got Ollie Martin. He *couldn't* have more poise, and what do *I* care if he *is* one? *Can't* decide whether to wear the green crepe or the red wool. Every time I look at my finger nails, I could *spit. Damn* Miss Rose.

TUESDAY. Joe came barging in my room this morning at *practically nine o'clock. Couldn't* have been more furious. Started to fight, but *too* dead. Know he said he wouldn't be home to dinner. Absolutely *cold* all day; couldn't *move.* Last night *couldn't* have been more perfect. Ollie and I dined at Thirty-Eight East, absolutely *poisonous* food, and not one *living* soul that you'd be seen *dead* with, and "Run like a Rabbit" was *the* world's worst. Took Ollie up to the Barlows' party and it *couldn't*

191

have been more attractive—*couldn't* have been more people absolutely *stinking*. They had those Hungarians in the green coats, and Stewie Hunter was leading them with a fork—everybody simply *died*. He had *yards* of green toilet paper hung around his neck like a lei; he *couldn't* have been in better form. Met a *really new number,* very tall, *too* marvelous, and one of those people that you can *really* talk to them. I told him sometimes I get so *nauseated* I could *yip,* and I felt I absolutely *had* to do something like write or paint. He said why didn't I write or paint. Came home alone; Ollie passed out *stiff.* Called up the new number three times today to get him to come to dinner and go with me to the opening of "Never Say Good Morning," but first he was out and then he was all tied up with his mother. Finally got Ollie Martin. Tried to read a book, but couldn't sit still. *Can't* decide whether to wear the red lace or the pink with the feathers. Feel *too* exhausted, but what *can* you do?

WEDNESDAY. The most terrible thing happened *just this minute.* Broke one of my finger nails *right off short.* Absolutely *the* most horrible thing I ever had happen to me in my life. Called up Miss Rose to come over and shape it for me, but she was out for the day. I do have *the* worst luck in the *entire* world. Now I'll have to go around like this all day and all night, but what *can* you do? *Damn* Miss Rose. Last night *too* hectic. "Never Say Good Morning" *too* foul, *never* saw more poisonous clothes on the stage. Took Ollie up to the Ballards' party; *couldn't* have been better. They had those Hungarians in the green coats and Stewie Hunter was leading them with a freesia—*too* perfect. He had on Peggy Cooper's ermine coat and Phyllis Minton's silver turban; *simply* unbelievable. Asked simply *sheaves* of *divine* people to come here Friday night; got the address of those Hungarians in the green coats from Betty Ballard. She says just engage them until four, and then whoever gives them another three hundred dollars, they'll stay till five. *Couldn't* be cheaper. Started home with Ollie, but had to drop him at his house; he *couldn't* have been sicker. Called up the new number today to get him to come to dinner and go to the opening of "Everybody Up" with me tonight, but he was tied up. Joe's going to be out; he didn't *condescend* to say *where, of course.* Started to read the papers, but nothing in them except that Mona Wheatley is in Reno charging *intolerable cruelty.* Called up Jim Wheatley to see if he had anything to do tonight, but he was tied up. Finally got Ollie Martin. *Can't* decide whether to wear the white satin or the black chiffon or the yellow pebble crepe. Simply *wrecked* to the *core* about my finger nail. Can't *bear* it. *Never* knew *anybody* to have such *unbelievable* things happen to them.

THURSDAY. Simply *collapsing* on my *feet*. Last night *too* marvelous. "Everybody Up" *too* divine, *couldn't* be filthier, and the new number was there, *too* celestial, only he didn't see me. He was with Florence Keeler in that *loathsome* gold Schiaparelli model of hers that every *shop-girl* has had since *God* knows. He must be out of his *mind;* she wouldn't *look* at a man. Took Ollie to the Watsons' party; *couldn't* have been more thrilling. Everybody simply *blind.* They had those Hungarians in the green coats and Stewie Hunter was leading them with a lamp, and, after the lamp got broken, he and Tommy Thomas did adagio dances—*too* wonderful. Somebody told me Tommy's doctor told him he had to absolutely get *right out of town,* he has *the* world's worst stomach, but you'd *never* know it. Came home alone, couldn't find Ollie *anywhere.* Miss Rose came at noon to shape my nail, *couldn't* have been more fascinating. Sylvia Eaton can't go *out the door* unless she's had a hypodermic, and Doris Mason *knows every single word* about Douggie Mason and that girl up in Harlem, and Evelyn North won't be *induced* to keep away from those three acrobats, and they don't *dare* tell Stuyvie Raymond *what* he's got the matter with him. *Never* knew anyone that had a more simply *fascinating* life than Miss Rose. Made her take that *vile* tangerine polish off my nails and put on dark red. Didn't notice until after she had gone that it's practically *black* in electric light; *couldn't* be in a worse state. *Damn* Miss Rose. Joe left a note saying he was going to dine out, so telephoned the new number to get him to come to dinner and go with me to that new movie tonight, but he didn't answer. Sent him three telegrams to *absolutely surely* come tomorrow night. Finally got Ollie Martin for tonight. Looked at the papers, but nothing in them except that the Harry Motts are throwing a tea with Hungarian music on Sunday. Think will ask the new number to go to it with me; they must have meant to invite me. Began to read a book, but too exhausted. *Can't* decide whether to wear the new blue with the white jacket or save it till tomorrow night and wear the ivory moire. Simply *heartsick* every time I think of my nails. *Couldn't* be wilder. Could *kill* Miss Rose, but what *can* you do?

FRIDAY. Absolutely *sunk; couldn't* be worse. Last night *too* divine, movie *simply* deadly. Took Ollie to the Kingslands' party, *too* unbelievable, everybody absolutely *rolling.* They had those Hungarians in the green coats, but Stewie Hunter wasn't there. He's got a *complete* nervous breakdown. Worried *sick* for fear he won't be well by tonight; will absolutely *never* forgive him if he doesn't come. Started home with Ollie, but dropped him at his house because he *couldn't* stop crying. Joe left word with the butler he's going to the country this afternoon for the week-end; *of course* he wouldn't *stoop* to say *what* country. Called up *streams* of marvelous numbers to get someone to come dine and go with me to the opening of "White Man's Folly," and then go somewhere after to dance for a while; can't *bear* to be the first one there at your own party. Everybody was tied up. Finally got Ollie Martin. *Couldn't* feel more depressed; never should have gone *anywhere near* champagne and Scotch together. Started to read a book, but too restless. Called up Anne Lyman to ask about the new baby and *couldn't* remember if it was a boy or girl—*must* get a secretary *next week*. Anne *couldn't* have been more of a help; she said she didn't know whether to name it Patricia or Gloria, so then of course I knew it was a girl *right away*. Suggested calling it Barbara; forgot she already had one. Absolutely *walking the floor* like a *panther* all day. Could *spit* about Stewie Hunter. Can't *face* deciding whether to wear the blue with the white jacket or the purple with the beige roses. Every time I look at those *revolting* black nails, I want to absolutely *yip*. I really have *the* most horrible things happen to me of anybody in the *entire* world. *Damn* Miss Rose.

The New Yorker, March 25, 1933

Sentiment

Oh, anywhere, driver, anywhere—it doesn't matter. Just keep driving.

It's better here in this taxi than it was walking. It's no good my trying to walk. There is always a glimpse through the crowd of someone who looks like him—someone with his swing of the shoulders, his slant of the hat. And I think it's he, I think he's come back. And my heart goes to scalding water and the buildings sway and bend above me. No, it's better to be here. But I wish the driver would go fast, so fast that people walking by would be a long gray blur, and I could see no swinging shoulders, no slanted hat. It's bad stopping still in the traffic like this. People pass too slowly, too clearly, and always the next one might be— No, of course it couldn't be. I know that. Of course I know it. But it might be, it might.

And people can look in and see me, here. They can see if I cry. Oh, let them—it doesn't matter. Let them look and be damned to them.

Yes, you look at me. Look and look and look, you poor, queer tired woman. It's a pretty hat, isn't it? It's meant to be looked at. That's why it's so big and red and new, that's why it has these great soft poppies on it. Your poor hat is all weary and done with. It looks like a dead cat, a cat that was run over and pushed out of the way against the curbstone. Don't you wish you were I and could have a new hat whenever you pleased? You could walk fast, couldn't you, and hold your head high and raise your feet from the pavement if you were on your way to a new hat, a beautiful hat, a hat that cost more than ever you had? Only I hope you wouldn't choose one like mine. For red is mourning, you know. Scarlet red for a love that's dead. Didn't you know that?

She's gone now. The taxi is moving and she's left behind forever. I wonder what she thought when our eyes and our lives met. I wonder did she envy me, so sleek and safe and young. Or did she realize how quick I'd be to fling away all I have if I could bear in my breast the still, dead heart that she carries in hers. She doesn't feel. She doesn't even wish. She is done with hoping and burning, if ever she burned and she hoped. Oh, that's quite nice, it has a real lilt. She is done with hoping and burning, if ever she— Yes, it's pretty. Well—I wonder if she's gone her slow way a little happier, or, perhaps, a little sadder for knowing that there is one worse off than herself.

This is the sort of thing he hated so in me. I know what he would say. "Oh, for heaven's sake!" he would say. "Can't you stop that fool sentimentalizing? Why do you have to do it? Why do you *want* to do it? Just because you see an old charwoman on the street, there's no need to get sobbing about her. She's all right. She's fine. 'When your eyes and your lives met'—oh, come on now. Why, she never even saw you. And her 'still, dead heart,' nothing! She's probably on her way to get a bottle of bad gin and have a roaring time. You don't have to dramatize *everything*. You don't have to insist that *everybody's* sad. Why are you always so sentimental? Don't *do* it, Rosalie." That's what he would say. I know.

But he won't say that or anything else to me, any more. Never anything else, sweet or bitter. He's gone away and he isn't coming back. "Oh, of course I'm coming back!" he said. "No, I don't know just when—I told you that. Ah, Rosalie, don't go making a national tragedy of it. It'll be a few months, maybe—and if ever two people needed a holiday from each other! It's nothing to cry about. I'll be back. I'm not going to stay away from New York forever."

But I knew. I knew. I knew because he had been far away from me long before he went. He's gone away and he won't come back. He's gone away and he won't come back, he's gone away and he'll never come back. Listen to the wheels saying it, on and on and on. That's sentimental, I suppose. Wheels don't say anything. Wheels can't speak. But I *hear* them.

I wonder why it's wrong to be sentimental. People are so contemptuous of feeling. "You wouldn't catch *me* sitting alone and mooning," they say. "Moon" is what they say when they mean remember, and they are so proud of not remembering. It's strange, how they pride themselves upon their lacks. "I never take anything seriously," they say. "I simply couldn't imagine," they say, "letting myself care so much that I could be hurt." They say, "No one person could be that important to *me*." And why, why do they think they're right?

Oh, who's right and who's wrong and who decides? Perhaps it was I who was right about that charwoman. Perhaps she *was* weary and still-hearted, and perhaps, for just that moment, she knew all about me. She needn't have been all right and fine and on her way for gin, just because he said so. Oh. Oh, I forgot. He didn't say so. He wasn't here; he isn't here. It was I, imagining what he would say. And I thought I heard him. He's always with me, he and all his beauty and his cruelty. But he mustn't be any more. I mustn't think of him. That's it, don't think of him. Yes. Don't breathe, either. Don't hear. Don't see. Stop the blood in your veins.

I can't go on like this. I can't, I can't. I cannot stand this frantic misery. If I knew it would be over in a day or a year or two months, I could endure it. Even if it grew duller sometimes and wilder sometimes, it could be borne. But it is always the same and there is no end.

> "Sorrow like a ceaseless rain
>   Beats upon my heart.
> People twist and scream in pain—
> Dawn will find them still again;
> This has neither wax nor wane,
>   Neither stop nor start."

Oh, let's see—how does the next verse go? Something, something, something, something, something to rhyme with "wear." Anyway, it ends:

> "All my thoughts are slow and brown:
>   Standing up or sitting down
> Little matters, or what gown
>   Or what shoes I wear."

Yes, that's the way it goes. And it's right, it's so right. What is it to me what I wear? Go and buy yourself a big red hat with poppies on it—that ought to cheer you up. Yes—go buy it and loathe it. How am I to go on, sitting and staring and buying big red hats and hating them, and then sitting and staring again—day upon day upon day upon day? Tomorrow and tomorrow and tomorrow. How am I to drag through them like this?

But what else is there for me? "Go out and see your friends and have a good time," they say. "Don't sit alone and dramatize yourself." Dramatize yourself! If it be drama to feel a steady—no, a *ceaseless* rain beating upon my heart, then I do dramatize myself. The shallow people, the little people, how can they know what suffering is, how could their thick hearts be torn? Don't they know, the empty fools, that I could not see again the friends we saw together, could not go back to the places where he and I have been? For he's gone, and it's ended. It's ended, it's ended. And when it ends, only those places where you have known sorrow are kindly to you. If you revisit the scenes of your happiness, your heart must burst of its agony.

And that's sentimental, I suppose. It's sentimental to know that you cannot bear to see the places where once all was well with you, that you cannot bear reminders of a dead loveliness. Sorrow is tranquillity remembered in emotion. It—oh, I think that's quite good. "Remembered in emotion"—that's a really nice reversal. I wish I could say it to him. But I won't say anything to him, ever again, ever, ever again. He's gone, and it's over, and I dare not think of the dead days. All my thoughts must be slow and brown, and I must—

Oh, no, no, no! Oh, the driver shouldn't go through this street! This was our street, this is the place of our love and our laughter. I can't do this, I can't, I can't. I will crouch down here, and hold my hands tight, tight over my eyes, so that I cannot look. I must keep my poor heart still, and I must be like the little, mean, dry-souled people who are proud not to remember.

But, oh, I see it, I see it, even though my eyes are blinded. Though I had no eyes, my heart would tell me this street, out of all streets. I know it as I know my hands, as I know his face. Oh, why can't I be let to die as we pass through?

We must be at the florist's shop on the corner now. That's where he used to stop to buy me primroses, little yellow primroses massed tight together with a circle of their silver-backed leaves about them, clean and cool and gentle. He always said that orchids and camellias were none of my affair. So when there were no spring and no primroses, he would give me lilies-of-the-valley and little, gay rosebuds and mignonette and bright blue cornflowers. He said he couldn't stand the thought of me without flowers—it would be all wrong; I cannot bear flowers near me, now. And the little gray florist was so interested and so glad—and there was the day he called me "madam"! Ah, I can't, I can't.

And now we must be at the big apartment house with the big gold doorman. And the evening the doorman was holding the darling puppy on a big, long leash, and we stopped to talk to it, and he took it up in his arms and cuddled it, and that was the only time we ever saw the doorman smile! And next is the house with the baby, and he always would take off his hat and bow very solemnly to her, and sometimes she would give him her little starfish of a hand. And then is the tree with the rusty iron bars around it, where he would stop to turn and wave to me, as I leaned out the window to watch him. And people would look at him, because people always had to look at him, but he never noticed. It was our tree, he said; it wouldn't dream of belonging to anybody else. And very few city people had their own personal tree, he said. Did I realize that, he said.

And then there's the doctor's house, and the three thin gray houses and then—oh, God, we must be at our house now! Our house, though we had only the top floor. And I loved the long, dark stairs, because he climbed them every evening. And our little prim pink curtains at the windows, and the boxes of pink geraniums that always grew for me. And the little stiff entry and the funny mail-box, and his ring at the bell. And I waiting for him in the dusk, thinking he would never come; and yet the waiting was lovely, too. And then when I opened the door to him— Oh, no, no, no! Oh, no one could bear this. No one, no one.

Ah, why, why, why must I be driven through here? What torture could there be so terrible as this? It will be better if I uncover my eyes and look. I will see our tree and our house again, and then my heart will burst and I will be dead. I will look, I will look.

But where's the tree? Can they have cut down our tree—*our* tree? And where's the apartment house? And where's the florist's shop? And where—oh, where's our house, where's—

Driver, what street is this? Sixty-Fifth? Oh. No, nothing, thank you. I—I thought it was Sixty-Third . . .

Harper's Bazaar, May 1933

Mrs. Carrington and Mrs. Crane

"My dear," Mrs. Carrington said, and she flicked a bead or two of caviar from her little fringed napkin, "I've got so I simply can't stand another minute of them. Not one single other minute."

"I know," Mrs. Crane said. She sighed and looked softly upon her friend. "Oh, don't I know. That's the way I feel all the time."

"Honestly," Mrs. Carrington said, "if I hadn't just simply dashed away from Angela's bridge and literally torn over here this afternoon, I—well, I don't know what I would have done."

"You don't have to tell me," Mrs. Crane said. "I know so well. You don't need to tell me."

"The emptiness," Mrs. Carrington needed to tell her. "And the silliness. And the eternal gossip, gossip, gossip. And all the talk about the clothes they have and the clothes they're going to get, and what they do to keep thin. Well, I'm fed up with it, that's all. No, thanks, dear, I don't dare take another sandwich; I'll have to roll all day tomorrow as it is."

"Rolling doesn't do a thing for me," Mrs. Crane said. "What I do is put my feet over my head thirty-five times every morning, and then, if I'm at home during the day, I don't have any lunch."

"That would simply kill me," Mrs. Carrington said. "That would be literally death to me. If I go without lunch, I simply lose control at dinner. Potatoes and everything. Angela's got a new diet; you know, one of those things where it doesn't matter so much how much you eat, it's what you eat with what. She's lost eight pounds."

"How does she look?" Mrs. Crane said.

"Oh, all right, I suppose," Mrs. Carrington said. "Honestly, I've got to the state where they all look alike to me. And talk alike. All those silly, empty women. Never a thought about anything except clothes and parties, never a discussion of anything really worth while. It isn't so bad in the winter. You can get away from them, a little bit, in New York. You can get off by yourself and do something really worth while— picture galleries, and the Philharmonic, and, oh, exhibitions of paintings, and concerts, and things like that. But in the summer, down here in the country—well, there's literally no getting away from them. That's all."

"I know," Mrs. Crane said. "You don't have to say it."

"Nothing but parties, parties, parties," Mrs. Carrington had to say. "Yes, and drinking, drinking, drinking. No, dear, please don't give me any more. After the way they all behaved at the Weldons' party last night, I feel as if I never wanted to see anything to drink again."

"Oh, please—it's really nothing but fruit juice," Mrs. Crane said. She refilled first her own glass, for she was a cozy hostess who shared rather than merely gave, and then her guest's, with a suave blending of gin, vermouth, and zest of lemon. "Oh, you went to the Weldons' last night? Was it any fun?"

"Fun!" Mrs. Carrington said. "The same old thing over again. Backgammon and gossip and diets and clothes. Oh, I nearly forgot to tell you, Betty had on that Florelle model, you know the one with the coat with little tails, only she had it in blue. I sort of thought I'd order it in black. What do you think? Don't you think it would be useful in black?"

"Oh, yes, lovely," Mrs. Crane said. "Was Betty tight?"

"Oh, of course," Mrs. Carrington said. "Blind."

"She's really getting tiresome," Mrs. Crane said. "I don't see how Jack stands her. Well, he's always so drunk himself, I suppose he doesn't notice. It's sickening, isn't it? Oh, my dear, just let me fill it up—it's really nothing but melted ice, anyway."

"No, don't, please don't," Mrs. Carrington said. "Well. Well, just that much, then. Oh, not all that, really. Well. Well, I literally need it, after that bridge party. And last night. What did you do last night?"

"We went to the Lockwoods'," Mrs. Crane said. "I don't have to tell you what it was like. I was so bored, I thought I couldn't last through the evening. But, my dear, it really was awfully amusing. Cynthia had on that white Cygnette model with the two little capes, and Maggie Chase had on the same model in green, and then Dorette came in later on with it in bright yellow."

"Oh, Lord," Mrs. Carrington said. "Now isn't that typical? Isn't that just the way their minds work? Never an original idea; even have to have clothes like one another's. I really don't see how I'm going to stand it until the end of the summer. I said as much to Freddy, coming home last night. 'Freddy,' I said, as we were coming home, 'Freddy,' I said, 'I literally cannot stand that silly, empty, drunken crowd any longer.'"

"I've said the same thing to Jim," Mrs. Crane said, "many a time. Many and many a time. What are you and Freddy doing tonight?"

"We're going to the Grays'," Mrs. Carrington said. "And it will be the same old thing. The same old silly talk. Never a new idea, never a moment's thought of worth-while things."

"Why, we're going, too," Mrs. Crane said. "Well, that will save my life, that you're going. We might get a moment to talk."

"If we don't," Mrs. Carrington said, "I'll never be able to get through it. Honestly, dear, you don't know how much you do for me. No, really no more—please. Well, if you're going to have another one, too. Oh, that's plenty, honestly. No, but what I was going to say is, a person of any intelligence at all simply has to have a certain amount of stimulation. You can't exist entirely on emptiness and silliness and clothes, day in, day out. Well, those people can, I suppose, but people like us—well, we die, that's all, we literally die."

"I know," Mrs. Crane said. "Oh, I know so well."

"I wish it were time to go back to New York," Mrs. Carrington said. "I want to make something of this winter; something worth while. I think I'll take some sort of course or other at Columbia. Hester Coles did, last year. Well, of course, she's a silly little fool, like all the rest of them. But I thought I might do it, too."

"I want to do something this winter," Mrs. Crane said. "If I can only find the time. What I'd really like to do is take up tap-dancing. Mary Morton did, last year, and she lost twelve pounds."

"Is that how she did it?" Mrs. Carrington said. "Did she really? Didn't she have to diet besides?"

"No," Mrs. Crane said. "She just gave up sweets and starches and she couldn't have any meat, except chicken once or twice a week. Twelve pounds, she lost."

"That's wonderful," Mrs. Carrington said. "That's just about what I'd like to lose."

"And it stays lost, when you do it that way," Mrs. Crane said.

"Well, I'm going to take tap-dancing the minute I go back," Mrs. Carrington said. "My dear, let's do it together. You will, really? You literally will? Oh, I think that will be wonderful. You see what you do for me—I never talk to you without being stimulated. Well, now I can really get through the rest of the summer, as long as I have something to look forward to, as long as I know I'm going to get something real out of the winter. Lord, the way the time drags, down here, doesn't it? Good heavens, is it honestly as late as that? Oh, I've got to literally tear home and get dressed. I'm whole hours late. What are you going to wear?"

"Oh, I haven't even given it a thought," Mrs. Crane said. "I did sort of think of the black net, but I don't know. Probably the dusty-pink Valérie model. You know. Betty has it in beige."

"Oh, yes, it's adorable," Mrs. Carrington said. "I suppose Betty'll be there tonight. She's probably tight already."

She rose and moved toward the door. For a moment, it seemed as if the fruit juice and melted ice that she had consumed were about to have their way with her. She stumbled slightly. "Oops!" she said, and had her balance again. Gently she smiled upon her hostess.

"Well, you don't know what this has done for me," she said. "I feel all lifted up. If I hadn't talked to you this afternoon, I could not have faced all the silliness again tonight. I just simply couldn't."

Mrs. Crane swayed delicately toward her friend.

"I know," she said. "It's such a comfort to know that there's somebody, even here in the country, who isn't like all the others. You don't have to tell me."

Affectionately they kissed, and, for a little time, they parted.

The New Yorker, July 15, 1933

The Little Hours

Now what's this? What's the object of all this darkness all over me?
They haven't gone and buried me alive while my back was turned, have
they? Ah, now would you think they'd do a thing like that! Oh, no, I
know what it is. I'm awake. That's it. I've waked up in the middle of
the night. Well, isn't that nice. Isn't that simply ideal. Twenty minutes
past four, sharp, and here's Baby wide-eyed as a marigold. Look at this,
will you? At the time when all decent people are just going to bed, I
must wake up. There's no way things can ever come out even, under
this system. This is as rank as injustice is ever likely to get. This is what
brings about hatred and bloodshed, that's what *this* does.

Yes, and you want to know what got me into this mess? Going
to bed at ten o'clock, that's what. That spells ruin. T-e-n-space-o-
apostrophe-c-l-o-c-k: ruin. Early to bed, and you'll wish you were dead.
Bed before eleven, nuts before seven. Bed before morning, sailors give
warning. Ten o'clock, after a quiet evening of reading. Reading—there's
an institution for you. Why, I'd turn on the light and read, right this
minute, if reading weren't what contributed toward driving me here. I'll
show it. God, the bitter misery that reading works in this world! Everybody knows that—everybody who *is* everybody. All the best minds
have been off reading for years. Look at the swing La Rochefoucauld
took at it. He said that if nobody had ever learned to read, very few
people would be in love. There was a man for you, and that's what *he*
thought of it. Good for you, La Rochefoucauld; nice going, boy. I wish
I'd never learned to read. I wish I'd never learned to take off my clothes.
Then I wouldn't have been caught in this jam at half-past four in the
morning. If nobody had ever learned to undress, very few people would
be in love. No, his is better. Oh, well, it's a man's world.

La Rochefoucauld, indeed, lying quiet as a mouse, and me tossing
and turning here! This is no time to be getting all steamed up about
La Rochefoucauld. It's only a question of minutes before I'm going to
be pretty darned good and sick of La Rochefoucauld, once and for all.
La Rochefoucauld this and La Rochefoucauld that. Yes, well, let me tell
you that if nobody had ever learned to quote, very few people would
be in love with La Rochefoucauld. I bet you I don't know ten souls who
read him without a middleman. People pick up those scholarly little

essays that start off "Was it not that lovable old cynic, La Rochefoucauld, who said . . ." and then they go around claiming to know the
master backwards. Pack of illiterates, that's all they are. All right,
let them keep their La Rochefoucauld, and see if I care. I'll stick to
La Fontaine. Only I'd be better company if I could quit thinking that
La Fontaine married Alfred Lunt.

I don't know what I'm doing mucking about with a lot of French
authors at this hour, anyway. First thing you know, I'll be reciting *Fleurs
du Mal* to myself, and then I'll be little more good to anybody. And I'll
stay off Verlaine too; he was always chasing Rimbauds. A person would
be better off with La Rochefoucauld, even. Oh, damn La Rochefoucauld. The big Frog. I'll thank him to keep out of my head. What's he
doing there, anyhow? What's La Rochefoucauld to me, or he to Hec-
uba? Why, I don't even know the man's first name, that's how close I
ever was to *him*. What am I supposed to be, a hostess to La Rochefoucauld? That's what *he* thinks. Sez he. Well, he's only wasting his time,
hanging around here. I can't help him. The only other thing I can remember his saying is that there is always something a little pleasing to
us in the misfortunes of even our dearest friends. That cleans me all up
with Monsieur La Rochefoucauld. *Maintenant c'est fini, ça.*

Dearest friends. A sweet lot of dearest friends I've got. All of them
lying in swinish stupors, while I'm practically up and about. All of them
stretched sodden through these, the fairest hours of the day, when man
should be at his most productive. Produce, produce, produce, for I tell
you the night is coming. Carlyle said that. Yes, and a fine one *he* was,
to go shooting off his face on production. *Oh*, Thomas Carl*i*-yill, what
I know about *you*-oo! No, that will be enough of that. I'm not going
to start fretting about Carlyle, at this stage of the game. What did he
ever do that was so great, besides founding a college for Indians? (That
one ought to make him spin.) Let him keep his face out of this, if he
knows what's good for him. I've got enough trouble with that lovable
old cynic, La Rochefoucauld—him and the misfortunes of his dearest
friends!

The first thing I've got to do is get out and whip me up a complete
new set of dearest friends; that's the first thing. Everything else can wait.
And will somebody please kindly be so good as to inform me how I am
ever going to meet up with any new people when my entire scheme of
living is out of joint—when I'm the only living being awake while the
rest of the world lies sleeping? I've got to get this thing adjusted. I must
try to get back to sleep right now. I've got to conform to the rotten
little standards of this sluggard civilization. People needn't feel that they

have to change their ruinous habits and come my way. Oh, no, no; no, indeed. Not at all. I'll go theirs. If that isn't the woman of it for you! Always having to do what somebody else wants, like it or not. Never able to murmur a suggestion of her own.

And what suggestion has anyone to murmur as to how I am going to drift lightly back to slumber? Here I am, awake as high noon what with all this milling and pitching around with La Rochefoucauld. I really can't be expected to drop everything and start counting sheep, at my age. I hate sheep. Untender it may be in me, but all my life I've hated sheep. It amounts to a phobia, the way I hate them. I can tell the minute there's one in the room. They needn't think that I am going to lie here in the dark and count their unpleasant little faces for them; I wouldn't do it if I didn't fall asleep again until the middle of next August. Suppose they never get counted—what's the worst that can happen? If the number of imaginary sheep in this world remains a matter of guesswork, who is richer or poorer for it? No, sir; *I'm* not their scorekeeper. Let them count themselves, if they're so crazy mad after mathematics. Let them do their own dirty work. Coming around here, at this time of day, and asking me to count them! And not even *real* sheep, at that. Why, it's the most preposterous thing I ever heard in my life.

But there must be *something* I could count. Let's see. No, I already know by heart how many fingers I have. I could count my bills, I suppose. I could count the things I didn't do yesterday that I should have done. I could count the things I should do today that I'm not going to do. I'm never going to accomplish anything; that's perfectly clear to me. I'm never going to be famous. My name will never be writ large on the roster of Those Who Do Things. I don't do anything. Not one single thing. I used to bite my nails, but I don't even do that any more. I don't amount to the powder to blow me to hell. I've turned out to be nothing but a bit of flotsam. Flotsam and leave 'em—that's me from now on. Oh, it's all terrible.

Well. This way lies galloping melancholia. Maybe it's because this is the zero hour. This is the time the swooning soul hangs pendant and vertiginous between the new day and the old, nor dares confront the one or summon back the other. This is the time when all things, known and hidden, are iron to weight the spirit; when all ways, traveled or virgin, fall away from the stumbling feet, when all before the straining eyes is black. Blackness now, everywhere is blackness. This is the time of abomination, the dreadful hour of the victorious dark. For it is always darkest— Was it not that lovable old cynic, La Rochefoucauld, who said that it is always darkest before the deluge?

There. Now you see, don't you? Here we are again, practically back where we started. La Rochefoucauld, we are here. Ah, come on, son— how about your going your way and letting me go mine? I've got my work cut out for me right here; I've got all this sleeping to do. Think how I am going to look by daylight if this keeps up. I'll be a seamy sight for all those rested, clear-eyed, fresh-faced dearest friends of mine—the rats! My *dear*, whatever have you been doing; I thought you were so good lately. Oh, I was helling around with La Rochefoucauld till all hours; we couldn't stop laughing about your misfortunes. No, this is getting too thick, really. It isn't right to have this happen to a person, just because she went to bed at ten o'clock once in her life. Honest, I won't ever do it again. I'll go straight, after this. I'll never go to bed again, if I can only sleep now. If I can tear my mind away from a certain French cynic, *circa* 1650, and slip into lovely oblivion. 1650. I bet I look as if I'd been awake since then.

How do people go to sleep? I'm afraid I've lost the knack. I might try busting myself smartly over the temple with the night-light. I might repeat to myself, slowly and soothingly, a list of quotations beautiful from minds profound; if I can remember any of the damn things. That might do it. And it ought effectually to bar that visiting foreigner that's been hanging around ever since twenty minutes past four. Yes, that's what I'll do. Only wait till I turn the pillow; it feels as if La Rochefoucauld had crawled inside the slip.

Now let's see—where shall we start? Why—er—let's see. Oh, yes, I know one. This above all, to thine own self be true and it must follow, as the night the day, thou canst not then be false to any man. Now they're off. And once they get started, they ought to come like hot cakes. Let's see. Ah, what avail the sceptered race and what the form divine, when every virtue, every grace, Rose Aylmer, all were thine. Let's see. They also serve who only stand and wait. If Winter comes, can Spring be far behind? Lilies that fester smell far worse than weeds. Silent upon a peak in Darien. Mrs. Porter and her daughter wash their feet in soda-water. And Agatha's Arth is a hug-the-hearth, but my true love is false. Why did you die when lambs were cropping, you should have died when apples were dropping. Shall be together, breathe and ride, so one day more am I deified, who knows but the world will end tonight. And he shall hear the stroke of eight and not the stroke of nine. They are not long, the weeping and the laughter; love and desire and hate I think will have no portion in us after we pass the gate. But none, I think, do there embrace. I think that I shall never see a poem lovely as a tree. I think I will not hang myself today. Ay tank Ay go home now.

Let's see. Solitude is the safeguard of mediocrity and the stern companion of genius. Consistency is the hobgoblin of little minds. Something is emotion remembered in tranquillity. A cynic is one who knows the price of everything and the value of nothing. That lovable old cynic is one who—oops, there's King Charles's head again. I've got to watch myself. Let's see. Circumstantial evidence is a trout in the milk. Any stigma will do to beat a dogma. If you would learn what God thinks about money, you have only to look at those to whom He has given it. If nobody had ever learned to read, very few people—

All right. That fixes it. I throw in the towel right now. I know when I'm licked. There'll be no more of this nonsense; I'm going to turn on the light and read my head off. Till the next ten o'clock, if I feel like it. And what does La Rochefoucauld want to make of that? Oh, he *will*, eh? Yes, he will! He and who else? La Rochefoucauld and *what* very few people?

The New Yorker, August 19, 1933

The Waltz

Why, thank you so much. I'd adore to.

I don't want to dance with him. I don't want to dance with anybody. And even if I did, it wouldn't be him. He'd be well down among the last ten. I've seen the way he dances; it looks like something you do on Saint Walpurgis Night. Just think, not a quarter of an hour ago, here I was sitting, feeling so sorry for the poor girl he was dancing with. And now *I'm* going to be the poor girl. Well, well. Isn't it a small world?

And a peach of a world, too. A true little corker. Its events are so fascinatingly unpredictable, are not they? Here I was, minding my own business, not doing a stitch of harm to any living soul. And then he comes into my life, all smiles and city manners, to sue me for the favor of one memorable mazurka. Why, he scarcely knows my name, let alone what it stands for. It stands for Despair, Bewilderment, Futility, Degradation, and Premeditated Murder, but little does he wot. I don't wot his name, either; I haven't any idea what it is. Jukes, would be my guess from the look in his eyes. How do you do, Mr. Jukes? And how is that dear little brother of yours, with the two heads?

Ah, now why did he have to come around me, with his low requests? Why can't he let me lead my own life? I ask so little—just to be left alone in my quiet corner of the table, to do my evening brooding over all my sorrows. And he must come, with his bows and his scrapes and his may-I-have-this-ones. And I had to go and tell him that I'd adore to dance with him. I cannot understand why I wasn't struck right down dead. Yes, and being struck dead would look like a day in the country, compared to struggling out a dance with this boy. But what could I do? Everyone else at the table had got up to dance, except him and me. There was I, trapped. Trapped like a trap in a trap.

What can you say, when a man asks you to dance with him? I most certainly will *not* dance with you, I'll see you in hell first. Why, thank you, I'd like to awfully, but I'm having labor pains. Oh, yes, *do* let's dance together—it's so nice to meet a man who isn't a scaredy-cat about catching my beri-beri. No. There was nothing for me to do, but say I'd adore to. Well, we might as well get it over with. All right, Cannonball, let's run out on the field. You won the toss; you can lead.

Why, I think it's more of a waltz, really. Isn't it? We might just listen

*to the music a second. Shall we? Oh, yes, it's a waltz. Mind? Why, I'm
simply thrilled. I'd love to waltz with you.*

I'd love to waltz with you. I'd love to waltz with you. I'd love to
have my tonsils out, I'd love to be in a midnight fire at sea. Well, it's
too late now. We're getting under way. *Oh.* Oh, dear. Oh, dear, dear,
dear. Oh, this is even worse than I thought it would be. I suppose that's
the one dependable law of life—everything is always worse than you
thought it was going to be. Oh, if I had any real grasp of what this
dance would be like, I'd have held out for sitting it out. Well, it will
probably amount to the same thing in the end. We'll be sitting it out
on the floor in a minute, if he keeps this up.

I'm so glad I brought it to his attention that this is a waltz they're
playing. Heaven knows what might have happened, if he had thought
it was something fast; we'd have blown the sides right out of the building. Why does he always want to be somewhere that he isn't? Why
can't we stay in one place just long enough to get acclimated? It's this
constant rush, rush, rush, that's the curse of American life. That's the
reason that we're all of us so—*Ow!* For God's sake, don't *kick*, you
idiot; this is only second down. Oh, my shin. My poor, poor shin, that
I've had ever since I was a little girl!

*Oh, no, no, no. Goodness, no. It didn't hurt the least little bit. And
anyway it was my fault. Really it was. Truly. Well, you're just being
sweet, to say that. It really was all my fault.*

I wonder what I'd better do—kill him this instant, with my naked
hands, or wait and let him drop in his traces. Maybe it's best not to
make a scene. I guess I'll just lie low, and watch the pace get him. He
can't keep this up indefinitely—he's only flesh and blood. Die he must,
and die he shall, for what he did to me. I don't want to be of the over-
sensitive type, but you can't tell me that kick was unpremeditated. Freud
says there are no accidents. I've led no cloistered life, I've known dancing partners who have spoiled my slippers and torn my dress; but when
it comes to kicking, I am Outraged Womanhood. When you kick me
in the shin, *smile.*

Maybe he didn't do it maliciously. Maybe it's just his way of showing
his high spirits. I suppose I ought to be glad that one of us is having
such a good time. I suppose I ought to think myself lucky if he brings
me back alive. Maybe it's captious to demand of a practically strange
man that he leave your shins as he found them. After all, the poor boy's
doing the best he can. Probably he grew up in the hill country, and
never had no larnin'. I bet they had to throw him on his back to get
shoes on him.

Yes, it's lovely, isn't it? It's simply lovely. It's the loveliest waltz. Isn't it? Oh, I think it's lovely, too.

Why, I'm getting positively drawn to the Triple Threat here. He's my hero. He has the heart of a lion, and the sinews of a buffalo. Look at him—never a thought of the consequences, never afraid of his face, hurling himself into every scrimmage, eyes shining, cheeks ablaze. And shall it be said that I hung back? No, a thousand times no. What's it to me if I have to spend the next couple of years in a plaster cast? Come on, Butch, right through them! Who wants to live forever?

Oh. Oh, dear. Oh, he's all right, thank goodness. For a while I thought they'd have to carry him off the field. Ah, I couldn't bear to have anything happen to him. I love him. I love him better than anybody in the world. Look at the spirit he gets into a dreary, commonplace waltz; how effete the other dancers seem, beside him. He is youth and vigor and courage, he is strength and gaiety and—*Ow!* Get off my instep, you hulking peasant! What do you think I am, anyway—a gang-plank? *Ow!*

No, of course it didn't hurt. Why, it didn't a bit. Honestly. And it was all my fault. You see, that little step of yours—well, it's perfectly lovely, but it's just a tiny bit tricky to follow at first. Oh, did you work it up yourself? You really did? Well, aren't you amazing! Oh, now I think I've got it. Oh, I think it's lovely. I was watching you do it when you were dancing before. It's awfully effective when you look at it.

It's awfully effective when you look at it. I bet I'm awfully effective when you look at me. My hair is hanging along my cheeks, my skirt is swaddled about me, I can feel the cold damp of my brow. I must look like something out of "The Fall of the House of Usher." This sort of thing takes a fearful toll of a woman my age. And he worked up his little step himself, he with his degenerate cunning. And it was just a tiny bit tricky at first, but now I think I've got it. Two stumbles, slip, and a twenty-yard dash; yes. I've got it. I've got several other things, too, including a split shin and a bitter heart. I hate this creature I'm chained to. I hated him the moment I saw his leering, bestial face. And here I've been locked in his noxious embrace for the thirty-five years this waltz has lasted. Is that orchestra never going to stop playing? Or must this obscene travesty of a dance go on until hell burns out?

Oh, they're going to play another encore. Oh, goody. Oh, that's lovely. Tired? I should say I'm not tired. I'd like to go on like this forever.

I should say I'm not tired. I'm dead, that's all I am. Dead, and in what a cause! And the music is never going to stop playing, and we're going on like this, Double-Time Charlie and I, throughout eternity. I suppose I won't care any more, after the first hundred thousand years. I suppose nothing will matter then, not heat nor pain nor broken heart nor cruel, aching weariness. Well. It can't come too soon for me.

I wonder why I didn't tell him I was tired. I wonder why I didn't suggest going back to the table. I could have said let's just listen to the music. Yes, and if he would, that would be the first bit of attention he has given it all evening. George Jean Nathan said that the lovely rhythms of the waltz should be listened to in stillness and not be accompanied by strange gyrations of the human body. I think that's what he said. I think it was George Jean Nathan. Anyhow, whatever he said and who-ever he was and whatever he's doing now, he's better off than I am. That's safe. Anybody who isn't waltzing with this Mrs. O'Leary's cow I've got here is having a good time.

Still if we were back at the table, I'd probably have to talk to him. Look at him—what could you say to a thing like that! Did you go to the circus this year, what's your favorite kind of ice cream, how do you spell cat? I guess I'm as well off here. As well off as if I were in a cement mixer in full action.

I'm past all feeling now. The only way I can tell when he steps on me is that I can hear the splintering of bones. And all the events of my life are passing before my eyes. There was the time I was in a hurricane in the West Indies, there was the day I got my head cut open in the taxi smash, there was the night the drunken lady threw a bronze ash-tray at her own true love and got me instead, there was that summer that the sailboat kept capsizing. Ah, what an easy, peaceful time was mine, until I fell in with Swifty, here. I didn't know what trouble was, before I got drawn into this *danse macabre*. I think my mind is beginning to wander. It almost seems to me as if the orchestra were stopping. It couldn't be, of course; it could never, never be. And yet in my ears there is a silence like the sound of angel voices. . . .

Oh, they've stopped, the mean things. They're not going to play any more. Oh, darn. Oh, do you think they would? Do you really think so, if you gave them fifty dollars? Oh, that would be lovely. And look, do tell them to play this same thing. I'd simply adore to go on waltzing.

The New Yorker, September 2, 1933

The Road Home

The girl in the deep right-hand corner of the taxicab seat looked steadily at the young man reclining against the left-hand wall of the cab. It was a fine dramatic glare that she was executing, but it went wasted. The rhythmic streaks of light from the street lamps showed only the young man's profile turned toward her; a large and handsome profile, the lips of which moved freely. Music, in an elemental form, issued from them and presently words came along with the gay and simple tune, and filled the dark spaces of the taxi.

> "Oh, Lord Jeffrey Amherst was a soldier of the king.
> And he came from acraw-woss the sea;
> To the Frenchmen and the Indians he didn't do a thing
> In the *wilds* of this *wild* coun-tree,
> In the WILDS of this WILD—"

The girl spoke. Her voice was low, but it struck across the song and stopped it there where it was.

"If I have to hear that again," she said, "if I have to hear that song just one more time, I'm going right smack out of my mind."

"What's the matter with that song?" the young man said. "That's a good song. That's the best song in the world, that's all that is. Shows how much you care about music. What's the matter with that song? What's the matter with you? What?"

"The matter with me?" she said. "Oh, there's nothing the matter with me, I assure you. Let me assure you of that. Not with *me*."

"Then what's the matter with you?" he said.

"Nothing whatever," she said. "What should be? Everything's been perfectly splendid, hasn't it? You had a wonderful time, didn't you?"

"When?" he said.

"Oh, 'when'!" she said. " 'When'! Why, tonight, of course. When did you think? Listen. I hate to ask you to strain yourself, but you might be so good as to recall that you took me to a party this evening. Can you remember that?"

"Certainly I can," he said. "What's the matter with it?"

"I'm so glad," she said, "that you *are* able to recollect that it was me you brought with you. That it was I you brought with you. It more or less seemed, all during the evening, as if that little matter had more or less slipped your memory."

"What little matter?" he said. "What's the matter with what?"

"But of course," she said, "as long as you were enjoying yourself, I'm sure nobody has any right to say anything. Just as long as you're having a good time, everything's perfectly all right. Naturally."

"Didn't you have a good time?" he said.

"Oh, perfect," she said. "Ideal. What girl wouldn't have, in my place? Naturally, it's my idea of a marvelous evening to sit in a corner all by myself, while a lot of loud-mouthed drunks go into a huddle and sing for four solid hours. Why, I had the time of my life. Logically."

"Who's a lot of loud-mouthed drunks?" he said.

"Oh, several people I could name," she said. "If I cared to."

"You didn't have to go sit in any corner," he said. "Why didn't you come over and sing?"

"Well, since you're so anxious to know," she said, "it was because nobody asked me to."

"My God, do you have to be asked to come on over and sing with a crowd of people?" he said.

"I most certainly do," she said. "And what do you think of that?"

"Nobody *asked* anybody," he said. "What's the matter with you, anyway, Marjorie?"

"Oh, nobody asked anybody?" she said. "Really? Well, you gave an awfully realistic imitation of begging that little Cronin girl to come over and join the singing. If you could call what she does 'singing,' and not be struck dead."

"She hasn't got a bad voice," he said. "Knows all the words, too."

"She certainly does," she said. "And of course, you had to stand close to her to hear them, because it would be terrible if you missed a syllable of 'Lord Jeffrey Amherst' or 'The Caissons Go Rolling Along.' Naturally, you had to put your arm around her so you could hear better. Of course."

"Oh, so that's what's the matter," he said. "Oh, God."

"I'm sure," she said, "that it doesn't make any difference to me who you put your arm around. Whom you put your arm around. Let me assure you of that. If you prefer someone like that hard, cheap, common little Cronin girl to someone that has a certain amount of depths and sensitiveness and has occasionally read a book, why, that's what you prefer. That's all."

"Oh, God," he said. "Oh, God."

"The only thing that hurts me," she said, "is absolute neglect. Doubtless that would seem strange to you and the little Cronin girl, but it just so happens that it absolutely kills me to be absolutely neglected. I just happen to be that sort of person, that's all. And there I sat, all evening, without anyone saying one word to me. Charming manners some people have, I must say. Why, when I wanted a drink, I had to go way into the other room and get it for myself."

"You seem to have made the trip quite a few times," he said.

"Well, I had to do something, didn't I?" she said. "Just sitting there, alone in a corner. While you sang. The only bit of attention you paid me the entire evening was when you spilled your entire drink all over my dress. I don't mean that I minded that. Of course, it's the first new dress I've had in ages, and there isn't the least sense in sending it to the cleaner's, because the kind of liquor those people have never comes out. I'll just have to go on wearing it the way it is, that's all. Miss Marjorie Reeves was in white satin trimmed with bathtub gin. Yes. But I certainly don't care anything about that."

"Ah, I'm sorry about that, Marjie," he said. "I feel like the devil about spoiling your dress."

"Oh, please don't think of it," she said. "*That* isn't what troubles me. What hurts me is to have you take me to a party, and then never give another darn about me all evening. And that's what happens, night after night—I sit, while you sing. Well, I can spare myself any such humiliation in future, thank heaven. I'm sorry, but this is the last time I'll ever go out with *you*, my dear!"

"You haven't said that since Tuesday," he said.

"Yes, and I had every right to say it Tuesday!" she said. "It was exactly the same thing Tuesday night. Me sitting in a corner alone, and you singing 'Lord Jeffrey Amherst' with your arm around people."

"And it was exactly the same thing coming home in the taxi Tuesday night," he said. "My God, can't we ever have a regular evening, like anybody else? We go to a party, and I keep looking forward to it all day, and then we go, and I think we're having a swell time, and you know damn well I'd rather be out with you than anybody in the world, and then there's always something I've done or something I haven't done, and then there's always this stuff on the way home. Good God!"

"Well, you'll be spared it in future, my dear," she said. "You don't ever have to see *me* again. That's what you want, isn't it? I'll keep out of your way—you don't have to trouble about that. Of course, there are people that might think of all the time I'd given them, when I'd never even *looked* at anyone else, but don't think about that. Everything is perfectly fine for you now. You can go right ahead and have a glorious time with the little Cronin girl, every night. Go singing with her, or whatever else you want to do. If that's what you want."

"Oh, shut your face!" he said.

"Listen to me, you big louse!" she said. "Please remember who you're talking to. Whom. You're not with the little Cronin girl now, you know. It just so happens that you're with somebody who happens to have a little sensitiveness, God help her, and a little breeding and a few depths, instead of a hard, ordinary little rat that you'd much rather be out singing with than—"

"Oh, nuts!" he said.

The girl swung her left arm back and struck him across the mouth with the back of her hand. As if by a reflex, his right hand sprang up, and its palm slapped her face, hard.

There was silence. After a while, there was a little shuffling sound, as the young man left his wall and edged along the seat toward the girl. Slowly and timidly he put his arms around her, and she could feel them tremble. If she had been looking, the streaks of light from the street lamps would have shown her the concern in his large and handsome face.

"Ah, I'm so sorry, Marjie," he said. "I'm so sorry. Gee, I—I never did a thing like that before in my life."

"I didn't, either," she said, and her voice was broken. "I—it wasn't very nice. I won't ever do a thing like that again."

"I won't, either," he said. "I—I can be different, Marjie. Honestly I can. If—well, if you'd ever see me again, maybe I could show you."

"I can be different, too," she said. "I guess."

After a minute she raised her face from his shoulder.

"But you see," she said, "it really was awful for me tonight. And Tuesday night. And all the nights. All you want to do is sing. But—well, you see, I wanted to sing, too. And you never asked me."

"But, baby, it never occurred to me," he said. "I thought you'd know that whatever I was doing, I'd want you there, too. And I never knew you liked to sing."

"I love it," she said.

"I love it, too," he said.

"I know all the words, too," she said.

"Why, of course you do," he said.

"You see," she said, "I don't mind you singing. Or even who you sing with. Whom you sing with. It's just the feeling of being left out of things. Anybody hates that. You would, too. I guess that's what's made me this way on the way home, every time."

"But I never knew you liked to sing," he said.

"Well, you know now," she said. "And maybe some time we could work up some other songs. I counted tonight, on account of not having anything else to do, and 'Lord Jeffrey Amherst' was thirteen times, and 'The Caissons Go Rolling Along' was eight."

"It must have been great for you!" he said.

"And she didn't have the words of 'The Caissons' right, either," she said. "She had them all bugged up."

"Really?" he said. "Why, that's terrible. Why, that's awful. Why, the dumb little cluck. And what a good song, too. That's one of the best songs in the world, that's what that is.

> "Da da da, da da da.
> Da da dum de da da da,
>   The caissons go rolling along—"

"No, listen," she said. "I know all the words. Listen.

> "Over hill, over dale,
> All along the dusty trail,
>   The caissons go rolling along.
> In and out, round about,
> Hear them something, hear them shout,
>   And the caissons go rolling along."

"Oh, yes, sure," he said. "That's the right way. Ah, Marjie, you've got a good voice." And he added his music to hers.

> "Then it's hi, hi, hee, the field ar-till-er-ee,
> Lift up your voices loud and strong,
> Where'er you go, you will always know
> That the caissons are rolling along—
>   Keep 'em rolling—
>   The caissons are—"

There was harmony in the taxicab.

The New Yorker, September 16, 1933

Glory in the Daytime

Mr. Murdock was one who carried no enthusiasm whatever for plays and their players, and that was too bad, for they meant so much to little Mrs. Murdock. Always she had been in a state of devout excitement over the luminous, free, passionate elect who serve the theater. And always she had done her wistful worshiping, along with the multitudes, at the great public altars. It is true that once, when she was a particularly little girl, love had impelled her to write Miss Maude Adams a letter beginning "Dearest Peter," and she had received from Miss Adams a miniature thimble inscribed "A kiss from Peter Pan." (That was a day!) And once, when her mother had taken her holiday shopping, a limousine door was held open and there had passed her, as close as *that,* a wonder of sable and violets and round red curls that seemed to tinkle on the air; so, forever after, she was as good as certain that she had been not a foot away from Miss Billie Burke. But until some three years after her marriage, these had remained her only personal experiences with the people of the lights and the glory.

Then it turned out that Miss Noyes, new come to little Mrs. Murdock's own bridge club, knew an actress. She actually knew an actress; the way you and I know collectors of recipes and members of garden clubs and amateurs of needlepoint.

The name of the actress was Lily Wynton, and it was famous. She was tall and slow and silvery; often she appeared in the role of a duchess, or of a Lady Pam or an Honorable Moira. Critics recurrently referred to her as "that great lady of our stage." Mrs. Murdock had attended, over years, matinee performances of the Wynton successes. And she had no more thought that she would one day have opportunity to meet Lily Wynton face to face than she had thought—well, than she had thought of flying!

Yet it was not astounding that Miss Noyes should walk at ease among the glamorous. Miss Noyes was full of depths and mystery, and she could talk with a cigarette still between her lips. She was always doing something difficult, like designing her own pajamas, or reading Proust, or modeling torsos in plasticine. She played excellent bridge. She liked little Mrs. Murdock. "Tiny one," she called her.

"How's for coming to tea tomorrow, tiny one? Lily Wynton's going to drop up," she said, at a therefore memorable meeting of the bridge club. "You might like to meet her."

The words fell so easily that she could not have realized their weight. Lily Wynton was coming to tea. Mrs. Murdock might like to meet her. Little Mrs. Murdock walked home through the early dark, and stars sang in the sky above her.

Mr. Murdock was already at home when she arrived. It required but a glance to tell that for him there had been no singing stars that evening in the heavens. He sat with his newspaper opened at the financial page, and bitterness had its way with his soul. It was not the time to cry happily to him of the impending hospitalities of Miss Noyes; not the time, that is, if one anticipated exclamatory sympathy. Mr. Murdock did not like Miss Noyes. When pressed for a reason, he replied that he just plain didn't like her. Occasionally he added, with a sweep that might have commanded a certain admiration, that all those women made him sick. Usually, when she told him of the temperate activities of the bridge club meetings, Mrs. Murdock kept any mention of Miss Noyes's name from the accounts. She had found that this omission made for a more agreeable evening. But now she was caught in such a sparkling swirl of excitement that she had scarcely kissed him before she was off on her story.

"Oh, Jim," she cried. "Oh, what do you think! Hallie Noyes asked me to tea tomorrow to meet Lily Wynton!"

"Who's Lily Wynton?" he said.

"Ah, Jim," she said. "Ah, really, Jim. Who's Lily Wynton! Who's Greta Garbo, I suppose!"

"She some actress or something?" he said.

Mrs. Murdock's shoulders sagged. "Yes, Jim," she said. "Yes. Lily Wynton's an actress."

She picked up her purse and started slowly toward the door. But before she had taken three steps, she was again caught up in her sparkling swirl. She turned to him, and her eyes were shining.

"Honestly," she said, "it was the funniest thing you ever heard in your life. We'd just finished the last rubber—oh, I forgot to tell you, I won three dollars, isn't that pretty good for me?—and Hallie Noyes said to me, 'Come on in to tea tomorrow. Lily Wynton's going to drop up,' she said. Just like that, she said it. Just as if it was anybody."

"Drop up?" he said. "How can you drop *up*?"

"Honestly, I don't know what I said when she asked me," Mrs. Murdock said. "I suppose I said I'd love to—I guess I must have. But I was so simply— Well, you know how I've always felt about Lily Wynton.

Why, when I was a little girl, I used to collect her pictures. And I've seen her in, oh, everything she's ever been in, I should think, and I've read every word about her, and interviews and all. Really and truly, when I think of *meeting* her— Oh, I'll simply die. What on earth shall I say to her?"

"You might ask her how she'd like to try dropping down, for a change," Mr. Murdock said.

"All right, Jim," Mrs. Murdock said. "If that's the way you want to be."

Wearily she went toward the door, and this time she reached it before she turned to him. There were no lights in her eyes.

"It—it isn't so awfully nice," she said, "to spoil somebody's pleasure in something. I was so thrilled about this. You don't see what it is to me, to meet Lily Wynton. To meet somebody like that, and see what they're like, and hear what they say, and maybe get to know them. People like that mean—well, they mean something different to me. They're not like this. They're not like me. Who do I ever see? What do I ever hear? All my whole life, I've wanted to know—I've almost prayed that someday I could meet— Well. All right, Jim."

She went out, and on to her bedroom.

Mr. Murdock was left with only his newspaper and his bitterness for company. But he spoke aloud.

" 'Drop up!' " he said. " 'Drop *up*,' for God's sake!"

The Murdocks dined, not in silence, but in pronounced quiet. There was something straitened about Mr. Murdock's stillness; but little Mrs. Murdock's was the sweet, far quiet of one given over to dreams. She had forgotten her weary words to her husband, she had passed through her excitement and her disappointment. Luxuriously she floated on innocent visions of days after the morrow. She heard her own voice in future conversations. . . .

I saw Lily Wynton at Hallie's the other day, and she was telling me all about her new play—no, I'm, terribly sorry, but it's a secret, I promised her I wouldn't tell anyone the name of it . . . Lily Wynton dropped up to tea yesterday, and we just got to talking, and she told me the most interesting things about her life; she said she'd never dreamed of telling them to anyone else. . . . Why, I'd love to come, but I promised to have lunch with Lily Wynton. . . . I had a long, long letter from Lily Wynton. . . . Lily Wynton called me up this morning. . . . Whenever I feel blue, I just go and have a talk with Lily Wynton, and then I'm all right again. . . . Lily Wynton told me . . . Lily Wynton and I . . . "Lily," I said to her . . .

The next morning, Mr. Murdock had left for his office before Mrs. Murdock rose. This had happened several times before, but not often. Mrs. Murdock felt a little queer about it. Then she told herself that it was probably just as well. Then she forgot all about it, and gave her mind to the selection of a costume suitable to the afternoon's event. Deeply she felt that her small wardrobe included no dress adequate to the occasion; for, of course, such an occasion had never before arisen. She finally decided upon a frock of dark blue serge with fluted white muslin about the neck and wrists. It was her style, that was the most she could say for it. And that was all she could say for herself. Blue serge and little white ruffles—that was she.

The very becomingness of the dress lowered her spirits. A nobody's frock, worn by a nobody. She blushed and went hot when she recalled the dreams she had woven the night before, the mad visions of intimacy, of equality with Lily Wynton. Timidity turned her heart liquid, and she thought of telephoning Miss Noyes and saying she had a bad cold and could not come. She steadied, when she planned a course of conduct to pursue at teatime. She would not try to say anything; if she stayed silent, she could not sound foolish. She would listen and watch and worship and then come home, stronger, braver, better for an hour she would remember proudly all her life.

Miss Noyes's living-room was done in the early modern period. There were a great many oblique lines and acute angles, zigzags of aluminum and horizontal stretches of mirror. The color scheme was sawdust and steel. No seat was more than twelve inches above the floor, no table was made of wood. It was, as has been said of larger places, all right for a visit.

Little Mrs. Murdock was the first arrival. She was glad of that; no, maybe it would have been better to have come after Lily Wynton; no, maybe this was right. The maid motioned her toward the living-room, and Miss Noyes greeted her in the cool voice and the warm words that were her special combination. She wore black velvet trousers, a red cummerbund, and a white silk shirt, opened at the throat. A cigarette clung to her lower lip, and her eyes, as was her habit, were held narrow against its near smoke.

"Come in, come in, tiny one," she said. "Bless its little heart. Take off its little coat. Good Lord, you look easily eleven years old in that dress. Sit ye doon, here beside of me. There'll be a spot of tea in a jiff."

Mrs. Murdock sat down on the vast, perilously low divan, and, because she was never good at reclining among cushions, held her back straight. There was room for six like her, between herself and her hostess. Miss Noyes lay back with one ankle flung upon the other knee, and looked at her.

"I'm a wreck," Miss Noyes announced. "I was modeling like a mad thing, all night long. It's taken everything out of me. I was like a thing bewitched."

"Oh, what were you making?" cried Mrs. Murdock.

"Oh, Eve," Miss Noyes said. "I always do Eve. What else is there to do? You must come pose for me some time, tiny one. You'd be nice to do. Ye-es, you'd be very nice to do. My tiny one."

"Why, I—" Mrs. Murdock said, and stopped. "Thank you very much, though," she said.

"I wonder where Lily is," Miss Noyes said. "She said she'd be here early—well, she always says that. You'll adore her, tiny one. She's really rare. She's a real person. And she's been through perfect hell. God, what a time she's had!"

"Ah, what's been the matter?" said Mrs. Murdock.

"Men," Miss Noyes said. "Men. She never had a man that wasn't a louse." Gloomily she stared at the toe of her flat-heeled patent leather pump. "A pack of lice, always. All of them. Leave her for the first little floozie that comes along."

"But—" Mrs. Murdock began. No, she couldn't have heard right. How could it be right? Lily Wynton was a great actress. A great actress meant romance. Romance meant Grand Dukes and Crown Princes and diplomats touched with gray at the temples and lean, bronzed, reckless Younger Sons. It meant pearls and emeralds and chinchilla and rubies red as the blood that was shed for them. It meant a grim-faced boy sitting in the fearful Indian midnight, beneath the dreary whirring of the *punkahs*, writing a letter to the lady he had seen but once; writing his poor heart out, before he turned to the service revolver that lay beside him on the table. It meant a golden-locked poet, floating face downward in the sea, and in his pocket his last great sonnet to the lady of ivory. It meant brave, beautiful men, living and dying for the lady who was the pale bride of art, whose eyes and heart were soft with only compassion for them.

A pack of lice. Crawling after little floozies; whom Mrs. Murdock swiftly and hazily pictured as rather like ants.

"But—" said little Mrs. Murdock.

"She gave them all her money," Miss Noyes said. "She always did. Or if she didn't, they took it anyway. Took every cent she had, and then spat in her face. Well, maybe I'm teaching her a little bit of sense now. Oh, there's the bell—that'll be Lily. No, sit ye doon, tiny one. You belong there."

Miss Noyes rose and made for the archway that separated the living-room from the hall. As she passed Mrs. Murdock, she stooped suddenly, cupped her guest's round chin, and quickly, lightly kissed her mouth.

"Don't tell Lily," she murmured, very low.

Mrs. Murdock puzzled. Don't tell Lily what? Could Hallie Noyes think that she might babble to the Lily Wynton of these strange confidences about the actress's life? Or did she mean— But she had no more time for puzzling. Lily Wynton stood in the archway. There she stood, one hand resting on the wooden molding and her body swayed toward it, exactly as she stood for her third-act entrance of her latest play, and for a like half-minute.

You would have known her anywhere, Mrs. Murdock thought. Oh, yes, anywhere. Or at least you would have exclaimed, "That woman looks something like Lily Wynton." For she was somehow different in the daylight. Her figure looked heavier, thicker, and her face—there was so much of her face that the surplus sagged from the strong, fine bones. And her eyes, those famous dark, liquid eyes. They were dark, yes, and certainly liquid, but they were set in little hammocks of folded flesh, and seemed to be set but loosely, so readily did they roll. Their whites, that were visible all around the irises, were threaded with tiny scarlet veins.

"I suppose footlights are an awful strain on their eyes," thought little Mrs. Murdock.

Lily Wynton wore, just as she should have, black satin and sables, and long white gloves were wrinkled luxuriously about her wrists. But there were delicate streaks of grime in the folds of her gloves, and down the shining length of her gown there were small, irregularly shaped dull patches; bits of food or drops of drink, or perhaps both, sometime must have slipped their carriers and found brief sanctuary there. Her hat— oh, her hat. It was romance, it was mystery, it was strange, sweet sorrow; it was Lily Wynton's hat, of all the world, and no other could dare it. Black it was, and tilted, and a great, soft plume drooped from it to follow her cheek and curl across her throat. Beneath it, her hair had the various hues of neglected brass. But, oh, her hat.

"Darling!" cried Miss Noyes.

"Angel," said Lily Wynton. "My sweet."

It was that voice. It was that deep, soft, glowing voice. "Like purple velvet," someone had written. Mrs. Murdock's heart beat visibly.

Lily Wynton cast herself upon the steep bosom of her hostess, and murmured there. Across Miss Noyes's shoulder she caught sight of little Mrs. Murdock.

"And who is this?" she said. She disengaged herself.

"That's my tiny one," Miss Noyes said. "Mrs. Murdock."

"What a clever little face," said Lily Wynton. "Clever, clever little face. What does she do, sweet Hallie? I'm sure she writes, doesn't she? Yes, I can feel it. She writes beautiful, beautiful words. Don't you, child?"

"Oh, no, really I—" Mrs. Murdock said.

"And you must write me a play," said Lily Wynton. "A beautiful, beautiful play. And I will play in it, over and over the world, until I am a very, very old lady. And then I will die. But I will never be forgotten, because of the years I played in your beautiful, beautiful play."

She moved across the room. There was a slight hesitancy, a seeming insecurity, in her step, and when she would have sunk into a chair, she began to sink two inches, perhaps, to its right. But she swayed just in time in her descent, and was safe.

"To write," she said, smiling sadly at Mrs. Murdock, "to write. And such a little thing, for such a big gift. Oh, the privilege of it. But the anguish of it, too. The agony."

"But, you see, I—" said little Mrs. Murdock.

"Tiny one doesn't write, Lily," Miss Noyes said. She threw herself back upon the divan. "She's a museum piece. She's a devoted wife."

"A wife!" Lily Wynton said. "A wife. Your first marriage, child?"

"Oh, yes," said Mrs. Murdock.

"How sweet," Lily Wynton said. "How sweet, sweet, sweet. Tell me, child, do you love him very, very much?"

"Why, I—" said little Mrs. Murdock, and blushed. "I've been married for ages," she said.

"You love him," Lily Wynton said. "You love him. And is it sweet to go to bed with him?"

"Oh—" said Mrs. Murdock, and blushed till it hurt.

"The first marriage," Lily Wynton said. "Youth, youth. Yes, when I was your age I used to marry, too. Oh, treasure your love, child, guard it, live in it. Laugh and dance in the love of your man. Until you find out what he's really like."

There came a sudden visitation upon her. Her shoulders jerked upward, her cheeks puffed, her eyes sought to start from their hammocks. For a moment she sat thus, then slowly all subsided into place. She lay back in her chair, tenderly patting her chest. She shook her head sadly, and there was grieved wonder in the look with which she held Mrs. Murdock.

"Gas," said Lily Wynton, in the famous voice. "Gas. Nobody knows what I suffer from it."

"Oh, I'm so sorry," Mrs. Murdock said. "Is there anything—"

"Nothing," Lily Wynton said. "There is nothing. There is nothing that can be done for it. I've been everywhere."

"How's for a spot of tea, perhaps?" Miss Noyes said. "It might help." She turned her face toward the archway and lifted up her voice. "Mary! Where the hell's the tea?"

"You don't know," Lily Wynton said, with her grieved eyes fixed on Mrs. Murdock, "you don't know what stomach distress is. You can never, never know, unless you're a stomach sufferer yourself. I've been one for years. Years and years and years."

"I'm terribly sorry," Mrs. Murdock said.

"Nobody knows the anguish," Lily Wynton said. "The agony."

The maid appeared, bearing a triangular tray upon which was set an heroic-sized tea service of bright white china, each piece a hectagon. She set it down on a table within the long reach of Miss Noyes and retired, as she had come, bashfully.

"Sweet Hallie," Lily Wynton said, "my sweet. Tea—I adore it. I worship it. But my distress turns it to gall and wormwood in me. Gall and wormwood. For hours, I should have no peace. Let me have a little, tiny bit of your beautiful, beautiful brandy, instead."

"You really think you should, darling?" Miss Noyes said. "You know—"

"My angel," said Lily Wynton, "it's the only thing for acidity."

"Well," Miss Noyes said. "But do remember you've got a performance tonight." Again she hurled her voice at the archway. "Mary! Bring the brandy and a lot of soda and ice and things."

"Oh, no, my saint," Lily Wynton said. "No, no, sweet Hallie. Soda and ice are rank poison to me. Do you want to freeze my poor, weak stomach? Do you want to kill poor, poor Lily?"

"Mary!" roared Miss Noyes. "Just bring the brandy and a glass." She turned to little Mrs. Murdock. "How's for your tea, tiny one? Cream? Lemon?"

"Cream, if I may, please," Mrs. Murdock said. "And two lumps of sugar, please, if I may."

"Oh, youth, youth," Lily Wynton said. "Youth and love."

The maid returned with an octagonal tray supporting a decanter of brandy and a wide, squat, heavy glass. Her head twisted on her neck in a spasm of diffidence.

"Just pour it for me, will you, my dear?" said Lily Wynton. "Thank you. And leave the pretty, pretty decanter here, on this enchanting little table. Thank you. You're so good to me."

The maid vanished, fluttering. Lily Wynton lay back in her chair, holding in her gloved hand the wide, squat glass, colored brown to the brim. Little Mrs. Murdock lowered her eyes to her teacup, carefully carried it to her lips, sipped, and replaced it on its saucer. When she raised her eyes, Lily Wynton lay back in her chair, holding in her gloved hand the wide, squat, colorless glass.

"My life," Lily Wynton said, slowly, "is a mess. A stinking mess. It always has been, and it always will be. Until I am a very, very old lady. Ah, little Clever-Face, you writers don't know what struggle is."

"But really I'm not—" said Mrs. Murdock.

"To write," Lily Wynton said. "To write. To set one word beautifully beside another word. The privilege of it. The blessed, blessed peace of it. Oh, for quiet, for rest. But do you think those cheap bastards would close that play while it's doing a nickel's worth of business? Oh, no. Tired as I am, sick as I am, I must drag along. Oh, child, child, guard your precious gift. Give thanks for it. It is the greatest thing of all. It is the only thing. To write."

"Darling, I told you tiny one doesn't write," said Miss Noyes. "How's for making more sense? She's a wife."

"Ah, yes, she told me. She told me she had perfect, passionate love," Lily Wynton said. "Young love. It is the greatest thing. It is the only thing." She grasped the decanter; and again the squat glass was brown to the brim.

"What time did you start today, darling?" said Miss Noyes.

"Oh, don't scold me, sweet love," Lily Wynton said. "Lily hasn't been naughty. Her wuzzunt naughty dirl 't all. I didn't get up until late, late, late. And though I parched, though I burned, I didn't have a drink until after my breakfast. 'It is for Hallie,' I said." She raised the glass to her mouth, tilted it, and brought it away, colorless.

"Good Lord, Lily," Miss Noyes said. "Watch yourself. You've got to walk on that stage tonight, my girl."

"All the world's a stage," said Lily Wynton. "And all the men and women merely players. They have their entrance and their exitses, and each man in his time plays many parts, his act being seven ages. At first, the infant, mewling and puking—"

"How's the play doing?" Miss Noyes said.

"Oh, lousily," Lily Wynton said. "Lousily, lousily, lousily. But what isn't? What isn't, in this terrible, terrible world? Answer me that." She reached for the decanter.

"Lily, listen," said Miss Noyes. "Stop that. Do you hear?"

"Please, sweet Hallie," Lily Wynton said. "Pretty please. Poor, poor Lily."

"Do you want me to do what I had to do last time?" Miss Noyes said. "Do you want me to strike you, in front of tiny one, here?"

Lily Wynton drew herself high. "You do not realize," she said, icily, "what acidity is." She filled the glass and held it, regarding it as though through a lorgnon. Suddenly her manner changed, and she looked up and smiled at little Mrs. Murdock.

"You must let me read it," she said. "You mustn't be so modest."

"Read—?" said little Mrs. Murdock.

"Your play," Lily Wynton said. "Your beautiful, beautiful play. Don't think I am too busy. I always have time. I have time for everything. Oh, my God, I have to go to the dentist tomorrow. Oh, the suffering I have gone through with my teeth. Look!" She set down her glass, inserted a gloved forefinger in the corner of her mouth, and dragged it to the side. "Oogh!" she insisted. "Oogh!"

Mrs. Murdock craned her neck shyly, and caught a glimpse of shining gold.

"Oh, I'm so sorry," she said.

"As wah ee id a me ass ime," Lily Wynton said. She took away her forefinger and let her mouth resume its shape. "That's what he did to me last time," she repeated. "The anguish of it. The agony. Do you suffer with your teeth, little Clever-Face?"

"Why, I'm afraid I've been awfully lucky," Mrs. Murdock said. "I—"

"You don't know," Lily Wynton said. "Nobody knows what it is. You writers—you don't know." She took up her glass, sighed over it, and drained it.

"Well," Miss Noyes said. "Go ahead and pass out, then, darling. You'll have time for a sleep before the theater."

"To sleep," Lily Wynton said. "To sleep, perchance to dream. The privilege of it. Oh, Hallie, sweet, sweet Hallie, poor Lily feels so terrible. Rub my head for me, angel. Help me."

"I'll go get the Eau de Cologne," Miss Noyes said. She left the room, lightly patting Mrs. Murdock's knee as she passed her. Lily Wynton sat in her chair and closed her famous eyes.

"To sleep," she said. "To sleep, perchance to dream."

"I'm afraid," little Mrs. Murdock began. "I'm afraid," she said, "I really must be going home. I'm afraid I didn't realize how awfully late it was."

"Yes, go, child," Lily Wynton said. She did not open her eyes. "Go to him. Go to him, live in him, love him. Stay with him always. But when he starts bringing them into the house—get out."

"I'm afraid—I'm afraid I didn't quite understand," Mrs. Murdock said.

"When he starts bringing his fancy women into the house," Lily Wynton said. "You must have pride, then. You must go. I always did. But it was always too late then. They'd got all my money. That's all they want, marry them or not. They say it's love, but it isn't. Love is the only thing. Treasure your love, child. Go back to him. Go to bed with him. It's the only thing. And your beautiful, beautiful play."

"Oh, dear," said little Mrs. Murdock. "I—I'm afraid it's really terribly late."

There was only the sound of rhythmic breathing from the chair where Lily Wynton lay. The purple voice rolled along the air no longer.

Little Mrs. Murdock stole to the chair upon which she had left her coat. Carefully she smoothed her white muslin frills, so that they would be fresh beneath the jacket. She felt a tenderness for her frock; she wanted to protect it. Blue serge and little ruffles—they were her own.

When she reached the outer door of Miss Noyes's apartment, she stopped a moment and her manners conquered her. Bravely she called in the direction of Miss Noyes's bedroom.

"Good-by, Miss Noyes," she said. "I've simply got to run. I didn't realize it was so late. I had a lovely time—thank you ever so much."

"Oh, good-by, tiny one," Miss Noyes called. "Sorry Lily went by-by. Don't mind her—she's really a real person. I'll call you up, tiny one. I want to see you. Now where's that damned Cologne?"

"Thank you ever so much," Mrs. Murdock said. She let herself out of the apartment.

Little Mrs. Murdock walked homeward, through the clustering dark. Her mind was busy, but not with memories of Lily Wynton. She thought of Jim; Jim, who had left for his office before she had arisen that morning, Jim, whom she had not kissed good-by. Darling Jim. There were no others born like him. Funny Jim, stiff and cross and silent; but only because he knew so much. Only because he knew the silliness of seeking afar for the glamour and beauty and romance of living. When they were right at home all the time, she thought. Like the Blue Bird, thought little Mrs. Murdock.

Darling Jim. Mrs. Murdock turned in her course, and entered an enormous shop where the most delicate and esoteric of foods were sold for heavy sums. Jim liked red caviar. Mrs. Murdock bought a jar of the shiny, glutinous eggs. They would have cocktails that night, though they had no guests, and the red caviar would be served with them for a surprise, and it would be a little, secret party to celebrate her return to contentment with her Jim, a party to mark her happy renunciation of all the glory of the world. She bought, too, a large, foreign cheese. It would give a needed touch to dinner. Mrs. Murdock had not given much attention to ordering dinner, that morning. "Oh, anything you want, Signe," she had said to the maid. She did not want to think of that. She went on home with her packages.

Mr. Murdock was already there when she arrived. He was sitting with his newspaper opened to the financial page. Little Mrs. Murdock ran into him with her eyes a-light. It is too bad that the light in a person's eyes is only the light in a person's eyes, and you cannot tell at a look what causes it. You do not know if it is excitement about you, or about something else. The evening before, Mrs. Murdock had run in to Mr. Murdock with her eyes a-light.

"Oh, hello," he said to her. He looked back at this paper, and kept his eyes there. "What did you do? Did you drop up to Hank Noyes's?"

Little Mrs. Murdock stopped right where she was.

"You know perfectly well, Jim," she said, "that Hallie Noyes's first name is Hallie."

"It's Hank to me," he said. "Hank or Bill. Did what's-her-name show up? I mean drop up. Pardon me."

"To whom are you referring?" said Mrs. Murdock, perfectly.

"What's-her-name," Mr. Murdock said. "The movie star."

"If you mean Lily Wynton," Mrs. Murdock said, "she is not a movie star. She is an actress. She is a great actress."

"Well, did she drop up?" he said.

Mrs. Murdock's shoulders sagged. "Yes," she said. "Yes, she was there, Jim."

"I suppose you're going on the stage now," he said.

"Ah, Jim," Mrs. Murdock said. "Ah, Jim, please. I'm not sorry at all I went to Hallie Noyes's today. It was—it was a real experience to meet Lily Wynton. Something I'll remember all my life."

"What did she do?" Mr. Murdock said. "Hang by her feet?"

"She did no such thing!" Mrs. Murdock said. "She recited Shake-speare, if you want to know."

"Oh, my God," Mr. Murdock said. "That must have been great."

"All right, Jim," Mrs. Murdock said. "If that's the way you want to be."

Wearily she left the room and went down the hall. She stopped at the pantry door, pushed it open, and spoke to the pleasant little maid.

"Oh, Signe," she said. "Oh, good evening, Signe. Put these things somewhere, will you? I got them on the way home. I thought we might have them some time."

Wearily little Mrs. Murdock went on down the hall to her bedroom.

Harper's Bazaar, September 1933

Cousin Larry

The young woman in the crepe de Chine dress printed all over with little pagodas set amid giant cornflowers flung one knee atop the other and surveyed, with an enviable contentment, the tip of her scrolled green sandal. Then, in a like happy calm, she inspected her finger nails of so thick and glistening a red that it seemed as if she but recently had completed tearing an ox apart with her naked hands. Then she dropped her chin abruptly to her chest and busied herself among the man-made curls, sharp and dry as shavings, along the back of her neck; and again she appeared to be wrapped in cozy satisfaction. Then she lighted a fresh cigarette and seemed to find it, like all about her, good. Then she went right on with all she had been saying before.

"No, but really," she said. "Honestly. I get so darn sick of all this talk about Lila—'Oh, poor Lila' this, and 'Oh, the poor thing' that. If they want to be sorry for her—well, it's a free country, I suppose, but all I can say is I think they're crazy. I think they're absolutely cock-eyed wild. If they want to be sorry for anybody, go be sorry for Cousin Larry, why don't they? Then they'd be making some sense, for a change. Listen, nobody has to be sorry for Lila. She has a marvelous time; she never does one solitary thing she doesn't want to do. She has the best time of anybody I know. And anyway, it's all her own fault, anyway. It's just the way she is; it's her rotten, vile disposition. Well, you can't be expected to feel sorry for anybody when it's their own fault, can you? Does that make any sense? Now I ask you!

"Listen. I know Lila. I've known her for years. I've seen her practically day in, day out. Well, you know how often I've visited them, down in the country. You know how well you know a person after you've visited them; well, that's the way I know Lila. And I like her. Honestly I do. I like Lila all right when she's decent. It's only when she starts feeling sorry for herself and begins whining and asking questions and spoiling everybody's fun that she makes me throw up. A lot of the time she's perfectly all right. Only she's selfish, that's all. She's just a rotten, selfish woman. And then the way people talk about Larry for staying in town and going around places without her! Listen to me, she stays home because she wants to. She'd *rather* go to bed early. I've seen her do it night after night, when I've been down there visiting. I know her like a book. Catch *that* one doing anything she doesn't feel like doing!

"Honestly. It just makes me boil to hear anyone say anything against Larry. Just let them try criticizing him to me, that's all. Why, that man's a living saint, that's what he is. How on earth he's got anything at all left, after ten years with that woman, I *don't* see. She can't let him alone a second; always wants to be in on everything, always wants to know what's the joke and what's he laughing about, and oh, tell her, tell her, so she can laugh too. And she's one of those damn serious old fools that can't see anything funny, and can't kid or anything, and then she tries to get cute and play, too, and—well, you just can't *look,* that's all. And poor Larry, who couldn't be funnier or have more of a sense of humor and all. I should think she'd have driven him cock-eyed wild, years ago.

"And then when she sees the poor soul having a little bit of fun with anybody for a few minutes, she gets—well, she doesn't get jealous, she's too self-centered ever to have a jealous moment—she's so rotten suspicious, she's got such a vile, dirty mind, she just gets mean. And to me, of all people. Now I ask you! Me, that's known Larry practically all my life, practically. Why, I've called him Cousin Larry for years—that shows you how I've always felt about him. And the very first time I went down there to stay with them, she started in about why did I call him Cousin Larry, and I said, oh, I'd known him so well, I felt sort of related, and then she got kittenish, the old fool, and said, well, I'd have to take her into the family, too, and I said, yes, that would be great, or something. And I *did* try to call her Aunt Lila, but I just simply couldn't seem to *feel* that way. And it didn't seem to make her any happier, anyway. Well, she's just one of those kind she's never happy unless she's miserable. She *enjoys* being miserable. That's why she does it. Catch her doing anything she doesn't want to do!

"Honestly. Poor Cousin Larry. Imagine that dirty old thing trying to work up something, because I call him Cousin Larry. Well, I certainly didn't let her stop me; I guess my friendship with Larry is worth a little more than *that.* And he calls me Little Sweetheart, too, just the way he always did. He's always called me his little sweetheart. Wouldn't you think she could see, if there was anything in it, he wouldn't call me that right in front of her face all the time?

"Really. It isn't that she means anything in my young life, it's just that I feel so terribly sorry for Larry. I wouldn't set foot in the house again if it wasn't for him. But he says—of course, he's never said one single word against her, he's the kind would always be just like a clam about any woman that happened to be his wife—he says nobody has any idea of what it's like to be there alone with Lila. So that's why I went down in the first place. And I saw what he meant. Why, the first night I was in the house, she went up to bed at ten o'clock. Cousin Larry and I were playing some old phonograph records—well, we had to do *something*, she wouldn't laugh or kid or do anything we were doing, just sat there like an old stick—and it just happened I happened to find a lot of old songs Larry and I used to sing and go dancing to, and everything. Well, you know how it is when you know a man awfully well, you always have things that remind you of things, and we were laughing and playing these records and sort of saying, 'Do you remember the time?' and 'What does that remind you of?' and all, the way everybody does; and the first thing you know, Lila got up and said she was sure we wouldn't mind if she went to bed—she felt so awfully tired. And Larry told me then, that's what she always does when anybody around is having a good time. If there's a guest in the house when she feels so awfully tired, that's just too bad, that's all. A little thing like that doesn't put *that* one out. When she wants to go to bed, she *goes*.

"So that's why I've gone down there so much. You don't know what a real godsend it is for Larry to have someone he can sit up with, after dear Lila goes to bed at ten o'clock. And then I'm somebody the poor soul can play golf with in the daytime, too; Lila can't play—oh, she's got something wrong with her insides, *wouldn't* she have? I wouldn't go near the place if it wasn't such a help to Larry. You know how crazy he is about having a good time. And Lila's *old*—she's an *owe-wuld* woman! Honestly. Larry—well, of course it doesn't make any difference how old a man is, anyway—years, I mean; it's the way he feels that counts. And Larry's just like a kid. I keep telling Lila, trying to clean up her nasty, evil mind, that Cousin Larry and I are nothing but a couple of crazy kids together. Now I ask you, wouldn't you think she'd have sense enough to see she's all through and the only thing for her to do is to sit back and let people have a good time that *can*? *She* had a good time; going to bed early, that's what she likes. Nobody interferes with her—wouldn't you think she'd mind her own business and stop asking questions and wanting to know what everything's about?

"Well, now look. Once I was down there, and I happened to be wearing orchids. And so Lila said oh, weren't they lovely and all, and who sent them to me. Honestly. She *deliberately* asked me who sent them to me. So I thought, well, it will just do you good, and I told her Cousin Larry did. I told her it was a sort of a little anniversary of ours—you know how it is, when you know a man a long time, you always have sort of little anniversaries, like the first time he ever took you to lunch, or the first time he sent you flowers or something. So anyway, this was one of those, and I told Lila what a wonderful friend Cousin Larry was to me, and how he always remembered things like that, and how much fun it was for him to do them, he seemed to get such pleasure out of doing sweet things. Now I ask you. Wouldn't you think anybody in the *world* would see how innocent it was if you told them that? And do you know what she said? Honestly. She said, 'I like orchids, too.' So I just thought, well, maybe if you were fifteen years younger you might get some man to send you some, baby, but I didn't say a thing. I just said, 'Oh, wear these, Lila, won't you?' Just like that; and Lord knows, I didn't *have* to say it, did I? But oh, no, she wouldn't. No, she thought she'd just go and lie down a while, if I didn't mind. She was feeling so awfully tired.

"And then—oh, my dear, I nearly forgot to tell you. You'll simply die over this, you'll absolutely collapse. Well, the last time I was there, Cousin Larry had sent me some little chiffon drawers; they couldn't have been cuter. You know, it was just a joke, these little pink chiffon things with *'Mais l'amour viendra'* embroidered on them in black. It means 'Love will come.' You know. He saw them in some window and he just sent them to me, just for this joke. He's always doing things like—hey, for goodness' sake, don't tell anyone, will you? Because, Lord knows if it *meant* anything, I wouldn't be telling you, you *know* that, but you know how people are. And there's been enough talk, just because I go out with him sometimes, to keep the poor soul company while Lila's in bed.

"Well, so anyway, he sent me these things, and so when I came down to dinner—there were just the three of us; that's another thing she does, she doesn't have anybody in unless he absolutely insists—I said to Larry, 'I've got them on, Cousin Larry.' So of course Lila had to hear and she said, 'What have you got on?' and she kept asking and asking, and naturally I wasn't going to tell *her*, and it just struck me so funny I nearly died trying not to laugh and every time I caught Larry's eye we'd both bust right out. And Lila kept saying oh, what was the joke, and oh, tell her, tell her. And so finally, when she saw we wouldn't tell, she had to go to bed, no matter how it made *us* feel. My God, can't people have jokes? This is a free country, isn't it?

"Honestly. And she's getting worse and worse all the time. I'm simply *sick* about Larry. I can't see what he's ever going to do. You know a woman like that wouldn't give a man a divorce in a million years, even if he was the one that had the money. Larry never says a word, but I

bet there are times when he just wishes she'd *die*. And everybody saying
'Oh, poor Lila,' 'Oh, poor, dear Lila, isn't it a shame?' That's because
she gets them off in corners, and starts sobbing about not having any
children. Oh, how she wishes she had a baby. Oh, if she and Larry only
had a baby, blah, blah, blah, blah, blah. And then the eyes filling with
tears—you know, you've seen her do it. Eyes filling with tears! A lot
she's got to cry about, always doing what she wants all the time. I bet
that's just a line, about not having a baby. That's just to get sympathy.
She's just so rotten selfish she wouldn't have ever given up her own
convenience to have one, that's what's the matter with her. She might
have had to stay up after ten o'clock.

"Poor Lila! Honestly, I could lose my lunch. Why don't they say
poor Larry, for a change? He's the one to feel sorry for. Well. All *I*
know is, I'll always do anything I can for Cousin Larry. That's all *I*
know."

The young woman in the printed crepe de Chine dress removed her
dead cigarette from its pasteboard holder and seemed, as she did so, to
find increased enjoyment in the familiar sight of her rich-hued finger
nails. Then she took from her lap a case of gold or some substance near
it, and in a minute mirror scanned her face as carefully as if it were
verse. She knit her brows, she drew her upper eyelids nearly to those
below them, she turned her head as one expressing regretful negation,
she moved her mouth laterally in the manner of a semi-tropical fish;
and when all this was done, she seemed even cooler in confidence of
well-being. Then she lighted a fresh cigarette and appeared to find that,
too, impeccable. Then she went right on over all she had been saying
before.

The New Yorker, June 30, 1934

Mrs. Hofstadter on Josephine Street

That summer, the Colonel and I leased a bungalow named 947 West Catalpa Boulevard, rumored completely furnished: three forks, but twenty-four nutpicks. Then we went to an employment agency, to hunt for treasure. The lady at the employment agency was built in terraces; she was of a steady pink, presumably all over, and a sky-wide capability. She bit into each of her words and seemed to find it savory, and she finished every sentence to the last crumb. When I am in the presence of such people I am frequently asked, "And what's the matter with Sister today? Has the cat got her tongue?" But they make the Colonel want to tell them what he done to Philadelphia Jack O'Brien.

So the Colonel did the talking for our team. The lady at the employment agency was of the prompt impression that I was something usually kept in the locked wing; she gave me a quick, kind nod, as who should say "Now you just sit there quietly and count those twelve fingers of yours," and then she and the Colonel left me out of the whole project. We wanted, the Colonel said, a man; a man to market, to cook, to serve, to remember about keeping the cigarette-boxes filled, and to clean the little house. We wanted a man, he said, because maids, at least those in our experience, talked a good deal of the time. We were worn haggard with unsolicited autobiographies. We must insist, he said, that our servant be, before all things, still.

"My wife," said the Colonel—the lady and I waited for him to add, "the former Miss Kallikak"—"my wife must never be disturbed."

"*I* see," the lady said. She sighed a little.

"She writes," the Colonel said.

"And pretty soon now," the lady and I inferred, "we must look around for someone to come in a couple of hours a week and teach her to read."

The Colonel went on talking about what we wanted. It was but little. The simplest food, he said. The lady nodded compassionately at him; surely she pictured him standing with extended dish trying to coax me in from eating clay. The quietest life, he said, the earliest hours, the fewest guests—it was a holiday, really, to live with us. We asked only someone to stand between us and the telephone, someone to flick from the doorstep young gentlemen soliciting subscriptions to magazines, someone to keep, at other times and in so far as possible, his face shut.

"Don't you say another word!" the lady said. She smacked that "say" as if it had been delicious with salt and onion. "Not one other word. I've got just the thing!"

Horace Wrenn, she said, was the thing. He was colored, she said, but fine. I was so deeply pondering the selection of "but" that I missed several courses in her repast of words. When next I heard her, a new name had sprung in.

"He's been with Mrs. Hofstadter off and on," she said. She looked triumphant. I looked as if all my life I had heard that anybody who had ever been with Mrs. Hofstadter, either off or on, was beyond question the thing. The Colonel looked much as usual.

"Mrs. Hofstadter on Josephine Street," the lady explained. "That's our loveliest residential district. She has a lovely home there. She's one of our loveliest families. Mrs. Hofstadter—well, wait till you see what *she* says!"

She took from her desk a sheet of notepaper spread with a handwriting like the lesser rivers on maps. It was Mrs. Hofstadter on Josephine Street's letter of recommendation of Horace Wrenn, and it must have been a sort of blending of the Ninety-Eighth Psalm with Senator Vest's tribute to his dog. Whatever it was, it was too good for the likes of us to see. The lady held it tight and slipped her gaze along its lines with clucks and smacks of ecstasy and cries of "Well, look at this, will you—'honest, economical, good carver'—well!" and "My, this *is* a reference for you!"

Then she locked the letter in her desk, and she talked to the Colonel. He is to be had only with difficulty, but she got him, and good. She congratulated him upon the softness of his fortune. She marveled that it was given him to find, and without effort, the blue rose. She envied him the life that would be his when perfection came to house with him. She sighed for the exquisite dishes, the smooth attentions that were to be offered him, ever in silence, by competence and humility, blent and incarnate. He was to have, she told him, just everything, and that without moving a hand or answering a question. There was only one little catch to it, she said; and the Colonel went gray. Horace could not come to us until the day after the next one. Mrs. Hofstadter on Josephine Street's daughter was to be married, and Horace had charge of the breakfast. It was touching to hear the Colonel plead his willingness to wait.

"Well, then I guess that's all," the lady said, briskly. She rose. "If you aren't the luckiest! You just run right along home now, and wait for Horace." Her air added, "And take Soft Susie, the Girl Who Is Like Anybody Else Till the Moon Comes Up, with you. We want no naturals here!"

We went home, sweet in thought of the luxury to come; though the Colonel, who is of a melancholy cast, took to worrying a little because Horace might not go back to New York with us when the summer was over.

Until the arrival of Horace, we did what is known as making out somehow, which is a big phrase for it. It was found to be best, after fair trial, for me to stay out of the kitchen altogether. So the Colonel did the cooking, and tomatoes kept creeping into everything, which gave him delusions of persecution. It was also found better for me to avoid any other room. The last time I made the bed, the Colonel came in and surveyed the result.

"What is this?" he inquired. "Some undergraduate prank?"

Horace arrived in the afternoon, toward the cool of the day. No bell or knocker heralded his coming; simply, he was with us in the living-room. He carried a suitcase of some leathery material, and upon his head he retained a wide white straw hat with drooping brim, rather like something chosen by a duchess for garden-party wear. He was tall and broad, with an enormous cinder-colored face crossed by gold-encircled spectacles.

He spoke to us. As if coated with grease, words slid from his great lips, and his tones were those of one who cozens the sick.

"Here," he said, "is Horace. Horace has come to take care of you."

He set down his suitcase and removed his hat, revealing oiled hair, purple in the sunlight, plaided over with thin, dusty lines; Horace employed a hair-net. He laid his hat upon a table. He advanced and gave to each of us one of his hands. I received the left, the middle finger of which was missing, leaving in its stead a big, square gap.

"I want you to feel," he said, "that I am going to think of this as my home. That is the way I will think of it. I always try to think the right thing. When I told my friends I was coming here, I said to them, I said, 'That is my home from now on.' You are going to meet my friends; yes, you are. I want you to meet my friends. My friends can tell you more about me than I can. Mrs. Hofstadter always says to me, 'Horace,' she says, 'I never heard anything like it,' she says. 'Your friends just can't say enough for you.' I have a great many friends, boy friends and lady friends. Mrs. Hofstadter always tells me, 'Horace,' she says, 'I never seen anybody had so many friends.' Mrs. Hofstadter on Josephine Street. She has a lovely home there; I want you to see her home. When I told her I was coming here, 'Oh, my, Horace,' she said, 'what'm I ever going to do without you?' I have served Mrs. Hofstadter for years, right there on Josephine Street. 'Oh, my, Horace,' she said, 'how'm I going to get along without Horace?' But I had promised to come to you folks, and Horace never goes back on his word. I am a big man, and I always try to do the big thing."

"Well, look," said the Colonel, "suppose I show you where your room is and you can—"

"I want you," Horace said, "to get to know me. And I'm going to get to know you, too; yes, I am. I always try to do the right thing for the folks I serve. I want you to get to know that girl of mine, too. When I tell my friends I have a daughter twelve years of age in September, 'Horace,' they say, 'I can hardly believe it!' You're going to meet that girl of mine; yes, you are. She'll come up here, and she'll talk right up to you; yes, and she'll sit down and play that piano there—play it all day long. I don't say it because I'm her father, but that's the brightest girl *you* ever seen. People say she's Horace all over. Mrs. Hofstadter on Josephine Street, she said to me, 'Horace,' she said, 'I can't hardly tell which is the girl and which is Horace.' Oh, there's nothing of her mother's side about *that* girl! I never could get on with her mother. I try never to say an unkind thing about nobody. I'm a big man, and I always try to do the big thing. But I never could live with her mother more than fifteen minutes at a time."

"Look," the Colonel said, "the kitchen's right in there, and your room is just off it, and you can—"

"Why, do you know," Horace said, "that girl of mine, she's taken for white every day in the week. Yes, sir. I bet you there's a hundred people, right in this town, never dreams that girl of mine's a colored girl. And you're going to meet my sister, too, some of these days pretty soon. My sister's just about the finest hairdresser *you* ever set *your* eyes on. And never touches a colored head, either. She's just about like what I am. I try never to say an unkind thing, I don't hold nothing against the colored race, but Horace just doesn't mix up with them, that's all."

I thought of a man I had known once named Aaron Eisenberg, who changed his name to Erik Colton. Nothing ever became of him.

"Look," the Colonel said, "your room's right off the kitchen, and if you've got a white coat with you you can—"

"Has Horace got a white coat!" Horace said. "Has he got a white coat! Why, when you see Horace in that white coat of his, you're going to say, just like Mrs. Hofstadter on Josephine Street says, 'Horace,' you're going to say, 'I never seen anybody look any nicer.' Yes, *sir,* I've got that white coat. I never forget anything; that's one thing I *don't* do. Now do you know what Horace is going to do for you? Do you *know* what he's going to do? Well, he's going out there in that kitchen, just like it was Mrs. Hofstadter's lovely big kitchen of hers, and he's going to fix you the best dinner *you* ever et in *your* life. I always try to make everybody happy; when people are happy, then I'm happy. That's the way I am. Mrs. Hofstadter said to me, sitting right there in her lovely home on Josephine Street, 'Horace,' she said, 'I don't know who these people are you're going to's,' she said, 'but I can tell you,' Mrs. Hofstadter said, 'they're going to be happy.' I just said, 'Thank you, Mrs. Hofstadter.' That's all I said. I've served her many years. And you're going to see that lovely home of hers, some of these days; yes, you are."

He gathered up his hat and his suitcase, smiled slowly upon us, and went into the kitchen.

The Colonel walked over to the window and stood for a while, looking out of it.

I said, "You know, I think if we play our cards right we can find out who Horace used to work for."

"For whom Horace used to work," the Colonel said, mechanically.

Horace returned. He wore a white coat and an apron that covered him in front to his shoe-leather. My mind went to Pullman dining-cars, and I remembered, with no pleasure, preserved figs and cream.

"Here's Horace," he said. "Now Horace is all ready to try and make you happy. Do you know what Horace is going to do for you, some of these days? Do you *know* what he's going to do? Well, he's just going to make you one of those mint juleps of his, that's what *he's* going to do! Mrs. Hofstadter of Josephine Street always says, 'Horace,' she says, 'when you going to make one of those mint juleps of yours?' Well, I'll tell you what Horace does; he doesn't care how much trouble he takes, when he's making people happy. First he goes to work and he takes some pineapple syrup and he puts it in a glass, and then he puts in just a liddle, lid-dle bit of that juice off them bottles full of red cherries, and then he puts in the gin and the ginger ale, and then he gets him a big, long piece of pineapple and he lays *that* in, and then when he gets the orange in and puts that old red cherry on top—well! That's the way *Horace* does when he fixes a mint julep."

The Colonel is from the old South. He left the room.

Horace came at me with his head lowered and a great forefinger pointed at the level of my eyes. I was terrified for only a moment. Then I saw it for gigantic archness.

"Wait'll you hear," he said, "wait'll you hear how that telephone is

going to ring, soon as my friends find out this is Horace's home. Why
I bet you right this minute, Mrs. Hofstadter on Josephine Street's telephone is ringing away, first this one and then that one, 'Where's Horace?' 'How'm I going to reach Horace?' I don't talk about myself, I
always try to be just the way I'd want you to be with me, but you're
going to say you never seen anybody had so many lady friends. Yes,
sir, and when you meet them, you're going to say, 'Horace,' you're
going to say, 'why, Horace, I'd take any one of them for as white as I
am any day in the week.' That's what *you're* going to say. Wait'll you
hear the fun there's going to be around this place when that telephone
starts, 'How are you, Horace?' 'What are you doing, Horace?' 'When'm
I going to see you, Horace?' I'm not going to talk about myself any
more than I'd want you to talk about *yourself,* but you wait'll you see
all those friends I have. Why, Mrs. Hofstadter on Josephine Street always says, 'Horace,' she says, 'I never—' "

The Colonel came back. "Look, Horace," he said, "would you—"

"Well, now, say, if you want to talk about friends," Horace said, "I
just don't mind telling you that out at Mrs. Hofstadter on Josephine
Street's daughter's wedding here yesterday, there wasn't a guest there
wasn't a friend of Horace's. There they all was, oh, a hundred, a hundred fifty people, all of them talking right up, 'Hello, Horace,' 'Glad to
see you, Horace.' Yes, sir, and not a colored face there, either. I just
said, 'Thank you.' I always try to say the right thing, and that's what I
said. Mrs. Hofstadter, she said to me, 'Horace,' she said—"

"Horace," I said, nor knew, perhaps, that it would stand my only
complete speech with him, "may I have a glass of water, please?"

"Can you have a glass of water!" Horace said. "Can you have a
glass of water! Well, I'll tell you just what Horace is going to do. He's
going out there in that kitchen, and he's going to bring you just the
biggest, coldest glass of water *you* ever had in *your* life. There's going
to be nothing too good for *you,* now Horace is here. Why, he's going
to do for you just like you was Mrs. Hofstadter, out in her lovely home
on Josephine Street; yes, he is."

He left, turning his head archly back over his shoulder to bestow his
parting smile.

The Colonel said, "I wonder which Mrs. Hofstadter that is."

"I keep getting her mixed up with the one that lives somewhere near
Josephine Street," I said.

Horace returned with the water, and spoke to us. Through his prep-
arations for dinner, he spoke to us. Through dinner, which was held at
six o'clock, according to the custom obtaining in Mrs. Hofstadter on

Josephine Street's lovely home, he spoke to us. We sat there. Once the Colonel asked Horace for something, and so learned his lesson forever. Better go without a service than bring on rich and recommended assurances of the tender perfection of its fulfillment.

I cannot remember the menu. I can bring back, while faintness spirals upward through me, an impression of waxen gray gravy, loose pink gelatine, and butter at blood-heat, specialties finer than which Mrs. Hofstadter on Josephine Street had never et. Over more definite items, memory draws her merciful gray curtain. She does, for that matter, over all the events of Horace's stay with us. I do not know how long that was. There were no days, there were no nights, there was no time. There was only space; space filled with Horace.

The Colonel, for it is a man's world, was away from the bungalow during the day. Horace was there. Horace was always there. I have known no being so present in a house as was Horace. I never knew him to open a door, I never heard his approaching footfall; Horace was out of the room and then, a thousand times more frequently, Horace was in it. I sat at my typewriter, and Horace stood across from it and spoke to me.

And in the evenings, when the Colonel returned, Horace spoke to us. All his conversation was for us, for none of his friends, boy friends or lady friends, ever called him to hold talk; it may be that Mrs. Hofstadter on Josephine Street could not bring herself to share his telephone number. The Colonel and I did not look at each other; after a little while we avoided each other's eyes. Perhaps it was that we did not wish to see each other in our shame. I do not know; I know nothing about those days. I am sure, after confirmation, that we did not think, either of us, "In heaven's name, what manner of worm is this I have married?" We had no thoughts, no spirits, no actions. We ceased to move from room to room, even from chair to chair. We stayed where we were, two vile, dead things, slowly drowned in warmish, sweetish oil. There we were, for eternity, world without end, with Horace.

But an end came. I have never known what brought it on, nor have I wanted to learn. Once your pardon arrives, what's it to you what induced the governor's signature? The Colonel said, afterward, that Horace said it once too often; but that is all I ever knew. All I know is that I came into the living-room one morning, one heavenly morning of sunshine, and heard the Colonel's voice upraised in the kitchen. People who happened to be passing through the town on trains at that time could also have heard the Colonel's voice upraised in the kitchen.

He was giving, it seemed, advice to Horace. "You go," it ran, "and you go now!"

I heard Horace's tones, those of one quieting a problem child, but they were so low I received few words. "—spoken to this way," I distinguished, and "—loveliest people in this town. Why, Mrs. Hofstadter on Josephine Street, she wouldn't never—"

Then the Colonel's voice had everything its way again. He gave a fresh piece of advice. He suggested, as a beginning, that Horace take Mrs. Hofstadter and take her lovely home and take her whole goddam Josephine Street—

The Colonel was free. He was so free that he stood, straight-shouldered on the sunlit porch, and sated his eyes on the back of Horace, receding down the path. Mrs. Hofstadter on Josephine Street's words had come true. She had not known who those people were that Horace was going to's, but she had known they were going to be happy. We were alone; tomatoes might start following us around again, but that was the worst that could happen to us.

So it was ten minutes before the telephone rang. Crazed with joy at the return of my tongue, I answered it. I heard a large voice, slithering along the wire like warm cottonseed oil.

"This," it said, "is Horace. Horace is speaking. I am a big man and I always try to do the big thing, and I want to tell you that I am sorry Horace left your home so impetuous; yes, I am: I want you to know that Horace is going to come back to your home again and serve you, just like for so many years he served—"

But somehow the receiver clicked into place and I never had to hear her name again.

The New Yorker, August 4, 1934

Clothe the Naked

Big Lannie went out by the day to the houses of secure and leisured ladies, to wash their silks and their linens. She did her work perfectly; some of the ladies even told her so. She was a great, slow mass of a woman, colored a sound brown-black save for her palms and the flat of her fingers that were like gutta-percha from steam and hot suds. She was slow because of her size, and because the big veins in her legs hurt her, and her back ached much of the time. She neither cursed her ills nor sought remedies for them. They had happened to her; there they were.

Many things had happened to her. She had had children, and the children had died. So had her husband, who was a kind man, cheerful with the little luck he found. None of their children had died at birth. They had lived to be four or seven or ten, so that they had had their ways and their traits and their means of causing love; and Big Lannie's heart was always wide for love. One child had been killed in a street accident and two others had died of illnesses that might have been no more than tedious, had there been fresh food and clear spaces and clean air behind them. Only Arlene, the youngest, lived to grow up.

Arlene was a tall girl, not so dark as her mother but with the same firm flatness of color. She was so thin that her bones seemed to march in advance of her body. Her little pipes of legs and her broad feet with jutting heels were like things a child draws with crayons. She carried her head low, her shoulders scooped around her chest, and her stomach slanted forward. From the time that she was tiny, there were men after her.

Arlene was a bad girl always; that was one of the things that had happened to Big Lannie. There it was, and Big Lannie could only keep bringing her presents, surprises, so that the girl would love her mother and would want to stay at home. She brought little bottles of sharp perfume, and pale stockings of tinny silk, and rings set with bits of green and red glass; she tried to choose what Arlene would like. But each time Arlene came home she had bigger rings and softer stockings and stronger perfume than her mother could buy for her. Sometimes she would stay with her mother over a night, and sometimes more than a week; and then Big Lannie would come back from work one evening, and the girl would be gone, and no word of her. Big Lannie would go on bringing surprises, and setting them out along Arlene's bed to wait a return.

Big Lannie did not know it, when Arlene was going to have a baby. Arlene had not been home in nearly half a year; Big Lannie told the time in days. There was no news at all of the girl until the people at the hospital sent for Big Lannie to come to her daughter and grandson. She was there to hear Arlene say the baby must be named Raymond, and to see the girl die. For whom Raymond was called, or if for anyone, Big Lannie never knew.

He was a long, light-colored baby, with big, milky eyes that looked right back at his grandmother. It was several days before the people at the hospital told her he was blind.

Big Lannie went to each of the ladies who employed her and explained that she could not work for some while; she must take care of her grandson. The ladies were sharply discommoded, after her steady years, but they dressed their outrage in shrugs and cool tones. Each arrived, separately, at the conclusion that she had been too good to Big Lannie, and had been imposed upon, therefore. "Honestly, those niggers!" each said to her friends. "They're all alike."

Big Lannie sold most of the things she lived with, and took one room with a stove in it. There, as soon as the people at the hospital would let her, she brought Raymond and tended him. He was all her children to her.

She had always been a saving woman, with few needs and no cravings, and she had been long alone. Even after Arlene's burial, there was enough left for Raymond and Big Lannie to go on for a time. Big Lannie was slow to be afraid of what must come; fear did not visit her at all, at first, and then it slid in only when she waked, when the night hung motionless before another day.

Raymond was a good baby, a quiet, patient baby, lying in his wooden box and stretching out his delicate hands to the sounds that were light and color to him. It seemed but a little while, so short to Big Lannie, before he was walking about the room, his hands held out, his feet quick and sure. Those of Big Lannie's friends who saw him for the first time had to be told that he could not see.

Then, and it seemed again such a little while, he could dress himself, and open the door for his granny, and unlace the shoes from her tired feet, and talk to her in his soft voice. She had occasional employment—now and then a neighbor would hear of a day's scrubbing she could do, or sometimes she might work in the stead of a friend who

was sick—infrequent, and not to be planned on. She went to the ladies
for whom she had worked, to ask if they might not want her back again;
but there was little hope in her, after she had visited the first one. Well,
now, really, said the ladies; well, really, now.

The neighbors across the hall watched over Raymond while Big Lannie looked for work. He was no trouble to them, nor to himself. He sat
and crooned at his chosen task. He had been given a wooden spool
around the top of which were driven little brads, and over these with a
straightened hairpin he looped bright worsted, working faster than sight
until a long tube of woven wool fell through the hole in the spool. The
neighbors threaded big, blunt needles for him, and he coiled the woolen
tubes and sewed them into mats. Big Lannie called them beautiful, and
it made Raymond proud to have her tell him how readily she sold them.
It was hard for her, when he was asleep at night, to unravel the mats
and wash the worsted and stretch it so straight that even Raymond's
shrewd fingers could not tell, when he worked with it next day, that it
was not new.

Fear stormed in Big Lannie and took her days and nights. She might
not go to any organization dispensing relief, for dread that Raymond
would be taken from her and put in—she would not say the word to
herself, and she and her neighbors lowered their voices when they said
it to one another—an institution. The neighbors wove lingering tales of
what happened inside certain neat, square buildings on the cindery skirts
of the town, and, if they must go near them, hurried as if passing grave-
yards, and came home heroes. When they got you in one of those places,
whispered the neighbors, they laid your spine open with whips, and then
when you dropped, they kicked your head in. Had anyone come into
Big Lannie's room to take Raymond away to an asylum for the blind,
the neighbors would have fought for him with stones and rails and
boiling water.

Raymond did not know about anything but good. When he grew big
enough to go alone down the stairs and into the street, he was certain
of delight each day. He held his head high, as he came out into the little
yard in front of the flimsy wooden house, and slowly turned his face
from side to side, as if the air were soft liquid in which he bathed it.
Trucks and wagons did not visit the street, which ended in a dump for
rusted bedsprings and broken boilers and staved-in kettles; children
played over its cobbles, and men and women sat talking in open windows and called across to one another in gay, rich voices. There was
always laughter for Raymond to hear, and he would laugh back, and
hold out his hands to it.

At first, the children stopped their play when he came out, and gathered quietly about him, and watched him, fascinated. They had been told of his affliction, and they had a sort of sickened pity for him. Some of them spoke to him, in soft, careful tones. Raymond would laugh with pleasure, and stretch his hands, the curious smooth, flat hands of the blind, to their voices. They would draw sharply back, afraid that his strange hands might touch them. Then, somehow ashamed because they had shrunk from him and he could not see that they had done so, they said gentle good-bys to him, and backed away into the street again, watching him steadily.

When they were gone, Raymond would start on his walk to the end of the street. He guided himself by lightly touching the broken fences along the dirt sidewalk, and as he walked he crooned little songs with no words to them. Some of the men and women at the windows would call hello to him, and he would call back and wave and smile. When the children, forgetting him, laughed again at their games, he stopped and turned to the sound as if it were the sun.

In the evening, he would tell Big Lannie about his walk, slapping his knee and chuckling at the memory of the laughter he had heard. When the weather was too hard for him to go out in the street, he would sit at his worsted work, and talk all day of going out the next day.

The neighbors did what they could for Raymond and Big Lannie. They gave Raymond clothes their own children had not yet worn out, and they brought food, when they had enough to spare and other times. Big Lannie would get through a week, and would pray to get through the next one; and so the months went. Then the days on which she could find work fell farther and farther apart, and she could not pray about the time to come because she did not dare to think of it.

It was Mrs. Ewing who saved Raymond's and Big Lannie's lives, and let them continue together. Big Lannie said that then and ever after; daily she blessed Mrs. Ewing, and nightly she would have prayed for her, had she not known, in some dimmed way, that any intercession for Mrs. Delabarre Ewing must be impudence.

Mrs. Ewing was a personage in the town. When she went to Richmond for a visit, or when she returned from viewing the azalea gardens in Charleston, the newspaper always printed the fact. She was a woman rigorously conscious of her noble obligation; she was prominent on the Community Chest committee, and it was she who planned and engineered the annual Bridge Drive to raise funds for planting salvia around the cannon in front of the D.A.R. headquarters. These and many others were her public activities, and she was no less exacting of herself in her

private life. She kept a model, though childless, house for her husband
and herself, relegating the supervision of details to no domestic lieutenant, no matter how seemingly trustworthy.

Back before Raymond was born, Big Lannie had worked as laundress
for Mrs. Ewing. Since those days, the Ewing wash tubs had witnessed
many changes, none for the better. Mrs. Ewing took Big Lannie back
into her employment. She apologized for this step to her friends by the
always winning method of self-deprecation. She knew she was a fool,
she said, after all that time, and after the way that Big Lannie had
treated her. But still, she said—and she laughed a little at her own
ways—anyone she felt kind of sorry for could always get round her,
she said. She knew it was awful foolish, but that, she said, was the way
she was. Mr. Ewing, she said behind her husband's hearing, always
called her just a regular little old easy mark.

Big Lannie had no words in which to thank Mrs. Ewing, nor to tell
her what two days' assured employment every week could mean. At
least, it was fairly assured. Big Lannie, as Mrs. Ewing pointed out to
her, had got no younger, and she had always been slow. Mrs. Ewing
kept her in a state of stimulating insecurity by referring, with perfect
truth, to the numbers of stronger, quicker women who were also in
need of work.

Two days' work in the week meant money for rent and stovewood
and almost enough food for Raymond and Big Lannie. She must depend, for anything further, on whatever odd jobs she could find, and
she must not stop seeking them. Pressed on by fear and gratitude, she
worked so well for Mrs. Ewing that there was sometimes expressed
satisfaction at the condition of the lady's household linen and her own
and her husband's clothing. Big Lannie had a glimpse of Mr. Ewing
occasionally, leaving the house as she came, or entering it as she was
leaving. He was a bit of a man, not much bigger than Raymond.

Raymond grew so fast that he seemed to be taller each morning.
Every day he had his walk in the street to look forward to and experience, and tell Big Lannie about at night. He had ceased to be a sight
of the street; the children were so used to him that they did not even
look at him, and the men and women at the windows no longer noticed
him enough to hail him. He did not know. He would wave to any gay
cry he heard, and go on his way, singing his little songs and turning
toward the sound of laughter.

Then his lovely list of days ended as sharply as if ripped from some
bright calendar. A winter came, so sudden and savage as to find no
comparison in the town's memories, and Raymond had no clothes to

wear out in the street. Big Lannie mended his outgrown garments as long as she could, but the stuff had so rotted with wear that it split in new places when she tried to sew together the ragged edges of rents.

The neighbors could give no longer; all they had they must keep for their own. A demented colored man in a near-by town had killed the woman who employed him, and terror had spread like brush fire. There was a sort of panic of reprisal; colored employees were dismissed from their positions, and there was no new work for them. But Mrs. Ewing, admittedly soft-hearted certainly to a fault and possibly to a peril, kept her black laundress on. More than ever Big Lannie had reason to call her blessed.

All winter, Raymond stayed indoors. He sat at his spool and worsted, with Big Lannie's old sweater about his shoulders and, when his tattered knickerbockers would no longer hold together, a calico skirt of hers lapped around his waist. He lived, at his age, in the past; in the days when he had walked, proud and glad, in the street, with laughter in his ears. Always, when he talked of it, he must laugh back at that laughter.

Since he could remember, he had not been allowed to go out when Big Lannie thought the weather unfit. This he had accepted without question, and so he accepted his incarceration through the mean weeks of the winter. But then one day it was spring, so surely that he could tell it even in the smoky, stinking rooms of the house, and he cried out with joy because now he might walk in the street again. Big Lannie had to explain to him that his rags were too thin to shield him, and that there were no odd jobs for her, and so no clothes and shoes for him.

Raymond did not talk about the street any more, and his fingers were slow at his spool.

Big Lannie did something she had never done before; she begged of her employer. She asked Mrs. Ewing to give her some of Mr. Ewing's old clothes for Raymond. She looked at the floor and mumbled so that Mrs. Ewing requested her to talk *up*. When Mrs. Ewing understood, she was, she said, surprised. She had, she said, a great, great many demands on her charity, and she would have supposed that Big Lannie, of all people, might have known that she did everything she could, and, in fact, a good deal more. She spoke of inches and ells. She said that if she found she could spare anything, Big Lannie was kindly to remember it was to be just for this once.

When Big Lannie was leaving at the end of her day's work, Mrs. Ewing brought her a package with her own hands. There, she said, was a suit and a pair of shoes; beautiful, grand things that people would think she was just a crazy to go giving away like that. She simply didn't know, she said, what Mr. Ewing would say to her for being such a crazy. She explained that that was the way she was when anyone got around her, all the while Big Lannie was trying to thank her.

Big Lannie had never before seen Raymond behave as he did when she brought him home the package. He jumped and danced and clapped his hands, he tried to speak and squealed instead, he tore off the paper himself, and ran his fingers over the close-woven cloth and held it to his face and kissed it. He put on the shoes and clattered about in them, digging with his toes and heels to keep them on; he made Big Lannie pin the trousers around his waist and roll them up over his shins. He babbled of the morrow when he would walk in the street, and could not say his words for laughing.

Big Lannie must work for Mrs. Ewing the next day, and she had thought to bid Raymond wait until she could stay at home and dress him herself in his new garments. But she heard him laugh again; she could not tell him he must wait. He might go out at noon next day, she said, when the sun was so warm that he would not take cold at his first outing; one of the neighbors across the hall would help him with the clothes. Raymond chuckled and sang his little songs until he went to sleep.

After Big Lannie left in the morning, the neighbor came in to Raymond, bringing a pan of cold pork and corn bread for his lunch. She had a call for a half-day's work, and she could not stay to see him start out for his walk. She helped him put on the trousers and pinned and rolled them for him, and she laced the shoes as snug as they would go on his feet. Then she told him not to go out till the noon whistles blew, and kissed him, and left.

Raymond was too happy to be impatient. He sat and thought of the street and smiled and sang. Not until he heard the whistles did he go to the drawer where Big Lannie had laid the coat, and take it out and put it on. He felt it soft on his bare back, he twisted his shoulders to let it fall warm and loose from them. As he folded the sleeves back over his thin arms, his heart beat so that the cloth above it fluttered.

The stairs were difficult for him to manage, in the big shoes, but the very slowness of the descent was delicious to him. His anticipation was like honey in his mouth.

Then he came out into the yard, and turned his face in the gentle air. It was all good again; it was all given back again. As quickly as he could, he gained the walk and set forth, guiding himself by the fence. He could not wait; he called out, so that he would hear gay calls in return, he laughed so that laughter would answer him.

He heard it. He was so glad that he took his hand from the fence and turned and stretched out his arms and held up his smiling face to welcome it. He stood there, and his smile died on his face, and his welcoming arms stiffened and shook.

It was not the laughter he had known; it was not the laughter he had lived on. It was like great flails beating him flat, great prongs tearing his flesh from his bones. It was coming at him, to kill him. It drew slyly back, and then it smashed against him. It swirled around and over him, and he could not breathe. He screamed and tried to run out through it, and fell, and it licked over him, howling higher. His clothes unrolled, and his shoes flapped on his feet. Each time he could rise, he fell again. It was as if the street were perpendicular before him, and the laughter leaping at his back. He could not find the fence, he did not know which way he was turned. He lay screaming, in blood and dust and darkness.

When Big Lannie came home, she found him on the floor in a corner of the room, moaning and whimpering. He still wore his new clothes, cut and torn and dusty, and there was dried blood on his mouth and his palms. Her heart had leapt in alarm when he had not opened the door at her footstep, and she cried out so frantically to ask what had happened that she frightened him into wild weeping. She could not understand what he said; it was something about the street, and laughing at him, and make them go away, and don't let him go in the street no more, never in the street no more. She did not try to make him explain. She took him in her arms and rocked him, and told him, over and over, never mind, don't care, everything's all right. Neither he nor she believed her words.

But her voice was soft and her arms warm. Raymond's sobs softened, and trembled away. She held him, rocking silently and rhythmically, a long time. Then gently she set him on his feet, and took from his shoulders Mr. Ewing's old full-dress coat.

Scribner's, January 1938

Soldiers of the Republic

That Sunday afternoon we sat with the Swedish girl in the big café in Valencia. We had vermouth in thick goblets, each with a cube of honeycombed gray ice in it. The waiter was so proud of that ice he could hardly bear to leave the glasses on the table, and thus part from it forever. He went to his duty—all over the room they were clapping their hands and hissing to draw his attention—but he looked back over his shoulder.

It was dark outside, the quick, new dark that leaps down without dusk on the day; but, because there were no lights in the streets, it seemed as set and as old as midnight. So you wondered that all the babies were still up. There were babies everywhere in the café, babies serious without solemnity and interested in a tolerant way in their surroundings.

At the table next ours, there was a notably small one; maybe six months old. Its father, a little man in a big uniform that dragged his shoulders down, held it carefully on his knee. It was doing nothing whatever, yet he and his thin young wife, whose belly was already big again under her sleazy dress, sat watching it in a sort of ecstasy of admiration, while their coffee cooled in front of them. The baby was in Sunday white; its dress was patched so delicately that you would have thought the fabric whole had not the patches varied in their shades of whiteness. In its hair was a bow of new blue ribbon, tied with absolute balance of loops and ends. The ribbon was of no use; there was not enough hair to require restraint. The bow was sheerly an adornment, a calculated bit of dash.

"Oh, for God's sake, stop that!" I said to myself. "All right, so it's got a piece of blue ribbon on its hair. All right, so its mother went without eating so it could look pretty when its father came home on leave. All right, so it's her business, and none of yours. All right, so what have you got to cry about?"

The big, dim room was crowded and lively. That morning there had been a bombing from the air, the more horrible for broad daylight. But nobody in the café sat tense and strained, nobody desperately forced forgetfulness. They drank coffee or bottled lemonade, in the pleasant, earned ease of Sunday afternoon, chatting of small, gay matters, all talking at once, all hearing and answering.

There were many soldiers in the room, in what appeared to be the uniforms of twenty different armies until you saw that the variety lay in the differing ways the cloth had worn or faded. Only a few of them had been wounded; here and there you saw one stepping gingerly, leaning on a crutch or two canes, but so far on toward recovery that his face had color. There were many men, too, in civilian clothes—some of them soldiers home on leave, some of them governmental workers, some of them anybody's guess. There were plump, comfortable wives, active with paper fans, and old women as quiet as their grandchildren. There were many pretty girls and some beauties, of whom you did not remark, "There's a charming Spanish type," but said, "What a beautiful girl!" The women's clothes were not new, and their material was too humble ever to have warranted skillful cutting.

"It's funny," I said to the Swedish girl, "how when nobody in a place is best-dressed, you don't notice that everybody isn't."

"Please?" the Swedish girl said.

No one, save an occasional soldier, wore a hat. When we had first come to Valencia, I lived in a state of puzzled pain as to why everybody on the streets laughed at me. It was not because "West End Avenue" was writ across my face as if left there by a customs officer's chalked scrawl. They like Americans in Valencia, where they have seen good ones—the doctors who left their practices and came to help, the calm young nurses, the men of the International Brigade. But when I walked forth, men and women courteously laid their hands across their splitting faces and little children, too innocent for dissembling, doubled with glee and pointed and cried, *"Olé!"* Then, pretty late, I made my discovery, and left my hat off; and there was laughter no longer. It was not one of those comic hats, either; it was just a hat.

The café filled to overflow, and I left our table to speak to a friend across the room. When I came back to the table, six soldiers were sitting there. They were crowded in, and I scraped past them to my chair. They looked tired and dusty and little, the way that the newly dead look little, and the first things you saw about them were the tendons in their necks. I felt like a prize sow.

They were all in conversation with the Swedish girl. She has Spanish, French, German, anything in Scandinavian, Italian, and English. When she has a moment for regret, she sighs that her Dutch is so rusty she can no longer speak it, only read it, and the same is true of her Rumanian.

They had told her, she told us, that they were at the end of forty-eight hours' leave from the trenches, and, for their holiday, they had all pooled their money for cigarettes, and something had gone wrong, and the cigarettes had never come through to them. I had a pack of American cigarettes—in Spain rubies are as nothing to them—and I brought it out, and by nods and smiles and a sort of breast stroke, made it understood that I was offering it to those six men yearning for tobacco. When they saw what I meant, each one of them rose and shook my hand. Darling of me to share my cigarettes with the men on their way back to the trenches. Little Lady Bountiful. The prize sow.

Each one lit his cigarette with a contrivance of yellow rope that stank when afire and was also used, the Swedish girl translated, for igniting grenades. Each one received what he had ordered, a glass of coffee, and each one murmured appreciatively over the tiny cornucopia of coarse sugar that accompanied it. Then they talked.

They talked through the Swedish girl, but they did to us that thing we all do when we speak our own language to one who has no knowledge of it. They looked us square in the face, and spoke slowly, and pronounced their words with elaborate movements of their lips. Then, as their stories came, they poured them at us so vehemently, so emphatically that they were sure we must understand. They were so convinced we would understand that we were ashamed for not understanding.

But the Swedish girl told us. They were all farmers and farmers' sons, from a district so poor that you try not to remember there is that kind of poverty. Their village was next that one where the old men and the sick men and the women and children had gone, on a holiday, to the bullring; and the planes had come over and dropped bombs on the bullring, and the old men and the sick men and the women and the children were more than two hundred.

They had all, the six of them, been in the war for over a year, and most of that time they had been in the trenches. Four of them were married. One had one child, two had three children, one had five. They had not had word from their families since they had left for the front. There had been no communication; two of them had learned to write from men fighting next them in the trench, but they had not dared to write home. They belonged to a union, and union men, of course, are put to death if taken. The village where their families lived had been captured, and if your wife gets a letter from a union man, who knows but they'll shoot her for the connection?

They told about how they had not heard from their families for more than a year. They did not tell it gallantly or whimsically or stoically. They told it as if—Well, look. You have been in the trenches, fighting, for a year. You have heard nothing of your wife and your children. They do not know if you are dead or alive or blinded. You do not know where they are, or if they are. You must talk to somebody. That is the way they told about it.

One of them, some six months before, had heard of his wife and his three children—they had such beautiful eyes, he said—from a brother-in-law in France. They were all alive then, he was told, and had a bowl of beans a day. But his wife had not complained of the food, he heard. What had troubled her was that she had no thread to mend the children's ragged clothes. So that troubled him, too.

"She has no thread," he kept telling us. "My wife has no thread to mend with. No thread."

We sat there, and listened to what the Swedish girl told us they were saying. Suddenly one of them looked at the clock, and then there was excitement. They jumped up, as a man, and there were calls for the waiter and rapid talk with him, and each of them shook the hand of each of us. We went through more swimming motions to explain to them that they were to take the rest of the cigarettes—fourteen cigarettes for six soldiers to take to war—and then they shook our hands again. Then all of us said *"Salud!"* as many times as could be for six of them and three of us, and then they filed out of the café, the six of them, tired and dusty and little, as men of a mighty horde are little.

Only the Swedish girl talked, after they had gone. The Swedish girl has been in Spain since the start of the war. She has nursed splintered men, and she has carried stretchers into the trenches and, heavier laden, back to the hospital. She has seen and heard too much to be knocked into silence.

Presently it was time to go, and the Swedish girl raised her hands above her head and clapped them twice together to summon the waiter. He came, but he only shook his head and his hand, and moved away.

The soldiers had paid for our drinks.

The New Yorker, February 5, 1938

The Custard Heart

No living eye, of human being or caged wild beast or dear, domestic animal, had beheld Mrs. Lanier when she was not being wistful. She was dedicated to wistfulness, as lesser artists to words and paint and marble. Mrs. Lanier was not of the lesser; she was of the true. Surely the eternal example of the true artist is Dickens's actor who blacked himself all over to play Othello. It is safe to assume that Mrs. Lanier was wistful in her bathroom, and slumbered soft in wistfulness through the dark and secret night.

If nothing should happen to the portrait of her by Sir James Weir, there she will stand, wistful for the ages. He has shown her at her full length, all in yellows, the delicately heaped curls, the slender, arched feet like elegant bananas, the shining stretch of the evening gown; Mrs. Lanier habitually wore white in the evening but white is the devil's own hue to paint, and could a man be expected to spend his entire six weeks in the States on the execution of a single commission? Wistfulness rests, immortal, in the eyes dark with sad hope, in the pleading mouth, the droop of the little head on the sweet long neck, bowed as if in submission to the three ropes of Lanier pearls. It is true that, when the portrait was exhibited, one critic expressed in print his puzzlement as to what a woman who owned such pearls had to be wistful about; but that was doubtless because he had sold his saffron-colored soul for a few pennies to the proprietor of a rival gallery. Certainly, no man could touch Sir James on pearls. Each one is as distinct, as individual as is each little soldier's face in a Meissonier battle scene.

For a time, with the sitter's obligation to resemble the portrait, Mrs. Lanier wore yellow of evenings. She had gowns of velvet like poured country cream and satin with the lacquer of buttercups and chiffon that spiraled about her like golden smoke. She wore them, and listened in shy surprise to the resulting comparisons to daffodils, and butterflies in the sunshine, and such; but she knew.

"It just isn't me," she sighed at last, and returned to her lily draperies. Picasso had his blue period, and Mrs. Lanier her yellow one. They both knew when to stop.

In the afternoons, Mrs. Lanier wore black, thin and fragrant, with the great pearls weeping on her breast. What her attire was by morning,

256

only Gwennie, the maid who brought her breakfast tray, could know; but it must, of course, have been exquisite. Mr. Lanier—certainly there was a Mr. Lanier; he had even been seen—stole past her door on his way out to his office, and the servants glided and murmured, so that Mrs. Lanier might be spared as long as possible from the bright new cruelty of the day. Only when the littler, kinder hours had succeeded noon could she bring herself to come forth and face the recurrent sorrows of living.

There was duty to be done, almost daily, and Mrs. Lanier made herself brave for it. She must go in her town car to select new clothes and to have fitted to her perfection those she had ordered before. Such garments as hers did not just occur; like great poetry, they required labor. But she shrank from leaving the shelter of her house, for everywhere without were the unlovely and the sad, to assail her eyes and her heart. Often she stood shrinking for several minutes by the baroque mirror in her hall before she could manage to hold her head high and brave, and go on.

There is no safety for the tender, no matter how straight their route, how innocent their destination. Sometimes, even in front of Mrs. Lanier's dressmaker's or her furrier's or her lingère's or her milliner's, there would be a file of thin girls and small, shabby men, who held placards in their cold hands and paced up and down and up and down with slow, measured steps. Their faces would be blue and rough from the wind, and blank with the monotony of their treadmill. They looked so little and poor and strained that Mrs. Lanier's hands would fly to her heart in pity. Her eyes would be luminous with sympathy and her sweet lips would part as if on a whisper of cheer, as she passed through the draggled line into the shop.

Often there would be pencil-sellers in her path, a half of a creature set upon a sort of roller-skate thrusting himself along the pavement by his hands, or a blind man shuffling after his wavering cane. Mrs. Lanier must stop and sway, her eyes closed, one hand about her throat to support her lovely, stricken head. Then you could actually see her force herself, could see the effort ripple her body, as she opened her eyes and gave these miserable ones, the blind and the seeing alike, a smile of such tenderness, such sorrowful understanding, that it was like the exquisite sad odor of hyacinths on the air. Sometimes, if the man was not too horrible, she could even reach in her purse for a coin and, holding it as lightly as if she had plucked it from a silvery stem, extend her slim arm and drop it in his cup. If he was young and new at his life, he would offer her pencils for the worth of her money; but Mrs. Lanier wanted no returns. In gentlest delicacy she would slip away, leaving him with mean wares intact, not a worker for his livelihood like a million others, but signal and set apart, rare in the fragrance of charity.

So it was, when Mrs. Lanier went out. Everywhere she saw them, the ragged, the wretched, the desperate, and to each she gave her look that spoke with no words.

"Courage," it said. "And you—oh, wish me courage, too!"

Frequently, by the time she returned to her house, Mrs. Lanier would be limp as a freesia. Her maid Gwennie would have to beseech her to lie down, to gain the strength to change her gown for a filmier one and descend to her drawing-room, her eyes darkly mournful, but her exquisite breasts pointed high.

In her drawing-room, there was sanctuary. Here her heart might heal from the blows of the world, and be whole for its own sorrow. It was a room suspended above life, a place of tender fabrics and pale flowers, with never a paper or a book to report the harrowing or describe it. Below the great sheet of its window swung the river, and the stately scows went by laden with strange stuff in rich tapestry colors; there was no necessity to belong to the sort who must explain that it was garbage. An island with a happy name lay opposite, and on it stood a row of prim, tight buildings, naïve as a painting by Rousseau. Sometimes there could be seen on the island the brisk figures of nurses and internes, sporting in the lanes. Possibly there were figures considerably less brisk beyond the barred windows of the buildings, but that was not to be wondered about in the presence of Mrs. Lanier. All those who came to her drawing-room came in one cause: to shield her heart from hurt.

Here in her drawing-room, in the lovely blue of the late day, Mrs. Lanier sat upon opalescent taffeta and was wistful. And here to her drawing-room, the young men came and tried to help her bear her life.

There was a pattern to the visits of the young men. They would come in groups of three or four or six, for a while; and then there would be one of them who would stay a little after the rest had gone, who presently would come a little earlier than the others. Then there would be days when Mrs. Lanier would cease to be at home to the other young men, and that one young man would be alone with her in the lovely blue. And then Mrs. Lanier would no longer be at home to that one young man, and Gwennie would have to tell him and tell him, over the telephone, that Mrs. Lanier was out, that Mrs. Lanier was ill, that Mrs. Lanier could not be disturbed. The groups of young men would come again; that one young man would not be with them. But there would be, among them, a new young man, who presently would stay a little later and come a little earlier, who eventually would plead with Gwennie over the telephone.

Gwennie—her widowed mother had named her Gwendola, and then, as if realizing that no other dream would ever come true, had died— was little and compact and unnoticeable. She had been raised on an upstate farm by an uncle and aunt hard as the soil they fought for their lives. After their deaths, she had no relatives anywhere. She came to New York, because she had heard stories of jobs; her arrival was at the time when Mrs. Lanier's cook needed a kitchen-maid. So in her own house, Mrs. Lanier had found her treasure.

Gwennie's hard little farm-girl's fingers could set invisible stitches, could employ a flatiron as if it were a wand, could be as summer breezes in the robing of Mrs. Lanier and the tending of her hair. She was as busy as the day was long; and her days frequently extended from day-break to daybreak. She was never tired, she had no grievance, she was cheerful without being expressive about it. There was nothing in her presence or the sight of her to touch the heart and thus cause discomfort.

Mrs. Lanier would often say that she didn't know what she would do without her little Gwennie; if her little Gwennie should ever leave her, she said, she just couldn't go on. She looked so lorn and fragile as she said it that one scowled upon Gwennie for the potentialities of death or marriage that the girl carried within her. Yet there was no pressing cause for worry, for Gwennie was strong as a pony and had no beau. She had made no friends at all, and seemed not to observe the omission. Her life was for Mrs. Lanier; like all others who were permitted close, Gwennie sought to do what she could to save Mrs. Lanier from pain.

They could all assist in shutting out reminders of the sadness abroad in the world, but Mrs. Lanier's private sorrow was a more difficult matter. There dwelt a yearning so deep, so secret in her heart that it would often be days before she could speak of it, in the twilight, to a new young man.

"If I only had a little baby," she would sigh, "a little, little baby, I think I could be almost happy." And she would fold her delicate arms, and lightly, slowly rock them, as if they cradled that little, little one of her dear dreams. Then, the denied madonna, she was at her most wistful, and the young man would have lived or died for her, as she bade him.

Mrs. Lanier never mentioned why her wish was unfulfilled; the young man would know her to be too sweet to place blame, too proud to tell. But, so close to her in the pale light, he would understand, and his blood would swirl with fury that such clods as Mr. Lanier remained unkilled.

He would beseech Mrs. Lanier, first in halting murmurs, then in rushes of hot words, to let him take her away from the hell of her life and try to make her almost happy. It would be after this that Mrs. Lanier would be out to the young man, would be ill, would be incapable of being disturbed.

Gwennie did not enter the drawing-room when there was only one young man there; but when the groups returned she served unobtrusively, drawing a curtain or fetching a fresh glass. All the Lanier servants were unobtrusive, light of step and correctly indistinct of feature. When there must be changes made in the staff, Gwennie and the housekeeper arranged the replacements and did not speak of the matter to Mrs. Lanier, lest she should be stricken by desertions or saddened by tales of woe. Always the new servants resembled the old, alike in that they were unnoticeable. That is, until Kane, the new chauffeur, came.

The old chauffeur had been replaced because he had been the old chauffeur too long. It weighs cruelly heavy on the tender heart when a familiar face grows lined and dry, when familiar shoulders seem daily to droop lower, a familiar nape is hollow between cords. The old chauffeur saw and heard and functioned with no difference; but it was too much for Mrs. Lanier to see what was befalling him. With pain in her voice, she had told Gwennie that she could stand the sight of him no longer. So the old chauffeur had gone, and Kane had come.

Kane was young, and there was nothing depressing about his straight shoulders and his firm, full neck to one sitting behind them in the town car. He stood, a fine triangle in his fitted uniform, holding the door of the car open for Mrs. Lanier and bowed his head as she passed. But when he was not at work, his head was held high and slightly cocked, and there was a little cocked smile on his red mouth.

Often, in the cold weather when Kane waited for her in the car, Mrs. Lanier would humanely bid Gwennie to tell him to come in and wait in the servants' sitting-room. Gwennie brought him coffee and looked at him. Twice she did not hear Mrs. Lanier's enameled electric bell.

Gwennie began to observe her evenings off; before, she had disregarded them and stayed to minister to Mrs. Lanier. There was one night when Mrs. Lanier had floated late to her room, after a theater and a long conversation, done in murmurs, in the drawing-room. And Gwennie had not been waiting, to take off the white gown, and put away the pearls, and brush the bright hair that curled like the petals of forsythia. Gwennie had not yet returned to the house from her holiday. Mrs. Lanier had had to arouse a parlor-maid and obtain unsatisfactory aid from her.

Gwennie had wept, next morning, at the pathos of Mrs. Lanier's eyes; but tears were too distressing for Mrs. Lanier to see, and the girl stopped them. Mrs. Lanier delicately patted her arm, and there had been nothing more of the matter, save that Mrs. Lanier's eyes were darker and wider for this new hurt.

Kane became a positive comfort to Mrs. Lanier. After the sorry sights of the streets, it was good to see Kane standing by the car, solid and straight and young, with nothing in the world the trouble with him. Mrs. Lanier came to smile upon him almost gratefully, yet wistfully, too, as if she would seek of him the secret of not being sad.

And then, one day, Kane did not appear at his appointed time. The car, which should have been waiting to convey Mrs. Lanier to her dress-maker's, was still in the garage, and Kane had not appeared there all day. Mrs. Lanier told Gwennie immediately to telephone the place where he roomed and find out what this meant. The girl had cried out at her, cried out that she had called and called and called, and he was not there and no one there knew where he was. The crying out must have been due to Gwennie's loss of head in her distress at this disruption of Mrs. Lanier's day; or perhaps it was the effect on her voice of an appalling cold she seemed to have contracted, for her eyes were heavy and red and her face pale and swollen.

There was no more of Kane. He had had his wages paid him on the day before he disappeared, and that was the last of him. There was never a word and not another sight of him. At first, Mrs. Lanier could scarcely bring herself to believe that such betrayal could exist. Her heart, soft and sweet as a perfectly made crème renversée, quivered in her breast, and in her eyes lay the far light of suffering.

"Oh, how could he do this to me?" she asked piteously of Gwennie. "How could he do this to poor mè?"

There was no discussion of the defection of Kane; it was too painful a subject. If a caller heedlessly asked whatever had become of that nice-looking chauffeur, Mrs. Lanier would lay her hand over her closed lids and slowly wince. The caller would be suicidal that he had thus uncon-sciously added to her sorrows, and would strive his consecrated best to comfort her.

Gwennie's cold lasted for an extraordinarily long time. The weeks went by, and still, every morning, her eyes were red and her face white and puffed. Mrs. Lanier often had to look away from her when she brought the breakfast tray.

She tended Mrs. Lanier as carefully as ever; she gave no attention to her holidays, but stayed to do further service. She had always been quiet, and she became all but silent, and that was additionally soothing. She worked without stopping and seemed to thrive, for, save for the effects of the curious cold, she looked round and healthy.

"See," Mrs. Lanier said in tender raillery, as the girl attended the group in the drawing-room, "see how fat my little Gwennie's getting! Isn't that cute?"

The weeks went on, and the pattern of the young men shifted again. There came the day when Mrs. Lanier was not at home to a group; when a new young man was to come and be alone with her, for his first time, in the drawing-room. Mrs. Lanier sat before her mirror and lightly touched her throat with perfume, while Gwennie heaped the golden curls.

The exquisite face Mrs. Lanier saw in the mirror drew her closer attention, and she put down the perfume and leaned toward it. She drooped her head a little to the side and watched it closely; she saw the wistful eyes grow yet more wistful, the lips curve to a pleading smile. She folded her arms close to her sweet breast and slowly rocked them, as if they cradled a dream-child. She watched the mirrored arms sway gently, caused them to sway a little slower.

"If I only had a little baby," she sighed. She shook her head. Delicately she cleared her throat, and sighed again on a slightly lower note. "If I only had a little, little baby, I think I could be almost happy."

There was a clatter from behind her, and she turned, amazed. Gwennie had dropped the hair-brush to the floor and stood swaying, with her face in her hands.

"Gwennie!" said Mrs. Lanier. "Gwennie!"

The girl took her hands from her face, and it was as if she stood under a green light.

"I'm sorry," she panted. "Sorry. Please excuse me. I'm—oh, I'm going to be sick!"

She ran from the room so violently that the floor shook.

Mrs. Lanier sat looking after Gwennie, her hands at her wounded heart. Slowly she turned back to her mirror, and what she saw there arrested her; the artist knows the masterpiece. Here was the perfection of her career, the sublimation of wistfulness; it was that look of grieved bewilderment that did it. Carefully she kept it upon her face as she rose from the mirror and, with her lovely hands still shielding her heart, went down to the new young man.

Here Lies, April 1939

Song of the Shirt, 1941

It was one of those extraordinarily bright days that make things look somehow bigger. The Avenue seemed to stretch wider and longer, and the buildings to leap higher into the skies. The window-box blooms were not just a mass and a blur; it was as if they had been enlarged, so that you could see the design of the blossoms and even their separate petals. Indeed you could sharply see all sorts of pleasant things that were usually too small for your notice—the lean figurines on radiator caps, and the nice round gold knobs on flagpoles, the flowers and fruits on ladies' hats and the creamy dew applied to the eyelids beneath them. There should be more of such days.

The exceptional brightness must have had its effect upon unseen objects, too, for Mrs. Martindale, as she paused to look up the Avenue, seemed actually to feel her heart grow bigger than ever within her. The size of Mrs. Martindale's heart was renowned among her friends, and they, as friends will, had gone around babbling about it. And so Mrs. Martindale's name was high on the lists of all those organizations that send out appeals to buy tickets and she was frequently obliged to be photographed seated at a table, listening eagerly to her neighbor, at some function for the good of charity. Her big heart did not, as is so sadly often the case, inhabit a big bosom. Mrs. Martindale's breasts were admirable, delicate yet firm, pointing one to the right, one to the left; angry at each other, as the Russians have it.

Her heart was the warmer, now, for the fine sight of the Avenue. All the flags looked brand-new. The red and the white and the blue were so vivid they fairly vibrated, and the crisp stars seemed to dance on their points. Mrs. Martindale had a flag, too, clipped to the lapel of her jacket. She had had quantities of rubies and diamonds and sapphires just knocking about, set in floral designs on evening bags and vanity boxes and cigarette-cases; she had taken the lot of them to her jeweller, and he had assembled them into a charming little Old Glory. There had been enough of them for him to devise a rippled flag, and that was fortunate, for those flat flags looked sharp and stiff. There were numbers of emeralds, formerly figuring as leaves and stems in the floral designs, which were of course of no use to the present scheme and so were left over, in an embossed leather case. Some day, perhaps, Mrs. Martindale would confer with her jeweller about an arrangement to employ them. But there was no time for such matters now.

There were many men in uniform walking along the Avenue under the bright banners. The soldiers strode quickly and surely, each on to a destination. The sailors, two by two, ambled, paused at a corner and looked down a street, gave it up and went slower along their unknown way. Mrs. Martindale's heart grew again as she looked at them. She had a friend who made a practice of stopping uniformed men on the street and thanking them, individually, for what they were doing for *her*. Mrs. Martindale felt that this was going unnecessarily far. Still, she did see, a little bit, what her friend meant.

And surely no soldier or sailor would have objected to being addressed by Mrs. Martindale. For she was lovely, and no other woman was lovely like her. She was tall, and her body streamed like a sonnet. Her face was formed all of triangles, as a cat's is, and her eyes and her hair were blue-gray. Her hair did not taper in its growth about her forehead and temples; it sprang suddenly, in great thick waves, from a straight line across her brow. Its blue-gray was not premature. Mrs. Martindale lingered in her fragrant forties. Has not afternoon been adjudged the fairest time of the day?

To see her, so delicately done, so finely finished, so softly sheltered by her very loveliness, you might have laughed to hear that she was a working-woman. "Go on!" you might have said, had such been your unfortunate manner of expressing disbelief. But you would have been worse than coarse; you would have been wrong. Mrs. Martindale worked, and worked hard. She worked doubly hard, for she was unskilled at what she did, and she disliked the doing of it. But for two months she had worked every afternoon five afternoons of every week, and had shirked no moment. She received no remuneration for her steady services. She gave them because she felt she should do so. She felt that you should do what you could, hard and humbly. She practiced what she felt.

The special office of the war-relief organization where Mrs. Martindale served was known to her and her coworkers as Headquarters; some of them had come to call it H.Q. These last were of the group that kept agitating for the adoption of a uniform—the design had not been thoroughly worked out, but the idea was of something nurselike, only with a fuller skirt and a long blue cape and white gauntlets. Mrs. Martindale was not in agreement with this faction. It had always been hard for her to raise her voice in opposition, but she did, although softly. She said that while of course there was nothing *wrong* about a uniform, certainly nobody could possibly say there was anything *wrong* with the idea, still it seemed—well, it seemed not quite right to make the work an excuse, well, for fancy dress, if they didn't mind her saying so. Naturally, they wore their coifs at Headquarters, and if anybody wanted to take your photograph in your coif, you should go through with it, because it was good for the organization and publicized its work. But please, not whole uniforms, said Mrs. Martindale. Really, *please,* Mrs. Martindale said.

Headquarters was, many said, the stiffest office of all the offices of all the war-relief organizations in the city. It was not a place where you dropped in and knitted. Knitting, once you have caught the hang of it, is agreeable work, a relaxation from what strains life may be putting upon you. When you knit, save when you are at those bits where you must count stitches, there is enough of your mind left over for you to take part in conversations, and for you to be receptive of news and generous with it. But at Headquarters they sewed. They did a particularly difficult and tedious form of sewing. They made those short, shirt-like coats, fastened in back with tapes, that are put on patients in hospitals. Each garment must have two sleeves, and all the edges must be securely bound. The material was harsh to the touch and the smell, and impatient of the needle of the novice. Mrs. Martindale had made three and had another almost half done. She had thought that after the first one the others would be easier and quicker of manufacture. They had not been.

There were sewing machines at Headquarters, but few of the workers understood the running of them. Mrs. Martindale herself was secretly afraid of a machine; there had been a nasty story, never traced to its source, of somebody who put her thumb in the wrong place, and down came the needle, right through nail and all. Besides, there was something—you didn't know quite how to say it—something more of sacrifice, of service, in making things by hand. She kept on at the task that never grew lighter. It was wished that there were more of her caliber.

For many of the workers had given up the whole thing long before their first garment was finished. And many others, pledged to daily attendance, came only now and then. There was but a handful like Mrs. Martindale.

All gave their services, although there were certain doubts about Mrs. Corning, who managed Headquarters. It was she who oversaw the work, who cut out the garments, and explained to the workers what pieces went next to what other pieces. (It did not always come out as intended. One amateur seamstress toiled all the way to the completion of a coat that had one sleeve depending from the middle of the front.

It was impossible to keep from laughing; and a sharp tongue suggested that it might be sent in as it was, in case an elephant was brought to bed. Mrs. Martindale was the first to say "Ah, don't! She worked so hard over it.") Mrs. Corning was a cross woman, hated by all. The high standards of Headquarters were important to the feelings of the workers, but it was agreed that there was no need for Mrs. Corning to scold so shrilly when one of them moistened the end of her thread between her lips before thrusting it into her needle.

"Well, really," one of the most spirited among the rebuked had answered her. "If a little clean spit's the worst they're ever going to get on them . . ."

The spirited one had returned no more to Headquarters, and there were those who felt that she was right. The episode drew new members into the school of thought that insisted Mrs. Corning was paid for what she did.

When Mrs. Martindale paused in the clear light and looked along the Avenue, it was at a moment of earned leisure. She had just left Headquarters. She was not to go back to it for many weeks, nor were any of the other workers. Somewhere the cuckoo had doubtless sung, for summer was coming in. And what with everybody leaving town, it was only sensible to shut Headquarters until autumn. Mrs. Martindale, and with no guilt about it, had looked forward to a holiday from all that sewing.

Well, she was to have none, it turned out. While the workers were gaily bidding farewells and calling out appointments for the autumn, Mrs. Corning had cleared her throat hard to induce quiet and had made a short speech. She stood beside a table piled with cut-out sections of hospital coats not yet sewn together. She was a graceless woman, and though it may be assumed that she meant to be appealing, she sounded only disagreeable. There was, she said, a desperate need, a dreadful need, for hospital garments. More were wanted right away, hundreds and thousands of them; the organization had had a cable that morning, urging and pleading. Headquarters was closing until September—that meant all work would stop. Certainly they had all earned a vacation. And yet, in the face of the terrible need, she could not help asking—she would like to call for volunteers to take coats with them, to work on at home.

There was a little silence, and then a murmur of voices, gaining in volume and in assurance as the owner of each realized that it was not the only one. Most of the workers, it seemed, would have been perfectly willing, but they felt that they absolutely must give their entire time to

their children, whom they had scarcely *seen* because of being at Headquarters so constantly. Others said they were just plain too worn out,
and that was all there was to it. It must be admitted that for some
moments Mrs. Martindale felt with this latter group. Then shame waved
over her like a blush, and swiftly, quietly, with the blue-gray head held
high, she went to Mrs. Corning.

"Mrs. Corning," she said. "I should like to take twelve, please."

Mrs. Corning was nicer than Mrs. Martindale had ever seen her. She
put out her hand and grasped Mrs. Martindale's.

"Thank you," she said, and her shrill voice was gentle.

But then she had to go and be the way she always had been before.
She snatched her hand from Mrs. Martindale's and turned to the table,
starting to assemble garments.

"And please, Mrs. Martindale," she said, shrilly, "kindly try and
remember to keep the seams straight. Wounded people can be made
terribly uncomfortable by crooked seams, you know. And if you could
manage to get your stitches even, the coat would look much more professional and give our organization a higher standing. And time is terribly important. They're in an awful hurry for these. So if you could
just manage to be a little quicker, it would help a lot."

Really, if Mrs. Martindale hadn't offered to take the things, she
would have . . .

The twelve coats still in sections, together with the coat that was half
finished, made a formidable bundle. Mrs. Martindale had to send down
for her chauffeur to come and carry it to her car for her. While she
waited for him, several of the workers came up, rather slowly, and
volunteered to sew at home. Four was the highest number of garments
promised.

Mrs. Martindale did say good-by to Mrs. Corning, but she expressed
no pleasure at the hope of seeing her again in the autumn. You do what
you can, and you do it because you should. But all you can do is all
you can do.

Out on the Avenue, Mrs. Martindale was herself again. She kept her
eyes from the great package the chauffeur had placed in the car. After
all, she might, and honorably, allow herself a recess. She need not go
home and start sewing again immediately. She would send the chauffeur
home with the bundle, and walk in the pretty air, and not think of
unfinished coats.

But the men in uniform went along the Avenue under the snapping
flags, and in the sharp, true light you could see all their faces; their clean
bones and their firm skin and their eyes, the confident eyes of the sol-

diers and the wistful eyes of the sailors. They were so young, all of them, and all of them doing what they could, doing everything they could, doing it hard and humbly, without question and without credit. Mrs. Martindale put her hand to her heart. Some day, maybe, some day some of them might be lying on hospital cots . . .

Mrs. Martindale squared her delicate shoulders and entered her car. "Home, please," she told her chauffeur. "And I'm in rather a hurry."

At home, Mrs. Martindale had her maid unpack the clumsy bundle and lay the contents in her up-stairs sitting-room. Mrs. Martindale took off her outdoor garments and bound her head, just back of the first great blue-gray wave, in the soft linen coif she had habitually worn at Headquarters. She entered her sitting-room, which had recently been redone in the color of her hair and her eyes; it had taken a deal of mixing and matching, but it was a success. There were touches, splashes rather, of magenta about, for Mrs. Martindale complemented brilliant colors and made them and herself glow sweeter. She looked at the ugly, high pile of unmade coats, and there was a second when her famous heart shrank. But it swelled to its norm again as she felt what she must do. There was no good thinking about those twelve damned new ones. Her job immediately was to get on with the coat she had half made.

She sat down on quilted blue-gray satin and set herself to her task. She was at the most hateful stretch of the garment—the binding of the rounded neck. Everything pulled out of place, and nothing came out even, and a horrid starchy smell rose from the thick material, and the stitches that she struggled to put so prettily appeared all different sizes and all faintly gray. Over and over, she had to rip them out for their imperfection, and load her needle again without moistening the thread between her lips, and see them wild and straggling once more. She felt almost ill from the tussle with the hard, monotonous work.

Her maid came in, mincingly, and told her that Mrs. Wyman wished to speak to her on the telephone; Mrs. Wyman wanted to ask a favor of her. Those were two of the penalties attached to the possession of a heart the size of Mrs. Martindale's—people were constantly telephoning to ask her favors and she was constantly granting them. She put down her sewing, with a sigh that might have been of one thing or of another, and went to the telephone.

Mrs. Wyman, too, had a big heart, but it was not well set. She was a great, hulking, stupidly dressed woman, with flapping cheeks and bee-stung eyes. She spoke with rapid diffidence, inserting apologies before she needed to make them, and so was a bore and invited avoidance.

"Oh, my dear," she said now to Mrs. Martindale, "I'm so sorry to bother you. Please do forgive me. But I do want to ask you to do me the most tremendous favor. Please do excuse me. But I want to ask you, do you possibly happen to know of anybody who could possibly use my little Mrs. Christie?"

"Your Mrs. Christie?" Mrs. Martindale asked. "Now, I don't think —or do I?"

"You know," Mrs. Wyman said. "I wouldn't have bothered you for the world, with all you do and all, but you know my little Mrs. Christie. She has that daughter that had infantile, and she has to support her, and I just don't know *what* she's going to do. I wouldn't have bothered you for the world, only I've been sort of thinking up jobs for her to do for me right along, but next week we're going to the ranch, and I really don't know *what* will become of her. And the crippled daughter and all. They just won't be able to *live*!"

Mrs. Martindale made a soft little moan. "Oh, how awful," she said. "How perfectly awful. Oh, I wish I could—tell me, what can I do?"

"Well, if you could just think of somebody that could use her," Mrs. Wyman said. "I wouldn't have bothered you, honestly I wouldn't, but I just didn't know who to turn to. And Mrs. Christie's really a wonderful little woman—she can do anything. Of course, the thing is, she has to work at home, because she wants to take care of the crippled child—well, you can't blame her, really. But she'll call for things and bring them back. And she's so quick, and so good. Please do forgive me for bothering you, but if you could just think——"

"Oh, there must be somebody!" Mrs. Martindale cried. "I'll think of somebody. I'll rack my brains, truly I will. I'll call you up as soon as I think."

Mrs. Martindale went back to her blue-gray quilted satin. Again she took up the unfinished coat. A shaft of the exceptionally bright sunlight shot past a vase of butterfly orchids and settled upon the waving hair under the gracious coif. But Mrs. Martindale did not turn to meet it. Her blue-gray eyes were bent on the drudgery of her fingers. This coat, and then the twelve others beyond it. The need, the desperate, dreadful need, and the terrible importance of time. She took a stitch and another stitch and another stitch and another stitch; she looked at their wavering line, pulled the thread from her needle, ripped out three of the stitches, rethreaded her needle, and stitched again. And as she stitched, faithful to her promise and to her heart, she racked her brains.

The Standard of Living

Annabel and Midge came out of the tea room with the arrogant slow
gait of the leisured, for their Saturday afternoon stretched ahead of
them. They had lunched, as was their wont, on sugar, starches, oils, and
butter-fats. Usually they ate sandwiches of spongy new white bread
greased with butter and mayonnaise; they ate thick wedges of cake lying
wet beneath ice cream and whipped cream and melted chocolate gritty
with nuts. As alternates, they ate patties, sweating beads of inferior oil,
containing bits of bland meat bogged in pale, stiffening sauce; they ate
pastries, limber under rigid icing, filled with an indeterminate yellow
sweet stuff, not still solid, not yet liquid, like salve that has been left in
the sun. They chose no other sort of food, nor did they consider it. And
their skin was like the petals of wood anemones, and their bellies were
as flat and their flanks as lean as those of young Indian braves.

Annabel and Midge had been best friends almost from the day that
Midge had found a job as stenographer with the firm that employed
Annabel. By now, Annabel, two years longer in the stenographic department, had worked up to the wages of eighteen dollars and fifty cents
a week; Midge was still at sixteen dollars. Each girl lived at home with
her family and paid half her salary to its support.

The girls sat side by side at their desks, they lunched together every
noon, together they set out for home at the end of the day's work. Many
of their evenings and most of their Sundays were passed in each other's
company. Often they were joined by two young men, but there was no
steadiness to any such quartet; the two young men would give place,
unlamented, to two other young men, and lament would have been
inappropriate, really, since the newcomers were scarcely distinguishable
from their predecessors. Invariably the girls spent the fine idle hours of
their hot-weather Saturday afternoons together. Constant use had not
worn ragged the fabric of their friendship.

They looked alike, though the resemblance did not lie in their features. It was in the shape of their bodies, their movements, their style,
and their adornments. Annabel and Midge did, and completely, all that
young office workers are besought not to do. They painted their lips
and their nails, they darkened their lashes and lightened their hair, and
scent seemed to shimmer from them. They wore thin, bright dresses,

tight over their breasts and high on their legs, and tilted slippers, fancifully strapped. They looked conspicuous and cheap and charming.

Now, as they walked across to Fifth Avenue with their skirts swirled by the hot wind, they received audible admiration. Young men grouped lethargically about newsstands awarded them murmurs, exclamations, even—the ultimate tribute—whistles. Annabel and Midge passed without the condescension of hurrying their pace; they held their heads higher and set their feet with exquisite precision, as if they stepped over the necks of peasants.

Always the girls went to walk on Fifth Avenue on their free afternoons, for it was the ideal ground for their favorite game. The game could be played anywhere, and, indeed, was, but the great shop windows stimulated the two players to their best form.

Annabel had invented the game; or rather she had evolved it from an old one. Basically, it was no more than the ancient sport of whatwould-you-do-if-you-had-a-million dollars? But Annabel had drawn a new set of rules for it, had narrowed it, pointed it, made it stricter. Like all games, it was the more absorbing for being more difficult.

Annabel's version went like this: You must suppose that somebody dies and leaves you a million dollars, cool. But there is a condition to the bequest. It is stated in the will that you must spend every nickel of the money on yourself.

There lay the hazard of the game. If, when playing it, you forgot, and listed among your expenditures the rental of a new apartment for your family, for example, you lost your turn to the other player. It was astonishing how many—and some of them among the experts, too— would forfeit all their innings by such slips.

It was essential, of course, that it be played in passionate seriousness. Each purchase must be carefully considered and, if necessary, supported by argument. There was no zest to playing wildly. Once Annabel had introduced the game to Sylvia, another girl who worked in the office. She explained the rules to Sylvia and then offered her the gambit "What would be the first thing you'd do?" Sylvia had not shown the decency of even a second of hesitation. "Well," she said, "the first thing I'd do, I'd go out and hire somebody to shoot Mrs. Gary Cooper, and then . . ." So it is to be seen that she was no fun.

But Annabel and Midge were surely born to be comrades, for Midge played the game like a master from the moment she learned it. It was she who added the touches that made the whole thing cozier. According to Midge's innovations, the eccentric who died and left you the money was not anybody you loved, or, for the matter of that, anybody you even knew. It was somebody who had seen you somewhere and had thought, "That girl ought to have lots of nice things. I'm going to leave her a million dollars when I die." And the death was to be neither untimely nor painful. Your benefactor, full of years and comfortably ready to depart, was to slip softly away during sleep and go right to heaven. These embroideries permitted Annabel and Midge to play their game in the luxury of peaceful consciences.

Midge played with a seriousness that was not only proper but extreme. The single strain on the girls' friendship had followed an announcement once made by Annabel that the first thing she would buy with her million dollars would be a silver-fox coat. It was as if she had struck Midge across the mouth. When Midge recovered her breath, she cried that she couldn't imagine how Annabel could do such a thing— silver-fox coats were common! Annabel defended her taste with the retort that they were not common, either. Midge then said that they were so. She added that everybody had a silver-fox coat. She went on, with perhaps a slight loss of head, to declare that she herself wouldn't be caught dead in silver fox.

For the next few days, though the girls saw each other as constantly, their conversation was careful and infrequent, and they did not once play their game. Then one morning, as soon as Annabel entered the office, she came to Midge and said that she had changed her mind. She would not buy a silver-fox coat with any part of her million dollars. Immediately on receiving the legacy, she would select a coat of mink.

Midge smiled and her eyes shone. "I think," she said, "you're doing absolutely the right thing."

Now, as they walked along Fifth Avenue, they played the game anew. It was one of those days with which September is repeatedly cursed; hot and glaring, with slivers of dust in the wind. People drooped and shambled, but the girls carried themselves tall and walked a straight line, as befitted young heiresses on their afternoon promenade. There was no longer need for them to start the game at its formal opening. Annabel went direct to the heart of it.

"All right," she said. "So you've got this million dollars. So what would be the first thing you'd do?"

"Well, the first thing I'd do," Midge said, "I'd get a mink coat." But she said it mechanically, as if she were giving the memorized answer to an expected question.

"Yes," Annabel said, "I think you ought to. The terribly dark kind of mink." But she, too, spoke as if by rote. It was too hot; fur, no matter how dark and sleek and supple, was horrid to the thoughts.

They stepped along in silence for a while. Then Midge's eye was caught by a shop window. Cool, lovely gleamings were there set off by chaste and elegant darkness.

"No," Midge said, "I take it back. I wouldn't get a mink coat the first thing. Know what I'd do? I'd get a string of pearls. Real pearls."

Annabel's eyes turned to follow Midge's.

"Yes," she said, slowly. "I think that's kind of a good idea. And it would make sense, too. Because you can wear pearls with anything."

Together they went over to the shop window and stood pressed against it. It contained but one object—a double row of great, even pearls clasped by a deep emerald around a little pink velvet throat.

"What do you suppose they cost?" Annabel said.

"Gee, I don't know," Midge said. "Plenty, I guess."

"Like a thousand dollars?" Annabel said.

"Oh, I guess like more," Midge said. "On account of the emerald."

"Well, like ten thousand dollars?" Annabel said.

"Gee, I wouldn't even know," Midge said.

The devil nudged Annabel in the ribs. "Dare you to go in and price them," she said.

"Like fun!" Midge said.

"Dare you," Annabel said.

"Why, a store like this wouldn't even be open this afternoon," Midge said.

"Yes, it is so, too," Annabel said. "People just came out. And there's a doorman on. Dare you."

"Well," Midge said. "But you've got to come too."

They tendered thanks, icily, to the doorman for ushering them into the shop. It was cool and quiet, a broad, gracious room with paneled walls and soft carpet. But the girls wore expressions of bitter disdain, as if they stood in a sty.

A slim, immaculate clerk came to them and bowed. His neat face showed no astonishment at their appearance.

"Good afternoon," he said. He implied that he would never forget it if they would grant him the favor of accepting his soft-spoken greeting.

"Good afternoon," Annabel and Midge said together, and in like freezing accents.

"Is there something—?" the clerk said.

"Oh, we're just looking," Annabel said. It was as if she flung the words down from a dais.

The clerk bowed.

"My friend and myself merely happened to be passing," Midge said, and stopped, seeming to listen to the phrase. "My friend here and myself," she went on, "merely happened to be wondering how much are those pearls you've got in your window."

"Ah, yes," the clerk said. "The double rope. That is two hundred and fifty thousand dollars, Madam."

"I see," Midge said.

The clerk bowed. "An exceptionally beautiful necklace," he said. "Would you care to look at it?"

"No, thank you," Annabel said.

"My friend and myself merely happened to be passing," Midge said.

They turned to go; to go, from their manner, where the tumbrel awaited them. The clerk sprang ahead and opened the door. He bowed as they swept by him.

The girls went on along the Avenue and disdain was still on their faces.

"Honestly!" Annabel said. "Can you imagine a thing like that?"

"Two hundred and fifty thousand dollars!" Midge said. "That's a quarter of a million dollars right there!"

"He's got his nerve!" Annabel said.

They walked on. Slowly the disdain went, slowly and completely as if drained from them, and with it went the regal carriage and tread. Their shoulders dropped and they dragged their feet; they bumped against each other, without notice or apology, and caromed away again. They were silent and their eyes were cloudy.

Suddenly Midge straightened her back, flung her head high, and spoke, clear and strong.

"Listen, Annabel," she said. "Look. Suppose there was this terribly rich person, see? You don't know this person, but this person has seen you somewhere and wants to do something for you. Well, it's a terribly old person, see? And so this person dies, just like going to sleep, and leaves you ten million dollars. Now, what would be the first thing you'd do?"

The New Yorker, September 20, 1941

The Lovely Leave

Her husband had telephoned her by long distance to tell her about the leave. She had not expected the call, and she had no words arranged. She threw away whole seconds explaining her surprise at hearing him, and reporting that it was raining hard in New York, and asking was it terribly hot where he was. He had stopped her to say, look, he didn't have time to talk long; and he had told her quickly that his squadron was to be moved to another field the next week and on the way he would have twenty-four hours' leave. It was difficult for her to hear. Behind his voice came a jagged chorus of young male voices, all crying the syllable "Hey!"

"Ah, don't hang up yet," she said. "Please. Let's talk another minute, just another——"

"Honey, I've got to go," he said. "The boys all want a crack at the telephone. See you a week from today, around five. 'By."

Then there had been a click as his receiver went back into place. Slowly she cradled her telephone, looking at it as if all frustrations and bewilderments and separations were its fault. Over it she had heard his voice, coming from far away. All the months, she had tried not to think of the great blank distance between them; and now that far voice made her know she had thought of nothing else. And his speech had been brisk and busy. And from back of him had come gay, wild young voices, voices he heard every day and she did not, voices of those who shared his new life. And he had heeded them and not her, when she begged for another minute. She took her hand off the telephone and held it away from her with the fingers spread stiffly apart, as if it had touched something horrid.

Then she told herself to stop her nonsense. If you looked for things to make you feel hurt and wretched and unnecessary, you were certain to find them, more easily each time, so easily, soon, that you did not even realize you had gone out searching. Women alone often developed into experts at the practice. She must never join their dismal league.

What was she dreary about, anyway? If he had only a little while to talk, then he had only a little while to talk, that was all. Certainly he had had time to tell her he was coming, to say that they would be together soon. And there she was, sitting scowling at the telephone, the

275

kind, faithful telephone that had brought her the lovely news. She would see him in a week. Only a week. She began to feel, along her back and through her middle, little quivers of excitement, like tiny springs uncoiling into spirals.

There must be no waste to this leave. She thought of the preposterous shyness that had fallen upon her when he had come home before. It was the first time she had seen him in uniform. There he stood, in their little apartment, a dashing stranger in strange, dashing garments. Until he had gone into the army, they had never spent a night apart in all their marriage; and when she saw him, she dropped her eyes and twisted her handkerchief and could bring nothing but monosyllables from her throat. There must be no such squandering of minutes this time. There must be no such gangling diffidence to lop even an instant from their twenty-four hours of perfect union. Oh, Lord, only twenty-four hours. . . .

No. That was exactly the wrong thing to do; that was directly the wrong way to think. That was the way she had spoiled it before. Almost as soon as the shyness had left her and she felt she knew him again, she had begun counting. She was so filled with the desperate consciousness of the hours sliding away—only twelve more, only five, oh, dear God, only one left—that she had no room for gaiety and ease. She had spent the golden time in grudging its going.

She had been so woebegone of carriage, so sad and slow of word as the last hour went, that he, nervous under the pall, had spoken sharply and there had been a quarrel. When he had had to leave for his train, there were no clinging farewells, no tender words to keep. He had gone to the door and opened it and stood with it against his shoulder while he shook out his flight cap and put it on, adjusting it with great care, one inch over the eye, one inch above the ear. She stood in the middle of the living-room, cool and silent, looking at him.

When his cap was precisely as it should be, he looked at her.

"Well," he said. He cleared his throat. "Guess I'd better get going."

"I'm sure you had," she said.

He studied his watch intently. "I'll just make it," he said.

"I'm sure you will," she said.

She turned, not with an actual shrug, only with the effect of one, and went to the window and looked out, as if casually remarking the weather. She heard the door close loudly and then the grind of the elevator.

When she knew he was gone, she was cool and still no longer. She ran about the little flat, striking her breast and sobbing.

Then she had two months to ponder what had happened, to see how she had wrought the ugly small ruin. She cried in the nights.

She need not brood over it any more. She had her lesson; she could forget how she had learned it. This new leave would be the one to remember, the one he and she would have, to keep forever. She was to have a second chance, another twenty-four hours with him. After all, that is no short while, you know; that is, if you do not think of it as a thin little row of hours dropping off like beads from a broken string. Think of it as a whole long day and a whole long night, shining and sweet, and you will be all but awed by your fortune. For how many people are there who have the memory of a whole long day and a whole long night, shining and sweet, to carry with them in their hearts until they die?

To keep something, you must take care of it. More, you must understand just what sort of care it requires. You must know the rules and abide by them. She could do that. She had been doing it all the months, in the writing of her letters to him. There had been rules to be learned in that matter, and the first of them was the hardest: never say to him what you want him to say to you. Never tell him how sadly you miss him, how it grows no better, how each day without him is sharper than the day before. Set down for him the gay happenings about you, bright little anecdotes, not invented, necessarily, but attractively embellished. Do not bedevil him with the pinings of your faithful heart because he is your husband, your man, your love. For you are writing to none of these. You are writing to a soldier.

She knew those rules. She would have said that she would rather die, and she would have meant something very near the words, than send a letter of complaint or sadness or cold anger to her husband, a soldier far away, strained and weary from his work, giving all he had for the mighty cause. If in her letters she could be all he wanted her to be, how much easier to be it when they were together. Letters were difficult; every word had to be considered and chosen. When they were together again, when they could see and hear and touch each other, there would be no stiltedness. They would talk and laugh together. They would have tenderness and excitement. It would be as if they had never been separated. Perhaps they never had been. Perhaps a strange new life and strange empty miles and strange gay voices had no existence for two who were really one.

She had thought it out. She had learned the laws of what not to do. Now she could give herself up to the ecstasy of waiting his coming.

It was a fine week. She counted the time again, but now it was sweet to see it go. Two days after tomorrow, day after tomorrow, tomorrow. She lay awake in the dark, but it was a thrilling wakefulness. She went tall and straight by day, in pride in her warrior. On the street, she looked with amused pity at women who walked with men in civilian suits.

She bought a new dress; black—he liked black dresses—simple—he liked plain dresses—and so expensive that she would not think of its price. She charged it, and realized that for months to come she would tear up the bill without removing it from its envelope. All right—this was no time to think of months to come.

The day of the leave was a Saturday. She flushed with gratitude to the army for this coincidence, for after one o'clock, Saturday was her own. She went from her office without stopping for lunch, and bought perfume and toilet water and bath oil. She had a bit of each remaining in bottles on her dressing table and in her bathroom, but it made her feel desired and secure to have rich new stores of them. She bought a nightgown, a delightful thing of soft chiffon patterned with little bouquets, with innocent puffs of sleeves and a Romney neck and a blue sash. It could never withstand laundering, a French cleaner must care for it—all right. She hurried home with it, to fold it in a satin sachet.

Then she went out again and bought the materials for cocktails and whiskies-and-sodas, shuddering at their cost. She went a dozen blocks to buy the kind of salted biscuits he liked with drinks. On the way back she passed a florist's shop in the window of which were displayed potted fuchsia. She made no attempt to resist them. They were too charming, with their delicate parchment-colored inverted cups and their graceful magenta bells. She bought six pots of them. Suppose she did without lunches the next week—all right.

When she was done with the little living-room, it looked gracious and gay. She ranged the pots of fuchsia along the window sill, she drew out a table and set it with glasses and bottles, she plumped the pillows and laid bright-covered magazines about invitingly. It was a place where someone entering eagerly would find delighted welcome.

Before she changed her dress, she telephoned downstairs to the man who tended both the switchboard and the elevator.

"Oh," she said, when he eventually answered. "Oh, I just want to say, when my husband, Lieutenant McVicker, comes, please send him right up."

There was no necessity for the call. The wearied attendant would have brought up anyone to any flat without the additional stress of a telephoned announcement. But she wanted to say the words. She wanted to say "my husband" and she wanted to say "lieutenant."

She sang, when she went into the bedroom to dress. She had a sweet, uncertain little voice that made the lusty song ludicrous.

> "Off we go, into the wild blue yonder,
>   Climbing high into the sun, sun, sun, sun.
> Here they come: zooming to meet our thunder—
>   At 'em boys, give 'er the gun!"

She kept singing, in a preoccupied way, while she gave close attention to her lips and her eyelashes. Then she was silent and held her breath as she drew on the new dress. It was good to her. There was a reason for the cost of those perfectly plain black dresses. She stood looking at herself in the mirror with deep interest, as if she watched a chic unknown, the details of whose costume she sought to memorize.

As she stood there, the bell rang. It rang three times, loud and quick. He had come.

She gasped, and her hands fluttered over the dressing table. She seized the perfume atomizer and sprayed scent violently all about her head and shoulders, some of it reaching them. She had already perfumed herself, but she wanted another minute, another moment, anything. For it had taken her again—the outrageous shyness. She could not bring herself to go to the door and open it. She stood, shaking, and squirted perfume.

The bell rang three times loud and quick again, and then an endless peal.

"Oh, *wait,* can't you?" she cried. She threw down the atomizer, looked wildly around the room as if for a hiding-place, then sternly made herself tall and sought to control the shaking of her body. The shrill noise of the bell seemed to fill the flat and crowd the air out of it.

She started for the door. Before she reached it, she stopped, held her hands over her face, and prayed, "Oh, please let it be all right," she whispered. "Please keep me from doing wrong things. Please let it be lovely."

Then she opened the door. The noise of the bell stopped. There he stood in the brightly lighted little hall. All the long sad nights, and all the strong and sensible vows. And now he had come. And there she stood.

"Well, for heaven's sake!" she said. "I had no idea there was anybody out here. Why, you were just as quiet as a little mouse."

"Well! Don't you ever open the door?" he said.

"Can't a woman have time to put on her shoes?" she said.

He came in and closed the doors behind him. "Ah, darling," he said. He put his arms around her. She slid her cheek along his lips, touched her forehead to his shoulder, and broke away from him.

"Well!" she said. "Nice to see you, Lieutenant. How's the war?"

"How are you?" he said. "You look wonderful."

"Me?" she said. "Look at you."

He was well worth looking at. His fine clothes complemented his fine body. The precision of his appointments was absolute, yet he seemed to have no consciousness of it. He stood straight, and he moved with grace and assurance. His face was browned. It was thin, so thin that the bones showed under the cheeks and down the jaws; but there was no look of strain in it. It was smooth and serene and confident. He was the American officer, and there was no finer sight than he.

"Well!" she said. She made herself raise her eyes to his and found suddenly that it was no longer difficult. "Well, we can't just stand here saying 'well' at each other. Come on in and sit down. We've got a long time ahead of us—oh, Steve, isn't it wonderful! Hey. Didn't you bring a bag?"

"Why, you see," he said, and stopped. He slung his cap over onto the table among the bottles and glasses. "I left the bag at the station. I'm afraid I've got sort of rotten news, darling."

She kept her hands from flying to her breast.

"You—you're going overseas right away?" she said.

"Oh, Lord, no," he said. "Oh, no, no, no. I said this was rotten news. No. They've changed the orders, baby. They've taken back all leaves. We're to go right on to the new field. I've got to get a train at six-ten."

She sat down on the sofa. She wanted to cry; not silently with slow crystal tears, but with wide mouth and smeared face. She wanted to throw herself stomach-down on the floor, and kick and scream, and go limp if anyone tried to lift her.

"I think that's awful," she said. "I think that's just filthy."

"I know," he said. "But there's nothing to do about it. This is the army, Mrs. Jones."

"Couldn't you have said something?" she said. "Couldn't you have told them you've had only one leave in six months? Couldn't you have said all the chance your wife had to see you again was just this poor little twenty-four hours? Couldn't you have explained what it meant to her? Couldn't you?"

"Come on, now, Mimi," he said. "There's a war on."

"I'm sorry," she said. "I was sorry as soon as I'd said it. I was sorry while I was saying it. But—oh, it's so hard!"

"It's not easy for anybody," he said. "You don't know how the boys were looking forward to their leaves."

"Oh, I don't give a damn about the boys!" she said.

"That's the spirit that'll win for our side," he said. He sat down in the biggest chair, stretched his legs and crossed his ankles.

"You don't care about anything but those pilots," she said.

"Look, Mimi," he said. "We haven't got time to do this. We haven't got time to get into a fight and say a lot of things we don't mean. Everything's all—all speeded up, now. There's no time left for this."

"Oh, I know," she said. "Oh, Steve, don't I know!"

She went over and sat on the arm of his chair and buried her face in his shoulder.

"This is more like it," he said. "I've kept thinking about this." She nodded against his blouse.

"If you knew what it was to sit in a decent chair again," he said.

She sat up. "Oh," she said. "It's the chair. I'm so glad you like it."

"They've got the worst chairs you ever saw, in the pilots' room," he said. "A lot of busted-down old rockers—honestly, rockers—that big-hearted patriots contributed, to get them out of the attic. If they haven't better furniture at the new field, I'm going to do something about it, even if I have to buy the stuff myself."

"I certainly would, if I were you," she said. "I'd go without food and clothing and laundry, so the boys would be happy sitting down. I wouldn't even save out enough for air mail stamps, to write to my wife once in a while."

She rose and moved about the room.

"Mimi, what's the matter with you?" he said. "Are you—are you jealous of the pilots?"

She counted as far as eight, to herself. Then she turned and smiled at him.

"Why—I guess I am—" she said. "I guess that's just what I must be. Not only of the pilots. Of the whole air corps. Of the whole Army of the United States."

"You're wonderful," he said.

"You see," she said with care, "you have a whole new life—I have half an old one. Your life is so far away from mine, I don't see how they're ever going to come back together."

"That's nonsense," he said.

"No, please wait," she said. "I get strained and—and frightened, I guess, and I say things I could cut my throat for saying. But you know what I really feel about you. I'm so proud of you I can't find words for it. I know you're doing the most important thing in the world, maybe the only important thing in the world. Only—oh, Steve, I wish to heaven you didn't love doing it so much!"

"Listen," he said.

"No," she said. "You mustn't interrupt a lady. It's unbecoming an officer, like carrying packages in the street. I'm just trying to tell you a little about how I feel. I can't get used to being so completely left out. You don't wonder what I do, you don't want to find out what's in my head—why, you never even ask me how I am!"

"I do so!" he said. "I asked you how you were the minute I came in."

"That was white of you," she said.

"Oh, for heaven's sake!" he said. "I didn't have to ask you. I could see how you look. You look wonderful. I told you that."

She smiled at him. "Yes, you did, didn't you?" she said. "And you sounded as if you meant it. Do you really like my dress?"

"Oh, yes," he said. "I always liked that dress on you."

It was as if she turned to wood. "This dress," she said, enunciating with insulting distinctness, "is brand-new. I have never had it on before in my life. In case you are interested, I bought it especially for this occasion."

"I'm sorry, honey," he said. "Oh, sure, now I see it's not the other one at all. I think it's great. I like you in black."

"At moments like this," she said, "I almost wish I were in it for another reason."

"Stop it," he said. "Sit down and tell me about yourself. What have you been doing?"

"Oh, nothing," she said.

"How's the office?" he said.

"Dull," she said. "Dull as mud."

"Who have you seen?" he said.

"Oh, nobody," she said.

"Well, what do you *do*?" he said.

"In the evenings?" she said. "Oh, I sit here and knit and read detective stories that it turns out I've read before."

"I think that's all wrong of you," he said. "I think it's asinine to sit here alone, moping. That doesn't do any good to anybody. Why don't you go out more?"

"I hate to go out with just women," she said.

"Well, why do you have to?" he said. "Ralph's in town, isn't he? And John and Bill and Gerald. Why don't you go out with them? You're silly not to."

"It hadn't occurred to me," she said, "that it was silly to keep faithful to one's husband."

"Isn't that taking rather a jump?" he said. "It's possible to go to dinner with a man and stay this side adultery. And don't use words like 'one's.' You're awful when you're elegant."

"I know," she said. "I never have any luck when I try. No. You're the one that's awful, Steve. You really are. I'm trying to show you a glimpse of my heart, to tell you how it feels when you're gone, how I don't want to be with anyone if I can't be with you. And all you say is, I'm not doing any good to anybody. That'll be nice to think of when you go. You don't know what it's like for me here alone. You just don't know."

"Yes, I do," he said. "I know, Mimi." He reached for a cigarette on the little table beside him, and the bright magazine by the cigarette-box caught his eye. "Hey, is this this week's? I haven't seen it yet." He glanced through the early pages.

"Go ahead and read if you want to," she said. "Don't let me disturb you."

"I'm not reading," he said. He put down the magazine. "You see, I don't know what to say, when you start talking about showing me glimpses of your heart, and all that. I know. I know you must be having a rotten time. But aren't you feeling fairly sorry for yourself?"

"If *I'm* not," she said, "who would be?"

"What do you want anyone to be sorry for you for?" he said. "You'd be all right if you'd stop sitting around alone. I'd like to think of you having a good time while I'm away."

She went over to him and kissed him on the forehead.

"Lieutenant," she said, "you are a far nobler character than I am. Either that," she said, "or there is something else back of this."

"Oh, shut up," he said. He pulled her down to him and held her there. She seemed to melt against him, and stayed there, still.

Then she felt him take his left arm from around her and felt his head raised from its place against hers. She looked up at him. He was craning over her shoulder, endeavoring to see his wrist watch.

"Oh, now, really!" she said. She put her hands against his chest and pushed herself vigorously away from him.

"It goes so quickly," he said softly, with his eyes on his watch. "We've—we've only a little while, darling."

She melted again. "Oh, Steve," she whispered. "Oh, dearest."

"I do want to take a bath," he said. "Get up, will you, baby?"

She got right up. "You're going to take a bath?" she said.

"Yes," he said. "You don't mind, do you?"

"Oh, not in the least," she said. "I'm sure you'll enjoy it. It's one of the pleasantest ways of killing time, I always think."

"You know how you feel after a long ride on a train," he said.

"Oh, surely," she said.

He rose and went into the bedroom. "I'll hurry up," he called back to her.

"Why?" she said.

Then she had a moment to consider herself. She went into the bedroom after him, sweet with renewed resolve. He had hung his blouse and necktie neatly over a chair and he was unbuttoning his shirt. As she came in, he took it off. She looked at the beautiful brown triangle of his back. She would do anything for him, anything in the world.

"I—I'll go run your bath water," she said. She went into the bathroom, turned on the faucets of the tub, and set the towels and mat ready. When she came back into the bedroom he was just entering it from the living-room, naked. In his hand he carried the bright magazine he had glanced at before. She stopped short.

"Oh," she said. "You're planning to read in the tub?"

"If you knew how I'd been looking forward to this!" he said. "Boy, a hot bath in a tub! We haven't got anything but showers, and when you take a shower, there's a hundred boys waiting, yelling at you to hurry up and get out."

"I suppose they can't bear being parted from you," she said.

He smiled at her. "See you in a couple of minutes," he said, and went on into the bathroom and closed the door. She heard the slow slip and slide of water as he laid himself in the tub.

She stood just as she was. The room was lively with the perfume she had sprayed, too present, too insistent. Her eyes went to the bureau drawer where lay, wrapped in soft fragrance, the nightgown with the little bouquets and the Romney neck. She went over to the bathroom door, drew back her right foot, and kicked the base of the door so savagely that the whole frame shook.

"What, dear?" he called. "Want something?"

"Oh, nothing," she said. "Nothing whatever. I've got everything any woman could possibly want, haven't I?"

"What?" he called. "I can't hear you, honey."

"Nothing," she screamed.

She went into the living-room. She stood, breathing heavily, her finger nails scarring her palms, as she looked at the fuchsia blossoms, with their dirty parchment-colored cups, their vulgar magenta bells.

Her breath was quiet and her hands relaxed when he came into the living-room again. He had on his trousers and shirt, and his necktie was admirably knotted. He carried his belt. She turned to him. There were things she had meant to say, but she could do nothing but smile at him, when she saw him. Her heart turned liquid in her breast.

His brow was puckered. "Look, darling," he said. "Have you got any brass polish?"

"Why, no," she said. "We haven't even got any brass."

"Well, have you any nail polish—the colorless kind? A lot of the boys use that."

"I'm sure it must look adorable on them," she said. "No, I haven't anything but rose-colored polish. Would that be of any use to you, heaven forbid?"

"No," he said, and he seemed worried. "Red wouldn't be any good at all. Hell, I don't suppose you've got a Blitz Cloth, have you? Or a Shine-O?"

"If I had the faintest idea what you were talking about," she said, "I might be better company for you."

He held the belt out toward her. "I want to shine my buckle," he said.

"Oh . . . my . . . dear . . . sweet . . . gentle . . . Lord," she said. "We've got about ten minutes left, and you want to shine your belt buckle."

"I don't like to report to a new C.O. with a dull belt buckle," he said.

"It was bright enough for you to report to your wife in, wasn't it?" she said.

"Oh, stop that," he said. "You just won't understand, that's all."

"It isn't that I won't understand," she said. "It's that I can't remember. I haven't been with a Boy Scout for so long."

He looked at her. "You're being great, aren't you?" he said. He looked around the room. "There must be a cloth around somewhere—oh, this will do." He caught up a pretty little cocktail napkin from the table of untouched bottles and glasses, sat down with his belt laid over his knees, and rubbed at the buckle.

She watched him for a moment, then rushed over to him and grasped his arm.

"Please," she said. "Please, I didn't mean it, Steve."

"Please let me do this, will you?" he said. He wrenched his arm from her hand and went on with his polishing.

"You tell me I won't understand!" she cried. "You won't understand anything about anybody else. Except those crazy pilots."

"They're all right!" he said. "They're fine kids. They're going to make great fighters." He went on rubbing at his buckle.

"Oh, I know it!" she said. "You know I know it. I don't mean it when I say things against them. How would I dare to mean it? They're risking their lives and their sight and their sanity, they're giving every-thing for——"

"Don't do that kind of talk, will you?" he said. He rubbed the buckle.

"I'm not doing any kind of talk!" she said. "I'm trying to tell you something. Just because you've got on that pretty suit, you think you should never hear anything serious, never anything sad or wretched or disagreeable. You make me sick, that's what you do! I know, I know— I'm not trying to take anything away from you, I realize what you're doing, I told you what I think of it. Don't, for heaven's sake, think I'm mean enough to grudge you any happiness and excitement you can get out of it. I know it's hard for you. But it's never lonely, that's all I mean. You have companionships no—no wife can ever give you. I suppose it's the sense of hurry, maybe, the consciousness of living on borrowed time, the—the knowledge of what you're all going into together that makes the comradeship of men in war so firm, so fast. But won't you please try to understand how I feel? Won't you understand that it comes out of bewilderment and disruption and—and being frightened, I guess? Won't you understand what makes me do what I do, when I hate myself while I'm doing it? Won't you please understand? Darling, won't you please?"

He laid down the little napkin. "I can't go through this kind of thing, Mimi," he said. "Neither can you." He looked at his watch. "Hey, it's time for me to go."

She stood tall and stiff. "I'm sure it is," she said.

"I'd better put on my blouse," he said.

"You might as well," she said.

He rose, wove his belt through the loops of his trousers, and went into the bedroom. She went over to the window and stood looking out, as if casually remarking the weather.

She heard him come back into the room, but she did not turn around. She heard his steps stop, knew he was standing there.

"Mimi," he said.

She turned toward him, her shoulders back, her chin high, cool, regal. Then she saw his eyes. They were no longer bright and gay and confident. Their blue was misty and they looked troubled; they looked at her as if they pleaded with her.

"Look, Mimi," he said, "do you think I want to do this? Do you think I want to be away from you? Do you think that this is what I thought I'd be doing now? In the years—well, in the years when we ought to be together."

He stopped. Then he spoke again, but with difficulty. "I can't talk about it. I can't even think about it—because if I did I couldn't do my job. But just because I don't talk about it doesn't mean I want to be doing what I'm doing. I want to be with you, Mimi. That's where I belong. You know that, darling. Don't you?"

He held his arms open to her. She ran to them. This time, she did not slide her cheek along his lips.

When he had gone, she stood a moment by the fuchsia plants, touching delicately, tenderly, the enchanting parchment-colored caps, the exquisite magenta bells.

The telephone rang. She answered it, to hear a friend of hers inquiring about Steve, asking how he looked and how he was, urging that he come to the telephone and say hello to her.

"He's gone," she said. "All their leaves were canceled. He wasn't here an hour."

The friend cried sympathy. It was a shame, it was simply awful, it was absolutely terrible.

"No, don't say that," she said. "I know it wasn't very much time. But oh, it was lovely!"

Woman's Home Companion, December 1943

The Game

A week after the Linehams came back from their honeymoon, they gave their first dinner party. The fete was by way of warming the new apartment, which awaited them completely furnished down to the last little gilded silver shell for individual portions of salted almonds.

It was in a big building on Park Avenue, not so far uptown as to make theater-going a major event; not so far downtown as to be assailed by the rumble and honk of *native* traffic and the screaming sirens of motorcycles, the spearheads for UN delegates quartered at the Waldorf.

The apartment was of many rooms, each light, high, and honorably square. Each, with its furnishings, might one day be moved intact to the American wing of some museum, labeled, "Room in Dwelling of Well-to-Do Merchant, New York, *Circa* Truman Administration"; and spectators, crowded behind the velvet rope which prevents their actual entrance, might murmur, according to their schools of thought, either, "Ah, it's darling!" or else, "Did people really live like that?"

Each room, in fact, already had museum qualities: impersonality, correctness, and rigidity. In the drawing room, indeed, the decorator had made chalk marks on the carpet to indicate where each leg of each piece of furniture must rest. The drawing room was done in mirrors that looked as if they had hung for months in hickory smoke, and its curtains and carpets and cushions were a muted green, more chaste than any white. There were flowers with that curious waxen look flowers have when they come from the florist already arranged in the vase. On the ceiling were pools of soft radiance; light, delicate and genteel, issued from massive lamps by routes so indirect they seemed rather more like detours. It was impossible to imagine the room with a fallen petal on a table, or with an open magazine face down on a sofa, or a puppy mark in a far corner of the carpet. It was utterly impeccable, and it was impossible not to imagine the cost of making it so and keeping it so. Happily enough in this blemished world, perfection is not unique; in the radius of twelve Park Avenue streets there must have been twenty rooms like it; all, like it, the property of nervous youngish men newly arrived at high positions in nervous youngish industries.

In the dining room—silver wall paper patterned with leafy shoots of bamboo—the Linehams and their six guests arrived at the finish of dinner. The dinner itself might well have been planned by the same mind that had devised the *décor:* black bean soup, crab meat and slivers of crab shell done in cream, roasted crown of lamb with bone tips decently encased in little paper drawers, tiny hard potatoes, green peas ruined by chopped carrots, asparagus instead of salad, and the dessert called, perhaps a shade hysterically, cherries Jubilee. It would have been safe to say that, within the before-mentioned radius of twelve streets, there occurred that night fifteen other dinners for eight, all consisting of bean soup, crab meat, crown of lamb, potatoes, peas and carrots, asparagus, and cherries Jubilee. That morning the same butcher and the same grocer, rubbing their hands, had made out the bills for all sixteen of them.

There was no division of men and women for the quarter hour after dinner. They went all together into the living room for their coffee and brandy. Little Mrs. Lineham poured the coffee, and her hand scarcely shook at all. She had the accepted and appealing timidity of the bride at her first appearance as hostess, and the condition was enhanced by the fact that the guests were her husband's friends, whom he had known before he had ever seen or thought of her; but they had been so kind in their praises of the apartment, the food, the tableware, the champagne, her dress, and her husband's newly gained ten pounds that she was almost entirely at ease. She felt all warm with gratitude to them.

"Oh, I think," she said suddenly, "you're all just lovely."

"Cute thing," two of the women said, and the third one, the one she liked best, smiled at her.

The drawing room was better for the presence of people, and this was a good-looking group, expensively dressed and carefully tended. The men wore the garb they could by now easily call Black Tie. (The steps in social ascent may be gauged by the terms employed to describe a man's informal evening dress: the progression goes Tuxedo, Tux, dinner jacket, Black Tie.) The women wore gowns of such immediate mode they would have to be cast off long before the opulent materials had lost their gloss. Only Thelma Chrystie, the one little Mrs. Lineham liked best, evaded the mark of the moment; her gown was so classic in design that it might have been worn six months before the date or six months after; nor were her jewels in the current vogue. The others wore bands and chunks of massed stones and bright metals that made each lady look rather as if she had spent a night with an openhanded admirer from the deep jungle. Mrs. Chrystie's ornaments were few and as delicate as frost.

Mrs. Chrystie was tall, pale, and still, three things that little Mrs. Lineham had always wanted to be. Emmy Lineham had always been described as a cute little trick, and she was therefore obliged to be rosy and to twitter. She admired Mrs. Chrystie for her looks, but loved her for a quality all her own, a peculiar warmth that seemed to flow from her, that melted all reserve and drew to her the trust of your heart. The gracious glow pervaded all those about her, even her husband, and made little Mrs. Lineham admire her all the more.

Not that Mrs. Lineham did not like Thelma Chrystie's husband. Who could dislike him? Sherm Chrystie—doubtless they had started him off as Sherman, but that had been long forgotten—was a youngish man, though not of a nervous kind. Indeed, he had little to be nervous about, for unlike the other men he was not unsteady in a new business. He had no business, and there is nothing like a whopping big inheritance to abort apprehensions. He was a big pink man, and nowhere, save in the street, could he be seen without a glass in his hand. But drink only made him somewhat endearingly silly—that is, until late in the evening, when sometimes he would awaken refreshed after an audible and public nap, steal heavily to the liquor tray to fix himself a drink, and, in preparing it, would somehow break every glass but his own.

Never once had Mrs. Chrystie been known to protest his excesses. Part of her peculiar warmth must have been her consideration for every human being. Never would she humiliate him before others by telling him he had had enough and urging him to have no more. Never would she be so cruel as to ask him to come home when he was having a good time. She had even been seen—when he was incapable of pouring a drink for himself—to mix one and, with her warm gentle smile, put it in his hand.

Mr. McDermott, the male half of another couple among the Linehams' guests, went to no such extremes in his pleasures as did Sherm. Mr. McDermott was in all things cautious almost to the point of timidity. He had achieved his present title and position in a vast spider web of radio networks by means of both hard work and the constant proffering of figurative red apples. But he had not attained his ease. He could not forget the many other men who had previously risen to the tall stature that was now his. He had seen them crash like oaks. Any day he expected to hear the cry "Timber!" for his own fall. His wife was a handsome, healthy woman, voluble and fond of giving information.

The other guests were Mr. and Mrs. Bain. The Bains were the Bains, in no way singular.

Bob Lineham, the host and bridegroom, was still lean despite the ten pounds acquired on the honeymoon. He was the tallest man there and the most pleasing to look at, but he was not so uncommonly beautiful as to warrant the utter adoration with which the little bride seemed almost to swoon as eyes followed him. His voice was so quiet that one must lean toward him to listen; you would sit back again not quite fulfilled but always expectant of his next utterance.

Sherm had scarcely had time to be empty-handed after his second great bowl of brandy when the Linehams' butler and waitress entered, single file, with trays of various whiskies, additional brandy, ice, water, and soda.

Bob went to the table to serve his guests, Emmy trotting after him, but Sherm was there first. Mrs. Chrystie, on a sofa, listened warmly while Mr. McDermott quoted Hooper ratings to Mr. Bain. Across the room Mrs. Bain, regardless of chalk marks, drew her chair close to Mrs. McDermott's.

"That little thing just worships the ground Bob Lineham walks on," Mrs. Bain said.

"I think it's lovely," Mrs. McDermott said. "That poor boy certainly deserves some happiness after what he's had."

"He's simply blossomed. He's blossomed like a flower. And after that broken life of his for two years."

"Nearly three," Mrs. McDermott said. "I thought he'd never pull out of it. They usually don't, if they don't marry again right away."

"I never knew his first wife," Mrs. Bain said. "We didn't meet Bob till after——"

"Oh, Alice was a wonderful girl," Mrs. McDermott said. "Not exactly pretty but awfully *nice*-looking. My, she used to get such a wonderful tan. She was a wonderful athlete. She had all kinds of cups and things for tennis and golf and swimming. That was the strangest thing about it. She was such a wonderful swimmer. Why, she swam like a man!"

"Well, that's the way it always happens," Mrs. Bain said. "The good ones get careless, I suppose, and even the best of them can get a cramp or something. Poor man, I don't see how he ever got over it."

"Oh, the Chrysties have been wonderful to him," Mrs. McDermott said. "He just depended on them."

"Weren't they there when it happened?" Mrs. Bain asked.

"It was up at their place at the lake," Mrs. McDermott said. "Alice and Bob were there for Bob's vacation. They didn't have a nickel, you know. Thelma was Alice's best friend."

"She's been awfully good to this one," Mrs. Bain said, meaning the second Mrs. Lineham.

"They can all say Emmy's none too bright," Mrs. McDermott said, "but, after all, her dad's head of Davis, McCord, Marsh and Welty, and all they are is the biggest agency in the advertising business. Now look at Bob; Emmy's father made him a vice-president *just like that*. Thelma must be really delighted about it. She's been a wonderful, wonderful friend, and I *know* she's going to be just as nice to this little thing as she was to Alice."

Their eyes went to Mrs. Chrystie, who had risen from the sofa and gone over to Emmy. She was giving certain tender pats and gentle pulls to the little bride's coiffure.

Mrs. Bain turned back to Mrs. McDermott and suddenly giggled. "It's terrible," she said. "Whenever something awful's happened in a family, I just can't seem to stay off the subject. It's as if something was *making* me do it. Did you *hear* what I said at dinner? Bob and I were talking about movies, and I asked him if he'd seen *Lady in the Lake*. I just thought I'd die."

"Oh, my dear, I know," Mrs. McDermott said. "Every time I see Bob I start talking about drowning and accidents in the water and artificial respiration too late and—ordinarily I never talk about things like that. Things I wouldn't dream of talking about. I only hope he doesn't notice it. I must say, he certainly doesn't seem to. But, of course, he's so polite."

"Isn't it terrible?" Mrs. Bain said. "What makes people do things like that?"

They both laughed and shook their heads indulgently.

Bob Lineham came up to them, a glass in each hand. "Scotch and soda *pour Madame*," he said, giving one to Mrs. McDermott. "And a little something for our bourbon-and-water girl." He offered the other glass to Mrs. Bain.

"Oh, Bob, you bad boy," she said. "It's much too strong. You should've given me just a teeny bit, absolutely *drowned* in water—oh, Bob, I just can't get over how wonderful you look. I simply can't get *over* it!"

"Palm Springs certainly agreed with you," Mrs. McDermott said.

"Oh, I've always been crazy to go there," Mrs. Bain said. "They say it's terribly attractive. Where'd you stay?"

"Emmy's father and mother lent us the house they have there," he said. "Cutest little place you ever saw."

"Palm Springs is real desert, isn't it?" Mrs. McDermott said.

"Sure is," he said. "There we were, right in the heart of the desert."

"My, what a *real* change that must've been for you," Mrs. Bain said—and wished she were dead.

"Let's see, who else needs drinks?" Bob said, looking around. "Sherm's all right, I see." He went over to his wife and Thelma Chrystie.

"See what Thelma did to my hair, Bob," Emmy said.

"Doesn't she look darling now?" Thelma said.

"She wasn't so dusty before," Bob said. He cupped Emmy's chin in his hand and kissed her little pink mouth. "This is the way she looks when she wakes up in the morning." He kissed her again.

"Don't mind me," Thelma said. "You two go right ahead."

Bob disengaged his bride. "How about a drink, Thelma? Oh, I forgot, you never——"

"Yes, I will have a drink," she said. "Whisky, brandy, anything— straight."

"Why, Thelma," Emmy said. "I never saw you drink anything before."

"Oh, my dear child," Thelma said, "the things and things and things you never saw!" He brought a glass of plain whisky. "Thank you, Bob."

"Quite all right," he said.

"Is it?" murmured Thelma.

Bob returned to the liquor tray. Emmy followed him. "Oh, darling," she said, "is it a good party?"

"I think it's great," he said.

"Are you sure?" she said. "Do you think they're having fun? Honestly, am I doing all right?"

"You couldn't do anything else if you tried your little head off," he said. He smoothed her hair back the way it had been before Mrs. Chrystie had attended to it. "There," he said, "that's my girl." He kissed her lightly on the top of her head.

Unseen and unheard, Thelma glided close. Bob looked into her eyes. They stood there for a second regarding each other over Emmy's smoothed head.

Emmy turned to Thelma. "I was just asking Bob—do you think they're really having a good time?"

"What do you think they want, my dear, paper hats and a magician?" Thelma said, smiling. "You haven't a thing to worry about, child. Has she, Bob?"

"I don't know," Emmy said. "They all look so sort of separated." She gestured vaguely at Mrs. McDermott and Mrs. Bain sitting together, Mr. Bain and Mr. McDermott sitting together across the room from them, and Sherm wandering about independently, holding his glass perilously tilted, and humming something from *The Chocolate Soldier*. "I wish we could sort of all get together and do something."

"How about a little bridge?" Thelma said.

"Oh, dear!" Emmy said. "I don't know one card from another."

"Well, shall we throw in the towel and play The Game?" Bob said.

"We've got enough people," Thelma said.

"Thelma's a whiz at The Game," Bob said to Emmy.

"Oh, I'm terrible at games. I'll never be any good," Emmy said. "I'll never learn anything. Never at all."

Thelma smiled at her. "You will, Oscar, you will," she said.

Sherm came over to them from the table where he had been replenishing his glass. He waved it in waltz time, " 'Come, hero, mine,' " he caroled. "Wonderful brandy, Bob, ole boy, ole boy," he said. "Marry the boss's daughter and ossify your friends, what?"

"Bob says let's play The Game, Sherm," Thelma said. "Want to play?"

"Sure I want to play The Game," Sherm said. "Emmy and I will take you all on. What do you say, Boss's Daughter?"

"Oh, I couldn't," Emmy said. "I'm scared stiff to play. I'm scared stiff anyway in front of all these people."

"Of course you're not," Thelma said. "Bob will be playing on your side. When you've got him, you won't think about anybody else." As she moved away, she added, not quite audibly, "And you can quote me on that."

The Game has never had a more specific title, nor has it needed one. It is a pastime lightly based on "Charades." It does not bring out the best in its players and it is, goodness knows, no sport for introverts. Nevertheless, in the Linehams' drawing room The Game got under way. Bob was made captain of one team, Thelma of the other. Thelma had selected Mrs. McDermott and the Bains; Bob had taken first Emmy, then Mr. McDermott, and last—his usual position—Sherm.

Sherm's feelings were never outraged by any such slight; he thriftily employed the time required for the selection of the more desirable players in making himself a fresh drink.

Sheets of paper were produced in record-breaking time; little Mrs. Lineham was so proud of her note paper with the new monogram. But there was pencil trouble.

Mrs. Bain smoothed things over for her hostess. "Dear," she said to her husband, "let Bob have your pen." Dear obliged. "It's a dream of a pen," she said; "it's one of those ones that write under water." She laughed. "I can't imagine what good they think that is; who wants to be under——" She stopped just in time.

Thelma took her cohorts into a smaller room called the study, though the origin of the name was obscure. They clustered around her in silence and watched her bite her pencil.

"Let's make them terribly hard," Mrs. McDermott said.

"Ah, no, we mustn't be mean," Thelma said. "Think of Sherm and poor little Emmy."

"Let's see," Mr. Bain said, "how about *War and Peace*?"

"Oh, everybody's done that," Mrs. McDermott said.

"Yes," Mrs. Bain said. "All anybody would have to do is to signal 'book' and then signal 'beard.' " She made a gesture as if she were drawing an invisible goatee to a point. "And they'd guess the author like a shot. And there they'd have it."

Thelma shuddered slightly, but she smiled at Mrs. Bain. "Anybody got any good quotations?" she said.

"Oh, I know a beauty," Mrs. McDermott said. " 'Get with child a mandrake root.' John Donne."

Mr. Bain shook his head, "Too easy," he said. "All you'd have to do is——"

"Oh, I know," Mrs. Bain interrupted with excitement. "A second marriage is the 'triumph of hope over experience.' Dr. Samuel Johnson."

Mrs. McDermott looked at her with wide eyes. "Mercy!" she whispered.

"Mr. B," Thelma said, "would you get me a drink of plain whisky?"

"Plain whisky!" he said. "You want plain whisky?"

"Yes," she said. "The stuff they drink at wakes."

Mr. Bain went into the other room to fetch the drink. "Time out," he called, as he entered.

"Thank you," Thelma said, taking the refilled glass from him when he returned. "W-e-l-l, what about songs? Anybody got any songs?"

" 'Chi-Baba, Chi-Baba, Chi-Wawa,' " Mr. Bain said. "That ought to hold them."

"W-e-l-l," Thelma said again. "How do you spell it?"

For the next few minutes Mr. Bain insisted the initial letter was "S." Mrs. McDermott said she had never heard of the thing. Thelma wrote it down as best she could and said, "We haven't any quotations yet."

"Wait a minute," Mrs. McDermott said. " 'Too much of water hast thou, poor Ophelia, and therefore I forbid my tears.' It's in *Hamlet*, where they say Ophelia's drowned."

Mrs. Bain giggled, "That's cute," she said. "You're worse than I am."

"Oh, what *makes* me do it?" Mrs. McDermott said. "Oh, that would be awful if Bob got it."

"What about poor little Emmy?" Mrs. Bain said. "We just couldn't do anything to hurt her. Bob would never speak to us again if we did."

"It would be brutal to remind them of anything unpleasant," Mrs. McDermott said.

"Unpleasant is putting it rather mildly, isn't it?" Thelma said.

"Listen," Mr. Bain said, "How about a play? *Billion Dollar Baby*?"

"*Really,* dear!" Mrs. Bain said. "You needn't hand it to them on a platter."

"Well, I don't know," Thelma said. "It would be rather nice to give them something darling Emmy might be able to get."

"If she gets that one to act out," Mrs. Bain said, "all she'd have to do is to get up and point to herself."

"Ah, come," Thelma said. "It isn't the poor child's fault."

"I don't see why she'd mind," Mrs. McDermott said. "I'd take it as a compliment if anyone thought I had a billion dollars. After all, it isn't as if Bob married her for her money. Of course, a lot of people may have thought so at first. He certainly is crazy mad about her now. I never saw a man so much in love with a woman, did you, Thelma?"

"My dear, let's not go into the beautiful love life of the Linehams." Thelma said. "We're supposed to be thinking up things for the other side to guess."

"Well, I never saw anything like it," Mrs. McDermott said. "I actually feel we're all butting in on them. We ought to leave them alone."

"Really?" Thelma said. "Let's see, what were we doing?" She wrote "*Billion Dollar Baby*" on a slip of paper and folded it.

There came shouts from the other room. "Hey, what are you doing in there? We've been ready for hours."

Mrs. McDermott called back, "All right, all right, just another minute."

"We are taking much too long," Thelma said. "We haven't any quotations, have we? What was that thing from *Hamlet*? 'Too much of water hast thou . . .' Oh, yes." She began to write.

"You're not going to use that one, are you?" Mrs. McDermott said.

"I'm just putting it down in case we can't think of anything else," Thelma said.

"Everything I've thought of is wrong," Mrs. Bain said. "You can't mention water, you can't mention rich girls, you can't mention second marriages. What can you do?"

"Oh, here's one," Thelma said. "More Shakespeare." She wrote hurriedly.

There were renewed shouts from the other room.

"Oh, bless you, Thelma," Mrs. McDermott said. "What is it?"

"I'll tell you when we get in there," Thelma said. She raised her voice and called, "We're coming."

They went into the other room where the opposing team awaited them, looking patient. Their group too had had certain difficulties in making their selections. Sherm had had a bit of Mrs. Bain's compulsion trouble. He had urged that they choose the song "Don't You Remember Sweet Alice, Ben Bolt?" and sought to advance his cause by singing it over and over. Nervously quelled by Mr. McDermott, he then suggested "Asleep in the Deep," and finding no enthusiasm went on to "Roll Out the Barrel." It was then that Emmy had replenished his drink for him.

The captains exchanged papers, and the teams sat down facing each other. When Sherm was a player, it was understood that his side was to take precedence. More, it was accepted that Sherm was to be the opening actor. It was imperative that he perform his solo before he fell asleep.

Sherm, happy and confident, drew a folded slip of paper, faced his team, and bowed so low that helpful hands were outstretched toward him and solicitous voices cried, "Whoo-oo-ps!" He regained his balance and, at the word "Go" from his chieftain, unfolded the slip. He accomplished this one-handed, for his other hand was curled about his glass. He read what was written on the paper, and went into his act.

After some time, his team gathered that he was attempting to convey the idea that he was to interpret a song. He did this by opening his mouth and pulling something invisible, possibly music, out of it. Then inspiration came to him; he went through a pantomime as if he were lathering his face and scraping his beard. It was difficult, however, for his comrades to divine his purpose, as the hand that held the glass obscured what the other hand was doing. They sat with their elbows on their knees and their chins in their hands, watching with varying degrees of frustration, until Mr. Bain, the timekeeper, called gaily, "All right, Sherm. Time's up!"

"What's the matter with you?" Sherm inquired in a hurt voice. "You all asleep or something?" He turned to the enemy for support. "It was perfectly clear what I was doing, wasn't it?" he said. "First I acted 'song,' and then I acted the name of it. Besides, it wasn't fair, anyhow."

"Certainly it's fair," Mr. Bain said. "It's 'Chi-Baba, Chi-Baba, Chi-Wawa.' Every kid in the street sings it. Only what in heaven's name were you doing to your face?"

"That was shaving," Sherm said with dignity. "I was a barber."

Cries of derision arose from all over the room. Sherm retired moodily to the liquor tray.

Mrs. McDermott volunteered to go first for her side. She opened her paper, gave the conventional blank look to the opposition, indicated that she was going to do an excerpt from a poem. In a matter of seconds her side guessed that the selection was:

" 'Twas brillig, and the slithy toves
   Did gyre and gimble in the wabe."

This speed was due less to Mrs. McDermott's dramatic gifts—although she did gyre and gimble quite acceptably—than to the fact that a bit of the "Jabberwocky" is an almost inevitable part of any session of The Game. The contestants are always ready and waiting for it.

"Wonderful, wonderful," Sherm pronounced bitterly. "I never draw a pushover like 'slithy toves.' Oh, no, I have to get 'Chi-Baba, Chi-Baba, Chi-Wawa'!"

Then Mr. McDermott got up, weighted with the responsibility of retrieving the honor of his team. He read his directions, gave the accepted sign, indicating he was to perform a title of a play, that it was in three words, and it was his intention to do the last word first. He folded his arms and rocked them gently.

"Belly-ache," Sherm said.

The others of the team fired guesses at Mr. McDermott.

" 'Lullaby'? Is it 'lullaby'?"

" 'Child'? 'Infant'? 'Baby'? . . . It's something something baby!"

Mr. McDermott giddy with his quick success threw precedent to the winds and essayed to do two words at once. He rubbed his thumb back and forth over his fingers. Nobody guessed that this was a symbol for money. Nobody guessed anything. Mr. McDermott sought to make matters plainer by moistening his thumb and moving it rapidly across the palm of his other hand in imitation of one who counts bank notes.

" 'Money'? Is it 'money'?"

Mr. McDermott stopped just short of paroxysms in pantomiming to his comrades that they were warm.

"No, it can't be 'money.' How can it be 'money'? It's got 'baby' in it. He's doing something about a 'baby.' "

Mr. McDermott counted more invisible money in savage abandon.

"*Billion Dollar Baby*," Emmy said suddenly.

Mr. McDermott threw out his arms to her and relaxed.

There were cries of "Wonderful! Why, she's wonderful!" and Bob, beaming with pride, kissed her as if they were alone in the room.

From the sofa opposite, Thelma Chrystie watched them.

"Why, I didn't do anything," Emmy said, when Bob released her. "It was just an accident."

"Oh, no, Emmy," Thelma said, "there are no such things as accidents. Are there, Bob?"

It was strange that the slow quiet words should have made Bob start as if she had screamed them at him.

Next, Mrs. Bain took her turn. After the conventional preliminaries, she indicated to her teammates that she had been allotted a quotation of eight words, and she was about to dramatize the first one. She vigorously and repeatedly pointed downward. The guesses came in a rush.

" 'Floor'?"

" 'Carpet'?"

" 'Earth'?"

Mrs. Bain pointed insistently, seeming to suggest greater depths.

" 'Underground'?"

"Hell hath no fury like a woman scorned," Thelma said, so rapidly the sentence sounded like one long word.

The players awarded her the highest of all praise, a stunned silence. When they found their voices, their cries ranged from "Marvelous!" to "I'll be damned!"

"Honestly," Emmy said, "it's absolutely scary."

Thelma smiled at her. "Well, it really wasn't all guess work," she said. "I recognized Mr. Lineham's gentle touch. The quotation was his idea, wasn't it?"

"Why, yes," Emmy said. "How on earth did you know?"

Thelma smiled again. "You see," she said, "Bob and I have played together so much."

Sherm, who had risen to pay a visit to the liquor tray, found tragedy there. "The brandy's all gone," he said. "Now, who could've done a thing like that? Oh, well, I'm the Spartan type. I'll pig it with whisky."

"Do you want to go next, dear heart?" Bob asked Emmy.

"No, you," she said. "I want to put it off as long as possible. I'm frightened to death. Why, darling, you look frightened too . . . Look at Bob, he's absolutely *white*!"

Bob regarded the two remaining slips of paper, hesitating between them.

"Take either one, my dear," Thelma said, "they're both just made for you."

"Hey," said Mr. Bain, "you mustn't talk to him. You mustn't have anything to do with him. It's against the rules."

"Ah, yes," Thelma said. "This year's rules." She went over to the liquor tray and filled her glass.

Bob chose one of the slips and, at the command to go ahead, he opened it and read what was written on it. In the customary manner he immediately turned toward the other team, but he did not include the whole troupe in his glance. He looked only at Thelma. She smiled at him her slow smile that showed her beautiful teeth, but there was something different about it; there was something different about all of her. Her glow, her own peculiar glow, was gone; it was as if the radiance that came from within her had suddenly been quenched and, as is always so when a precious light goes out, the new darkness was cold and menacing.

Bob turned back to his team, lifted his fingers to signify a quotation, then dropped his arms. "I—I can't—do it."

A great complaint rose from his own ranks. "Oh, Bob, what do you mean, you can't?" "Sure you can, go ahead," and over them all, Emmy's little voice calling, "Why, darling, you can do anything."

"Sorry," Bob said, "it's too hard."

"What's so hard about it, Bob, ole boy, ole boy, ole boy?" Sherm said. "Look what I got. I had to do 'Chi-klobba, Chi-blobba, Chi-schmobba.' Whatever you've got, you're on velvet."

"How many words?" Emmy said.

He held up ten fingers, then four.

"Look, I quit," he said, and his voice shook. "It's all right to play The Game decently, but this kind of stuff I'm damned if I'm going to stand for."

The opposing side immediately went into action.

Mr. Bain rushed to Bob and snatched the paper from his hand and read the words on it. "Is this what all the excitement's about? What's the matter with you, Bob, anyway? It's a quotation from *Hamlet*. Any school child knows it. It's perfectly fair."

"The hell it's fair!" Bob said. "Nobody has to take this stuff."

The company sat in silent discomfort. Slow and smooth and sweet, Thelma came and looked at the paper.

"Oh, that's the one he got," she said. "Listen," she said to Bob's teammates, "I ask you. It isn't very nice to be called unfair, you know, particularly by someone who for years was your—particularly by an old friend. Here's the quotation. It's where they break the news that poor little Ophelia's dead. 'Too much of water hast thou, poor Ophelia, and therefore I forbid my tears.' " She turned to Emmy, "Now will you tell me why your husband should get so upset about that?"

"Well, it's awfully long," Emmy said, "and it's hard and—you know."

She looked pleadingly at Thelma, the tall still woman, the woman of peculiar radiance, the woman who had been so kind to her, the woman she liked best—and she saw a stranger. A stranger who stood outside her house, looked through the window and saw something she herself did not have and hated Emmy for having it.

"Oh, come on," Mrs. McDermott said. "If he doesn't want to do it, he doesn't want to do it. I never thought it was so good anyway. Remember, I told you, Thelma. All right, Bob, you're out. Let's finish up the game. Come on, Mr. B, it's your turn."

The teams settled down again. Bob, still shaken after his outburst, sat down beside Emmy. She patted his wrist and kept her hand there.

Mr. Bain opened his paper and read on it, ". . . weary, stale, flat and unprofitable." (It had turned out to be quite a night for *Hamlet*, as are many nights on which The Game is played.)

Mr. Bain performed "weary" according to his own ideas, with no results from his audience; the same was true of his rendition of "stale," so he let that go for a time and sought an easy role in "flat." He drew his hands across each other parallel to the floor.

" 'Smooth'?"

" 'Level'?"

" 'Flat'?"

Mr. Bain indicated their correctness and went back to another try at the word "weary." He laid his cheek on his folded hands like a tired child.

" 'Tired'?" they said. " 'Tired'?"

" 'Sandman'?"

" 'Sleep'?"

"Let's see, he did 'flat' before," Thelma said. Perhaps it was the influence of *Hamlet* that made her speak as if in soliloquy. "But what kind of 'flat' was he trying to show? Was it just *flat* 'flat'? . . . Or was it the other kind? . . . A place? . . . Two rooms, perhaps . . . Sanctuary? . . . Where two people might meet sometimes when they could steal away—a secret haven—through the years . . ."

The Game was much quieter than it had been at first. Possibly Bob's conduct had had a dampening effect on the company. Bob's side sat silent.

Thelma's words came across the room to them as her voice went dreamily on. "And if that's 'sleep' he's doing now . . . 'sleep' . . . then

I don't think he means just *flat* 'flat' . . . I think he means a secret place. . . ."

Slowly little Mrs. Lineham took her hand from her husband's wrist.

Mr. Bain canceled further speculations by returning to his second word. He pantomimed slicing bread, went graphically on to spread a slice with butter, began to munch it, spat it out with every manifestation of distaste.

"I think that's bread he's eating," Thelma said, "and something's the matter with it. Maybe it's stale. Hateful word. Love gone stale. It is 'stale,' isn't it?"

"Oh, wait a minute, wait a minute," Mrs. McDermott said. "That's out of *Hamlet* too. 'Weary, stale, flat'—and something else. It's one of those gloomy numbers."

"Oh, I know," Thelma said. "The last word is 'unprofitable.' 'Weary, stale, flat and unprofitable.' "

"As the girl said to the sailor," Sherm said. He rose and pigged it with a little more whisky.

"Go on, Emmy," Mrs. McDermott said. "It's your turn."

"You don't have to do it, Emmy," Bob said, "if you don't want to."

"I'll do it," Emmy said.

She took the last paper. Mr. McDermott, in sudden recollection, whispered to Thelma, "Oh, that's the one you did. What is it? You didn't tell us."

"It's something from *Henry V*," Thelma said.

"Oh, I saw the movie. Laurence Olivier," Mrs. McDermott said.

Emmy opened the paper and looked at it and stood helplessly before her team. "Oh, dear," she said. "I just don't know how to do it. I don't even know what it means."

They sought to reassure her by telling her, "Of course, you can do it. Go ahead, just try. We're all with you, Emmy," and so on.

Hopelessly she looked again at the paper. " 'Give dreadful note of preparation.' From *Henry V* by William Shakespeare," she read.

"I can't," she told her audience pitiably. "I just don't know."

"Come on," they said. "What is it? Is it a song, a book, is it a person, what? Oh, it's a quotation . . . How many words? . . . Five. What's the first word? Go on. You can do it."

Emmy went through small uncertain motions of taking invisible objects from an invisible container presenting them to her team.

"What's she doing?"

"She's handing out something."

"Is she giving us something?"

" 'Give,' " Bob said. "You're giving, aren't you, dear heart?"

"Why, the little girl is going great guns," Sherm said.

"Okay. 'Give,' " Mr. McDermott said. "Next word."

"Second word?"

"Two syllables."

"First syllable."

"You're doing 'scared.' You're 'frightened.' "

"Is it something you dread? . . . Oh, the first syllable is 'dread.' "

"Is the word 'dreaded'?"

"Is it 'dreadful'?"

"Second word is 'dreadful.' Why, the girl's a whizz!"

"Come on, third word."

"One syllable?"

"What's she doing?"

"She's scratching the palm of her hand," Sherm said. "Something itches. Mosquitoes. DDT."

"Oh, Sherm, get out of the way."

"Come on, Emmy. Do it again."

"Are you writing? Is that what you're doing on your hand?"

"Writing a book? A book? A novel?"

"A letter?"

"Feelthy postcard," said Sherm.

"Is it a letter you're writing?"

"No. It can't be a 'letter,' it's only one syllable."

" 'Note'! It's 'note.' "

"Okay. 'Give dreadful note . . .' "

Emmy stood with her knuckles pressed to her temple, trying desperately to plan out her next move. " 'Give dreadful note,' " she murmured. " 'Give . . . dreadful . . . note.' "

(The players are not supposed to speak, but no one stopped her; she was so little and a bride besides.)

" 'Dreadful note,' " she said. She looked at Bob pleadingly, as if he could send her telepathic aid. " 'Dreadful note'!" she said. " 'Give— dreadful—note——' *Bob. Bob! What's the matter with you? Don't you feel well?*"

"No, darling, I just . . . Hot in here. I'll . . . get a drink."

"Come on, Emmy, forget the bridegroom for a minute!"

"He's all right. Do the fourth word. Oh, you're going to do the fifth."

"How many syllables? Oh, you're going to do the whole word?"

"What's she doing *now*?"

"You're folding something. Is that what you're doing? Folding clothes?"

"You're putting them in a drawer?"

"You're putting them in a bag. You're packing. Is that the word? Is it 'packing'?"

"Oh, it's nowhere's near it," Emmy said. "I wish I knew how to do it."

Thelma drained her glass. "I'll tell her how to do it," she said. "Let me coach her. I have to stay out anyway to balance Bob. Come here, dear, I'll whisper to you."

"No," Bob said, "let her alone. Let her do it her own way."

"Oh, but I need help so, Bobby," Emmy said, and she went to receive Thelma's instructions.

"Oh," she said in a moment, "Do you really think that's how?"

"It's the only way," Thelma said.

"Well, thanks ever so much," Emmy said. She began to act again.

"You're taking off your clothes. Is it 'strip'? 'Strip-tease'?"

"No, she's putting something on. She's tying her head in something."

"Getting ready to go somewhere?"

"You're putting your toe in something. Something cold. Is it water? Are you putting your foot in cold water . . . Yes, she's shivering."

Mrs. McDermott gasped, "Thelma, make her stop. *Make* her."

Thelma paid no attention to her. The other side went on guessing.

"Are you getting ready for a swim?"

There was a sound of breaking glass. At first it was accepted that Sherm had been at his late evening activities, but when the company looked, they found Bob had set his glass down so hard he'd smashed it.

"Yes, she's getting ready for a swim," Bob said roughly. "That's right, isn't it, Thelma?"

"Well, what's the word?" Sherm said.

" 'Preparation,' " Thelma said.

"What kind of talk is that?" Sherm said. " 'Give dreadful note of preparation.' What the hell does it mean?"

"Why, anybody would know what it means the way she did it," Thelma said. "She did it beautifully. She did 'note' like a written note. It really means 'note' like sound—she did it better. I suppose the word 'preparation' put written note in her mind. You know, someone preparing to do something. Someone writing a note to show that they intended to do something, that it didn't just *happen*. Or maybe it was the word 'dreadful' that did it. A dreadful note. A note that mustn't be seen. A last note, that this person, whoever it was, left to show that she—that *they*—had found out something, something that had been going on for years, something they'd never dreamed of—and just couldn't bear. And then 'preparation.' Wasn't she cute getting ready to go into the water? Why, you could just see the whole story."

Wildly Emmy turned to Bob. "What's she talking about?" she said. "What's she talking about? Who is the someone she's talking about? Who went into the cold water? Who was the someone who found out something and wrote a dreadful note to tell what they were going to do, to show that there aren't any accidents? She said you knew there weren't any accidents. *Bob, what is she talking about? What's she saying?*"

"Everything but Alice's name," Bob said. There was not a sound as he walked out of the room.

Thelma, dissipating awkwardness as the early sun dissipates gray mists, came over to Emmy, warm and gracious.

"Pay no attention to him," Thelma said. "He's just overwrought. Naturally, he's nervous. His first party in his new house. Don't worry about him." She put her arm around Emmy. But Emmy wrenched herself away as if the cool pale flesh sullied her shoulders.

"Don't you touch me!" she said between her teeth. "Don't you come near me again, ever, ever, ever!"

Sherm, with his nearly empty glass tilted in his hand, pulled himself up to his full height and weight. He stood over Emmy. "Now wait just a minute, kiddy," he said. "You're a good girl, and I like you, but you can't talk to Thelma that way. Anybody who doesn't want her around can go take a jump in the lake!"

"Oh, my God!" Mrs. McDermott said. "Oh, my God!"

Cosmopolitan, December 1948

I Live on Your Visits

The boy came into the hotel room and immediately it seemed even smaller.

"Hey, it's cool in here," he said. This was not meant as a comment on the temperature. "Cool," for reasons possibly known in some department of Heaven, was a term then in use among many of those of his age to express approbation.

It was indeed cool in the room, after the hard gray rain in the streets. It was warm, and it was so bright. The many-watted electric bulbs his mother insisted upon were undimmed by the thin frilled shades she had set on the hotel lamps, and there were shiny things everywhere: sheets of mirror along the walls; a square of mirror backing the mirror-plated knob on the door that led to the bedroom; cigarette boxes made of tiny bits of mirror and matchboxes slipped into little mirror jackets placed all about; and, on consoles and desk and table, photographs of himself at two and a half and five and seven and nine framed in broad mirror bands. Whenever his mother settled in a new domicile, and she removed often, those photographs were the first things out of the luggage. The boy hated them. He had had to pass his fifteenth birthday before his body had caught up with his head; there was that head, in those presentments of his former selves, that pale, enormous blob. Once he had asked his mother to put the pictures somewhere else—preferably some small, dark place that could be locked. But he had had the bad fortune to make his request on one of the occasions when she was given to weeping suddenly and long. So the photographs stood out on parade, with their frames twinkling away.

There were twinklings, too, from the silver top of the fat crystal cocktail shaker, but the liquid low within the crystal was pale and dull. There was no shine, either, to the glass his mother held. It was cloudy from the clutch of her hand, and on the inside there were oily dribbles of what it had contained.

His mother shut the door by which she had admitted him, and followed him into the room. She looked at him with her head tilted to the side.

"Well, aren't you going to kiss me?" she said in a charming, wheedling voice, the voice of a little, little girl. "Aren't you, you beautiful big ox, you?"

"Sure," he said. He bent down toward her, but she stepped suddenly away. A sharp change came over her. She drew herself tall, with her shoulders back and her head flung high. Her upper lip lifted over her teeth, and her gaze came cold beneath lowered lids. So does one who has refused the white handkerchief regard the firing squad.

"Of course," she said in a deep, iced voice that gave each word its full due, "if you do not wish to kiss me, let it be recognized that there is no need for you to do so. I had not meant to overstep. I apologize. *Je vous demande pardon.* I had no desire to force you. I have never forced you. There is none to say I have."

"Ah, Mom," he said. He went to her, bent again, and this time kissed her cheek.

There was no change in her, save in the slow, somehow offended lifting of her eyelids. The brows arched as if they drew the lids up with them. "Thank you," she said. "That was gracious of you. I value graciousness. I rank it high. *Mille grazie.*"

"Ah, Mom," he said.

For the past week, up at his school, he had hoped—and coming down in the train he had hoped so hard that it became prayer—that his mother would not be what he thought of only as "like that." His prayer had gone unanswered. He knew by the two voices, by the head first tilted then held high, by the eyelids lowered in disdain then raised in outrage, by the little lisped words and then the elegant enunciation and the lofty diction. He knew.

He stood there and said, "Ah, Mom."

"Perhaps," she said, "you will award yourself the privilege of meeting a friend of mine. She is a true friend. I am proud that I may say it."

There was someone else in the room. It was preposterous that he had not seen her, for she was so big. Perhaps his eyes had been dazzled, after the dim-lit hotel corridor; perhaps his attention had been all for his mother. At any rate, there she sat, the true friend, on the sofa covered with embossed cotton fabric of the sickened green that is peculiar to hotel upholsteries. There she sat, at one end of the sofa, and it seemed as if the other end must fly up into the air.

"I can give you but little," his mother said, "yet life is still kind enough to let me give you something you will always remember. Through me, you will meet a human being."

Yes, oh, yes. The voices, the stances, the eyelids—those were the signs. But when his mother divided the race into people and human beings—that was the certainty.

He followed her the little way across the room, trying not to tread on the train of her velvet tea gown that slid along the floor after her and slapped at the heels of her gilt slippers. Fog seemed to rise from his raincoat and his shoes cheeped. He turned out to avoid the coffee table in front of the sofa, came in again too sharply and bumped it.

"Mme. Marah," his mother said, "may I present my son?"

"Christ, he's a big bastard, isn't he?" the true friend said.

She was a fine one to talk about anybody's being big. Had she risen, she would have stood shoulder against shoulder with him, and she must have outweighed him by sixty pounds. She was dressed in quantities of tweedlike stuff ornamented, surprisingly, with black sequins set on in patterns of little bunches of grapes. On her massive wrists were bands and chains of dull silver, from some of which hung amulets of discolored ivory, like rotted fangs. Over her head and neck was a sort of caul of crisscrossed mauve veiling, splattered with fuzzy black balls. The caul caused her no inconvenience. Puffs of smoke issued sporadically from behind it, and, though the veiling was crisp elsewhere, around the mouth it was of a marshy texture, where drink had passed through it.

His mother became the little girl again. "Isn't he wonderful?" she said. "This is my baby. This is Crissy-wiss."

"*What* is his name?" the true friend said.

"Why, Christopher, of course," his mother said.

Christopher, of course. Had he been born earlier, it would have been Peter; earlier again, Michael; he had been not much too late for Jonathan. In the lower forms of his school, there were various Nicholases, several Robins, and here and there a Jeremy coming up. But the members of his own class were in the main Christophers.

"Christopher," the true friend said. "Well, that's not too bad. Of course, that downward stroke of the 'p' is bound to give him trouble, and I'm never really happy about an 'r' and an 'i' together. But it's not too bad. Not too. When's your birthday?" she asked the boy.

"The fifteenth of August," he said.

His mother was no longer the little girl. "The heat," she said, "the cruel August heat. And the stitches. Oh, God, the stitches!"

"So he's a Leo," the true friend said. "Awfully big for a Leo. You want to be pretty careful, young man, from October 22nd to November 13th. Keep away from anything electrical."

"I will," the boy said. "Thank you," he added.

"Let me see your hand," the true friend said.

The boy gave her his hand.

"Mm," she said, scanning the palm. "M-hmm, m-hmm, m-hmm. Oh. Well—*that* can't be helped. Well, you'll have pretty good health, if you just watch that chest of yours. There's a long sickness in your twenties and a bad accident some time around forty-five, but that's about all. There's going to be an unhappy love affair, but you'll get over it. You'll marry and—I can't see if there's two or three children. Probably two and one born dead, or something like that. I don't see much money, any time. Well, you watch your chest." She gave him back his hand.

"Thank you," he said.

The little girl came back to his mother. "Isn't he going to be famous?" she said.

The true friend shrugged. "It's not in his hand," she said.

"I always thought he'd write," his mother said. "When he was so small you could hardly see him, he used to write little verses. Crissy, what was the one about the bumpety bunny?"

"Oh, Mother!" he said. "I don't remember!"

"Oh, you do so, too!" she said. "You're just being modest. It was all about how the bunny went bumpety, bumpety all day long. Of course you remember. Well, you don't seem to write verses any more—at least none you show to *me*. And your letters—they're like telegrams. When you write at all, that is. Oh, Marah, why do they have to grow up? And now he's going to be married and have all those children."

"Two, anyway," the true friend said. "I'm not too happy about that third one."

"I suppose I'll never see him then," his mother said. "A lonely old woman, sick and trembling, and no one to take care of me."

She picked up the true friend's empty glass from the coffee table, filled it and her own from the cocktail shaker, and returned the friend's. She sat down near the sofa.

"Well, sit down, Crissy," she said. "And why don't you take off your coat?"

"Why, I don't think I'd better, Mom," he said. "You see—"

"He wants to keep his wet coat on," the true friend said. "He likes to smell like low tide."

"Well, you see," the boy said, "I can stay just a minute. You see, the train was late and everything, and I told Dad I'd be sure to be there early."

"Oh?" his mother said. The little girl ran off abruptly. The eyelids came into play.

"It's because the train was late," he said. "If it had been on time, I could have stayed awhile. But it had to go and be late, and they're having dinner awfully early tonight."

"I see," his mother said. "I see. I had thought that you would have dinner with me. With your mother. Her only son. But no, that is not to be. I have only an egg, but I would have shared it with you so gladly. So happily. But you are wise, of course. You must think first of your own comfort. Go and fill your stomach with your father. Go eat stalled ox with him."

"Mother, don't you see?" he said. "We have to have dinner early because we have to go to bed early. We've got to get up at daybreak because we're driving to the country. You know. I wrote you."

"Driving?" she said. "Your father has a new car, I presume."

"It's the same old heap," he said. "Nearly eight years old."

"Really?" she said. "Naturally, the buses in which I am obliged to ride are all this year's models."

"Ah, Mom," he said.

"Is your father well?" she said.

"He's fine," he said.

"Why not?" she said. "What is there could pierce that heart? And how is Mrs. Tennant? As I suppose she calls herself."

"Let's not do this again, will you, Mom?" he said. "She's Mrs. Tennant. You know that. She and Dad have been married for six years."

"To me," she said, "there is only one woman who may rightfully wear a man's name; the one whose son he has sired. But that is only my humble opinion. Who is to listen to it?"

"You get along all right with your stepmother?" the true friend said.

As always, it took him a moment before he could connect the term. It seemed to have nothing to do with Whitey, with her gay little monkey's face and her flying straw-colored hair.

A laugh fell from his mother's lips, hard, like a pellet of ice. "Such women are sly," she said. "They have ways."

"Well, born on a cusp," the true friend said. "You've got to keep considering that."

His mother turned to the boy. "I am going to do something that you will agree, in any honesty, that I have never done before," she said. "I am going to ask a favor of you. I am going to ask you to take off your coat and sit down, so that for just a few poor minutes it will seem as if you were not going to leave me. Will you let me have that illusion? Do not do it out of affection or gratitude or consideration. Just in simple pity."

"Yes, sit down, for God's sake," the true friend said. "You make people nervous."

"All right, sure," the boy said. He took off his raincoat, hung it over his arm, and sat on a small, straight chair.

"He's the biggest damn thing I ever saw," the true friend said.

"Thank you," his mother said. "If you think I ask too much, I plead guilty. *Mea culpa.* Well, now that we are cozy, let us talk, shall we? I see so little of you—I know so little about you. Tell me some things. Tell me what there is about this Mrs. Tennant that causes you to rank her so high above me. Is she more beautiful than I am?"

"Mom, please," he said. "You know Whitey isn't beautiful. She's just sort of funny-looking. Nice funny."

"Nice funny," she said. "Oh, I'm afraid I could never compete with that. Well, looks aren't everything, I suppose. Tell me, do you consider her a human being?"

"Mother, I don't know," he said. "I can't do that kind of talk."

"Let it pass," she said. "Let it be forgotten. Is your father's country place attractive at this time of year?"

"It isn't a place," he said. "You know—it's just a big sort of shack. There isn't even any heat. Just fireplaces."

"Ironic," she said. "Bitterly, cruelly ironic. I, who so love an open fire; I, who could sit all day looking into its leaping golds and purples and dreaming happy dreams. And I haven't even a gas log. Well. And who is going to this shack, to share the lovely, glowing fires?"

"Just Dad and Whitey and me," he said. "Oh, and the other Whitey, of course."

His mother looked at the true friend. "Is it growing dark in here?" she said. "Or is it just that I think I am going to faint?" She looked again at the boy. "The *other* Whitey?"

"It's a little dog," he said. "Not any particular kind. It's a nice little dog. Whitey saw it out in the street, when it was snowing, and it followed her home, and so they kept it. And whenever Dad—whenever anybody called Whitey, the dog would come, too. So Dad said well, if he thought that was his name, then that was going to *be* his name. So that was why."

"I am afraid," his mother said, "that your father is not aging with dignity. To me, whimsey after forty-five is a matter of nausea."

"It's an awfully nice little dog," he said.

"The management does not allow dogs here," she said. "I suppose that will be held against me. Marah—this drink. It is as weak as the beating of my heart."

"Why doesn't he make us some fresh ones?" the true friend said.

"I'm sorry," the boy said. "I don't know how to make cocktails."

"What do they teach you, anyway, in that fancy school of yours?" the true friend said.

His mother tilted her head at the boy. "Crissy," she said, "want to be a big, brave man? Take the bowl and get some nice, cold ice out of the kitchen."

He took the ice bowl, went into the minuscule kitchen, and took a tray of ice cubes from the tiny refrigerator. When he replaced the tray, he could hardly close the refrigerator door, the shelves were so crowded. There were a cardboard box of eggs, a packet of butter, a cluster of glossy French rolls, three artichokes, two avocados, a plate of tomatoes, a bowl of shelled peas, a grapefruit, a tin of vegetable juices, a glass of red caviar, a cream cheese, an assortment of sliced Italian sausages, and a plump little roasted Cornish Rock hen.

When he returned, his mother was busied with bottles and shaker. He set the bowl of cubes beside them.

"Look, Mom," he said, "honestly I've got to—"

His mother looked at him and her lip trembled. "Just two more minutes," she whispered. "Please, oh, please."

He went and sat again.

She made the drinks, gave one to the true friend, and kept one. She sank into her chair; her head drooped and her body looked as boneless as a skein of yarn.

"Don't you want a drink?" the true friend said.

"No, thanks," the boy said.

"Might do you good," the true friend said. "Might stunt your growth. How long are you going to stay up in this country where you're going?"

"Oh, just over tomorrow night," he said. "I have to be back at school Sunday evening."

His mother stiffened and straightened. Her former coldnesses were as tropical heat to that which took her now.

"Do I understand you to say that you will not be coming in to see me again?" she said. "Do I understand you aright?"

"I can't, Mom," he said. "I won't have a chance. We've got to drive back, and then I have to get the train."

"I quite comprehend," she said. "I had thought, in my tenderness, I would see you again before your return to your school. I had thought, of course, that if you must rush away like a mad thing today, then I would see you again, to make up for it. Disappointments—I thought I had had them all, I thought life could bring forth no new ones. But this—this. That you will not take a little bit of your time from your relatives, who have so much of it, to give to me, your mother. How it must please them that you do not want to see me. How they must laugh together. What a triumph. How they must howl in merriment."

"Mother, don't say things like that," he said. "You shouldn't, even when you're—"

"Please!" she said. "The subject is closed. I will say no more about your father, poor, weak man, and that woman with the dog's name. But you—you. Have you no heart, no bowels, no natural instincts? No. You have not. I must face the fact. Here, in the presence of my friend, I must say what I had thought never, never to say. My son is not a human being!"

The true friend shook her caul and sighed. The boy sat still.

"Your father," his mother said. "Does he still see his old friends? *Our* old friends?"

"Why, I don't know, Mom," he said. "Yes, they see a lot of people, I guess. There's almost always somebody there. But they're alone a lot of the time. They like it that way."

"How fortunate," she said. "They like being alone. Smug, content, no need— Yes. And the old friends. They do not see me. They are all in twos, they have lives, they know what they're going to be doing six months from now. Why should they see me? Why should they have memories, kindnesses?"

"Probably most of them Pisces," the true friend said.

"Well, you must go," the boy's mother said. "It is late. Late—when is it ever late for me, when my son is with me? But you have told me. I know. I understand, and so I bow my head. Go, Christopher. Go."

"I'm terribly sorry, Mom," the boy said. "But I told you how it is." He rose and put on his coat.

"Christ, he gets bigger and bigger," the true friend said.

This time, the eyelids of the boy's mother were lowered at her friend. "I have always admired tall men," she said. She turned again to the boy. "You must go," she said. "It is so written. But take happiness with you. Take sweet memories of our little time together. See—I shall show you that I bear no vengefulness. I shall show you that I wish only well to those who have wrought but evil to me. I shall give you a present to take one of them."

She rose, moved about the room, touched boxes and tables fruit-lessly. Then she went to the desk, moved papers and inkstands, and brought forth a small, square box, on top of which was a little plaster poodle, sitting on its hind legs, its front paws curved endearingly, begging.

"This is a souvenir of happier times," she said. "But I need no reminders. Take this dear, happy thing to one you love. See! See what it is!"

She touched a spring at the back of the box and the "Marseillaise" tinkled forth, hesitantly.

"My little music box," she said. "That moonlit night, the ship so brilliant, the ocean so still and beckoning."

"Hey, that's cool, Mom," he said. "Thanks ever so much. Whitey'll love it. She loves things like that."

"Things like that?" she said. "There are no other things like that, when one gives from one's heart." She stopped and seemed to ponder. "*Whitey* will love it?" she said. "Are you telling me that you propose giving it to that so-called Mrs. Tennant?" She touched the box; the tinkling ceased.

"I thought you said—" the boy said.

She shook her head at him, slowly. "Curious," she said. "Extraordinary. That my son should have so little perception. This gift, from my poor little store, is not for her. It is for the little dog. The little dog that I may not have."

"Why, thanks, Mom," he said. "Thanks."

"So go," she said. "I would not hold you. Take with you my wishes for your joy, among your loved ones. And when you can, when they will release you for a little while—come to me again. I wait for you. I light a lamp for you. My son, my only child, there are but desert sands for me between your comings. I live on your visits—Chris, I live on your visits."

The New Yorker, January 15, 1955

Mrs. Ewing was a short woman who accepted the obligation borne by so many short women to make up in vivacity what they lack in number of inches from the ground. She was a creature of little pats and prods, little crinklings of the eyes and wrinklings of the nose, little runs and ripples of speech and movement, little spirals of laughter. Whenever Mrs. Ewing entered a place, all stillness left it.

Her age was a matter of guesswork, save for those who had been at school with her. For herself, she declared that she paid no attention to her birthdays—didn't give a hoot about them; and it is true that when you have amassed several dozen of the same sort of thing, it loses that rarity which is the excitement of collectors. In the summertime, she wore little cotton play suits, though her only game was bridge, and short socks, revealing the veins along the backs of her legs. For winter, she chose frocks of audible taffeta, frilled and frilled again, and jackets made of the skins of the less-sought-after lower animals. Often, of an evening, she tied a pale ribbon in her hair. Through shimmering heat or stabbing wind Mrs. Ewing trudged to her hairdresser's; her locks had been so frequently and so drastically brightened and curled that to caress them, one felt, would be rather like running one's fingers through julienne potatoes. She decorated her small, square face in a manner not unusual among ladies of the South and the Southwest, powdering the nose and chin sharp white and applying circles of rouge to the cheeks. Seen from an end of a long, softly lighted room, Mrs. Ewing was a pretty woman.

She had long been a widowed lady. Even before her widowhood, she and Mr. Ewing had lived separately, while the sympathy of the town dwelt with her. She had dallied with the notion of divorce, for it is well known that the thought, much less the presence, of a merry divorcée sets gentlemen to pawing the ground and snorting. But before her plans took form, Mr. Ewing, always a devout believer in the doctrine of one more for the road, was killed in an automobile accident. Still, a widow, too, a soft little widow, has repute the world over for causing the hearts of gentlemen to beat warm and fast. Mrs. Ewing and her friends felt sure that she would marry again. Time slid on, and this did not happen.

Mrs. Ewing never vaunted her lorn condition, never shut herself within the shaded chambers of bereavement. She went right along, skip-

ping and tinkling through all the social events of the town, and no week
went by without her presiding in her own house over cheerful little
dinners or evenings of passionate bridge. She was always the same, and
always the same to everyone, although she reached her heights when
there were men present. She coquetted with the solid husbands of her
friends, and with the two or three bachelors of the town, tremulous
antiques pouring pills into their palms at the dinner table, she was
sprightly to the verge of naughtiness. To a stranger observing her might
have come the thought that Mrs. Ewing was not a woman who easily
abandoned hope.

Mrs. Ewing had a daughter: Lolita. It is, of course, the right of parents to name their offspring what they please, yet it would sometimes
be easier if they could glimpse the future and see what the little one was
going to look like later on. Lolita was of no color at all; she was thin,
with insistent knobs at the ends of her bones, and her hair, so fine that
it seemed sparse, grew straight. There was a time when Mrs. Ewing,
probably hostess to fantasies about a curly-headed tot, took to wetting
the child's hair severely and rolling it up on strips of rags when she went
to bed. But when the strips were untied in the morning, down fell the
hair again, straight as ever. All that came of the project was a series of
white nights for Lolita, trying to rest her head on the hard knots of the
rags. So the whole thing was given up, and her hair hung as it must
thereafter. In her early days at school, the little boys would chase her
around the schoolyard at recess, snatching at the limp strands and crying, "Oh, Lolita, give us a curl, willya? Ah, Lolita, give us one of your
pretty curls!" The little girls, her little friends, would gather in a group
to watch and say "Oo, aren't they terrible?" and press their hands
against their mouths to control their giggles.

Mrs. Ewing was always her own sparkling self with her daughter,
but her friends, mothers of born belles, tried to imagine themselves in
her place and their hearts ached for her. Gallant in their own way, they
found cases to relate to her, cases of girls who went through periods of
being plain and then turned suddenly into dazzling beauties; some of
the more scholarly brought up references to the story of the ugly duck-
ling. But Lolita passed through young girlhood and came of age and
the only difference in her was that she was taller.

The friends did not dislike Lolita. They spoke sweetly to her and
when she was not present always inquired of her mother about her,
although knowing there would be no news. Their exasperation was not
with her but with the Fates, who had foisted upon Mrs. Ewing that pale
gawk—one, moreover, with no spirit, with never a word to say for

herself. For Lolita was quiet, so quiet that often you would not realize she was in the room, until the light shone on her glasses. There was nothing to do about it; there were no hopeful anecdotes to cover the condition. The friends, thinking of their own winging, twittering young, sighed again for Mrs. Ewing.

There were no beaux draped along the railing of the Ewing porch in the evening; no young male voices asked for Lolita over the telephone. At first seldom, then not at all, did the other girls ask her to their parties. This was no mark of dislike; it was only that it was difficult to bear her in mind, since school was done with for all of them and they no longer saw her daily. Mrs. Ewing always had her present at her own little soirees, though the Lord knew she added nothing to them, and, dauntless, took her along to the public events attended by both old and young, festivals for the benefit of church or charity or civic embellishment. Even when brought into such festivities, Lolita would find a corner and stay there in her quiet. Her mother would call to her across the big public room, carolling high and clear above the social clatter: "Well, come on there, little old Miss Stick-in-the-Mud! Get up on your feet and start mixing around with people!" Lolita would only smile and stay where she was, quiet as she was. There was nothing morose about her stillness. Her face, if you remembered to see it, had a look of shy welcoming, and her smile might have been set high in the tiny list of her attractions. But such attributes are valuable only when they can be quickly recognized; who has time to go searching?

It often happens in the instance of an unsought maiden daughter and a gay little mother that the girl takes over the running of the house, lifting the burden from the mother's plump shoulders. But not Lolita. She had no domestic talents. Sewing was a dark mystery to her, and if she ventured into the kitchen to attempt some simple dish, the results would be, at best, ludicrous. Nor could she set a room in pretty order. Lamps shivered, ornaments shattered, water slopped out of flower vases before her touch. Mrs. Ewing never chided the girl for her clumsiness; she made jokes about it. Lolita's hands shook under railleries, and there would be only more spilled water and more splintered shepherdesses.

She could not even do the marketing successfully, although armed with a résumé of the needs of the day in her mother's curly handwriting. She would arrive at the market at the proper hour, the time it was filled with women, and then seem to be unable to push her way through them. She stood aside until later arrivals had been served before she could go to the counter and murmur her wants; and so Mrs. Ewing's lunch would be late. The household would have tottered if it had not been for the

maid Mrs. Ewing had had for years—Mardy, the super-cook, the de-
mon cleaner. The other ladies lived uneasily with their servants, ridden
with fears that they might either leave or become spoiled, but Mrs.
Ewing was cozy with Mardy. She was as vigorously winsome with the
maid as with the better-born. They enjoyed laughing together, and right
at hand was the subject of Lolita's incompetences.

Experiments palled, and finally Lolita was relieved of domestic offices. She stayed still and silent; and time went on and Mrs. Ewing went
on and on, bright as a bubble in the air.

Then there bloomed a certain spring, not gradually but all in a day, a
season long to be referred to as the time John Marble came. The town
had not before seen the like of John Marble. He looked as if he had
just alighted from the chariot of the sun. He was tall and fair, and he
could make no awkward move or utter no stumbling phrase. The girls
lost all consciousness of the local young men, for they were nowhere as
against John Marble. He was older than they—he had crossed thirty—
and he must have been rich, for he had the best room at the Wade
Hampton Inn and he drove a low, narrow car with a foreign name, a
thing of grace and power. More, there was about him the magic of the
transitory. There were the local young men, day after day, year in, year
out. But John Marble had come on some real-estate dealings for his
firm, some matters of properties outside the town limits, and when his
business was done, he would go back to the great, glittering city where
he lived. Time pressed; excitement heightened.

Through his business John Marble met important men of the town,
the fathers of daughters, and there was eager entertaining for the brilliant stranger. The girls put on the fluffiest white, and tucked bunches
of pink roses in their pale-blue sashes; their curls shone and swung like
bells. In the twilight they sang little songs for John Marble, and one of
them had a guitar. The local young men, whose evenings hung like wet
seaweed around their necks, could only go in glum groups to the bowl-
ing alley or the moving-picture theater. Though the parties in John Marble's honor slackened, for he explained that because of the demands of
his business he must regret invitations, still the girls impatiently refused
appointments to the local young men, and stayed at home alone on the
chance of a telephone call from John Marble. They beguiled the time
of waiting by sketching his profile on the telephone pad. Sometimes they
threw away their training and telephoned him, even as late as ten
o'clock at night. When he answered, he was softly courteous, charmingly distressed that his work kept him from being with them. Then,

more and more frequently, there was no answer to their calls. The switchboard operator at the inn merely reported that Mr. Marble was out.

Somehow, the difficulties in the way of coming nearer to John Marble seemed to stimulate the girls. They tossed their fragrant curls and let their laughter soar, and when they passed the Wade Hampton Inn, they less walked than sashayed. Their elders said that never in their memories had the young girls been so pretty and so spirited as they were that spring.

And with the whole townful of bright blossoms bended for his plucking, John Marble chose Lolita Ewing.

It was a courtship curiously without detail. John Marble would appear at the Ewing house in the evening, with no preliminary telephoning, and he and Lolita would sit on the porch while Mrs. Ewing went out among her friends. When she returned, she shut the gate behind her with a clang, and as she started up the brick path she uttered a loud, arch *"A-hem,"* as if to warn the young people of her coming, so that they might wrench themselves one from the other. But there was never a squeal of the porch swing, never a creak of a floor board—those noises that tell tales of scurryings to new positions. The only sound was of John Marble's voice, flowing easily along; and when Mrs. Ewing came up on the porch, John Marble would be lying in the swing and Lolita would be sitting in a wicker chair some five feet away from him, with her hands in her lap, and, of course, not a peep out of her. Mrs. Ewing's conscience would smite her at the knowledge of John Marble's one-sided evening, and so she would sit down and toss the ball of conversation in the air and keep it there with reports of the plot of the moving picture she had seen or the hands of the bridge game in which she had taken part. When she, even she, came to a pause, John Marble would rise and explain that the next day was to be a hard one for him and so he must go. Mrs. Ewing would stand at the porch steps and as he went down the path would call after him roguish instructions that he was not to do anything that she would not do.

When she and Lolita came in from the dark porch to the lighted hall, Mrs. Ewing would look at her daughter in an entirely new way. Her eyes narrowed, her lips pressed together, and her mouth turned down at the corners. In silence she surveyed the girl, and still in silence not broken by even a good night, she would mount to her bedroom, and the sound of her closing door would fill the house.

The pattern of the evenings changed. John Marble no longer came to sit on the porch. He arrived in his beautiful car and took Lolita driving through the gentle dark. Mrs. Ewing's thoughts followed them. They would drive out in the country, they would turn off the road to a smooth dell with thick trees to keep it secret from passersby, and there the car would stop. And what would happen then? Did they—Would they— But Mrs. Ewing's thoughts could go no farther. There would come before her a picture of Lolita, and so the thoughts would be finished by her laughter.

All the days, now, she continued to regard the girl under lowered lids, and the downturn of her mouth became a habit with her, though not among her prettier ones. She seldom spoke to Lolita directly, but she still made jokes. When a wider audience was wanting, she called upon Mardy. "Hi, Mardy!" she would cry. "Come on in here, will you? Come in and look at her, sitting there like a queen. Little Miss High-and-Mighty, now she thinks she's caught her a beau!"

There was no announcement of engagement. It was not necessary, for the town sizzled with the news of John Marble and Lolita Ewing. There were two schools of thought as to the match: one blessed Heaven that Lolita had gained a man and the other mourned the callousness of a girl who could go away and leave her mother alone. But miracles were scarce in the annals of the town, and the first school had the more adherents. There was no time for engagement rites. John Marble's business was concluded, and he must go back. There were scarcely hours enough to make ready for the wedding.

It was a big wedding. John Marble first suggested, then stated, that his own plan would be for Lolita and him to go off alone, be married, and then start at once for New York; but Mrs. Ewing paid him no heed. "No, *sir*," she said. "Nobody's going to do *me* out of a great big lovely wedding!" And so nobody did.

Lolita in her bridal attire answered her mother's description of looking like nothing at all. The shiny white fabric of her gown was hostile to her colorless skin, and there was no way to pin the veil becomingly on her hair. But Mrs. Ewing more than made up for her. All in pink ruffles caught up with clusters of false forget-me-nots, Mrs. Ewing was at once bold sunlight and new moonlight, she was budding boughs and opening petals and little, willful breezes. She tripped through the throngs in the smilax-garlanded house, and everywhere was heard her laughter. She patted the bridegroom on arm and cheek, and cried out, to guest after guest, that for two cents she would marry him herself. When the time came to throw rice after the departing couple, she was positively devil-may-care. Indeed, so extravagant was her pitching that one hard-packed handful of the sharp little grains hit the bride squarely in the face.

But when the car was driven off, she stood still looking after it, and there came from her downturned mouth a laugh not at all like her usual trill. "Well," she said, "we'll see." Then she was Mrs. Ewing again, running and chirping and urging more punch on her guests.

Lolita wrote to her mother every week without fail, telling of her apartment and the buying and placing of furniture and the always new adventure of shopping; each letter concluded with the information that John hoped Mrs. Ewing was well and sent her his love. The friends eagerly inquired about the bride, wanting to know above all if she was happy. Mrs. Ewing replied that well, yes, she said she was. "That's what I tell her every time I write to her," she said. "I say, 'That's right, honey, you go ahead and be happy just as long as you can.' "

It cannot be said in full truth that Lolita was missed in the town; but there was something lacking in the Ewing house, something lacking in Mrs. Ewing herself. Her friends could not actually define what it was, for she went on as always, flirting the skirts of her little dresses and trying on her little hair ribbons, and there was no slowing of her movements. Still, the glister was not quite so golden. The dinners and the bridge games continued, but somehow they were not as they had been.

Yet the friends must realize she had taken a stunning blow, for Mardy left her; left her, if you please, for the preposterous project of getting married; Mardy, after all the years and all Mrs. Ewing's goodness to her. The friends shook their heads, but Mrs. Ewing, after the first shock, could be gay about it. "I declare," she said, and her laugh spiralled out, "everybody around me goes off and gets married. I'm just a regular little old Mrs. Cupid." In the long line of new maids there were no Mardys; the once cheerful little dinners were gloomy with grease.

Mrs. Ewing made several journeys to see her daughter and son-in-law, bearing gifts of black-eyed peas and tins of herring roe, for New Yorkers do not know how to live and such delicacies are not easily obtained up North. Her visits were widely spaced; there was a stretch of nearly a year between two of them, while Lolita and John Marble travelled in Europe and then went to Mexico. ("Like hens on hot griddles," Mrs. Ewing said. "People ought to stay put.")

Each time she came back from New York, her friends gathered about her, clamoring for reports. Naturally, they quivered for news of oncoming babies. There was none to tell them. There was never any issue of those golden loins and that plank of a body. "Oh, it's just as well," Mrs. Ewing said comfortably, and left the subject there.

John Marble and Lolita were just the same, the friends were told.

John Marble was as devastating as he had been when he first came to the town, and Lolita still had not a word to say for herself. Though her tenth wedding anniversary was coming close, she could not yet give shape to her dresses. She had closets of expensive clothes—when Mrs. Ewing quoted the prices of some of the garments, the friends sucked in their breath sharply—but when she put on a new dress it might as well have been the old one. They had friends, and they entertained quite nicely, and they sometimes went out. Well, yes, they did seem so; they really did seem happy.

"It's just like I tell Lolita," Mrs. Ewing said. "Just like I always say to her when I write: 'You go ahead and be happy as long as you can.' Because—Well, you know. A man like John Marble married to a girl like Lolita! But she knows she can always come here. This house is her home. She can always come back to her mother."

For Mrs. Ewing was not a woman who easily abandoned hope.

The New Yorker, August 27, 1955

The Banquet of Crow

It was a crazy year, a year when things that should have run on schedule went all which ways. It was a year when snow fell thick and lasting in April, and young ladies clad in shorts were photographed for the tabloids sunbathing in Central Park in January. It was a year when, in the greatest prosperity of the richest nation, you could not walk five city blocks without being besought by beggars; when expensively dressed women loud and lurching in public places were no uncommon sight; when drugstore counters were stacked with tablets to make you tranquil and other tablets to set you leaping. It was a year when wives whose position was only an inch or two below that of the saints—arbiters of etiquette, venerated hostesses, architects of memorable menus—suddenly caught up a travelling bag and a jewel case and flew off to Mexico with ambiguous young men allied with the arts; when husbands who had come home every evening not only at the same hour but at the same minute of the same hour came home one evening more, spoke a few words, and then went out their doors and did not come in by them again.

If Guy Allen had left his wife at another period, she would have held the enduring interest of her friends. But in that year of lunacy so many marital barks were piled up on Norman's Woe that the friends had become overly familiar with tales of shipwreck. At first they flocked to her side and did their practiced best to medicine her wound. They clicked their tongues in sorrow and shook their heads in bewilderment; they diagnosed the case of Guy Allen as one of insanity; they made blistering generalizations about men, considered as a tribe; they assured Maida Allen that no woman could have done more for a man and been more to a man; they pressed her hand and promised her, "Oh, he'll come back—you'll see!"

But time went on, and so did Mrs. Allen, who never in her life before had been known to keep to a subject—on and on with her story of the desperate wrong that had been done her, and she so blameless. Her friends had no energy left to interpolate coos of condolence into the recital, for they were weak with hearing it—it, and others like it; it is the terrible truth that the sagas of the deserted are deplorably lacking in variety. There came a day, indeed, when one lady slammed down her teacup, sprang to her feet, and shrieked, "For Christ's *sake,* Maida, talk about something else!"

Mrs. Allen saw no more of that lady. She began to see less and less of her other friends, too, though that was their doing, not hers. They took no pride in their dereliction; they were troubled by the lurking knowledge that the most ruthless bore may still be genuinely in anguish.

They tried—each tried once—inviting her to pleasant little dinners, to take her out of herself. Mrs. Allen brought her King Charles's head right along with her, and stuck it up, so to say, in the middle of the table, a grisly centerpiece. Several male guests, strangers to her, were provided. In their good humor at meeting a new and pretty woman, they made small flirtatious sorties. Her return was to admit them to her tragedy, going on, past the salad and through the Mocha mousse, with her list of proven talents as wife, chum, and lover, and pointing out, with cynical laughter, just where *those* had got her. When the guests were gone, the hostess miserably accepted the host's ultimatum on who was not to be asked again.

They did invite her, though, to their big cocktail parties, the grand mop-ups of social obligations, thinking that Mrs. Allen could not pit her soft voice against the almighty noise of such galas and so her troubles, unspoken, might be for a while unthought of. Mrs. Allen, on her entrance, went by straight line to acquaintances who had known her and her husband together, and inquired of them if they had seen anything of Guy. If they said they had, she asked them how he was. If they said, "Why, fine," she tendered them a forgiving smile and passed on. Her friends gave up the whole thing.

Mrs. Allen resented their behavior. She lumped them all together as creatures who could function in fair weather only, and uttered thanks that she had found them out in time—in time for what, she did not state. But there was no one to question her, for she spoke to herself. She had begun the practice while pacing the silent rooms of her apartment until deep into the night, and presently she carried it with her out to the street, on her daily walk. It was a year when there were many along the sidewalks mouthing soliloquies, and unless they talked loud and made gestures other pedestrians did not turn to look.

It was a month, then two months, then nearly four, and she had had no direct word from Guy Allen. A day or so after his departure, he had telephoned the apartment and, first inquiring about the health of the maid who answered (he was always the ideal of servants), had asked that his mail be forwarded to his club, where he would be staying. Later that day, he sent the club valet to gather his clothes, pack them, and fetch them to him. These incidents occurred while Mrs. Allen was out; there had been no mention of her, either to the maid or through the valet, and that made a bad time for her. Still, she told herself, at least she knew where he was. She did not pursue the further thought that at most she knew where he was.

On the first of each month, she received a check, in the amount it had always been, for household expenses and herself. The rent must have been sent to the owner of the apartment building, for she was never asked for it. The checks did not come to her from Guy Allen; they were enclosed in notes from his banker, a courtly, white-haired gentleman, whose communications gave the effect of having been written with a quill. Aside from the checks, there was nothing to indicate that Guy and Maida Allen were husband and wife.

Her present became intolerable to Mrs. Allen, and she could see her future only as a hideous prolonging of it. She turned to the past. She did not let memory lead her; it was she who steered memory back along the sunny bypaths of her marriage. Eleven years of marriage, years of happiness—perfect happiness. Oh, Guy had had a man's little moods sometimes, but she could always smile him out of them, and such minute happenings only brought them more sweetly together; lovers' quarrels wax the way to bed. Mrs. Allen shed April tears for times gone by; and nobody ever came along and explained to her that if she had had eleven years of perfect happiness, she was the only human being who ever did.

But memory is a tacit companion. Silence banged on Mrs. Allen's ears. She wanted to hear gentle voices, especially her own. She wanted to find understanding—that thing so many spend their lives in seeking, though surely it should be easy to come upon, for what is it but mutual praise and pity? Her friends had let her down; then she must collect others. It is surprisingly difficult to assemble a fresh circle. It cost Mrs. Allen time and trouble to track down ladies of old acquaintance, which for years she had succeeded in never bringing to mind, and to trace fellow-travellers once pleasantly met with on shipboard and in planes. However, she had some responses, and there followed intimate sessions at her apartment in the afternoons.

They were unsatisfactory. The ladies brought her not understanding but exhortation. They told her to buck up, to pull herself together, to get on her toes; one of them actually slapped her on the back. The sessions came to take on much of the character of the fight talk in the

locker room between the halves of the big game, and when it was finally
urged that she tell Guy Allen to go to hell, Mrs. Allen discontinued
them.

Yet good came of them, for it was through one of the benighted
advisers that Mrs. Allen met Dr. Langham.

Though Dr. Marjorie Langham earned her own living, she had lost none
of her femininity—doubtless because she had never trod the bloody
halls of medical school or strained her bright eyes studying for an M.D.
With one graceful leap she had landed on her slender feet as a healer
of troubled minds. It was a year when the couches of such healers had
not time to grow cool between patients. Dr. Langham was enormously
successful.

She was full of anecdotes about her patients. She had her own way
of telling them, so that the case histories not only were killingly comic
in themselves but gave you, the listener, the fine feeling that you weren't
so crazy after all. On her deeper side, she was a woman of swift com-
prehensions, and of firm sympathy with the hard lot of sensitive members of her sex. She was made for Mrs. Allen.

Mrs. Allen did not go direct to the couch on her first visit to Dr.
Langham. In the office filled with chintzes and cheer, she and the Doctor
sat opposite each other, woman and woman; Mrs. Allen found it easier
that way to pour forth all. The Doctor, during the relating of Guy
Allen's outrageous behavior, nodded repeatedly; when she was told, on
request, Guy Allen's age, she wore an amused little smile. "Well, of
course, that's what it is," she said. "Oh, those middle forties! That dear
old dangerous age! Why, that's all that's the matter with him—he's
going through the change."

Mrs. Allen pounded her temples with her fists, for being such a fool
as not to have thought of that before. There she had been weeping and
wailing because it had completely slipped her mind that men, too, are
born into the world with the debt of original sin laid on them; Guy
Allen, as must everyone else, had reached the age of paying it; there was
the whole matter. (In the last two cases of broken marriages of which
Mrs. Allen had heard, that year, one of the outgoing husbands was
twenty-nine and the other sixty-two, but she did not recall them to
memory.) The Doctor's explanation so relieved Mrs. Allen that she went
and lay down on the couch.

"That's the girl—relax," Dr. Langham said. "Oh, all the poor
women, the poor idiot women! Tearing their hearts out, beating them-

selves with their 'Why, why, why?'s, breaking their necks to find a fancy reason for it when their husbands walk out, when it's just the traditional case of temporarily souped-up nerves and the routine change in metabolism."

The Doctor gave Mrs. Allen books to take home with her, to read before her next appointment; some of their authors, she said, were close friends of hers, women recognized as authorities on their subject. The books were written, as if by one pen, in a fluid, conversational style, comfortable for laymen. There was a sameness about their contents; each was a collection of instances of married men who had rushed out from their beds and boards in mad revolt against middle age. The revolts, as such, were rather touching. The wild-eyed mobs were without plan or direction, the nights were bitter cold, they sickened for home. Back came the revolutionaries, one after one, with hanging heads and supplicating palms, back to their wise, kind wives.

Mrs. Allen was impressed by these works. She came upon many a passage which, if the books had belonged to her, she would have underscored heavily.

She felt that she might properly be listed among those wives who waited at home, so kind, so wise. She could say, in all humility, that many people had told her she was almost too kind for her own good, and she could point to an act of true wisdom. In the first black days of her misery, she had sworn an oath to herself that she would make no move toward Guy Allen: Might her right hand wither and drop off if she employed it to dial his telephone number! No one could count the number of miles she had walked, up and down her carpets, fighting to hold to her vow. She did it, but the sight of her saved right hand, fresh and fair, brought no comfort to her; it simply reminded her of the use to which it might have been put. From there, she thought of another hand on another dial, always with new pain that Guy Allen had never called her.

Dr. Langham gave her high marks for keeping away from the telephone, and brushed aside her grief at Guy Allen's silence.

"Certainly he hasn't called you," she said. "Exactly as I expected—yes, and the best sign we've had that he's doing a little suffering on his own hook. He's afraid to talk to you. He's ashamed of himself. He knows what he did to you—he doesn't know why he did it, the way we do, but he knows what a terrible thing it was. He's doing a lot of thinking about you. His not daring to call you up shows that."

It was a big factor in Dr. Langham's success that she had the ability to make wet straws seem like sturdy logs to the nearly submerged.

Maida Allen's cure was not effected in a day. It was several weeks before she was whole. She gave all credit to her doctor. Dr. Langham, by simply switching the cold light of science on the reason for Guy Allen's apparent desertion, had given her back to herself. She was no more the lone, lorn creature, rejected like a faded flower, a worn glove, a stretched garter. She was a woman brave and humane, waiting, with the patience that was her crown jewel, for her poor, muddled man to get through his little indisposition and come home to her to be cheered through convalescence and speeded to recovery. Daily, on Dr. Langham's couch, talking and listening, she gained in strength. She slept through the nights, and when she went out to the street, her straight back and her calm, bright face made her seem like a visitor from a fairer planet, among those of the bowed shoulders and the twitching mouths who thronged the pavements.

The miracle happened. Her husband telephoned to her. He asked if he might come to the apartment that evening to pick up a suitcase that he wanted. She suggested that he come to dinner. He was afraid he couldn't do that; he had to dine early with a client, but he would come about nine o'clock. If she was not going to be at home, would she please to leave the suitcase with Jessie, the maid. She said it was the one night in she didn't know how long that she was not going out. Fine, he said, then he'd see her later; and rang off.

Mrs. Allen was early for her doctor's appointment. She gave Dr. Langham the news in a sort of carol. The Doctor nodded, and her amused smile broadened until virtually all of her exceptionally handsome teeth showed.

"So there you are," she said. "And there he is. And who is the one that told you so? Now listen to me. This is important—maybe the most important part of your whole treatment. Don't lose your head tonight. Remember that this man has put one of the most sensitive creatures I ever saw in my life through hell. Don't soften up. Don't fall all over him, as if he was doing you a favor coming back to you. Don't be too easy on him."

"Oh-h-h, I won't!" Mrs. Allen said. "Guy Allen will eat crow!"

"That's the girl," Dr. Langham said. "Don't make any scene, you know; but don't let him think that all is forgiven. Just be cool and sweet. Don't let him know that you've missed him for a moment. Just let him see what *he's* been missing. And for God's sake, don't ask him to stay all night."

"Not for anything on this earth," Mrs. Allen said. "If that's what he wants, he'll ask me. Yes, and on his knees!"

The apartment looked charming; Mrs. Allen saw to it that it did, and saw that she did herself. She bought masses of flowers on her way home from the Doctor's, and arranged them exquisitely—she had always been good at that—all about the living room.

He rang the bell at three minutes past nine. Mrs. Allen had let the maid off that evening. She opened the door to him herself.

"Hi!" she said.

"Hello, there," he said. "How are you?"

"Oh, simply fine," she said. "Come on in. I think you know the way, don't you?"

He followed her into the living room. He held his hat in his hand, and carried his coat over his arm.

"You've got a lot of flowers," he said. "Pretty."

"Yes, aren't they lovely?" she said. "Everybody's been so kind to me. Let me take your things."

"I can stay just a minute," he said. "I'm meeting a man at the club."

"Oh, that's too bad," she said.

There was a pause. He said, "You're looking fine, Maida."

"I can't imagine why," she said. "I'm about to drop in my tracks. I've been going out day and night."

"It agrees with you," he said.

"Notice anything new in this room?" she said.

"Why—I said about all the flowers," he said. "Is there something else?"

"The curtains, the curtains," she said. "New last week."

"Oh, yes," he said. "They look great. Pink."

"Rose," she said. "The room does look nice with them, don't you think?"

"Great," he said.

"How's your room at the club?" she said.

"It's all right," he said. "I have everything I want."

"Everything?" she said.

"Oh, sure," he said.

"How's the food?" she said.

"Pretty good now," he said. "Much better than it used to be. They've got a new chef."

"What fun!" she said. "So you really like it, living at the club?"

"Oh, yes," he said. "I'm very comfortable there."

"Why don't you sit down," she said, "and tell me what was the matter with it here? Food? Shaving mirror? What?"

"Why, everything was fine," he said. "Look, Maida, I've really got to run. Is my bag here?"

"It's in your closet in the bedroom, where it always was," she said. "Sit down—I'll get it for you."

"No, don't you bother," he said. "I'll get it."

He went toward the bedroom. Mrs. Allen started to follow, then thought of Dr. Langham and stayed where she was. The Doctor would surely consider it somewhat lenient, to go into the bedroom with him, the minute he came back.

He returned, carrying the suitcase.

"Surely you can sit down and have a drink, can't you?" she said.

"I wish I could, but I've really got to go," he said.

"I thought we might exchange just a few gracious words," she said. "The last time I heard your voice, it was not saying anything very agreeable."

"I'm sorry," he said.

"You stood right there, by the door—and very attractive you looked," she said. "I've never seen you awkward in your life. If you were ever going to be, that was the time to be it. Saying what you did. Do you remember?"

"Do you?" he said.

"I do indeed," she said. " 'I don't want to do this any more, Maida. I'm through.' Do you really feel that was a pretty thing to say to me? It seemed to me rather abrupt, after eleven years."

"No. It wasn't abrupt," he said. "I'd been saying it to you for six of those eleven years."

"I never heard you," she said.

"Yes, you did, my dear," he said. "You interpreted it as a cry of 'Wolf,' but you heard me."

"Could it be possibly that you had been planning this dramatic exit for six years?" she said.

"Not planning," he said. "Just thinking. I had no plans. Not even when I spoke those doubtless ill-chosen words of farewell."

"And have you now?" she said.

"I'm going to San Francisco in the morning," he said.

"How nice of you to confide in me," she said. "How long will you be away?"

"I really don't know," he said. "We opened that branch office out there—you know. Things got rather messed up, and I've got to go do some straightening. I can't tell how long it will take."

"You like San Francisco, don't you?" she said.

"Oh, sure," he said. "Good town."

"And so nice and far away, too," she said. "You really couldn't get any farther off and still stay in America the Beautiful, could you?"

"That's right, at that," he said. "Look, I've really got to dash. I'm late."

"Couldn't you give me a quick idea of what you've been doing with yourself?" she said.

"Working all day and most nights," he said.

"That interests you?" she said.

"Yes, I like it fine," he said.

"Well, good for you," she said. "I'm not trying to keep you from your date. I just would like to see a very small gleam of why you've done what you have. Were you that unhappy?"

"Yes, I was, really," he said. "You needn't have made me say it. You knew it."

"Why were you unhappy?" she said.

"Because two people can't go on and on and on, doing the same things year after year, when only one of them likes doing them," he said, "and still be happy."

"Do you think *I* can be happy, like this?" she said.

"I do," he said. "I think you will. I wish there were some prettier way of doing it, but I think that after a while—and not a long while, either—you will be better than you've ever been."

"Oh, you think so?" she said. "I see, you can't believe I'm a sensitive person."

"That's not for the lack of your telling me—eleven years' worth," he said. "Look, this is no use. Goodbye, Maida. Take care of yourself."

"I will," she said. "Promise."

He went out the door, down the hall, and rang the elevator bell. She stood holding the door open looking after him.

"You know what, my dear?" she said. "You know what's the matter with you? You're middle-aged. That's why you've got these ideas."

The elevator stopped at the floor, and the attendant slid the door back.

Guy Allen looked back, before he entered the car. "I wasn't middle-aged six years ago," he said. "And I had them then. Goodbye, Maida. Good luck."

"Have a nice trip," she said. "Send me a picture postcard of the Presidio."

Mrs. Allen closed the door and went back into the living room. She stood quite still in the middle of the floor. She did not feel as she had thought she would.

Well. She had behaved with perfect coolness and sweetness. It must have been that Guy was still not over his common illness. He'd get over it; yes, he would. Yes, he would. When he got out there, stumbling up and down those San Francisco hills, he would come to his well senses. She tried a little fantasy; he would come back, and his hair would have gone gray all in a night—the night he realized the anguish of his folly—and gray hair would not be becoming to him. He'd come back to eat crow, yes, and she'd see that he did. She made a little picture of him, gray and shabby and broken down, gnawing at a leg of cold crow, which she saw with all its feathers left on it, black and shining and disgusting.

No. Fantasy was no good.

She went to the telephone and called Dr. Langham.

The Bolt Behind the Blue

Miss Mary Nicholl was poor and plain, which afflictions compelled her, when she was in the presence of a more blessed lady, to vacillate between squirming humility and spitting envy. The more blessed lady, her friend Mrs. Hazelton, enjoyed Miss Nicholl's visits occasionally; humility is a seemly tribute to a favorite of fate, and to be the cause of envy is cozy to the ego. The visits had to be kept only occasional, though. With the years, Miss Nicholl grew no less flat in the purse and no more delightful to the eye, and it is a boresome business to go on and on feeling tenderness for one whose luck never changes.

Miss Nicholl worked as secretary to a stern and sterling woman. For seven hours a day she sat in a small room lined with filing cabinets where at half-past twelve precisely was put upon her desk, next to her typewriter, a tray set forth with the produce of the stern and sterling one's favorite health-food shop. The job was permanent and the lunches insured Miss Nicholl against constipation, yet it is to be admitted that her daily round lacked color and height. Those were fine occasions for her when, her work done, she might cover her typewriter and go to call on Mrs. Hazelton, to tread the gleaming halls, to sit in the long blue drawing room, to stroke the delicate cocktail glass and warm her spirit in its icy contents.

And her enjoyment did not die with her leave-taking; indeed, it took on strong new life. She would go home to the house where she roomed, summon Miss Christie who lived across the hall, and tell about her excursion into elegance. Miss Nicholl had a keen eye and a magnetic memory; she described every curve of furniture, every stretch of fabric, every ornament, every arrangement of flowers. She went long and full into the details of Mrs. Hazelton's costume, and all but called each pearl by name. Miss Christie was employed in a combined lending library and gift shop, all a-twist with potted philodendron; in her life there was none such as Mrs. Hazelton. She hung on every word of the recital. So did Miss Nicholl.

Fortune had upended her cornucopia to hurtle gifts upon Alicia Hazelton. She was beautiful, modeled after the design of an earlier day, when there were not just good-looking women, there were great beauties. She would have been perfectly placed in a victoria, holding a tiny jointed parasol, or tooling down the avenue on the box of a coach, seated next the gentleman in the grey topper who managed the reins. She was large and soft and white and golden. Though she was quite complacent about her massive shoulders and bosom, her real pride lay in her exquisite feet and ankles. Mrs. Hazelton knew too much about her style to essay short skirts, and she never would have slung one knee over the other, but each time she sat she tweaked up her draperies and left on view those ankles, lightly crossed. And she was rich. She was not wealthy or well-to-do or comfortably off; in the popular phrase, Mrs. Hazelton was loaded. And she had had three husbands and three divorces. To Miss Nicholl, whose experiences had not encompassed so much as a furtive pressure of the hand, there seemed to be always present behind Mrs. Hazelton's chair an invisible trio of the adoring and discarded.

If Mrs. Hazelton had been asked, she would have answered that she had known Miss Nicholl for, oh, Lord, ages and ages—so long she couldn't remember how the acquaintanceship had begun. Miss Nicholl could have reminded her. Once, the stern and sterling one had sent Miss Nicholl to Mrs. Hazelton with tickets for a charity benefit, under orders to see the lady in person and get the money for them right then. Mrs. Hazelton, warmed with the altruistic exercise of writing a check, had invited Miss Nicholl to sit down, had given her a cocktail, and, as she left, had bidden her to drop in any time.

Miss Christie had not had these circumstances explained to her. Exact words were never spoken, but Miss Christie had come to live in the belief that Miss Nicholl and Mrs. Hazelton had grown up together, would in fact have made a joint debut had it not been for the death of Miss Nicholl's father, too innocent a soul to mistrust the dastard who managed his financial affairs; so Miss Nicholl had had to go to work and, naturally, her path had split wide from Mrs. Hazelton's. But they always kept in touch with each other. Miss Christie thought that was simply lovely.

As fervently as she cherished Mrs. Hazelton's invitation given at their first meeting, Miss Nicholl did not presume on it. She never did drop in. She always telephoned to inquire if she might come in for a little while the next day or the day after it, on her way from work. If she was told that Mrs. Hazelton would be out or occupied or ill, she let weeks go by before she tried again. Frequently there were long dry reaches between her visits.

It was after such a lapse that Miss Nicholl telephoned one day and heard Mrs. Hazelton answer the call herself and warmly tell her to come that very afternoon. When Miss Nicholl had replaced the receiver, she went through three different sorts of glow. The first was of pure pleasure, the next of exasperation that the blouse she had on was well into its second day, and the third of stormy frustration that Miss Christie had been summoned to New Jersey to attend the sickbed of someone spoken of as Auntie Dee-dee, and would be away at least overnight.

Still, Miss Nicholl could depend on her memory never to slack; as soon as Miss Christie returned, after Auntie Dee-dee had either recovered or done whatever it was she was going to do, Miss Nicholl would be quite ready with the account of the appointment with Mrs. Hazelton. So the glow of pleasure came back and stayed. It was high in her when she arrived at Mrs. Hazelton's and caroled to the maid who opened the door, "Well, Dellie, it's been a long time since we've seen each other, hasn't it?"

It is heartening to speak easily with the servants. It shows how solidly you are accepted in the house.

Miss Nicholl had made her telephone call at a most fortunate time for herself. For four days, Mrs. Hazelton had not stirred beyond her own walls. For four days, she had heard no voices save those of the maids and that of her little daughter, who was kept at home by a cold. Worse, she had heard scarcely a word of her own. The servants were too adept to require spoken orders, and there are limits to the number of times you can ask a child if she has any fever. Miss Nicholl's proposed visit took on something in the nature of a godsend. The Nicholl admiration was thick and sweet, and Mrs. Hazelton craved honey. Besides, Miss Nicholl was older than Mrs. Hazelton by a year or so and looked it by a decade. A thing like that can be a comfort on a dismal day.

Yet, as she awaited her guest, Mrs. Hazelton's anticipation was not without alloy. The thought of Miss Nicholl always brought with it a nasty little guilt. She supposed she really ought to do more for the poor thing. But what more could she do? It was unthinkable that you could tuck a folded twenty-dollar bill into her dry palm; such people were so impossibly sensitive about being objects of charity. You could have her come to see you, feed her a drink, let her look at your pretty flowers, maybe give her some little thing you were through with—such a donation, unlike cash, wounded no feelings. Perhaps she might let her come oftener, and she must remember to keep Mary Nicholl's name on the Christmas list. Such plans were soothing to a degree, but still the guilt sneaked back, and with it came, of course, the irritation toward the one that caused it. Mrs. Hazelton, sitting waiting for Miss Nicholl, tapped her foot.

But when Miss Nicholl came into the drawing room, she was welcomed charmingly. The two ladies exchanged embraces—Mrs. Hazelton smelled like a summer afternoon in Heaven—and sat down opposite each other, smiling. It was no trouble to smile when looking at Mrs. Hazelton. With the folds of her chiffon tea gown flowing along her figure and her little Yorkshire terrier lying curled at her feet beside the high-heeled tapering slippers that were made for her in Rome, she was like an admirably composed canvas. The dog, Bonne Bouche—she had been christened before Mrs. Hazelton bought her—wore on her head, in the manner of the fashionables among her tribe, a bow of satin ribbon holding back her silvery bangs. Bonne Bouche was all that Mrs. Hazelton could ask of a pet. She was tiny, she was noiseless, and she had a real talent for sleeping. Mrs. Hazelton loved her truly.

Mrs. Hazelton's view from across the room was less agreeable. Before her eyes was Miss Nicholl, sitting there, as was her way, with no part of her touching the back of the chair.

"Dreadful the way we never see each other," Mrs. Hazelton said. "Oh, this city, this city! So rushed you don't have a chance to lay eyes on an old friend. It's been so long, I honestly thought you might have changed—I swear I did. But nothing like that. You never do change, you lucky thing, you."

With the exception of the last four, Mrs. Hazelton could not have uttered truer words. Miss Nicholl had not altered in appearance since back beyond her school days; it is possible, indeed, that those who had gazed on her infant face had found her a seamy baby. Her features were less chiseled than hewn, and long lines ran beside her mouth and across her grainy brow. She was of a ruthless trimness. Her belt was cinched so tight that, looking at it, you could hardly draw your own breath, the stiff waves of her hair were netted to her skull, her skirt snapped sharply at her legs. She wore, to pin the collar of her blouse all shipshape, a pansy of lavender enamel with a minute diamond forming an unconvincing dewdrop on one petal. Mrs. Hazelton had never seen her without this ornament. Nor had anybody else.

"Oh, I'm the same tacky old me," Miss Nicholl said. "But you— well, you're lovelier than ever."

"You really think I don't look too awful?" Mrs. Hazelton said.

"I never heard such talk," Miss Nicholl said. "You're just plain gorgeous, that's all you are."

"Oh, now really!" Mrs. Hazelton said.

The maid entered, carrying a tray on which were cocktail glasses and a crystal shaker. She set the tray on a table, filled two glasses, gave one to Miss Nicholl—who cried out, "Why, Dellie, how *nice*!"—and the other to the hostess. The ladies sipped. Dellie, as quietly as she had come, left them alone together again.

"Oooo—yummy!" Miss Nicholl said. "What a treat! I haven't had a cocktail since—why it must be since the last time I was here. Sometimes I simply long for one—times when it's just beginning to get dark. Well, one thing about being poor—I'll never fill a drunkard's grave. When you can't afford cocktails, you have to get along without, that's all. Oh, I'm not complaining. I'd be a fine one to complain, now wouldn't I, when I can sit here with you. There you are, just the way I always think about you. No, wait a minute! Isn't there something different? I can't quite decide what it is. Now, don't you go tell me. Oh, I know! Didn't you used to wear two long strings of pearls?"

Mrs. Hazelton had done so; now she wore only one long rope, while around her neck were three tight strands. Some time before, she had chanced to look in her mirror when there was a mean light falling on it. She saw signs, and chilled as she saw them, of certain swags under her chin, if not yet reality, then certainly warning. So she had taken one length of pearls to her jeweler's where it was cut into the triple neckband, to clasp her throat and keep its secret.

"I had the other long one made into these," she said. "They're smarter. So many women are wearing them like this."

"Naturally, after you started the style," Miss Nicholl said. "Yes, they do look smart, I suppose. But if I must be brutally frank, I'd have to say I think I like them better the way they were."

"Oh, you do?" Mrs. Hazelton said.

"I always feel that pearls show up better in a long string," Miss Nicholl said. "You know—like flowing. I suppose it's because I love them so much—well, you know me and pearls. Really, there are times I've thought to myself, if I ever decide to go wrong, I'd do it for pearls."

"Fortunately, I've never had to do quite that," Mrs. Hazelton said. Miss Nicholl laughed. Mrs. Hazelton joined her, courteously, after a moment.

"Just to look at you," Miss Nicholl said, "a person would know you'd always had them."

"Of course, such things are a matter of luck," Mrs. Hazelton said.

"Some people seem to have all of it," Miss Nicholl said. She took rather more than a sip of her cocktail. "Well, tell me about everything. How's our little girl?"

"She's fine," Mrs. Hazelton said. "Oh, no, she isn't, either. She's got a cold."

"Poor little trick!" Miss Nicholl said. "She must be pretty big now, isn't she? It's so long since I've seen her." Miss Nicholl's pause let it be known that the time lag was no fault of hers.

"Yes, she's enormous," Mrs. Hazelton said. "Well, after all, she's eleven."

"Such a fascinating age!" Miss Nicholl said. "You and she must have high old times together."

"Yes, Ewie's great fun," Mrs. Hazelton said.

"You still call her Ewie?" Miss Nicholl asked.

"Everyone does," Mrs. Hazelton said.

"Well, it's kind of cute, of course," Miss Nicholl said. "Still, it does seem a shame. Stephanie is such an adorable name."

"Not," Mrs. Hazelton said, "when you remember that her father's name was Stephen."

"Do you ever talk to her about her father?" Miss Nicholl asked.

"My dear, the child is only eleven years old," Mrs. Hazelton said.

"Now tell me what you've been up to, while my back was turned," Miss Nicholl said. "For all I knew, you might have gone and got yourself married again."

"No, thank you," Mrs. Hazelton said. "No more marrying for me, thank you very much. You know the old saying: once bit, twice shy." She sat back mysteriously confident that the adage applied to her case.

"Oh, you're wise!" Miss Nicholl said. "Wise *and* beautiful—you've got everything. What do you need a husband for? Now me, I don't for a moment regret I never tried marriage. People say, 'But don't you ever get lonely?' I wouldn't pay them the compliment of listening to them. All I do, I just simply say to them, 'If a woman can't think of something to do to keep herself from being lonely, it's her own fault.' "

"That's what *I* think, certainly," Mrs. Hazelton said.

But she did not. She did not know what she thought about such things lately. She had been back from her last visit to Nevada for a long while during which she had done nothing startling to keep herself vivid before her friends—God, how people do get used to you! On her previous returns from her quests for freedom, invitations had whirled about her like blown snow; now they trickled in, slow and thin. Oh, of course there were various bids for her presence, but there was no excitement to them. And actually, once or twice, the plea that she come to dine had concluded with those words that are like the thud of clods on a coffin-lid: "Just us, you know—you don't mind if we don't get a man for you, do you, darling?" Lord in Heaven, was she, Alicia Hazelton, becoming an extra woman?

"You'll never have to worry about being alone," Miss Nicholl said. "You—with the whole town clamoring after you."

"Oh—that," Mrs. Hazelton said. Suddenly she looked closely at Miss Nicholl. "Mary," she said, "tell me. What do you do evenings?"

"Why, I don't know," Miss Nicholl said. "Different things—" She broke off in a high, wild cry; Mrs. Hazelton's daughter had come into the room. "There she is!" shrieked Miss Nicholl. "There her was! There's her mother's ewe lamb!"

Ewie was a pretty thing, tall and slender, with skin white as cherry bloom, waving red-gold hair cut close to her fine head, and long, straight red-gold eyelashes.

"You remember Miss Nicholl, Ewie," Mrs. Hazelton said. "Go say how-do-you-do to her."

Ewie went to Miss Nicholl, let her hand touch Miss Nicholl's hand, and kicked a little curtsy, the very awkwardness of which would have been irresistible in a smaller child.

"She's simply beautiful—the picture of her mother!" Miss Nicholl said. "Well, aren't I going to get a kiss, Ewie? Just for old times' sake?"

"I've got a head cold," Ewie said. She left Miss Nicholl and rushed to the dog. She picked her up and pressed kisses on her infinitesimal nose.

"Ah, de Bouchie-wouchie," she said. "Ah, de baby angel."

"Ewie!" Mrs. Hazelton said. "Stop kissing the dog. With your cold."

Ewie replaced Bonne Bouche, who immediately returned to slumber. Then she sat down on a sofa and began humming a private, tuneless selection.

"Don't slump like that," Mrs. Hazelton said. "Look at Miss Nicholl. See how nice and straight she sits."

Ewie looked at Miss Nicholl and looked away again.

"I'm so sorry you have a cold," Miss Nicholl said. "It's a shame."

"Oh, it's much better," Mrs. Hazelton said.

"It'll be worse tonight," Ewie said. "Dellie says that's the dangerous thing about head colds, they always get worse at night. They go up into your sinuses or something. She says sometimes they get so bad you have to have a terrible operation."

"Well, you won't have to have anything like that," Mrs. Hazelton said.

"I might," Ewie said. She hummed again.

"Oh, this beautiful room!" Miss Nicholl said. "Those flowers! You always have white flowers, don't you, lady fair?"

"Yes, always," Mrs. Hazelton said. She always did, ever since she had read of a leader of society who permitted none but white blossoms in her home.

"They're just like you," Miss Nicholl said. She looked at an array of stock like a great white fountain, started to count the sprays, felt vertigo coming on, and gave it up.

"These are on their last legs," Mrs. Hazelton said. "The florist will be here tomorrow. He changes them every three days."

"Three days, you extravagant pussy-cat!" Miss Nicholl cried. "Oh, why can't I take care of your flowers? I've got a green thumb."

Ewie's eyelashes sprang apart. She looked eagerly at Miss Nicholl.

"You have?" she breathed. "Is it on the hand you shook hands with me with? Ah, I didn't see it. Show it to me."

"Oh, no, dear," Miss Nicholl said. "It isn't a real one. It's just a way of saying that flowers will do anything for you."

"Oh, shoot!" Ewie said. She went back to her musical abstraction.

"Ewe lamb, if you could manage to stop that singing, somehow," Mrs. Hazelton said. "Pour some fresh in Miss Nicholl's glass."

Ewie rose, gave Miss Nicholl a drink ("Why, *thank* you, you sweet thing!"), and watched her sip.

"Do you like that stuff?" she said. "I think it tastes like medicine."

"Well, it is a kind of medicine, you know," Miss Nicholl said. "A lovely kind. It does so much good for poor sick people."

Ewie drew closer. "Are you sick?" she asked. "What've you got the matter with you?"

"I'm not sick, precious," Miss Nicholl said. "I only said that. It was just a sort of figure of speech. Have you had figures of speech in school?"

"That's next year," Ewie said. "With Miss Fosdeck; I hate her. What kind of sick people is it good for?"

"Oh, Ewie, for heaven's sake!" Mrs. Hazelton said.

"I didn't mean really sick," Miss Nicholl said. "I meant people who are, well—people who are blue."

"You know what?" Ewie said. "Dellie knew this baby and it got born too soon, and it was blue. Dark blue. All over."

"But I'm sure Dellie said it's all right now, didn't she?" Miss Nicholl said.

"It died," Ewie said. "Dellie says all those cases are doomed.

Doomed from the womb." The remembered phrase caught her fancy, and she chuckled.

"Oh, Dellie says, Dellie says!" Mrs. Hazelton said. "You'll turn into a Dellie-says one of these fine days if you don't watch out. Why don't you go and sit down and be sweet?"

Ewie went and sat down and was sweet, save that she resumed her song, this time adding as a lyric "doomed from the womb, oh-h, doomed from the womb," until her mother's voice drowned her out.

"Ewie, *stop that!*" Mrs. Hazelton screamed.

"You still haven't told me what you've been doing," Miss Nicholl said quickly to Mrs. Hazelton. "But I can guess—I know you, lady fair. Nothing but parties, parties, parties, every day and every night. Aren't I right?"

"No, my dear," Mrs. Hazelton said. "I've taken a vow to let up. Daytime things, lunch and fashion openings and cocktails and all that, yes, but oh, those late nights, every blessed night!"

"Oh, you haven't been out at night for ages," Ewie said.

"Naturally," Mrs. Hazelton said. "When my only child is sick, I'm not going to leave her here alone."

"Dellie was here," Ewie said. "Anyway, you haven't gone out at night since before I got my head cold."

"If I choose to stay at home for an evening of quiet now and then, I can do it without any comment from you," Mrs. Hazelton said.

Ewie took up her aria again, but with no words. She also occupied herself with forming tiny pleats in the skirt of her frock, pressing them sharp with a thumbnail.

"I bet you've been doing a lot of entertaining, yourself," Miss Nicholl said.

"Oh, it's so hard to get up the energy," Mrs. Hazelton said. "And this season's crop of extra men! They're about the right age for Ewie. They make me feel a hundred years old."

"You! Old!" Miss Nicholl said.

"I can't stand them hanging around the house, messing on my carpets," Mrs. Hazelton said. "I know lots of women invite them, but—well, let them. It's their funeral."

Ewie ceased her activities. "You know what?" she said. "I was in a funeral once."

"You were no such thing!" Mrs. Hazelton said.

"Oh, I was so, too!" Ewie said. "There was this big long funeral going down Fifth Avenue, and it was so long some of the last cars had to wait for a light, and so, why, I started to walk across to go to the park, and so there I was, right in the middle of it. Only Dellie yelled and yanked me back. She says it's terrible luck to go through a funeral. Once she had a cousin that did, and in two weeks, right smack to the day, her cousin died."

"I'm not sure that I like all this about Dellie yelling and yanking on Fifth Avenue," Mrs. Hazelton said. "That's the way they get when they've been with you so long—think they can do anything. Still, I can't imagine how I'd have ever got along without her. She practically brought Ewie up, you know."

"Yes, I can see the marks," Miss Nicholl said. "Oh, only fooling, lady fair, just my little joke. I've always said Dellie's a real treasure. Well, you always have perfect servants."

"There I was, bang in the middle of a funeral," Ewie said.

"I don't know what makes Ewie this way," Mrs. Hazelton said.

"Oh, all children are like that," Miss Nicholl said.

"I never was," Mrs. Hazelton said.

"Come to think of it, I don't believe I was either," Miss Nicholl said. "And you couldn't have been anything but perfect. Ever."

They considered Ewie, now both pleating and humming.

"So active," Miss Nicholl said. "Always busy."

"She never got that from her father," Mrs. Hazelton said. "That or anything else."

Ewie hummed higher.

"Ewe lamb, you don't think you've got any fever, do you?" Mrs. Hazelton said.

Ewie felt the back of her neck. "Not yet," she said.

"You're just about all well," Mrs. Hazelton said. "If it's a decent day tomorrow, you and Dellie can go to the park."

"Oh, what fun!" Miss Nicholl cried.

"It's Dellie's day off tomorrow," Ewie said. "She's going over to see her sister. Her sister's husband's terribly sick."

"Hasn't Dellie got any healthy friends, honey-bunny?" Miss Nicholl said.

"Oh, she's got zillions of them," Ewie said. "There was seventeen, right in her family, only twelve of them died. Some of them were born dead, and the others had a liver condition. Dellie said it was nothing but bile, bile, bile—"

"Ewie, please," Mrs. Hazelton said. "No details, if you don't mind."

"Dellie says all the alive ones feel fine," Ewie said. "It's just this husband of her sister's. He can't work or anything, but Dellie says you wouldn't want to meet a lovelier man. He's good and sick. Dellie says her sister says she wouldn't be surprised if he started spitting blood, any day."

"Kindly stop that disgusting talk," Mrs. Hazelton said. "While we're trying to drink our cocktails."

"Well, I was only answering *her*," Ewie said, jerking her head in the direction of Miss Nicholl. "She asked me if Dellie had any healthy friends, and I told her all except that husband of her sister's and he—"

"That will do," Mrs. Hazelton said. "Now why don't you run along and ask Dellie to take your temperature? And then you can stay in the kitchen and talk to her and Ernestine."

"Can I take Bonne Bouche with me?" Ewie asked.

"I suppose so," Mrs. Hazelton said. She picked up the little dog. "But don't let Ernestine give her anything to eat besides her supper. She's beginning to lose her figure." She kissed Bonne Bouche on her hair ribbon. "Aren't you, darling?"

Ewie joyously received the dog into her arms. "Can we stay in the kitchen to have our supper?" she asked.

"Oh, all right, all right!" Mrs. Hazelton said.

"Oo brother!" Ewie said. She started for the door.

"Ewie, what's the matter with you, anyway?" Mrs. Hazelton said. "I tell you, I'm thinking seriously of changing that school of yours, next year. You have no more manners than a moose. Say good-by to Miss Nicholl, for heaven's sake."

Ewie turned toward Miss Nicholl and smiled at her—her smile, that had the rarity of all truly precious things. "Good-by, Miss Nicker," she said. "Please do come again very soon, won't you?"

"Oh, I will, you angel-pie," Miss Nicholl said.

Ewie, cooing to Bonne Bouche, left them.

"She's simply adorable!" Miss Nicholl said. "Oh, lady fair, why do you have to have everything in the world? Well, you deserve it, that's all I can say. That's what keeps me from murdering you, right this minute."

"Oh, you mustn't do that," Mrs. Hazelton said.

"If I could only have a sweet, happy little girl like Ewie, that's all I would ask," Miss Nicholl said. "You don't know how I've always wanted to have a child all my own. Without having any old man mixed up in it."

"I'm afraid that would be rather hard to accomplish," Mrs. Hazelton said. "I guess you'd just have to take the bitter along with the sweet, like the rest of us. Well. What were we talking about before Ewie barged in? Oh, yes—what *do* you do in the evenings?"

"Why, after I'm through work," Miss Nicholl said, "I really feel I've earned a little enjoyment. So when I get home, after I've cleaned up, Idabel and I—"

"Who?" Mrs. Hazelton said.

"Idabel Christie," Miss Nicholl said. "That has the room across the hall from me. You know—I've told you about her."

"Oh, yes, of course," Mrs. Hazelton said. "I forgot for a moment her name was Idabel. I don't know how I came to."

"It's an odd name," Miss Nicholl said. "But I think it's rather sweet, don't you?"

"Yes, charming," Mrs. Hazelton said.

"Anyway, we do all sorts of things," Miss Nicholl said. "When we're feeling rich, we go to dinner at the Candlewick Tea Room—terribly nice, and just around the corner from us. It's so pretty—candles, and yellow tablecloths and a little bunch of different-colored immortelles, dyed I guess they are, on every table. It's those little touches that make the place. And the food! Idabel and I always say to each other when we go in, 'All diet abandon, ye who enter here.'"

"*You* don't have to diet," Mrs. Hazelton said. "You're one of those fortunate people."

"Me fortunate! Well, that's a new picture of yours truly," Miss Nicholl said. "One thing, though, I don't want to flesh up, if I can help it. But oh, those yummy sticky rolls, served in little baskets, and that prune spin with maraschino cherries in it! Idabel Christie likes the fudge cup-custard, but I can't resist the prune spin."

Only a tiny ripple along her chiffons told that Mrs. Hazelton shuddered.

"Well, of course the Candlewick couldn't be farther away from this," Miss Nicholl said. "You'd probably laugh at it."

"Why, I wouldn't at all," Mrs. Hazelton said.

"Yes, you would," Miss Nicholl said. "You don't know about how, when you can have so few things, you have to like the thing you *can* have. We can't go to the Candlewick very often. It's not at all cheap, I mean for us. You can hardly get out of there much under two dollars apiece with the tip. Listen to me! I bet you never heard of as little as two dollars."

"Now stop it," Mrs. Hazelton said.

"There's another thing about the Candie—we call it the Candie to ourselves," Miss Nicholl said. "You have to get there pretty fairly early. It's so small and it's grown so popular you haven't a chance of a table after six o'clock."

"But when you're through dinner doesn't that make an awfully long evening for you?" Mrs. Hazelton asked.

"That's what we like," Miss Nicholl said. "We have to get up in the morning—we're woiking goils, you know. Usually, when we go to the Candie, we make a real binge of it and go to a movie afterward. And sometimes, when we feel just wild, we go to the theater. But that's pretty seldom. The price of tickets, these days!"

"You do?" Mrs. Hazelton asked. "You go to the theater alone together? Oh, I wouldn't dare do that!"

"I don't think anybody would try to hold us up," Miss Nicholl said. "And if they did, there's two of us."

"I didn't mean holdups," Mrs. Hazelton said. "It's only I've always been told nothing ages a woman so much as being seen at the theater in the evening with just another woman."

"Oh, really?" Miss Nicholl said.

"Oh, it certainly doesn't work with *you*," Mrs. Hazelton said. "Probably some silly old wives' tale, anyway. Well, but look. Suppose you don't go to the movies or the theater. Then what do you do?"

"We just stay home and do our nails and put up our hair and talk," Miss Nicholl said.

"That must be a comfort," Mrs. Hazelton said. "To have somebody to talk to whenever you feel like it right there in the house. A great comfort."

"Well, yes, it is, you know," Miss Nicholl cried.

"It's the only thing that could possibly make me give a thought to having another husband," Mrs. Hazelton said, slowly. "Somebody here, somebody to talk to you."

"Why, you've got Ewie!" Miss Nicholl cried.

"You've heard Ewie," Mrs. Hazelton said.

"Then some evenings," Miss Nicholl said, "when we don't feel like going out or talking or anything, we just go to our own rooms and read. Idabel Christie, oh, she's a wicked one! She works in a library, the way I've told you, and when she sees a book she knows I'd like, she hides it away for me, even if there's a long waiting list. I suppose I'm as bad as she is, for taking it."

"I simply must order some books," Mrs. Hazelton said. "There's not a new book in this house."

"Think of buying books, instead of borrowing them from a library!"

Miss Nicholl said. "Think of being the first one to read them! Think of never having to touch another plastic jacket! Well, there's not much use dreaming about buying books, when you haven't got a decent rag to your back, is there? Oh, what a curse it is to be poor!"

"Mary Nicholl, no one would ever think about your being poor if you didn't talk about it so much," Mrs. Hazelton said.

"I don't care if they know," Miss Nicholl said. "I never heard that poverty was any disgrace. I'm not ashamed of it. However little money I may have, I earn every cent of it. There are some people who can't say that much for themselves."

"I'm sure you ought to be very proud," Mrs. Hazelton said.

"Well, I am," Miss Nicholl said. "But I'd like to have just *some* clothes. The coat I've got to wear with this suit doesn't belong to the skirt. The skirt it belongs to—moths ate the whole seat right out of it. That makes you feel chic, going around with your—with the whole seat out of your skirt."

"I thought what you have on looks awfully nice," Mrs. Hazelton said.

"Well, let's talk about something prettier than my old rags," Miss Nicholl said. "I bet you've been getting yourself heaps and heaps of lovely new clothes, haven't you?"

"Oh, I've picked up a few little things," Mrs. Hazelton said. "Nothing very interesting. Would you like to see them?"

"*Would* I!" Miss Nicholl said.

"Well, come along," Mrs. Hazelton said. She rose, beautifully.

"Could I—" Miss Nicholl said. "I mean would I be awfully greedy if I just took what's left in the shaker of the lovely little cocktails?"

"Oh, of course," Mrs. Hazelton said. "I hope it's still cold."

Bearing her glass, which the remnant in the shaker could fill only partway, Miss Nicholl followed her hostess to a room dedicated to great deep closets. She stood close as Mrs. Hazelton slid along poles hangers bearing dress after dress, the cost of the least of which would have been two years' rent to Miss Nicholl.

"But, they're all new!" she cried. "All of them! Oh, what did you do with the old ones—the ones that weren't even old, I mean. What did you *do* with them?"

"Oh, I don't know," Mrs. Hazelton said. "Told Dellie to get rid of them somehow, I suppose. I was sick of the sight of them." It was apparent that the question had not interested her.

Miss Nicholl went to work, and put her shoulders into it. She piled up praises until she seemed to be building them into dizzy towers. Mrs. Hazelton did not speak, but there was encouragement in the way she looked distractedly about, as if searching her stores for something to give.

Higher and higher Miss Nicholl raised her towers; admiration glugged from her lips like syrup from a pitcher, and Mrs. Hazelton seemed again to be searching. Her quest stopped when she opened a drawer and took from it an evening purse covered with iridescent sequins. She insisted upon Miss Nicholl's accepting it.

Mrs. Hazelton was not an ungenerous lady, but she was not subject to imagination. Her most recent Christmas gift to Miss Nicholl had been a big jar of bath salts and a tall flagon of after-shaving lotion. The four women who lived on Miss Nicholl's floor shared its one bathroom. They all rose at the same hour in the morning; they retired at the same hour at night. To have commandeered the bathroom for the time required for lolling and anointing would have been considered, in their mildest phrase, piggish. So Miss Nicholl had set the unopened jar and flagon on her bureau, where they looked rich indeed and were much admired by Miss Christie. And now a sequinned purse, perfect to be carried with a ball gown.

Still, a present is a present, and Miss Nicholl positively writhed with gratitude.

She took the purse back to the drawing room when they returned from reviewing the wardrobe, and put it in her big black oilcloth handbag which, half a block away, could hardly be told from patent leather. Dellie had been in, removed the cocktail tray, and left no replacement. Miss Nicholl gave a little yelp as she saw darkness beyond the windows, and said she really ought to go. Mrs. Hazelton's protest was neither voiced nor worded stiffly enough to cause her to change her mind. Mrs. Hazelton seemed, in fact, somewhat languid, almost, if it was conceivable that anyone like her could have had anything to make her tired, a trifle weary.

"Mustn't take a chance on wearing out my welcome," Miss Nicholl said. "I always come dangerously near it, when I'm here—I can't tear myself away." She looked around the room. "I just want to take the picture of this room away with me. Oh, I simply revel in all this wonderful space!"

"Yes, space is the greatest luxury to me," Mrs. Hazelton said.

Miss Nicholl made a small laugh. "It would be to me, too," she said, "but it's the costliest, isn't it? Or wouldn't you know, lady fair? Well, fare thee well. Lovely, lovely time."

"Be sure to come again," Mrs. Hazelton said. "Don't forget."

"I couldn't do that, ever," Miss Nicholl said. "I'm that regular old bad penny. I'll be turning up again before you know it."

"Well, I've got myself rather tangled up, all next week," Mrs. Hazelton said. "The week after, perhaps. Call up anyway."

"Oh, I will, never fear," Miss Nicholl said. "And thanks again, a zillion, for the wonderful evening purse. I'll think of you every time I use it."

Miss Nicholl was going home by bus; before she reached the bus stop, a vicious rain and an ugly wind attacked her. Such demonstrations worked evilly upon her spirit. As she fought through the elements, she talked to herself furiously, though her lips never moved.

"Well, that was a fine visit, I must say. A half-a-shaker of cocktails, and not even a cheese cracker. You'd think a person could do better than that, with all her money. And pushing me out in the pouring rain—never even suggesting staying to dinner. I suppose she's got a lot of her rich society friends coming, and I'm not good enough to associate with them. Not that I would have stayed, if she'd got down on her knees and begged me. I don't want anything to do with those people, thank you very much. I'd just be bored sick.

"And those faded flowers. And that awful Dellie, with never a smile out of her, no matter how democratic you try to be to her. The first thing I'd have, if I was rich, would be nice-mannered servants. You can always tell a lady by her servants' manners. And that little dog—acts to me as if it was drugged.

"And all those clothes, on all those hangers. Why, it would take a girl twenty years old the rest of her life to wear half of them. Yes, and that's just who they're appropriate for, too—someone twenty years old. If there's anything I hate to see, it's a woman trying to keep young by dressing like a girl. Simply makes a laughing-stock of herself. And giving me that sequinned purse. What does she think I'm going to do with it, except stick it away in my bottom drawer? Because that's where it's going to go, with not even tissue paper around it—no, not even news-paper. Well, maybe I'll show it to Idabel first. It must have cost a mint; Idabel will enjoy seeing it. Oh, my God, Idabel won't be home. My whole afternoon, just wasted.

"Yes, and the gorgeous Mrs. Hazelton is putting on weight, too. She must be five pounds heavier than she was last time. My, it will just kill her to get fat. Just absolutely finish her. Well, she'll put on many a pound before I telephone her again. She can call me when she wants to see me. And I'm not so sure I'll come, either.

"And that child. That child doesn't look right to me. So pale, and all. And all that talk about sickness and funerals. There's no good behind that. It's like some sort of sign. It will be a big surprise to me if that child ever makes old bones.

"Not that it's the poor thing's fault. Her mother doesn't do a thing about her. Nothing but 'Stop that, Ewie,' and, 'Don't do that, Ewie.' Ewie, indeed—what a name! Sheer affectation. It's no wonder the poor thing likes that Dellie better than her mother. Oh, what a frightful thing it must be to have your own child turn from you! I don't see how she can sleep nights.

"What kind of life is that, sitting around in a teagown, counting her pearls? Pearls that size are nothing but vulgar, anyway. Why should she have all those things? She's never done anything—couldn't even keep a husband. It's awful to think of that empty existence; nothing to do but have breakfast in bed and spend money on herself. No, *sir*, she can have her pearls and her hangers and her money and her twice-a-week florist, and welcome to them. I swear, I wouldn't change places with Alicia Hazelton for anything on earth!"

It is a strange thing, but it is a fact. Though it had every justification, a bolt did not swoop from the sky and strike Miss Nicholl down, then and there.

Mrs. Hazelton, when Miss Nicholl was gone, sank into her chair, crossed her incomparable ankles, and smoothed her chiffon folds. She breathed the soft long sigh that comes after duty well done, though with effort. That was the trouble with such as Miss Nicholl—once they came, God, how they stayed. Well. The poor thing was so delighted with that purse; how little it took! Those binges with Miss What's-her-name from across the hall, in that tearoom with the little touches, prune spin with cherries in it!

Ewie came in. "You know what?" she said. "Dellie's sister's husband is lots worse. Dellie's sister telephoned, and Dellie says it sounds to her as if her sister's husband is as good as a goner from what her sister says."

"I'm not interested," Mrs. Hazelton said. "It's quite enough to listen to what Dellie says, all day long, without having to hear what her sister says too."

Ewie sat down, mainly on her shoulders and the back of her neck. "Miss Nicker isn't very pretty, is she?" she said.

"Beauty isn't everything," Mrs. Hazelton said.

"I think she's the most terrible-looking person I ever saw," Ewie said. "And her clothes are something awful."

"They're not awful at all," Mrs. Hazelton said. "She dresses herself very sensibly, for her type. You're not to say a word against her, do you hear, Ewie? She's a wonderful woman."

"Why is she?" Ewie asked.

"Well, she works very hard," Mrs. Hazelton said, "and she doesn't do anybody any harm, and people like to do things for her because it gives her so much pleasure."

"I sort of feel sorry for her," Ewie said.

"You needn't," Mrs. Hazelton said. "She has more than a good many people. Much more."

She looked around the big, beautiful room, sweet with shimmering blossoms. She touched the pearls about her throat, twined her fingers in the long rope, and glanced down at the delicate slippers that were made for her in Rome.

"What's she got that's so much more?" Ewie asked.

"Why," Mrs. Hazelton said, "she hasn't any responsibilities, and she has a job that gives her something to do every day, and a nice room, and a lot of books to read, and she and her friend do all sorts of things in the evenings. Oh, let me tell you, I'd be more than glad to change places with Mary Nicholl!"

And again that bolt, though surely sufficiently provoked, stayed where it was, up in back of the blue.

Esquire, December 1958

SKETCHES

Our Tuesday Club

MISS HARRIET MEEKER

For the last decade, now, every time that Miss Meeker's friends are gathered together—in the absence of Miss Meeker—someone is certain to "wonder why it is that Hettie Meeker has never married; she'd make such a splendid wife for some man." From constant repetition the speculation has rather lost its initial zest; in fact, the remark has come to be delivered a bit perfunctorily, and the responses it reaps, if any, are merely preoccupied nods or half-hearted generalities about man's international stupidity in the matter of mate choosing. Indeed, only the loyalty of Miss Meeker's friends keeps the ancient formula of wonder still in use, for the reason for her celibacy is as well known to them as it is to Miss Meeker herself. In so many words, no one has ever asked Miss Meeker to make any radical change in her mode of living. Yet Miss Meeker would, indeed, make a splendid wife for some man. No man would ever have a moment's uncertainty about her affections. She would be the most enthusiastically exemplary of helpmates, almost aggressively contented with her home, resolutely good-humored, violently proud of her spouse, fiercely faithful, breathlessly interested in his every concern.

It is, indeed, in the quality of enthusiasm that Miss Meeker excels. She is vivacious to the verge of hysteria about everything; life is a succession of superlatives to her. Every jest, be it never so feeble, is the funniest thing she ever heard; every bit of gossip, be it never so mild, is the most thrilling thing she ever listened to. Her iron-bound high spirits have never been known to weaken. One cannot help but wonder if sometimes, in the maiden fastnesses of her chamber, Miss Meeker's rigid exuberance ever relaxes, if her gleaming smile vanishes for a while, and her high laughter is temporarily stilled. But as to that, no one will ever be able to render a true report.

Somehow, there is about Miss Meeker the faintly unpleasant suggestion of an overzealous salesman. Her wares of good humor and vivacity are spread out a little too obtrusively; potential customers are intimidated by such a lavish display. Then, too, Miss Meeker is a victim of injudicious advertising. The publicity campaign which her friends have carried on for her has been along too broad lines. With admirable loyalty her friends long ago volunteered to put Miss Meeker's matrimonial drive over the top; but in the excitement of the campaign they lost their heads and overdid things. They ceaselessly hymned her praises to every eligible man that they encountered; they doggedly had her to dinner and the theater and bridge and weekends with their husbands' unmarried friends; they constantly stressed her unparalleled fitness for the post of somebody's wife. They lost no opportunities and they overlooked no bets. And all their devoted and conscientious work brought absolutely no results. Just a little more subtlety in publicity methods might have made a world of difference to Miss Meeker.

For the fact remains that she would make a splendid wife for some man.

MRS. FELIX THROOP

It is one of Mrs. Throop's most frequent remarks that she hasn't had a well day since that period in the dim past which she refers to as "I don't know when." It is not always the same complaint that prevents her feeling really herself; her scope of ailments is practically limitless. Sometimes she is attacked by one of the standard illnesses, spoken of by her in an affectionate possessive as "my rheumatism" or "one of my headaches." Again, it is a coy affliction, eluding the most expert diagnosis, a shooting pain, a heaviness, or a sort of a funny dull feeling. Whatever it may be, however, she is never unaccompanied by an ill of some sort. As she says herself, she really doesn't see how she stands it.

In appearance Mrs. Throop is what has aptly been called the picture of health; she might be classified as belonging to the extreme milkmaid type. To comment on this, though, is markedly to ruffle Mrs. Throop's feelings, as well it may. For that healthy look, she explains, is the most insidious feature of her collective diseases. No matter what she may be suffering, she is always blooming to the eye. But, as she asseverates, never were appearances more deceptive than they are in her case; to use her own whimsical phrase, she could be dying and nobody would ever know it, to look at her. And it is indeed hard, as you can readily imagine, to be so defrauded of sympathy by an unfortunately buxom physique.

Another deplorable phase of her condition is her craving for food—abnormal, she feels it to be. When the refreshments are served at the club meetings Mrs. Throop sighs gloomily, as if at the ordeal that she must face. She protests courageously at first, insisting that "half of that is more than enough for me." The proved futility of protest depressing her, she lingeringly abandons it, and, once she gets under way, performs some really spectacular feats of consumption. Yet even at such inspired times she cannot wholly give herself over to the pleasures of the moment; always mindful of her afflictions, she murmurs darkly that she knows she will suffer for it tomorrow.

What remnant of health remains to her Mrs. Throop guards jealously. It is her favorite axiom that one cannot take too good care of oneself. It is impossible to enjoy her company without being conscious of the heady scent of camphorated oil, by which, as by an aura, she is always surrounded. She never under any condition omits her rubbers, and she is no believer in saving her umbrella for a rainy day. In fair weather as in foul it is her constant companion. The merest intangible rumor of an epidemic suffices to keep her cowering for weeks within doors. Her panic at the thought of germs is pitiful to behold. If she were ever brought face to face with a germ she would promptly lose consciousness from sheer terror.

So, one rather imagines, would the germ.

MRS. ALBERT CHENEY

In appearance Mrs. Cheney is strikingly like Queen Mary of England, without the parasol. She is justifiably proud of this resemblance and heightens it by following as closely as possible in her dress the fashions set by her royal prototype, which means that she can buy nothing ready-made. She carries herself with a royal rigidity, holding her mouth shut, in a thin and slightly puckered line; yet this is not due to emulation of royalty so much as to the realization of her exalted position of wife of the head of the Cheney drop forge works and, as such, of her acknowledged leadership of society.

To listen to Mrs. Cheney's abundant conversation is to marvel at the practiced ease with which she puts every subject in its place. When she speaks, it is as though the language contained no such weak-kneed phrases as "I think" or "It seems to me"; in her crisp statements a thing is so or it is not so; that is all. Uncompromisingly, she voices her opinions, as if well knowing that there could be no permissible others.

Mrs. Cheney is a positive genius at disposing of world problems in a single scathing sentence. Take, for instance, her attitude on the issue of woman suffrage. "Perfectly ridiculous!" she is wont to exclaim contemptuously. "What should *I* want to vote for?" And there you have it. What, indeed, should Mrs. Albert Cheney want to vote for? So much for suffrage.

So does Mrs. Cheney settle all other problems. As there is no issue too great, so is there none too small for her attention. She can find time to settle the little problems of everyday life also. If asked about a play that she has seen, Mrs. Cheney will succinctly reply that it is good or it is bad. There is no quibbling, no allowance for personal biases, no concession to the possible taste of others. It is a good play or it is not a good play.

In like manner does Mrs. Cheney deal with all other questions, whether of literature or art, of servant keeping or child rearing, of etiquette or ethics. She pronounces her dictum, and the subject is closed.

It is but natural, therefore, that Mrs. Cheney should wield the chief executive powers in our Tuesday Club. The members often remark, sagely, that you could go a long way before you could find a cleverer woman than Mrs. Cheney.

In which opinion they are heartily indorsed by Mrs. Cheney herself.

MISS IDA ODDIE

Miss Oddie is one of those rare women who are born to be unmarried; one cannot possibly conceive of her in any other capacity. She makes little innocuous jokes about her spinsterhood, and in a spirit of gentle banter frequently refers to herself as an old maid. It is typical of Miss Oddie that any little jests which she might make would be at her own expense. She would perish rather than run the least chance of hurting anybody else's feelings.

There is a persistent sweetness about Miss Oddie that will not be downed. In fact, she is so consistently sweet in her attitude toward everything that one cannot help but detect a slight savor of monotony about her. This determined saccharinity of Miss Oddie's is a phenomenon observable in many extremely unmarried women of a—as the saying goes—certain age; her unused affections have, as it were, turned to sugar; one might say that she has diabetes of the emotions.

Miss Oddie's habitual attitude is one of apology. She flutters timidly about, asking pardon by her manner for being in a state of existence. It is her laborious efforts to efface herself that render Miss Oddie so noticeable. It is she who insists on sitting upon the uncomfortable chair, who is always last through the door, who persistently holds the umbrella over her companion, reserving the drippings for herself. She will sit in a draft for hours at a stretch rather than trouble anyone to close the window. If by so doing she contracts a heavy cold, she bears it uncomplainingly, sweetly making the best of it.

Her attire admirably expresses Miss Oddie's personality. She is given to neutral tones, to self-effacing styles, to modest little tuckers, and unobtrusive hats. She wears a tender little smile, which from constant use has become a trifle set, and her eyes are finely wrinkled at the corners, as if from the effects of a constant glare.

It comes, perhaps, from looking too persistently on the sunny side.

MRS. SYDNEY SWAIN

The extraordinary thing about Mrs. Swain is the perpetual state of exhaustion in which she exists. No human eye has ever beheld her when she felt fresh and rested. Her head droops with weary grace as she relates, in her soft, tired voice, how completely worn out she is. She is constantly having to go and lie down, and it is no unusual occurrence for her to have to give up everything and go away for a good rest.

Exactly what it is that has so tired her or just what she is resting up for has never been cleared up, for all strain has been removed from her life by the force of Mr. Swain's inherited money, and she need face no greater drain upon her strength than the lifting to her mouth of her limousine's speaking tube.

Perhaps it is her maternal cares that have so heavily taken their toll of her vitality. Mrs. Swain's is what might be called an indirect motherhood, carried on by a chain of nurse, governess and aunt, but she is the nominal head of the system and, as such, has a full sense of her responsibilities. She often observes that no one in the world has any idea what a care young children are.

Which does seem as if she were somewhat misinformed in her statistics.

MISS FRANCES PARSONS

Mrs. Swain's goodness to her elder sister, Miss Frances Parsons, is one of the favorite topics of conversation among members of our club. They love to recall how Frances was slaving away in a bank, as secretary to the president, when Sydney Swain married her sister; how the new Mrs. Swain insisted on Frances' leaving her position and coming to live in the big Swain house; how Mrs. Swain allowed Frances to plan all the meals, to supervise the servants, to assume charge of all the household accounts; how, in addition to even that important position, now that there are two little Swains, Frances has been assigned to the post of resident maiden aunt and, as such, is assured of a home and every luxury and has absolutely nothing to worry about—well, until the children grow up, anyway.

The club members are continually finding fresh evidences of Mrs. Swain's generosity. When Mrs. Swain got her new fur coat Frances came to the very next club meeting wearing the old one. Now that the Swains take the children with them on their trips to New York, they take Frances along, too, and she stays with them at the very best hotels and goes to all the most exclusive shops with Mrs. Swain and the children.

Her very presence in the club is due to her sister. When one of the members moved out of town, and the club was confronted with the necessity of finding someone to take her place, Mrs. Swain was the first to suggest Frances. It really is a great thing for Frances. She loves society and it gives her a chance to get out once in a while. Frances doesn't go out in the evening; but then, as Mr. Swain is at the office all day, the only opportunity that Mrs. Swain and he have to go out together is in the evening, and Mrs. Swain is, by her own admission, far too good a mother to leave her children alone with the servants.

So Frances is in the club and, whenever it meets at the Swain house, Mrs. Swain lets her see about the refreshments and buy the prizes. It has come to be a popular saying among members of the club: "Well, Frances Parsons certainly is a lucky girl!"

But there! Isn't it true that some people never know when they are well off? When Mrs. Throop walked into her room unannounced the other day, there was Frances crying her eyes out, with her head on the cover of that old typewriter that she used to have down at the bank.

MRS. PERCY PUGH

Mrs. Pugh specializes in youthfulness; she is a professed Peter Pan. She acknowledges, frequently, that she just never will grow up. She gleefully relates somewhat tenuous anecdotes, all a trifle anti-climactical as to point, dealing with occasions when she has been mistaken for her own daughter. The club members listen to these enthusiastic recitals with the not entirely undivided attention one lends to an oft-heard tale.

It is, doubtless, her extreme naïveté that creates the impression of guileless youth in Mrs. Pugh. Her naïveté is like some cherished heirloom, not only in that it has been in the family for years, but in that it is carefully guarded, proudly exhibited, the subject of many quaint narratives, told, it must be added, by Mrs. Pugh herself, who can do them

full justice. She is perhaps at her best when retailing the startlingly un-
studied things she has said and their effect upon certain staid listeners.
She is simply bubbling over—the phrase is her own—with ingenuous-
ness. Though she has had the usual education, she receives every stray
bit of information with little cries of wonder that such things can be
out in the great, big world.

Mrs. Pugh has constantly to fight against temptations that do not
often trouble other women. When she passes children coasting down a
hill, she exclaims that she would give anything to coast with them; when
her daughter goes off to schoolgirl parties Mrs. Pugh affirms that it
nearly makes her cry because she can't go too. However, she makes the
best of things by bringing a prettily childlike manner to her own grown-
up entertainments. She claps her hands and jumps up and down in her
seat quaintly when the refreshments appear, and she assumes a cunning
pout if she fails to win a prize. Into her conversation she injects piquant
words of youthful slang, and, while she has never quite dared baby talk
at firsthand, Mrs. Pugh frequently makes opportunity to quote literally
from remarks of infants of her acquaintance.

It is really a concession on Mrs. Pugh's part to belong to our club at
all. Indeed, it is only her youthful enthusiasm for games that has brought
her into the club and kept her there. As she repeatedly observes, her
idea of fun isn't staying indoors with a lot of grown-ups; if she had her
way she would be with the young people all the time.

Quite a formidable barrier to her ever attaining her wish is the feeling
of the young people in the matter.

MRS. LUCIUS KING

Mrs. King has an amazingly wide acquaintance among the newly departed. She never picks up a newspaper without finding some familiar
name among the obituary notices; it is an off day for her when she can
discover only one or two. It need not necessarily be one of her immediate circle; although the name be only that of some relation by marriage
of a distant acquaintance, say, or even that of some person whom she
has heard vaguely mentioned at some time, Mrs. King takes as flatter-
ingly personal an interest as if it were one of her own relatives. Naturally, when the obituary column yields her such a lavish supply of
absorbing current events, Mrs. King confines her newspaper reading
almost entirely to it, although her attention may occasionally wander
over to the front page, if any particularly striking fatalities are reported
thereon.

In her attire, Mrs. King strikes a prolonged minor note. She runs to heavy veils, somber draperies, gun-metal ornaments and black gloves. It almost seems as if she were holding herself ready, so that if she were ever called upon to attend a funeral at a moment's notice, she would be perfectly dressed for the occasion. She carefully hoards crêpe veils and black-bordered handkerchiefs, for, as she so justly says, one never can tell what may happen and it does no harm to be prepared. Mrs. King even carries this admirable truism into her most intimate feminine concerns; carefully put away, in an obscure bureau drawer, is a complete outfit, simple yet becoming, in which she has given explicit directions that she shall be arrayed when her own hour comes.

Mrs. King has a turn of observation which, although it has become almost mechanical to her, is inclined to render those about her somewhat subdued in spirit. For example, at a large social gathering, Mrs. King will look mournfully around and sighingly wonder how many of the assembled guests will still be alive and well ten years hence. At the theater, although the play may be a side-splitting farce, Mrs. King injects a somber note by the reminder that, for all the audience knows, the actors' hearts may be breaking beneath their gaudy costumes. When asked to make any engagement for the near future, Mrs. King never fails to include in her acceptance the stipulation "if I'm spared," although it would seem, to the captious, as if that contingency might be taken for granted.

The best of company is Mrs. King when in an anecdotal mood; her listeners never know a moment's boredom. Her stories keep one on the edge of one's chair, nerves taut, hair erect, eyes glazed with horror. She enjoys a large circle of friends whose lives have been singularly rich in blood-curdling tragedies. Her tales are all of their hideous experiences— how this one's husband went suddenly mad at the dinner table; how that one's child accidentally hanged itself with a jumping rope; how a third, while fainting from the shock of the news of an uncle's demise, fell into the bathtub and was drowned. Such as these are only the mildest of Mrs. King's repertory. Never repeating herself, she can wander on for hours along these lines.

After a period of her society, the listener is apt to wonder if Mrs. King ever knew any people who lived normally healthy, pleasant, unmarred lives, terminating restfully in bed. If she ever did, Mrs. King obviously doesn't consider them worth talking about.

Ladies' Home Journal, July 1920

As the Spirit Moves

Any day, now, I expect to read in the paper that Sir Oliver Lodge, or somebody else who keeps right in touch with all the old crowd, has received a message from the Great Beyond announcing that the spirits have walked out for a forty-four-hour week, with time and a half for overtime, and government control of ouija boards. And it would be no more than fair, when you come right down to it; something ought to be done to remedy the present working conditions among the spirits. Since this wave of spiritualism has broken over the country it has got so that a spirit doesn't have a minute to himself. The entire working force has to come trooping back to earth every night to put in a hard night's labor knocking on walls, ringing bells, playing banjos, pushing planchettes round, and performing such parlor specialties. The spirits have not had a quiet evening at home for months. The Great Beyond must look as deserted as an English lecture platform.

No spirit could object to coming back now and then in the way of business, so to speak, through a professional medium. That sort of thing is more or less expected; it's all in an eternity, as you might say. But the entrance of all these amateurs into the industry has been really too much. It is the ouija-board trade in particular that is so trying. Now that every family has installed its own private ouija board and expects immediate service on it at any hour of the day or night, the sting has been put into death. It's enough to wear a poor spirit to a shadow, that's what it is.

THE AGE OF THE OUIJA BOARD

Of course there may not be any particular connection, but nation-wide spiritualism seems to have come in like a lion at just about the time that nation-wide alcoholism was going out like a lamb. The séance room has practically become the poor man's club. After all, people have to do something with their evenings; and it can always be argued on the side of the substitute pastime that it does not cut into the next morning, anyway. There was a time when ouija-board operating was looked upon only as an occupation for highly unmarried elderly ladies of pronounced religious tendencies; prohibition was regarded in much the same light, if you remember. And now the ouija board has replaced the corkscrew as the national emblem. Times surely do change, as I overheard someone saying only yesterday.

It has certainly been a great little fiscal year for stockholders in ouija-board plants. A census to show the distribution of ouija boards would prove that they average at least one to a family. There is every reason for their popularity as a family institution; their initial cost can soon be scraped together, their upkeep amounts to practically nothing, they take up little space, and anybody can run them. They are the Flivvers among psychical appliances. No home can conscientiously feel that it is supplied with all modern conveniences, lacking one; there is even some talk, I hear, of featuring built-in ouija boards in the more luxurious of the proposed new apartment houses.

A strong factor in the popularity of the ouija board as a domestic utensil is the prevalence of ouija-board agencies throughout the country. No shopping round is necessary; you can buy one anywhere, from a notion counter to a used-car emporium. Its purchase used to involve much secret diplomacy. You had to worm the manufacturer's address from some obscure acquaintance who was rumored to go in for all that sort of thing, and then you had to send to some vague place in the West, whence your ouija board came to you, f. o. b., in a plain wrapper. Now there is not the slightest hitch—you can pick one up anywhere on the way home. Our own corner drug store has been celebrating Ouija Week for the past month or so, and I understand that the boards are going like hot cakes—after all, you can't better the old similies. They certainly make a tasteful window display, combined, as they are, with garlands of rubber bath hose, with notes of color introduced by a few hot-water bags here and there. I imagine that the exhibit was arranged by the same person who thinks up names for the drinks served at the soda fountain.

What a simple matter this thing of communicating with the spirits has turned out to be, since the ouija board made its entrance into the great American family life. There is practically nothing to it—anybody can do it in the privacy of his own room. Look at the results that the members of our little circle have been getting, for instance, since we took up the ouija board in a really thorough way. And we never had a lesson in our lives, any of us. It has been a rough season, locally, for the professional-medium trade; I doubt if the professionals have even made expenses, since we learned that we could do it ourselves.

Home spirit communication has completely revolutionized our local social life. I often wonder what we should ever do with our evenings if it weren't for the spirits. Since they have taken to dropping in for an informal chat over the ouija board we never lack a lively parlor game for one and all—metaphysical, yet clean.

And then just look at the money we save on amusement taxes! You know how it is yourself; the minute you leave home to make an evening of it, it runs right into expense. What with the cost of theater tickets, cabaret food and taxicab charter—good night, as the saying goes. Even such wholesome community activities as interapartment poker games, wives welcome, come under the head of outgo sooner or later. Of course this is a relatively free country, and no one has a better right than you to your own opinion of the ouija board as a medium of communication with the next world; but considering it solely as a means of after-dinner entertainment you must concede that the price is right, anyway.

Where would our little circle be of an evening if the spirits had not grown so clubby? Sitting round, that's where we would be, trying to figure out if the William Hart picture round at the Elite Motion-Picture Palace was the same one that they showed the week before over at the Bijou Temple of Film Art. Since we got our ouija board I have so completely lost touch with the movies that Theda Bara may have got religion, for all I know about it.

WHEN THE BRIDGE HOUNDS WERE UNLEASHED

Of course, we did have our bits of the higher life once in a while in the old days. Whenever the husbands could be argued into it we used to take up the rugs and devote the evening to Terpsichore, as the boys say. But we got little or nothing out of it, considering all the effort involved. The talent for dancing among the male element of our set would, if pooled, be about equal to the histrionic ability of Mr. Jack Dempsey. The only one who really worked up any enthusiasm about it was old Mr. Emery, who as a parlor Maurice had one foot in the grave and the other on his partner's instep. He had taken up dancing along about the time that the waltz was being condemned by press and pulpit, and his idea of a really good jazz number was "Do You See My New Shoes?"

The community dances never went over really big, that you could mention; by the time the second fox trot had reached the place where the record was scratched the men had all gathered in one corner and were arguing about how long you ought to let it stand before you put it in the still; and the women were settled along the other side of the room, telling each other how you could reduce without exercising or dieting. Those evenings were apt to cause hard feeling between husband

and wife, and one word frequently led to another on the way home.

Then there was the time that we went in rather heavily for bridge. The bridge hounds were unleashed on Tuesday evenings, and at eleven o'clock chicken salad and lettuce sandwiches would be served and the one who had the highest score could choose between a blue glass candy jar with a glass crab apple on its top, and a hive-shaped honey pot of yellow china with china bees that you'd swear were just about to sting you swarming all over it; in either case what was left went without any argument to the holder of the next highest score.

On the next Tuesday the club would meet again, and play till eleven o'clock, at which time chicken salad and cream cheese and olive sandwiches would be provided, and the winner had to make up his mind between one of those handy little skating girls made of painted wood with a ball of colored twine instead of a bodice, and a limp-leather copy of *Gitanjali*, by Rabindranath Tagore, the well-known hyphenated Indian.

The bridge club would doubtless have still been tearing things wide open every Tuesday, but the ouija board came in, and the hostesses' imagination in the selection of prizes gave out, at about the same time.

Mrs. Both, who is awfully good at all that kind of thing, tried to inaugurate a series of Sunday evening intellectual festivals, but they were never what you could really call a riot. The idea was that everyone should meet at her house, and the more gifted among us should entertain and at the same time elevate the majority. But Mrs. Both could never get enough backing from the rest of the home talent. She herself read several papers that she had written on such subjects as "The New Russia, and Why"; and "Modern Poetry—What of Its Tomorrow?"

HENRY G. TAKES TO VERSE

And Mrs. Curley, who is always so agreeable about doing anything like that, did some of her original child impersonations, in her favorite selections, "Don't Tell the Daisies I Tolded You, 'Cause I Pwomised Them Not to Tell"; and "Little Girls Must Always Be Dwessed up Clean—Wisht I Was a Little Boy." As an encore she always used to give, by request, that slightly rough one about "Where Did Baby Bruvver Tum Fwom, That's What Me Wants to Know," in which so many people think she is at her best. Mrs. Curley never makes the slightest change in costume for her specialty—she doesn't even remove her chain-drive eyeglasses—yet if you closed your eyes you'd really almost think that a little child was talking. She has often been told that she should have gone on the stage. Then Mr. Bliss used to sing "Rocked in the Cradle of the Deep," and would gladly have done more, except that it was so hard to find songs that suited his voice.

Those were about the only numbers that the program ever comprised. Mr. Smalley volunteered to make shadow pictures and give an imitation of a man sawing wood, including knots, but Mrs. Both somehow did not quite feel that this would have been in the spirit of the thing. So the intellectual Sunday evenings broke up, and the local mental strain went down to normal again.

Mrs. Both is now one of the leaders in the home-research movement. She has been accomplishing perfect wonders on the ouija board; she swung a wicked planchette right from the start. Of course she has been pretty lucky about it. She got right in touch with one spirit, and she works entirely with him. Henry G. Thompson, his name is, and he used to live a long time ago, up round Cape Cod way, when he was undeniably a good fellow when he had it. It seems that he was interested in farming in a small way, while he was on earth, but now that he has a lot of time on his hands he has taken up poetry. Mrs. Both has a whole collection of poems that were dictated to her by this spirit. From those that I have seen I gather that they were dictated but not read.

But then, of course, she has not shown me all of them.

Anyway, they are going to be brought out in book form in the fall, under the title *Heart Throbs From the Hereafter*. The publishers are confident of a big sale, and are urging Mrs. Both to get the book out sooner, while the public is still in the right mood. But she has been having some sort of trouble with Henry, over the ouija board. I don't know if I have it quite straight, but it seems that Henry is behaving in a pretty unreasonable way about the percentage of royalties that he insists must go to the Thompson estate.

But aside from this little hitch—and I dare say that she and Henry will patch it up between them somehow—Mrs. Both has got a great deal out of spiritualism. She went about it in the really practical way. She did not waste her own time and the spirits' asking the ouija board questions about who is going to be the next President, and whether it will rain tomorrow, and what the chances are for a repeal of the Volstead Act. Instead she sat right down and got acquainted with one particular spirit, and let him do the rest. That is really the best way to go about it; get your control, and make him work your ouija board for you, and like it. Some of our most experienced mediums agree that that is the only way to get anywhere in parlor spiritualism.

But when you come right down to it there are few who can get more out of a ouija board than our own Aunt Bertha. Her work is not so highly systematized as that of Mrs. Both, but it is pretty fairly spectacular, in its way.

I knew that Aunt Bertha was going to get in some snappy work on the ouija board; I could have told you that before I ever saw her in action. She has always been good at anything anywhere nearly like that. Now you take solitaire, for instance. I don't think I ever saw a prettier game of solitaire than that which Aunt Bertha puts up. You may be looking over her shoulder while she deals out the cards for a game of Canfield, and from the layout before her you would swear that she had not a chance of getting more than one or two aces up, at most. In fact, it looks so hopeless that you lose interest in the game, and go over to the other end of the room to get a magazine. And when you come back Aunt Bertha will have all the cards in four stacks in front of her, and she will smile triumphantly and exclaim: "What do you think of that? I got it again!"

AUNT BERTHA'S SNAPPY WORK

I have known that to happen over and over again; I never saw such luck in my life. I would back Aunt Bertha against any living solitaire player for any amount of money you want, only providing that the judges leave the room during the contest.

It was no surprise to me to find that she had just the same knack with a ouija board. She can take a ouija board that would never show the least signs of life for anybody else and make it do practically everything but a tail spin. She can work it alone or she can make a duet of it—it makes no difference to her. She is always sure of results, either way. The spirits seem to recognize her touch on the board immediately. You never saw such a remarkable thing; it would convert anybody to spiritualism just to see her.

Aunt Bertha asks a question of the spirits, and the words are no more than out of her mouth when the planchette is flying about, spelling out the answer almost faster than you can read it. The service that she gets is perfectly wonderful. And, as she says herself, you can see that there is no deception about it, because she does not insist upon asking the question herself; anyone can ask whatever he can think of—there are no limits. Of course, the answers have occasionally turned out to be a trifle erratic, but then, to quote Aunt Bertha again, what does that prove? The spirits never claimed to be right all the time. It is only human of them to make a slip once in a while.

She can go deeper into the affairs of the Other Side than a mere game of questions and answers, if you want her to. Just say the word, and Aunt Bertha will get you in touch with anybody that you may name, regardless of how long ago he or she may have lived. Only the other night, for instance, someone suggested that Aunt Bertha summon Noah Webster's spirit, and in scarcely less time than it takes to tell it, there he was talking to her on the ouija board, as large as life. His spelling wasn't all that it used to be, but otherwise he seemed to be getting along splendidly.

Again, just to show you what she can do when she sets her mind to it, she was asked to try her luck at getting connected with the spirit of Disraeli—we used up Napoleon and Cleopatra and Julius Cæsar and all the other stock characters the very first week that Aunt Bertha began to work the ouija board, and we had to go in pretty deep to think up new ones. The planchette started to move the minute that Aunt Bertha put her hands on it, if you will believe me, and when she asked, "Is this Disraeli?" it immediately spelled out, "This is him." I tell you, I saw it with my own eyes. Uncanny, it really was.

There seems to be nobody whom Aunt Bertha cannot make answer her on the ouija board. There is even a pretty strong chance that she may be able to get Central, after she has had a little more practice.

Mrs. Crouch, too, has been having some pleasant chats with the spirits. And it is only natural that they should treat her as practically one of the family, for she has been doing propaganda work for the Other Side for years. I often think that one of the big undertaking corporations is overlooking a great little advance agent in Mrs. Crouch. She has a way of asking you how you feel that would make you swear you could smell lilies.

Mrs. Crouch frequently states that she takes but little interest in the things of this world, and she dresses the part. There is a quaint style about her which lends to everything that she wears an air of its having been bequeathed to her by some dear one who went over round 1889.

There is a certain snap to her conversation, too, for which she is noted among our set. Perhaps her favorite line is the one about in the midst of life, which she has been getting off for so long that she has come to take an author's pride in it. You never saw anyone so clever as Mrs. Crouch is at tracing resemblances to close friends of hers who passed on at what she calls, in round numbers, an early age; you would be surprised at the number of persons with whom she comes in contact who have just that same look round the eyes. In fact, you might call Mrs. Crouch the original Glad Girl, and not be much out of the way.

So the ouija-board operations have been right along in her line. Scarcely a day passes, she tells me, that she does not receive a message from at least one of her large circle of spirit friends, saying that everything is fine, and how is she getting on, herself? It has really been just like Old Home Week for Mrs. Crouch ever since she got her ouija board.

Miss Thill is another of our girls who has made good with the spirits. Spiritualism is no novelty to her; she has been a follower of it, as she says, almost all her life, and by now she has fairly well caught up with it. In her case, also, it is no surprise to find her so talented with the ouija board. She has always been of a markedly mediumistic turn of mind—there are even strong indications of clairvoyant powers. Time and time again Miss Thill has had the experience of walking along the street thinking of some friend of hers, and whom will she meet, not two hours afterward, but that very same friend! As she says, you cannot explain such things away by calling them mere coincidence. Sometimes it really almost frightens Miss Thill to think about it.

You would know that Miss Thill was of a spiritualistic trend only to look at her. She has a way of suddenly becoming oblivious of all that is going on about her and of looking far off into space, with an intent expression, as of one seeking, seeking; materialists, at their first sight of her in this condition, are apt to think that she is trying to remember whether she really did turn off the hot water before leaving home. Her very attire is suggestive of the occult influence. What she saves on corsets she lavishes on necklaces of synthetic jade, carved with mystic signs, which I'll wager have no good meaning behind them if the truth were known.

Miss Thill is a pretty logical candidate for the head of the local branch of the Ouija Board Workers of the World. She has an appreciable edge on the other contestants in that she once attended a lecture given by Sir Oliver Lodge himself. Unfortunately she chose rather an off day; Sir Oliver was setting them right as to the family life of the atom, and it went right on over Miss Thill's head; she couldn't even jump for it. There were none of those little homy touches about Sir Oliver's intimacies with the spirits which Miss Thill had been so eager to hear, and I believe that there was quite a little bitterness on her part about it. She has never felt really the same toward Sir Oliver since. So far as she is concerned he can turn right round and go back to England—back to his old haunts, as you might put it.

HARDENED HUSBANDS

By means of her ouija board Miss Thill, as might have been expected, has worked her way right into the highest intellectual circles of spirit society. As if recognizing an equal some of the greatest celebrities of the Great Beyond have taken her up. It seems that it is no uncommon occurrence for her to talk to such people as Tennyson and Sir Walter Scott on the ouija board; she has come to think scarcely anything of it. I hear that she has been receiving several messages from Shakspere only lately. His spirit is not what a person could call really chatty, as I understand it; he doesn't seem to be one to do much talking about himself. Miss Thill has to help him out a good deal. She asks him one of her typically intellectual questions, such as what he thinks of the modern drama, and all he has to do to answer her is to guide the planchette to either "Yes" or "No"; or, at most, both. Still, his spirit is almost an entire stranger to her, when you stop to think of it, so you really cannot expect anything of a more inside nature just yet, anyway.

Unfortunately several of the husbands among our little circle have been markedly out of sympathy with the spirit movement. They have adopted a humorous attitude toward it which has seemed to be almost coarse to the more enthusiastic of the women workers. They use the ouija board only to ask it such frivolous questions as "Where is the nearest place where you can still get it?"—which is particularly trying to those who realize the true seriousness of the thing. It is small wonder that they get no answer from the spirits when they go about it that way; no spirit is going to stand for that sort of stuff. There are too many demands on the spirits' time for them to bother about calls which are not absolutely necessary.

Attempts to convince the more hardened husbands of the supernatural powers of the ouija board have ended in nothing. Some of them when told, by way of positive proof, of the amazing messages which their own wives have received from the board, have even made open accusations of pushing, which have almost led to an even division of the children, and a parting of the ways. Not since the dance craze came in has there been so much really notable matrimonial friction as there is over this matter of spirit communication. The ouija board is not without—or, in fact, is with, if you do not mind plain speaking—its somber side.

TOO MUCH IS ENOUGH

Personally I find that I am rather out of things at the neighborhood social festivals. When the others gather round to exchange bright sayings of their ouija boards I am left nowhere as regards adding anything to the general revelry. The spirits have not done the right thing by me; I can never get any action on the ouija board. It isn't as if I had not given the spirits a fair chance. No one was any readier than I to be one of the boys; the flesh was willing, but the spirits weakened, if you could put it that way. There I was, so anxious to make friends with them, and find out how all the folks were, and if they were still with the same people, and how they liked their work. And they would never even say so much as "Haven't we had a poisonous winter?" to me. So if that is the way they are going to be about it—why, all right. I can take a hint as well as the next one.

As for the community ouija boards, any time the research workers want to store them away in the spare bedrooms with the rest of the bird's-eye-maple furniture it will be quite all right for me. I am willing to call it a day and give the spirits a rest any time that the others are. I am not fanatical about the ouija board; I am perfectly able to take it or let it alone. In fact, I think that a reasonable amount of daily exercise on it is a good thing. It is not the actual manual labor that I object to—it is the unexpurgated accounts of all the messages received and their meanings, if any.

Sometimes I even feel that I could moil along through life if I never had to hear another discourse on the quaint things that some local ouija board has said. To put it in so many words—at a rough estimate—I am just about all through.

In fact, if I thought that you would stand for it I would even go so far as to say that I am ouija bored.

The Saturday Evening Post, May 22, 1920

A Dinner Party Anthology

MRS. CHARLES FRISBIE

As hostess, Mrs. Frisbie is present at the dinner table in body only; her spirit wings afar to the unseen realms of kitchen and pantry, where she fain would be. For, as she sadly explains, only if she were there to supervise could she be assured that things would go smoothly. Unwatched by a stern eye, the cook is apt to serve the fish after the roast or, whimsically, to omit the salad altogether. True, Mrs. Frisbie's cook, during their four years' cooperation, has always faithfully followed the old traditions in such matters, but that, according to Mrs. Frisbie, is no proof of what she might do. It would not be the slightest surprise to Mrs. Frisbie to have her break out into the wildest unconventionalities at any moment. Servants, she avers, would do anything; they cannot be trusted to do the simplest task correctly unless you stand right over them while they are doing it.

One is inclined to wonder just why Mrs. Frisbie considers the giving of a dinner party worth while, for the wear and tear upon her nervous system which it entails must be appalling. With hawklike intensity she watches every movement of the waitress, waiting breathlessly for a mistake. A moment's delay in the service brings her to the verge of a mental breakdown; she bursts into rapid, irrelevant discourse, while her eyes are fixed in a desperate glare and her fingers play soundless tarantellas on the tablecloth. She apologizes continually to her guests for mishaps which have not yet occurred, plaintively relating how hopeless it is for one so handicapped by her servants to attempt any form of hospitality. It is impossible for the more sensitively organized among Mrs. Frisbie's guests not to take all this to heart and feel depressingly guilty about it.

But it is not alone at dinner parties that the behavior of her servants so affects Mrs. Frisbie. Her whole life, one gathers from her conversation, has been practically wrecked by their caprices. So heavy is the pall that they have cast over her that she can talk of nothing else. She has an inexhaustible fund of anecdotes illustrating their grotesquely unreasonable demands—how a certain one insisted upon a room to herself; how another reserved the top of the bottle for her own coffee; how still another wanted to be always running off to church. Each transitory chambermaid or fleeting laundress that passes through her employ serves as the heroine of another narrative.

With the piteous air of those whose spontaneous generosity has met only with imposition in this world, Mrs. Frisbie admits that all her trouble with servants is directly traceable to the fact that she is too good to them; she really feels, she says, that the only way to get anything out of them is to treat them as so many cattle. Sometimes, she adds wistfully, she yearns to give up her entire ménage and go to live in some little shanty in the backwoods where she could do all her own work and be freed from any effort at entertaining.

It would really amaze Mrs. Frisbie to learn how many people of her acquaintance are wholly in sympathy with the idea.

MR. CHARLES FRISBIE

Mr. Frisbie's Christian name was a truly superb bit of foresight by his parents; one cannot imagine his answering to any other appellation than Charlie.

Mr. Frisbie has built up for himself quite an enviable local reputation as an amateur comedian. And, assuredly, there is no one more deserving of success in this line; it is the result of years of earnest endeavor and unflagging application. He is an inspiring example of what hard work can accomplish. Never, in the memories of those who know him, has he let slip the opportunity for a pun or a dialect story.

The real point of Mr. Frisbie's humor lies in its expectedness. There is a soothing certainty about all his quips; one can see them coming minutes ahead. He is also unsparing of himself in his jesting; though he may have made the same joke a hundred times before, he unflinchingly goes all through it again should a chance offer. No one could estimate what a boon prohibition and a certain motor car have been to him; it would almost seem as if they had both been instituted solely to afford him a field for drolleries.

Mr. Frisbie is also adept at the playing of elfish pranks. It is at the telephone, perhaps, that this quality best asserts itself. He never prosaically gives his correct name over the wire; he invariably waggishly announces himself as some national celebrity, such as Charlie Chaplin or William Jennings Bryan. He still tells about the time when he called up Mr. Partridge at three o'clock in the morning and, having brought him stumbling sleepily down through the drafty darkness from his top-floor bedroom, roguishly told him to go back to bed again. This feat probably marked the climax of Mr. Frisbie's career. Some people, indeed, feel that he has gone downhill since.

Naturally Mr. Frisbie revels in his opportunities as host at the dinner. Between sallies he performs quaint tricks with olives, silverware and lumps of sugar, leading the laughter on every occasion. Well may his guests remark, as they frequently do, that Charlie is a regular case.

But of what they neglect to add.

MRS. LEWIS WILCOX

The authority with which Mrs. Wilcox settles all questions of what is, or is not, the correct thing to do would lead one to believe that she must have collaborated on the drawing up of the conventions. To her it is not life that matters; it is the etiquette with which one faces it that counts. The pangs of birth mean, to her, worrying over whether the announcement cards will be correctly engraved; the fear of death is the dread that the funeral may not be conducted according to the best usage.

She is in constant terror of being forced into contact with those who are not her social equals; she must be ceaselessly on guard lest any of the bourgeoisie worm their way into her visiting list. This dread of the middle classes she feels not only for herself but for her family.

The Wilcox children lead practically cloistered lives for fear that, in the regrettable democracy of childhood, they may become acquainted with little ones less well-bred than themselves. For it is upon good breeding that Mrs. Wilcox plumes herself; it is a topic of which she seems never to tire. To the overcritical, it seems, perhaps, as if good breeding is much like a sense of humor, in that its possessor never considers it necessary to call attention to it. But any such caviling may doubtless be set down to jealousy of Mrs. Wilcox's exalted position.

Mrs. Wilcox herself would be the first to ascribe it to that cause.

MR. LEWIS WILCOX

There is no more accurate summary of Mr. Wilcox in appearance, habits and opinions than his own word picture of himself. In his graphic, though somewhat redundant, phrase, he is a he-man.

From listening to his dissertations upon the topic one might gather that Mr. Wilcox was a publicity agent for the cold bath. He talks of it with salesmanlike enthusiasm, rather as if he were seeking to popularize it. It would seem from the way he speaks as if he were the only living exponent of its daily use. His contempt for those cheats who underhandedly temper their baths with warm water is beyond the power of even his bluffest Anglo-Saxon words to express.

Mr. Wilcox prides himself—and with justice—upon the size of his appetite. He speaks almost boastfully of the hordes of chops which he habitually consumes at breakfast, of the pounds of thick red meat which regularly buoy him up at lunch and dinner. Given time, he will enlarge upon the subject and cite complete menus of typical repasts as examples of his prowess. It is not necessary to inquire directly as to Mr. Wilcox's habits in order to elicit this information; he volunteers it gladly, without needing any reference to the topic to start him upon his recital.

Mr. Wilcox is for open air openly arrived at. His first action on entering a room is to fling up the windows, letting in great blasts of wholesome atmosphere. That this might cause hard feeling on the part of others in the room never deters him in his activities; he loudly explains to the discomforted ones that the air will do them good, and lets them enjoy a good, healthful shiver. It is characteristic of Mr. Wilcox that he feels himself cramped by ornaments and dim lights. He can breathe freely only when he has turned on every light in the room and has swept aside with an impatient hand all flowers, vases, pillows and such fripperies as may be near him. Any sensitiveness that the hostess may display on such occasions Mr. Wilcox nobly disregards.

His red-blooded exuberance is carried into his business life. Mr. Wilcox never speaks of his employment as work. Ask him his occupation and he will breezily reply that he is in the adding-machine game. Thus lightheartedly does he speak of any industry—the ball-bearing game, the renewable-fuse game, the motor-truck-belting game—as if it were some great national sport.

Mr. Wilcox stands unalterably for law and order; he is even willing to resort to violence to bring them about; he is, in fact, an earnest advocate of the firing squad as a corrective for social unrest. Mr. Wilcox goes on record as saying, two or three times a day at least, that the only way to treat these Bolsheviki is to shoot them. The vast breadth of this statement can be appreciated only when one understands that under the term Bolsheviki—which form of the word he uses interchangeably for both the singular and the plural—Mr. Wilcox lists anybody who asks for a raise in wages.

In his zeal for order Mr. Wilcox strongly urges military discipline. In fact, he verges on the fanatical on this subject. He ardently believes that the louder an argument is uttered the more convincing it is; therefore, he is wont almost to shout, with accompanying virile thumps on a neighboring table, that the only thing which can save this country from ruin is three months' compulsory military training, annually, for all men between the ages of eighteen and forty.

Mr. Wilcox was forty-one last January.

MRS. HOMER PARTRIDGE

Motherhood claims Mrs. Partridge's undivided attention. She concentrates exclusively upon Homer Partridge, Junior, aged six; Titus Partridge (Mrs. Partridge was a Miss Titus), aged four; and Whittlesley Partridge (the maiden name of Mrs. Partridge's mother was Whittlesley), aged eighteen months. She takes not the faintest interest in anything outside of their concerns; she makes not the least pretense, as she often confesses, of keeping abreast of anything that is going on in the world beyond their nursery. Mrs. Partridge makes this confession in no spirit of apology; on the contrary, it is her proudest boast. There may be some women, she admits, who are able to combine with their motherhood an interest in current events, both local and international, but her tone indicates that, if indeed such women do exist, she would not care to make their acquaintance.

All those about her are regarded by Mrs. Partridge merely in the relation in which they stand to her children. She never calls or refers to any one of her friends just by his or her first name; she always prefaces the name with the word "Auntie" or "Uncle," which purely courtesy title the children are wont to employ. Her husband is known to her only as "Daddy."

On those rare occasions when she tears herself from a cribside long enough to attend a social gathering, Mrs. Partridge takes part in the conversation only when it touches upon her progeny. She will address the entire dinner party upon the boys, ranging in her discourse from the deeply serious, such as excerpts from the doctor's report on Junior's adenoids, to the light and frivolous, such as accounts of the reactions of little Titus to his first day in Sunday school. Warming to her theme, she will even give impersonations of the baby making cooing sounds in his bathtub. Delightful as this performance no doubt is in the original, much of the illusion is unfortunately lost in the imitation.

Should the conversation veer to more general topics, Mrs. Partridge becomes restless and preoccupied. Only when the talk is brought back to her young—by her own efforts if necessary—does Mrs. Partridge really give herself over to enjoying the evening; she can go on indefinitely, never losing any whit of her interest in the subject.

In which respect she is wholly unique among those present.

MR. HOMER PARTRIDGE

It is always with a start of surprise that one recalls Mr. Partridge's presence in the room. He has a way of effacing himself so completely that, without straining the memory, it is almost impossible to bear in mind that he is among the company. He has probably been addressed by more names that are not his own than has any other man of like age in the community. Try as they may, people seem to be wholly unable to remember what his name is.

His most frequently recurring experience is that of being put, by some mutual friend, through the ceremony of an introduction to someone whom he has met several times before. Not for worlds would he chance causing any embarrassment by suggesting that they have already been repeatedly introduced. He politely shakes hands, sincerely glad to meet the one in question on each separate occasion, yet knowing that as soon as he goes away his new acquaintance's mind will retain absolutely no impression of him and the whole process will only have to be gone through again. In the same way, Mr. Partridge is too desirous of saving discomfort to correct those who miscall him. Rather, he will answer willingly to any name whatever, thankful at being addressed at all.

If one determinedly seeks out Mr. Partridge in his unobtrusive corner at some social gathering and draws him into conversation, he will be found the most sympathetic of companions. He hangs on every syllable, making little wordless murmurs of commiseration, approbation or amazement as the nature of the recital prompts, laughing long and heartily at humorous touches and nearly breaking down over strokes of pathos. One leaves Mr. Partridge reluctantly, vowing to seek him out again at the very next opportunity and have another good long talk.

The unfortunate part of it is that one forgets all about him long before the next opportunity of seeking him out occurs.

MRS. MORRIS PRESSEY

The trouble with Mrs. Pressey—for, as she assures you, it is really a great trouble to her—is that she has too much soul. Her soulfulness is continually getting in her way, causing her to feel things and to yearn for things of which the more materially minded are totally unconscious. Other painful afflictions of Mrs. Pressey's are her extreme sensitiveness and her too highly strung nerves.

Besides all this, Mrs. Pressey is psychic to a high degree. It is no unusual occurrence for her to dream about some friend from whom she has not heard for a long time and then within the very next week to receive a letter from that friend. Mrs. Pressey has become accustomed to such phenomena as this. She has come to accept them as only additional evidences of her intense spirituality. This quality, which so differentiates her from those about her, she would like to express in her dress, but has met with little if any encouragement in her desires. In a town of less than one hundred thousand people it is difficult to wear garments which interpret one's soul without causing talk. So Mrs. Pressey is forced to content herself with leaving off hair nets and having her gowns made with mildly flowing sleeves.

Mrs. Pressey is given to sitting alone at twilight, gazing out over the darkening world. If spoken to suddenly at such times she starts and has some difficulty in bringing herself back to everyday affairs. It is understood that she is thinking great thoughts on these occasions. Many of her friends are firm in their belief that Mrs. Pressey could create a furore in the literary world should she ever commit her impressions to paper; indeed, Mrs. Pressey acknowledges that she would write if only she had the time.

But what with her walking to school with the children in the morning, calling for them at noon and having only the remainder of the day to herself, it looks as if Mrs. Pressey's Alice-blue quill pen must stand forever idle in its glassful of buckshot.

MR. MORRIS PRESSEY

The present seems to hold nothing for Mr. Pressey and the future can offer but little promise. He dwells entirely in the roseate past, in that glorious period when he used to live in Chicago. True, it was for only two brief years, but it was enough.

A change in his business, marriage and the desirability of bringing up the children in the semicountry air conspired, in the order mentioned, to bring Mr. Pressey to the town of his present residence and to keep him there. But his ten years' establishment has in no degree robbed him of his metropolitan viewpoint. Mr. Pressey has not become as the other inhabitants; his attitude is that of a transient visitor from some mighty city.

Of course, knowing as they do Mr. Pressey's feelings toward their efforts, his associates strain to pass muster in his sophisticated sight. They labor to carry off all their activities—particularly those of a social nature—in such a manner that Mr. Pressey may not be too deeply struck with the difference in the way those things are done in Chicago. Curiously enough, the decade which has elapsed since he was in direct contact with the whirl of life in a great city has not clouded his memory in the least; as a matter of fact, with the passing of time he grows more and more authoritative in his statements of what is done in the Windy City.

His metropolitan residence has given Mr. Pressey quite a standing as an authority on the stage and its people, and the ladies of his acquaintance depend upon him for bits of information as to who is who, and why, in Chicago society. A further result of his experience is his election to the office of president of the country club, a position which he holds with indulgent good nature, as a grown-up humors children by taking part in their game.

Only once has the glamour which surrounds Mr. Pressey been dimmed in the eyes of the townspeople. That was the time when the Frisbies had as a house guest a man who had lived for sixteen years in New York.

Ladies' Home Journal, August 1920

A Summer Hotel Anthology

MISS ABBEY FINCH

In this self-centered world it is indeed refreshing to chance upon one so insistently altruistic as Miss Finch. Her entire life is given lavishly over to the furthering of innocent merrymaking for others; her whole endeavor is to draw together all those about her and to plunge them into a happy round of stimulating yet impeccable divertisements. To Miss Finch that day is counted as practically thrown away whose sunset finds her unsuccessful in having imbued some of her fellow creatures with the get-together spirit. A predilection on the part of anyone to sit quietly apart, reading or merely resting, she regards as little short of unwholesome; her conscience gives her no rest until she has approached such a one and, with her cheery smile and playfully commanding manner, induced him or her to drag over a rocking-chair and join some convivial game or neighborly tourney of gossip.

As surely as welcome summer comes around again each year Miss Finch blossoms forth, reliable as one of the hardier annuals, each season a little more energetic, a little more executive, a little more determinedly brisk and cheerful, than the season before. Voluntarily she assumes all responsibility for the organizing and carrying out of the hotel's social activities; it is almost as if she regarded herself as the hostess, so conscientiously does she strive to see to it that the guests are provided with congenial entertainment. Indeed, more than one new arrival, until definitely set right, has labored under the delusion that Miss Finch is the proprietress of the establishment.

It is Miss Finch who instigates the biweekly bridge parties, collecting the entrance fees—in itself no mean undertaking—and selecting the prizes. It is she who engineers the various tournaments of the more active sports; who soothes the usual hard feeling caused by the handicap awards; who presents the silver-finished cups, accompanying each by a humorously apt speech, composed of sly yet inoffensive hits at the prize winner. She arranges the annual straw ride, the beach party, the moonlight sail, cheerfully deferring each from the appointed date to the next clear night; she intimidates faint-hearted male guests into attending the midsummer masquerade. If a time arrives for which no special event is scheduled, Miss Finch collects a gathering about the hotel piano and, seating herself firmly upon the stool, plays formerly popular airs strictly according to note and in rigid time, thus endeavoring to inspire a spontaneous outburst of song.

In short, Miss Finch gives unstintingly of her time, spirits and ingenuity, so that every moment of the long summer may be replete with entertainment. It is safe to say that the social life of the hotel would be virtually nowhere without her. And it is pleasant to record that her efforts are thoroughly appreciated by the guests. One could walk scarcely half the length of the porch without overhearing some tribute to her abilities. Perhaps the compliment oftenest repeated is that Miss Finch's gift for bringing people together amounts to a real talent.

Where she soars to positive genius is in her unerring instinct for bringing together those who, from their first glimpse of one another, have been straining every effort to keep apart.

MRS. HENRY LARKIN

There is but one interest in life for Mrs. Larkin; she admits freely that nothing else can ever be of the slightest importance to her. She exists solely, as she almost constantly explains, for the sake of her daughter. Her own life, continues the gently flowing recital, is, as a unit, not worth the living, so cruelly straitened is it by the extreme delicacy of her health. Year after year Mrs. Larkin visits the hotel, seeking in vain for recovery in the abundant sea air. There is, fortunately, nothing organically wrong; hers is an intangible affection, hopelessly permanent, which necessitates complete rest, congenial surroundings, soothing medicines, tempting food, exemption from any responsibility or worry, and the elimination of all effort.

It is a lesson by which many a one might profit to see how courageously Mrs. Larkin bears up; it plucks at the heartstrings to see her resting wearily in her rocking-chair, fragile as fine porcelain in her semi-invalid robes of delicate lavender, yet always wearing a brave little smile as she answers: "Not any worse, thank you," to anxious inquiries about her condition. She feels that she must make the best of it, as she tells one, so that her daughter may not be made unhappy. Sometimes, while the tears rise becomingly to her slightly faded blue eyes, Mrs. Larkin even hints that were it not for her little girl—as she tenderly, though in an entirely reminiscent sense, refers to her daughter—she would give up the struggle and pass almost imperceptibly away.

What little can be done to make things more bearable for Mrs. Larkin her friends conscientiously try to do. There is always a solicitous group about her chair, seeking to beguile her with chat or with rubbers of bridge. It is amazing what a revivifying effect this seems to have upon Mrs. Larkin; she joins animatedly in the talk or plays an exceptionally shrewd game. Yet, in quiet moments during some rare interval when the group about her has dispersed, she will take one into her somewhat overcrowded confidence and explain that such things would mean nothing to her had she not her daughter's happiness always on her mind. It is only that she feels she must nerve herself up to seeing people for her little girl's sake. Then, too, Mrs. Larkin admits that her friends would be wholly at a loss should she not see them. Were it not for disappointing them Mrs. Larkin often says that she would much prefer to be left quietly alone.

How true it is that a great sacrifice is grossly unappreciated in this world.

MISS ANNA LARKIN

It is difficult to pass on any definite description of Mrs. Larkin's daughter. There is an indistinct impression as of a mild someone in the last twenties, with neatly unobtrusive dress and rapidly forgotten features, but anything clearer is almost impossible to discern; she never remains still long enough to permit study. Her chair is usually empty, still rocking violently from her last hurried exit. Almost as soon as she regains her place in it Miss Larkin jumps up again, in obedience to a plaintively sweet request, and runs up to their fourth-floor suite to fetch her mother's scarf, her mother's sweater, her mother's embroidery silk, her mother's book or her mother's digestive tablets.

In the brief intervals between her dashes upstairs Miss Larkin knits desperately, as if making up for time out, on other scarfs or sweaters, all in that pale tint of lavender which is so subtly flattering to Mrs. Larkin's exquisitely delicate pallor. When each garment is finished Mrs. Larkin gracefully accepts it; it then becomes one more thing that her daughter may run upstairs to fetch. Upon infrequent occasions Miss Larkin has stolen time from her usual knitting to make a baby carriage robe for one of her school friends; Mrs. Larkin's wistful smile during these periods of neglect rends the heart of the beholder.

Outside interests are palpably impracticable for Miss Larkin; they would cut in too heavily on her personal messenger service. If, in a spirit of mild and kindly meant roguery, someone playfully mentions matrimony in connection with Miss Larkin, tears start in Mrs. Larkin's eyes and her lips tremble piteously with unspoken appeals.

It ends, always, in Miss Larkin's having to put down her knitting and run upstairs to bring her mother a fresh handkerchief and the smelling salts.

MRS. VIRGIL COMEE

Mrs. Comee is unanimously admitted to be the outstanding figure in hotel intellectual circles. She is, as she herself not infrequently concedes, a woman of broad knowledge and high cultural attainments. This, she acknowledges with a deprecatory smile, is not solely due to her natural gifts; she owes not a little of it to her habitual environment of lofty culture and her exceptional opportunities of keeping in touch with the great contemporary minds.

From her plentiful discourse on the fascinating subject one learns that Mrs. Comee's home suburb—that favored place where she spends all of her year save the two hottest months—is inhabited almost entirely by people who do things. The verb *to do* and the noun *things* are not, in this connection, to be taken in any merely physical sense; it is understood that they refer to intellectual pursuits. As but a few examples of the types of *intelligentsia* who are her fellow residents in the community Mrs. Comee cites an artist whose drawings ornament some of the most widely circulated mail-order catalogues; an authoress who writes the descriptive rhapsodies under the pictured costumes in an important fashion magazine; and a composer, more than one of whose songs have been used as encores by a professional singer. Mrs. Comee speaks of these personages with perfect composure; it is plain to see that such people are her accustomed acquaintances.

And even among such lions one understands that Mrs. Comee has no difficulty in holding her own. She speaks with natural pride of the culture club of which she is the presiding officer, and which suspends its activities during her absence, thus giving the less intellectual members a chance to relax the mental strain during the torrid months. Mrs. Comee seldom tires of describing the notable work accomplished by the club. Its members have taken up, and, one gathers, put lingeringly down again, art, literature, eugenics, the drama and civic improvement. Logically, since Mrs. Comee has thus thoroughly plumbed these subjects, hers is the last word upon the porch on all of them.

But there is an even greater glamour about her. She has had the inestimable advantage of travel. Shortly after her honorable graduation from high school Mrs. Comee spent the month of July, 1896, in touring Europe. It follows, therefore, that she is a recognized authority upon European history, geography and customs, and she often gives little impromptu lectures upon them, while rocking gently on the porch. When really warmed to her subject Mrs. Comee will even fetch her photograph album and give illustrated travelogues. In the snapshots Europe figures chiefly as a background for Mrs. Comee, wearing the costume of her post-high-school period. She is shown feeding the doves in front of St. Mark's, standing by the lion of Lucerne, about to climb the Eiffel Tower, just completing the descent of the Eiffel Tower, and doing countless other appropriate and instructive things. These views do much to give the Continent that note of personal interest which one so often misses in professional photographs.

The hotel guests say that it is indeed a treat to listen to Mrs. Comee's conversation. Mrs. Comee, herself, generously grants one every possible opportunity of enjoying the privilege.

MRS. EARLE STALEY

Almost immediately after one has met Mrs. Staley—with but the conventional interlude for the usual speculation that the day must be a scorching one in the city, and the customary concurrence in the opinion that humidity is infinitely harder to cope with than heat—she will put aside all generalities and explain, at some length, that the most arresting thing about her is her remarkable frankness. Half jokingly, she warns new acquaintances that they had best avoid her, if they are seeking for pleasing flattery; it is her invariable habit to speak her mind. In more serious vein Mrs. Staley goes on to say that it is at once her pride and her comfort always to know that, be the remainder of the world as deceitful as it may, her mind will, so long as she retains her faculties, be spoken.

It may not always be pleasant, Mrs. Staley avers, but she is not the one to let that cow her. She refuses to cover her true opinions with any cloak of evasion or ambiguity merely for the sake of easing some one's foolishly sensitive feelings. Thus, should her judgment of a friend's new frock be solicited, Mrs. Staley, if she thinks it unbecoming, promptly speaks her mind; more, she adds gratuitous bits of frankness by declaring that the color is unflattering, the material unattractive, the cut unskilled; and she ends by remarking that her friend must have been mentally unbalanced to have made such an ill-advised purchase.

If, on the contrary, Mrs. Staley does approve of the dress, she does not hesitate to admit it, frankly saying that it is infinitely less unsightly than many another in the friend's wardrobe. Should any friend not be looking her best, Mrs. Staley tells her of it immediately, with her refreshing bluntness. This procedure may, and often does, cause some little hard feeling, but Mrs. Staley generously overlooks it. As it is her whimsy to phrase it, if people don't like her frankness they can lump it. She must either speak her mind or else she must not speak at all.

There are many who feel that she makes an unfortunate choice.

MRS. WILMOT HOPPING

Her health, so Mrs. Hopping says, is the main thing. Obviously, she deems any other consideration so poor a second that she does not even admit it into her scheme of living. Her life is arranged to the sole end of fostering that enviably excellent health with which beneficent nature has so liberally endowed her.

Naturally a life of such devotion entails its sacrifices. At the table, for instance, Mrs. Hopping can take no part in the light conversation around her. Her attention is concentrated upon choosing only those foods which go directly into nourishment, upon masticating each mouthful an impressively high number of times, and upon keeping score of the exact number of calories which she consumes at a sitting. On the porch Mrs. Hopping cannot settle down to soothing idleness; her daily schedule has it otherwise. She must spring up, when the time set for exercise arrives, and take a rapid walk, always over the same course, which she enlivens by inhaling deeply for six steps and exhaling grudgingly during the next six.

When her daily bathing hour, scheduled at just the correct distance from her last meal, comes around, Mrs. Hopping does not permit herself any indulgence in haphazard immersion. She walks determinedly to the water's edge, and stooping over—without bending the knees—applies a handful of the salt liquid to each wrist and to her forehead; not till then does she feel that she can safely give herself over to Neptune. While she disports herself amid the health-giving billows, a daughter, stationed on the beach with a watch, sees that she does not overstay her allotted time.

The most diverting entertainment cannot hold Mrs. Hopping one minute past her self-appointed bedtime; nor can she linger blissfully in bed of a morning. She bounds up immediately, when the tinkle of her alarm clock tells her that the last second of the hours of sleep necessary to perfect health has elapsed. Her rising and retiring, as everything else throughout her day, must be done at the physiological moment.

Mrs. Hopping shows herself a woman of adamant will power in her rigid adherence to the stringent régime under which she has placed herself. But it has its rewards, as Mrs. Hopping so proudly enumerates, in her cheerily brisk circulation, her imperturbable blood pressure, her undeviatingly correct pulse and her lavishly open pores. Indeed, if one were to make the deduction solely from her conversation, one would think that to Mrs. Hopping there were no other events of importance in the world. There are times, truthfully, when one finds oneself wishing that she might, if but for a brief interval, touch upon some other, and perhaps some more general, topic of the day.

But her health, so Mrs. Hopping says, is the main thing.

MRS. RAMSAY BRACKET

Her truly remarkable memory is perhaps the most striking of the many admirable traits with which Mrs. Bracket is equipped. It must undoubtedly have been of unusual retentiveness congenitally, and she has so developed it by many summers of rigorous training that she is now able to perform, without an effort, feats of recollection which are little short of startling. With never a moment's brain racking Mrs. Bracket can give you the name, address, approximate age, marital condition, social status and financial rating of every guest in the hotel, down to the most obscure transient; she can even add to each account intimate details of the subject's most personal concerns—details so minute that they would slip unperceived from any memory less highly schooled.

Figures themselves hold no terror for her; she has all the latest statistics at her tongue's tip—the number of times an evening that the Hopping girl dances with the Comee boy; the number of suitors imported from the city by the elder Miss Staley; the number of hours, to date, that the visiting belle from New Orleans has spent on the moonlit pier. Mrs. Bracket, as she sits at her pleasant task of punching holes in a potential centerpiece and carefully sewing them up again, is cordially ready to quote you the correct figures in any of such cases.

It is Mrs. Bracket who is the acknowledged head of the rocking-chair board of censorship. Thus far, none among the hotel guests has been stamped with her approval.

In fact, the only guest upon whom she can conscientiously bestow her thorough approval in every way is Mrs. Ramsay Bracket.

MR. GEORGE WILLIS

It would be in no way overstating the case to call Mr. Willis, as many another admirer has called him before, the life of the hotel. It is impossible to conjure up a mental picture of the hotel front without visualizing his figure in its specially reserved rocking-chair on the end.

The gay frocks and sweaters of the ladies are given value by the dark note of his blue serge suit. To show that he has a fitting sense of appropriate attire for a seaside resort Mr. Willis affects navy blue serge suits, vaguely suggestive in cut of the uniform of a sea captain. He heightens this effect by wearing a crisp white yachting cap with a glistening black vizor and, as a concession to the summery weather, completes his costume with such cool touches as white canvas shoes and a white necktie fresh from the capable hands of the laundress.

No business drags him away to the city; an adequate income assures his being dependably on hand all summer long, standing ever ready to fetch a chair, to open a parasol, to pick up a dropped knitting needle, to make a fourth at bridge, to hold yarn, or to read aloud from the headlines—and to do it all with a geniality that verges on the jocose.

In fact, as a joker he is highly thought of. His humor depends almost entirely upon his personality; it is not, as the ladies agree, so much what Mr. Willis says as the way he says it. He has a trick of looking upon a sunny sky and saying: "A pretty nice day, if I do say so myself," which fairly convulses his hearers; while his dry dismissal of a rainy day as "Fine weather—for ducks" must really be heard to be appreciated.

He is in no way appalled by being oftentimes, for a stretch of midweek days, the only man about the porch; indeed, Mr. Willis seems to thrive on it. It is with enormous tact that he distributes his attentions, so that no one lady may read unintended meanings into them. Common talk has it that many wily spinsters have sought to draw him into matrimony, and some of the more optimistic element even hold to the idea that he will succumb yet.

But the summers flit by, changing Mr. Willis' hair from an interesting gray to a distinguished white, and he still doggedly remains a bachelor—thus conferring an inestimable boon upon some fortunate woman.

An Apartment House Anthology

THE GROUND FLOOR

Mr. and Mrs. Cuzzens much prefer living on the ground floor, they often say. Sometimes, when Mrs. Cuzzens is really warmed up to it, she puts the thing even stronger, and announces to the world that she would turn down flat all offers to live on an upper floor, in this or any other apartment house in New York City, even if you were to become desperate at her firmness and present her with an apartment rent free.

In the first place Mrs. Cuzzens is never wholly at her ease in an elevator. One of her liveliest anecdotes concerns an aunt of hers on her mother's side who was once a passenger in an elevator which stopped short midway between floors, and doggedly refused to move either up or down. Fortunately it all ended happily. Cries for help eventually caught the attention of the janitor—it seemed little short of providential that he had always had quite a turn for messing around with machinery—and he succeeded in regulating the power so that Mrs. Cuzzens' aunt reached her destination practically as good as new. But the episode made a terrific impression on Mrs. Cuzzens.

Of course it is rather dark on the ground floor, but Mr. and Mrs. Cuzzens regard that as one of the big assets of their apartment. Mrs. Cuzzens had a pretty nasty example of the effects of an oversunshiny place happen right in her own family. Her sister-in-law—not, Mrs. Cuzzens is careful to specify, the wife of the brother in the insurance business, but the wife of the brother who is on the road for a big tire concern, and is doing very well at it—hung some French-blue draperies at her living-room windows. And in less than a year the sunlight turned those curtains from their original color to an unwholesome shade of greenish yellow. Why, the change was so marked that many people, seeing them in this state, almost refused to believe that they had ever been blue. Mrs. Cuzzens' sister-in-law, as is perfectly understandable, was pretty badly broken up about it. Naturally Mrs. Cuzzens would hate to have a thing like that happen in her own home.

There is another advantage to living on the ground floor. The rent there is appreciably smaller than it is on the stories above, although Mr. and Mrs. Cuzzens seldom if ever work this into the conversation. Well, it is easy to overlook it, in the press of more important reasons for occupying their apartment.

A Mean Eye for Freak News

Mrs. Cuzzens has a fund, to date inexhaustible, of clean yet stimulating anecdotes, of which the one about the elevator and the one about the curtains are representative. She specializes in the unique. Hers is probably the largest collection in the country of stories of curious experiences, most of them undergone by members of her intimate circle. She is generous almost to a fault in relating them too. About any topic that happens to come up will be virtually certain to remind her of the funny thing that once happened to her Aunt Anna or the queer experience her Cousin Beulah had that time in Springfield.

Her repertory of anecdotes undoubtedly had much to do with attracting Mr. Cuzzens to her, for Mr. Cuzzens leans heavily to the out-of-the-ordinary himself. In his after-dinner reading of the newspaper he cheats a bit on the front-page items, just murmuring the headlines over, and gathering from them a rough idea—if you could really speak of Mr. Cuzzens as harboring a rough idea—of what is going on in the way of the conventional hold-ups and graft inquiries. But he casts a mean eye over the oddities in the day's news. He never misses the little paragraph about the man in Winsted, Connecticut, who intrusts a family of orphaned eggs to the care of a motherly cat, with gratifying results to one and all; or the report of the birth on an ocean liner, to a couple prominent in steerage circles, of a daughter, named Aquitania Wczlascki in commemoration of the event.

These specialties of Mr. and Mrs. Cuzzens work in together very prettily. They provide many an evening of instructive and harmless entertainment, while so far as expense goes, the only overhead is three cents for an evening paper.

Mr. Cuzzens puts on the slippers he got last birthday, and Mrs. Cuzzens unhooks a bit here and there as the evening wears on and she can feel reasonably sure that no one will drop in. As they sit about the grained-oak table in the glow of the built-in chandelier Mr. Cuzzens will read aloud some such fascinating bit of current history as the announcement of the birth, in Zanesville, Ohio, of a calf with two heads, both doing well. Mrs. Cuzzens will cap it with the description, guaranteed authentic, of a cat her mother's cousin once possessed which had a double set of claws on each foot.

Clever Mr. Cuzzens

When the excitement of this has died down Mr. Cuzzens will find an item reporting that a famous movie star has taken a load off the public's mind by having her eyelashes insured for one hundred thousand dollars. That will naturally lead his wife to tell the one about the heavy insurance her Uncle David carried, and the perfectly terrible red tape his bereaved family had to go through before they could collect.

After twenty minutes or so passed in their both listening attentively to Mrs. Cuzzens' recital, Mr. Cuzzens' eye, sharpened by years of training, will fall on an obscure paragraph telling how an apple tree near Providence was struck by lightning, which baked all the fruit. Mrs. Cuzzens will come right back with the story of how her little nephew once choked on a bit of the core of a baked apple, and the doctor said it might have been fatal if he had got there half an hour later.

And so it goes, back and forth, all evening long.

But the Cuzzens have their light side too. They often make a night of it at the movies. In fact Mr. Cuzzens, who is apt to be pretty slangy at times, says that he and the little woman are regular movie fans. Mr. Cuzzens loses himself so completely in the display that he reads each subtitle aloud. If it seems to him worthy, and if the operator leaves it on long enough, he reads it through twice. Both he and his wife take deeply to heart the news pictures, showing a grain elevator destroyed by fire in Florence, Georgia; or the living head of Uncle Sam formed by a group of Los Angeles school children.

Any trick effects on the screen leave Mrs. Cuzzens bewildered. She can never figure out how, for example, they make a man seem to walk up the side of a house. However, Mr. Cuzzens is awfully clever at all that sort of thing—more than one person has told him he should have gone in for mechanical work—and he explains the process on the way home.

Occasionally Mr. and Mrs. Cuzzens patronize the drama. There is a theater near them to which come plays almost direct from their run lower down on Broadway. The casts are only slightly changed; just substitutions in five or six of the leading roles. Both the Cuzzenses prefer comedies of the wholesome type, setting themselves on record as going to the theater to be amused. They say that they wouldn't go around the corner to see one of those unpleasant plays, for there is enough trouble in this world, anyway. And after all, who is there that can give them any argument on that one?

Now and then they devote an evening to cards, playing a little interfamily game with Mr. Cuzzens' married sister and her husband. The sport is kept absolutely clean. No money changes hands.

In the daytime, while Mr. Cuzzens is busy at his office—he is with a firm that makes bathroom scales, and it's as good as settled that they are going to do something really worth while for him the first of the year—Mrs. Cuzzens is occupied with her own activities. She often complains that the days aren't half long enough for her, but nothing really satisfactory has been done to remedy this, as yet. Much of her time is devoted to shopping, for there are always button molds to be matched, or a strip of linoleum for the washtubs to be priced, or a fresh supply of trick paper for the pantry shelves to be laid in. She is almost over-conscientious about her shopping. It is no unusual thing for her to spend an entire day in a tour of the department stores, searching for a particular design of snap fastener or the exact match of a spool of silk. She reaches home at the end of one of these days of toil pretty well done up, but still game.

And then there are her social duties. She is one of the charter members of a bridge club which numbers just enough to fill two tables comfortably. The club meets every fortnight, giving the players a chance to compete for the brocade-covered candy box—the winner must supply her own candy, which is no more than fair—or the six embroidered, guest-room-size handkerchiefs, which the hostess donates in the interest of sport.

During these functions Mrs. Cuzzens takes part in a great deal of tense conversation about the way the skirt was gathered over the hips and came down longer in front. She also gives, and receives, ideas on novel fillings for sandwiches, effective patterns for home-knit sweaters, and simple yet snappy dishes for Sunday-night supper.

Neither Mr. nor Mrs. Cuzzens is a native of New York. Up to a year or so after their marriage they helped swell the population of a town in Illinois which at the last census had upward of one hundred thousand inhabitants. They celebrate Old Home Week by a visit to the folks every year, but they congratulate themselves heartily that Mr. Cuzzens' business prevents their staying more than a week. For they agree that after eight years' residence in what Mr. Cuzzens aptly calls the big city they could never bring themselves to live in a small town again.

As Mrs. Cuzzens puts it, life in New York is so much broader.

THE SECOND FLOOR EAST

The Parmalees are always intending to move, but somehow they never get around to it. Several times Mrs. Parmalee has come out flat with the statement that the very next day she is going to look for an apartment farther downtown. But what with one thing and another coming up, she never seems to be able to make it.

Yet after all, as they argue, they might be a whole lot worse off than staying right where they are. Of course they are pretty far uptown, away from the theaters and restaurants; but everybody in their crowd, including themselves, has a car. So, to use Mr. Parmalee's very words, they should worry! It has often been remarked of Mr. Parmalee that it is not so much what he says as the way he says it.

Again, Mrs. Parmalee points out that it doesn't really matter much where they live, for they are hardly ever home, anyway. To which Mr. Parmalee retorts, just like a flash, that she has said a forkful!

And when you come right down to it, Mrs. Parmalee has seldom said a truer thing. It is indeed a cold night for the Parmalees when they have nothing to gather around but their own gas logs. The evening begins to hang heavy along around half past seven, and from then on things get no better rapidly.

The Parmalees are not ones to lose themselves in reading. Just let Mr. Parmalee see who won the first race, and give him a look at the financial page to ascertain whether Crucible Steel is plucking at the coverlet, and he is perfectly willing to call it a day as far as the pursuit of literature is concerned. As for Mrs. Parmalee, she masters the really novel murders and the better-class divorce cases, while for her heavier reading she depends on the current installment of the serial running in one of the more highly sexed magazines. That done with, she is through for the month.

Conversation could not be spoken of as a feature of the evening, either. Mr. Parmalee has been called, over and over again, a perfect scream when he is out on a party. But at home he doesn't really extend himself. A couple of half-hearted assents to his wife's comments on the shortcomings of the janitor and the unhealthful effects of such changeable weather—and that's, as someone has phrased it, that.

Life in the Parmalee Set

So you can see for yourself about the only thing left in the way of parlor entertainment is to come to the mat. The Parmalees' battles are not mere family events; they come more under the head of community affairs. The entire apartment house takes an interest, almost a pride in them. Take them when they get going really strong and you won't miss a syllable, even as far off as the top-floor apartment on the other side of the house. On a clear night with the wind in the right direction the people living three houses down have been able to enjoy every word of it.

The bouts almost invariably end in a draw. Mr. Parmalee, it is true, has a somewhat broader command of language than his wife, but she has perfected a short contemptuous laugh which is the full equivalent of a nasty crack. It leaves Mr. Parmalee practically flat, with nothing more inspired to offer than an "Is that so?" or a "Yeah, you're perfect—you are!"

But these sporting events take place only rarely. The Parmalees have little time to indulge in home pleasures. Theirs is a full and sociable life. Mr. Parmalee is in what he jocosely calls the automobile game, and most of his friends are engaged in the same pursuit. And as their wives are Mrs. Parmalee's intimates, you can just imagine how nice and clubby that makes everything.

Their social day begins around five o'clock, when the dozen or so members of their set meet at one or another's apartment, for cocktails. The Parmalee coterie has been seriously inconvenienced since prohibition went into what has been called effect. It means that they can no longer meet at a hotel or a restaurant, as they used to in the old days. It is badly out of their way to gather at someone's house, for it often involves their having to go all the way downtown again for dinner. But they have to make the best of it, just like you or me.

And it is comforting to know that the gentlemen still manage, as a rule, to pick up a little something here and there before they are met by what Mr. Parmalee calls, with screaming effect, their better seven-eighths. The ladies, collectively, are usually referred to, by their husbands and by one another, as the girls—which is something of an understatement.

Up to the time of meeting, Mrs. Parmalee, like the rest of the girls, has put in a crowded afternoon at a matinee, the hairdresser's or the manicure's; a blinding polish on the finger nails is highly thought of by both the male and female members of the Parmalees' set. There is usually a great deal of trying on to be done, also, which does much toward taking up Mrs. Parmalee's time and Mr. Parmalee's money. He likes to see his wife dressed as elaborately as the wives of his friends. He is pretty fairly reasonable about the price of her clothes, just so long as

they look as if they cost a lot. Neither of the Parmalees can see the point
of this thing of paying high prices for unobtrusive garments. What they
are after, Mr. Parmalee says, is their money's worth. As is only just.

Mrs. Parmalee and her friends dress with a soothing uniformity. They
all hold the same ideas about style; really you'd seldom find a more
congenial group in every way. All the girls, including Mrs. Parmalee,
are fundamentally large and are increasing in weight almost daily. They
are always going to start dieting next Monday.

In general style and get-up the girls resemble a group of very clever
female impersonators. They run to rather larger and more densely
plumed hats than the fashion absolutely insists upon, and they don't go
in for any of your dull depressing colors. Always heavily jeweled, they
have an adroit way of mingling an occasional imitation bracelet or necklace with the genuine articles, happily confident that the public will be
fooled. In the warm weather their dresses are of transparent material
about the arms and shoulders, showing provocative glimpses of very
pink ribbons and of lace that you could hardly tell from the real.

There is a great deal of hearty gayety at the afternoon meetings of
the crowd. You couldn't ask to see people among whom it is easier to
get a laugh. Any popular line, such as "You don't know the half of it,"
or "You'd be surprised," is a sure-fire hit, no matter in what connection
it is used. You might think that these jests would lose a little of their
freshness after months of repetition, but you were never so wrong in
your life. They never fail to go over big.

After a couple of hours of crackling repartee and whole-hearted
drinking the Parmalees and their crowd set out for dinner. They dine at
a downtown restaurant, if they plan going en masse to the theater afterwards. Otherwise they group themselves in their cars—most of the
motors, like Mr. Parmalee's, are perquisites of being in the automobile
game—and drive to some favorite road house, where they not only dine
but get in some really constructive drinking during the evening. Mr.
Parmalee is the life and soul of these parties. It is, his friends often say,
as good as a show to hear him kid the waiter.

Guess-What-It-Cost-Sports

Dancing occurs sporadically after dinner, but most of the time is devoted
to badinage. There is much good-natured banter, impossible to take in
bad part, about the attentions paid by various of the husbands to the
wives of various of the other husbands.

Often the conversation takes a serious turn among the men, as they tell about how much they had to pay for the last case of it. Stories are related of the staggering prices exacted for highballs at some restaurant where they will still listen to reason; and someone is sure to tell about the dinner he gave the night before, giving the menu in full detail, and as a climax calling upon his audience to guess what the grand total of the check was. These anecdotes are told with the pride that other sportsmen exhibit in telling about the size of the fish they caught.

The ladies spend what could be figured up to be the greater part of the evening in going out to the dressing room to keep their color schemes up to the mark.

In the warmer months the Parmalees make no radical change in their way of living. But though they do not go away for any long vacation they get a welcome glimpse of Nature by motoring to Long Beach for dinner three or four times a week with the rest of their crowd. They also manage to get a lot of wholesome country air and a refreshing eyeful of green grass down at the Belmont Park track.

What with all this talk of hard times and tight money wherever you go, it is cheering to see the Parmalees, who seem always to have it to spend. In his homey little chats with his wife Mr. Parmalee often gets quite worked up over where the money to meet their expenses is coming from; but he never lets it trouble him in his social life. Mr. Parmalee is a great advocate of being a good fellow when you have it. After all, as he has it figured out, the last places you can cut down are on theater tickets and restaurant checks and liquor.

It is also pleasant, in these days of change and restlessness, to think of the Parmalees going right along, never so much as thinking of wanting anything different. I wouldn't want to be the one to say that there is never just a dash of hard feeling between certain members of the crowd; the Parmalees never claimed to be any more than human. But such little differences as may spring up from time to time are easily dissolved in alcohol, and the crowd goes right on again, as usual.

After all, it takes Mr. Parmalee, with that wit of his, to sum up their whole existence in one clear-cut phrase. He says that it is a great life if you don't weaken.

THE SECOND FLOOR WEST

The minute you step into her apartment you realize that Mrs. Prowse is a woman of fine sensibilities. They stick out, as you might say, all over the place. You can see traces of them in the handmade candles dripping artistically over the polychrome candlesticks; in the single perfect blossom standing upright in a roomy bowl; in the polychrome bust of Dante on the mantel—taken, by many visitors, to be a likeness of William Gibbs McAdoo; most of all in the books left all about, so that Mrs. Prowse, no matter where she is sitting, always can have one at hand, to lose herself in. They are, mainly, collections of verse, both free and under control, for Mrs. Prowse is a regular glutton for poetry. She is liable to repeat snatches of it at almost any time. There are heavier volumes, too, just as there are greater depths to Mrs. Prowse. Henry Adams, Conan Doyle in his latter manner, Blasco Ibáñez, Clare Sheridan—all the boys and girls are represented.

Mrs. Prowse has not quite made up her mind as to whether it is more effective to have her books look well-thumbed or new and bright, though she rather inclines to the latter as being more decorative and less tiring. Most of the volumes are bound in red, which is, as Mrs. Prowse would put it, rather amusing with her orange curtains. If you were to pick up a book at random and go systematically through it you would find that, oddly enough, many of the pages, along after the middle, are uncut. But Mrs. Prowse's guests are not apt to go through her books, and the effect is, as I was saying only a minute ago, great.

It is not only literature that Mrs. Prowse patronizes. Beauty in any form gets a big hand from her. She can find it, too, in places where you or I would never think of looking. The delicate brown of a spoiled peach, the calm gray of a puddle on the sidewalk—such things never escape her.

Perhaps it is because she is so used to directing attention to things you might otherwise miss that Mrs. Prowse follows up the idea and coaxes you to notice those beauties which you couldn't very well avoid. She is always putting in a good word for the sunset or the sky or the moon, never letting slip an opportunity to get in a little press work for Nature.

She feels such things considerably more than most people. Sometimes, indeed, her appreciation of the beautiful stops just short of knocking her for what is academically called a goal. In the midst of a friendly conversation, or perhaps when it is her turn to bid in a bridge game, Mrs. Prowse will suddenly be rendered speechless, and lean tensely forward, gazing hungrily out the window at a lonely star or a wind-tossed cloud. She has quite a bad time in pulling herself together on these occasions. She must start perceptibly, look dazedly around the room, and press her hand against her eyes for a moment before she can return to the commonplace.

It is a blow to Mrs. Prowse and her husband that there has never been what Mrs. Prowse refers to as the patter of little feet about the house. But she manages to get a bit of comfort out of the situation. With no children to tie her down she is free to do all the worth-while things that beckon her. Look, for example, at what she accomplished during the past winter alone. She heard several lectures by visiting poets; went to two New Thought meetings; had her horoscope read and learned that her name should have been Valda; attended the annual luncheon of a club devoted to translating Browning into English; went to tea in Greenwich Village three times; took a lesson in lampshade making; heard a debate on whether or not a woman should take her husband's name, and what of it; and had her hair permanently waved.

But at that, Mrs. Prowse does not feel that her time is fully occupied. What she would really like, she admits, is to work, and work hard. And there are several jobs for which she is forced to confess that she is just as well fitted as the next one.

She would consider, for instance, giving readings from the modern poets or doing selections from Maeterlinck to a soft accompaniment on the piano. She has thought, and pretty seriously, too, of the stage, which, she can't help feeling, she could do much to raise from its present commercialism. It is really just a matter of ethics that keeps her from rushing right out and going to work at one of these positions. She doesn't feel that it would be quite fair for her to take the job away from someone who might be in real need of the money.

You wouldn't want to say right out that Mr. Prowse is not in sympathy with his wife's ideas, but then again you would scarcely be justified in saying that he cheered her on. Mr. Prowse is apt to let things take their course, and not do any worrying about them.

He is fond of his business, golf, the Yankees, meat cooked rather rare, musical comedies and his friends. Mrs. Prowse accompanies him to the theater, and often tells his friends that they must come up sometime soon. But there is about her at these times an air of gentle martyrdom. You'd almost think you could hear the roar of the waiting lions, she does it so realistically.

Mr. Prowse's policy of going about just as cheerfully as if his wife had no sensibilities whatever is a uniquely annoying one to her. Some of her most effective moods are absolutely frittered away on him. Mrs. Prowse has feelings which are almost always being severely injured; you run a chance of stepping on them if you come within ten feet of her. She is too delicately strung to come bluntly out and say what has hurt her. She seeks refuge in a brooding silence, and you must guess what it is all about.

Misunderstood but Faithful

Mr. Prowse is particularly bad at the game. He never seems to realize that anything is wrong. Sometimes she even has to call attention to her mental suffering and its cause. Even then he cannot be drawn into a really satisfactory battle. And it is, you will agree, practically impossible to work up any dramatic interest in married life when one of the principals won't take part in the big scenes.

It is little wonder that Mrs. Prowse, though never actually saying that her marriage is anything but happy, sometimes intimates that she is not always understood.

She has always been somewhat taken with the idea of having an assortment of tame young men about her—nothing really out of the way, of course, just have them come to tea, and take her to picture galleries, and send flowers, and maybe write verses, which she could drop where her husband would find them. She has even gone so far, in the privacy of her room, as to invent a rather nice little scene, in which she mapped out what she would say to some smitten young tea-hound should he become too serious. It is a credit to Mrs. Prowse to report that her answer was to the effect that she could never forget the vows she made to Mr. Prowse at the altar.

In all the books, as it is useless to tell you, it is no trouble at all for a married woman to gather a flock of attentive young men about her. But Mrs. Prowse has found it rather rough going. The young men don't seem to fall in with the idea. There was, it is true, a young man she met at a tea who was interested in interior decoration. In answer to her invitation he did call one afternoon—it was just by luck that she was wearing her beaded Georgette crêpe—and told her all about how she ought to live with purples. But when he found out that she really didn't feel they could have the living room done over for another year anyway he faded gently out of her life.

And that, as a matter of fact, was about as far as Mrs. Prowse ever got along those lines.

As is no more than you would expect, Mrs. Prowse admits but few to her circle of intimates. She is constantly being disappointed in people, finding out that they have no depths. Perhaps the sharpest blow, though one frequently experienced, is in having people whom she had accepted as kindred spirits turn out to be clever on the surface, but with no soul when you came right down to it. Mrs. Prowse often says that somehow she can never bring herself to be intimate with people who are only clever.

And that really works out awfully well, for it makes it mutual.

THE THIRD FLOOR EAST

You couldn't find, if you were to take the thing really to heart and make a search of the city, a woman who works harder, day in and day out, than Mrs. Amy. She says so herself.

In the first place there are two young Amys to occupy her attention. Everyone in the building is conscious of the presence of the two young Amys, but the Parmalees, in the apartment below, are most keenly aware of it.

It is in the fresh morning, when the Parmalees are striving to fulfill a normal desire for sleep, that the young Amys seem particularly near. The Amy children are early risers, and they have none of that morning languor from which office workers are so apt to suffer. Mrs. Parmalee, whose bedroom is directly beneath theirs, has often said that she would be the last one to feel any surprise if at any moment they were to come right on through.

Of course there is a resident nurse who looks after the little ones, but Mrs. Amy seems to find little or no relief in this. The nurse watches over them all day, and sleeps in the bed between their cribs at night, but, as Mrs. Amy says, she cannot worry over them as a mother would.

It is in worrying that Mrs. Amy accomplishes some of her most strenuous work. She confesses that there is scarcely a minute when her mind is at rest. Her worries even cut in on her nights, and she describes graphically how, tossing from side to side, she hears the clock strike twelve, half past twelve, one, half past one—sometimes it goes on that way up to three.

The past months have been especially trying to her, for the older Amy child has lately started school. He attends the public school around the corner, where his mother cannot help but feel that his time is devoted less to acquiring education than to running a splendid chance of contracting diseases and bringing them home, to share with his sister. During his first term Mrs. Amy has at different times detected in him symptoms of mumps, measles, chicken pox, scarlet fever, whooping cough and infantile paralysis. It is true that none of these ever developed, but that's not the point. The thing is that his mother was just as much worried as if he had had record cases of them all.

Then there are her household cares to prey upon her. Annie, a visiting maid, arrives before breakfast and stays till after dinner, but Mrs. Amy frequently sighs that she is far from satisfactory. Twice, now, her gravy has been distinctly lumpy, and just the other day she omitted to address Mrs. Amy as "ma'am" in answering her. There may be those who can throw off such things, but Mrs. Amy takes them hard. Only the fact that she worries so over the prospect of not being able to get another maid prevents her from marching right out into the kitchen and formally presenting Annie with the air.

It seems as if there were some great conspiracy to prevent things' breaking right for Mrs. Amy. Misfortunes pile up all through the day, so that by evening she has a long hard-luck story with which to greet Mr. Amy.

All through dinner she beguiles him with a recital of what she has had to endure that day—how the milkman didn't come and she was forced to send out to the grocer's; how she hurried to answer the telephone at great personal inconvenience, only to find it was someone for Annie; how the butcher had no veal cutlets; how the man didn't fix the pantry sink; how Junior refused to take his cereal; how the druggist omitted to send the soap she ordered; how—but you get the idea. There is always enough material for her to continue her story all through dinner and carry it over till bedtime with scarcely a repetition.

Mr. Amy would be glad to do what he could to lighten her burdens, but Mrs. Amy, though she all but hints in her conversation that many of her troubles may be laid at her husband's door, refuses to let him crash in on her sphere.

He has a confessed longing, for instance, to take the children out on the nurse's Sundays off. But Mrs. Amy cannot be induced to see it. Her feeling is that he would be just as apt as not to take them in a street car, or to the zoo, where they would get themselves simply covered with germs. As she says, she would worry so while they were gone that she would be virtually no good by the time they got back.

Mr. Amy often seeks to persuade his wife to join him in an evening's revelry at the movies or the theater, but she seldom consents. Her mind cannot come down to the pleasures before her when it is all taken up with what might be going on at home at that very minute. The house might burn up, the children might run temperatures, a sudden rain might come up and spoil the bedroom curtains; anything is liable to happen while she is away. So you can see how much there is on her side when she tells Mr. Amy that she feels safer at home.

Occasionally the Amys have a few friends in to dinner. Mrs. Amy obliges at these functions with one of her original monologues on the things that have gone wrong in her household during that day alone. They would entertain oftener, but what with the uncertainty of Annie's gravy and the vagaries of the tradespeople, the mental strain is too great for Mrs. Amy.

Mr. Amy often has to take a man out for dinner, in the way of business. He used to bring his business acquaintances to dine with him at home, but it got on Mrs. Amy's nerves to that degree that she had to put a stop to the practice.

She said it just bored her to death to have to sit there and listen to them talk about nothing but their business.

THE THIRD FLOOR WEST

What is really the keynote of the Tippetts' living room is the copy of the *Social Register* lying temptingly open on the table. It is as if Mrs. Tippett had been absorbed in it, and had only torn herself from its fascinating pages in order to welcome you.

It is almost impossible for you to overlook the volume, but if you happen to, Mrs. Tippett will help you out by pointing to it with an apologetic little laugh. No one knows better than she, she says, that its orange-and-black binding is all out of touch with the color scheme of the room; but, you see, she uses it for a telephone book and she is simply lost without it. Just what Mrs. Tippett does when she wants to look up the telephone number of her laundress or her grocer is not explained. And few people have the strength to go into the subject unassisted.

Some day when you happen to be reading the *Social Register* and come to the T's, you will find that Mr. and Mrs. Tippett's names are not there. Naturally you will take this for a printer's error. But it is only too intentional. The Tippetts do not yet appear in the register, though they have every hope of eventually making the grade.

As soon as Mrs. Tippett feels that the one about using the *Social Register* as a telephone book has sunk in, she will begin to laugh off her apartment. She says that it is the greatest joke, their living way up here in this funny old house that has been made over into flats. You have no idea how the Tippetts' friends simply howl at the thought of their living up on the West Side.

Whimsically Mrs. Tippett adds that what with so many social leaders moving down to Greenwich Village and over by the East River, it seems to her that the smart thing to do nowadays is to live in the most out-of-the-way place you can find.

Mr. Tippett will enlarge on the thing for you, if you stay until he comes home from business. Mr. Tippett solicits advertising for one of the excessively doggy magazines. There is not much in it, but it gives him an opportunity to come in contact with some awfully nice people. He will put over some perfect corkers about living so far uptown that he goes to work by the Albany boat; or he may even refer to his place of residence as Canada for you.

He bears out his wife's statements as to their friends' amusement at the apartment; in fact you gather from the chat that the Tippetts' chief reason for occupying the place is the good laugh it affords their friends.

The Tippetts are exceedingly well connected, as you will learn just as soon as they get a chance to tell you. Mr. Tippett's own cousin is not only included in the *Social Register* but has been referred to in the society weeklies—oh, not a breath of scandal, of course!—and often figures in the morning papers under the head of "among those present were." The Tippetts are deeply devoted to her. She is seldom absent from their conversation. If she is ill their calls are more regular than the doctor's. When she is away they carry her letters about and read them aloud to you at a moment's notice. Way back in midsummer they start planning her Christmas present.

The Tippetts are kept busy the year round. Sometimes Mrs. Tippett says wistfully she almost wishes they were not quite so much in demand. Almost every day she has to keep an appointment with some friend, to have tea at one of the more exclusive hotels. She keeps a sharp lookout for any smart people that may be hanging around, so that at dinner she can breathlessly tell her husband whom they were with and what they had on.

It is great fun to be out with Mrs. Tippett. She can tell you who everybody is, where they originated, whom they married, what their incomes are, and what is going the rounds about them. From a close following of the society papers she really feels that she knows intimately all those who figure in their columns. She goes right ahead with the idea, and speaks of them by the nicknames under which they appear in the society press.

Mrs. Tippett is inclined to be a trifle overpunctual; haven't you heard it called a good fault? She often arrives rather early for her tea engagements, and so, not being one to waste time, she dashes off a few notes on the hotel stationery while waiting.

Mr. Tippett—it may be from three years of close association—has got from her this admirable habit of catching up with his correspondence at odd times. For instance, when he drops in at some club, as the guest of a member, he frequently finds a few minutes to sit down at a desk and scribble off a letter on the convenient paper.

The Tippetts have many obligations to fulfill. They are so fond of Mr. Tippett's cousin that they try never to disappoint her when she invites them to anything. This means they must spend two or three week-ends at her country place, dine with her several times during the winter, and use her opera tickets once or even oftener. You'd really be amazed at the supply of subsequent conversation that the Tippetts can get out of any of these events.

Besides all this, they usually manage to attend one or two of the large charity affairs, for which tickets may be purchased at a not-so-nominal sum, and they always try to work in one session at the horse show.

This past season has been particularly crowded for Mrs. Tippett. Twice her volunteered aid has been accepted by a woman she met at Mr. Tippett's cousin's house, and she has helped arrange the counters at rummage sales. In short, things are coming along nicely with the Tippetts. They have every reason to be satisfied with their life.

Which is remarkably like Mr. Tippett's business, in that, though there is not much in it, it brings them in contact with some awfully nice people.

THE TOP FLOOR EAST

There was a time when Mrs. Huff kept her own carriage and lived in a three-story house with a conservatory between the dining room and the pantry. I don't feel that I am violating any confidence in telling you this, because Mrs. Huff would be the first one to say so.

All this was some time ago, when Mrs. Huff's daughter Emma was still in school—in private school, Mrs. Huff is careful to say. And one good look at Mrs. Huff's daughter Emma will convince you that her schooldays must have been indeed some time ago.

Shortly before Mr. Huff did what his widow refers to as passed on, the fortune began to meet with reverses, due mainly to Mr. Huff's conviction that he could put Wall Street in its place during his spare time. Mrs. Huff clung as long as possible to her own carriage and the three-story house with the conservatory, but she had eventually to let them go, in the order named. For a good many years, now, she has been settled in this apartment, in the midst of as much of her palmy-days furniture as could be wedged into the place.

But to Mrs. Huff those good old days are as yesterday. They are as fresh in her mind and her conversation. She can—does, even—go on for hours about how often they had to have the palms in the conservatory replaced, and how much they paid for the fountain, which represented a little girl and boy holding a pink iron umbrella over themselves—she can see it now. From there she drifts into reminiscences of all the trouble they had with drunken coachmen before they got their old Thomas, who was with them twelve years.

Mrs. Huff and her daughter live the calm and ladylike life befitting former conservatory owners. They are attended by one maid, Hannah by name, who was once Emma's nurse. She does the housework, washing, marketing and cooking; arranges Mrs. Huff's hair and corsets; remodels the ladies' clothes in the general direction of the styles; and is with difficulty persuaded to accept her wages each month—the same wages—which is rather a pretty touch of sentiment—as she was getting when she first entered Mrs. Huff's employ. As Mrs. Huff says, Hannah is really quite a help to them.

Mrs. Huff relies chiefly for her diversion on the funerals of her many acquaintances and connections. She reads the obituary column each morning in much the same spirit that other people look over the What Is Going on Today section. Occasionally if the day is fine and there is no really important funeral on hand she takes a little jaunt out to a favorite cemetery and visits various friends there.

Her minor amusements include calls on many sick and a few healthy acquaintances, and an occasional card party. Her stories of how often they had to change the palms and how much they paid for the fountain are the features of these affairs.

Miss Emma Huff suffers slightly from hallucinations; no, suffers is hardly the word. She manages to get quite a good time out of them.

She is under the impression that she is the desired of every man with whom she comes in contact. She is always arriving home fluttering from her adventure with the overzealous clerk in the shoe shop, or the bus driver who was too careful about helping her alight, or the floorwalker who almost insisted on taking her arm to direct her to the notions. Miss Huff never dares stay late at a friend's house, for fear some man may spring from the shadows and abduct her on the way home.

Between adventures Miss Huff does a good deal of embroidery. If there were ever a contest in putting cross-stitch baskets on guest towels she would be entered scratch. Also, she is a mean hand at copying magazine covers in water colors. Last year she made all her own Christmas cards, and if all goes well she plans doing it again next Christmas.

Once or twice it has been suggested by relatives or overintimate friends that it might be rather nice for Miss Huff to commercialize her talents. Or, if her feeling for art would not allow that, she might find some light and ladylike employment—just to pass the time, is always hastily added.

Mrs. Huff awards these advisers with what, in anybody else, would be a dirty look. She does not waste words to reply to any suggestion that a daughter of hers should enter the business world. For Mrs. Huff can never forget that she once kept her own carriage and lived in a three-story house with a conservatory between the dining room and the pantry.

THE TOP FLOOR WEST

There are, of course, a Mr. and a Mrs. Plank, but they sink indistinguishably into the background. Mrs. Plank may be roughly summarized as a woman who always knows what you ought to do for that indigestion, while Mr. Plank is continually going into a new business where "none of us is going to get much money at first."

The real life of the Plank party is Arlette—Mrs. Plank let herself go, for the only time in her life, in the choosing of her daughter's name.

Arlette is, at the present writing, crowding nineteen summers, and she looks every day of it. As for her mode of living, just ask anybody in the apartment house.

Arlette stopped school three years ago by her own request. She had no difficulty in convincing her mother that she had enough education to get along with anywhere. Mrs. Plank is a firm believer in the theory that, unless she is going to teach, there is no earthly use of a girl's wasting her time in going all through high school. Men, says Mrs. Plank—and she has been married twenty-one years, so who could be a better judge—do not select as their wives these women who are all full of education. So for the past three years Arlette's intellectual decks have been cleared for matrimony.

But Arlette has not yet given a thought to settling down into marriage. There was a short season when she thought rather seriously of taking up a screen career, after someone had exclaimed over the startling likeness between her and Louise Lovely. But so far she has taken it out in doing her hair in the accepted movie-star manner, to look as if it had been arranged with an egg-beater.

Most of Arlette's time is spent in dashing about in motors driven by young men of her acquaintance. The cars were originally designed to accommodate two people, but they rarely travel without seven or eight on board. These motors, starting out from or drawing up to the apartment house, with their precious loads of human freight, are one of the big spectacles of the block.

The Skids for Eddie

It is remarkable how without the services of a secretary Arlette prevents her dates from becoming mixed. She deftly avoids any embarrassing overlapping of suitors. Her suitors would, if placed end to end, reach halfway up to the Woolworth Tower and halfway back.

They are all along much the same design—slim, not too tall, with hair shining like linoleum. They dress in suits which, though obviously new, have the appearance of being just outgrown, with half belts, and lapels visible from the back.

The average duration of Arlette's suitors is five weeks. At the end of that time she hands the favored one a spray of dewy raspberries and passes on to the next in line.

The present incumbent, Eddie to his friends, has lasted rather longer than usual. His greatest asset is the fact that he is awfully dry. He has a way of saying "absotively" and "posolutely" that nearly splits Arlette's sides. When he is introduced he says, with a perfectly straight face, "You're pleased to meet me," and Arlette can hardly contain herself. He interpolates a lot of Ed Wynn's stuff into the conversation, and Arlette thinks it is just as good as the original, if not better.

Then, too, he knows a perfectly swell step. You take three to the right, then three to the left, then toddle, then turn suddenly all the way around and end with a dip; the effect is little short of professional.

But Arlette has lately met a young man who has his own car and can almost always get his father's limousine when he takes you to the theater. Also, his father owns a chain of moving-picture houses, and he can get a pass for her.

So it looks from here as if the skids were all ready to be applied to Eddie.

Mrs. Plank worries a bit over her daughter's incessant activities. She hears stories of the goings-on of these modern young people that vaguely trouble her, and she does wish that Arlette would take more rest. Naturally, though, she hesitates to bring the matter to her daughter's attention. Occasionally she goes so far as to hint that Arlette might take a little interest in watching her do the housework, so that she can pick up some inside stuff on household matters that might be useful in her married life.

For all Mrs. Plank wants, she says, is to live to see her daughter making some good man happy.

Arlette's ideas, now, seem to be more along the lines of making some good men happy.

The Saturday Evening Post, August 20, 1921

Men I'm Not Married To

No matter where my route may lie,
   No matter whither I repair,
In brief—no matter how or why
   Or when I go, the boys are there.
On lane and byways, street and square,
   On alley, path and avenue,
They seem to spring up everywhere—
   The men I am not married to.

I watch them as they pass me by;
   At each in wonderment I stare,
And, "but for heaven's grace," I cry,
   "There goes the guy whose name I'd wear!"
They represent no species rare,
   They walk and talk as others do;
They're fair to see—but only fair—
   The men I am not married to.

I'm sure that to a mother's eye
   Is each potentially a bear.
But though at home they rank ace-high,
   No change of heart could I declare.
Yet worry silvers not their hair;
   They deck them not with sprigs of rue.
It's curious how they do not care—
   The men I am not married to.

L'Envoi

In fact, if they'd a chance to share
   Their lot with me, a lifetime through,
They'd doubtless tender me the air—
   The men I am not married to.

FREDDIE

"Oh, boy!" people say of Freddie. "You just ought to meet him some time! He's a riot, that's what he is—more fun than a goat."

Other, and more imaginative souls play whimsically with the idea, and say that he is more fun than a barrel of monkeys. Still others go at the thing from a different angle, and refer to him as being as funny as a crutch. But I always feel, myself, that they stole the line from Freddie. Satire—that is his dish.

And there you have, really, one of Freddie's greatest crosses. People steal his stuff right and left. He will say something one day, and the next it will be as good as all over the city. Time after time I have gone to him and told him that I have heard lots of vaudeville acts using his comedy, but he just puts on the most killing expression, and says, "Oh, say not suchly!" in that way of his. And, of course, it gets me laughing so that I can't say another word about it.

That is the way he always is, just laughing it off when he is told that people are using his best lines without even so much as word of acknowledgment. I never hear any one say "There is such a thing as being too good-natured" but that I think of Freddie.

You never knew any one like him on a party. Things will be dragging along, the way they do at the beginning of the evening, with the early arrivals sitting around asking one another have they been to anything good at the theatre lately, and is it any wonder there is so much sickness around with the weather so changeable. The party will be just about plucking at the coverlet when in will breeze Freddie, and from that moment on the evening is little short of a whirlwind. Often and often I have heard him called the life of the party, and I have always felt that there is not the least bit of exaggeration in the expression.

What I envy about Freddie is that poise of his. He can come right into a room full of strangers, and be just as much at home as if he had gone through grammar school with them. He smashes the ice all to nothing the moment he is introduced to the other guests by pretending to misunderstand their names, and calling them something entirely different, keeping a perfectly straight face all the time as if he never realized there was anything wrong. A great many people say he puts them in mind of Buster Keaton that way.

He is never at a loss for a screaming crack. If the hostess asks him to have a chair Freddie comes right back at her with "No, thanks; we have chairs at home." If the host offers him a cigar he will say just like

a flash, "What's the matter with it?" If one of the men borrows a cigarette and a light from him Freddie will say in that dry voice of his,
"Do you want the coupons too?" Of course his wit is pretty fairly
caustic, but no one ever seems to take offense at it. I suppose there is
everything in the way he says things.

And he is practically a whole vaudeville show in himself. He is never
without a new story of what Pat said to Mike as they were walking
down the street, or how Abie tried to cheat Ikie, or what old Aunt
Jemima answered when she was asked why she had married for the fifth
time. Freddie does them in dialect, and I have often thought it is a
wonder that we don't all split our sides. And never a selection that every
member of the family couldn't listen to, either—just healthy fun.

Then he has a repertory of song numbers, too. He gives them without
accompaniment, and every song has a virtually unlimited number of
verses, after each one of which Freddie goes conscientiously through the
chorus. There is one awfully clever one, a big favorite of his, with the
chorus rendered a different way each time—showing how they sang it
when grandma was a girl, how they sing it in gay Paree and how a
cabaret performer would do it. Then there are several along the general
lines of "Casey Jones," two or three about Negroes who specialized on
the banjo, and a few in which the lyric of the chorus consists of the
syllables "ha, ha, ha." The idea is that the audience will get laughing
along with the singer.

If there is a piano in the house Freddie can tear things even wider
open. There may be many more accomplished musicians, but nobody
can touch him as far as being ready to oblige goes. There is never any
of this hanging back waiting to be coaxed or protesting that he hasn't
touched a key in months. He just sits right down and does all his specialties for you. He is particularly good at doing "Dixie" with one hand
and "Home, Sweet Home" with the other, and Josef Hofmann himself
can't tie Freddie when it comes to giving an imitation of a fife-and-drum
corps approaching, passing, and fading away in the distance.

But it is when the refreshments are served that Freddie reaches the
top of his form. He always insists on helping to pass plates and glasses,
and when he gets a big armful of them he pretends to stumble. It is as
good as a play to see the hostess' face. Then he tucks his napkin into
his collar, and sits there just as solemnly as if he thought that were the
thing to do; or perhaps he will vary that one by folding the napkin into
a little square and putting it carefully in his pocket, as if he thought it
was a handkerchief. You just ought to see him making believe that
he has swallowed an olive pit. And the remarks he makes about the

food—I do wish I could remember how they go. He is funniest, though, it seems to me, when he is pretending that the lemonade is intoxicating, and that he feels its effects pretty strongly. When you have seen him do this it will be small surprise to you that Freddie is in such demand for social functions.

But Freddie is not one of those humorists who perform only when out in society. All day long he is bubbling over with fun. And the beauty of it is that he is not a mere theorist, as a joker; practical—that's Freddie all over.

If he isn't sending long telegrams, collect, to his friends, then he is sending them packages of useless groceries, C.O.D. A telephone is just so much meat to him. I don't believe any one will ever know how much fun Freddie and his friends get out of Freddie's calling them up and making them guess who he is. When he really wants to extend himself he calls up in the middle of the night, and says that he is the wire tester. He uses that one only on special occasions, though. It is pretty elaborate for everyday use.

But day in and day out, you can depend upon it that he is putting over some uproarious trick with a dribble glass or a loaded cigar or a pencil with a rubber point; and you can feel completely sure that no matter where he is or how unexpectedly you may come upon him, Freddie will be right there with a funny line or a comparatively new story for you. That is what people marvel over when they are talking about him—how he is always just the same.

It is right there, really, that they put their finger on the big trouble with him.

But you just ought to meet Freddie sometime. He's a riot, that's what he is—more fun than a circus.

MORTIMER

Mortimer had his photograph taken in his dress suit.

RAYMOND

So long as you keep him well inland Raymond will never give any trouble. But when he gets down to the seashore he affects a bathing suit fitted with little sleeves. On wading into the sea ankle-deep he leans over and carefully applies handfuls of water to his wrists and forehead.

CHARLIE

It's curious, but no one seems to be able to recall what Charlie used to talk about before the country went what may be called, with screaming effect, dry. Of course there must have been a lot of unsatisfactory weather even then, and I don't doubt that he slipped in a word or two when the talk got around to the insanity of the then-current styles of women's dress. But though I have taken up the thing in a serious way, and have gone about among his friends making inquiries, I cannot seem to find that he could ever have got any farther than that in the line of conversation. In fact, he must have been one of those strong silent men in the old days.

Those who have not seen him for several years would be in a position to be knocked flat with a feather if they could see what a regular little chatterbox Charlie has become. Say what you will about prohibition— and who has a better right?—you would have to admit, if you knew Charlie, that it has been the making of him as a conversationalist.

He never requires his audience to do any feeding for him. It needs no careful leading around of the subject, no tactful questions, no well-timed allusions, to get him nicely loosened up. All you have to do is say good evening to him, ask him how everybody over at his house is getting along, and give him a chair—though this last is not essential—and silver-tongued Charlie is good for three hours straight on where he is getting it, how much he has to pay for it, and what the chances are of his getting hold of a couple of cases of genuine pinch-bottle, along around the middle of next week. I have known him to hold entire dinner parties spellbound, from cocktails to finger bowls, with his monologue.

Now I would be well down among the last when it came to wanting to give you the impression that Charlie has been picked for the All-American alcoholic team. Despite the wetness of his conversation he is just a nice, normal, conscientious drinker, willing to take it or let it alone, in the order named. I don't say he would not be able to get along without it, but neither do I say that he doesn't get along perfectly splendidly with it. I don't think I ever saw any one who could get as much fun as Charlie can out of splitting the Eighteenth Amendment with a friend.

There is a glamour of vicarious romance about him. You gather from his conversation that he comes into daily contact with any number of picturesque people. He tells about a friend of his who owns three untouched bottles of the last absinthe to come into the country; or a lawyer he knows, one of whose grateful clients sent him six cases of champagne in addition to his fee; or a man he met who had to move to the country in order to have room for his Scotch.

Charlie has no end of anecdotes about the interesting women he meets, too. There is one girl he often dwells on, who, if you only give her time, can get you little bottles of Chartreuse, each containing an individual drink. Another gifted young woman friend of his is the inventor of a cocktail in which you mix a spoonful of orange marmalade. Yet another is the justly proud owner of a pet marmoset which becomes the prince of good fellows as soon as you have fed him a couple of teaspoonfuls of gin.

It is the next best thing to knowing these people yourself to hear Charlie tell about them. He just makes them live.

It is wonderful how Charlie's circle of acquaintances has widened during the last two years; there is nothing so broadening as prohibition. Among his new friends he numbers a conductor on a train that runs down from Montreal, and a young man who owns his own truck, and a group of chaps who work in drug stores, and I don't know how many proprietors of homey little restaurants in the basements of brownstone houses.

Some of them have turned out to be but fair-weather friends, unfortunately. There was one young man, whom Charlie had looked upon practically as a brother, who went particularly bad on him. It seems he had taken a pretty solemn oath to supply Charlie, as a personal favor, with a case of real Gordon, which he said he was able to get through his high social connections on the other side. When what the young man called a nominal sum was paid, and the case was delivered, its bottles were found to contain a nameless liquor, though those of Charlie's friends who gave it a fair trial suggested Storm King as a good name for the brand. Charlie has never laid eyes on the young man from that day to this. He is still unable to talk about it without a break in his voice. As he says—and quite rightly, too—it was the principle of the thing.

But for the most part his new friends are just the truest pals a man ever had. In more time than it takes to tell it, Charlie will keep you right abreast with them—sketch in for you how they are, and what they are doing, and what their last words to him were.

But Charlie can be the best of listeners, too. Just tell him about any little formula you may have picked up for making it at home, and you will find the most sympathetic of audiences, and one who will even go to the flattering length of taking notes on your discourse. Relate to him tales of unusual places where you have heard that you can get it or of grotesque sums that you have been told have been exchanged for it, and he will hang on your every word, leading you on, asking intelligent questions, encouraging you by references to like experiences of his own.

But don't let yourself get carried away with success and attempt to branch out into other topics. For you will lose Charlie in a minute if you try it.

But that, now I think of it, would probably be the very idea you would have in mind.

LLOYD

Lloyd wears washable neckties.

HENRY

You would really be surprised at the number of things that Henry knows just a shade more about than anybody else does. Naturally he can't help realizing this about himself, but you mustn't think for a minute that he has let it spoil him. On the contrary, as the French so well put it. He has no end of patience with others, and he is always willing to oversee what they are doing, and to offer them counsel. When it comes to giving his time and his energy there is nobody who could not admit that Henry is generous. To a fault, I have even heard people go so far as to say.

If, for instance, Henry happens to drop in while four of his friends are struggling along through a game of bridge he does not cut in and take a hand, thereby showing up their playing in comparison to his. No, Henry draws up a chair and sits looking on with a kindly smile. Of course, now and then he cannot restrain a look of pain or an exclamation of surprise or even a burst of laughter as he listens to the bidding, but he never interferes. Frequently, after a card has been played, he will lean over and in a good-humoured way tell the player what he should have done instead, and how he might just as well throw his hand down then and there, but he always refuses to take any more active part in the game. Occasionally, when a uniquely poisonous play is made, I have seen Henry thrust his chair aside and pace about in speechless excitement, but for the most part he is admirably self-controlled. He always leaves with a few cheery words to the players, urging them to keep at it and not let themselves get discouraged.

And that is the way Henry is about everything. He will stroll over to a tennis court, and stand on the side lines, at what I am sure must be great personal inconvenience, calling words of advice and suggestion for sets at a stretch. I have even known him to follow his friends all the way around a golf course, offering constructive criticism on their form as he goes. I tell you, in this day and generation, you don't find many people who will go as far out of their way for their friends as Henry does. And I am far from being the only one who says so, too.

I have often thought that Henry must be the boy who got up the idea of leaving the world a little better than he found it. Yet he never crashes in on his friends' affairs. Only after the thing is done does he point out to you how it could have been done just a dash better. After you have signed the lease for the new apartment Henry tells you where you could have got one cheaper and sunnier; after you are all tied up with the new firm Henry explains to you where you made your big mistake in leaving the old one.

It is never any news to me when I hear people telling Henry that he knows more about more things than anybody they ever saw in their lives.

And I don't remember ever having heard Henry give them any argument on that one.

JOE

After Joe had had two cocktails he wanted to go up and bat for the trap drummer. After he had had three he began to get personal about the unattractive shade of the necktie worn by the strange man at the next table.

OLIVER

Oliver had a way of dragging his mouth to one side, by means of an inserted forefinger, explaining to you, meanwhile, in necessarily obscured tones, the work which his dentist had just accomplished on his generously displayed back teeth.

ALBERT

Albert sprinkled powdered sugar on his sliced tomatoes.

The Saturday Evening Post, June 17, 1922

Welcome Home

If at any time you happened to be hunting around for an average New York couple you couldn't make a better selection than my friends the Lunts. They are just about as average as they come.

The Lunts may not go so far as to say that they helped buy the island from the Indians, but they do feel that they have every reason to regard themselves as dyed-in-the-wool New Yorkers. Mr. Lunt has been living here for going on fourteen years now, and Mrs. Lunt is virtually a native, having come on from the West with her family that time her father got the good offer, when she was twelve years old.

I shouldn't want to come out with the bald statement that the Lunts live as quiet a life as any couple in the city. You have to be pretty well up on your statistics before you can go around talking that way. But I will step right up and say that Mr. and Mrs. Joseph Watson Lunt plod along in about as homey and unspectacular a manner as you would want to see. In fact, their high point in riotous living was touched five years ago, when Mr. Lunt nerved himself up definitely to take the plunge and sign it J. Watson.

In the first place, they are not exactly in the position of having it to throw around. Mr. Lunt is in the advertising business, and anybody will be glad to tell you where that was shot to, during the past few seasons. He is generally considered quite a boy in his own line of work. It is practically an open secret that it was he who thought up the slogan, "Good-by, Button Troubles," for the Anti-Button Suit people; though it is perhaps not so widely known that the famous line, "Ask the Prince of Wales," used by the Never-Slip Sleeve-Garter Company, was one of his brain children. He would be the first to say that he deserves no particular credit; it is simply that his mind happens to work that way.

THRILLING HOURS WITH RADIO

He had been connected with a small and determinedly doggy advertising agency for some time. There was a stretch of months when the phrase "connected with" would have been putting it rather too firmly. It would have been more in line with the facts to say that he was hanging on to the agency. For things down there were looking so thin that the office force regarded itself as but one jump ahead of the boys on the park benches. Indeed, Mr. Lunt got into the habit—from which he will doubtless never wholly recover—of looking on every pay envelope that did not contain the official raspberry as just so much velvet.

Even now that business is beginning to get the roses back in its cheeks, Mr. Lunt is scarcely able to present any parks to the city. His is what you could call a fair salary, but couldn't really hail as fair enough. The Lunts make both ends meet, and let it pass at that. There is no chance of tying them in a large and dashing bow. What with the rent of the four-room apartment, and the wages of the handmaiden who returns to the bosom of her family every evening, Mr. Lunt is glad to be able to call it a month twelve times a year.

So you will be among the first to see for yourself that the Lunts can contribute little towards keeping the white lights blazing on Broadway of an evening. Eleven o'clock usually finds the apartment dark, and Mr. and Mrs. Lunt fairly into the swing of the night's gay round of sleep.

Now and then they run so wild as to go to a movie—the movie house around the corner from them gets all the big feature pictures only a month or so after the Broadway film palaces are through with them, and you are pretty nearly always sure of a seat, if you make the theater by quarter past seven—and twice a month, say, they attend, in a body, some show that they have heard highly spoken of by their friends. The Lunts conscientiously read the newspaper dramatic reviews every morning, and ache for them when they are out of town and unable to procure a New York paper. But they regard them purely as reading matter. When they want dramatic criticism they ask their friends.

Occasionally they break out in a game of bridge with some other average New York couple, for a stake of half a cent a point. The losing side carefully copies down the sum lost on a slip of paper, and carries it over till the next meet, to be played off then.

The radio, which has recently come into their lives, has done great things for the Lunts. Now that Mr. Lunt has, with considerable difficulty and frequent muttered mention of biblical characters, got the apparatus installed, they are never at a loss for an evening's stimulating pleasure. There they can sit, in their own living room, and listen to some kindly soul over in the Newark broadcasting station tell "How Johnny Musk-Ox Went to Old Daddy West Wind's Party," or they can hear a lecture on "Diseases of the Cranberry and How to Fight Them," that keeps them right on the edge of their seats. As Mrs. Lunt says, she hasn't the faintest idea what science is going to do next.

Every few weeks Mrs. Lunt puts on the black evening dress she picked up when one of the Fifty-seventh Street shops was having its sale, and Mr. Lunt dons his vintage dinner coat, and they go forth to a social gathering at the apartment of one of their friends. Conservative dancing is indulged in, to the strains of the phonograph. Between dances the ladies exchange amusing anecdotes of the bright things said by their children and the stupid things got off by their maids, while the gentlemen punctiliously offer one another cigarettes and solicitously ask if it doesn't seem to be getting pretty warm. Over the refreshments things open up appreciably, and there is much hearty laughter over references to purely local incidents. Any strangers to the crowd who happen to have been invited can do little about helping the banter along.

On Sunday mornings Mr. Lunt gets in a lot of good wholesome sleep, so that he will be in condition to grapple with the puzzle page of the Sunday paper. Once that is off his mind he and his wife make an exhaustive study of the newspapers. Then Mrs. Lunt gets caught up on her correspondence, and Mr. Lunt, with the interest of the dilettante, endeavors to make the mainspring of the living-room clock listen to reason, or has a try at nailing together the place where the bookshelves have sprung.

It sometimes happens that one of their more prosperous friends asks the Lunts to make a day of it and come for a motor ride in the country. The friends would be surprised did they know what a treat a Sunday in the country isn't, to the Lunts. As Mr. Lunt often says, there is no use talking, he likes his Sundays at home.

GAYETY ALWAYS ON TAP

Mrs. Lunt gets in a good deal more social life than her husband, for she can work it in in the afternoons. Intimates gather at her apartment, or she visits one of theirs, to put in a few rubbers of bridge or a few yards of sewing on lace-edged crêpe-de-chine underwear. In either case the afternoon comes to a climax in watercress sandwiches and tea.

You know, the curious thing about the Lunts, and the thing, perhaps, that goes farthest toward making them an average New York couple, is that they are not at all worked up over the calm of their existence. I don't recall ever having seen their eyes brim with bitter tears over all the widely advertised gayety going on about them, in which they have no part. In fact, they really seem to go ahead on the idea that they are sitting comparatively pretty.

There is to them, as to the other average New Yorkers, something strangely reassuring in knowing that the hotels, the theaters, the dance clubs and the restaurants are always right there, ready and waiting for the time when the Lunts may have the price and the inclination to give the gay life a fair trial. In the same way there is a pleasant security in the thought of all the museums and the art galleries, the concert halls and the lecture chambers, always in action. The Lunts are easily the next-to-the-last people to patronize them, but there is something soothing in the knowledge that, in case they should ever see the light, there they are, all set. It gives them a feeling like having money in the bank. Or at least something like that.

Once a year, however, the Lunts lay aside the cloistered life, and burn up Broadway. This is on the occasion of the annual metropolitan visit of Mr. Lunt's Aunt Caroline, from the town where he spent his boyhood days.

There are times when, dreaming idly in the gloaming, one finds oneself drifting into wondering why, barring acts of God and business trips, Mr. Lunt's Aunt Caroline should ever feel called upon to come to New York.

Of course she does want to see her nephew and niece, whom she groups under the general heading of "those poor children"—a little phrase of hers which does not imply that the Lunts are in a thin way financially or that they are in bad health; it simply expresses her kindly pity for them because they live in New York. But even allowing for her natural desire to be with her dear ones, it does not seem that the sacrifice involved is worth it.

For Aunt Caroline seems to have a peculiarly poisonous time of it in the big city. She is unalterably against New York—a feeling which she splits with the something over seventy thousand transients that daily knock at its portals. The city-by-the-Hudson's hem, all right to visit is to them, and it is nothing more.

Like them, Aunt Caroline sees in Manhattan nothing but a mammoth reminder of how much better things are done back home. The distress which her annual visit causes her would make the suffering in the Near East look like so much spirit of Mardi Gras.

And Aunt Caroline is not the girl to suffer in silence. She isn't going to store it up in her mind, to brood over during the long winter evenings. She comes clean with it then and there. It's a rather nice idea, too, because it gives her something to chat about all through her visit.

The big object of Aunt Caroline's journey to New York seems to be to put the city in short pants, if you might say so. The moment she sets foot in the Grand Central Terminal she compares it audibly and unfavorably with the new railroad station back home, built as soon as a decent interval had elapsed after the old one burned to the ground. Escorted to the street by Mrs. Lunt, Aunt Caroline, after becoming promptly and passionately in the wrong as to which is up town and which down, gazes tolerantly up at the buildings and is reminded to tell, at considerable length, of the new six-story Beehive Store recently erected at the corner of Elm Street and Maple Avenue. The taxicab in which she presently finds herself but brings back audible memories of the superior qualities of the jitney line owned by that nice Mr. Gooch, who used to own the livery stable over on State Street.

A CRITICAL GUEST

In the short ride to the Lunt apartment she manages to work in at least three times the line about "New York may be all right for a visit, but I wouldn't live here if you gave me the place." That is Aunt Caroline's favorite, really, though she is only slightly less fond of that other sparkler of hers—"We live, back home; you exist, in New York."

Epigrammatic—that's Aunt Caroline down to the ground. There can be little doubt but that she picked up the mantle of Wilde somewhere.

Aunt Caroline stays with the Lunts but three or four days, but in that brief while she tears their bank roll wide open. She is not the sort of visitor who gets along on a couple of bus rides, a jaunt up the Statue of Liberty, a ramble through the Aquarium and a trip to the Hippodrome, and then returns home, broadened with travel.

She goes in for being entertained on a large scale. In the first place, she wants—and only natural too—to mingle with the pleasure seekers and learn what goes on in what she looks upon as the Hollywood of the Atlantic Coast. And in the second place—or no, on thinking it over, it would really be better to put this one first—Mr. Lunt has an admirably normal desire to demonstrate to Aunt Caroline, and thus vicariously to the inhabitants of his native town, that he has got along so spectacularly since leaving the village green that money is little, if any, object to him.

And then, besides, Mr. and Mrs. Lunt do want to give Aunt Caroline just the best of good times. I keep forgetting that one.

So every evening of her stay Aunt Caroline and the Lunts attend a highly popular play—naturally Aunt Caroline wants to see the big successes—sitting somewhere along about the fifth row, center. As a tribute to his personality the ticket agency has taken Mr. Lunt in on the inside, and let twenty-five dollars cover the three tickets.

During the play's unfolding, Aunt Caroline sets up an opposition entertainment—a discourse in full detail on the higher merits of the productions given weekly by the Florence Hemingway–Lester De Vaux stock company at the Majestic Theater back home. Those about her gather from her remarks that people from all over the world flock there, as to Oberammergau. She frequently wishes aloud that Mr. and Mrs. Lunt could see Miss Hemingway's and Mr. De Vaux's company present *Lord and Lady Algy*. She even volunteers, out of the goodness of her heart, to send them word next time the comedy is revived, so that they can abandon everything and rush right up.

AUNTY MAKES THE MONEY FLY

Before the theater the Lunts, as is only fitting, have taken Aunt Caroline to dine at the Biltmore, the Knickerbocker Grill, the Commodore or the Pennsylvania; even on their annual outing they seldom feel quite up to making the grade at the Plaza or the Ritz.

Aunt Caroline takes it all pretty personally. She looks coldly about at the neighboring diners, and remarks that if you want to see a really stylish woman you should hurry and meet Mrs. Doctor Robbins, who lives in one of those new two-family houses out by Oak Park, and has every single stitch made in the house by a seamstress.

She all but runs a temperature over the prices that are demanded for the dishes she selects. But she courageously goes right ahead and orders them anyway, a dogged look about her mouth as if to say, "I'll put this management in its place!" I forget just who it was that got the bill passed through the Senate making it a misdemeanor for Aunt Caroline to eat anything but such foods as lobster thermidor, breast of guinea hen under glass, hearts of palm and baked Alaska when she is dining out. Certainly she never takes a chance on breaking the law.

During dinner she beguiles her host and hostess by comparing the food before her with that served by the Misses Amy and Lucretia Crouch at Ye Signe of Ye Greene Teapotte, which they are conducting over in the old Lewis house on Evergreen Street—food which, she asserts, is the finest that has ever passed her lips.

After the theater, Mr. Lunt suggests that they drop in at a restaurant or a roof show for a while. He does it awfully well too; you'd think he did it ten or twelve times every year of his life. If he is a little slow on his cue Aunt Caroline helps him along with the laughing suggestion that they go to one of those cabaret places, which is the name that she has got up for them. As is but natural, she wants to see what all the talk is about.

Established at a ringside table, for which Mr. Lunt has helped a head waiter on towards an independent old age, Aunt Caroline again goes the full course, for she has always had a fine appetite, thank goodness. While she sups she gives a talk on how terrible it is for New Yorkers to eat so much rich stuff late at night, and how the only thing she really enjoys at such an hour is the hot chocolate served at McGovern's drug store at the corner of Poplar Street. This light-hearted chatter makes it easier for Mr. Lunt to face the check for nineteen dollars and sixty cents.

With no kindly eye Aunt Caroline looks on the seething throng of exhilarated transients worming their way around the dance floor, and states that she simply does not know what the New People are thinking of, she declares she doesn't.

Nor is she overcome when the professional part of the entertainment is in progress and the spotlights are turned on some of America's Finest, costumed as the Twelve Leading Nonalcoholic Beverages or the Eight Most Popular Winter Resorts, or something along those lines—weaving sinuously around the tables and making a strong personal appeal to the gentlemen nearest them. Aunt Caroline blots out their singing by her somewhat protracted account of the much prettier divertisement given by the young ladies of the Lazy Daisy Club back home, who gave A Pageant of America's Heroines to raise money for new weather strips for the clubhouse.

The music of one of the highest-paid living orchestras only serves to call to her mind what a pleasurable experience it would be for the Lunts to hear Mrs. Topping's two boys, Earl and Royal, perform "The Jolly Haymakers' Quickstep," lively but not too fast, on mandolin and piano.

Time flies over those reminiscences, and it is not till somewhere around two o'clock that Aunt Caroline and the Lunts arrive at the silent apartment. Aunt Caroline frequently remarks on the way up that it is a mystery to her how New Yorkers stand the pace.

During the days of the visit Mrs. Lunt conducts her guest to a matinée or two, so that she may have other opportunities to get in press work for the actors back home. The remainder of the time she shops, piloted by Mrs. Lunt.

Aunt Caroline does not trust the New York shops for important things like hats or dresses or shoes. The best they can hope to do for her is to supply her with hooks and eyes, sewing cotton and assorted needles. One year she did go so far as to give one of the larger department stores a chance to sell her a hair net. But she found it so far below the standard of those sold at G. F. Newins' store on Spruce Street that ever since she has made a point of bringing quantities of hair nets down with her when she comes to New York. Nor has she ever allowed the unfortunate occurrence to die away in silence.

Yet Aunt Caroline likes to tour the more exclusive shops. It gives her many a laugh to look over the hats and gowns, and tell how much cheaper and more out of the ordinary are those shown by Miss Emma— Miss Emma Mullitt, in private life, and from a very nice family too—in her shops next door to the library on Grove Street.

VISITING AUNT CAROLINE

It is a wearing thing, this shopping, and Aunt Caroline is glad to drop in with Mrs. Lunt at Sherry's or the Ritz, afterwards. Over the teacups, between intervals of glancing about and remarking that she hasn't seen what she calls a really good-looking woman since she came to New York, she tells about the perfectly delicious tea—not anything like this—that you can get at the new Cozy Tea Room back home.

And so, what with one thing and another, the hours dash by, as on their hands and knees, and the time comes for Aunt Caroline to leave the white-light district flat for another year. Tearful at leaving those poor children behind her, she kisses her nephew and niece, urges them as a personal favor to her to take care of themselves, and departs for the great open spaces where men are men and there are no *couvert* charges, leaving the Lunts to make up the deficit in the next five or six months.

Once a year, when advertising in America can manage to stagger along without Mr. Lunt for three or four days, the Lunts do their share in the way of tightening up the home ties by paying a visit to Aunt Caroline. With her noted kindness of heart Aunt Caroline is logically aglow over her annual opportunity to give the poor children a chance to stop existing for a little while, and take a crack at living, for a change. She meets them at the train, beaming with welcome and bubbling with exclamations of how glad they must be to get out of that horrid old New York.

Her friends, too, get into the spirit of the thing, and congratulate the Lunts on their escape, on meeting them. The impression seems to have got around that they are up from North Brother Island for a day or two. Also, it seems as if Aunt Caroline had taken everybody aside and warned them that her nephew and niece would strive to press New York City on them for a gift, the only condition being that they establish residence there.

"Well," is their cheery greeting, "I guess you're pretty glad to get out of that New York, heh? I go down there once or twice a year, and I tell you I'm glad enough to get back home after a day or two. I wouldn't live there if you gave me the place."

You gather from the firmness of the tones that they have been turning down offers of Manhattan Island all day long, and are getting sick and tired of the thing.

They are interesting conversations, but somewhat one-sided. The Lunts have yet to get together and work up something notably snappy in the way of a come-back.

VILLAGE HIGH LIFE

The fun of visiting Aunt Caroline is not confined to exchanging friendly greetings with the natives. I don't mean by that you should go crashing to conclusions. I can't tell you how I should feel if you were to get the thing all wrong, and carry around the idea that Aunt Caroline's home life is one mad round of pleasures. Just one good look at her would put that thought out of your mind forever. In fact, if you want to find the ideal exponent of average small-town life, Aunt Caroline is the very girl for you.

In the first place, she really hasn't got it to burn. Though Mr. Lunt's Uncle Phil left enough always to keep the wolf at a respectful distance from the door, Aunt Caroline is in no position to give away any libraries.

Then, too, as she delicately puts it, she is not so young as she used to be. Even when she was, the wild life was not being done by the town's best families. And now, when after ten years of easy widowhood she has arrived comfortably at the middle fifties, she cares virtually nothing about making a habit of drinking champagne from slippers or being carried to the table in a pie. She has never had any desire to join the goings-on of the young married set, which she does hear are little short of scandalous, at the Country Club. Aunt Caroline seldom gives them a thought. Eleven o'clock, almost any night, finds her house dark, and her eight hours of sleep well under way.

Now I shouldn't want you to leap to the other extreme and believe that Aunt Caroline and her friends don't have plenty of wholesome enjoyment out of life. Indeed they do. And Aunt Caroline is only too glad to let the Lunts have a generous share of it when they come to visit her.

If they crave excitement there is a perfectly splendid moving-picture theater just three squares away from Aunt Caroline's, which shows all the big feature pictures just a month or so after they have been shown on Broadway. All you have to do is to be sure to get there around quarter past seven, so as to be certain of getting a seat.

If they want to patronize the drama Aunt Caroline inquires among her friends if the attraction then on view at the Majestic Theater is worthy of their attention. If she gets enough favorable replies she, her nephew and her niece make a family theater party of it.

To vary things Aunt Caroline asks in enough friends for a few tables of bridge one evening during the Lunts' stay. As a concession to the New York gambling spirit a stake of half a cent a point is agreed upon, with much laughter. When the rubbers are over, the losers put down the sum they have lost on a slip of paper, jokingly called a slate by the men, and all gayly agree to hold it over till the Lunts' next visit, and play it off then.

And then, of course, there is always the radio. Aunt Caroline's wealthy brother-in-law had it installed for her as a birthday gift, and you have hardly any idea of the comfort it has been to her. Sitting right there in Aunt Caroline's third-story guest room, the Lunts can hear all about "Tommy Woodchuck's Adventure with the Wishing Fairy" or listen to a discourse on "How Shall We Stop Our Forest Fires?" that they will never regret having heard. As Aunt Caroline often asks, Isn't it just wonderful what things science can do?

The big night of the visit comes when Aunt Caroline puts on the lavender-and-gray changeable taffeta dress she had sent her by her sister in Boston, and, accompanied by Mr. and Mrs. Lunt, who are dressed accordingly, attends a social gathering at the house of one of her friends. It is quite a wild night. The comparatively younger guests dance to the music of the phonograph. Between numbers the dancing ladies join the elder matrons and discuss the quaint sayings of their children and their maids, while the men exchange cigarettes and inquire if anybody doesn't want a window raised. Things grow pretty informal when the refreshments are served, and there are bursts of gayety over references to strictly local events.

The Lunts politely come in on the laughter, but they can't do much to adding any helpful lines to the somewhat specialized conversation.

Mr. Lunt sleeps long and deep on the Sunday morning of their visit. It is just as well, too, because then his mind is all fresh for the puzzle page which comes in the *Sunday Clarion*. The guests and their hostess devote a large part of the day to missing nothing in the papers, and then Mrs. Lunt, following Aunt Caroline's example, gets a few letters off her mind. Mr. Lunt, meanwhile, rambles about the house, striving to do something constructive about the limp G-flat on the piano, or seeking to discover what really is the matter with the hinge on the china-closet door.

Aunt Caroline often says that she loves her quiet Sundays at home. She really prefers them to the ones when her prosperous friends take her motoring through the surrounding country.

In the afternoons, while Mr. Lunt drops around at their various offices to talk over the old days with his one-time schoolmates, Aunt Caroline and Mrs. Lunt get in a little social intercourse. Some of Aunt Caroline's friends come in for the afternoon or else she takes Mrs. Lunt with her to spend a few hours at one of their houses. They may play a bit of bridge or they may devote the time to putting in some work on crêpe-de-chine lingerie—it costs practically nothing at all when you make it yourself; and when you think of what the shops ask for it!

Either occupation just leads up to lettuce sandwiches and tea.

And so the time goes by, till the Lunts must return to New York. Aunt Caroline is annually pretty badly broken up over their leaving for that awful city. Tears blur her vision as she waves them good-by from the station platform, and the only thing that keeps her from going completely to pieces is the thought that she has again brought into their sultry lives a breath of real life.

The Lunts blow the annual kisses to her from the parlor-car window, and settle back to watch the old town go sliding past, a tolerant light in their eyes. As Mr. Lunt sums it up, it's all right for a visit, but he wouldn't live there if you gave him the place.

The Saturday Evening Post, July 22, 1922

Our Own Crowd

Mr. and Mrs. Grew annually take it pretty personally when the end of the season arrives and they must call it a summer. Of course, Mrs. Grew feels it only due to society that she get back to the apartment and find out what steps, if any, the agent has taken about that crack in the dining-room ceiling; but she is just about unhinged at the idea of leaving the Pebbly Point House and facing the harsh realities of life once more. If Mr. Grew, who is a perfect wizard at ferreting out the sunny side of things, did not call to her attention the fact that it is but a matter of eight or ten months before another summer will be upon them and they will find themselves—barring acts of God and a rise in the hotel rates—at the Pebbly Point House once again, it is doubtful if she would be able to pull herself together for the journey home.

Mr. and Mrs. Grew do not by any means imply that every visitor to the Pebbly Point House gets as much out of it as they do. It all comes down to a question of getting in with the right set, that impeccable group picturesquely summed up by the Grews in the phrase "our own crowd." And, of course, you will find it pretty uphill work attempting to make the social grade at first. But once you get to be one of the boys, the Grews join in reassuring you that "fun" isn't half the word for it.

You couldn't ask for anything much fairer than the rates at the Pebbly Point House. The catch to it is that good news like that always gets around pretty quickly, and so the hotel is approximately as exclusive as the subway.

But do you know, the Grews laughingly ask you, that they regard that, really, as one of the assets of the place? It gives our own crowd, you glean, such a perfectly corking opportunity to see the screaming way the other half lives. In fact our own crowd gets so many hearty snickers out of the mannerisms and the sports clothes of the transients that the summer is practically a whirlwind of merriment. Mr. Grew, who has the driest way of playing on words, often speaks of this outer circle not as guests but as jests, and, as you can readily see, it's a riot.

Another splendid thing about the Pebbly Point House is that it is so unspoiled. The Grews as good as admit that, even if the rates were twice what they are, they would be simply tickled to death to pay them for the privilege of stopping at a place so refreshingly free from the Ritzy note. Mrs. Grew is just about on tenterhooks as each fresh summer approaches for fear she will get to the hotel only to find it utterly ruined by the introduction of city-chap ideas in regard to rooms, service and cuisine. What our own crowd loves to do, the members frequently declare, is to go up to the Pebbly Point House and just rough it. And good old Mr. Blatch, the genial on-and-off host, sees to it that they get their wish.

Our own crowd does not, really, assume the proportions of a mob scene. There are but six members, all charter—the Grews, Mr. and Mrs. Eddy and Mr. and Mrs. Rinse. As soon as the Grews explain to you the series of curious coincidences that threw them together you realize for yourself that they were slated from the very beginning to be fast friends, and could you meet them you would see at a glance that "fast" is used in the best sense of the word.

In the first place, all three couples made their initial visit to the Pebbly Point House seven summers ago. Then scarcely had they been there a month before Mrs. Grew discovered that Mrs. Rinse's sister-in-law lived in the exact same apartment house where the Grews had been during 1910–1911, and was just as dissatisfied with the elevator service and the hot-water supply as they were. As additional proof that the world is small to the point of stuffiness, it later came out that Doctor Creevy, who had been Mrs. Grew's family physician before she was married, was living not much more than a stone's throw from the Eddy's house in South Orange, and both Mr. and Mrs. Eddy knew him very well by sight. It is things like that that make you stop and think, as Mrs. Grew said at the time.

The real leader of our own crowd is Mrs. Eddy. She is a woman born to command, and brought up accordingly. Until she came to the Pebbly Point House she had never set so much as a foot in any summer resort where the rates were less than ten dollars a day for one. You know that for a positive fact, because she tells you so herself shortly after you have been introduced to her. Naturally, she enjoys tremendous prestige at the hotel. She has one of the rooms with running water.

Rocking gently on the porch, Mrs. Eddy gives a series of short talks on how she locks up her jewels in the safe-deposit vault during the summer months and just goes a-gypsying along without them. Also, she explains that it is her practice to leave at home her really good gowns and hats. It may seem a bit selfish of her, at first thought, to deprive the guests of the privilege of seeing the real hot dog, but when you consider all the bother about luggage she saves herself and the railroads you can see that it is the only sensible course for her to take. She really has to laugh, though, and pretty frequently, too, when she thinks of the bewilderment of her winter friends, could they see her at the Pebbly Point House, snuggling right up close to Nature in simple frock and canvas shoes, no more bejeweled than the day she was born.

Mrs. Eddy is one of the most interesting conversationalists on the entire porch. "Well informed" is but a lukewarm term for her. She might, really, be called the Girl With the Camera Eye. She can tell you without a moment's floundering just who was sitting on the moonlit pier with whom, how close and until when on any night you can name; precisely how far things have got between that Sisson girl and the Binney boy; what Mrs. Binney thinks of it and what she would do if she were Mrs. Binney; at exactly what hour and in what state the McBirch party got back from that motor ride to the Goldenrod Inn.

Try to catch her—that's all she asks. She has never been known to make a memory-slip. It is not too much to say that she is losing time out of vaudeville.

Mrs. Rinse, now, is less the intellectual type and more the fluffy. She runs to ruffled organdie dresses with naïve sashes, and when she is really willing to let herself go she tucks a rose into her hair over one ear, where it balances the delicate gold chain that fetters her glasses to the other ear. She is full of fluttery gestures, and often, before she can control herself, she breaks out skipping.

She is the envied possessor of a flutelike soprano, delightfully lilting but not quite massive enough to be called a parlor voice—a kitchenette voice, say. Oftentimes, of a Sunday evening, she may be cajoled into giving the guests a musical treat. Her selections are amorous, in a refined way. She has done much to make popular "Just A-Wearyin' for You" and "Little Gray Home in the West."

Mrs. Rinse makes a winsome picture standing there by the piano, gripping a property roll of music, her eyelids, behind the sparkling glasses, fluttering with the tender emotions caused by the lyrics. It has often been remarked what a shame it is that the hotel parlor, also used as a dance room, is so big and high-ceilinged. Those sitting back of the third row of camp chairs at Mrs. Rinse's recital might just as well be at the movies.

Mrs. Rinse is, also, a perfect shark with children. She explains it by admitting that she herself is nothing but a kiddie at heart. To put them at their ease, she employs baby talk in her conversations with them, which goes big with little boys of ten or twelve years old.

Annually she conceives and directs an entertainment given by the tiny guests in the dance room, with herself as prima donna. Two summers ago, for example, they did "The Woodsy Fairy's Birthday Party," Mrs. Rinse playing the lead, and the supporting company, cast as wild flowers, in crêpe-paper costumes.

The plot of the piece unfolded to show how the Woodsy Fairy bade the woodland folk to her birthday feast; and, loosening up over the rose leaves and dew, they all came right out and told what they were thankful for. Some were thankful for the sunbeams, others for the brooklets; and that's the way it went, one thing leading to another. The Woodsy Fairy—being the author and producer, it was only fair that she got the big line of the show—was thankful that there was just nothing but happiness in all this great big old world.

Sex interest was supplied by the love of Spring Beauty for Jack-in-the-Pulpit, and comedy relief was provided by Johnny Chickadee, a character part played by a somewhat hard-boiled actor of eleven years, who was merely adequate in the role.

The guests at the Pebbly Point House, however, were almost unanimous in declaring that last summer's Rinse production was even better. It was called "Vacation Days at the Pebbly Point House," and the theme was much less generic than that of the Woodsy Fairy drama. It was a revue composed of sly cracks, in more-or-less verse, at recent local events. A member of the company would step forward, and, bucked up by tremendous laughter and applause, recite such telling thrusts as:

Sherlock Holmes could do wonderful things,
But we doubt if he could find Mr. Armbruster's water wings.

When the audience were back in their seats again another performer would declaim:

Whenever you see Tommy MacWinch looking blue,
It's a sign Mildred won't go out with him in the canoe.

The song hit of the piece, rendered by Mrs. Rinse, had a generous number of topical verses and wound up with a stirring chorus of:

Then we'll give three cheers for the Pebbly Point,
And we'll all give three cheers more;
And we'll hope to all be back again
Next summertime once more.

It is, as you can see, a great thing for our own crowd to be able to list as a member one so feminine yet so full of fun as Mrs. Rinse.

She and Mrs. Eddy set each other off splendidly. And the beauty of it is that Mrs. Grew is entirely something else again—just a good fellow, she is; a regular pal to the college boys that spend their holidays at the Pebbly Point House, given to sailor hats and talk of cold showers, walking with the hands thrust deep in the sweater pockets, and even occasionally letting slip a goshdarn or a by golly before she catches herself.

The ladies of our own crowd do not go in any too heavily for athletics. Now and then, if it gives signs of being a reasonably cool day, they wander over the golf course, agreeing beforehand that there is no use in being fanatical about the thing and counting it as a stroke when you pick up your ball and toss it out of the rough. But usually a saunter into the sea as far as the waist, a conservative dip to get the shoulders wet, a good, rousing rock on the porch, and they are just about used up.

What energy remains goes into the knitting of sweaters or the crocheting of strips of lace for those guest towels that make such thoughtful Christmas gifts. The work goes easily, for the toilers are beguiled by Mrs. Eddy's tales of the troubles her maids give her, by Mrs. Grew's description of her trip to Bermuda, and by Mrs. Rinse's account of her sister-in-law's operation, from the day she first felt that peculiar shooting pain to the funny cracks she made on her way out of the ether.

In the evenings the ladies form a select group on the porch close to the dance-room windows, where they go off into perfect bursts of merriment at the remarks which Mrs. Eddy, who admittedly shook a mean schottish when she was a girl, makes about the technic of the dancers. Occasionally they participate in the hotel bridge parties. To Mrs. Eddy, as the brightest social light, falls the task of collecting the twenty-five-cent entrance fee from each of the players, which is no fool of a job either. She and her two friends form the committee which goes to the village and purchases the sweet-grass baskets for the prizes.

In short, or at least pretty short, the three female members of our own crowd are not out of one another's sight during the entire summer, save during the hours of sleep or during those few necessary moments when they are upstairs whitening their shoes. It is doubtful if they ever have a thought which they do not split three ways.

Each is constantly finding fresh words of encouragement to buoy up the others. If Mrs. Eddy remarks that she really must do something in the way of dieting, both Mrs. Grew and Mrs. Rinse are loud to reassure her that it's so much more becoming to her when her face is full, and that if they were in her shoes they would not cut out so much as a single calorie. If Mrs. Rinse knits a sweater, her two friends vow they have never seen a stitch so novel, without being *risqué*. If Mrs. Grew springs a new sports skirt, Mrs. Eddy and Mrs. Rinse can hardly wait to get the address of her seamstress. And so it goes, day in, day out. It's enough, really, to put your faith in human nature right back on its feet again.

The big day of the week for our own crowd is Friday. For on Friday night the ladies are joined by the boys, which is the name that they have worked out for their husbands. The aggregate age of the boys, at the present writing, is somewhere along around one hundred and twenty-five, but the nickname sticks.

The boys cannot conscientiously be said to do much in the way of snapping things up on Friday evenings. Each naturally has to reply in full to his wife's anxious inquiries as to how affairs at the homestead are staggering along without her. There must be detailed reports on the weather in the city, the behavior of the maid, the promptness of the laundry, the regularity of the iceman's visits and the stand the cleaner has taken about the return of the rugs. It is an evening given over to connubial confidences. And as a concession to the boys' five days of labor in the city, and their grueling ride up on the train, our own crowd drifts hayward at a rurally early hour.

All day Saturday the boys devote to golf, although a casual observer of their game might pick up the idea that it was just so much devotion thrown away. The ladies meanwhile forge ahead on the sweaters and the guest towels. It is not until Saturday night that our own crowd really gets into its stride.

It isn't as if the members have to house a family of cocktails before they can get going. With nothing more to work on than the tomato omelet and the tinned cherries served for supper, they are off on an evening of revelry. Continuous laughter resounds from their jolly big circle of chairs on the porch, while lesser guests brush apologetically past. Any remark is good for a laugh, particularly allusions to jokes and adventures of past summers.

The Grews and the Eddys and the Rinses are so closely knitted together that their repartee is of a local, not to say an intimate, nature which makes a newcomer feel as cozily at home as if they were speaking in code. But the members of our own crowd, with their background of seven seasons at the Pebbly Point House, can feel for newcomers nothing more than a flicker of amused resentment. As they all agree, they don't want any outsiders, anyway; so that makes it just fine for everybody.

Even Mr. Eddy unbends on these occasions and becomes practically
a boy again. Mr. Eddy, you can see at a glance, is a man weighted down
with affairs. As he strides down the porch in his stylish stout flannels
and the yachting cap which he wears out of compliment to the Pebbly
Point House's nearness to the water, it is whispered after him that he
is something down in the Street, and that his position is good for anywhere from ten thousand to twenty-two hundred a year.

He is not a constructive humorist, though he is loud in his appreciation of the cuttings-up of Mr. Grew and Mr. Rinse. He expresses his
convivial feelings by taking our own crowd right in on the inside with
him, and giving it some pretty strong hints on the business outlook. Mr.
Eddy, for all his dignity, is a regular little sunbeam in the matter of
point of view. He as good as blurts it right out that he considers it little
more than a question of time before business takes up its bed and walks.
It may require quite a while, he says in all fairness, or again, it may
not. And he suggests, less in words than in manner, that it would not
be a bad notion for the members of our own crowd to make their plans
accordingly.

Mr. Grew and Mr. Rinse are the twin lives of the party. Mr. Grew
is the more spontaneous comedian, great at impromptu cracks and
catch-as-catch-can punning. Mr. Rinse has a number of specialties, including an impersonation of "Dinkelspiel on the Telephone," and a
recitation of "How Tony Lose-a da Monk." He isn't one to push himself
forward and insist on doing his stunts on all occasions, either, like so
many of these home entertainers. Sometimes people even have to ask
him to do them.

You couldn't want to see a prettier picture of perfect clubbiness than
our own crowd at these Saturday-night meetings. No wonder that the
members declare, as each orgy breaks up, that they don't know when
they have had a better time or laughed themselves sicker. In the privacy
of their various rooms, later, each couple decides that never in the history of social intercourse has there been a more congenial or an altogether dandier group.

The clubby spirit lasts well over into the next day, when, after a jolly
morning on the beach, the ladies troop over to have an afternoon's golf
with their husbands. This makes it considerably easier for the boys to
tear themselves away and return home by the evening train.

Naturally, as the season crashes to a close, our own crowd is brim-
ming with plans for practically incessant reunions all during the winter.
Upon the heart of each member are graven the addresses and the telephone numbers of the others. There are promises of daily telephone

calls, and of evening gatherings at least twice weekly; the men are to get together about every other day for lunch and the women are to have afternoons of knitting and chat several times during the week.

It will not be, they must mournfully concede, quite the same as being up at the Pebbly Point House, but it will be the immediately next best thing.

And then, when they get back to their several homes, it is just as if all those golden plans went suddenly bad on them. No one seems to be able to say quite why it is. What Mrs. Grew lays it to, and a very good explanation at that, is the way that one thing after another comes up.

When Mrs. Grew first comes home she finds things at the apartment pretty nastily shot up. The curtains have to be hung, the chintz pajamas must be taken off the furniture, there is a bad delay in traffic somewhere in the pipes of the kitchen sink that requires attention, two of the blue dishes have got themselves broken and must be replaced. And, as you can see, it all runs into time.

Then she annually discovers that she has not so much as a single stitch to her back. Naturally, something has to be done to relieve her condition, and Mrs. Grew is just the girl to do it. And you could scarcely ask her to hurry through the assembling of her winter wardrobe.

Hardly can she feel that she is decently clad once more before the winter's social activities begin breaking out; and, as she often says, outsiders can have but little conception of the time and energy it takes to get Mr. Grew to put on his dinner coat and go out for an evening's bridge. Then, too, there are the movies to be caught up with, and Mrs. Grew is almost never without a bit of shopping that must be done immediately. So she is amply justified in saying that she really hasn't a minute that she can lawfully call her own.

Even during this long period of separation it is not as if the other members of our own crowd were not fresh in the memories of the Grews. *Au contraire,* if you'll pardon my French. They are almost always with them in conversation. In fact the Grews are quite celebrated among their city friends for their informal little travelogues on their adventures at the Pebbly Point House. Whenever they are among those present at a social gathering they contribute to the entertainment of the guests by giving spirited accounts of the unspoiled wholesomeness of the hotel itself, and the perfectly corking times that can be had there— provided, of course, that you belong to the right set.

Mrs. Grew's conscience gives her periodic bad spells, and she frequently remarks to Mr. Grew that she simply must call up the Eddys and the Rinses and have them up to dinner. She even goes to the length of setting dates for the function. First, she will have them when the new hall runner is laid down; then it shall be after she has had her georgette-crêpe dress dyed henna; then as soon as Helga learns how to make decent gravy.

But the first thing you know there it is Thanksgiving, and hardly have they parked the last of the minced turkey before Christmas is upon them.

Mrs. Grew sends cards to the Eddys and the Rinses, and feels a lot better for it. She and Mr. Grew receive from Mr. and Mrs. Rinse the cunningest card with a picture of a little boy and a little girl kissing permanently under the mistletoe, and a highly engraved sheet stating that Mr. and Mrs. Waldemere Newins Eddy extend appropriate greet-ings.

Finally comes the day when Mrs. Eddy is in town for a smattering of shopping, and Mrs. Grew runs virtually smack into her, right out in broad daylight on Forty-second Street. Her first idea is to turn and run, but she dismisses that as impracticable. She approaches her friend apol-ogetically, fearful that Mrs. Eddy has been so wounded by her neglect that the best she will draw is a cold nod.

But Mrs. Eddy is even at the moment writhing under like pangs of guilt. Both ladies cover their embarrassment with an almost hysterical cordiality, and rush into an embrace, crying in chorus, "My dear, I don't know what you must think of me! I've been meaning and meaning to call you up, but I simply haven't had a minute!"

Before they part, Mrs. Grew has got it over with, and the Eddys are pledged to come to dinner the very next week. Mrs. Grew also vows to get Mr. and Mrs. Rinse, so that our own crowd may be reunited in full.

When she telephones Mrs. Rinse, Mrs. Grew is not able to protest that she does not know what Mrs. Rinse must think of her before Mrs. Rinse herself has got off the line. It also comes out that Mrs. Rinse's intention to get in touch with the rest of our own crowd has seldom been off her mind, but what with one thing and another she has abso-lutely not had a minute in which to go about it.

She cordially accepts the invitation to the reunion, declaring that it will be almost like being up at the Pebbly Point House once again.

But the trick to it is that it isn't. Before her guests arrive on the big night, Mrs. Grew has a shivery presentiment that the party is going to be a complete dud. She even expresses to Mr. Grew her wish that it were over, which gets no argument out of him.

The fraternal spirit of our own crowd seems to go utterly democratic during the winter. The members, so bubbling with mirth and *camara-*

derie on the porch, are curiously diffident and constrained in the Grews'
living room. The boys, in particular, have all the ease of manner of
those wanted by the police. The ladies size up one another's costumes
with the cold and wary gaze suggestive of the mien of strange dogs
meeting for the first time.

The crowd's members even look odd to one another's unaccustomed
eyes. There is something strange, not to say bizarre, about Mrs. Eddy's
silhouette which never was apparent at the Pebbly Point House. There
is something just a bit off about her dress, too, and it escapes the attention of neither of the other two ladies that she has evidently not yet
got around to taking her jewels out of the safe-deposit vault. Mrs. Rinse,
so fluffy and appealing amid rural surroundings, goes, somehow, a little
sour in city clothes. The boys, so many glasses of fashion on the hotel
porch, have a peculiar look about the collar and the line of the haircut.

Gathered at the dinner table, our own crowd cracks perceptibly under the strain of thinking up something to say. The boys ask one another
with great heartiness if they have been getting any golf lately; but as
none of them have, that closes that up tight. Mr. Grew tries out a few
jokes here and there, but they cause scarcely a ripple. The ladies inquire
brightly as to one another's health during the time they have been separated; but that topic, even with Mrs. Rinse's recent case of grippe,
cannot be stretched out over more than twenty minutes. The snappiest
they can do in the line of conversation is to give reports on the plays
they have seen and agree on the distressing condition of the weather.

After dinner things go from bad to something terrible. Mr. Grew
abandons all effort, and Mr. Eddy sits in impressive silence, breathing
not a word of the business situation. Mr. Rinse, cajoled by his hostess,
does render "Dinkelspiel at the Telephone" for old sake's sake; but,
away from the salt air, it seems to have lost its tang. Even he gets the
idea, and does not give an encore.

Seeing that the party is about to sink into a decline, Mrs. Grew, in
a desperate effort, brings out the album with the word "Snapshots"
burned into its leather cover. It is crammed with photographs of interesting events at the Pebbly Point House, which ought to do much in the
way of bringing up jolly reminiscences. There are those snapped on the
beach, slightly groggy in effect owing to too bright a sun, of groups of
toweled young ladies drying their hair and mounds of athletic young
men stacked in human pyramids. There are the tennis-court groups,
with the principal humorist looking cock-eyed at the camera through
the mesh of his racquet. There are the views taken on that day when
the spirit of carnival was rife, and the men dressed up in women's

clothes and took on the girls at baseball. There are close-ups of the man who has charge of the rowboats—there's a character!—and of Mr. Armbruster holding aloft a freshly caught snapper, and of the winners in the water sports being presented by Mr. Blatch with suitably engraved silver eye cups.

The guests gather about the album and examine each snapshot dutifully. But when the photographs were taken each family of our own crowd had a set of prints made from the films, so any element of surprise is rather apt to be missing.

Eventually Mrs. Eddy glances at the clock and with an extravagant start of surprise declares they simply must run if they are to catch the 10:40. Mrs. Rinse also is overcome by the flight of time, and the only thing she can do about it is to make plans for immediate departure, explaining that if they don't make the 10:17 they may have to wait twenty minutes for the next one. Mr. Rinse backs her up by remarking that that's the way it is when you live on Long Island.

Mrs. Grew implores them not to think of going for hours to come, rising as she does so to lead the way to her bedroom for the ladies to get their wraps. It is there settled by Mrs. Eddy that our own crowd must get together the next week at her house. The news is passed on to the boys, who notably refrain from throwing their hats up in the air about it.

On their way to their trains Mrs. Eddy and Mrs. Rinse can find but sparing praise for the taste in which the Grews' apartment is decorated, and they agree that the dessert at dinner was a sharp disappointment to them.

It is somewhat difficult to get Mr. Grew into the spirit of the thing on the day of the Eddys' dinner, but he eventually listens to reason, and they embark for the Oranges in the evening. Our own crowd, they find, has not turned out in full force for the occasion. That afternoon Mrs. Rinse has telephoned that she is just about devastated at the incident, but an old school friend of hers, whom she hasn't seen for she doesn't know how many years, has dropped in to stay with her, and she cannot see any way out but for her and Mr. Rinse to forgo the reunion.

The evening whirls by almost exactly as did the one dedicated to the Grews' festival, even to the poring over the collection of snapshots. The Grews tear themselves away in time to catch the 9:26 back to town, explaining that they have been up late so much recently. Mrs. Eddy prays them to stay over for another two or three trains, but she is, after all, fairly reasonable about taking no for an answer.

It is while they are waiting at the station that Mrs. Grew announces to her husband that before she'd let herself get as fat as Ethel Eddy she doesn't know what she would do. Mr. Grew confines himself to asking, purely for the rhetorical effect, why the hell people who live in the suburbs think it's any treat to you to tramp out there to dinner.

This fête does not entirely clean up our own crowd's winter schedule. Still another get-together meet is held, this time at the Rinses'. But owing to the roughest kind of luck, the Grews find themselves unable to attend. Mrs. Grew telephones Mrs. Rinse the day before to tell, with a break in her voice, how a man has come on from Mr. Grew's firm's Chicago office, and they simply cannot get out of dining with him and his wife. The only thing that consoles her, she adds, is the confidence that Mrs. Rinse understands how those things are.

The crowd's winter sessions having closed, things get pretty well back to normalcy again, and the days roll by until, as is no more than to be expected, summer comes around. Somehow, the crowd's spirit of *camaraderie* seems to be closely tied up with the warm weather. Like the stirring of the sap, if you don't mind something rather radical in the way of a simile, is the feeling of tender warmth for the Eddys and the Rinses that rises in the Grews with the first balmy days of June. As the time approaches for them to leave the city it seems as if they could hardly wait to get up to the Pebbly Point House and join up with the right set once again.

And our own crowd never disappoints, once it is established on the porch. Seen there, Mrs. Eddy again becomes a striking figure of a woman; Mrs. Rinse and Mrs. Grew hurry to tell her how simply great she looks with her face fuller. Mrs. Rinse is as frilled and as frolicsome as ever; her friends are amazed at the ladylike strides she has made in her singing. Mrs. Grew's sports costumes are even more dashing; the other two ladies simply can't say enough in favor of them.

Mr. Grew and Mr. Rinse resume their places as undisputed screams, and Mr. Eddy sprinkles words of hope about the future of the financial world.

Even at the first moment of the first meeting of the summer it is just as though the members of our own crowd had never been parted. They go right on with their badinage from where they left off, and it seems to go over bigger every season. Really, so close do they go as the summer dashes by that when the day after Labor Day arrives it doesn't seem as if they could rip themselves apart.

Indeed, they probably couldn't, and still live, if they did not hold tight to the annual thought of the practically countless times that they would get together during the winter.

The Saturday Evening Post, October 21, 1922

Professional Youth

If you want to take home to the folks some of the real inside stuff about this younger generation that has been breaking into the news so much lately, you owe it to yourself to start the thing off right by meeting Tommy Clegg. He is just the boy to come stealing down the winding staircase and let you in on the ground floor. For Tommy is one of the charter members of the Younger Generation, Inc.

Now, I shouldn't want you to go away with the notion that Tommy is the boy who invented youth. He himself would laughingly deny it if you were to walk up to him on the street and ask him to tell you flatly, one way or the other, did he or didn't he.

But he was well up in the van when it came to cashing in on the idea. Tommy and his little playmates don't regard being young as just one of those things that are likely to happen to anybody. They make a business of it.

And Tommy Clegg did much to put the current younger generation on a business basis. He is in a practically perfect position to do some invaluable work in the way of getting the firm's name before the public. As a sort of side line to his regular job of being just a kiddie, Tommy is engaged in giving literature a series of shoves in the right direction. It was but three or four short years ago that he first toddled to his little desk, seized his pen in his chubby fist and proceeded to knock American letters for a row of cloth-covered volumes of Louisa M. Alcott. And just take a look at him today—one of the leading boy authors, hailed alike by friends and relatives as the thirty-one-year-old child wonder.

Perhaps you have read his collected works, that celebrated five-inch shelf. As is no more than fair, his books—*Annabelle Takes to Heroin, Gloria's Neckings,* and *Suzanne Sobers Up*—deal with the glamorous adventures of our young folks. Even if you haven't read them, though, there is no need for you to go all hot and red with nervous embarrassment when you are presented to their author. Tommy will take care of all that for you. He has the nicest, most reassuring way of taking it all cozily for granted that not a man or a woman and but few children in these loosely United States could have missed a word that he has written. It grinds the ice practically to powder the moment you meet him.

HOW TOMMY PREPARES FOR EMERGENCIES

Probably you have it all worked out by this time that Tommy is not his official title. You seldom said a truer word. He signs his works in full—almost to repletion, in fact—Thomas Warmington Clegg, Junior.

But he wants all the world to think of him as just Tommy. He presses you to try to be a child again, along with him, and go ahead. He bucks you up by explaining that everybody calls him just Tommy—and when he says "everybody" you get a more than fair idea that it is no mere figure of speech. There is a largeness about it that hints pretty strongly to you that he includes such people as Gloria Swanson and Secretary Hughes and all the severely crowned heads of Europe. You have to fight hard to keep the tears back when you realize that there he is, urging you to string right along with the big boys and call him Tommy too.

But democratic—that's Tommy all over. Scarcely 85 per cent of his success has gone to his head. He doesn't take any more credit for what he has done than if he were Thackeray.

There is a pleasingly boyish sound about "Tommy" that makes it, really, more a trade-mark than a name. And Tommy Clegg, who has one of the best little business heads you ever saw in your life, isn't the boy to overlook that. Youth, as we got to saying only about five minutes ago, is his dish. It was a rough day for him when he found it was no longer practicable for him to go about in rompers and carry a pail and shovel.

He can hardly keep from breaking down and taking a good laugh, he tells you, every time he thinks how funny it is for a child like him to be sending belles-lettres for a loop, the way he does. But you mustn't think he takes it too personally. He simply sets it down as additional proof of what the present younger generation can do, once it gets into its stride. Perhaps at the moment you may not be able to recall ever having seen any pictures of Keats with a long white beard, either; but that, as Pat said to Mike while they were walking down the street one day, is neither here nor there. I'm not quite sure if it was Tommy that started it, but there seems to be a pretty persistent rumor going the rounds of our boys and girls that nothing was ever written prior to a couple of years ago.

You will find it rather uphill work, at first, to draw Tommy out about himself and his achievements. He may even wait to be introduced to you before he tells you, with an almost fanatical regard for detail, who he is, what he does and how much he gets for it. From there he will go on and show you a full line of samples, just so there will be no chance of your getting any wrong ideas about his work.

For Tommy never runs the risk of going out without taking along a few manuscripts; an author never knows, these days, when somebody is going to rush up to him in the Subway or on Forty-second Street or up at the Polo Grounds and ask him to give a reading. And it doesn't do any harm to be prepared, so that he can start right off, the minute anybody drops a hat. In case of any tie he usually slips a couple of photographs in his pocket, too, for he might run into Jeritza or Queen Mary or Peggy Hopkins Joyce any time, on a ferry or at the movies, and there they would be, begging him for some little keepsake, and how would he feel if he had to confess that he had gone and left his photographs in his other clothes?

They are pretty striking, too, these pictures of Tommy. Taken in profile, they are, and so that there won't be any confusion in the beholder's mind he is shown holding a pen and bending musingly over a fair, broad sheet of paper—just as a barber, say, might be photographed dreamily regarding a razor and strop.

As special correspondent from the front line of the younger generation, Tommy naturally strives to give the public—his public, he calls it tenderly—a good all-round view of the boys and girls. Sometimes his stories show them as clear-eyed young rebels—Tommy loves that one—facing life with sparkling eyes, their shining eyes undimmed by mists of sentiment and conventionality. He intimates pretty definitely that they are so many white hopes, and now that they have come along to take hold of things it's going to be just the dandiest of all perfectly corking little worlds. Tommy uses these tales of his to get into circulation some of his more revolutionary ideas. It makes you stop and give a hearty gasp when you realize how daring is the viewpoint of these young ones of today. Looking facts squarely in the face isn't the half of it. These clear-eyed heroes and heroines as good as come right out and say that there are two sexes, that youth is not apt to last a lifetime, that parents are occasionally slightly out of touch with the activities of their children, that spring is one of the pleasantest of the seasons and that there have been several known cases where love did not endure after the first forty or fifty years. It gives all the old theories rather a nasty shake-up, that's what it does.

But startling as these stories are, there doesn't seem to be any noticeable clamor for the moving-picture rights to them. As publicity for the younger set they are all very well, of course, as far as they go, but they don't catch the out-of-town trade. There isn't, as you might say, a headache in a barrelful of them.

THE GOINGS-ON OF THE YOUNGER SET

Tommy, who has his lighter side, too, is better able to show some of his real stuff when he writes, not of clear-eyed young rebels but of cock-eyed ones. There are few that can tie him when it comes to describing night life in the country clubs and the merry romps of the light-hearted girls and boys, so full of mischief and gin. You get the impression from these works that an evening with the younger generation is like something between a Roman bath and one of King Alphonso's little vacations at Deauville. Rouge flows like water in Tommy's pages, and cigarettes and cocktails circulate as freely as hard-boiled eggs at brookside picnics. Things, according to the author, look pretty black; he broadcasts the grim warning that conditions are getting no better rapidly and that decadence, as those outside the younger generation know of it, is still in its infancy.

And as the farmer said when his wife, who had long been subject to deathlike epileptic seizures, finally died during one of them, "That's more like it." That's the stuff that got the boys and girls before the public. Those are the stories that have done much to make it common gossip that you never saw your mother behaving herself that way when she was a girl.

Tommy Clegg, being, as you might put it, one of the members of the firm, knows what he is talking about when he tells of the goings-on of the younger set. As soon as you meet some of his friends you can see that his characters are drawn practically from life.

He has several playmates who are carving out quite a name for themselves as lost souls. With the engaging frankness so characteristic of the modern young, they sit right down and tell you all about themselves without so much as a flinch; it just seems as if they couldn't bear to think of your going along from day to day without knowing the worst about them. They are too far gone to conceal their shame. It is almost as if they wore on their chests a large placard with "Look at me—I'm terrible" lettered upon it.

You cannot conscientiously feel that you have any working knowledge of what life among the Apaches is like until you have heard these boys repeat a few of their favorite selections. It comes out that one orgy after another is bogey for them and their regular bedtime is all hours, at the earliest. They confide that you could count on the thumbs of one hand the number of sober breaths that they have drawn since they got out of grammar school. Rather uncomfortably blood-chilling are the tales they tell of the crimes that they have committed when the beast in them was unleashed by the Haig boys; how they paid a hansom driver to let them climb up in his seat and take the reins, or went right up to a policeman and asked him how he got that way, or drove around and around the park in an open taxicab, singing "Lord Geoffrey Amherst" in harmony close to the point of stuffiness. You gather from the general trend of the conversation that the next step for them will be the gutter. It seems to be a hospitably wide-open secret that if it wasn't for them, bootlegging in America would be on the rocks today.

And it is little short of devastating to see how bitterly hardened they are to the effects of strong drink. You never in your life saw an uglier crack tendered than the old one about its taking more than one swallow to make a snootful. One high ball, and the boys get right up and do impersonations of Charlie Chaplin; two, and they have to be held back from going out and taking over the railroads. The person who got up the line about not knowing where the younger generation is coming to certainly worked the whole thing into a nut-shell.

Some of the young ladies of Tommy's circle, too, make it their whole career to drive home to you the startling truth that things are not what they used to be when grandma was a girl. "Daring" is no word for them. You can't steal a look at them any time of the day but what they are being just as daring and modern and unconventional as it is possible to be and still stay out of Bedford. And just as unconscious of the effect they are creating as if they were doing it all before a camera too.

GIRLS WILL BE GIRLS

The funny thing is that if you took only a quick glance at them you would think they were nothing more than regular girls. They may run a bit to trick earrings, and it is evident that much of this talk about rouge and lip sticks has its foundation in fact; but there is nothing, really, that you wouldn't see right in your own home. They seem to be coming along pretty nicely with their inhaling, yet it isn't anything to write to the papers about. It has been several years since there was any cause for any grave alarm about tobacco's stunting their growth.

It is in their conversation that the girls get in some of their snappiest work. Bright as a dollar bill, they are, every one of them; and frank— well, there isn't a slang phrase that they would stop at. It is pointed out at some length in many modern literary works that there are few things sweeter and more wholesome than the girl of today's attitude toward sex. She just looks unflinchingly at the thing with those widely advertised clear eyes of hers, remarks, in effect, "So that's what all the fuss is about!" and calls it a day. And you can see from these friends of Tommy's that the rumor has not been exaggerated in the least. There is no unwholesome mystery about sex to them; in fact so healthy, so buxom almost is their attitude toward it that they seldom if ever talk about anything else. If sex should suddenly be abolished the girls could never make another sapient crack.

They just work those little curly heads of theirs to the bone striving to get a shock into every sentence. It is rough going, this living up to all their press notices, but the girls never fall down on the job. They are conscientious to a somewhat grave fault about giving their audience its money's worth in thrills; but then, it's in one of the finest little causes in the world.

So they do their stuff valiantly, running on just the way the heroines do in the prom-girl school of fiction—for, after all, who are they that they should make a liar out of literature? It is rather evident that for all their appearance of fresh—to put it mildly—youth, there are some pretty fairly sable pasts attached to them. They let fall with many an ugly thud hints of hands held and dances cut, and they don't mind how far out of their way it takes them if they can bring it to your attention that they have plumbed life right to the depths and are fully able to fill in the missing letters in the word "d—n." They watch hopefully for any signs of grogginess that their unconventionalities may cause in the listener, pausing eloquently after each of their most telling nifties, as who should say, "Hear that one? Pretty snappy work, eh?" It is more fun to listen to them chattering away so freely and frankly; it is all just as impromptu as the Passion Play.

If you want to be as good as hand in glove with the intellectual side of things, too, Tommy can give you the chance of a lifetime to take a look at the younger intelligentsia. He counts any number of clear-eyed young rebels among his intimates.

NOTHING LEFT BUT THE RIVER

But I shouldn't, if I were you, go in expecting them to turn out to be regular little balls of fire. If at any time you entertained the idea of painting your district red they aren't really the boys that you would call in to help you out with the job. They are scarcely the logical persons that you would select for the post of trying out new steps on the table or holding up any silk hats to be kicked. They seem to be always rather low in their minds, and there is a general air about them as if the chambermaid had neglected to dust that morning. The farthest that they go in the way of whooping things up is to give an occasional short laugh of quiet contempt.

For you might just as well be all set, before you meet them, to find them pretty seriously displeased with the way things are being done. It is all very well for you to be apologetic and to beg them to give the world just one more chance to try to be a better boy, but it's no use. They are definitely off everything, and that's flat. You are given the choice between taking it and letting it alone, reading from left to right.

They are in an especially depressed state about America. They stack right up with its severest pals and best critics. The country has turned out to be a practically total loss—no art, no literature, no folk dancing, no James Joyce, no appreciation, no native basketry, nothing; just so much real estate, inhabited by a lot of people who follow the comic strips, present automobiles to baseball players and keep conscientious track of what film will be shown at the local Bijou Dream the week after next.

The boys can't even drag much hope out of the thought that their brave little band of youthful cognoscenti will put the country on its feet. After all they are but a thin red line; and Babbitts multiply so rapidly. It looks really as if there were nothing much left but the river.

Almost any night you can see the young intelligentsia gathered up at Tommy's, a sort of intellectual Kiddies' Klub, you might call it. There they all are, tots in their waning twenties and early thirties—the cunningest age, I often say it is; just the time when they're into everything—kidding back and forth about poetry and art and sex until it's long past the time for the sandman to come. And you will find things will work out considerably prettier for you if, when they get fairly started interchanging good ones, you don't even attempt to put up your glove and intercept the talk. Just let it whistle on over your head, and maybe if you sit quiet you will be able to pick up something rather snappy to take home to the family.

And the kiddies seldom fail to toss off a few ideas that are guaranteed to knock you, if not cold, at least pretty uncomfortably chilly. They usually start off in lighter vein with some comical cracks at the aged. There is not much in this life that can win a snicker from them, but they do have to indulge in a rousing smile when they think of those poor old souls of forty-five and forty-seven trying to stagger along in the wake of progress. Yet they are a bit worked up over it, too, even though they are the first to see its humorous side. You gather that grow-ing old is something that people do just to be mean.

Some of the boys, in fact, take the thing so much to heart that they come right out and say their highest hope is that someone will be public-spirited enough to come along and shoot them before they reach forty. And it looks from here like a pretty good ten-to-three bet that they will get their wish.

But it is when they cease bantering and get down to the really deep stuff that they will open your eyes for you. Many a night will you spend tossing on a hot pillow after these little ones have shown up life to you as it really is. Disillusioned is no name for them; you might just as well go right ahead and call them cynical, for short.

It all comes out with a rush, once they get started. They come clean with the news that war is a horrible thing, that injustice still exists in many parts of the globe even to this day, that the very rich are apt to sit appreciably prettier than the very poor. Even the tenderer matters are not smeared over with romance for them. They have taken a calm look at this marriage thing and they are there to report that it is not always a lifelong trip to Niagara Falls. You will be barely able to stagger when the evening is over. In fact, once you have heard the boys settling things it will be no surprise to you if any day now one of them works it all out that there is nothing to this Santa Claus idea.

What with keeping up with the Hollywood society notes and with remembering to feed Fluff and Chum, the family brace of goldfish, I don't, myself, have much time for sitting and dreaming in the candle-lit gloaming. But when I do get a moment to myself I lavish it upon wondering what people used to get excited about before the present younger generation came along. Maybe it is not safe to trust in mem-ories of departed youth, yet it seems that all this about things being so different from what they were when grandma was a girl is something of an overstatement. Where the boys and girls of grandma's day made their big mistake was in using the wrong kind of advertising. If ever a man deserved firing it was their press agent.

I don't know who it was that started the nation-wide publicity cam-paign for our present young folks. But you couldn't ask to see a sweeter job, no matter who did it. And all novel stuff too. Not a milk bath or a jewel robbery in the lot.

GETTING THEMSELVES CONDEMNED

The commercial genius who began the grand work of selling this younger generation to the public went right ahead on the principle that, after all, there is but one sure way to get people talking—simply give them something to talk about; and then you can retire to the country estate and go in for raising double petunias, comfortably sure that your work will be carried right along for you.

One hearty look back at the way things were done in grandma's day convinced the publicity agent for the modern young that that was no way to crash into the news. It may have been all very well, but it never set people to gathering in little knots on street corners, talking the matter over in hushed voices. Then, according to popular folklore, girls were gentle and low-voiced, ready to faint at the drop of a garter, unable to feel really themselves without their flannel petticoats, given to modest white muslin dresses, with perhaps a bunch of daisies at the belt if they wanted to go in strong for sex appeal. The young men of the period were honest and noble and true, kind to the antique and the bedridden, and lips that touched lip stick should never touch theirs. Nothing could have been sweeter of course in its way, but it never accomplished anything notable toward getting them into the contemporary topics of the day.

Once it was seen where the boys and girls of ye olden daye fell down it was virtually no trouble at all to get the current young out of the amateur class. All they had to do was to capitalize their goings-on instead of their virtues, and the thing was done. As soon as they could get themselves condemned by press and pulpit they would be all set. The only things they needed were a snappy trade name—"flapper" fixed half of that up fairly well, though they never did do the right thing by way of the male clients—and a couple of good catchy slogans, such as, "Well, I don't know what the young people are coming to, I'm sure" and "What on earth can their fathers and mothers be thinking of?"

There was nothing more to it. The business of being young ranked in American industries right after automobile manufacture.

And no one knows better than you yourself how prettily the drive worked. There has been nothing like it since the gold rush.

In the first place the news broke just at the right time. It was an off season, as you might say. Laddie Boy had barely come to his decision to take up a political career. There was nothing really worth while in the way of a war on the engagement pad—just a few bush-league events in the Balkans and the regular Turkish daily dozen. Hollywood was still regarded as one of those quaint little Western towns where men were men and women were women. The public was just about ripe for something to talk about after the children had gone upstairs to bed.

Then the incoming fashions helped the young people's cause along. Bobbed hair and short skirts were news items, and the you-just-know-she-doesn't-wear-them movement was budding into vogue. Rolled stockings appeared on every hand—there isn't the slightest need for being silly about it; you know perfectly well what I mean.

Women's clubs all over the country passed resolutions stating that they never in all their lives had seen anything like it, they declared they hadn't. People with a gift for looking on the bright side of things ascribed it to the general clutter left by the war and promised that everything would be all right as soon as business was able to come downstairs and sit up in an easy-chair propped up with pillows again.

SOFT FOR THE TIRED AUTHORS

And all the tired authors regarded the news about the younger set as being sent to them direct from heaven by special assignment. The market was all clogged up with stories about young A.E.F. lieutenants and beautiful Y.W.C.A. girls; stories full of such racy bits of army slang as "buddies" and "Sammies" and "Come on, men, it's the zero hour, so let's go over the top with the best of luck"; stories crowded with realistic word pictures of kindly old French peasants who refused to accept money from the grateful Yankee boys, and of privates who went about imploring a chance to die for their superior officers. It was like a day in the country for the overworked writers to fall on a nice timely topic, rough enough to have a widespread appeal, yet safely out of the asterisk class.

It is no news to you to say that they made the most of it. You couldn't pick up a magazine without finding a minimum of three stories founded on the scandalous doings of the modern young, all pointing the moral that things are not what they used to be when Madison Square was considered uptown.

As publicity it was so much velvet for the younger generation. And you have to admit that Tommy Clegg and his friends stood up under all the talk pretty gamely. They shrank from the blinding glare of the limelight much as Miss Pola Negri shudders back from it. If they felt from time to time that the service was beginning to slack up a bit they rushed right in just like one of the family and helped out by providing a little more advertising copy for the firm. You couldn't have wanted to see a nicer spirit of cooperation.

Even Constant Readers and Pro Bono Publicos got the idea of the thing and wrote indignant letters to their favorite papers, demanding that immediate steps be taken to do something about our boys and girls—put them out to sea in an open boat, say, or call out the militia and turn machine guns on them or give them some little hint like that.

The lurid doings of the younger set got into the circulating libraries, reached the footlights, eventually were taken up by the moving-picture scenario fitters. Unfortunately, by the time a national evil gets taken up by the movies in a serious way it is but tepid dog so far as its news interest is concerned. That is just the next step before it belongs to the ages.

But don't, whatever you do, utter any words of condolence to Tommy and his playmates on that score. For they still regard themselves and their activities as authentic front-page stuff.

The Saturday Evening Post, April 28, 1923